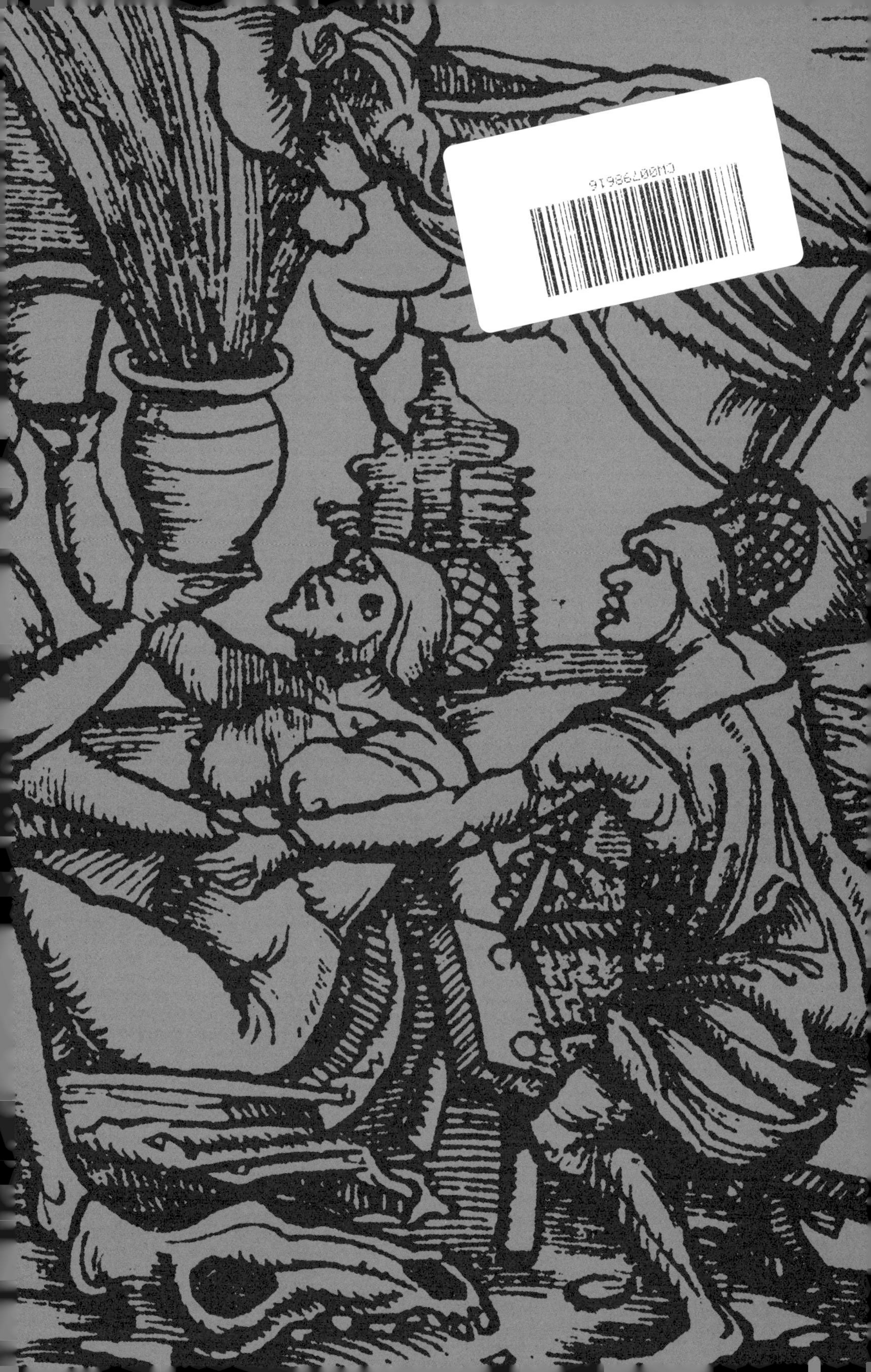

The Dark Horse Book of
Horror

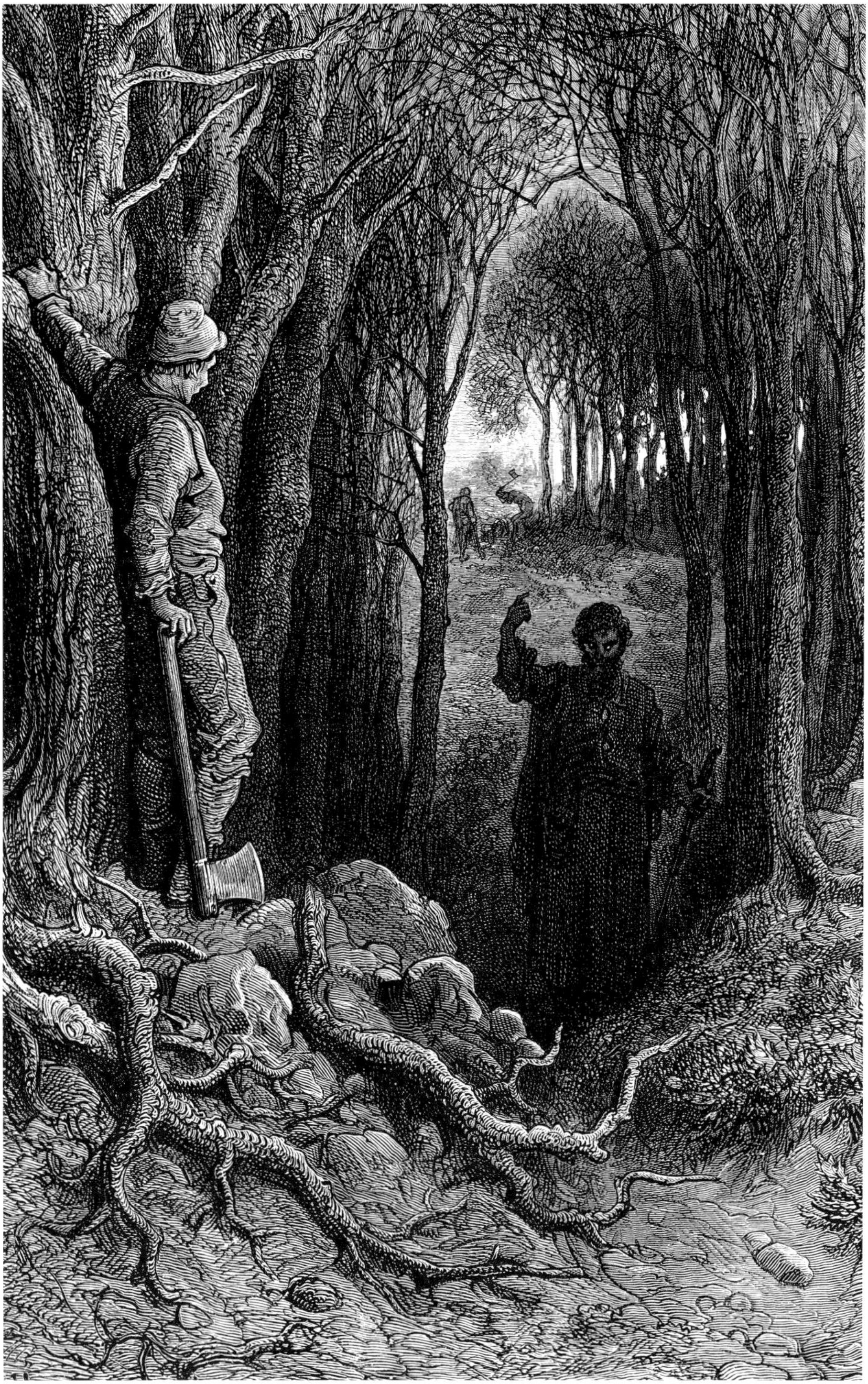

From Samuel Taylor Coleridge's *The Rime of the Ancient Mariner*, illustrated by Gustave Doré

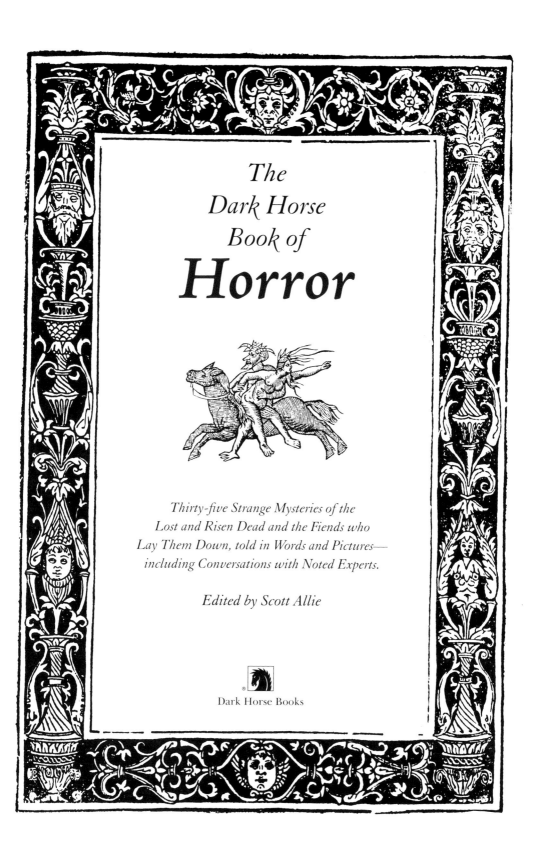

The
Dark Horse
Book of
Horror

Thirty-five Strange Mysteries of the
Lost and Risen Dead and the Fiends who
Lay Them Down, told in Words and Pictures—
including Conversations with Noted Experts.

Edited by Scott Allie

Dark Horse Books

Cover Illustration
Gary Gianni

Cover Design and Colors
Jim Keegan

Publisher
Mike Richardson

Associate Editor
Shawna Ervin-Gore

Assistant Editors
Matt Dryer, Dave Marshall, Katii O'Brien

Collection Designer
Patrick Satterfield

Digital Art Technician
Christina McKenzie

This volume collects *The Dark Horse Book of Hauntings*, *The Dark Horse Book of Witchcraft*, *The Dark Horse Book of the Dead*, *The Dark Horse Book of Monsters*, and "The Stain" from *Myspace Dark Horse Presents #15*.

DarkHorse.com
Published by Dark Horse Books
A division of Dark Horse Comics, Inc.
10956 SE Main Street
Milwaukie, OR 97222

First edition: August 2017
ISBN 978-1-50670-372-5

1 3 5 7 9 10 8 6 4 2
Printed in China

Library of Congress Cataloging-in-Publication Data

Names: Allie, Scott, editor.
Title: The Dark Horse book of horror : thirty-five strange mysteries of the lost and risen dead and the fiends who lay them down, told in words and pictures--including conversations with men and women versed in such matters ; edited by Scott Allie.
Description: First edition. | Milwaukie, OR : Dark Horse Books, 2017.
Identifiers: LCCN 2017010255 | ISBN 9781506703725 (hardback)
Subjects: LCSH: Comic books, strips, etc. | BISAC: COMICS & GRAPHIC NOVELS / Horror. | COMICS & GRAPHIC NOVELS / Fantasy. | FICTION / Occult & Supernatural.
Classification: LCC PN6726 .D34 2017 | DDC 741.5/973--dc23
LC record available at https://lccn.loc.gov/2017010255

Introduction

The book in your hands collects four separate anthologies that Dark Horse published from 2003 to 2006. First was *The Dark Horse Book of Hauntings*, and with the fourth, *The Dark Horse Book of Monsters*, it felt like we'd concluded a set, even though there was no serialized story running throughout the books to signal a resolution. No story had ended. Nevertheless, it felt like time to conclude the run, and for that same reason, it's satisfying to see all four together under one great Gary Gianni cover.

This project began when Mike Mignola told me about "Dr. Carp's Experiment," a short story for which we had no immediate home. Mike was gearing up for the first Hellboy movie, which would mean reduced output of Hellboy comics, something we wanted to handle wisely. Building an anthology around this story got us both excited. We agreed "Dr. Carp" was sort of a story about a haunting, and that finding stories that also broadly fit a theme would be the most interesting way to go. Hence *The Dark Horse Book of Hauntings* . . .

And so each year, Mike came up with a short story, and we decided how tightly or loosely to sketch out a theme around it, and went to our friends to flesh the book out. Evan Dorkin and Jill Thompson's entry in the first book was the breakout hit, even before the book was on sale—Dark Horse staffers were reduced to tears by "Stray," which won awards and led to Evan and Jill's *Beasts of Burden* series. To best take advantage of the variety implied in the word *anthology*, we stepped away from comics in the interviews and illustrated prose stories here, giving readers an even broader view of the theme.

After *The Dark Horse Book of Monsters*, in 2006, we were proud of what we'd done with the books, and felt that every good thing deserves to come to an end. By the time we might have started work on a fifth book, we were gearing up to launch *MySpace Dark Horse Presents*, the online anthology that filled our appetite for variety for the next few years.

Anthologies are beautiful books, and my career has revolved loosely around them, since my first professional work on the literary magazine

Glimmer Train Stories. Before that, it was the original *Dark Horse Presents* series that led me away from superhero comics into the endlessly varied world of independents. Anthologies have a unique power to open readers' eyes. Editors know that an anthology needs some hooks—a Hellboy story, a fan fave like Busiek—but the real wonder of anthologies, the victory for editor and reader alike, is the gem that catches you off guard, the way "Stray" affected our own staff almost fifteen years ago. If you picked this edition up for Mignola or Craig Russell or Jill Thompson, I hope you're surprised and pleased by work from someone you'd never heard of before, and that you can find more of their comics. Or if you're just a devotee of anthologies, and sought this one out wishing there were more on the shelves, I hope this assortment suits you. And for the horror buffs giving this a try, you are my people—this is for you.

Thanks to the fellow editors on the original editions, and to all of our contributors, some of whom I haven't gotten to work with since. And many thanks to you, the reader—please take your time with these stories. This isn't a comic you should get through in one sitting. I recommend reading it with only one light turned on, and if possible only at night.

Table of Contents

❧ Hauntings ❧

❧ Witchcraft ❧

The Dead

Monsters

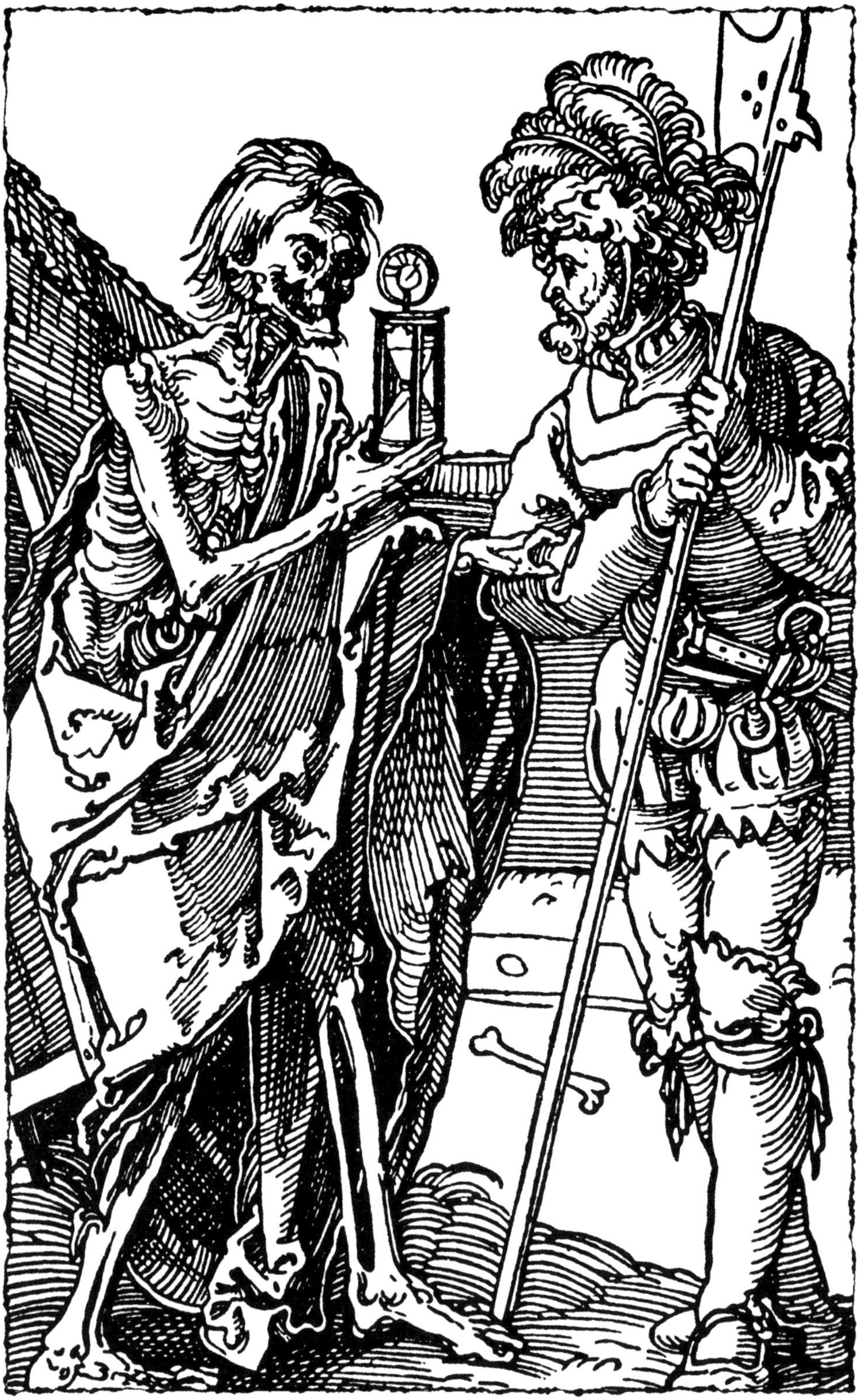

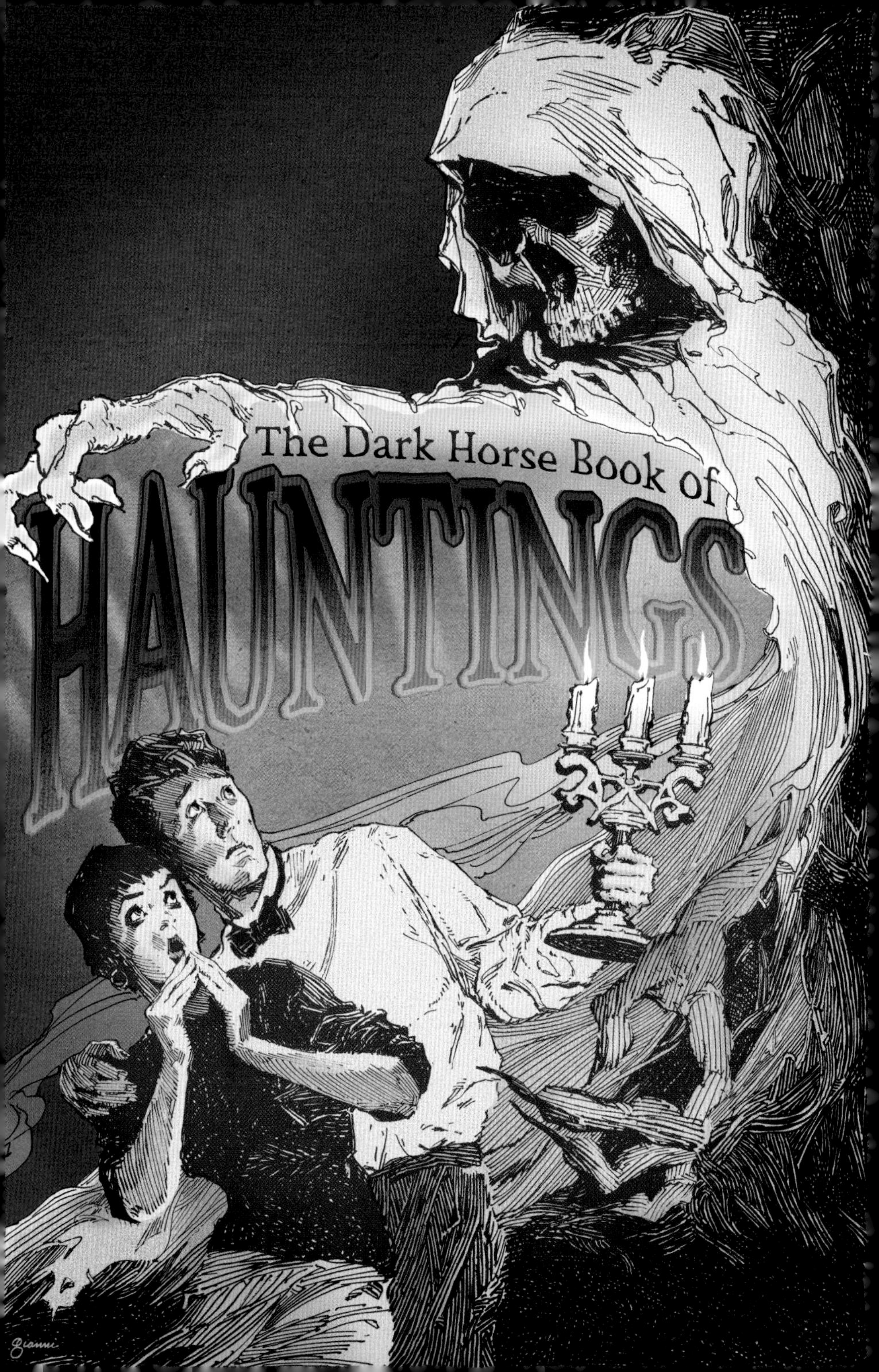
The Dark Horse Book of
HAUNTINGS
gianni

The
Dark Horse
Book of
Hauntings

*Eight uncanny tales of Spirit Manifestations,
Apparitions, and otherworldly Horrors—
told in Words and Pictures;
also, Séance Medium L. L. Dreller orates upon
his Occult Gift: Peculiar Stories from Beyond.*

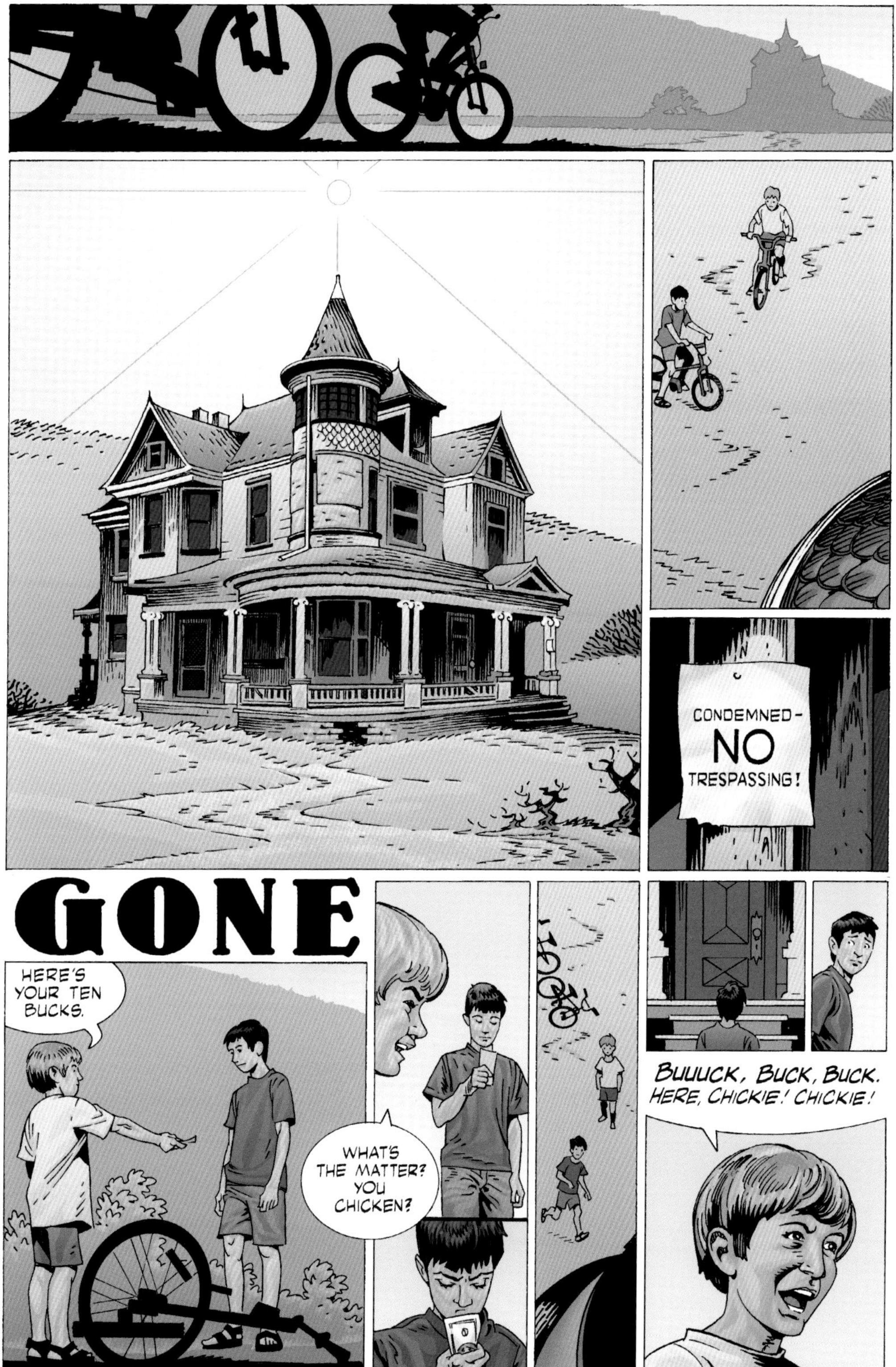
CONDEMNED - NO TRESPASSING!
GONE
PCR OP.55 — 2003
HERE'S YOUR TEN BUCKS.
WHAT'S THE MATTER? YOU CHICKEN?
BUUUCK, BUCK, BUCK. HERE, CHICKIE! CHICKIE!

BY P. CRAIG RUSSELL & MIKE RICHARDSON

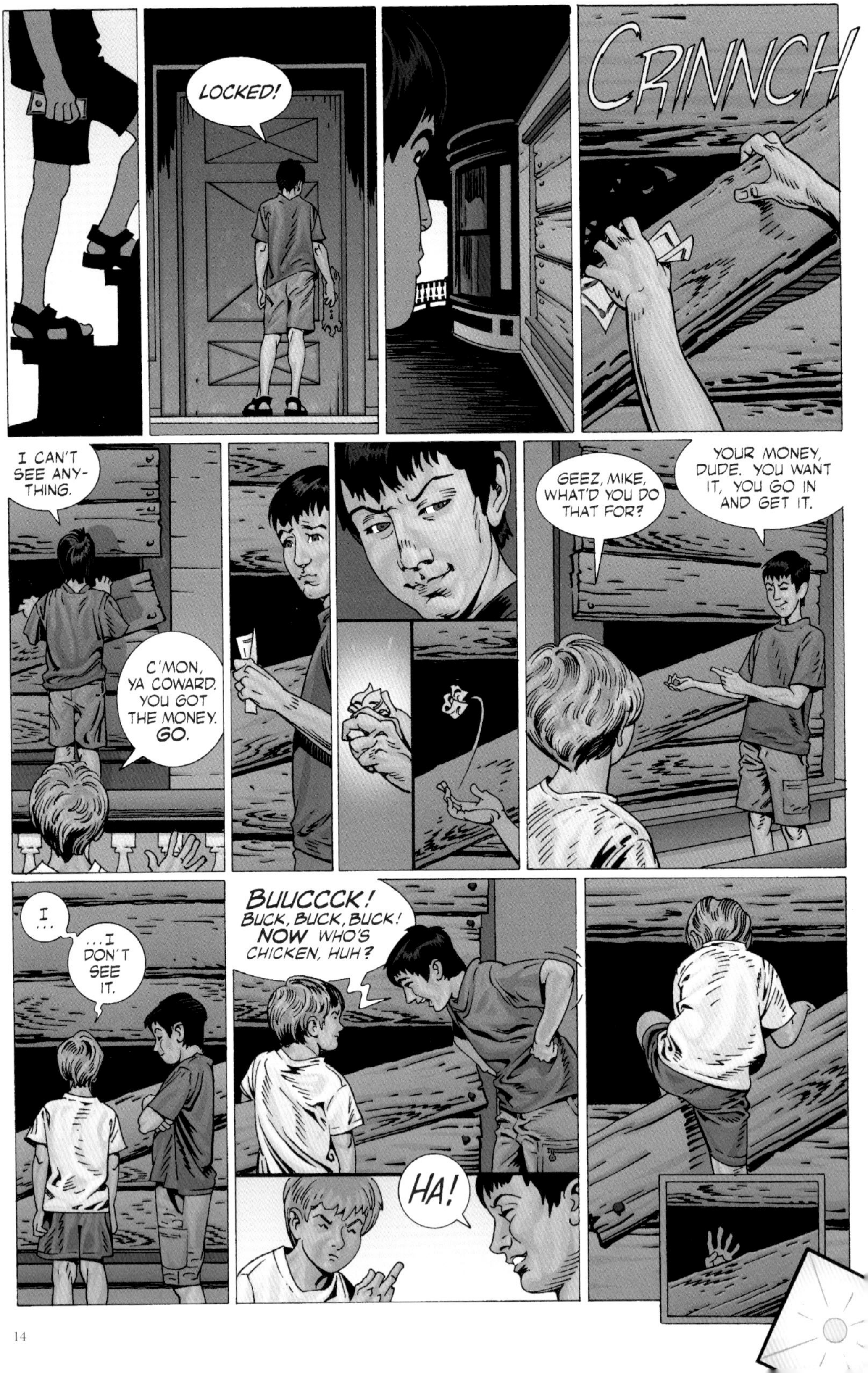
LOCKED!
CRINNCH
I CAN'T SEE ANY-THING.
C'MON, YA COWARD. YOU GOT THE MONEY. GO.
GEEZ, MIKE, WHAT'D YOU DO THAT FOR?
YOUR MONEY, DUDE. YOU WANT IT, YOU GO IN AND GET IT.
I...
...I DON'T SEE IT.
BUUCCCK! BUCK, BUCK, BUCK! NOW WHO'S CHICKEN, HUH?
HA!

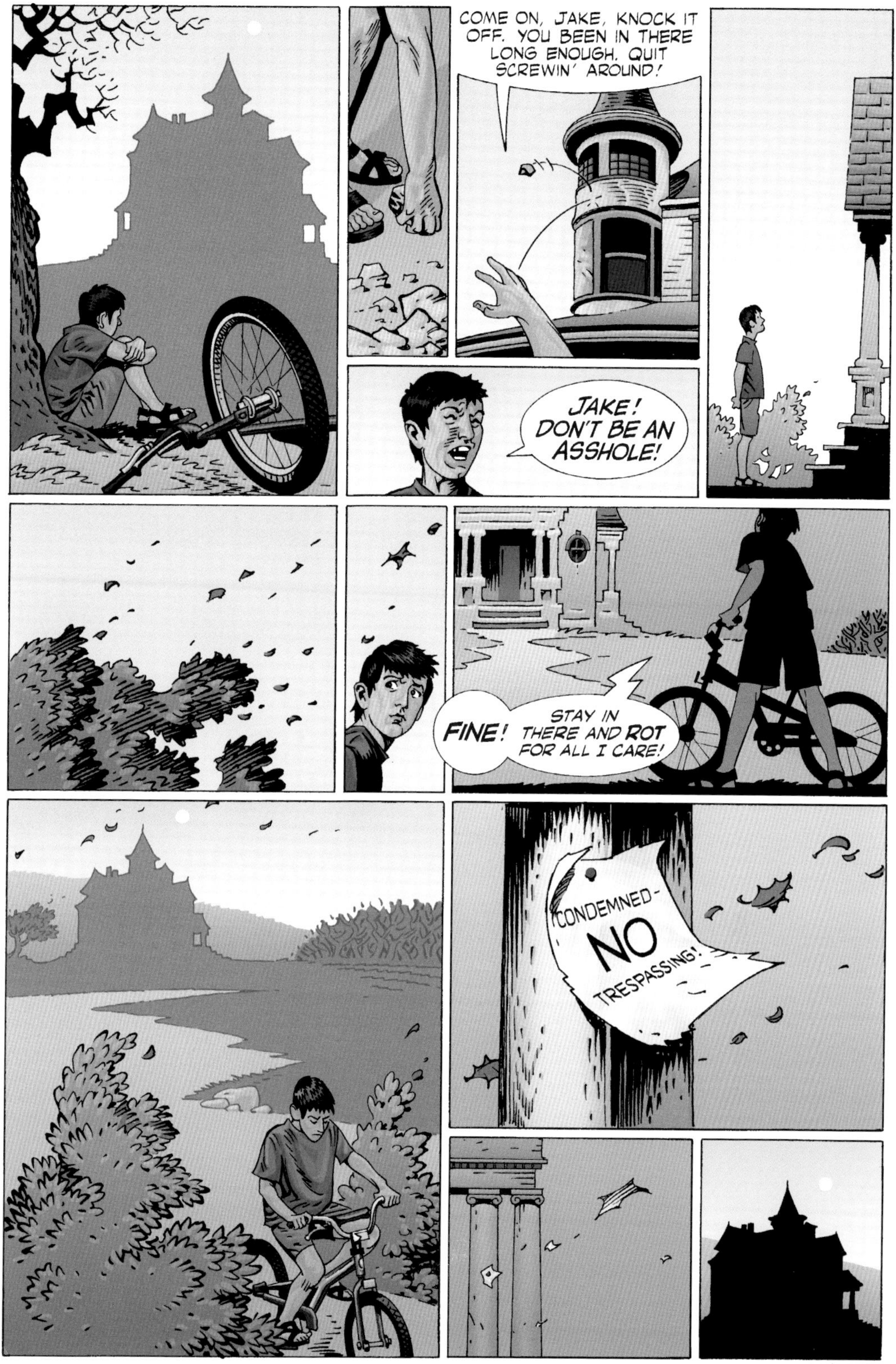
COME ON, JAKE, KNOCK IT OFF. YOU BEEN IN THERE LONG ENOUGH. QUIT SCREWIN' AROUND!
JAKE! DON'T BE AN ASSHOLE!
FINE! STAY IN THERE AND ROT FOR ALL I CARE!
CONDEMNED- NO TRESPASSING!

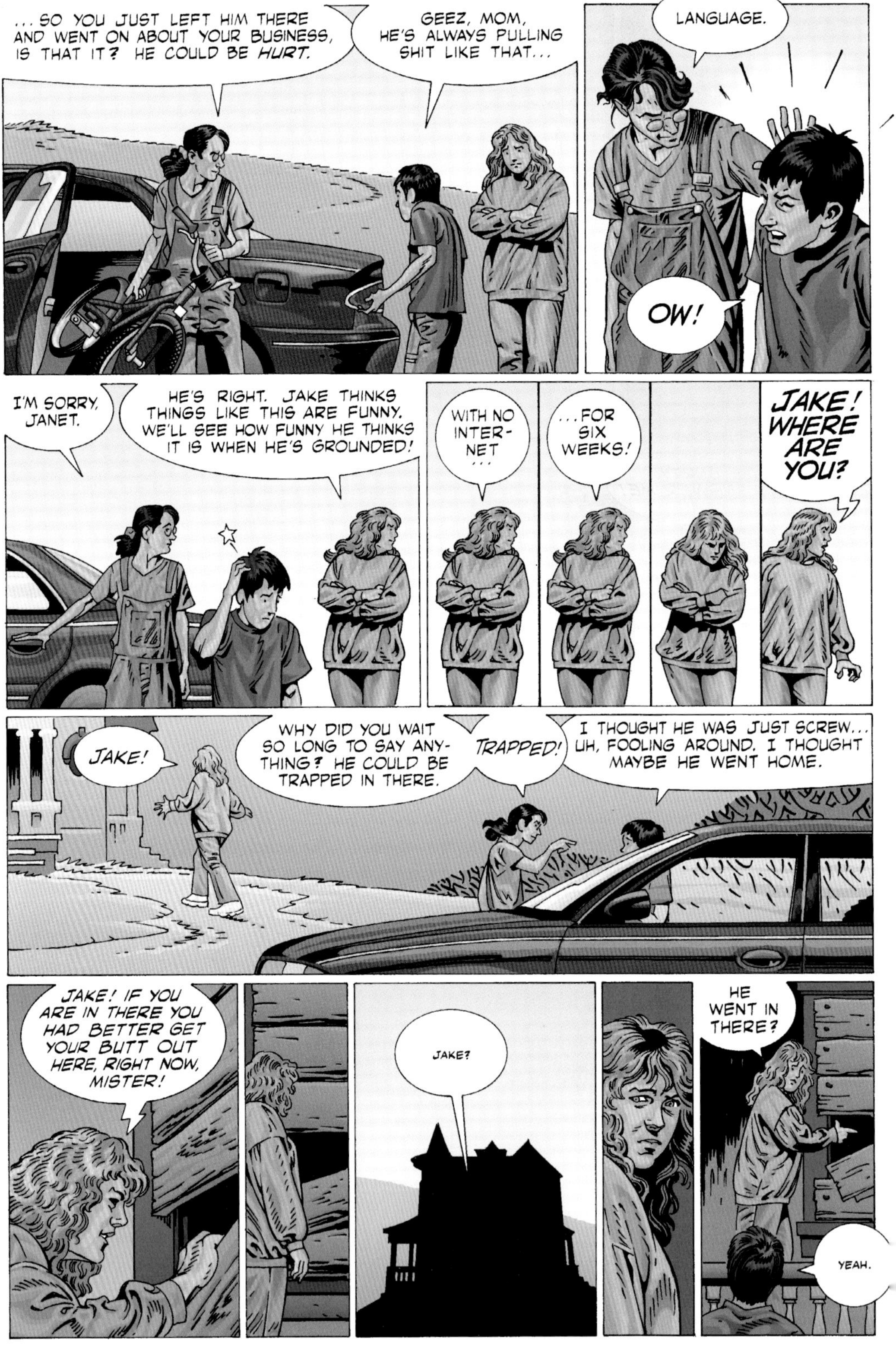
...SO YOU JUST LEFT HIM THERE AND WENT ON ABOUT YOUR BUSINESS, IS THAT IT? HE COULD BE HURT.
GEEZ, MOM, HE'S ALWAYS PULLING SHIT LIKE THAT...
LANGUAGE.
OW!
I'M SORRY, JANET.
HE'S RIGHT. JAKE THINKS THINGS LIKE THIS ARE FUNNY. WE'LL SEE HOW FUNNY HE THINKS IT IS WHEN HE'S GROUNDED!
WITH NO INTER-NET...
...FOR SIX WEEKS!
JAKE! WHERE ARE YOU?
JAKE!
WHY DID YOU WAIT SO LONG TO SAY ANY-THING? HE COULD BE TRAPPED IN THERE.
TRAPPED!
I THOUGHT HE WAS JUST SCREW... UH, FOOLING AROUND. I THOUGHT MAYBE HE WENT HOME.
JAKE! IF YOU ARE IN THERE YOU HAD BETTER GET YOUR BUTT OUT HERE, RIGHT NOW, MISTER!
JAKE?
HE WENT IN THERE?
YEAH.

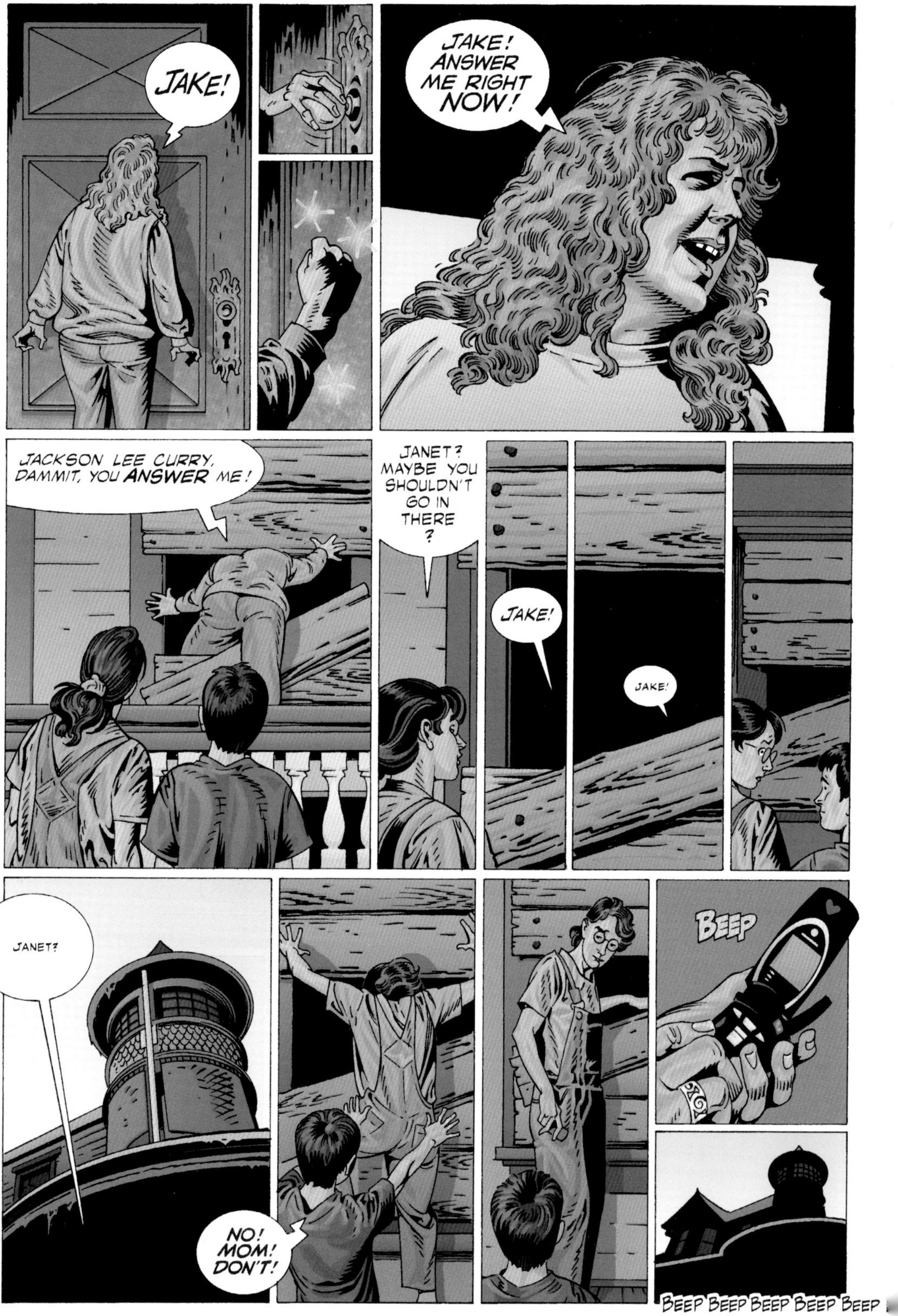

JAKE!
JAKE! ANSWER ME RIGHT NOW!
JACKSON LEE CURRY, DAMMIT, YOU ANSWER ME!
JANET? MAYBE YOU SHOULDN'T GO IN THERE?
JAKE!
JAKE!
JANET?
NO! MOM! DON'T!
BEEP
BEEP BEEP BEEP BEEP BEEP

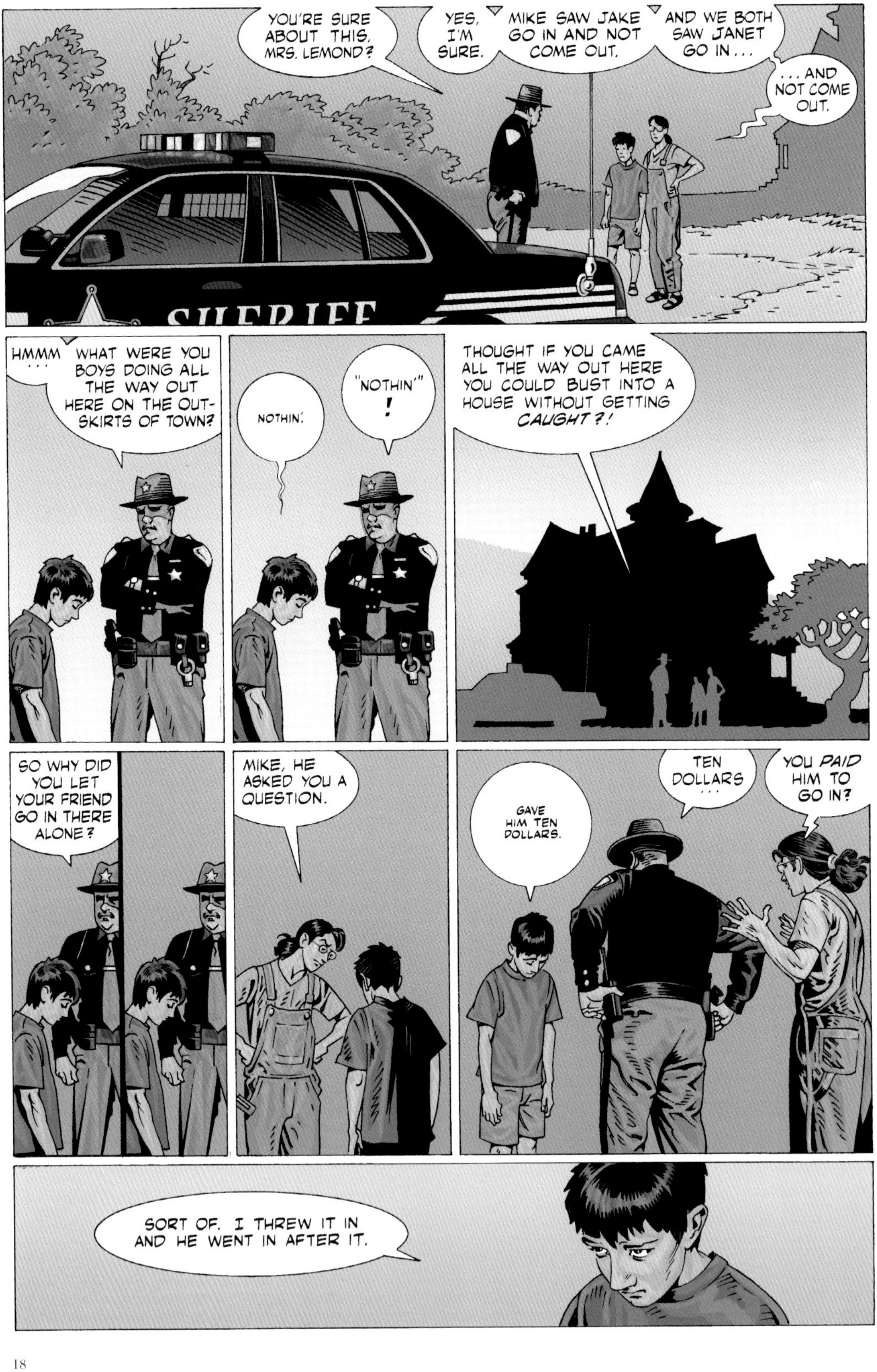
YOU'RE SURE ABOUT THIS, MRS. LEMOND?
YES, I'M SURE.
MIKE SAW JAKE GO IN AND NOT COME OUT.
AND WE BOTH SAW JANET GO IN...
...AND NOT COME OUT.
SHERIFF
HMMM...
WHAT WERE YOU BOYS DOING ALL THE WAY OUT HERE ON THE OUT-SKIRTS OF TOWN?
NOTHIN'.
"NOTHIN'" !
THOUGHT IF YOU CAME ALL THE WAY OUT HERE YOU COULD BUST INTO A HOUSE WITHOUT GETTING CAUGHT?!
SO WHY DID YOU LET YOUR FRIEND GO IN THERE ALONE?
MIKE, HE ASKED YOU A QUESTION.
GAVE HIM TEN DOLLARS.
TEN DOLLARS...
YOU PAID HIM TO GO IN?
SORT OF. I THREW IT IN AND HE WENT IN AFTER IT.

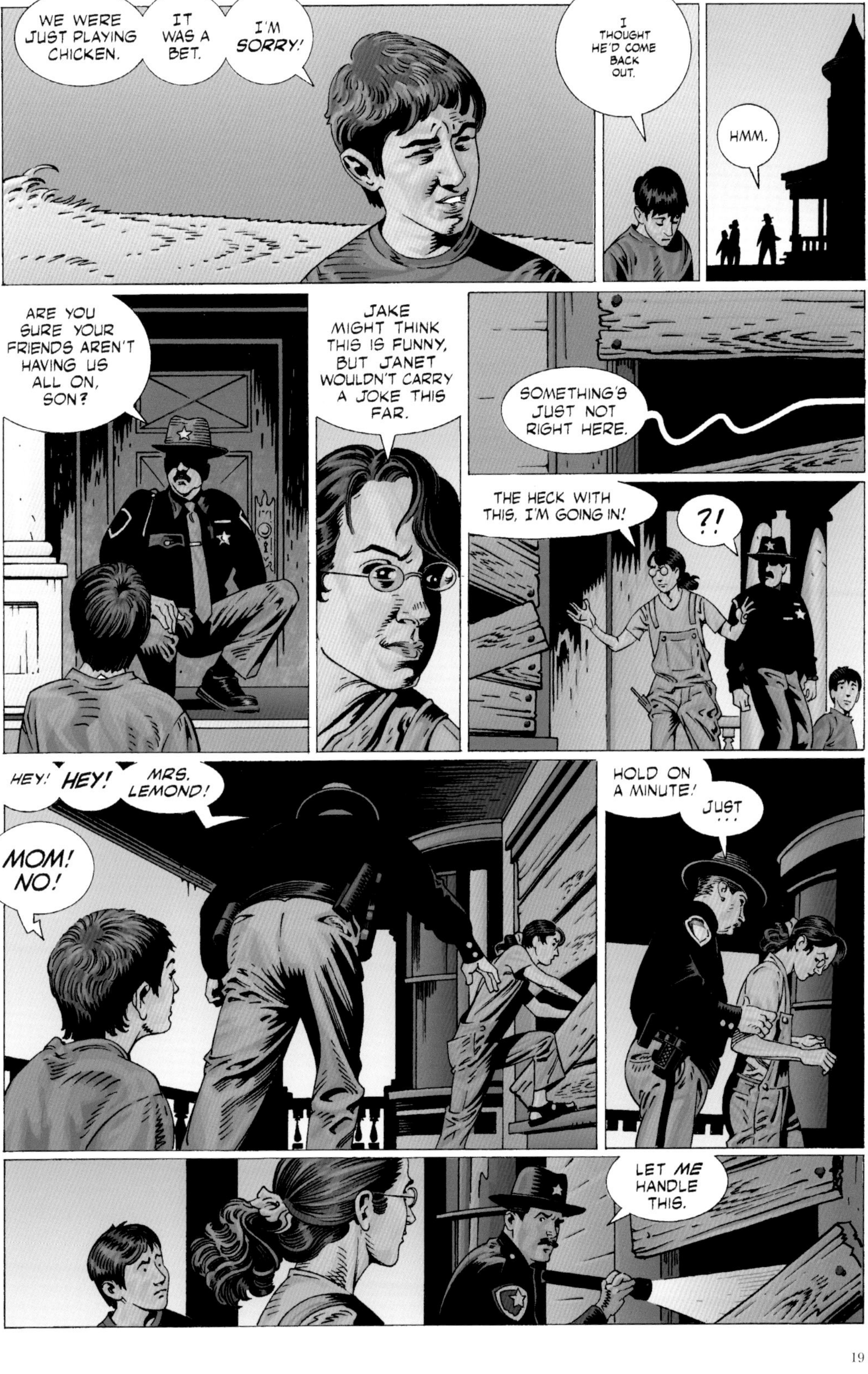
WE WERE JUST PLAYING CHICKEN.
IT WAS A BET.
I'M SORRY!
I THOUGHT HE'D COME BACK OUT.
HMM.
ARE YOU SURE YOUR FRIENDS AREN'T HAVING US ALL ON, SON?
JAKE MIGHT THINK THIS IS FUNNY, BUT JANET WOULDN'T CARRY A JOKE THIS FAR.
SOMETHING'S JUST NOT RIGHT HERE.
THE HECK WITH THIS, I'M GOING IN!
?!
HEY!
HEY!
MRS. LEMOND!
MOM! NO!
HOLD ON A MINUTE!
JUST . . .
LET ME HANDLE THIS.

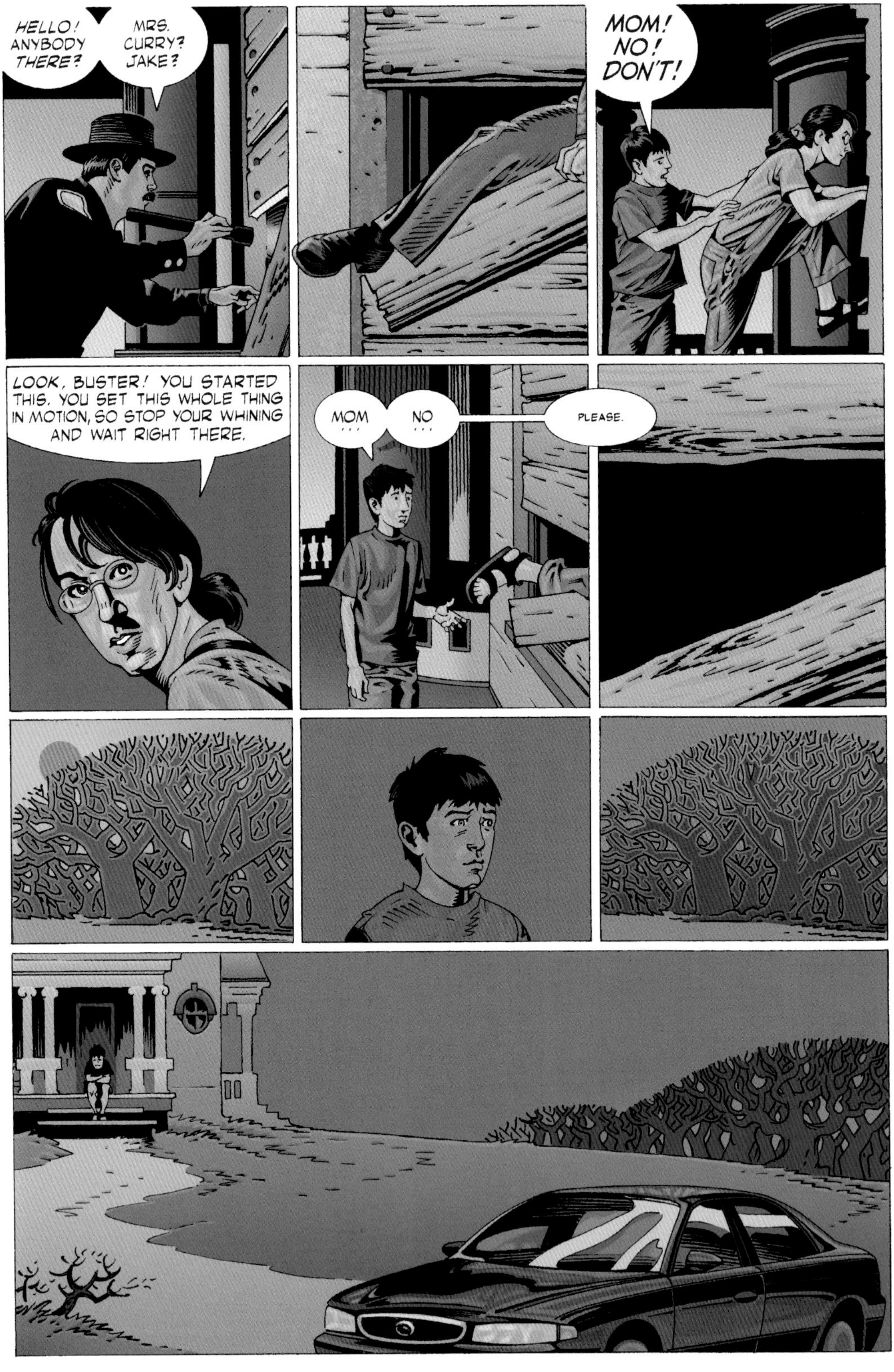
HELLO! ANYBODY THERE?
MRS. CURRY? JAKE?
MOM! NO! DON'T!
LOOK, BUSTER! YOU STARTED THIS. YOU SET THIS WHOLE THING IN MOTION, SO STOP YOUR WHINING AND WAIT RIGHT THERE.
MOM ...
NO ...
PLEASE.

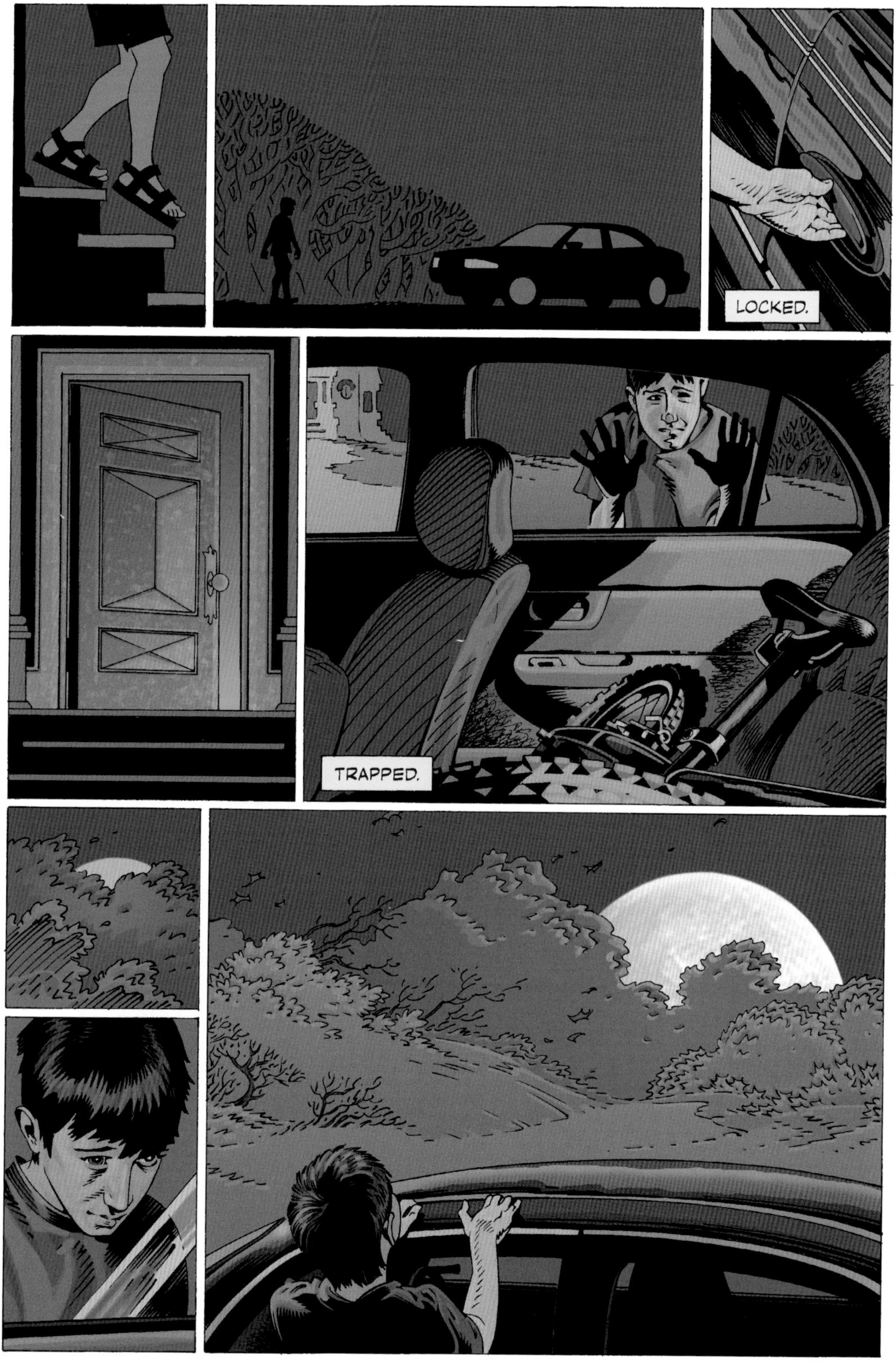
LOCKED.
TRAPPED.

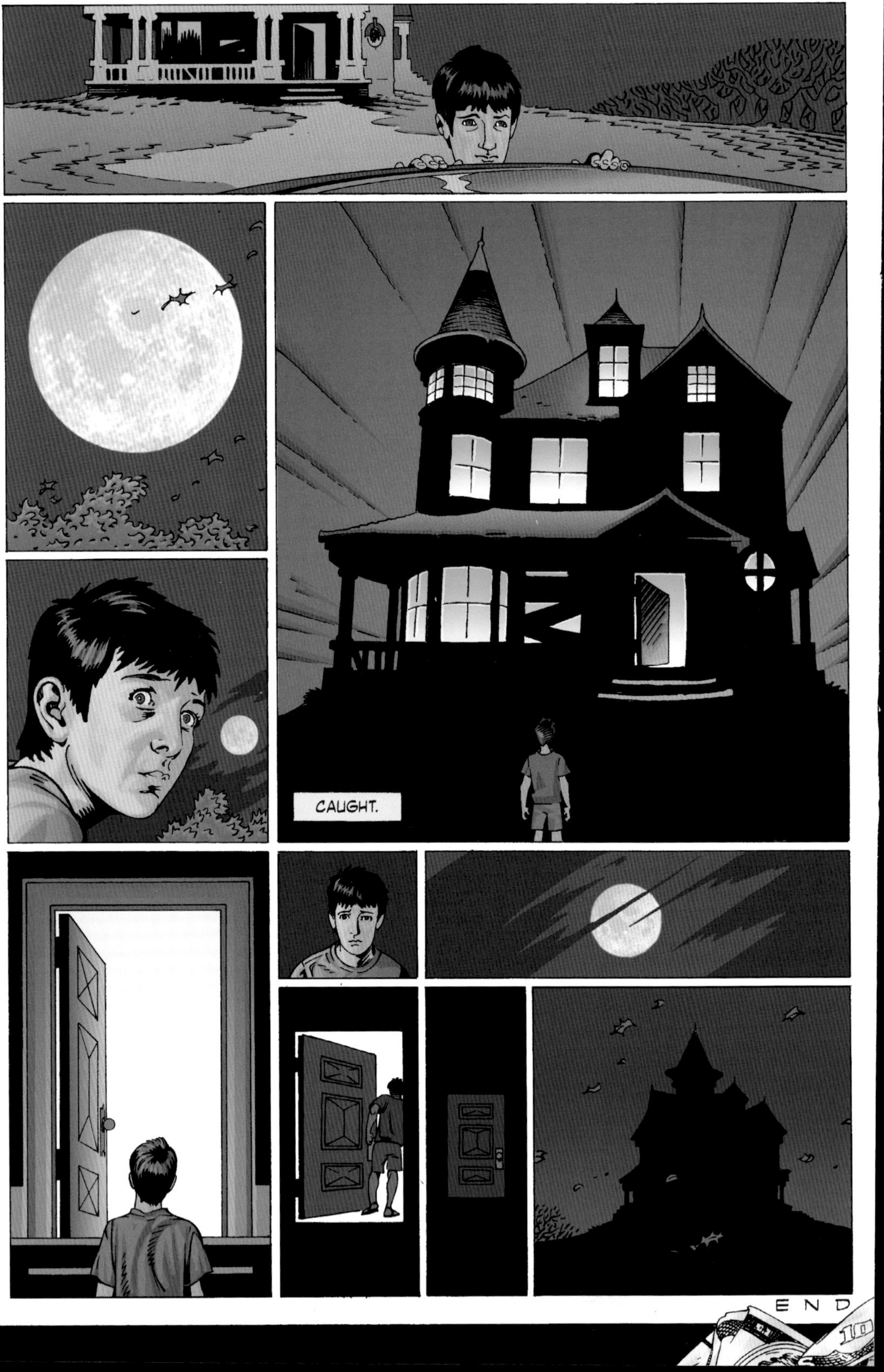
CAUGHT.
END

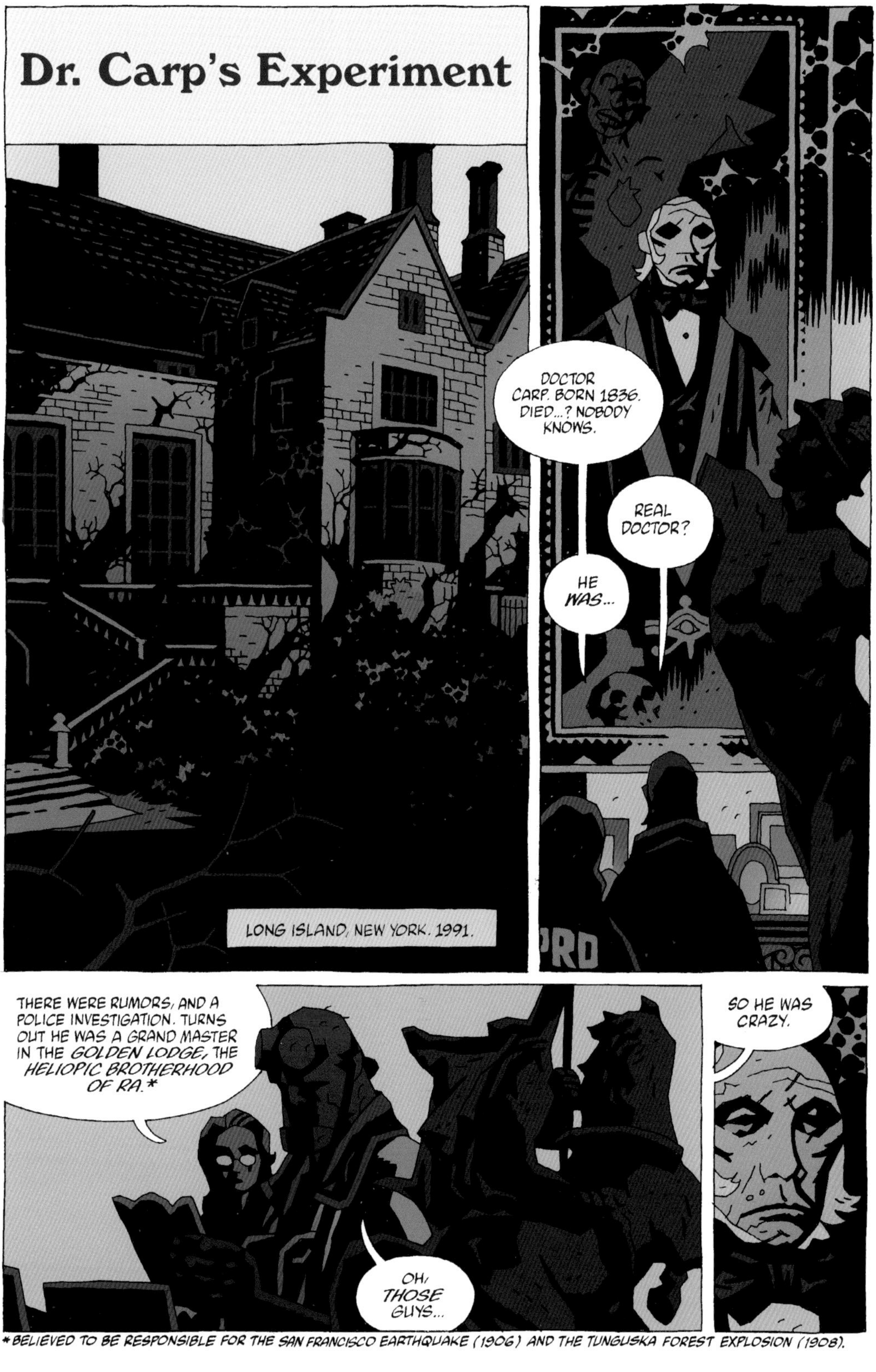
Dr. Carp's Experiment
LONG ISLAND, NEW YORK. 1991.
DOCTOR CARP. BORN 1836. DIED...? NOBODY KNOWS.
REAL DOCTOR?
HE *WAS*...
THERE WERE RUMORS, AND A POLICE INVESTIGATION. TURNS OUT HE WAS A GRAND MASTER IN THE *GOLDEN LODGE*, THE *HELIOPIC BROTHERHOOD OF RA*.*
OH, *THOSE* GUYS...
SO HE WAS CRAZY.

*BELIEVED TO BE RESPONSIBLE FOR THE SAN FRANCISCO EARTHQUAKE (1906) AND THE TUNGUSKA FOREST EXPLOSION (1908).

WHAT HAPPENED TO HIM?

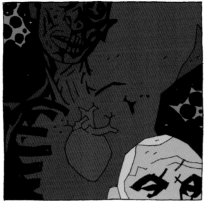

HE DISAPPEARED IN 1902, THEN HIS SISTER MOVED IN AND LIVED HERE, TILL SHE DIED IN 1911. THE HOUSE HAS BEEN PRETTY MUCH EMPTY SINCE THEN.

HOW HAUNTED IS IT?

NOT TOO BAD.

"THE USUAL STUFF..."

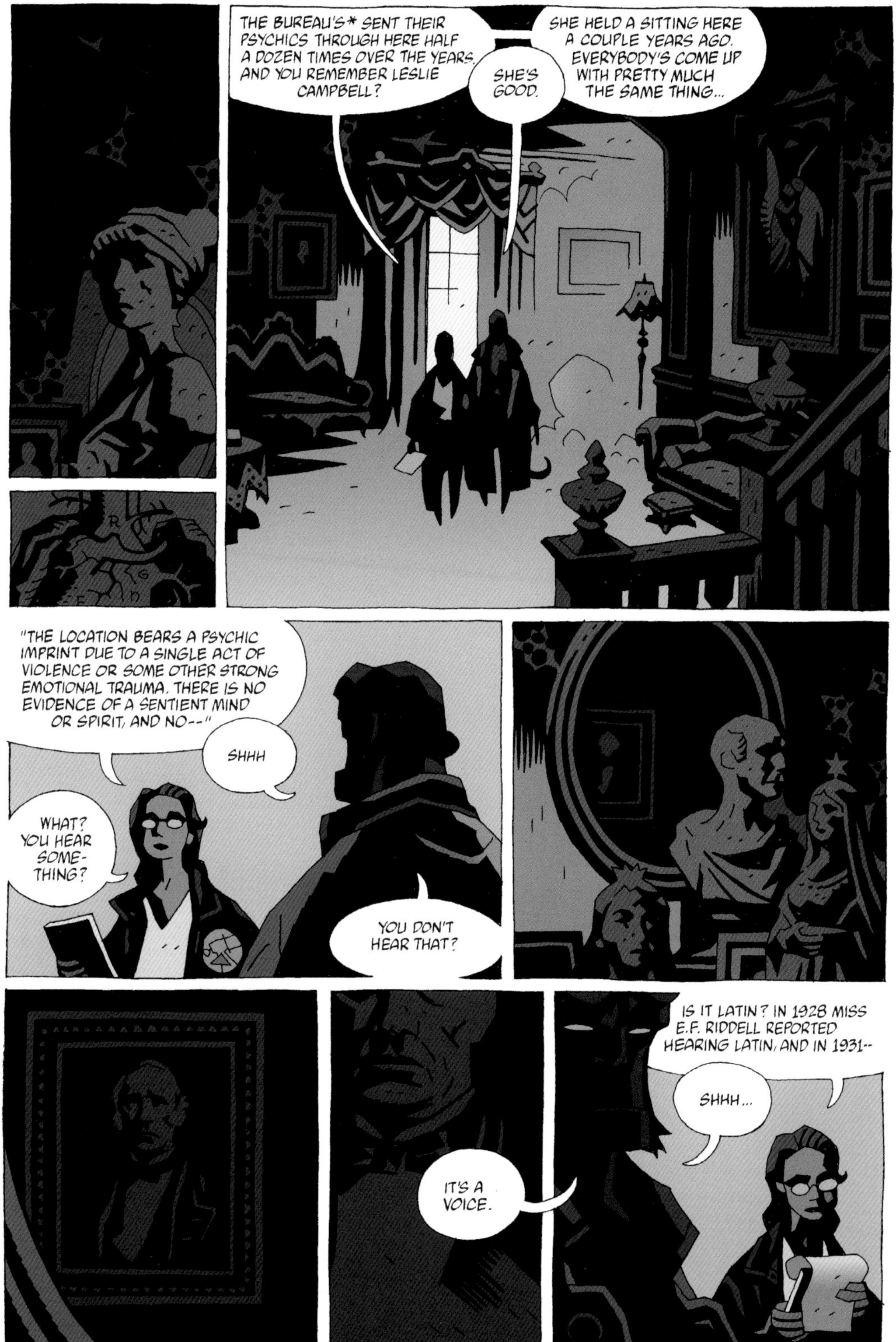
THE BUREAU'S* SENT THEIR PSYCHICS THROUGH HERE HALF A DOZEN TIMES OVER THE YEARS. AND YOU REMEMBER LESLIE CAMPBELL?
SHE'S GOOD.
SHE HELD A SITTING HERE A COUPLE YEARS AGO. EVERYBODY'S COME UP WITH PRETTY MUCH THE SAME THING...
"THE LOCATION BEARS A PSYCHIC IMPRINT DUE TO A SINGLE ACT OF VIOLENCE OR SOME OTHER STRONG EMOTIONAL TRAUMA. THERE IS NO EVIDENCE OF A SENTIENT MIND OR SPIRIT, AND NO--"
SHHH
WHAT? YOU HEAR SOME-THING?
YOU DON'T HEAR THAT?
IS IT LATIN? IN 1928 MISS E.F. RIDDELL REPORTED HEARING LATIN, AND IN 1931--
SHHH...
IT'S A VOICE.

*BUREAU FOR PARANORMAL RESEARCH AND DEFENSE

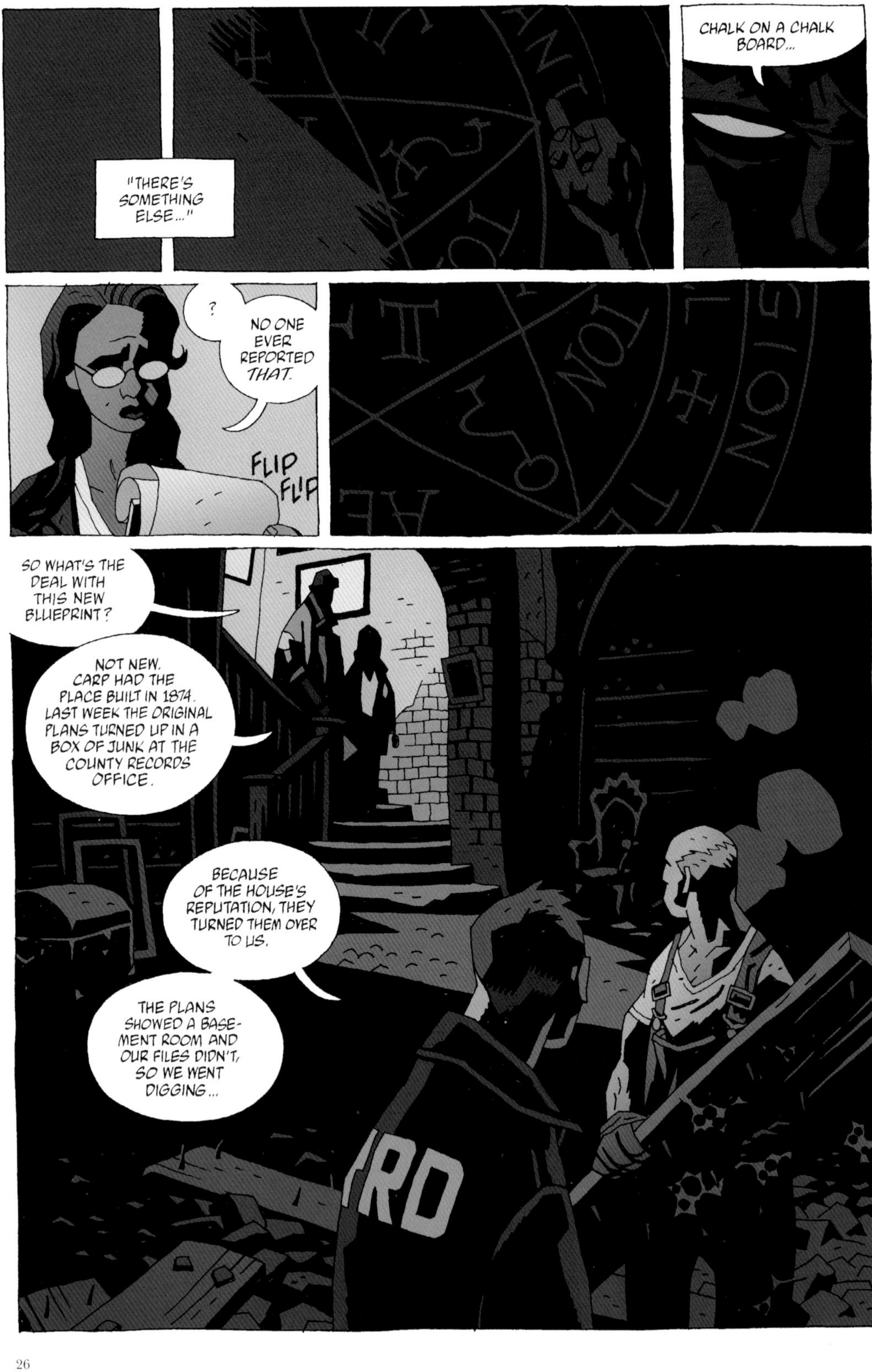
"THERE'S SOMETHING ELSE..."
CHALK ON A CHALK BOARD...
?
NO ONE EVER REPORTED THAT.
FLIP
FLIP
SO WHAT'S THE DEAL WITH THIS NEW BLUEPRINT?
NOT NEW. CARP HAD THE PLACE BUILT IN 1874. LAST WEEK THE ORIGINAL PLANS TURNED UP IN A BOX OF JUNK AT THE COUNTY RECORDS OFFICE.
BECAUSE OF THE HOUSE'S REPUTATION, THEY TURNED THEM OVER TO US.
THE PLANS SHOWED A BASEMENT ROOM AND OUR FILES DIDN'T, SO WE WENT DIGGING...
RD

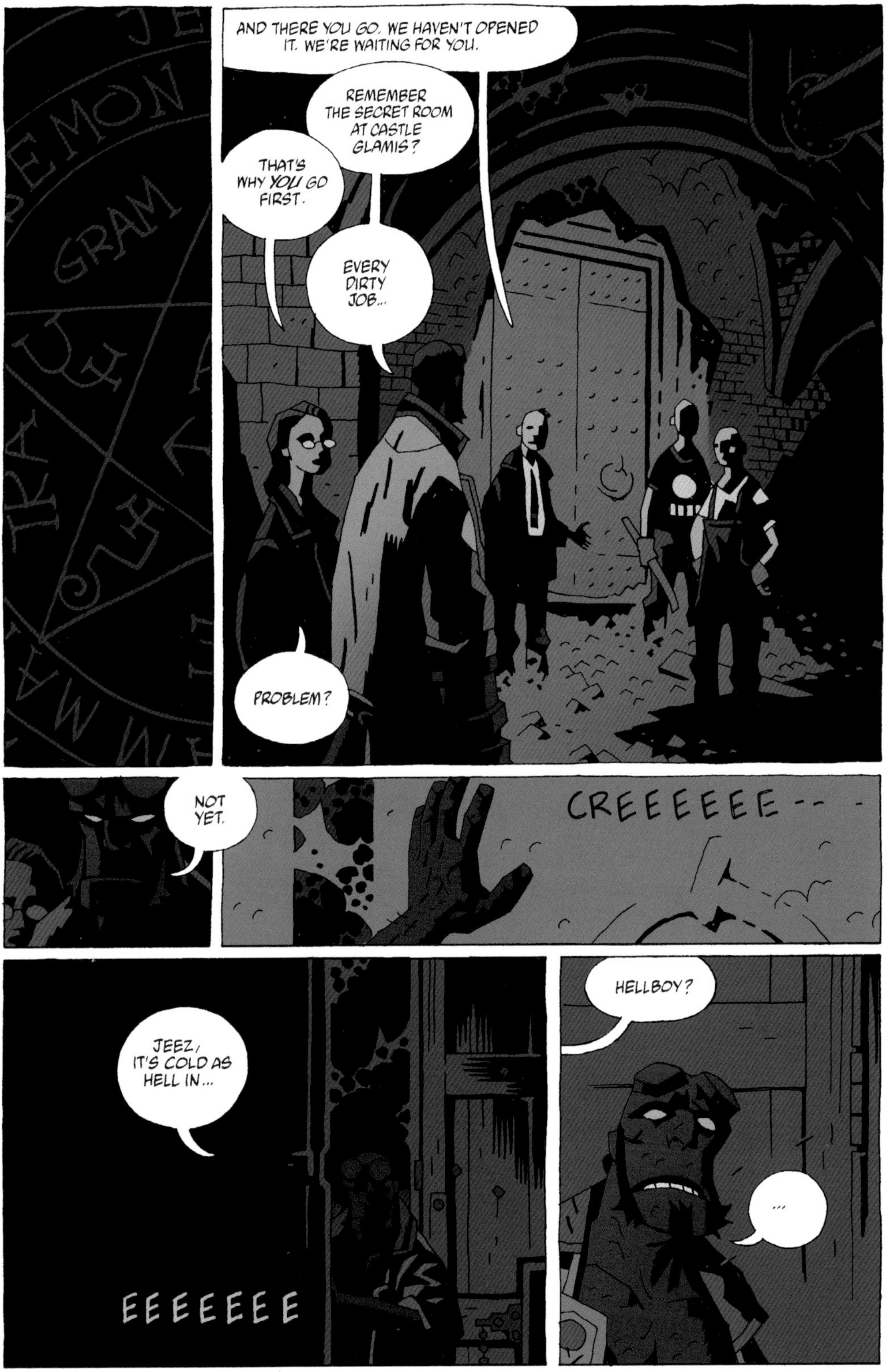
AND THERE YOU GO. WE HAVEN'T OPENED IT. WE'RE WAITING FOR YOU.
REMEMBER THE SECRET ROOM AT CASTLE GLAMIS?
THAT'S WHY YOU GO FIRST.
EVERY DIRTY JOB...
PROBLEM?
NOT YET.
CREEEEEE--
JEEZ, IT'S COLD AS HELL IN...
EEEEEEE
HELLBOY?
...

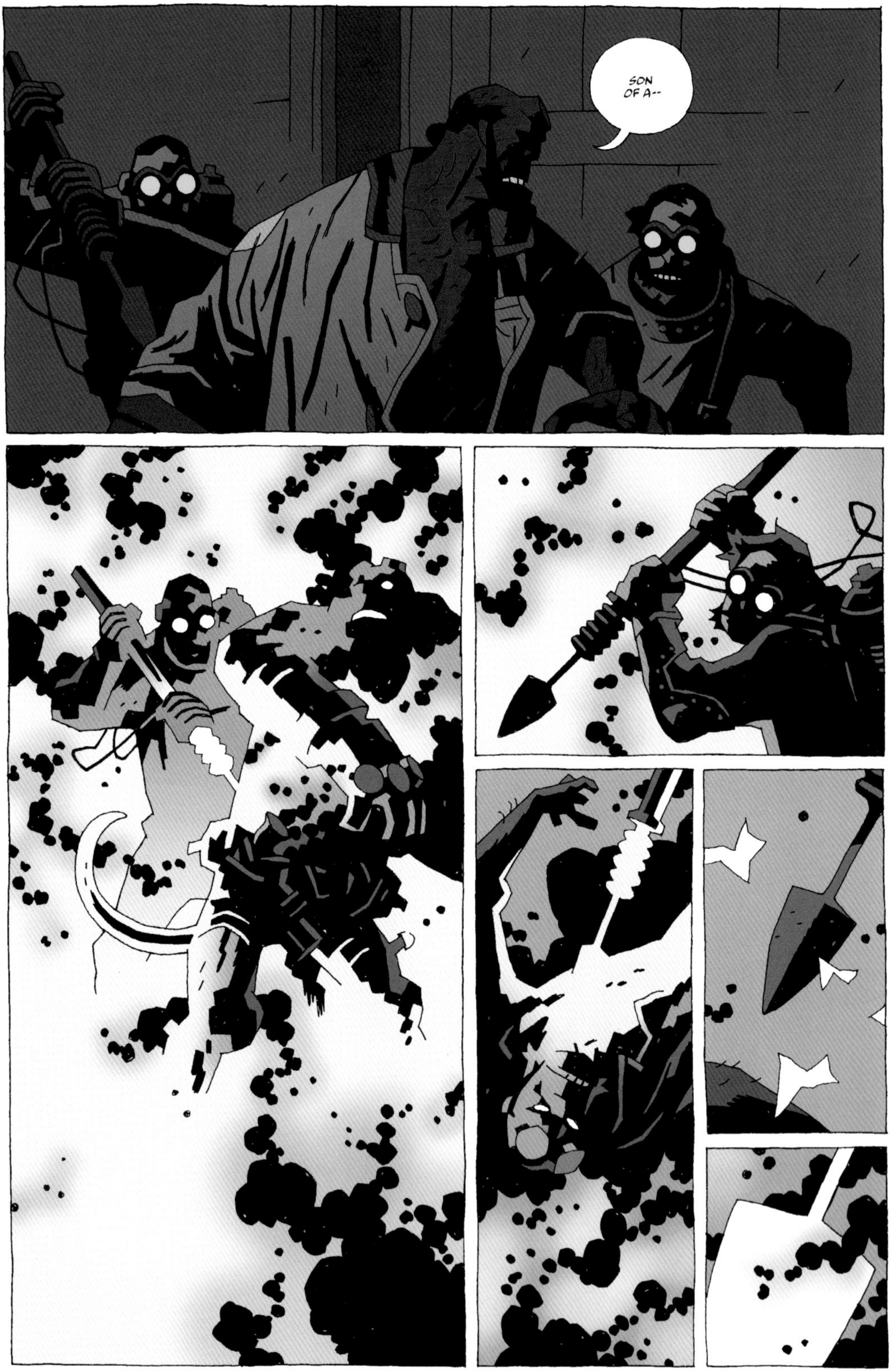
SON OF A--

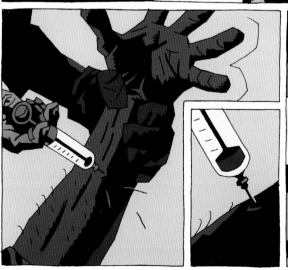

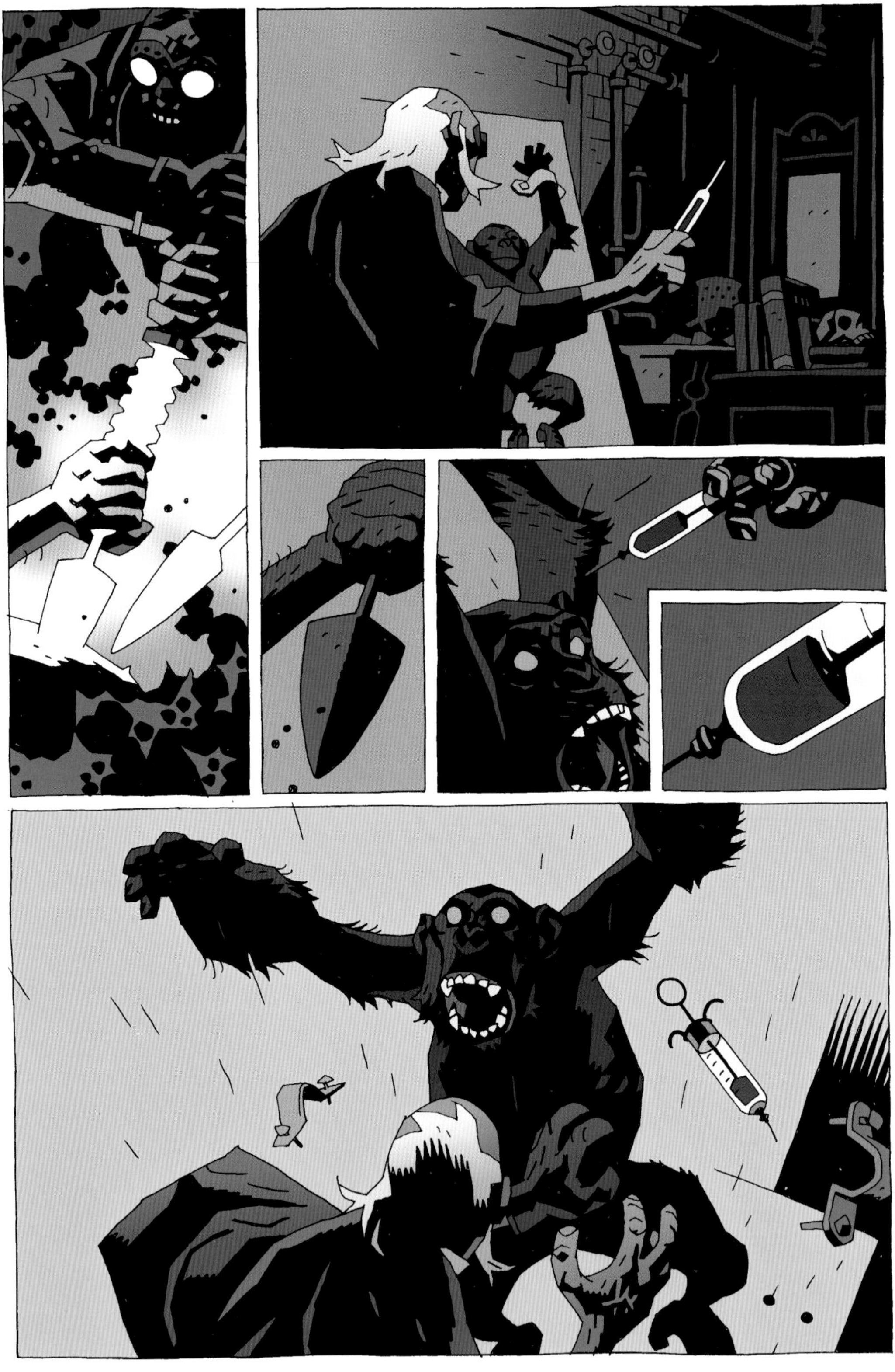

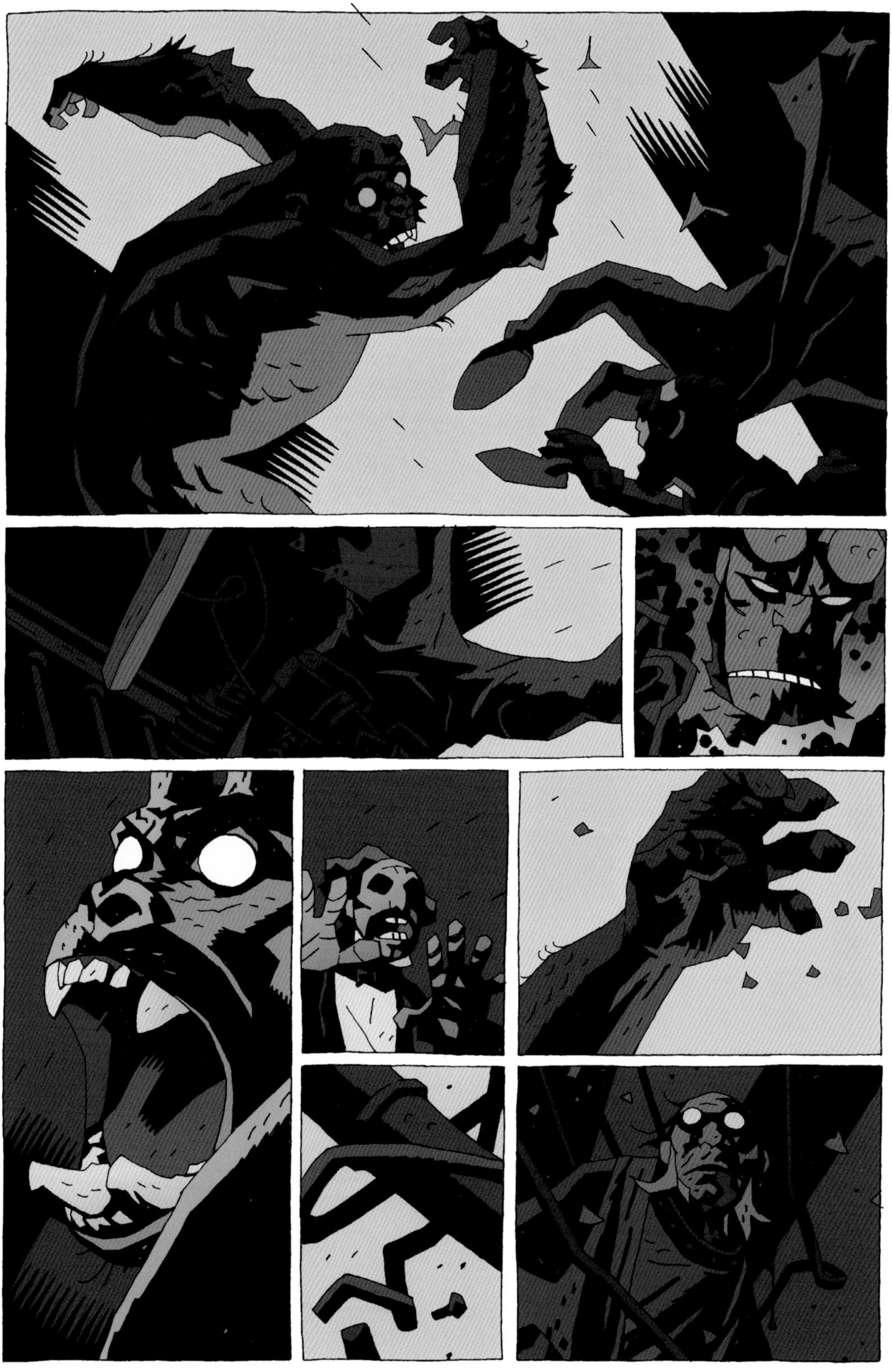

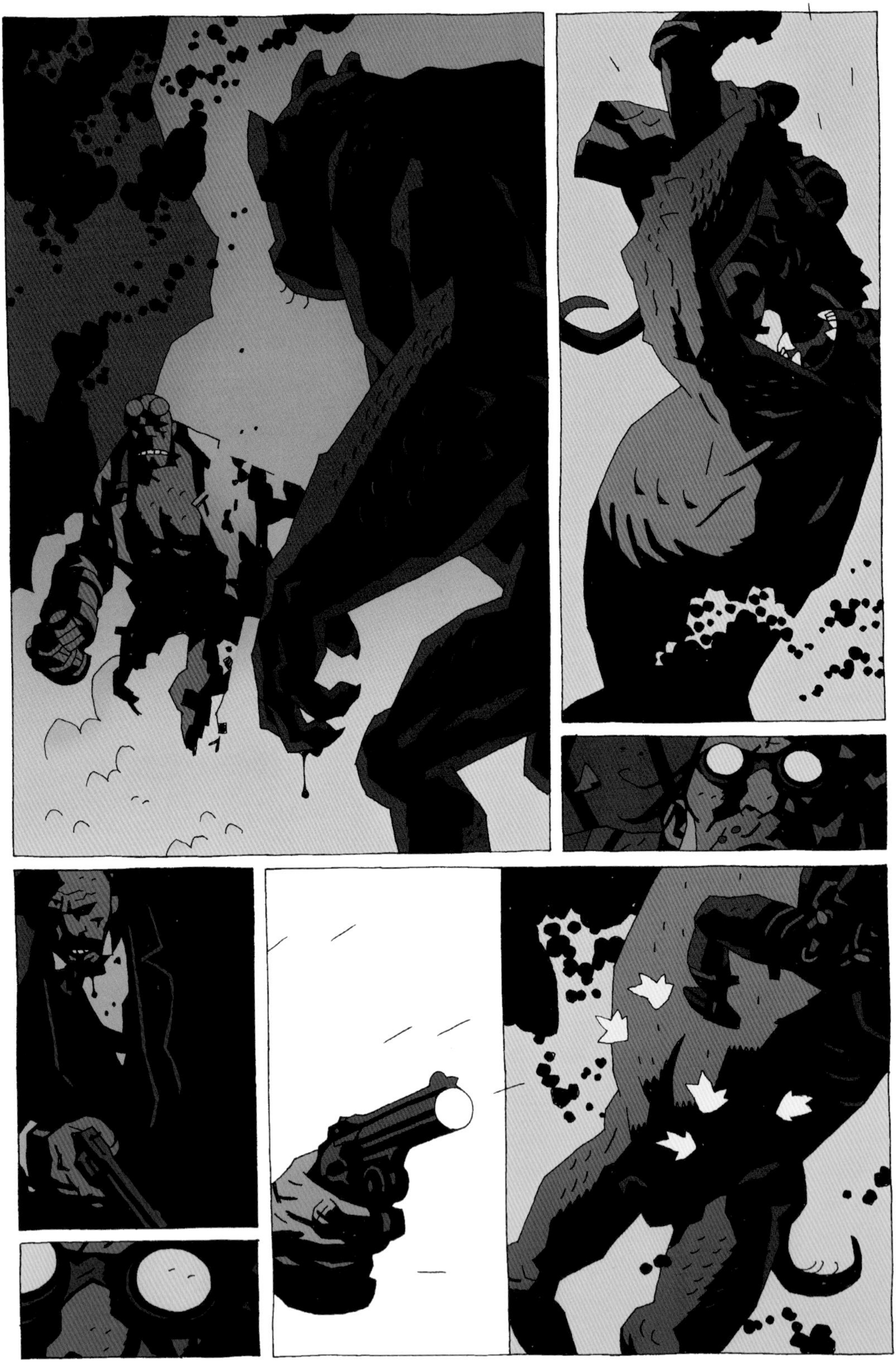

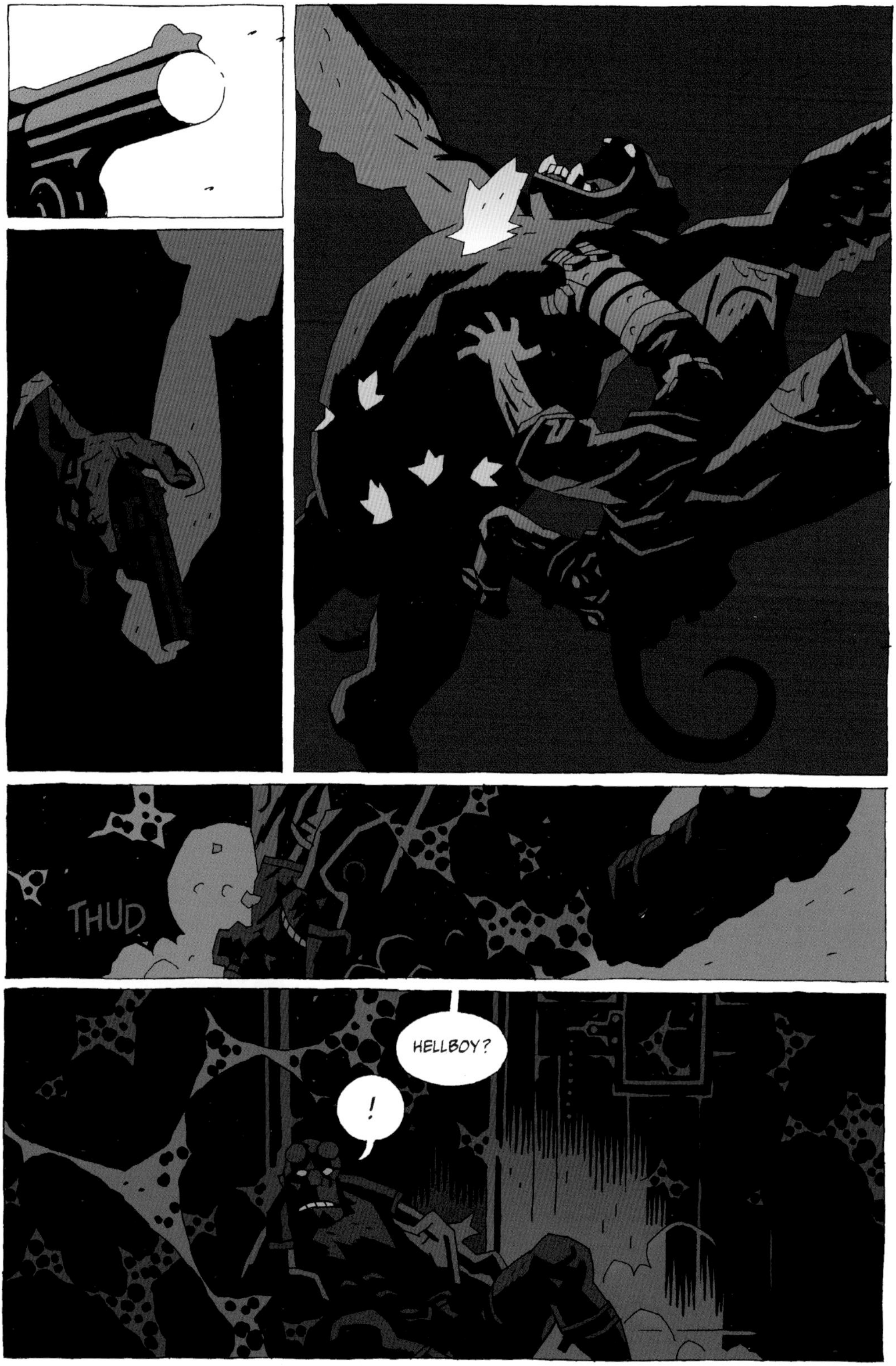
THUD
HELLBOY?
!

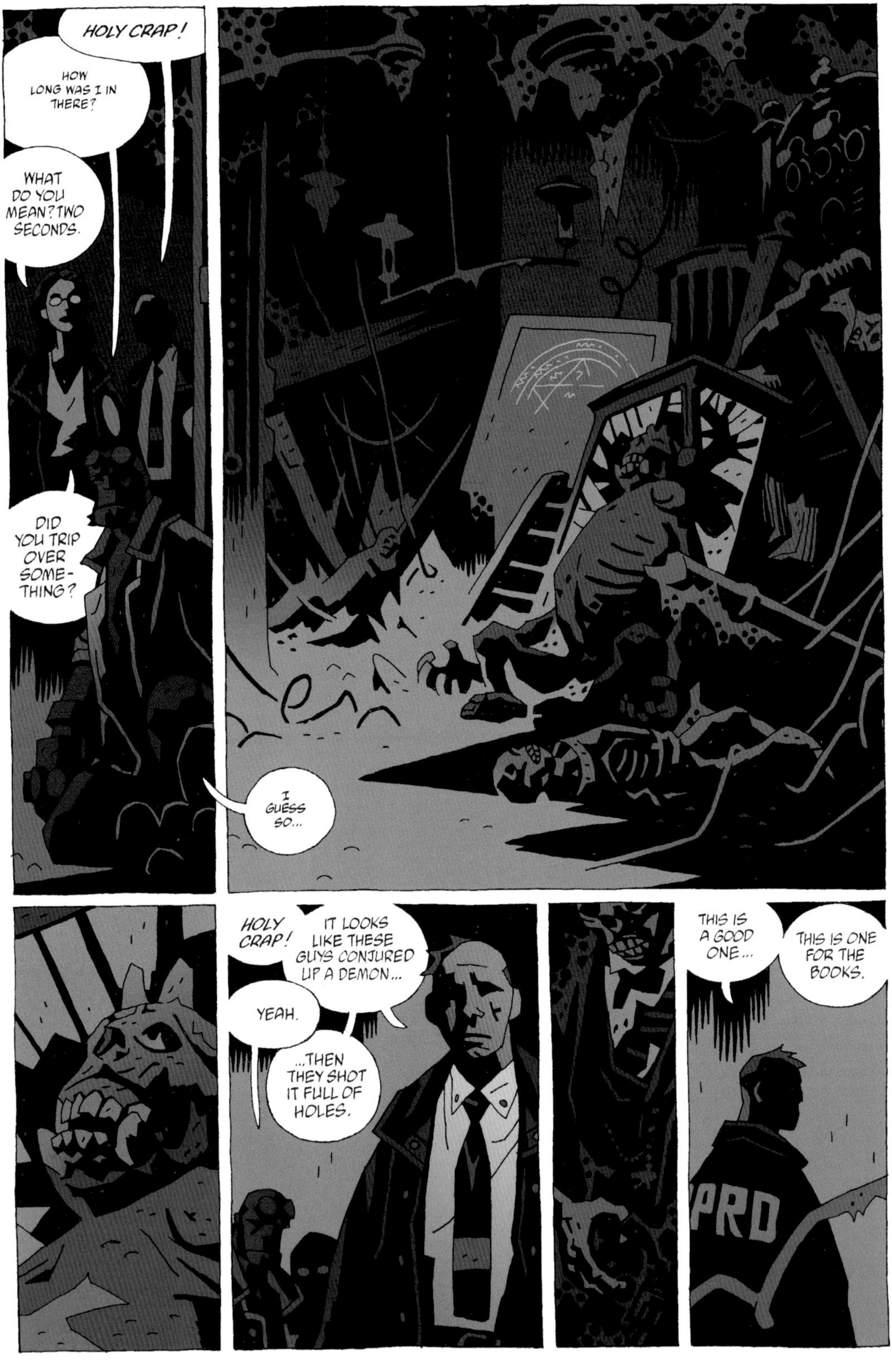
HOLY CRAP!
HOW LONG WAS I IN THERE?
WHAT DO YOU MEAN? TWO SECONDS.
DID YOU TRIP OVER SOME-THING?
I GUESS SO...
HOLY CRAP!
IT LOOKS LIKE THESE GUYS CONJURED UP A DEMON...
YEAH.
...THEN THEY SHOT IT FULL OF HOLES.
THIS IS A GOOD ONE...
THIS IS ONE FOR THE BOOKS.
PRD

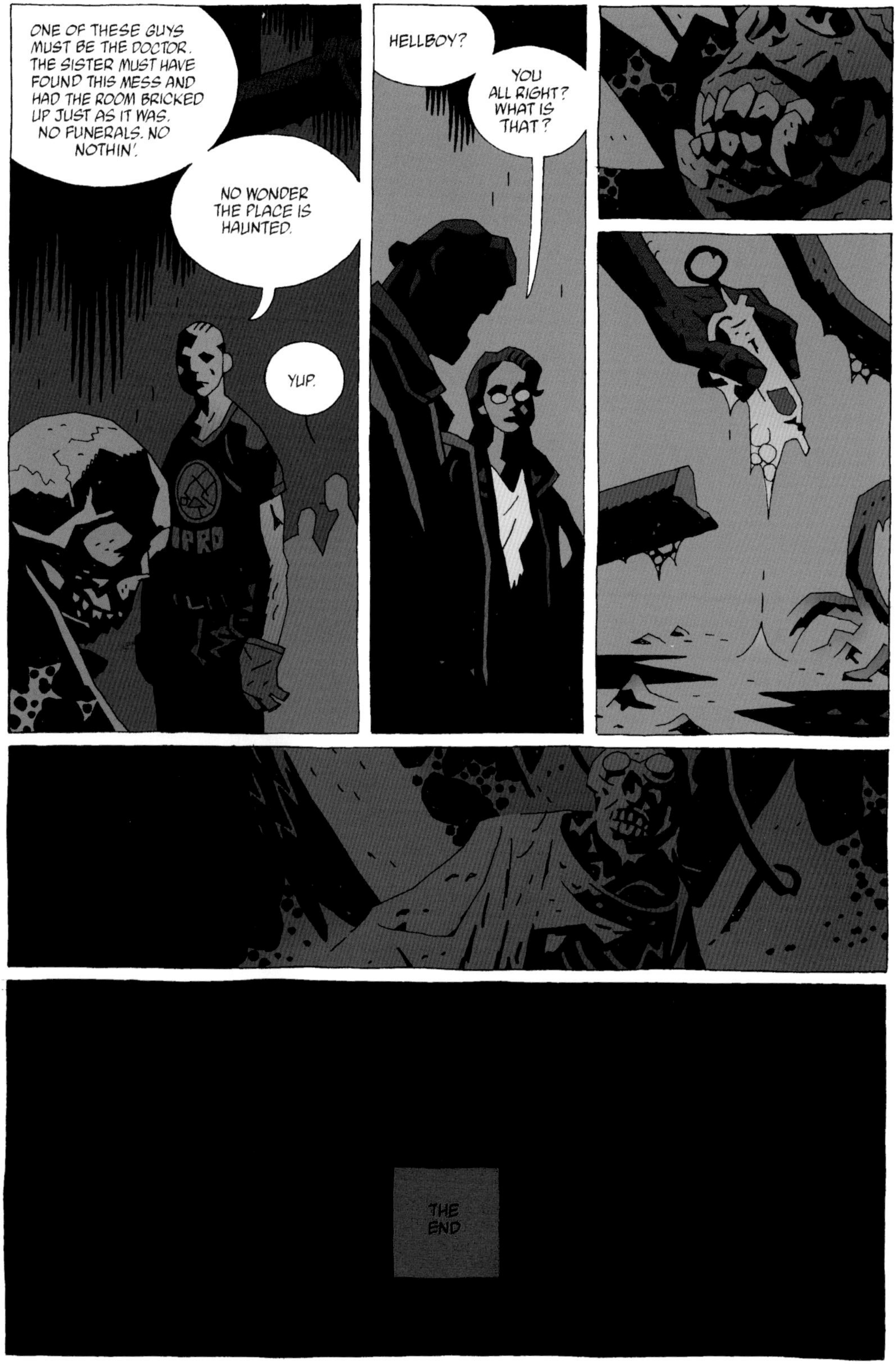
ONE OF THESE GUYS MUST BE THE DOCTOR. THE SISTER MUST HAVE FOUND THIS MESS AND HAD THE ROOM BRICKED UP JUST AS IT WAS. NO FUNERALS. NO NOTHIN'.
NO WONDER THE PLACE IS HAUNTED.
YUP.
HELLBOY?
YOU ALL RIGHT? WHAT IS THAT?
THE END

Thurnley Abbey

by PERCEVAL LANDON

ILLUSTRATIONS *by* GARY GIANNI

T hree years ago I was on my way out to the East, and as an extra day in London was of some importance, I took the Friday evening mail-train to Brindisi instead of the usual Thursday morning Marseilles express. Many people shrink from the long, forty-eight-hour train journey through Europe, and the subsequent rush across the Mediterranean on the nineteen-knot *Isis* or *Osiris*; but there is really very little discomfort on either the train or the mail-boat, and unless there is actually nothing for me to do, I always like to save the extra day and a half in London. This time—it was early in the shipping season, probably about the beginning of September— there were few passengers, and I had a compartment to myself in the P. & O. Indian Express all the way from Calais. The journey was just like any other. We slept after luncheon; we dawdled the afternoon away with yellow-backed novels; sometimes we exchanged platitudes in the smoking room, and it was there that I met Alastair Colvin.

Colvin was a man of middle height, with a resolute, well-cut jaw; his hair was turning grey; his moustache was sun whitened, but otherwise he was clean-shaven—obviously a gentleman, and obviously also a preoccupied man. He had no great wit. When spoken to, he made the usual remarks in the right way, and I dare say he refrained from banalities only because he spoke less than the rest of us.

Of course this did not seem to me to be of any importance. Most travelers by train become a trifle infirm of purpose after thirty-six hours' rattling. But Colvin's restless way I noticed in somewhat marked contrast with the man's personal importance and dignity, especially ill suited to his finely made large hand with strong, broad, regular nails and its few lines. As I looked at his hand I noticed a long, deep, and recent scar of ragged shape. However, it is absurd to pretend that I thought anything was unusual. I went off at five o'clock on Sunday afternoon to sleep away the hour or two that had still to be got through before we arrived at Brindisi.

Once there, we few passengers transhipped our hand baggage, verified our berths—there were only a score of us in all—and then, after an aimless ramble of half an hour in Brindisi, we returned to dinner at the Hotel International, not wholly surprised that the town had been the death of Virgil. After dinner I was looking with awe at a trellis overgrown with blue vines, when Colvin moved across the room to my table. He picked up *Il Secolo*, but almost immediately gave up the pretence of reading it. He turned squarely to me and said:

"Would you do me a favour?"

One doesn't do favours to stray acquaintances on Continental expresses without knowing something more of them than I knew of Colvin. But I smiled in a noncommittal way, and asked him what he wanted. I wasn't wrong in part of my estimate of him; he said bluntly:

"Will you let me sleep in your cabin on the *Osiris*?" And he coloured a little as he said it.

Now, there is nothing more tiresome than having to put up with a stable companion at sea, and I asked him rather pointedly:

"Surely there is room for all of us?" I thought that perhaps he had been partnered off with some mangy Levantine, and wanted to escape from him at all hazards.

Colvin, still somewhat confused, said, "Yes, I am in a cabin by myself. But you would do me the greatest favour if you would allow me to share yours."

This was all very well, but, besides the fact that I always sleep better when alone, there had been some recent thefts onboard English liners, and I hesitated, frank and honest and self-conscious as Colvin was. Just then the mail-train came in with a clatter and a rush of escaping steam, and I asked him to see me again about it on the boat when we started. He answered me curtly—I suppose he saw the mistrust in my manner—"I am a member of White's." I smiled to myself as he said it, but I remembered in a moment that the man—if he were really what he claimed to be, and I make no doubt that he was—must have been sorely put to it before he urged that fact as a guarantee of his respectability to a total stranger at a Brindisi hotel.

That evening, as we cleared the red and green harbor lights of Brindisi, Colvin explained. This is his story in his own words.

"When I was traveling in India some years ago, I made the acquaintance of a youngish man in the Woods and Forests. We camped out together for a week, and I found him a pleasant companion. John Broughton was a light-hearted soul when off duty, but a steady and capable man in any of the small emergencies that continually arise in that department. He was liked and trusted by the natives, and though a trifle over-pleased with himself when he escaped to civilization at Simla or Calcutta, Broughton's future was well assured in government service, when a fair-sized estate was unexpectedly left to him, and he joyfully shook the dust of the Indian plains from his feet and returned to England. For five years he drifted about London. I saw him now and then. We dined together about every eighteen months, and I could trace pretty exactly the gradual sickening of Broughton with a merely idle life. At last he told me that he had decided to marry and settle down at his place, Thurnley Abbey, which had long been empty. He spoke about looking after the property and standing for his constituency in the usual way. Vivien Wilde, his fiancée, had, I suppose, begun to take him in hand.

"Among other things, I asked him about Thurnley Abbey. He confessed that he hardly knew the place. The last tenant, a man called Clarke, had lived in one wing for fifteen years and seen no one. He had been a miser and a hermit. It was the rarest thing for a light to be seen at the Abbey after dark. Only the barest necessities of life were ordered, and the tenant himself received them at the side door. His one half-caste manservant, after a month's stay in the house, had abruptly left without warning, and had returned to the Southern States. One thing Broughton complained bitterly about: Clarke had wilfully spread the rumor among the villagers that the Abbey was haunted, and had even condescended to play childish tricks with spirit-lamps and salt in order to scare trespassers away at night. He had been detected in the act of this tomfoolery, but the story spread, and no one, said Broughton, would venture near the house except in broad daylight. The hauntedness of Thurnley Abbey was now, he said with a grin, part of the gospel of the countryside, but he and his young wife were going to change all that. Would I propose myself any time I liked? I, of course, said I would, and equally, of course, intended to do nothing of the sort without a definite invitation.

"The house was put in thorough repair, though not a stick of the old furniture and tapestry was removed. Floors and ceilings were relaid; the roof was made watertight again, and the dust of half a century was scoured out. It was called an Abbey, though as a matter of fact it had been only the infirmary of the long-vanished Abbey of Clouster some five miles away. The larger part of the building remained as it had been in pre-Reformation days, but a wing had been added in Jacobean times, and that part of the house had been kept in something like repair by Mr. Clarke. He had, in both the ground and first floors, set heavy timber doors, strongly barred with iron, in the passage between the earlier and the Jacobean parts of the house, and had entirely neglected the former. So there had been a good deal of work to be done.

"Broughton, whom I saw in London two or three times about this period, made a deal of fun over the positive refusal of the workmen to remain after sundown. Even after electric light had been put into every room, nothing would induce them to remain, though, as Broughton observed, electric light was death on ghosts. The legend of the Abbey's ghosts had gone far and wide,

and the men would take no risks. They went home in batches of five and six, and even during the daylight hours there was an inordinate amount of talking between one another, if either happened to be out of sight of his companion. On the whole, though nothing of any sort had been conjured up even by their heated imaginations during their five months' work upon the Abbey, the belief in the ghosts was rather strengthened than otherwise because of the men's confessed nervousness, and local tradition declared itself in favor of the ghost of an immured nun.

"'Good old nun!' said Broughton.

"I asked him whether in general he believed in the possibility of ghosts, and, rather to my surprise, he said that he couldn't say he entirely disbelieved in them. A man in India had told him one morning in camp that he believed that his mother was dead in England, as her vision had come to his tent the night before. He had not been alarmed, but had said nothing, and the figure vanished again. As a matter of fact, the next possible *dak-walla* brought on a telegram announcing the mother's death. 'There the thing was,' said Broughton. But at Thurnley he was practical enough. He roundly cursed the idiotic selfishness of Clarke, whose silly antics had caused all the inconvenience. At the same time, he couldn't refuse to sympathize to some extent with the ignorant workmen. 'My own idea,' said he, 'is that if a ghost ever does come in one's way, one ought to speak to it.'

"I agreed. Little as I knew of the ghost world and its conventions, I had always remembered that a spook was honor bound to wait to be spoken to. It didn't seem much to do, and I felt that the sound of one's own voice would at any rate reassure oneself as to one's wakefulness. But there are few ghosts outside Europe—few, that is, that a white man can see—and I had never been troubled with any. However, as I have said, I told Broughton that I agreed.

"So the wedding took place, and I went to it in a tall hat which I bought for the occasion, and the new Mrs. Broughton smiled very nicely at me afterwards. As it had to happen, I took the Orient Express that evening and was not in England again for nearly six months. Just before I came back, I got a letter from Broughton. He asked if I could see him in London or come to Thurnley, as he thought I should be better able to help him than anyone else he knew. I had nothing to do, so after dealing with some small accumulation of business during my absence, I packed a kit-bag and departed to Euston. I was met by Broughton's great limousine at Thurnley Road station, and after a drive of nearly seven miles, I could see the Abbey across a wide pasturage.

"Broughton had seen me coming from afar, and walked across from his other guests to welcome me. There was no doubt that the man was altered, gravely altered. He was nervous and fidgety, and I found him looking at me only when my eye was off him. I naturally asked him what he wanted of me. I told him I would do anything I could, but that I couldn't conceive what he lacked that I could provide. He said with a lusterless smile that there was, however, something, and that he would tell me the following morning. It struck me that he was somehow ashamed of himself, and perhaps ashamed of the part he was asking me to play. However, I dismissed the subject from my mind and went up to dress in my palatial room.

"It was a very large low room with oak beams projecting from the white ceiling. Every inch of the walls, including the doors, was covered with tapestry, and a remarkably fine Italian fourpost bedstead, heavily draped, added to the darkness and dignity of the place. All the furniture was old, well made, and dark. Underfoot there was a plain green pile carpet, the only new thing about the room except the electric-light fittings and the jugs and basins. Even the looking glass on the dressing table was an old pyramidal Venetian glass set in a heavy repoussé frame of tarnished silver.

"After a few minutes' cleaning up, I went downstairs. Nothing much happened at dinner. The people were very much like those of the garden party. A young

woman next to me
seemed anxious to know what
was being read in London. As she was
far more familiar than I with the most recent magazines and literary
supplements, I found salvation in being myself instructed in the tendencies of
modern fiction. She was a cheerless soul, yet nothing could have been less
creepy than the glitter of silver and glass, and the subdued lights and cackle of
conversation all around the dinner table.

"After the ladies had gone I found myself talking to the rural dean. He
was a thin, earnest man, who at once turned the conversation to old
Clarke's buffooneries. But, he said, Mr. Broughton had introduced such a
new and cheerful spirit, not only into the Abbey, but, he might say, into the
whole neighbourhood, that he had great hopes that the ignorant
superstitions of the past were henceforth destined to oblivion. Thereupon
his other neighbour, a portly gentleman of independent means and
position, audibly remarked, 'Amen,' which damped the rural dean, and we
talked of partridges past, partridges present, and pheasants to come. At the
other end of the table Broughton sat with a couple of his friends, red-faced
hunting men. Once I noticed that they were discussing me, but I paid no
attention to it at the time. I remembered it a few hours later.

"By eleven all the guests were gone, and Broughton, his wife, and I were
alone together under the fine plaster ceiling of the Jacobean drawing room.
Mrs. Broughton talked about one or two of the neighbours, and then, with

a smile, said that she knew I would excuse her, shook hands with me, and went off to bed. I am not very good at analyzing things, but I felt that she talked a little uncomfortably and with a suspicion of effort, smiled rather conventionally, and was obviously glad to go. These things seem trifling enough to repeat, but I had the faint feeling that everything was not quite square. Under the circumstances, this was enough to set me wondering what on earth the service could be that I was to render—wondering also whether the whole business were not some ill-advised jest in order to make me come down from London for a mere shooting party.

"Broughton said little after she had gone. But he was evidently laboring to bring the conversation around to the so-called haunting of the Abbey. As soon as I saw this, of course I asked him directly about it. He then seemed at once to lose interest in the matter. There was no doubt about it: Broughton was somehow a changed man, and to my mind he had changed in no way for the better. Mrs. Broughton seemed no sufficient cause. He was clearly very fond of her, and she of him. I reminded him that he was going to tell me what I could do for him in the morning, pleaded my journey, lit a candle, and went upstairs with him. At the end of the passage leading into the old house he grinned weakly and said, 'Mind, if you see a ghost, do talk to it; you said you would.' He stood irresolutely a moment and then turned away. At the door of his dressing room he paused once more: 'I'm here,' he called out, 'if you should want anything. Good night,' and he shut the door.

"I went along the passage to my room, undressed, switched on a lamp beside my bed, read a few pages of *The Jungle Book*, and then, more than ready for sleep, turned the light off and went fast asleep.

"Three hours later I woke up. There was not a breath of wind outside. There was not even a flicker of light from the fireplace. As I lay there, an ash tinkled slightly as it cooled, but there was hardly a gleam of the dullest red in the grate. An owl cried among the silent Spanish chestnuts on the slope outside. I idly reviewed the events of the day, hoping that I should fall off to sleep again before I reached dinner. But at the end I seemed as wakeful as ever. There was no help for it. I must read my *Jungle Book* again till I felt ready to go off, so I fumbled for the pear at the end of the cord that hung down inside the bed, and I switched on the bedside lamp. The sudden glory dazzled me for a moment. I felt under my pillow for my book with half-shut eyes. Then, growing used to the light, I happened to look down to the foot of my bed.

"I can never tell you really what happened then. Nothing I could ever confess in the most abject words could even faintly picture to you what I felt. I know that my heart stopped dead, and my throat shut automatically. In one instinctive movement I crouched back up against the headboards of the bed, staring at the horror. The movement set my heart going again, and the sweat dripped from every pore. I am not a particularly religious man, but I

had always believed that God would never allow any supernatural appearance to present itself to man in such a guise and in such circumstances that harm, either bodily or mental, could result to him. I can only tell you that at the moment both my life and my reason rocked unsteadily on their seats."

The other *Osiris* passengers had gone to bed. Only Colvin and I remained leaning over the starboard railing, which rattled uneasily now and then under the fierce vibration of the over-engined mail boat. Far over, there were the lights of a few fishing smacks riding out the night, and a great rush of white combing and seething water fell out and away from us overside.

At last Colvin went on:

"Leaning over the foot of my bed, looking at me, was a figure swathed in a rotten and tattered veiling. This shroud passed over the head, but left both eyes and the right side of the face bare. It then followed the line of the arm down to where the hand grasped the bed end. The face was not entirely that of a skull, though the eyes and the flesh of the face were totally gone. There was a thin, dry skin drawn tightly over the features, and there was some skin left on the hand. One wisp of hair crossed the forehead. It was perfectly still. I looked at it, and it looked at me, and my brains turned dry and hot in my head. I had still got the pear of the electric lamp in my hand, and I played idly with it; only I dared not turn the light out again. I shut my eyes, only to open them in a hideous terror the same second. The thing had not moved.

My heart was thumping, and the sweat cooled me as it evaporated. Another cinder tinkled in the grate, and a panel creaked in the wall.

"My reason failed me. For twenty minutes, or twenty seconds, I was able to think of nothing else but this awful figure, till there came, hurtling through the empty channels of my senses, the remembrances that Broughton and his friends had discussed with me furtively at dinner. The dim possibility of it being a hoax stole gratefully into my unhappy mind, and once there, pluck came creeping back along a thousand tiny veins. My first sensation was one of blind unreasoning thankfulness that my brain was going to stand the trial. I am not a timid man, but the best of us needs some human handle to steady him in time of extremity, and in this faint but growing hope that it might be only a brutal hoax, I found the fulcrum that I needed. At last I moved.

"How I managed to do it I cannot tell you, but with one spring toward the foot of the bed I got within arm's length and struck out one fearful blow with my fist at the thing. It crumbled under it, and my hand was cut to the bone. With a sickening revulsion after my terror, I dropped half-fainting across the end of the bed. So it was merely a foul trick after all. No doubt the trick had been played many a time before: no doubt Broughton and his friends had had some large bet among themselves as to what I should do when I discovered the gruesome thing. From my state of abject terror I found myself transported into an insensate anger. I shouted curses upon Broughton. I

dived rather than climbed over the bed-end of the sofa. I tore at the robed skeleton—how well the whole thing had been carried out, I thought—I broke the skull against the floor, and stamped upon its dry bones. I flung the head away under the bed, and rent the brittle bones of the trunk in pieces. I snapped the thin thigh bones across my knee, and flung them in different directions. The shin bones I set up against a stool and broke with my heel. I raged like a berserker against the loathly thing, and stripped the ribs from the backbone and slung the breastbone against the cupboard. My fury increased as the work of destruction went on. I tore the frail rotten veil into twenty pieces, and the dust went up over everything, over the clean blotting paper and the silver inkstand. At last my work was done. There was but a raffle of broken bones and strips of parchment and crumbling wool. Then, picking up a piece of the skull—it was the cheek and temple bone of the right side, I remember—I opened the door and went down the passage to Broughton's dressing room. I remember still how my sweat-dripping pajamas clung to me as I walked. At the door I kicked and entered.

"Broughton was in bed. He had already turned the light on and seemed shrunken and horrified. For a moment he could hardly pull himself together. Then I spoke. I don't know what I said. I know only that from a heart full and over full with hatred and contempt, spurred on by shame of my own recent cowardice, I let my tongue run on. He answered nothing. I was amazed at my own fluency. My hair still clung lankly to my wet temples, my hand was bleeding profusely, and I must have looked a strange sight. Broughton huddled himself at the head of the bed just as I had. Still he made no answer, no defense. He seemed preoccupied with something besides my reproaches, and once or twice moistened his lips with his tongue. He could say nothing, though he moved his hands now and then, just as a baby who cannot speak moves its hands.

"At last the door into Mrs. Broughton's rooms opened and she came in, white and terrified. 'What is it? What is it? Oh, in God's name! What is it?' she cried again and again, and then she went up to her husband and sat on the bed in her night-dress, and the two faced me. I told her what the matter was. I spared her husband not a word for her presence there. Yet he seemed hardly to understand. I told the pair that I had spoiled their cowardly joke for them. Broughton looked up.

"'I have smashed the foul thing into a hundred pieces,' I said. Broughton licked his lips again and his mouth worked. 'By God!' I shouted, 'it would serve you right if I thrashed you within an inch of your life. I will take care that not a decent man or woman of my acquaintance ever speaks to you again. And there,' I added, throwing the broken piece of the skull upon the floor beside his bed, 'there is a souvenir for you, of your damned work tonight!'

"Broughton saw the bone, and in a moment it was his turn to frighten me. He squealed like a hare caught in a trap. He screamed and screamed till Mrs. Broughton, almost as bewildered as myself, held on to him and coaxed him like a child to be quiet. But Broughton—and as he moved I thought that ten minutes ago I perhaps looked as terribly ill as he did—thrust her from him, and scrambled out of bed on to the floor, and, still screaming, put out his hand to the bone. It had blood on it from my hand. He paid no attention to me whatever. In truth I said nothing. This was a new turn indeed to the horrors of the evening. He rose from the floor with the bone in his hand and stood silent. He seemed to be listening. 'Time, time, perhaps,' he muttered, and almost at the same moment fell at full length on the carpet, cutting his head against the fender. The bone flew from his hand and came to rest near the door. I picked Broughton up, haggard and broken, with blood over his face. He whispered hoarsely and quickly, 'Listen, listen!' We listened.

"After ten seconds' utter quiet, I seemed to hear something. I could not be sure, but at last there was no doubt. There was a quiet sound as one moving along the passage. Little regular steps came toward us over the hard oak flooring. Broughton moved to where his wife sat, white and speechless, on the bed, and pressed her face into his shoulder.

"Then—the last thing that I could see as he turned the light out—he fell forward with his own head pressed into the pillow of the bed. Something in their company, something in their cowardice, helped me, and I faced the open doorway of the room, which was outlined fairly clearly against the dimly lit passage. I put out one hand and touched Mrs. Broughton's shoulder in the darkness, but at the last moment I too failed. I sank on my knees and put my face in the bed. Only we all heard. The footsteps came to the door and there they stopped. The piece of bone was lying a yard inside the door. There was a rustle of moving stuff, and the thing was in the room. Mrs. Broughton was silent: I could hear Broughton's voice praying, muffled in the pillow. I was cursing my own cowardice. Then the steps moved out again on the oak boards of the passage, and I heard the sounds dying away. In a flash of remorse I went to the door and looked out. At the end of the corridor I thought I saw something that moved away. A moment later the passage was empty. I stood with my forehead against the jamb of the door almost physically sick.

"'You can turn the light on,' I said, and there was an answering flare. There was no bone at my feet. Mrs. Broughton had fainted. Broughton was almost useless, and it took me ten minutes to bring her to. Broughton only said one thing worth remembering. For the most part he went on muttering prayers. But I was glad afterwards to recollect that he had said that thing. He said in a colourless voice, half as a question, half as a reproach, 'You didn't speak to her.'

"We spent the remainder of the night together. Mrs. Broughton actually fell off into a kind of sleep before dawn, but she suffered so horribly in her dreams that I shook her into consciousness again. Never was dawn so long in coming. Three or four times Broughton spoke to himself. Mrs. Broughton would then just tighten her hold on his arm, but she could say nothing. As for me, I can honestly say that I grew worse as the hours passed and the light strengthened. The two violent reactions had battered down my steadiness of view, and I felt that the foundations of my life had been built upon the sand. I said nothing, and after binding up my hand with a towel, I did not move. It was better so. They helped me and I helped them, and we all three knew that our reason had gone very near to ruin that night. At last, when the light came in pretty strongly, and the birds outside were chattering and singing, we felt that we must do something. Yet we never moved. You might have thought that we should particularly dislike being found as we were by the servants, yet nothing of that kind mattered a straw, and an overpowering listlessness bound us as we sat, until Chapman, Broughton's man, actually knocked and opened the door. None of us moved. Broughton,

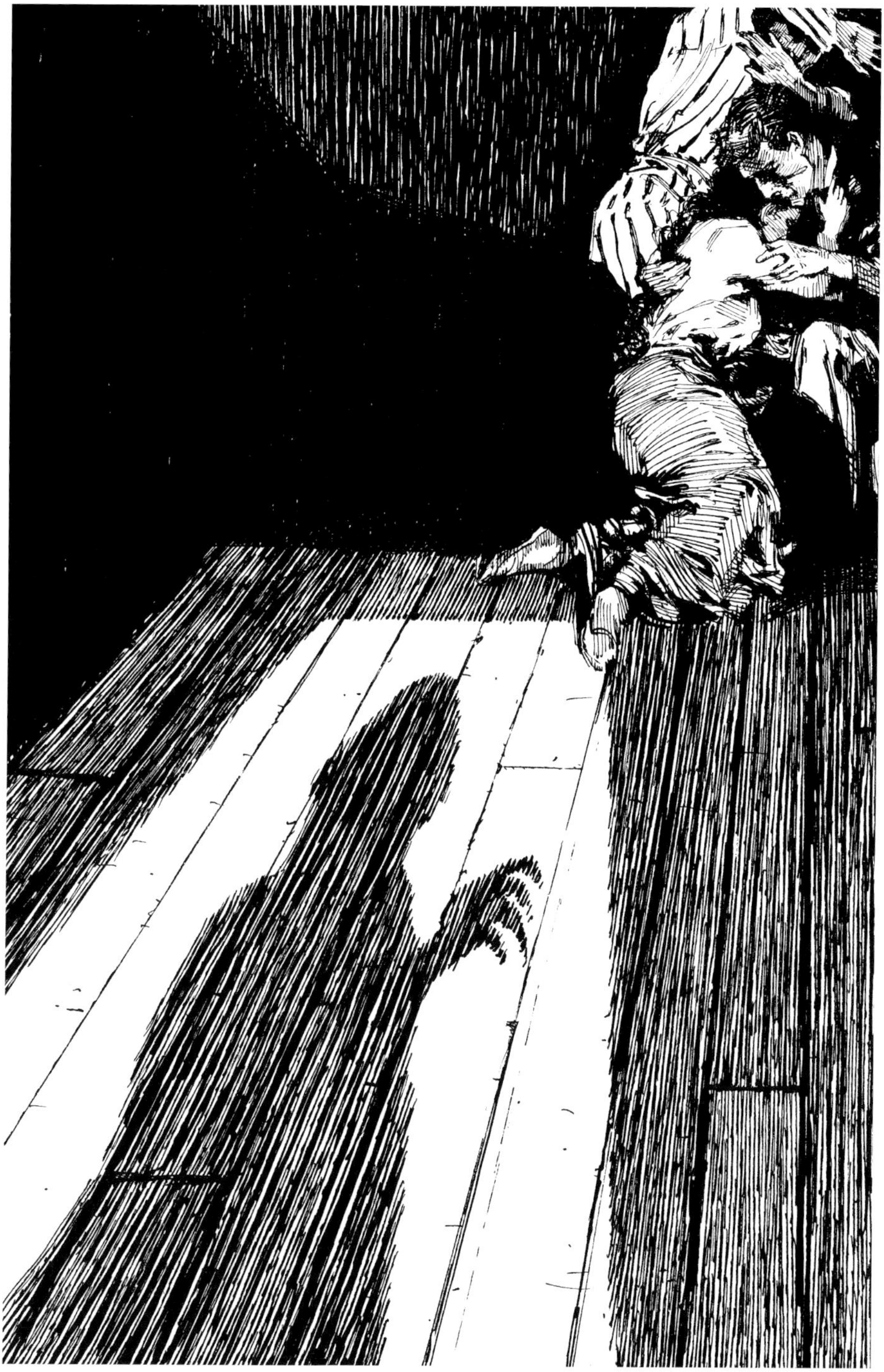

speaking hardly and stiffly, said, 'Chapman, you can come back in five minutes.' Chapman was a discreet man, but it would have made no difference to us if he had carried his news to the 'room' at once.

"We looked at each other and I said I must go back. I meant to wait outside till Chapman returned. I simply dared not re-enter my bedroom alone. Broughton roused himself and said that he would come with me. Mrs. Broughton agreed to remain in her own room for five minutes if the blinds were drawn up and all the doors left open.

"So Broughton and I, leaning stiffly one against the other, went down to my room. By the morning light that filtered past the blinds we could see our way, and I released the blinds. There was nothing wrong with the room from end to end, except smears of my own blood on the end of the bed, on the sofa, and on the carpet where I had torn the thing to pieces."

Colvin had finished his story. There was nothing to say. Seven bells stuttered out from the fo'c's'le, and the answering cry wailed through the darkness. I took him downstairs.

"Of course I am much better now, but it is a kindness of you to let me sleep in your cabin."

The End

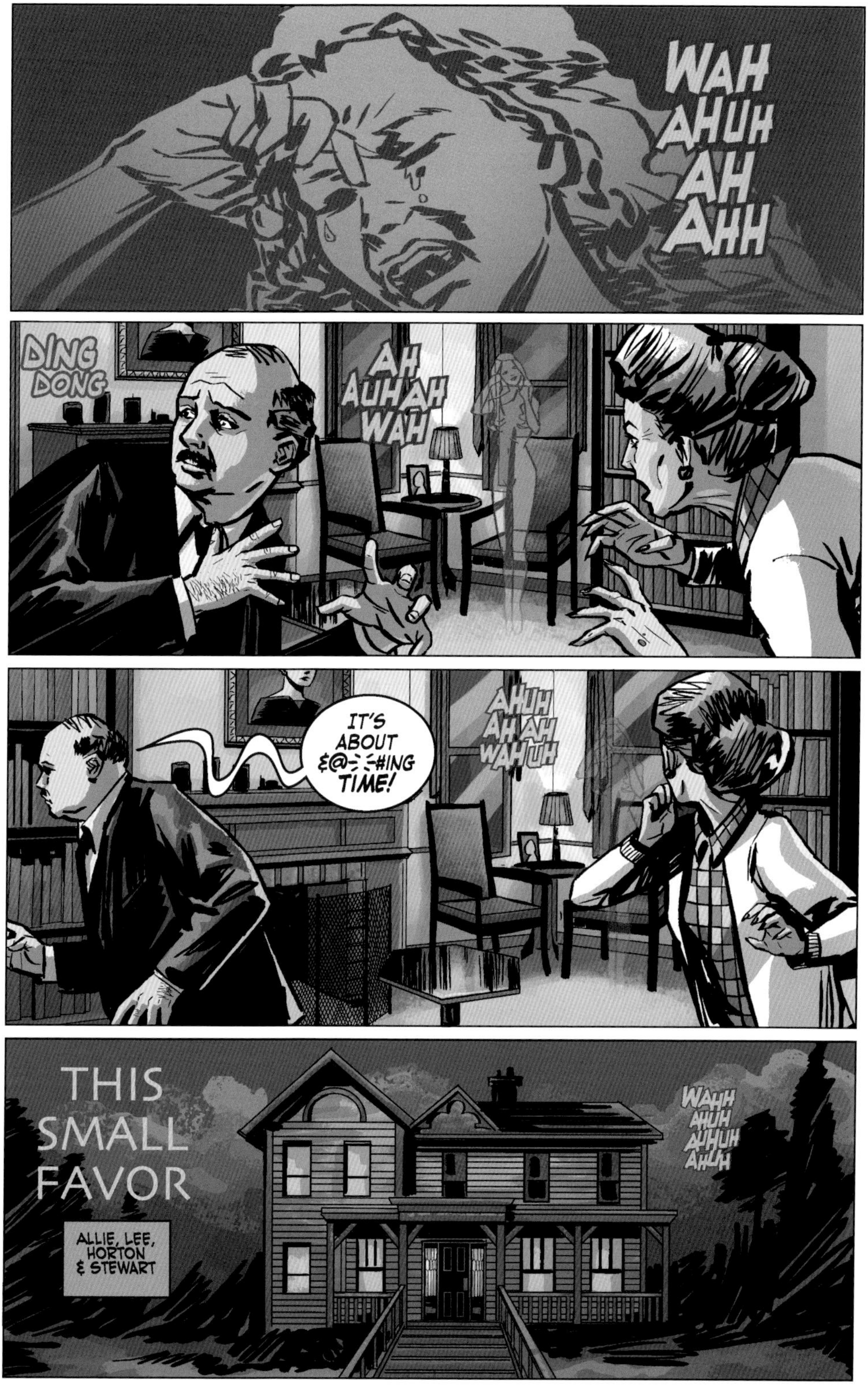
WAH AHUH AH AHH
DING DONG
AH AUHAH WAH
AHUH AH AH WAHUH
IT'S ABOUT &@#ING TIME!
THIS SMALL FAVOR
ALLIE, LEE, HORTON & STEWART
WAHH AHUH AHUH AHUH

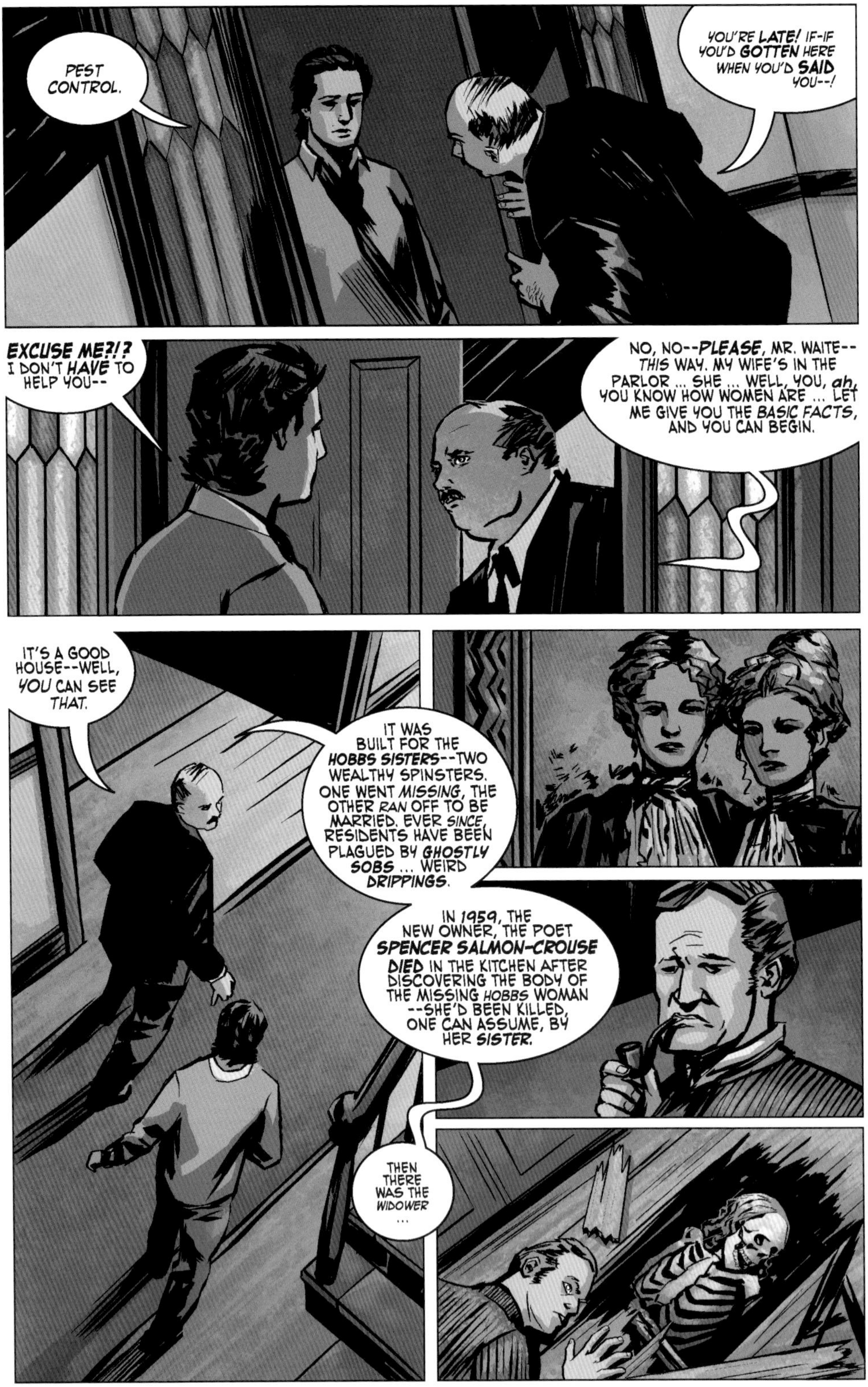
PEST CONTROL.
YOU'RE LATE! IF-IF YOU'D GOTTEN HERE WHEN YOU'D SAID YOU--!
EXCUSE ME?!? I DON'T HAVE TO HELP YOU--
NO, NO--PLEASE, MR. WAITE--THIS WAY. MY WIFE'S IN THE PARLOR ... SHE ... WELL, YOU, ah, YOU KNOW HOW WOMEN ARE ... LET ME GIVE YOU THE BASIC FACTS, AND YOU CAN BEGIN.
IT'S A GOOD HOUSE--WELL, YOU CAN SEE THAT.
IT WAS BUILT FOR THE HOBBS SISTERS--TWO WEALTHY SPINSTERS. ONE WENT MISSING, THE OTHER RAN OFF TO BE MARRIED. EVER SINCE, RESIDENTS HAVE BEEN PLAGUED BY GHOSTLY SOBS ... WEIRD DRIPPINGS.
IN 1959, THE NEW OWNER, THE POET SPENCER SALMON-CROUSE DIED IN THE KITCHEN AFTER DISCOVERING THE BODY OF THE MISSING HOBBS WOMAN --SHE'D BEEN KILLED, ONE CAN ASSUME, BY HER SISTER.
THEN THERE WAS THE WIDOWER ...

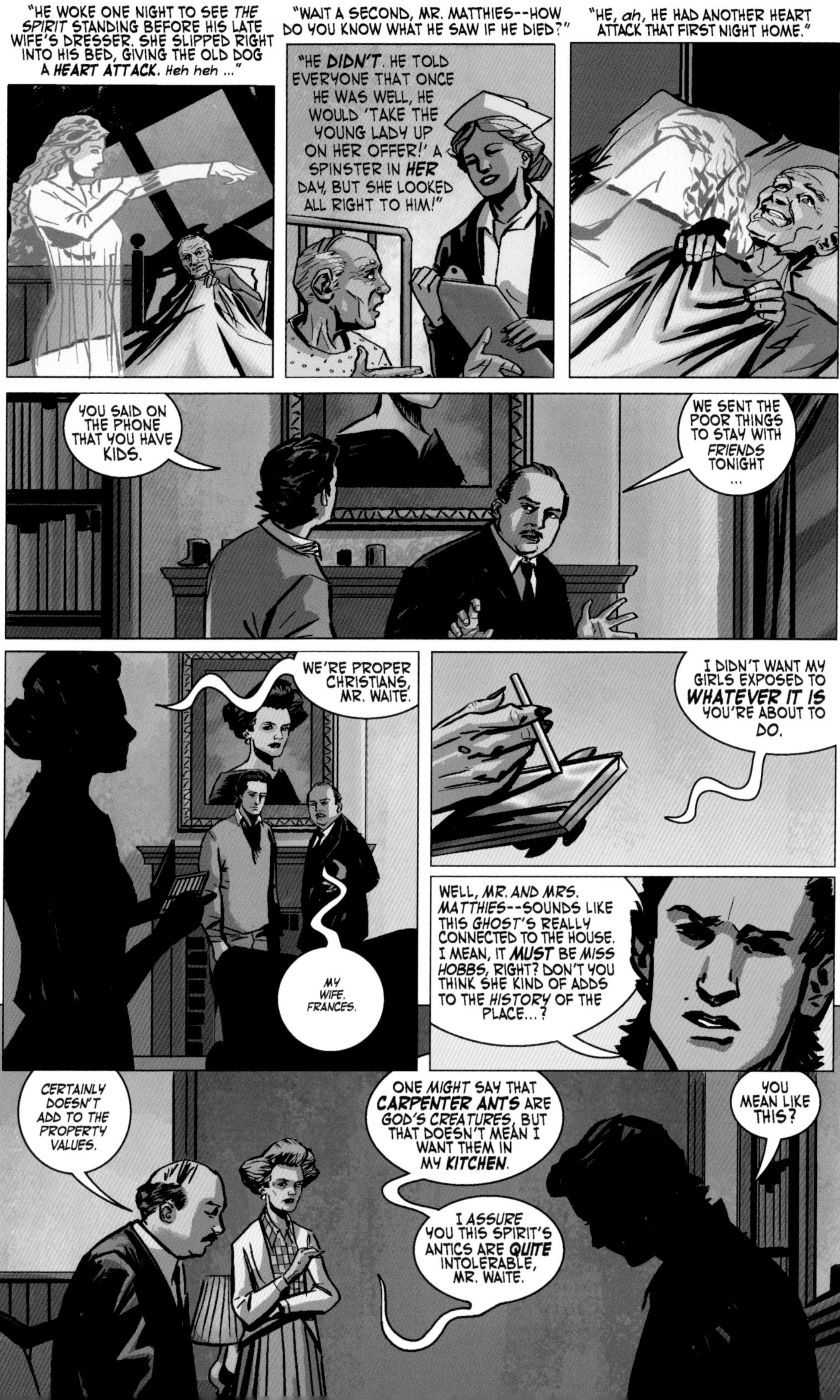
"HE WOKE ONE NIGHT TO SEE THE SPIRIT STANDING BEFORE HIS LATE WIFE'S DRESSER. SHE SLIPPED RIGHT INTO HIS BED, GIVING THE OLD DOG A HEART ATTACK. Heh heh ..."
"WAIT A SECOND, MR. MATTHIES--HOW DO YOU KNOW WHAT HE SAW IF HE DIED?"
"HE DIDN'T. HE TOLD EVERYONE THAT ONCE HE WAS WELL, HE WOULD 'TAKE THE YOUNG LADY UP ON HER OFFER!' A SPINSTER IN HER DAY, BUT SHE LOOKED ALL RIGHT TO HIM!"
"HE, ah, HE HAD ANOTHER HEART ATTACK THAT FIRST NIGHT HOME."
YOU SAID ON THE PHONE THAT YOU HAVE KIDS.
WE SENT THE POOR THINGS TO STAY WITH FRIENDS TONIGHT ...
WE'RE PROPER CHRISTIANS, MR. WAITE.
MY WIFE. FRANCES.
I DIDN'T WANT MY GIRLS EXPOSED TO WHATEVER IT IS YOU'RE ABOUT TO DO.
WELL, MR. AND MRS. MATTHIES--SOUNDS LIKE THIS GHOST'S REALLY CONNECTED TO THE HOUSE. I MEAN, IT MUST BE MISS HOBBS, RIGHT? DON'T YOU THINK SHE KIND OF ADDS TO THE HISTORY OF THE PLACE... ?
CERTAINLY DOESN'T ADD TO THE PROPERTY VALUES.
ONE MIGHT SAY THAT CARPENTER ANTS ARE GOD'S CREATURES, BUT THAT DOESN'T MEAN I WANT THEM IN MY KITCHEN.
I ASSURE YOU THIS SPIRIT'S ANTICS ARE QUITE INTOLERABLE, MR. WAITE.
YOU MEAN LIKE THIS?

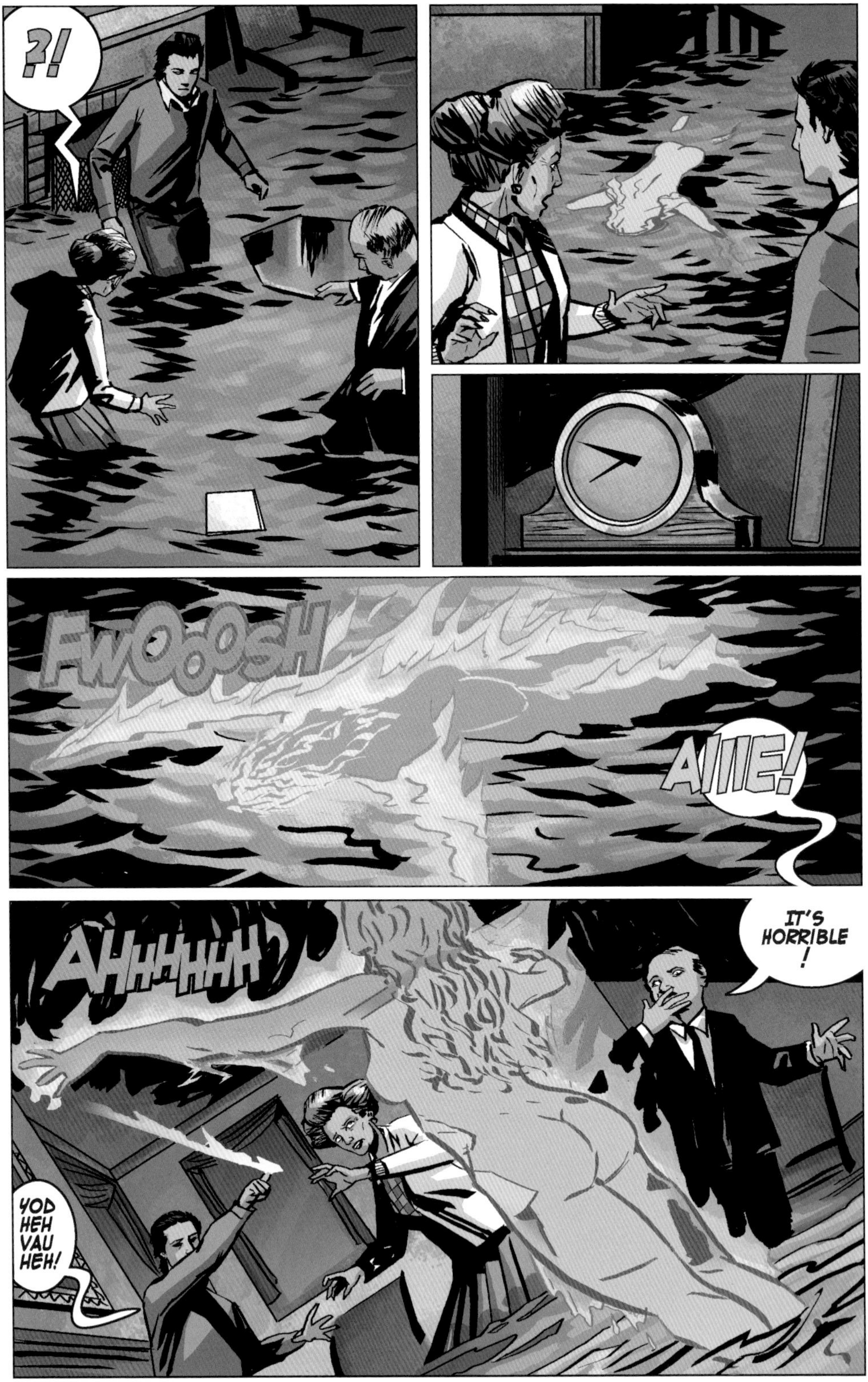
?!
FWOOOSH
AIIIE!
AHHHHHH
IT'S HORRIBLE!
YOD HEH VAU HEH!

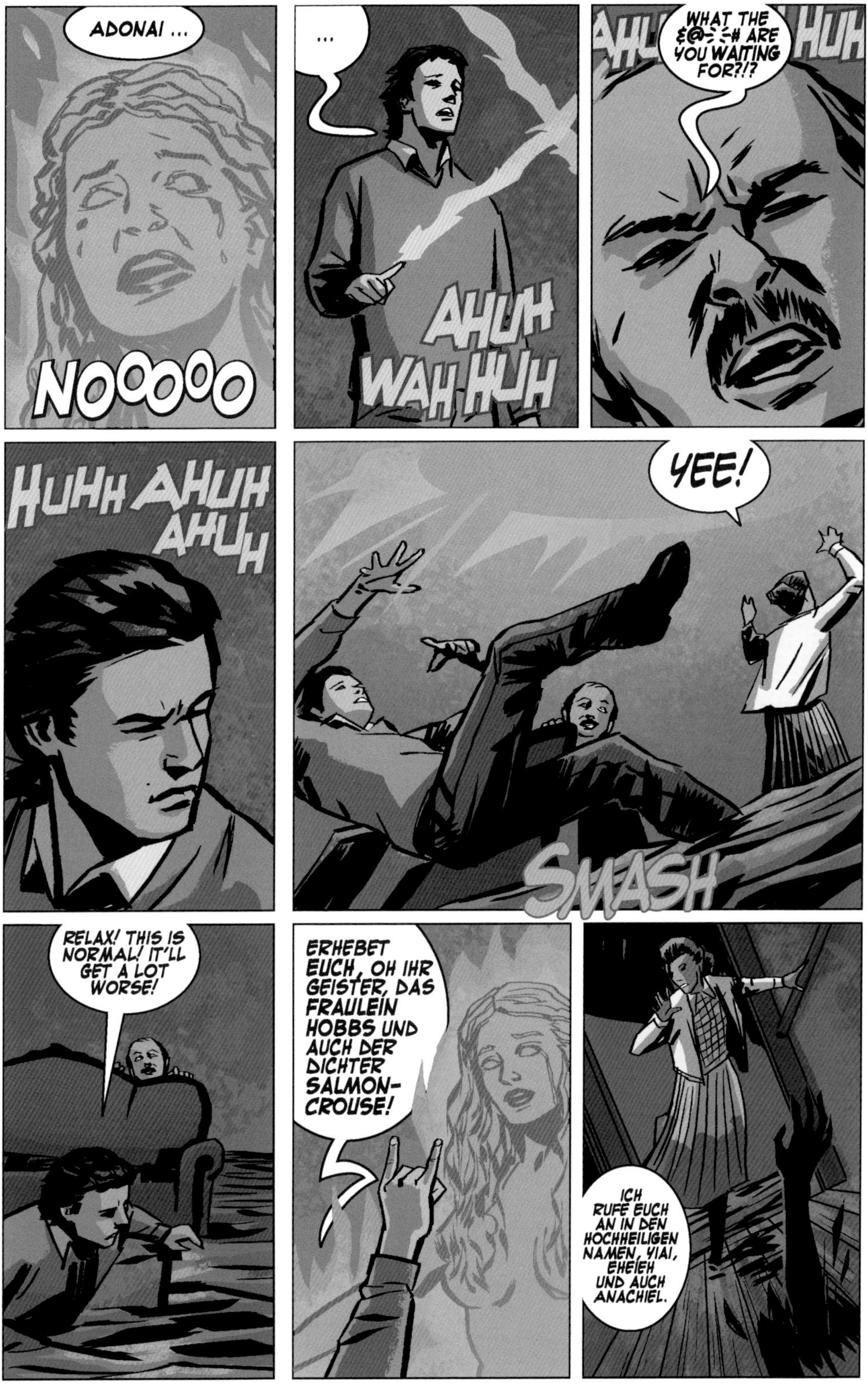
ADONAI ...
NOOOOO
...
AHUH WAH HUH
WHAT THE &@#!# ARE YOU WAITING FOR?!?
AHUH HUH
HUHH AHUH AHUH
YEE!
SMASH
RELAX! THIS IS NORMAL! IT'LL GET A LOT WORSE!
ERHEBET EUCH, OH IHR GEISTER, DAS FRAULEIN HOBBS UND AUCH DER DICHTER SALMON-CROUSE!
ICH RUFE EUCH AN IN DEN HOCHHEILIGEN NAMEN, YIAI, EHEIEH UND AUCH ANACHIEL.

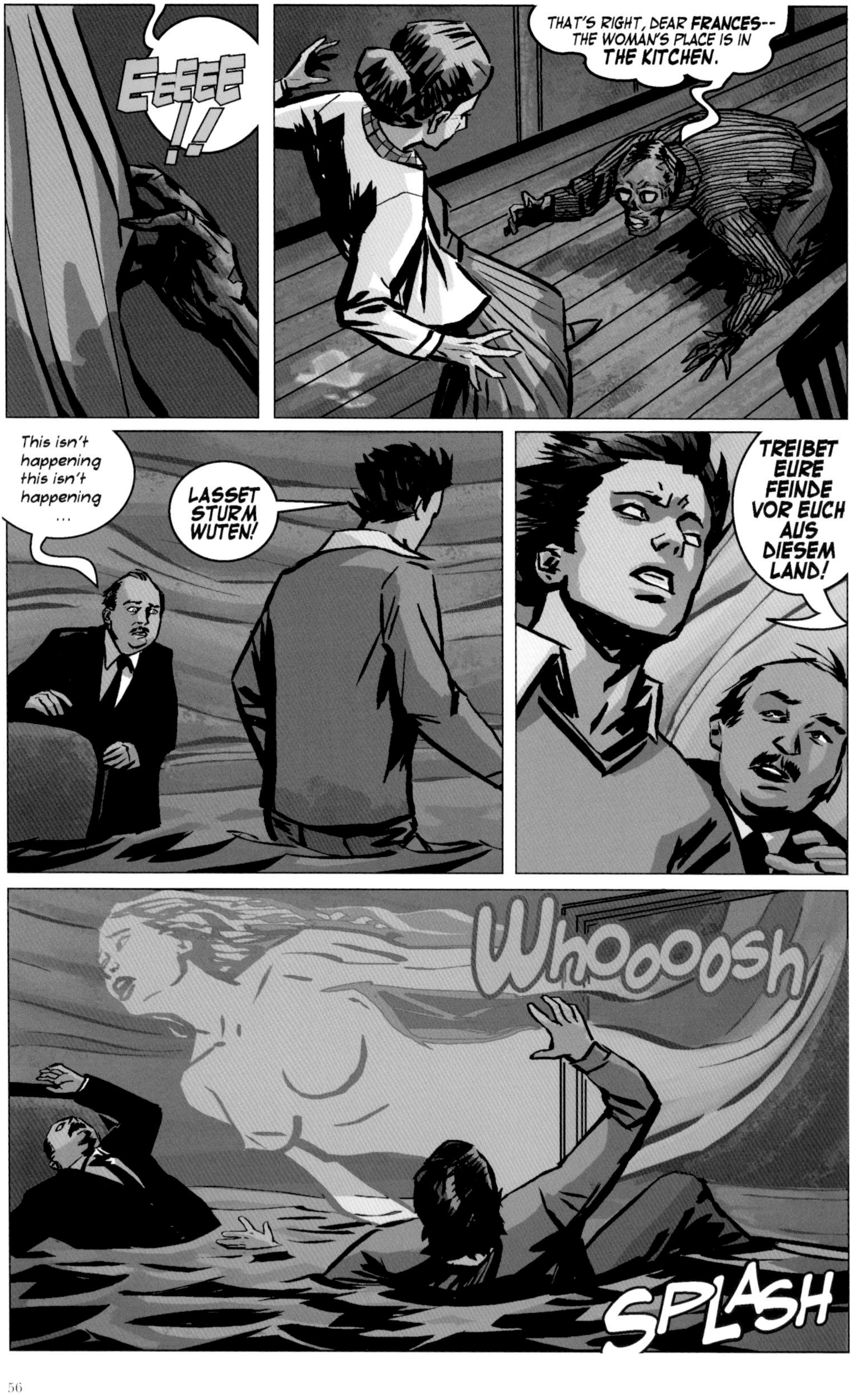
EEEEE!!
THAT'S RIGHT, DEAR FRANCES-- THE WOMAN'S PLACE IS IN THE KITCHEN.
This isn't happening this isn't happening ...
LASSET STURM WUTEN!
TREIBET EURE FEINDE VOR EUCH AUS DIESEM LAND!
Whoooosh
SPLASH

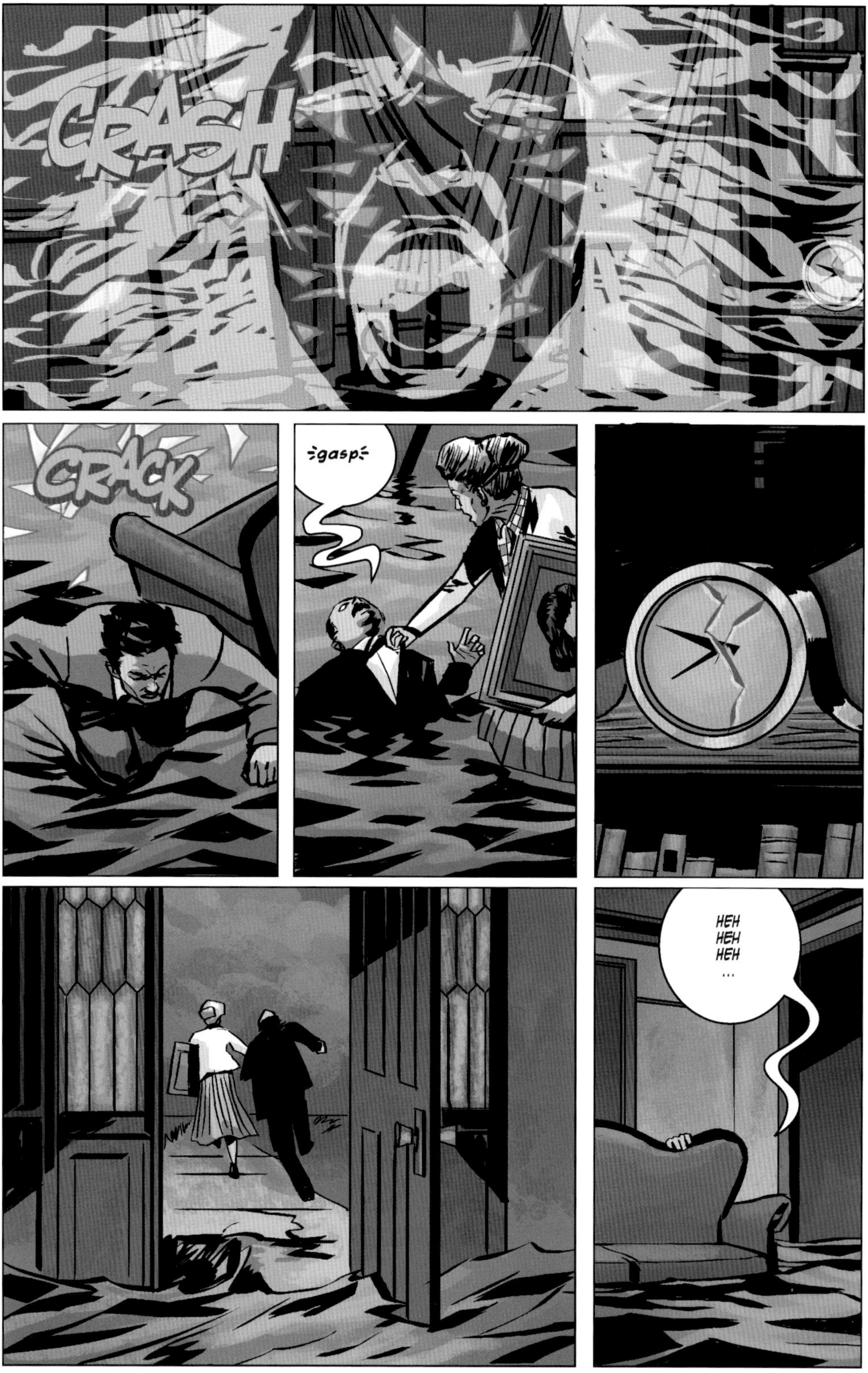
CRASH
CRACK
gasp
HEH HEH HEH ...

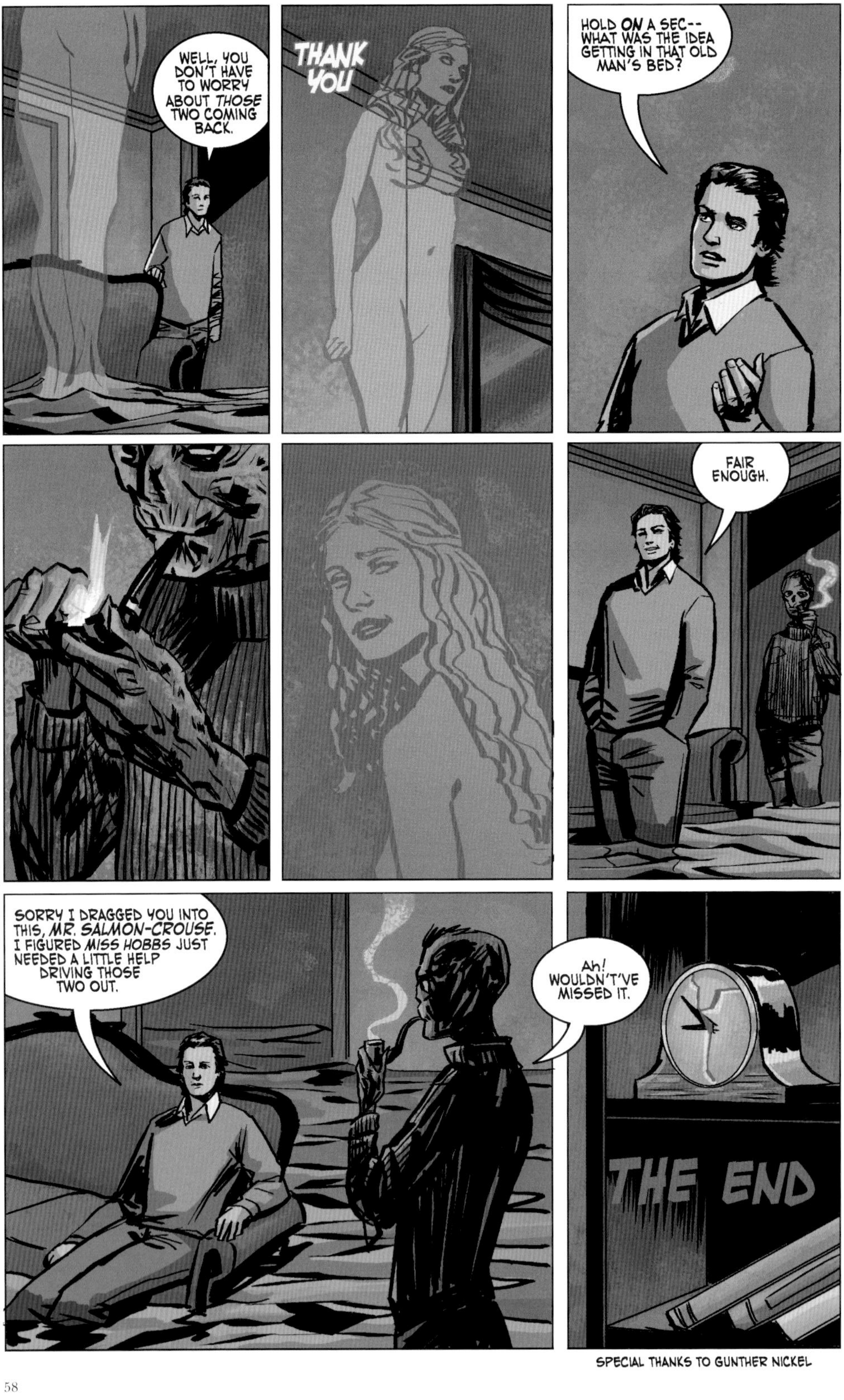
WELL, YOU DON'T HAVE TO WORRY ABOUT THOSE TWO COMING BACK.
THANK YOU
HOLD ON A SEC-- WHAT WAS THE IDEA GETTING IN THAT OLD MAN'S BED?
FAIR ENOUGH.
SORRY I DRAGGED YOU INTO THIS, MR. SALMON-CROUSE. I FIGURED MISS HOBBS JUST NEEDED A LITTLE HELP DRIVING THOSE TWO OUT.
AH! WOULDN'T'VE MISSED IT.
THE END

SPECIAL THANKS TO GUNTHER NICKEL

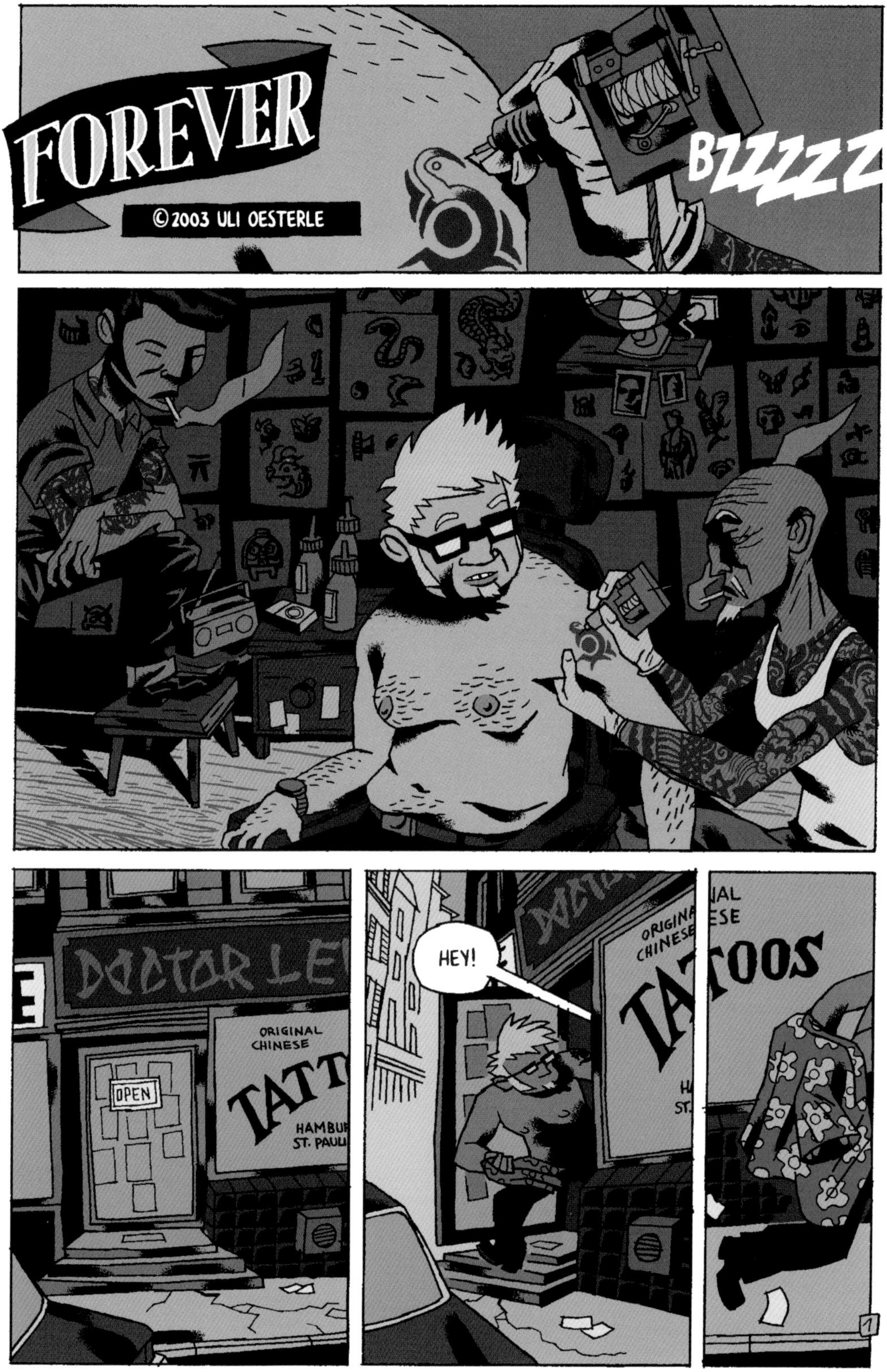
FOREVER
©2003 ULI OESTERLE
BZZZZZ
DOCTOR LE
OPEN
ORIGINAL CHINESE
TATT
HAMBUR
ST. PAULI
HEY!
ORIGINAL CHINESE
TATOOS
1

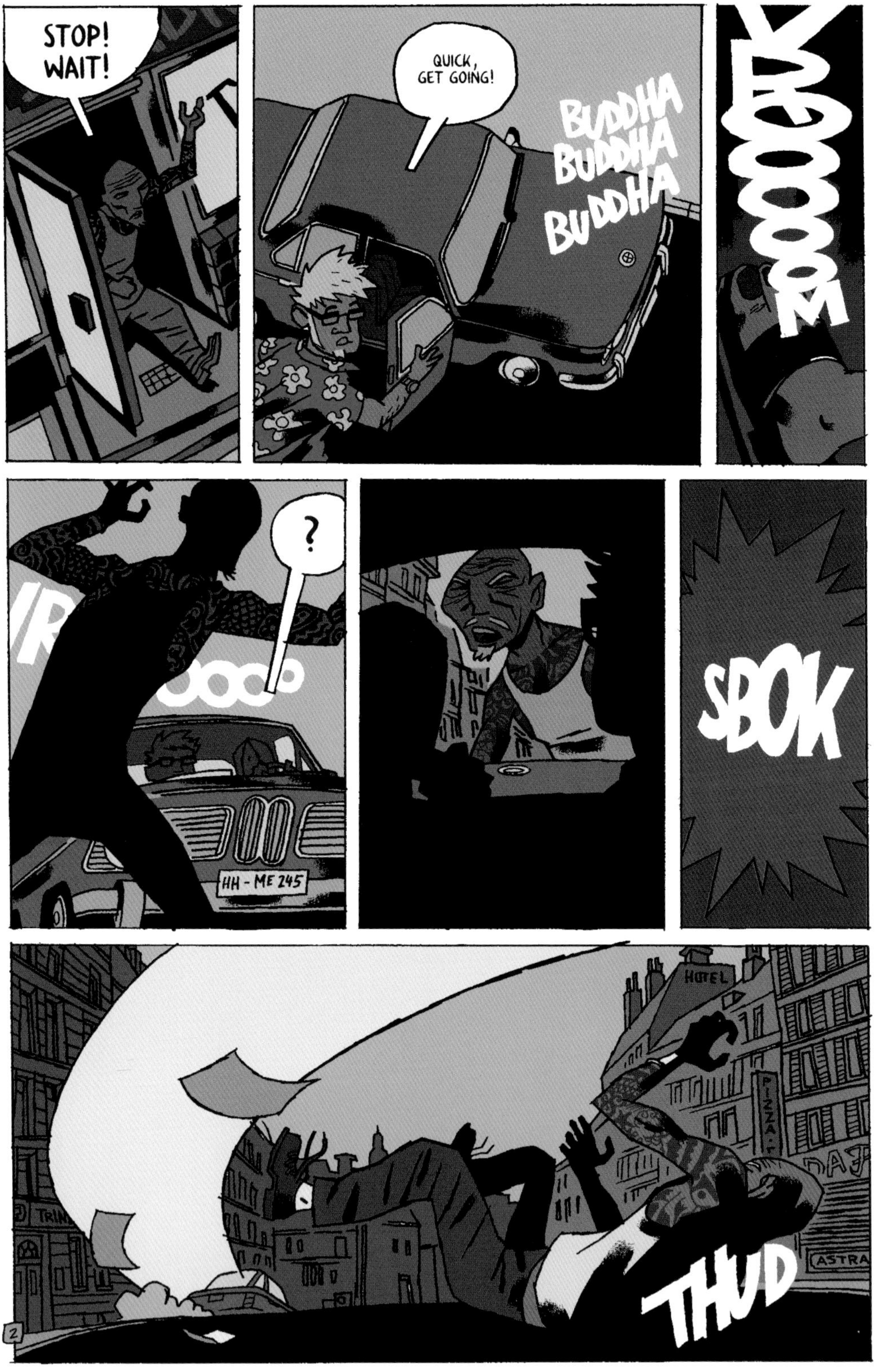
STOP! WAIT!
QUICK, GET GOING!
BUDDHA BUDDHA BUDDHA
VROOOOOM
?
SBOK
HH - ME 245
HOTEL
PIZZA
ASTRA
THUD

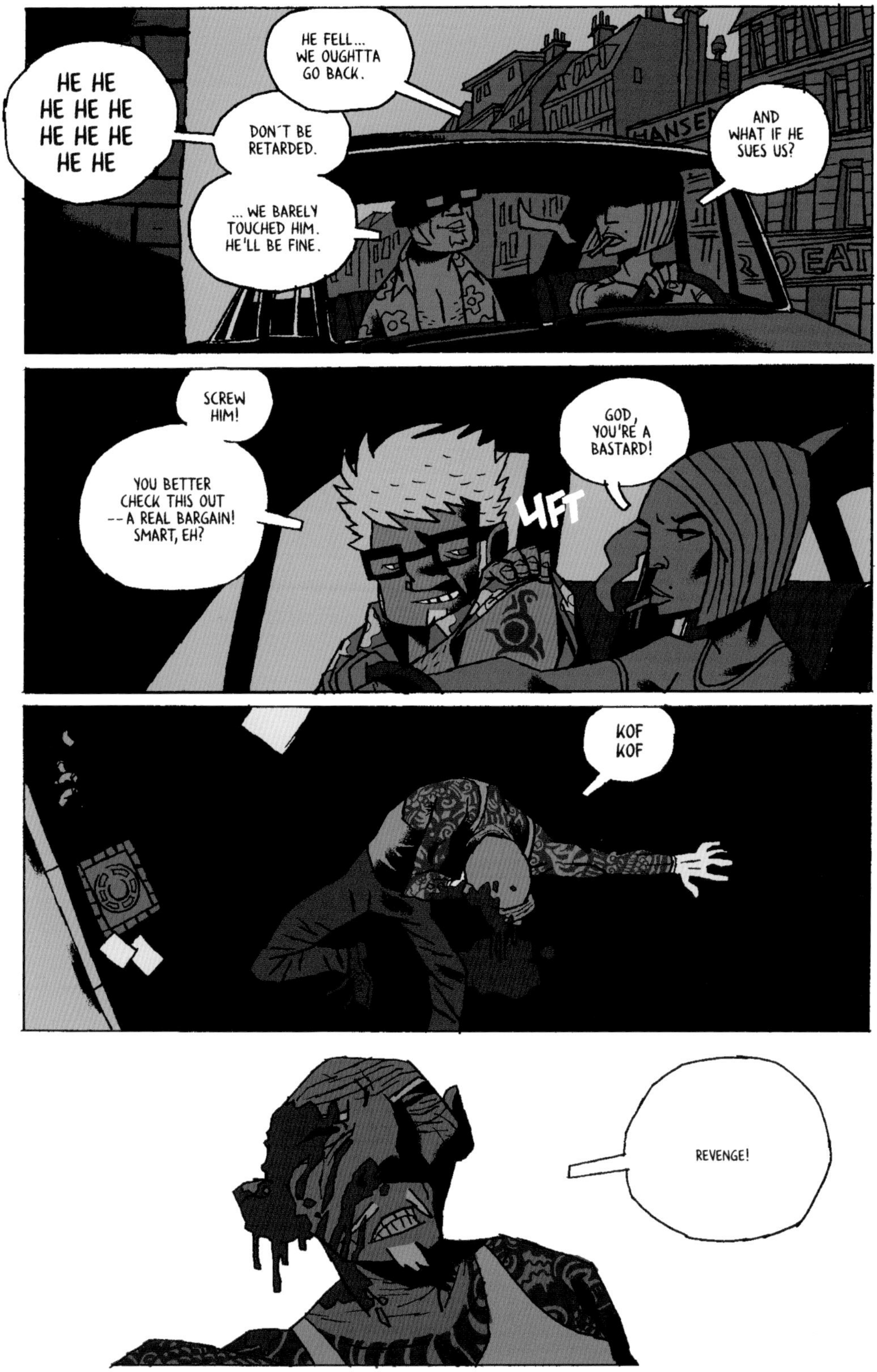
HE FELL... WE OUGHTTA GO BACK.
HE HE HE HE HE HE HE HE HE HE
DON´T BE RETARDED.
... WE BARELY TOUCHED HIM. HE'LL BE FINE.
AND WHAT IF HE SUES US?
SCREW HIM!
YOU BETTER CHECK THIS OUT --A REAL BARGAIN! SMART, EH?
LIFT
GOD, YOU'RE A BASTARD!
KOF KOF
REVENGE!

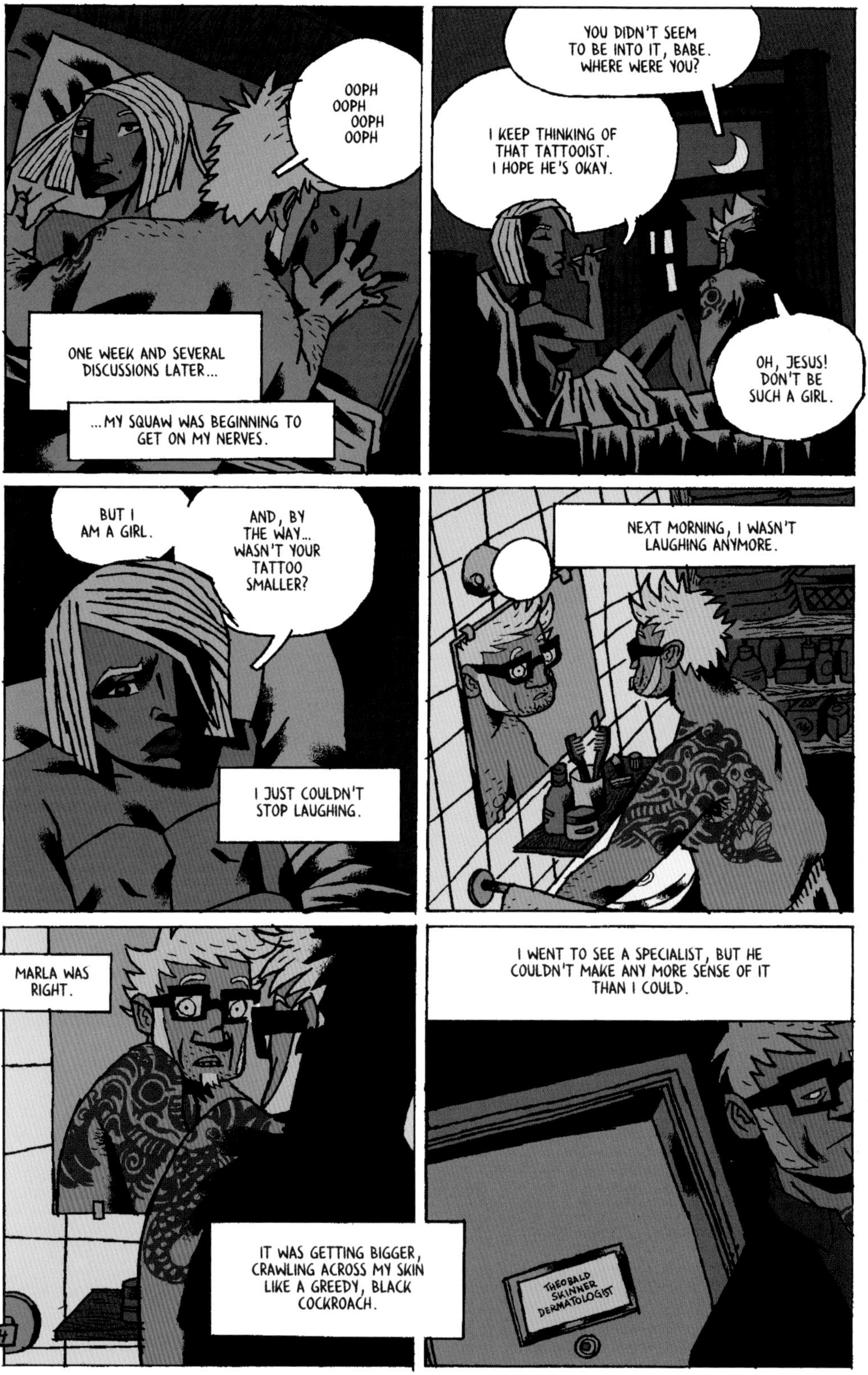
OOPH OOPH OOPH OOPH
ONE WEEK AND SEVERAL DISCUSSIONS LATER...
...MY SQUAW WAS BEGINNING TO GET ON MY NERVES.
YOU DIDN'T SEEM TO BE INTO IT, BABE. WHERE WERE YOU?
I KEEP THINKING OF THAT TATTOOIST. I HOPE HE'S OKAY.
OH, JESUS! DON'T BE SUCH A GIRL.
BUT I AM A GIRL.
AND, BY THE WAY... WASN'T YOUR TATTOO SMALLER?
I JUST COULDN'T STOP LAUGHING.
NEXT MORNING, I WASN'T LAUGHING ANYMORE.
MARLA WAS RIGHT.
IT WAS GETTING BIGGER, CRAWLING ACROSS MY SKIN LIKE A GREEDY, BLACK COCKROACH.
I WENT TO SEE A SPECIALIST, BUT HE COULDN'T MAKE ANY MORE SENSE OF IT THAN I COULD.
THEOBALD SKINNER DERMATOLOGIST

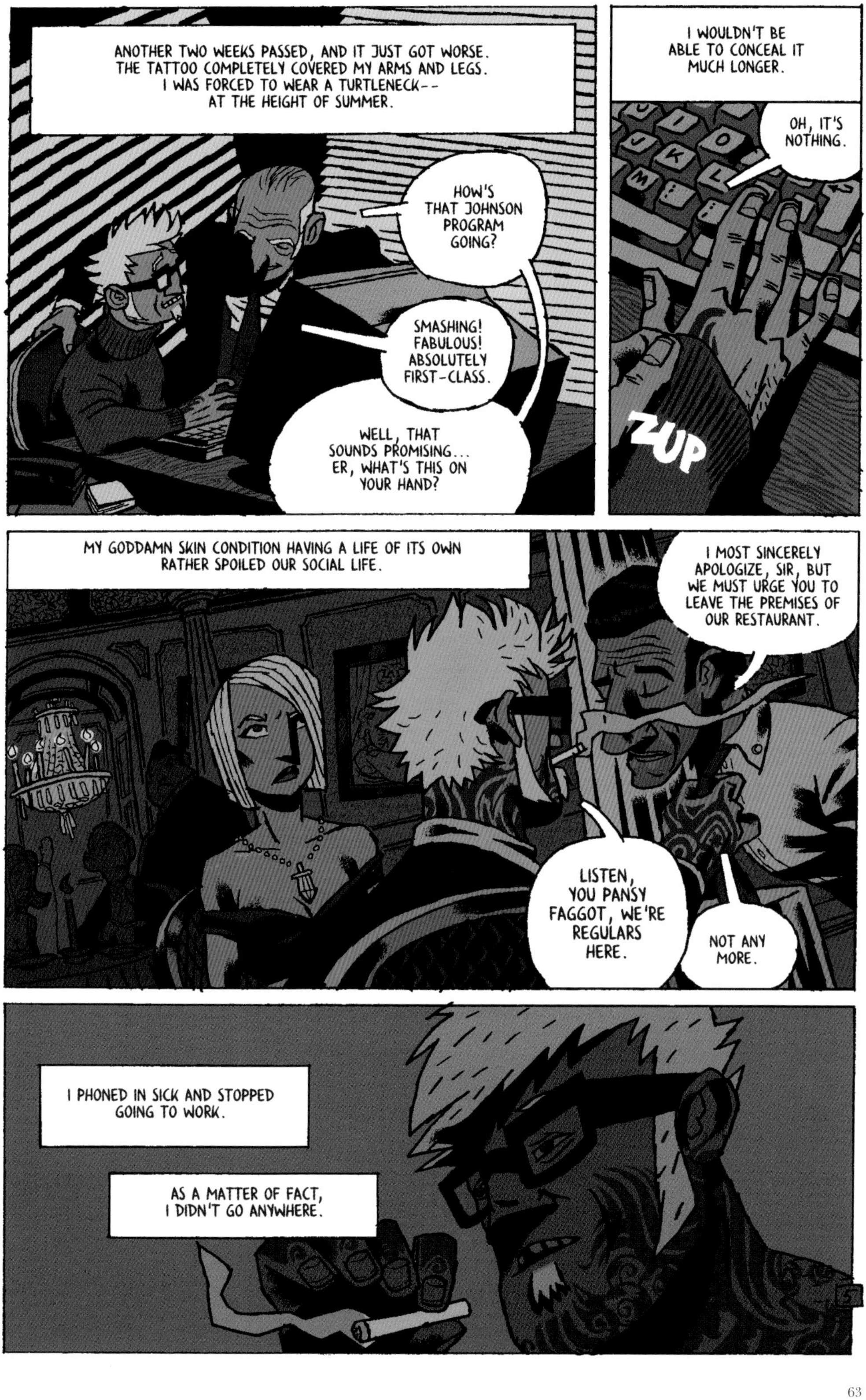
ANOTHER TWO WEEKS PASSED, AND IT JUST GOT WORSE. THE TATTOO COMPLETELY COVERED MY ARMS AND LEGS. I WAS FORCED TO WEAR A TURTLENECK-- AT THE HEIGHT OF SUMMER.
HOW'S THAT JOHNSON PROGRAM GOING?
SMASHING! FABULOUS! ABSOLUTELY FIRST-CLASS.
WELL, THAT SOUNDS PROMISING... ER, WHAT'S THIS ON YOUR HAND?
I WOULDN'T BE ABLE TO CONCEAL IT MUCH LONGER.
OH, IT'S NOTHING.
ZUP
MY GODDAMN SKIN CONDITION HAVING A LIFE OF ITS OWN RATHER SPOILED OUR SOCIAL LIFE.
I MOST SINCERELY APOLOGIZE, SIR, BUT WE MUST URGE YOU TO LEAVE THE PREMISES OF OUR RESTAURANT.
LISTEN, YOU PANSY FAGGOT, WE'RE REGULARS HERE.
NOT ANY MORE.
I PHONED IN SICK AND STOPPED GOING TO WORK.
AS A MATTER OF FACT, I DIDN'T GO ANYWHERE.

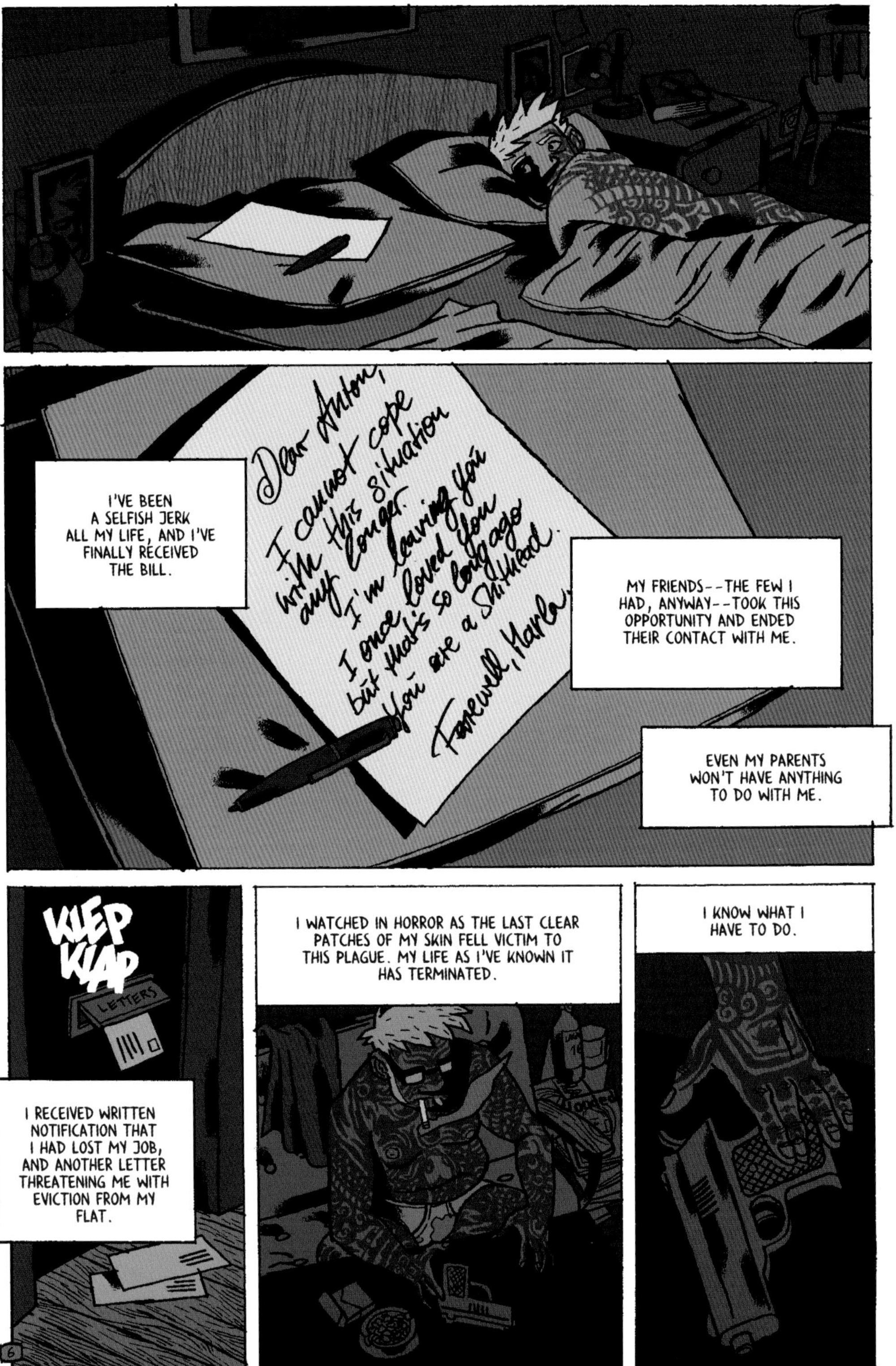

Dear Anton,
I cannot cope with this situation any longer.
I'm leaving you.
I once loved you but that's so long ago
You are a Shithead.
Farewell, Marla
I'VE BEEN A SELFISH JERK ALL MY LIFE, AND I'VE FINALLY RECEIVED THE BILL.
MY FRIENDS--THE FEW I HAD, ANYWAY--TOOK THIS OPPORTUNITY AND ENDED THEIR CONTACT WITH ME.
EVEN MY PARENTS WON'T HAVE ANYTHING TO DO WITH ME.
KLEP KLAP
LETTERS
I RECEIVED WRITTEN NOTIFICATION THAT I HAD LOST MY JOB, AND ANOTHER LETTER THREATENING ME WITH EVICTION FROM MY FLAT.
I WATCHED IN HORROR AS THE LAST CLEAR PATCHES OF MY SKIN FELL VICTIM TO THIS PLAGUE. MY LIFE AS I'VE KNOWN IT HAS TERMINATED.
I KNOW WHAT I HAVE TO DO.

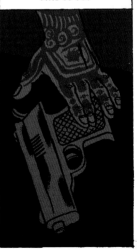

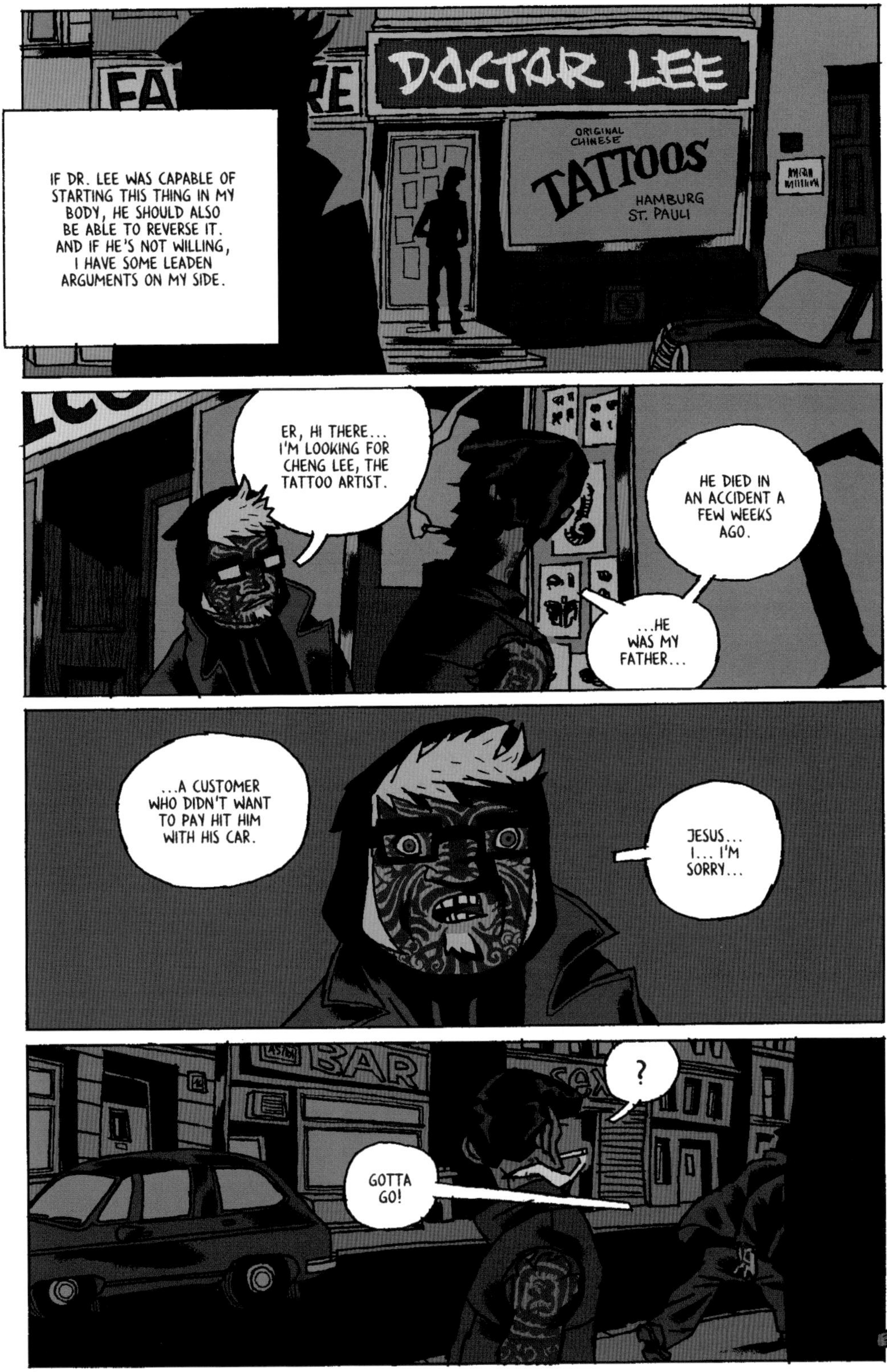
DOKTOR LEE
ORIGINAL CHINESE
TATTOOS
HAMBURG ST. PAULI
IF DR. LEE WAS CAPABLE OF STARTING THIS THING IN MY BODY, HE SHOULD ALSO BE ABLE TO REVERSE IT. AND IF HE'S NOT WILLING, I HAVE SOME LEADEN ARGUMENTS ON MY SIDE.
ER, HI THERE... I'M LOOKING FOR CHENG LEE, THE TATTOO ARTIST.
HE DIED IN AN ACCIDENT A FEW WEEKS AGO.
...HE WAS MY FATHER...
...A CUSTOMER WHO DIDN'T WANT TO PAY HIT HIM WITH HIS CAR.
JESUS... I... I'M SORRY...
BAR
?
GOTTA GO!

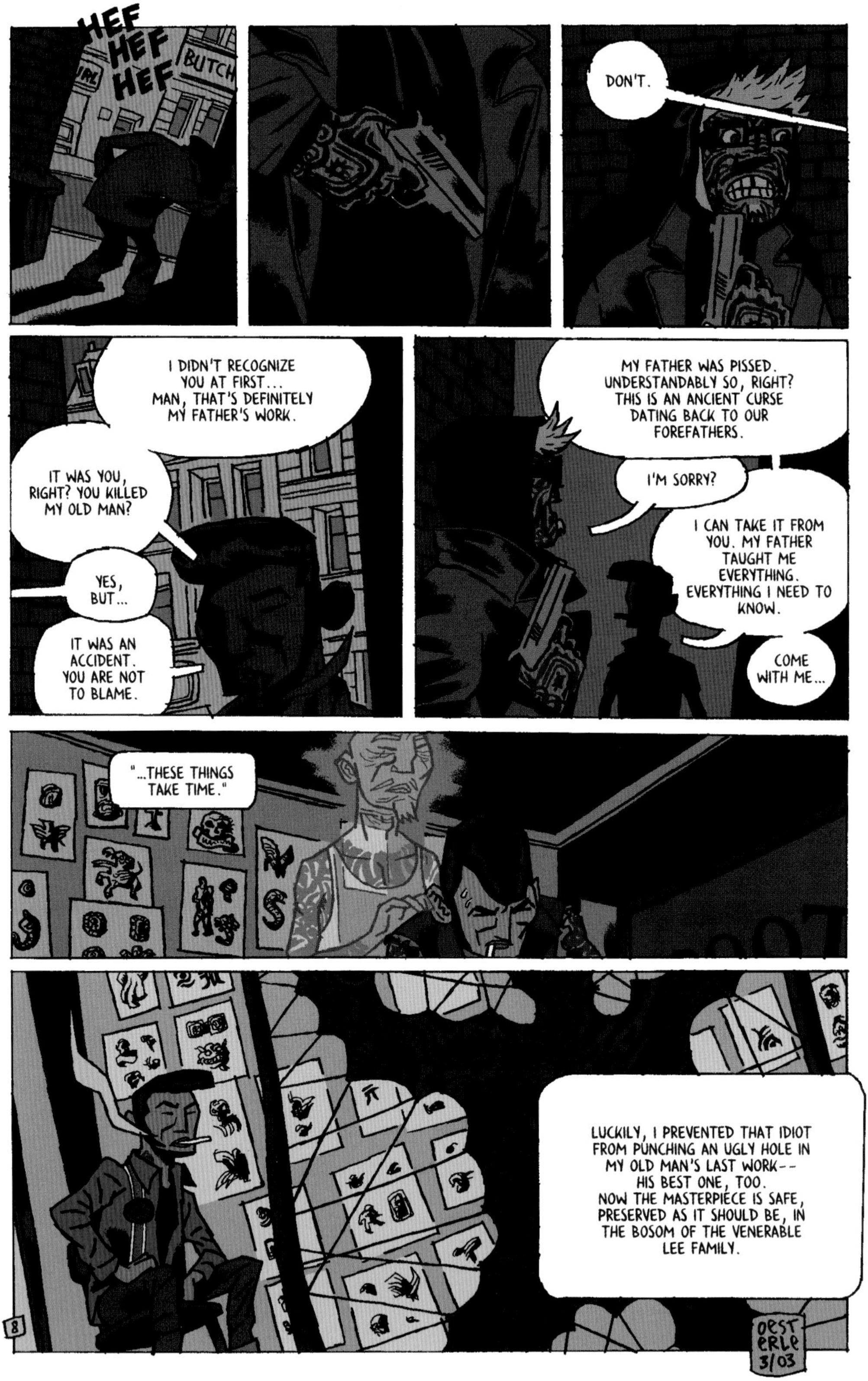
HEF HEF HEF
BUTCH
DON'T.
I DIDN'T RECOGNIZE YOU AT FIRST... MAN, THAT'S DEFINITELY MY FATHER'S WORK.
IT WAS YOU, RIGHT? YOU KILLED MY OLD MAN?
YES, BUT...
IT WAS AN ACCIDENT. YOU ARE NOT TO BLAME.
MY FATHER WAS PISSED. UNDERSTANDABLY SO, RIGHT? THIS IS AN ANCIENT CURSE DATING BACK TO OUR FOREFATHERS.
I'M SORRY?
I CAN TAKE IT FROM YOU. MY FATHER TAUGHT ME EVERYTHING. EVERYTHING I NEED TO KNOW.
COME WITH ME...
"...THESE THINGS TAKE TIME."
LUCKILY, I PREVENTED THAT IDIOT FROM PUNCHING AN UGLY HOLE IN MY OLD MAN'S LAST WORK-- HIS BEST ONE, TOO. NOW THE MASTERPIECE IS SAFE, PRESERVED AS IT SHOULD BE, IN THE BOSOM OF THE VENERABLE LEE FAMILY.
8
OESTERLE 3/03

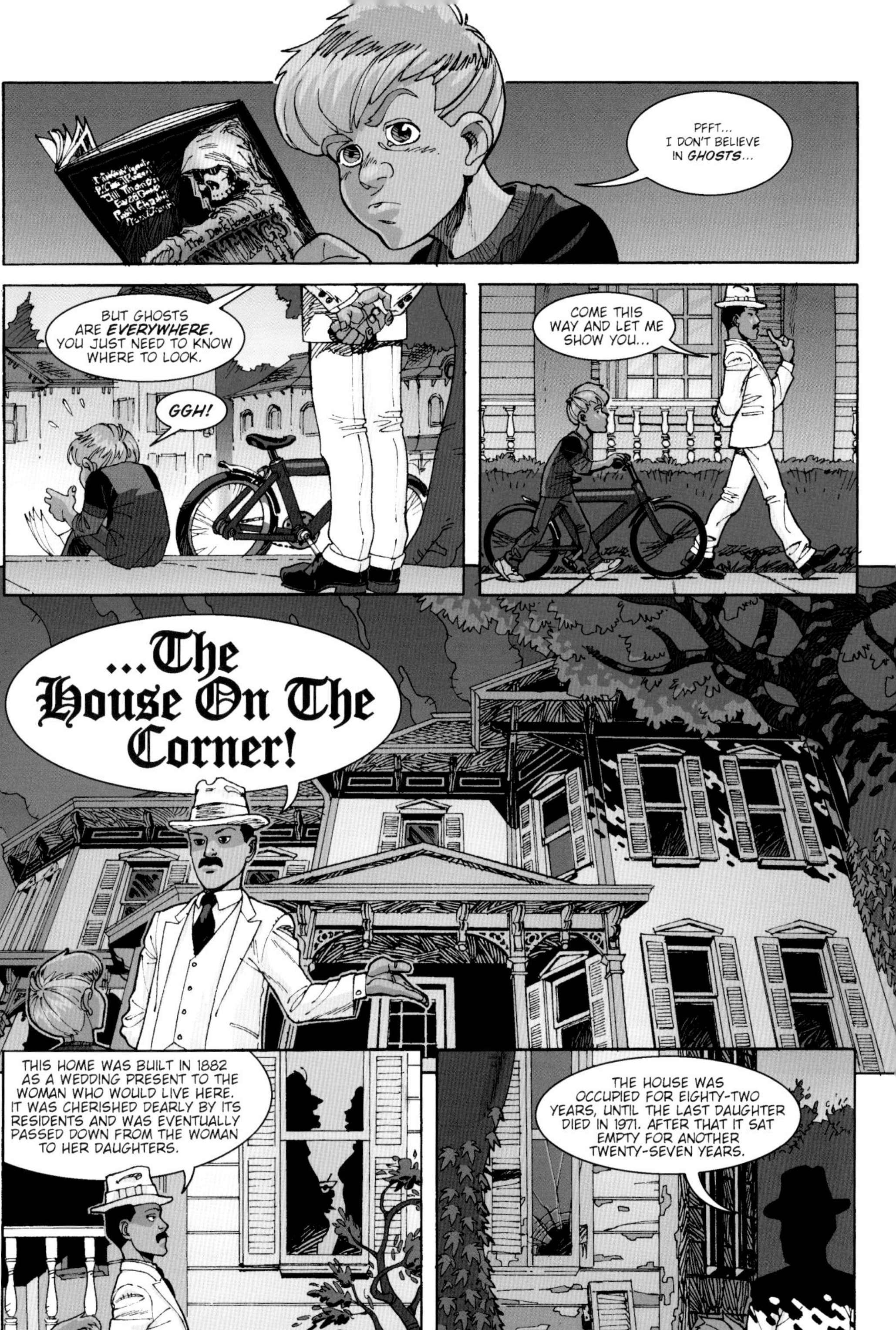
PFFT... I DON'T BELIEVE IN GHOSTS...
BUT GHOSTS ARE EVERYWHERE. YOU JUST NEED TO KNOW WHERE TO LOOK.
GGH!
COME THIS WAY AND LET ME SHOW YOU...
...The House On The Corner!
THIS HOME WAS BUILT IN 1882 AS A WEDDING PRESENT TO THE WOMAN WHO WOULD LIVE HERE. IT WAS CHERISHED DEARLY BY ITS RESIDENTS AND WAS EVENTUALLY PASSED DOWN FROM THE WOMAN TO HER DAUGHTERS.
THE HOUSE WAS OCCUPIED FOR EIGHTY-TWO YEARS, UNTIL THE LAST DAUGHTER DIED IN 1971. AFTER THAT IT SAT EMPTY FOR ANOTHER TWENTY-SEVEN YEARS.

BY FREEWATER & MARANGON

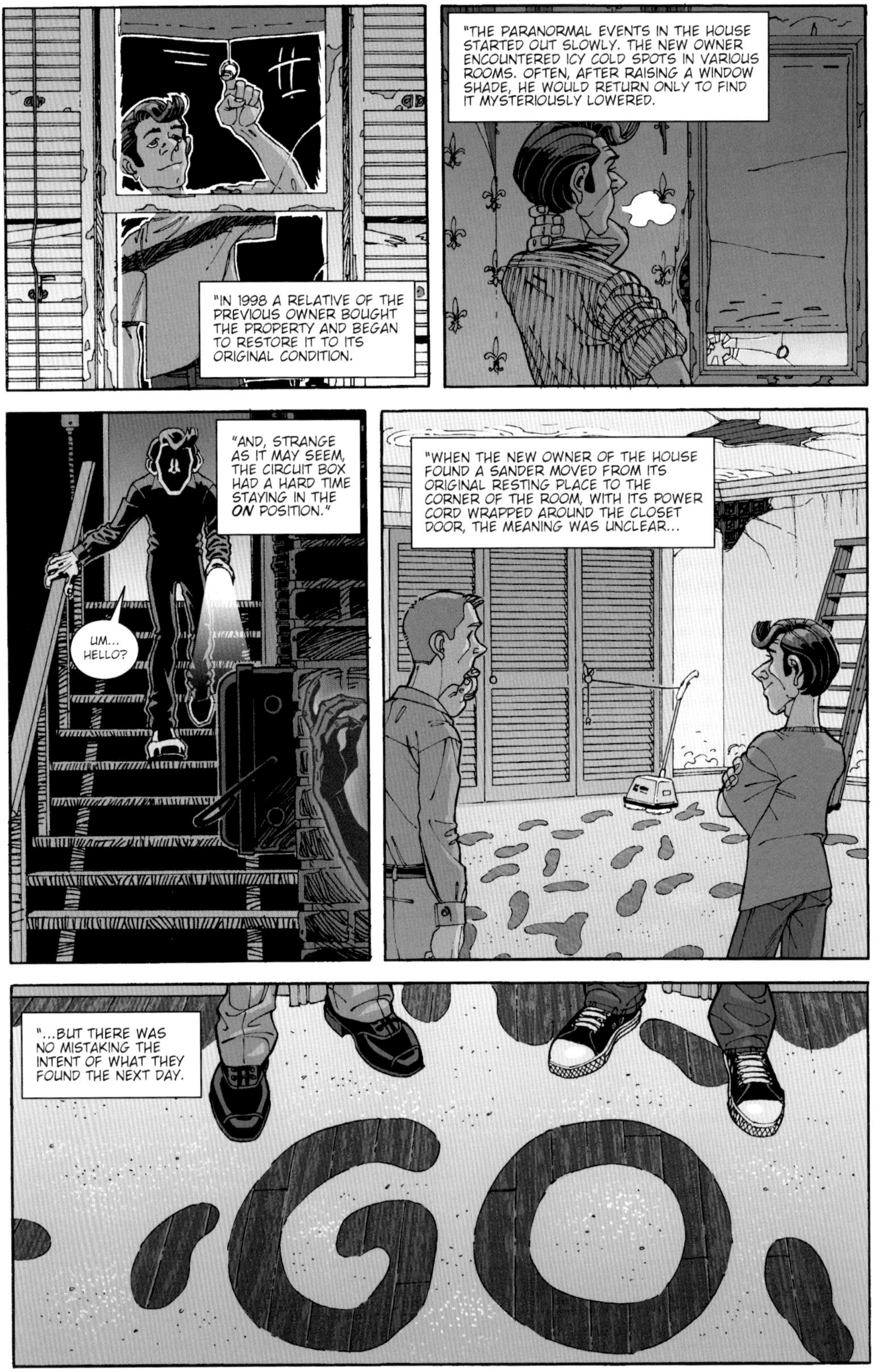

"IN 1998 A RELATIVE OF THE PREVIOUS OWNER BOUGHT THE PROPERTY AND BEGAN TO RESTORE IT TO ITS ORIGINAL CONDITION.
"THE PARANORMAL EVENTS IN THE HOUSE STARTED OUT SLOWLY. THE NEW OWNER ENCOUNTERED ICY COLD SPOTS IN VARIOUS ROOMS. OFTEN, AFTER RAISING A WINDOW SHADE, HE WOULD RETURN ONLY TO FIND IT MYSTERIOUSLY LOWERED.
"AND, STRANGE AS IT MAY SEEM, THE CIRCUIT BOX HAD A HARD TIME STAYING IN THE ON POSITION."
UM... HELLO?
"WHEN THE NEW OWNER OF THE HOUSE FOUND A SANDER MOVED FROM ITS ORIGINAL RESTING PLACE TO THE CORNER OF THE ROOM, WITH ITS POWER CORD WRAPPED AROUND THE CLOSET DOOR, THE MEANING WAS UNCLEAR...
"...BUT THERE WAS NO MISTAKING THE INTENT OF WHAT THEY FOUND THE NEXT DAY.
GO

"THIS OTHERWORLDLY MESSAGE WAS IGNORED, AND WORK ON THE HOUSE CONTINUED. AND SO DID THE HAUNTING."

HEY!

POP!

"IF THE GHOST COULDN'T GET THE NEW OWNER TO LEAVE, THEN AT LEAST IT COULD COMMENT ON THE REDECORATING CHOICES..."

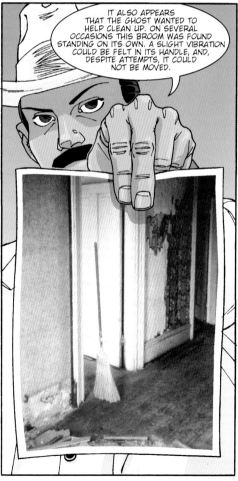

IT ALSO APPEARS THAT THE GHOST WANTED TO HELP CLEAN UP. ON SEVERAL OCCASIONS THIS BROOM WAS FOUND STANDING ON ITS OWN. A SLIGHT VIBRATION COULD BE FELT IN ITS HANDLE, AND, DESPITE ATTEMPTS, IT COULD NOT BE MOVED.

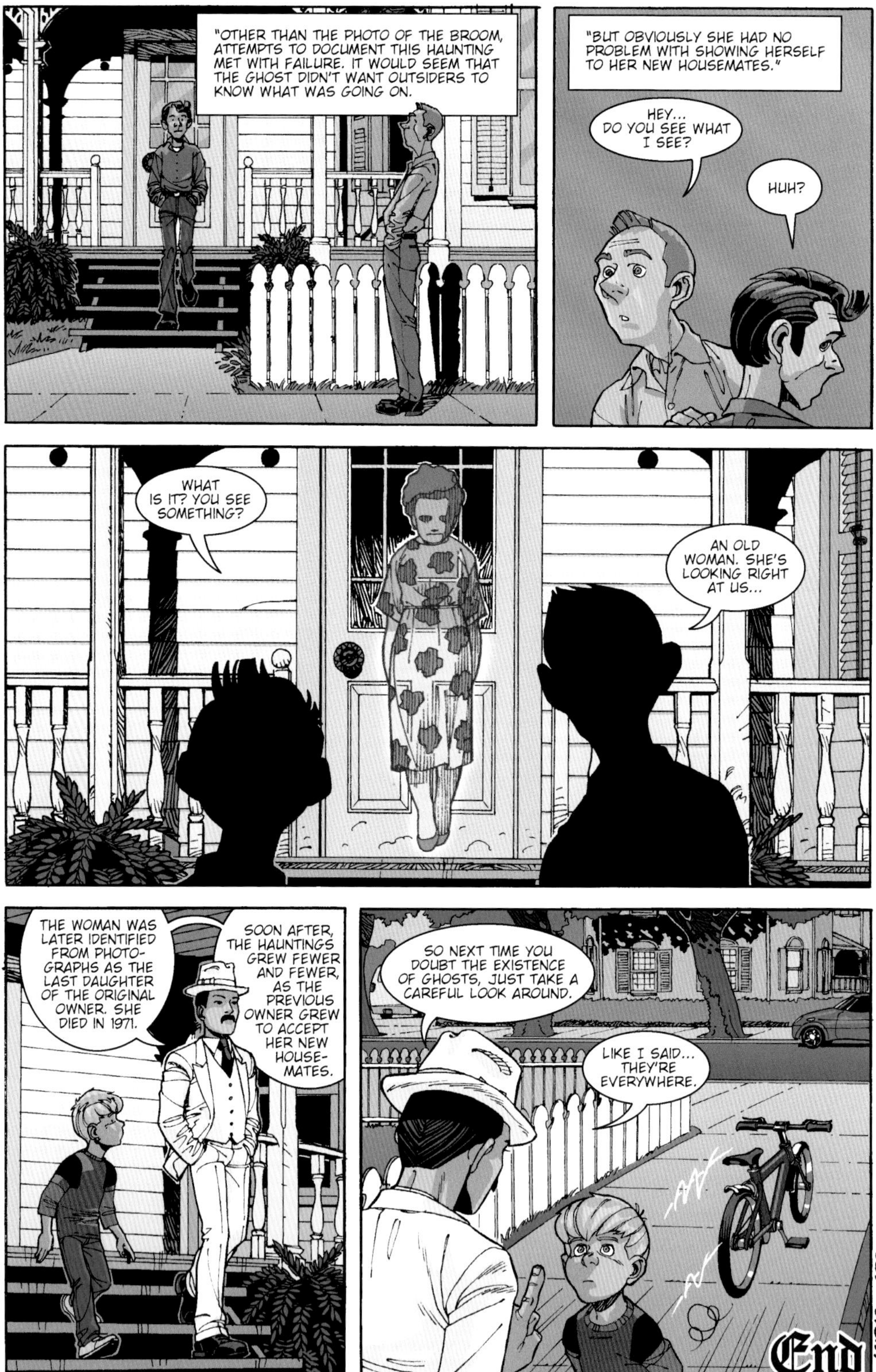
"OTHER THAN THE PHOTO OF THE BROOM, ATTEMPTS TO DOCUMENT THIS HAUNTING MET WITH FAILURE. IT WOULD SEEM THAT THE GHOST DIDN'T WANT OUTSIDERS TO KNOW WHAT WAS GOING ON.
"BUT OBVIOUSLY SHE HAD NO PROBLEM WITH SHOWING HERSELF TO HER NEW HOUSEMATES."
HEY... DO YOU SEE WHAT I SEE?
HUH?
WHAT IS IT? YOU SEE SOMETHING?
AN OLD WOMAN. SHE'S LOOKING RIGHT AT US...
THE WOMAN WAS LATER IDENTIFIED FROM PHOTO-GRAPHS AS THE LAST DAUGHTER OF THE ORIGINAL OWNER. SHE DIED IN 1971.
SOON AFTER, THE HAUNTINGS GREW FEWER AND FEWER, AS THE PREVIOUS OWNER GREW TO ACCEPT HER NEW HOUSE-MATES.
SO NEXT TIME YOU DOUBT THE EXISTENCE OF GHOSTS, JUST TAKE A CAREFUL LOOK AROUND.
LIKE I SAID... THEY'RE EVERYWHERE.
End
—LUCAS—'03

Spirit Rescue

An interview with séance medium
L. L. DRELLER

by SCOTT ALLIE

*A*fter failing out of college, Larry Dreller avoided the draft by joining the Navy. After seeing a bit of the world, he returned to college, at the University of Denver, majoring in education and world history. He taught a variety of high-school subjects in the U.S., Canada, Australia, and England, before returning to Denver. There he taught briefly in Catholic schools, before settling into work with the state of Colorado, first in youth services, and later with the Department of Employment. Somehow all of this led to his current occupation, as a retiree heavily involved with the First Spiritual Science Church, where he conducts trainings and séances. He's written two books on his experiences and his gift, both for Weiser Books.

ALLIE: *Was Catholicism your religion of origin?*

DRELLLER: No. I was brought up as a sort of hard-nosed Lutheran, and I converted to Roman Catholic because of my girlfriend. In those days you had to—I think you still do—and then she took off and became a nun. I really have some power there, don't I? But I just don't believe in organized religions. They're boring.

Even the Spiritualist church that you're part of now isn't actually the Spiritualist church—you said it was an off-branch?

It's an off-branch. The Spiritualists don't believe in reincarnation, and the church that I go to does, so they left the National Spiritualist church.

How did the Spiritualist church start?

It goes back roughly to 1848, with the Fox sisters. I believe the town was Hydesville, New York. Actually, there was some movement even before this. I can never remember his name, but there was a man about twenty-two years of age who had visions in New York. He coined a lot of phrases that eventually were taken over in the Spiritualist religion. But in 1848, Hydesville, New York, the Fox sisters heard noises in the basement, and found that they could communicate with the spirit. It was a traveling salesman named Charles Haynes, who was murdered and buried in the basement. This idea of contacting spirits became a sensation, which spread throughout the United States and into Europe. People threw in some Christianity and it became Spiritualism. Then came séances, table tipping, and eventually the Ouija board, which was very popular in the early 1900s. Spiritualism spread, and it really came to fruition around WWI when there was just a catastrophic loss of life. People wanted to find out if there is life after death. They didn't trust their organized religion.

I always thought the word Spiritualism referred to spirituality, but it's not merely spirituality as most people think of it, but—

Spirit communication. Life after death. The early Spiritualists started designing rituals, based on something called the power of the white light. The Spiritualists said the white light was sent from God, the universe, or Jesus, wherever. So you can see there's an intimate relationship between Christianity and Spiritualism. We have that ritual where we say that we believe in God, and we believe God is in everyone and everything, and God is love, and we are spiritual beings in a material existence. But mainly we create our own reality with our own thoughts. We also are very strong on the idea "question reality." Always question reality, because in our techno-materialist society, we're given a new reality, and we lose the reality and spirituality of ourselves.

In both books you talk a lot about different aspects of Zen discipline. Do distinctly Eastern traditions go all the way back to the origin of Spiritualism, or is that new?

That's a newer thing. A woman named Helen Blavatsky founded a movement called Theosophy, which helped bring Zen Buddhist meditation to the West. As with Spiritualists, Theosophists believe we go on to another place. In Buddhism, as you well know, we are reborn until we get rid of our negative karma. And that's in Spiritualism also.

Is that the Spiritualists' conflict with reincarnation—they believe we move beyond this life, rather than being reborn back into it?

Right—in Spiritualism, you go on to an astral plane, where you are learning the meaning of your previous life, and are now learning what the meaning of the universe is really about and how you fit into the scheme of things.

The first time you encountered a spirit, you were a teenager—is that right?

That was my grandfather, whom I never met in his life. He used to visit me in my dreams. A lot of the knowledge that you get from the spirit world does come through dreams. He told me to study harder and stop fighting my relatives. That there's more after this life. He taught me about spiritual baggage. You take all this stuff—who you are, your personality—with you. Do you want a negative personality, or do you want a positive personality? I told my grandmother about these dreams. She pulled out an old album, and there he was. And he was quite a dapper individual.

Then there was my grandmother's best friend who passed away. I went to her funeral and saw her. She was dressed up like a woman in the early fifties. The long gloves to the elbow, and a big picture hat. And she was young, and very, very pretty. Later I looked at the photos of her and she was a beauty, but not toward the end of her life.

From then on, my experiences really opened up. I think I had the gift very early. I supposedly suffered crib death twice. I can still remember the visions I saw as a baby—they stayed with me. To this day it scares the bejesus out of me. After you're in the craft for a long time, you know that life continues, but the thing is, when my time comes, I don't want to go. It's still mysterious. We're not given all the answers ...

This is where the readership has to drop skeptical thoughts and realize that life does continue. The thing is, Scott, we are energy, we are essence. You remember the first law of thermodynamics? Everything in our universe is comprised of matter, which essentially means electromagnetic atoms, small jewels—everything that occupies space has energy. It can switch back and forth. I like to use the analogy of how water can be frozen—it changes form, and it can evaporate into steam. It can dissipate entirely, but it's energy. All the energy that has ever been created is still here. We change form. We're just quickly moving molecules which take on the appearance of solidity. So my hypothesis is that when we pass away our energy goes on.

And those experiences led you to Spiritualism?

Well, I was busy being a teenager, you know, raging, surging hormones. I didn't think as much about this stuff. Then I went into the Navy. It was in San Diego. We used to put a lot of the World War II ships and Korean war ships in mothballs—all sealed up. We'd salvage equipment from these old ships. Sextants never really get old—signal flags, binoculars. Even their jackets. One night I was on the night watch, and I vaguely heard this music. On a ship when the hatches are closed, you really can't hear anything.

Were you on the ship at this point?

I was on the ship. It was moored next to ours. I opened the hatches on the quartermaster locker. I opened it up, and there were three young sailors. One had red hair, and one was down on the floor playing cards. He had them spread out, and the other two were laughing. On the radio receivers—beautiful radios back then—there was this big-band music I later identified as Glenn Miller. I said, What are you guys doing here? They looked up at me and disappeared. The cards stayed, and I put one in my pocket, and kept it for a long time. It was the queen of hearts.

It must have been a lot different than seeing the spirit of your grandfather in a dream, or seeing your grandmother's friend at a funeral. This must have been much more concrete.

Very, very personal. They weren't very far from me.

Was it scary for you, or were you getting accustomed to this sort of thing?

I was already used to having experiences. I could tell in high school whether a girl was going to turn me down. I could tell what the teacher was thinking. I did pretty well in school. You don't question it, because when you are a medium, or you're psychically aware, you have to be open and have a clear mind, and get rid of doubt.

Do you see a difference between a medium and a psychic?

Oh, they're really interrelated. A medium is a receiver between that higher world and this world. A séance medium contacts the departed, the deceased, or—ugly word—the dead! A psychic does things like readings, and has a precognitive skill. Sometimes they can have visions and so on, but they don't talk to the dead.

In the first book you talk about two kinds of mediums, referring to the particular methods the medium might use.

Right. The first is a mental medium, or trance medium, who uses his or her clairvoyant, clairaudient, or clairsentient gifts. Then you have your physical medium—or you did in the old days. They used to call them platform mediums, showbiz people. These are the ones that got into trouble with fraud. They had the ectoplasm—I saw a demonstration of that once, and I thought it was fascinating.

What was that like?

It's usually done in a soft light—red light is best, because it's an ethereal substance, as it's been explained to me. A deceased person gets into the physical medium's body, talks through their vocal chords, and then expels this ectoplasm. It comes out of the mouth and other body orifices. Sometimes it turns into little miniatures of the deceased person's head and face and arms, and so on. And talks. I've seen a demonstration where it came out of a person's mouth. It's not done much anymore because it was attacked by Harry Houdini and other people. But Sir Arthur Conan Doyle was very in awe of it. It's been reported that Queen Victoria held séances all the time.

When you were in the Navy, were you already starting to perform séances?

No. Oh, that came much later. It would be too strange in the Navy to go around and say, Let's have a séance.

How long ago was it that you started?

After the Navy I was a graduate student being tested by a graduate student in psychology. Someone from a long, long line of mediums trained me. His first name is Tim—I'll just let it be Tim. He came from generations of séance mediums in New Orleans, which seems to be America's most haunted place. We formed several study circles. We held a lot of séances, and talked to people.

You mentioned a ritual, but what does that consist of?

You should already know each other, you should have worked up to this for a little while before you really get into it, because some people have fear, some people are skeptical. You want to make sure that you're all singing from the same page. This is the way it was taught to me. We stand up, join hands, and then someone lights the candles, and convenes. We use white candles, lit with a wooden kitchen match. We bring these spirit forces into our bodies, asking for strength, protection, and guidance. They can make themselves known by odors, noise, temperature changes, and sighted appearances. When I've gotten really deeply into trance, I've called people in.

Is there a physical sensation that accompanies that?

There's a tingle. I have a tingling feeling; others have been flat, you know, nothing. You can't expect immediate results, but sometimes, boy, does it ever flow!

What happens when it is flowing? The whole group feels it?

Yes. Then we do the invocation—"The Spirits Above, the Spirits Below, the Spirits to the North of us, the Spirits to the South of us, the Spirits to the East of us, the Spirits to the West of us. Please attend us; answer our questions …" or do you have anything to say, or we would like to talk to you. It just all depends on what the group wants to accomplish.

Do you have a particular group that you work with?

I haven't been working with a group recently. I'm about to start some courses, and we're going over my second book now, doing corrections. There are several people here that are very gifted in astral projection, and have talked to spirits.

Beyond doing séances, you also purge unwanted spirits from homes.

I'm going to do one this weekend, as a matter of fact. It's simple. The Native Americans burned sage, cedar, and other natural plants, and I use that every so often. The Buddhists use incense, as do the Roman Catholics. The old

Spiritualists' way to purge starts with three cups of tap water and one cup of white vinegar—don't ask me why, it has to be white vinegar—and one cup of salt. I understand that sea salt works best. You bring it to boil in a pan, and you start from the bottom level of the building. All the windows, from bottom to top, must be open. You carry this steaming pan through each room.

That's basically a smudging.

Just like the Native Americans use. And in each room you ask that any spirit who is there leave this house in the holy white light and do not return. Go in peace. And that's a soul rescue.

So you're not so much chasing spirits out as helping them along?

Yes. When you want to get a spirit out of a haunting, you want to inform them that, yes, indeed, they're dead, and it's time to move on. It does no good to linger here.

What about unwanted spirits, or lower-level spirits? You say that these are the spirits of people who have kind of lived bad lives or who haven't—

Well, some of them are in paybacks. And you know, paybacks are a bitch. These malevolent spirits, or ghosts, are negative energy. That's the best way to put it. Scott, remember we talked about the revenants as well as the haunters? Revenants are people who have passed on, but are still sort of confused and have left behind vibrations and energy scars. There's a refusal to let go of who they were. They're confused and shocked, in a state of denial.

These are the angry ones. They don't want to go, or they had so much negative spiritual baggage, that they can't go. And they become haunters, which are angry, confused, and disbelieving spirits. They can become stronger and malevolent, feeding off the fear we project. They can linger around for centuries, because, remember, there is no concept of time.

Besides these sort of negative energies of humans who lived bad lives, do you encounter any other sort of spirits? Do you think there's such a thing as demons?

No, I think "demon" is a misused term. Demons are considered evil, but they weren't in ancient Greece—a demon was just a person that passed on—that's where the word comes from. Now we have the connotation that demons are evil, and ugly, and bad. I have, however, brushed shoulders several times with entities that I don't think had the best of intentions.

This is one thing that I haven't had enough personal experience with. The paranormal researchers have got to get in here and get it figured out. So far they've worked their way through ESP and precognition, but they have to really start investigating what these entities are.

So you think it's important to look at paranormal issues with the same kind of certainty that scientists look at their work?

Yes. But scientists are skeptics, because they rely on being able to weigh and classify, being able to see, touch, smell, hear—this type of thing. I never worry about skeptics. It will have to happen to them.

Scott, in the history of mankind, we have had hundreds of thousands to maybe millions of brushes with spirits. Is it all imagination? Come on. I know they exist. But how do you pull this out and let someone in a lab analyze it? The scientific community knows that something is amiss, and they are turning resources to it. They're looking at near death experiences, the whole light at the end of the tunnel we see. They say these experiences are due to medication, that the person isn't really dead, they had hypoxia, a lack of oxygen to the brain. And now they've come up with a new explanation, which I think is kind of cute—going through the tunnel and seeing the light is the brain revisiting the birth canal.

When we first spoke, I mentioned Hans Holzer, and you referred to him as the master—

He's the master.

He's no doubt the most famous ghost hunter in the twentieth century. But you're a lot more sympathetic to the spirits than Holzer. He was really chasing people—spirits—out of houses, in a much more old-fashioned way, treating spirits like pests. So I was a little surprised to hear you refer to him as the master, because it seems like what you do is very different. Also, he wasn't even a medium— he employed the services of others, like Sybil Leek, who also published a lot of books on her own adventures.

Well, Holzer is the intellectual scholar researcher. But let me ask you, how does he know so much? This man is obviously a medium, and just does not say that he is. He knows too much.

Why can't he just know from experience without actually having the sensitivity that you have?

I just feel from reading his books that he has brushed shoulders, or he wouldn't be in this area.

Well, he certainly brushed shoulders with a lot of entities. In his books he goes into great detail about the hauntings themselves. In a lot of instances, like the famous haunted hotel in San Diego, he didn't actually have the experiences—he relays the experiences of others, then brings in a medium to help him deal with it.

He just knows too much, and I think he has dabbled. That's why I feel he's the one who brought ghost investigation to the forefront. And in that, he is the master. There's a book that I would recommend very much. It's called, *Ghost: Investigating the Other Side*, by Katherine Ramsland. She's an investigative reporter. She was unconvinced in the first chapters, and in the end she knows it's so. Oh, I'm sure it has a lot to do with selling books, but I could tell from her tone that now she's a believer. The impartial, the distant, the skeptical—once they have one experience, it leads to the next, to the next, to the next.

Another big difference between you and Holzer is that your view of the entities is much more sympathetic. Holzer was a reflection of an older time, looking at ghosts simply as a problem. He'd just go in and get rid of them. What you do is more like therapy for the ghost, as well as therapy for the people there. You're very up-front that this approach to looking at the afterlife is a way for people to feel better about their present lives, to have a bigger picture about where their loved ones have gone, and maybe where they're going.

You hit it right on the head. We do have a survival of the personality, we take our essence with us, and you can call it a ghost, soul, spirit, energy, whatever. We let fear grow instead of trying to realize who these poor people were. But we can learn from them, which is what we do in the séances. I've been very lucky to be able to meet with one of my deceased relatives, my maternal grandmother, whom I loved very much, and to whom I dedicated my first book.

If a person believes that they are in a haunted house, that they're living with a spirit of some kind, what would your advice to them be?

If they feel they want to just get rid of it, they can then purge it with sea salt and vinegar. But I don't know if I'd want to call an exorcist. It's almost impossible—the Catholic Church looks the other way, and as Episcopalians go, it would really have to be proven. But if everything becomes really bad, deplorable and negative, move.

I thought you might say people shouldn't be scared, but you're saying it's natural to be afraid of these things.

Can you imagine, Scott, how many spirits, ghosts, essences, whatever, are with us right now? If we saw them all, we'd crack up.

My mother-in-law was living with us, my wife and children and me, and she said, You know that you're haunted here? She used to be kind of restless, an insomniac. She'd go downstairs to the family room and sleep on the couch. She said this man kept coming. He had red eyes, and was very, very tall. His head touched the ceiling. We had nine-foot-high ceilings, and he would stare at her. So she moved. After that, we were always visited at the same time, Wednesday evening about 9:00, by the smell of burned feathers or hair. Then it got very cold. The kids' clothes were always rearranged, thrown on the floor. Could have been a poltergeist. The kids were adolescent, and those teenage hormone surges are what they say brings on poltergeist activity. Anyway, this spirit would come and we'd smell this obnoxious odor. I had the electrician make sure there wasn't anything wrong, and it was at that particular time that we really got bombarded. It was warm, so there was no reason for the fireplaces in the neighborhood to be going. So it shouldn't be that odor of burning. But it would come through, and I thought, Well, let's get someone to deal with this. And that worked ... at first. Then it came back a few months later, so I started doing my ritual, and it worked for a while, but it kept coming back.

Did you ever see the spirit that your mother-in-law referred to?

No, but neighborhoods in the suburbs being what they are, the neighborhood kids told us that there had been a suicide in our house—in my study, as a matter of fact. A teenage girl had tried to commit suicide several times. We sold the house and moved. Luckily it didn't come along with us. Sometimes they will—they'll follow you.

I've had a lot of interesting experiences, but I haven't put those in the books, because they'd just go on and on. And people want proof—although there are a heck of a lot of people that I run across who say, Hey, I loved your book—let me tell you about my experience!

When my wife and I actually did see some spirits was when we were newlyweds, and we were living in an apartment in Capitol Hill, here in Denver. It's an older neighborhood, and we were visited several times by a young man standing at the foot of our bed. My wife finally saw it, so she became sort of a believer. And we moved. We found out from the landlord that the man had committed suicide in our place. Thanks for telling us! You know, because I would not have moved in! I'd thought the deal was awfully good. I didn't use any of my arts to get rid of him, I just said to Lana, my wife, Let's move!

Then two years ago we went to New Orleans, and we were staying with these friends in one of their timeshares, in one of the oldest sections of New Orleans. There was a hospital there dating back to the French. We were staying with this couple—in separate rooms, Scott. Anyway, the gal we were staying with—she's very scientific, very rational—she said, Boy, I feel uneasy here! And even her husband said, I just feel creepy and crawly. And they didn't sleep at all. Then one night there was a raging storm in New Orleans—you know what it's like down there when they get thunder and lightning? Well, the lightning lit up the window, and there was this young soldier in a strange outfit, very Battle of New Orleans—

A Civil War uniform?

Civil War or something like that. I vaguely recognized his bandolier and his hat, as he was standing at the end of the bed. We were in New Orleans for about five, six days, and he stayed there. He'd stare down at me, and it gave me the creeps. Poor kid. He wasn't more than sixteen or seventeen years of age. Well, anyway, I was talking to a lady down on the wharf—she was running a tourist booth, and she said, Where are you staying? And I told her, and she got big eyes and looked at me, and she said, Oh my God! She used to own that place, but she left it because the ghosts kept bothering her kids. One night she'd been washing the dishes, and the dishes started flying around, smashing against things. And she said it was time to get out of there.

We also went to several of the plantations—Oh, my God, the vibrations were so incredible. I got headaches, and I'd have to get out of the tour and go outside. I'd hear banjo music in one place. My hair was being touched— what little hair I have left was being stroked, and I could feel cobwebs over my face, breath blowing in my ears. I always get nervous, Scott, because I don't want them to come with me. I'm afraid they're going to piggyback on me. I kept thinking of white light, white light, white light. A misty white light surrounding me.

Scott, I've had so many wonderful things, been gifted with so many wonderful encounters. There comes a point, when you're at a cocktail party or something—I start talking about it, and you should see their eyes. I just say, Oh ho ho, just kidding. And I move on, because it's not fully acceptable. But when science devotes itself to investigating hauntings, my God, they get these wonderful sightings, some of which show up on the real high-speed film. I have a friend that is doing that. He's a commercial photographer, but he's going after spirits now. When they get these photographs, people say, Oh, it's been doctored! Or it's the light coming in through the drapes—we have a million excuses for why it can happen. Scott, think about when it becomes provable—we have a place to go to when we die. What a neat thing! Our personality does survive. It's not the end.

Larry Dreller is a practicing medium, and has been for several decades. His books on these experiences, Beginner's Guide to Mediumship *and* Secrets of a Medium, *are available from better bookstores, or the publisher, Red Wheel Weiser at redwheelweiser.com.*

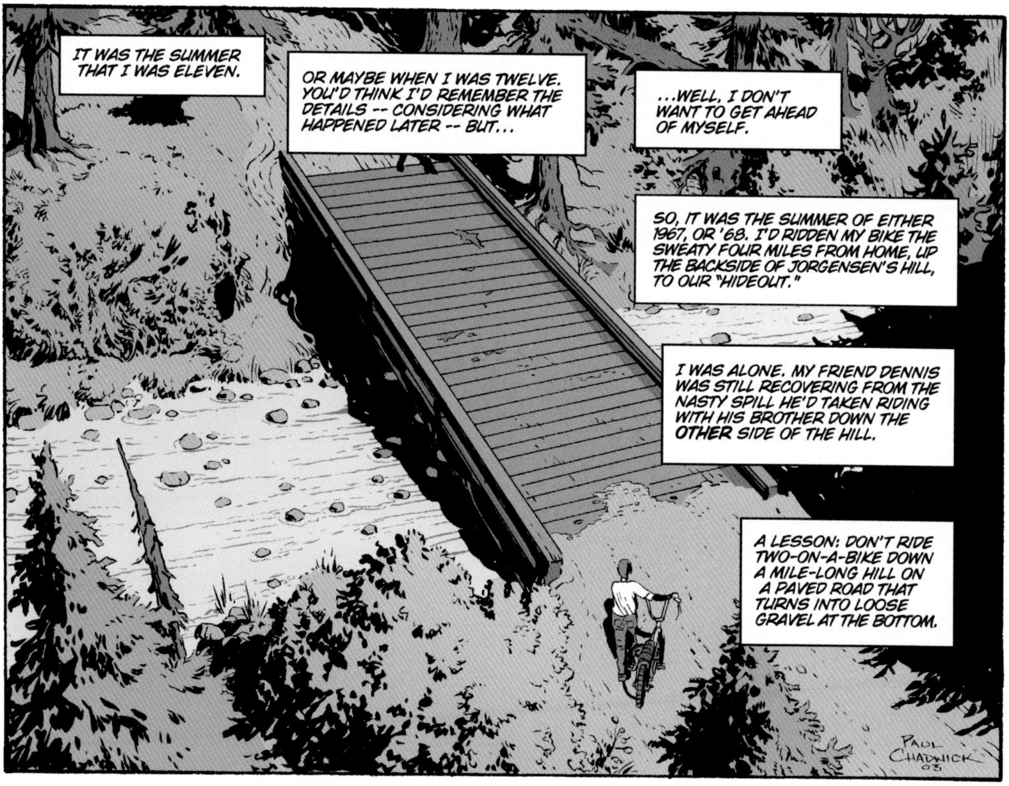
IT WAS THE SUMMER THAT I WAS ELEVEN.
OR MAYBE WHEN I WAS TWELVE. YOU'D THINK I'D REMEMBER THE DETAILS -- CONSIDERING WHAT HAPPENED LATER -- BUT...
...WELL, I DON'T WANT TO GET AHEAD OF MYSELF.
SO, IT WAS THE SUMMER OF EITHER 1967, OR '68. I'D RIDDEN MY BIKE THE SWEATY FOUR MILES FROM HOME, UP THE BACKSIDE OF JORGENSEN'S HILL, TO OUR "HIDEOUT."
I WAS ALONE. MY FRIEND DENNIS WAS STILL RECOVERING FROM THE NASTY SPILL HE'D TAKEN RIDING WITH HIS BROTHER DOWN THE OTHER SIDE OF THE HILL.
A LESSON: DON'T RIDE TWO-ON-A-BIKE DOWN A MILE-LONG HILL ON A PAVED ROAD THAT TURNS INTO LOOSE GRAVEL AT THE BOTTOM.
PAUL CHADWICK

Lies, Death, and Olfactory Delusions

Written by Randy Stradley   Art by Paul Chadwick   Colors and Letters by Michelle Madsen

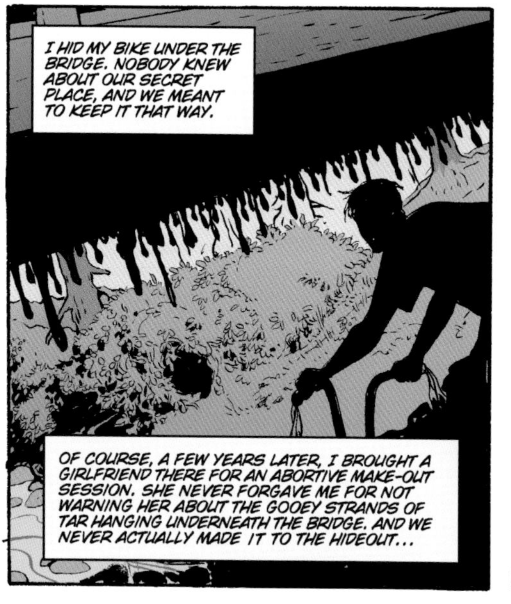
I HID MY BIKE UNDER THE BRIDGE. NOBODY KNEW ABOUT OUR SECRET PLACE, AND WE MEANT TO KEEP IT THAT WAY.
OF COURSE, A FEW YEARS LATER, I BROUGHT A GIRLFRIEND THERE FOR AN ABORTIVE MAKE-OUT SESSION. SHE NEVER FORGAVE ME FOR NOT WARNING HER ABOUT THE GOOEY STRANDS OF TAR HANGING UNDERNEATH THE BRIDGE. AND WE NEVER ACTUALLY MADE IT TO THE HIDEOUT...

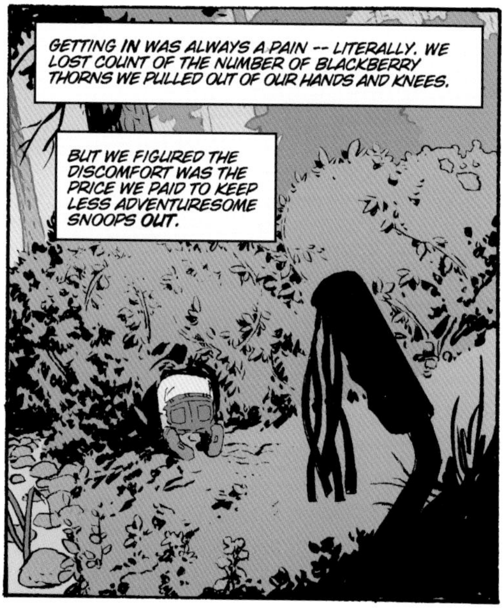
GETTING IN WAS ALWAYS A PAIN -- LITERALLY. WE LOST COUNT OF THE NUMBER OF BLACKBERRY THORNS WE PULLED OUT OF OUR HANDS AND KNEES.
BUT WE FIGURED THE DISCOMFORT WAS THE PRICE WE PAID TO KEEP LESS ADVENTURESOME SNOOPS OUT.

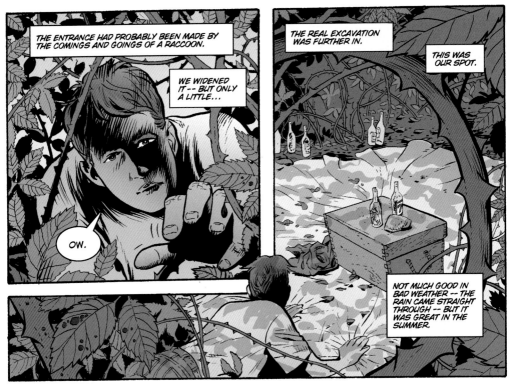

THE ENTRANCE HAD PROBABLY BEEN MADE BY THE COMINGS AND GOINGS OF A RACCOON.

WE WIDENED IT -- BUT ONLY A LITTLE...

OW.

THE REAL EXCAVATION WAS FURTHER IN.

THIS WAS OUR SPOT.

NOT MUCH GOOD IN BAD WEATHER -- THE RAIN CAME STRAIGHT THROUGH -- BUT IT WAS GREAT IN THE SUMMER.

I HAD NO REAL OBJECTIVE IN COMING TO THE HIDEOUT THAT DAY.

I HAD READ EVERY COMIC BOOK AND LOOKED AT EVERY PLAYBOY THAT WE HAD STASHED THERE UNTIL THEY WERE COMMITTED TO MEMORY.

I GUESS I JUST WANTED TO GET AWAY FROM MY SISTER AND HER FRIENDS.

"I'M 'DAPPLED,'" I REMEMBER THINKING.

AND THEN I NOTICED SOMETHING ELSE.

SNIFF SNIFF

I KNEW EXACTLY WHAT IT WAS.

I HAD SMELLED THAT SMELL OFTEN ENOUGH...

...BUT HE COULDN'T HAVE FOUND THIS PLACE... COULD HE?

LARRY?

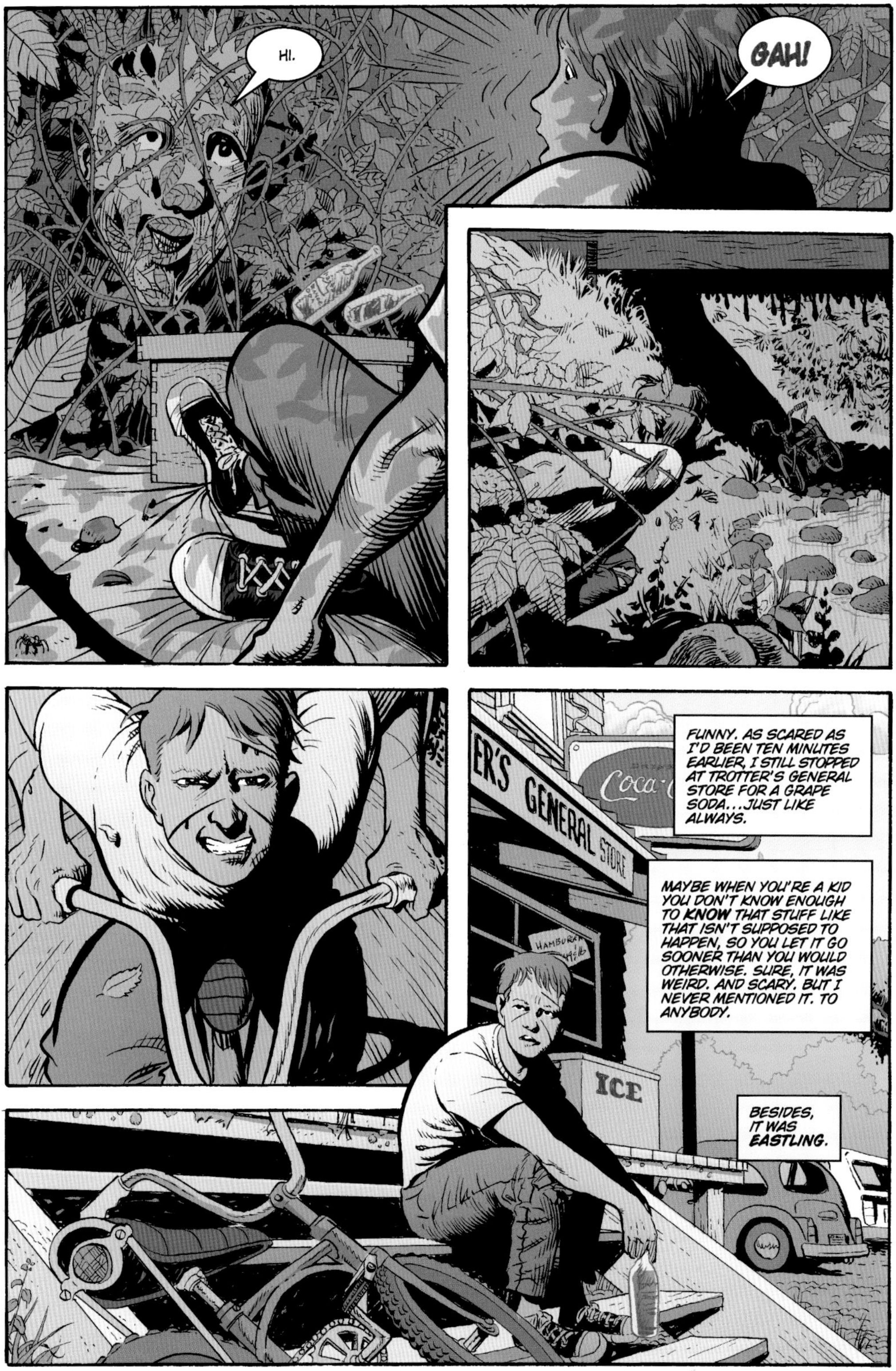
HI.
GAH!
ER'S GENERAL STORE
Coca-Co
FUNNY. AS SCARED AS I'D BEEN TEN MINUTES EARLIER, I STILL STOPPED AT TROTTER'S GENERAL STORE FOR A GRAPE SODA...JUST LIKE ALWAYS.
MAYBE WHEN YOU'RE A KID YOU DON'T KNOW ENOUGH TO **KNOW** THAT STUFF LIKE THAT ISN'T SUPPOSED TO HAPPEN, SO YOU LET IT GO SOONER THAN YOU WOULD OTHERWISE. SURE, IT WAS WEIRD. AND SCARY. BUT I NEVER MENTIONED IT. TO ANYBODY.
ICE
BESIDES, IT WAS **EASTLING**.

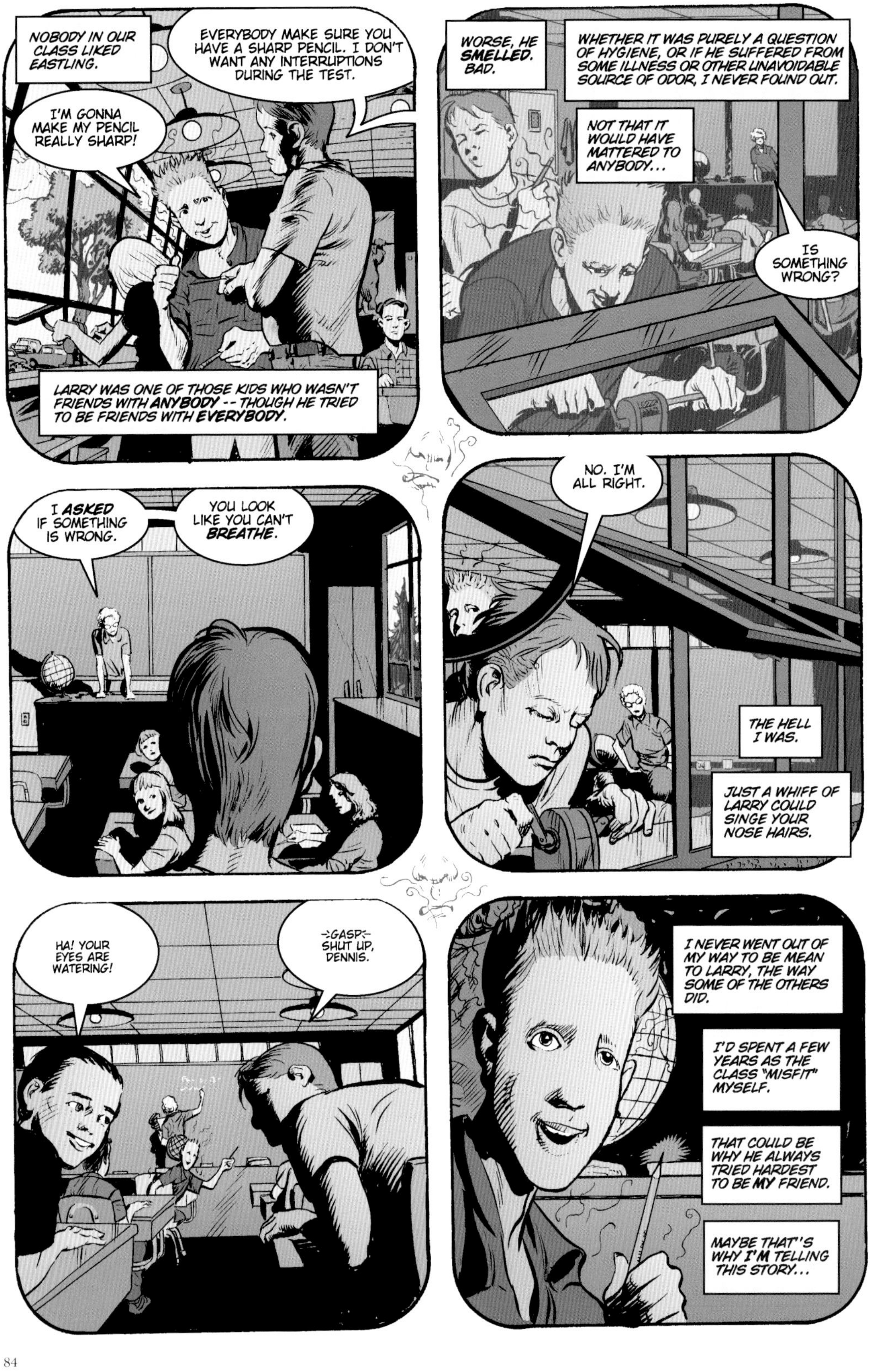
NOBODY IN OUR CLASS LIKED EASTLING.
EVERYBODY MAKE SURE YOU HAVE A SHARP PENCIL. I DON'T WANT ANY INTERRUPTIONS DURING THE TEST.
I'M GONNA MAKE MY PENCIL REALLY SHARP!
LARRY WAS ONE OF THOSE KIDS WHO WASN'T FRIENDS WITH ANYBODY -- THOUGH HE TRIED TO BE FRIENDS WITH EVERYBODY.
WORSE, HE SMELLED. BAD.
WHETHER IT WAS PURELY A QUESTION OF HYGIENE, OR IF HE SUFFERED FROM SOME ILLNESS OR OTHER UNAVOIDABLE SOURCE OF ODOR, I NEVER FOUND OUT.
NOT THAT IT WOULD HAVE MATTERED TO ANYBODY...
IS SOMETHING WRONG?
I ASKED IF SOMETHING IS WRONG.
YOU LOOK LIKE YOU CAN'T BREATHE.
NO. I'M ALL RIGHT.
THE HELL I WAS.
JUST A WHIFF OF LARRY COULD SINGE YOUR NOSE HAIRS.
HA! YOUR EYES ARE WATERING!
-GASP- SHUT UP, DENNIS.
I NEVER WENT OUT OF MY WAY TO BE MEAN TO LARRY, THE WAY SOME OF THE OTHERS DID.
I'D SPENT A FEW YEARS AS THE CLASS "MISFIT" MYSELF.
THAT COULD BE WHY HE ALWAYS TRIED HARDEST TO BE MY FRIEND.
MAYBE THAT'S WHY I'M TELLING THIS STORY...

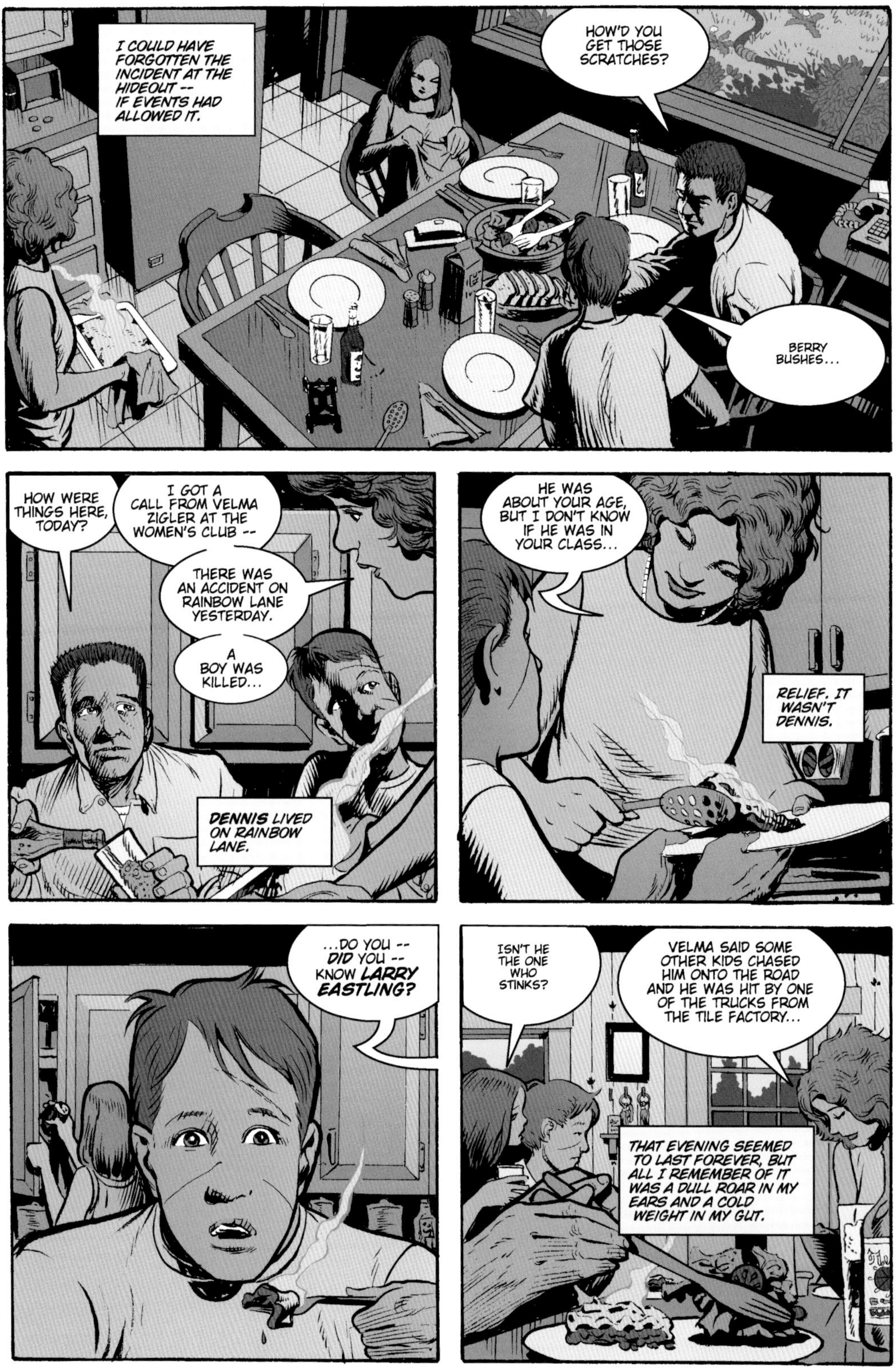
I COULD HAVE FORGOTTEN THE INCIDENT AT THE HIDEOUT -- IF EVENTS HAD ALLOWED IT.
HOW'D YOU GET THOSE SCRATCHES?
BERRY BUSHES...
HOW WERE THINGS HERE, TODAY?
I GOT A CALL FROM VELMA ZIGLER AT THE WOMEN'S CLUB --
THERE WAS AN ACCIDENT ON RAINBOW LANE YESTERDAY.
A BOY WAS KILLED...
DENNIS LIVED ON RAINBOW LANE.
HE WAS ABOUT YOUR AGE, BUT I DON'T KNOW IF HE WAS IN YOUR CLASS...
RELIEF. IT WASN'T DENNIS.
...DO YOU -- DID YOU -- KNOW LARRY EASTLING?
ISN'T HE THE ONE WHO STINKS?
VELMA SAID SOME OTHER KIDS CHASED HIM ONTO THE ROAD AND HE WAS HIT BY ONE OF THE TRUCKS FROM THE TILE FACTORY...
THAT EVENING SEEMED TO LAST FOREVER, BUT ALL I REMEMBER OF IT WAS A DULL ROAR IN MY EARS AND A COLD WEIGHT IN MY GUT.

LATER, I FOUND MOM DIGGING AROUND IN MY CLOSET.

WHAT'RE YOU LOOKING FOR?

MRS. ZIGLER SAYS THE EASTLING FAMILY DOESN'T HAVE MUCH MONEY.

YOU'VE OUTGROWN YOUR SUNDAY SUIT --

-- SO I'M DONATING IT TO THE EASTLINGS SO THEY CAN HAVE LARRY *BURIED* IN IT.

THOUGHTS OF LARRY AND DEATH STAYED WITH ME FOR THE NEXT FEW DAYS. THAT, AND *SOMETHING ELSE.*

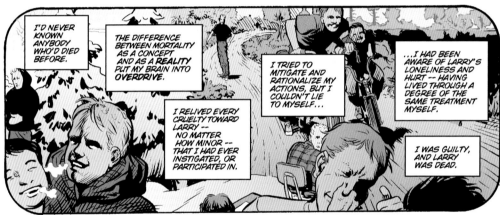

I'D NEVER KNOWN ANYBODY WHO'D DIED BEFORE.

THE DIFFERENCE BETWEEN MORTALITY AS A CONCEPT AND AS A *REALITY* PUT MY BRAIN INTO *OVERDRIVE.*

I RELIVED EVERY CRUELTY TOWARD LARRY -- NO MATTER HOW MINOR -- THAT I HAD EVER INSTIGATED, OR PARTICIPATED IN.

I TRIED TO MITIGATE AND RATIONALIZE MY ACTIONS, BUT I COULDN'T LIE TO MYSELF...

...I HAD BEEN AWARE OF LARRY'S LONELINESS AND HURT -- HAVING LIVED THROUGH A DEGREE OF THE SAME TREATMENT MYSELF.

I WAS GUILTY, AND LARRY WAS DEAD.

I WONDERED ABOUT LARRY.

I WONDERED IF DEATH HURT.

I MEAN, I WAS PRETTY SURE THAT BEING HIT BY A TRUCK HURT...

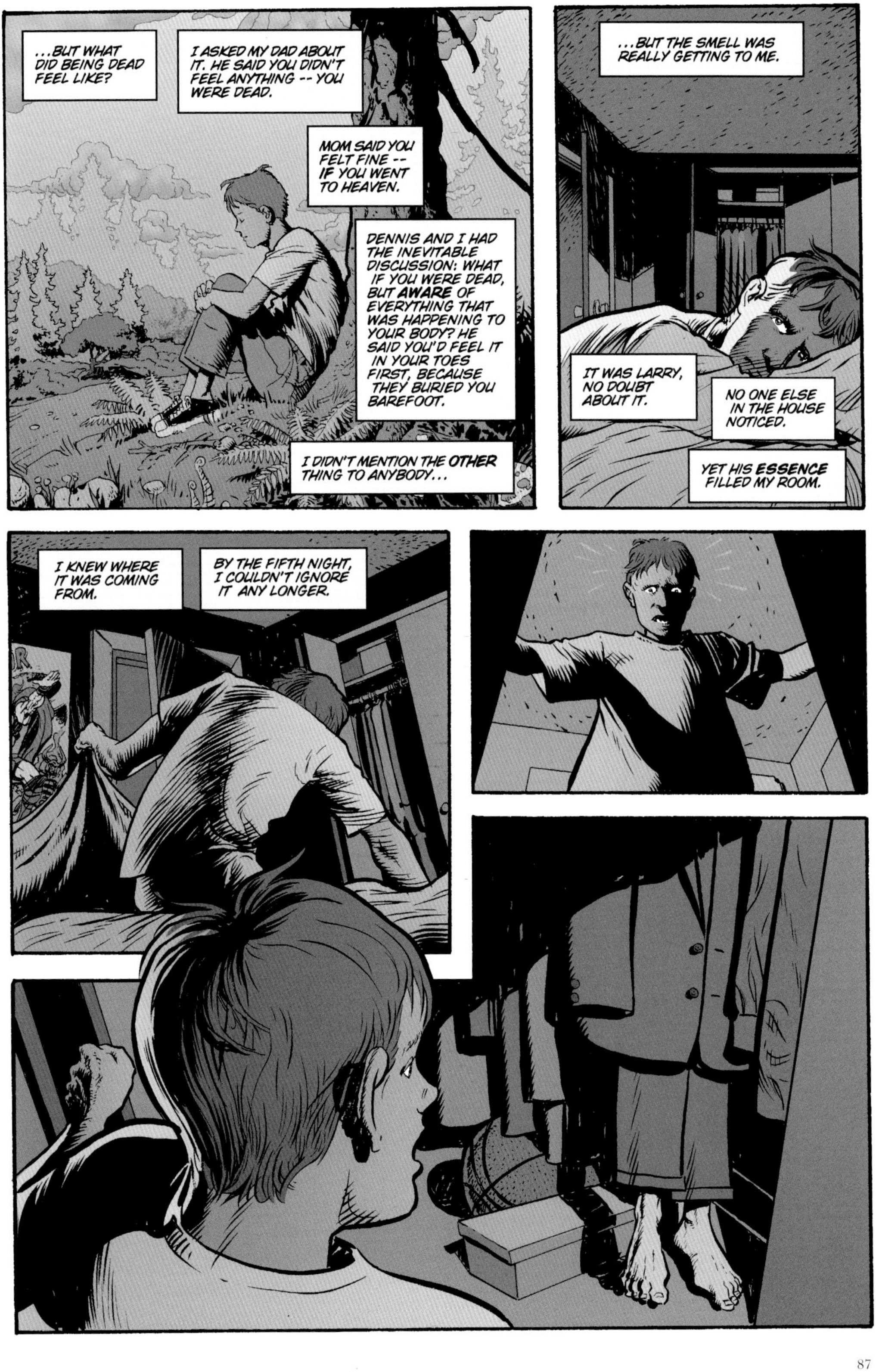
...BUT WHAT DID BEING DEAD FEEL LIKE?
I ASKED MY DAD ABOUT IT. HE SAID YOU DIDN'T FEEL ANYTHING -- YOU WERE DEAD.
MOM SAID YOU FELT FINE -- IF YOU WENT TO HEAVEN.
DENNIS AND I HAD THE INEVITABLE DISCUSSION: WHAT IF YOU WERE DEAD, BUT AWARE OF EVERYTHING THAT WAS HAPPENING TO YOUR BODY? HE SAID YOU'D FEEL IT IN YOUR TOES FIRST, BECAUSE THEY BURIED YOU BAREFOOT.
I DIDN'T MENTION THE OTHER THING TO ANYBODY...
...BUT THE SMELL WAS REALLY GETTING TO ME.
IT WAS LARRY, NO DOUBT ABOUT IT.
NO ONE ELSE IN THE HOUSE NOTICED.
YET HIS ESSENCE FILLED MY ROOM.
I KNEW WHERE IT WAS COMING FROM.
BY THE FIFTH NIGHT, I COULDN'T IGNORE IT ANY LONGER.

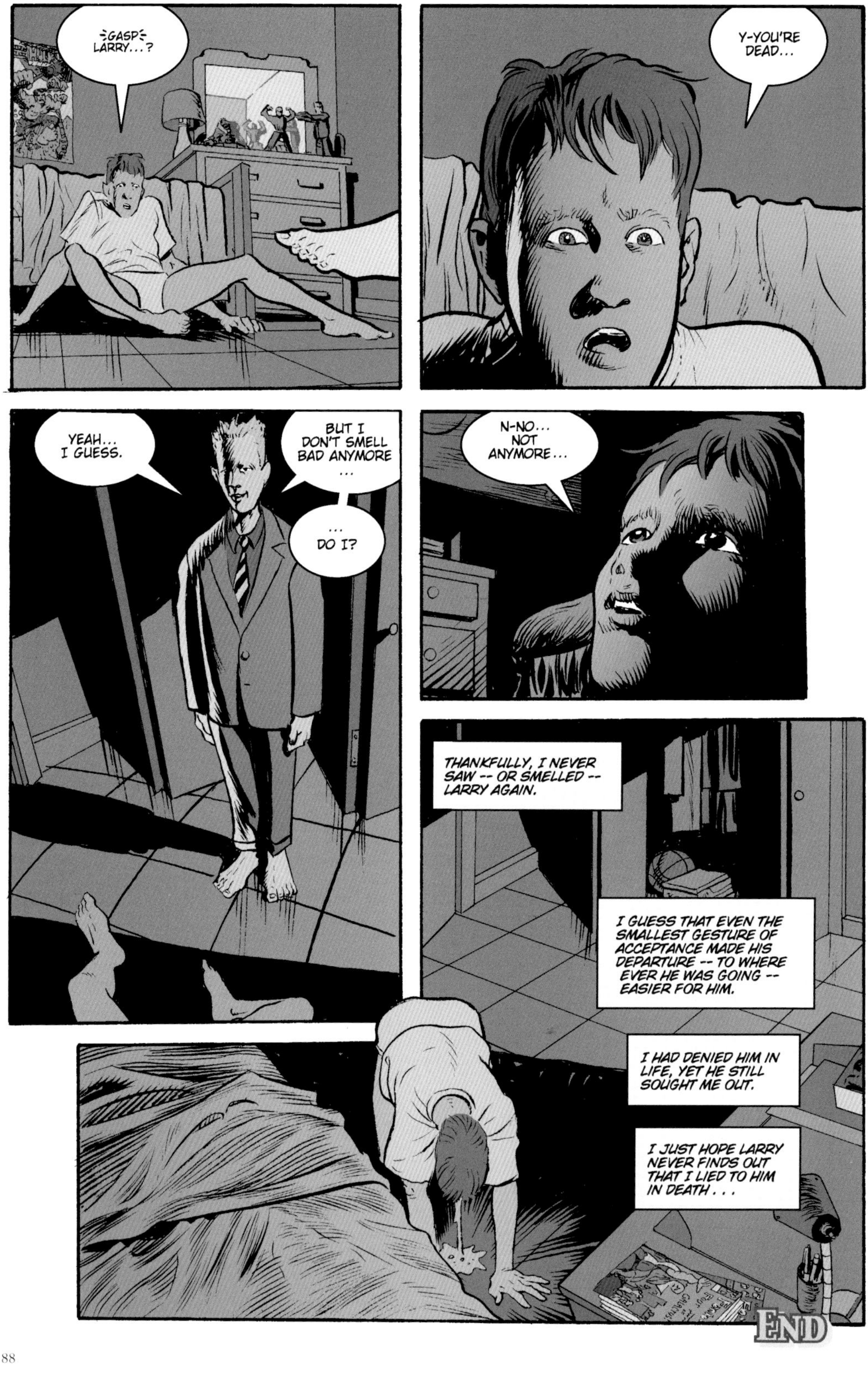
GASP
LARRY...?
Y-YOU'RE DEAD...
YEAH... I GUESS.
BUT I DON'T SMELL BAD ANYMORE ...
... DO I?
N-NO... NOT ANYMORE...
THANKFULLY, I NEVER SAW -- OR SMELLED -- LARRY AGAIN.
I GUESS THAT EVEN THE SMALLEST GESTURE OF ACCEPTANCE MADE HIS DEPARTURE -- TO WHERE EVER HE WAS GOING -- EASIER FOR HIM.
I HAD DENIED HIM IN LIFE, YET HE STILL SOUGHT ME OUT.
I JUST HOPE LARRY NEVER FINDS OUT THAT I LIED TO HIM IN DEATH . . .
END

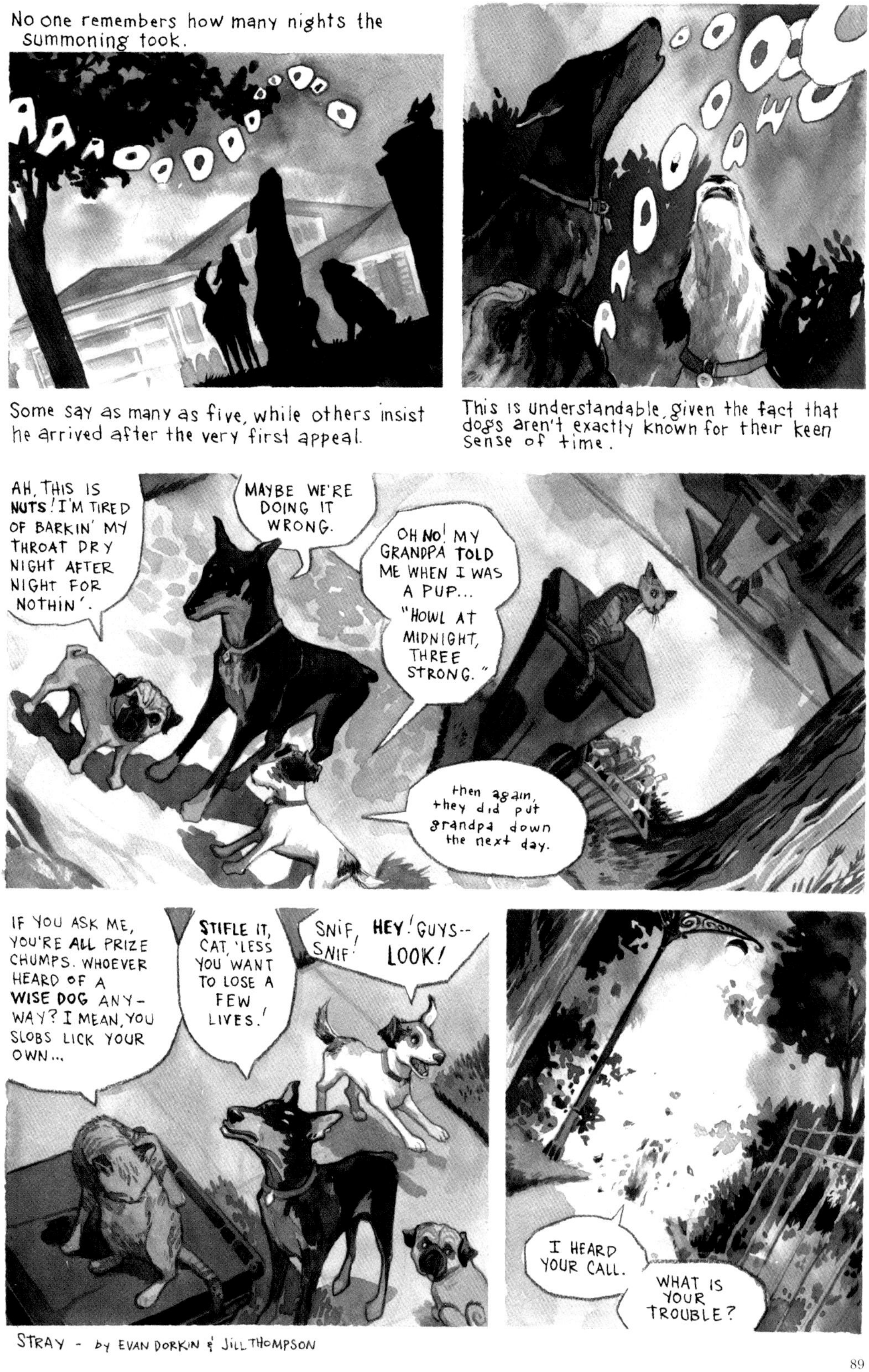
No one remembers how many nights the summoning took.
AAAROOOOOOOOOOO
Some say as many as five, while others insist he arrived after the very first appeal.
OOOOOAWOOOO
This is understandable, given the fact that dogs aren't exactly known for their keen sense of time.
AH, THIS IS NUTS! I'M TIRED OF BARKIN' MY THROAT DRY NIGHT AFTER NIGHT FOR NOTHIN'.
MAYBE WE'RE DOING IT WRONG.
OH NO! MY GRANDPA TOLD ME WHEN I WAS A PUP... "HOWL AT MIDNIGHT, THREE STRONG."
then again, they did put grandpa down the next day.
IF YOU ASK ME, YOU'RE ALL PRIZE CHUMPS. WHOEVER HEARD OF A WISE DOG ANY-WAY? I MEAN, YOU SLOBS LICK YOUR OWN...
STIFLE IT, CAT, 'LESS YOU WANT TO LOSE A FEW LIVES.'
SNIF, SNIF!
HEY! GUYS-- LOOK!
I HEARD YOUR CALL.
WHAT IS YOUR TROUBLE?
STRAY - by EVAN DORKIN & JILL THOMPSON

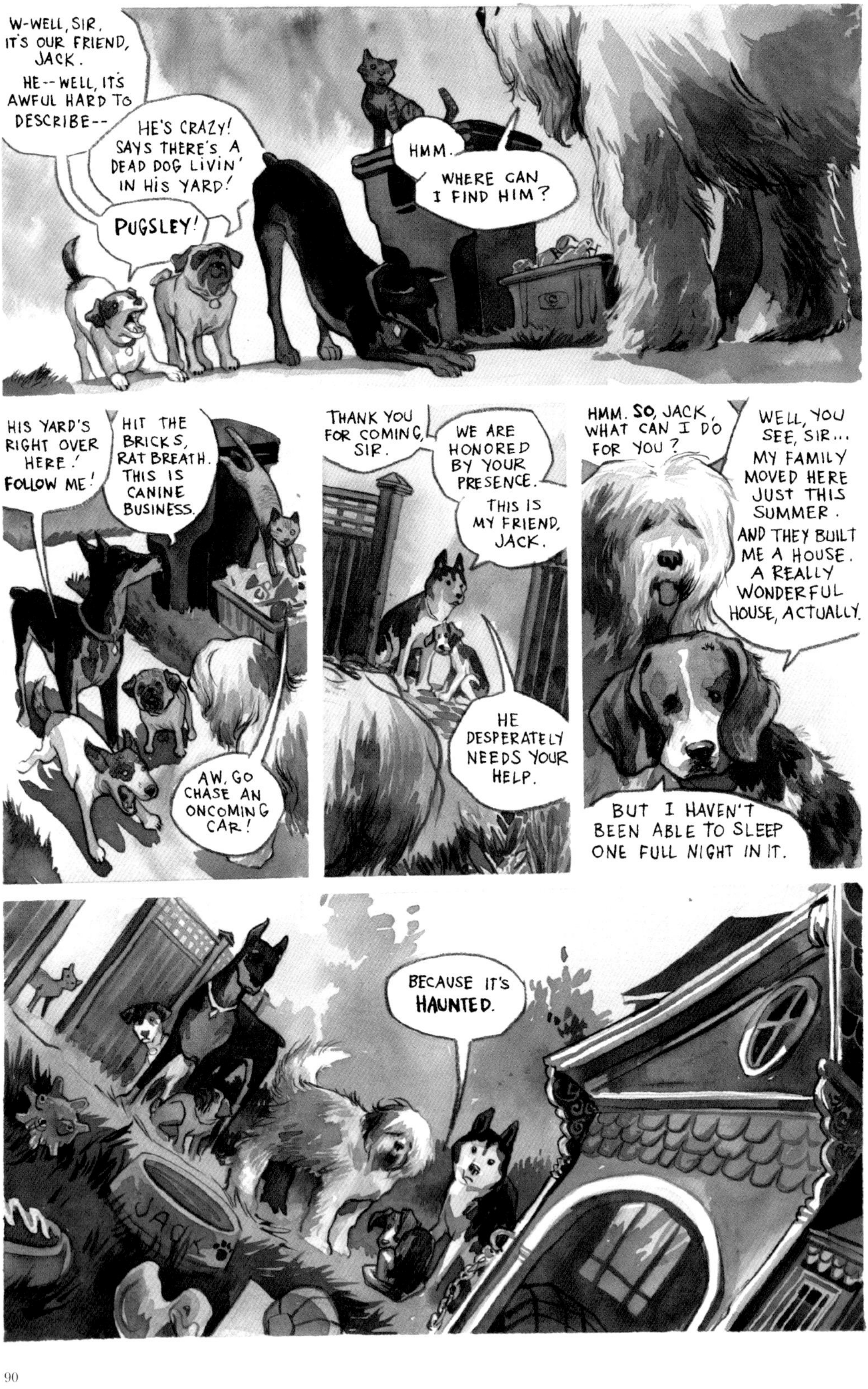
W-WELL, SIR, IT'S OUR FRIEND, JACK.
HE--WELL, IT'S AWFUL HARD TO DESCRIBE--
HE'S CRAZY! SAYS THERE'S A DEAD DOG LIVIN' IN HIS YARD!
PUGSLEY!
HMM.
WHERE CAN I FIND HIM?
HIS YARD'S RIGHT OVER HERE! FOLLOW ME!
HIT THE BRICKS, RAT BREATH. THIS IS CANINE BUSINESS.
AW, GO CHASE AN ONCOMING CAR!
THANK YOU FOR COMING, SIR.
WE ARE HONORED BY YOUR PRESENCE.
THIS IS MY FRIEND, JACK.
HE DESPERATELY NEEDS YOUR HELP.
HMM. SO, JACK, WHAT CAN I DO FOR YOU?
WELL, YOU SEE, SIR... MY FAMILY MOVED HERE JUST THIS SUMMER.
AND THEY BUILT ME A HOUSE. A REALLY WONDERFUL HOUSE, ACTUALLY.
BUT I HAVEN'T BEEN ABLE TO SLEEP ONE FULL NIGHT IN IT.
BECAUSE IT'S HAUNTED.
JACK

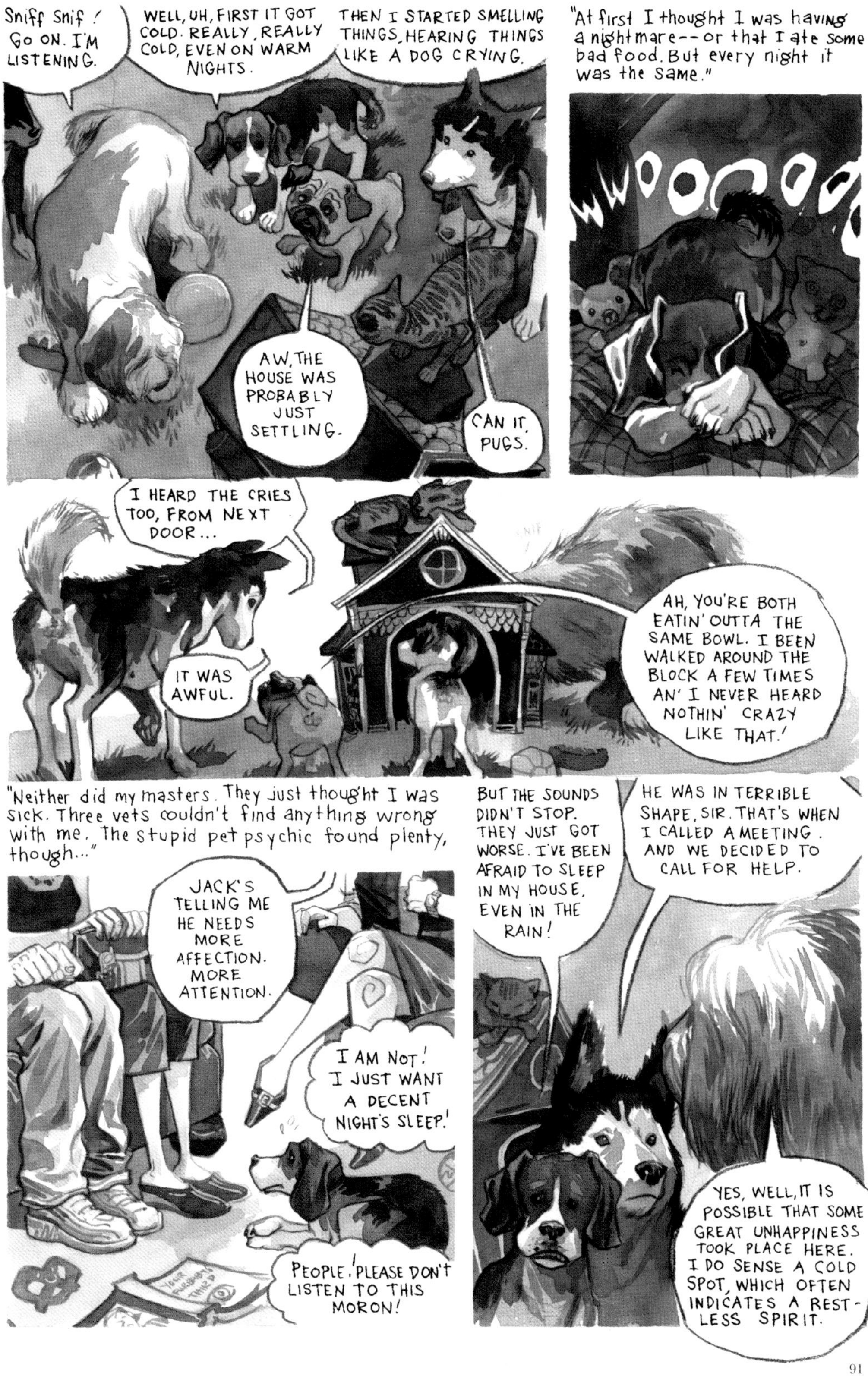
Sniff Snif! Go on. I'm listening.
WELL, UH, FIRST IT GOT COLD. REALLY, REALLY COLD, EVEN ON WARM NIGHTS.
THEN I STARTED SMELLING THINGS, HEARING THINGS LIKE A DOG CRYING.
AW, THE HOUSE WAS PROBABLY JUST SETTLING.
CAN IT, PUGS.
"At first I thought I was having a nightmare--or that I ate some bad food. But every night it was the same."
WWOOOOOOO
I HEARD THE CRIES TOO, FROM NEXT DOOR...
IT WAS AWFUL.
AH, YOU'RE BOTH EATIN' OUTTA THE SAME BOWL. I BEEN WALKED AROUND THE BLOCK A FEW TIMES AN' I NEVER HEARD NOTHIN' CRAZY LIKE THAT!
"Neither did my masters. They just thought I was sick. Three vets couldn't find anything wrong with me. The stupid pet psychic found plenty, though..."
JACK'S TELLING ME HE NEEDS MORE AFFECTION. MORE ATTENTION.
I AM NOT! I JUST WANT A DECENT NIGHT'S SLEEP!
PEOPLE! PLEASE DON'T LISTEN TO THIS MORON!
BUT THE SOUNDS DIDN'T STOP. THEY JUST GOT WORSE. I'VE BEEN AFRAID TO SLEEP IN MY HOUSE, EVEN IN THE RAIN!
HE WAS IN TERRIBLE SHAPE, SIR. THAT'S WHEN I CALLED A MEETING. AND WE DECIDED TO CALL FOR HELP.
YES, WELL, IT IS POSSIBLE THAT SOME GREAT UNHAPPINESS TOOK PLACE HERE. I DO SENSE A COLD SPOT, WHICH OFTEN INDICATES A REST-LESS SPIRIT.

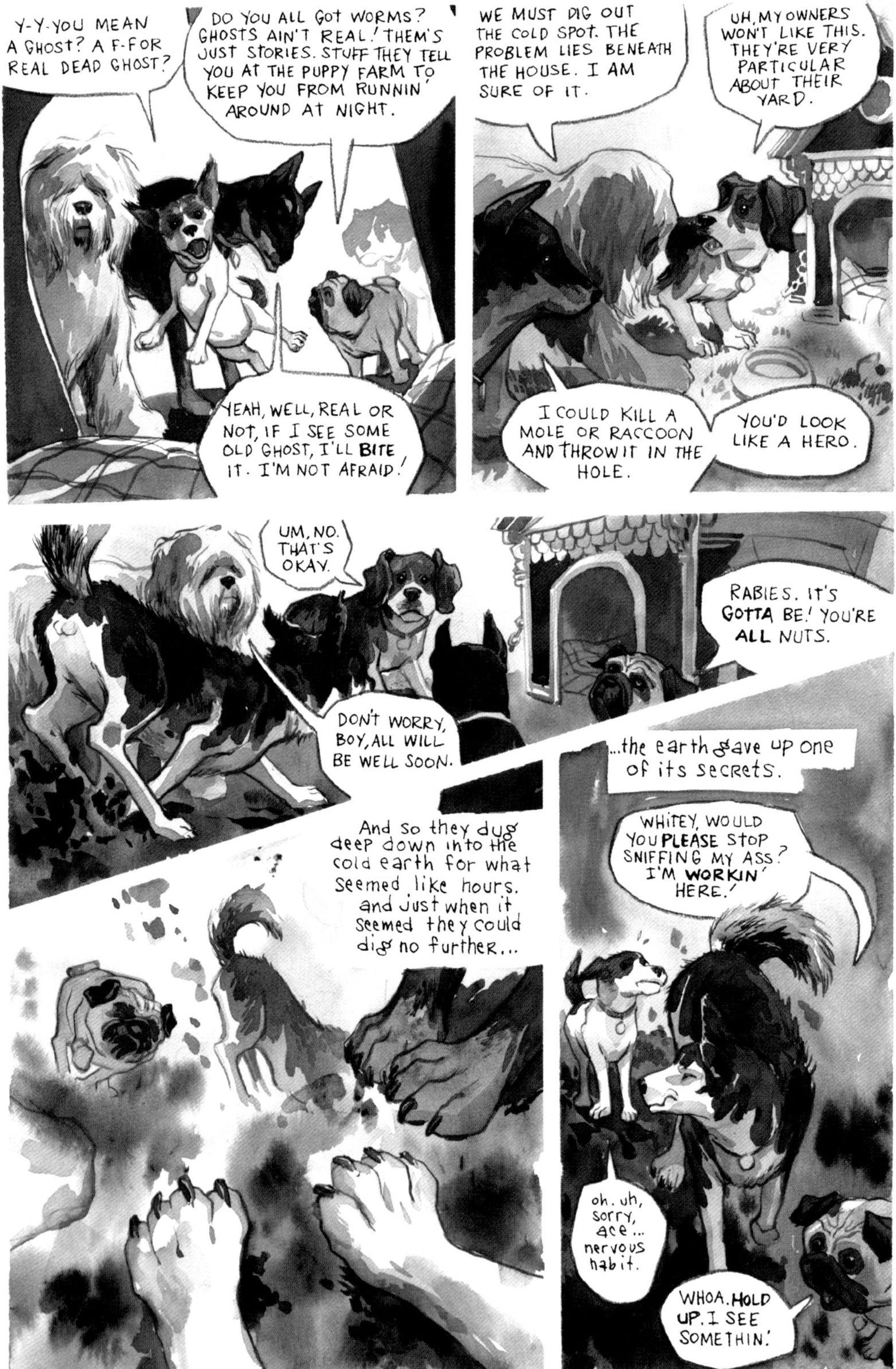

Y-Y-YOU MEAN A GHOST? A F-FOR REAL DEAD GHOST?
DO YOU ALL GOT WORMS? GHOSTS AIN'T REAL! THEM'S JUST STORIES. STUFF THEY TELL YOU AT THE PUPPY FARM TO KEEP YOU FROM RUNNIN' AROUND AT NIGHT.
YEAH, WELL, REAL OR NOT, IF I SEE SOME OLD GHOST, I'LL BITE IT. I'M NOT AFRAID!
WE MUST DIG OUT THE COLD SPOT. THE PROBLEM LIES BENEATH THE HOUSE. I AM SURE OF IT.
UH, MY OWNERS WON'T LIKE THIS. THEY'RE VERY PARTICULAR ABOUT THEIR YARD.
I COULD KILL A MOLE OR RACCOON AND THROW IT IN THE HOLE.
YOU'D LOOK LIKE A HERO.
UM, NO. THAT'S OKAY.
DON'T WORRY, BOY, ALL WILL BE WELL SOON.
RABIES. IT'S GOTTA BE! YOU'RE ALL NUTS.
And so they dug deep down into the cold earth for what seemed like hours. and just when it seemed they could dig no further...
...the earth gave up one of its secrets.
WHITEY, WOULD YOU PLEASE STOP SNIFFING MY ASS? I'M WORKIN' HERE!
oh. uh, sorry, ace... nervous habit.
WHOA. HOLD UP. I SEE SOMETHIN'.

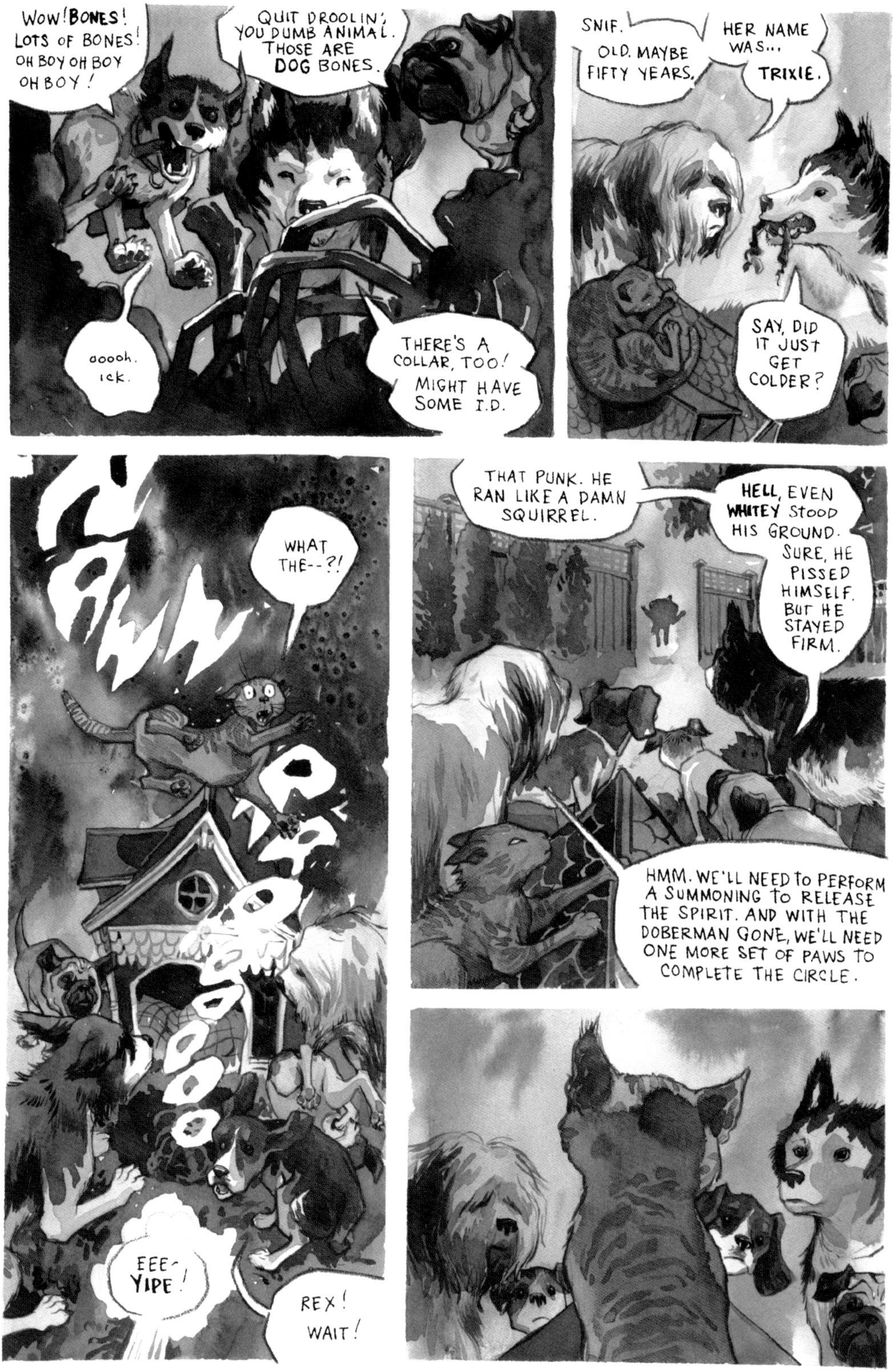
WOW! BONES! LOTS OF BONES! OH BOY OH BOY OH BOY!
QUIT DROOLIN', YOU DUMB ANIMAL. THOSE ARE DOG BONES.
ooooh. ick.
THERE'S A COLLAR, TOO! MIGHT HAVE SOME I.D.
SNIF.
OLD. MAYBE FIFTY YEARS.
HER NAME WAS... TRIXIE.
SAY, DID IT JUST GET COLDER?
WHAT THE--?!
EEE-YIPE!
REX! WAIT!
THAT PUNK. HE RAN LIKE A DAMN SQUIRREL.
HELL, EVEN WHITEY STOOD HIS GROUND. SURE, HE PISSED HIMSELF. BUT HE STAYED FIRM.
HMM. WE'LL NEED TO PERFORM A SUMMONING TO RELEASE THE SPIRIT. AND WITH THE DOBERMAN GONE, WE'LL NEED ONE MORE SET OF PAWS TO COMPLETE THE CIRCLE.

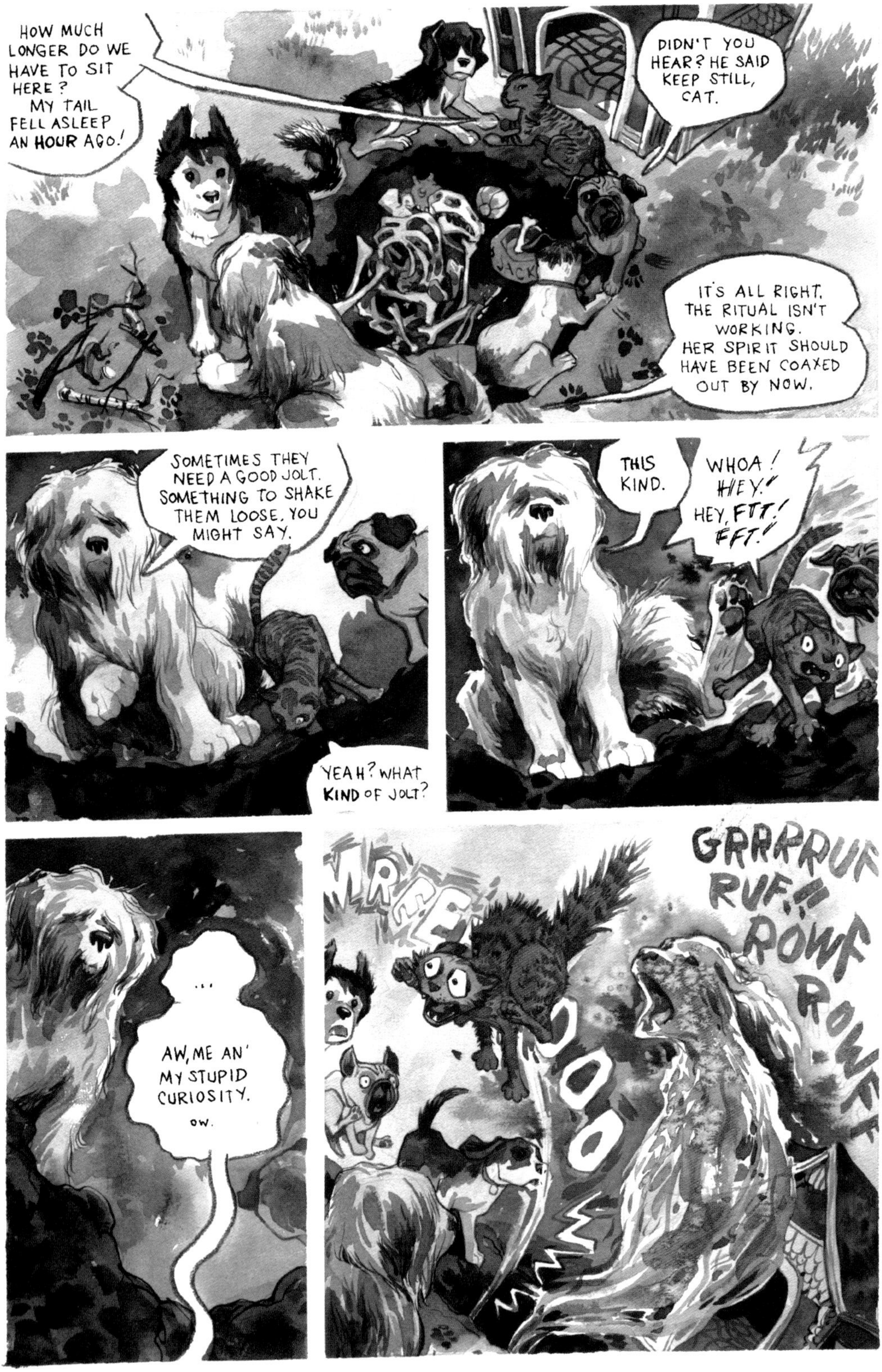
HOW MUCH LONGER DO WE HAVE TO SIT HERE? MY TAIL FELL ASLEEP AN HOUR AGO!
DIDN'T YOU HEAR? HE SAID KEEP STILL, CAT.
IT'S ALL RIGHT. THE RITUAL ISN'T WORKING. HER SPIRIT SHOULD HAVE BEEN COAXED OUT BY NOW.
SOMETIMES THEY NEED A GOOD JOLT. SOMETHING TO SHAKE THEM LOOSE, YOU MIGHT SAY.
YEAH? WHAT KIND OF JOLT?
THIS KIND.
WHOA! HEY! HEY, FTT! FFT!
...
AW, ME AN' MY STUPID CURIOSITY.
OW.
GRRRRUF
RUF!!
ROWF
ROWF

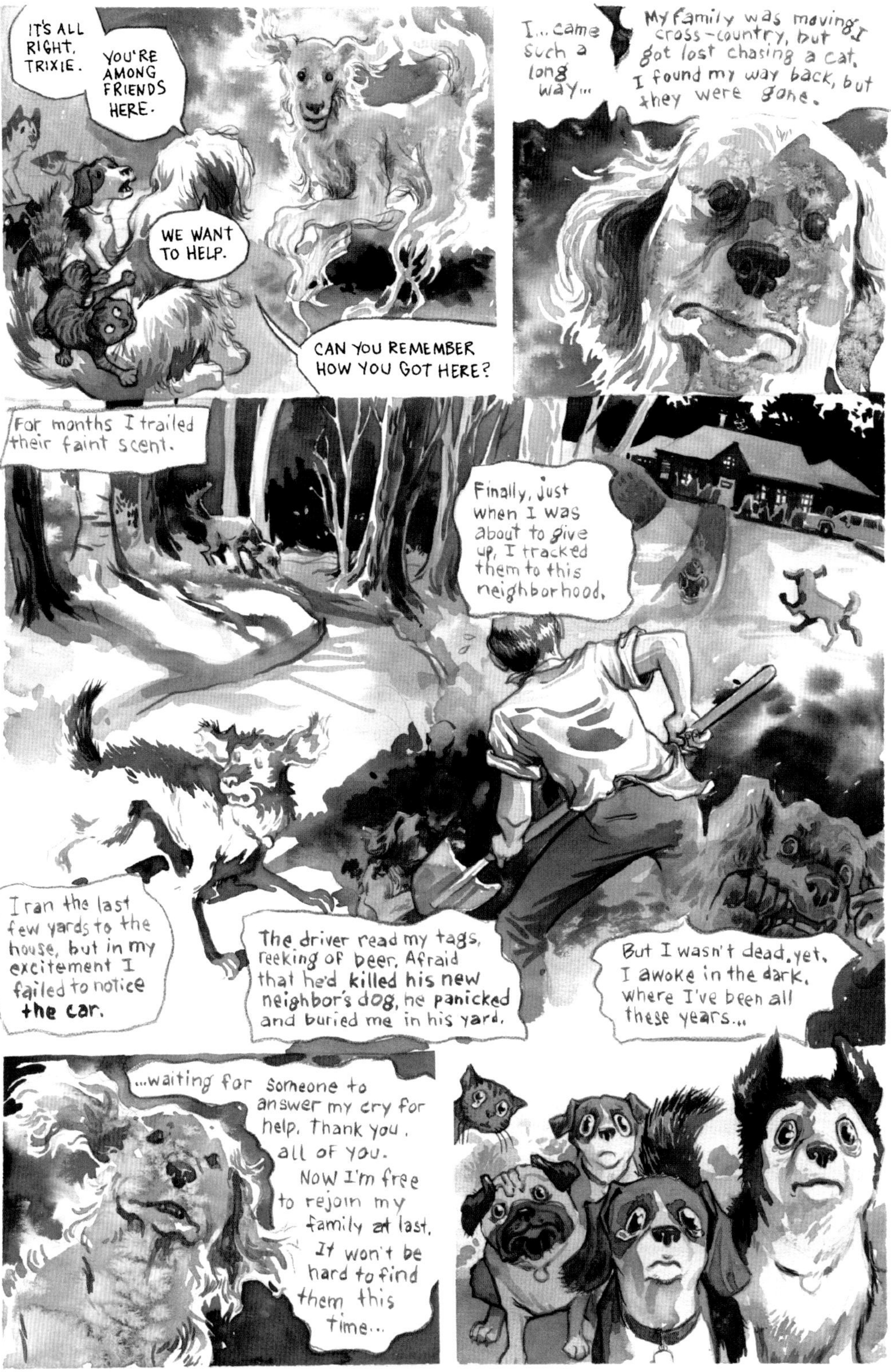
IT'S ALL RIGHT, TRIXIE.
YOU'RE AMONG FRIENDS HERE.
WE WANT TO HELP.
CAN YOU REMEMBER HOW YOU GOT HERE?
I... came such a long way...
My family was moving cross-country, but I got lost chasing a cat. I found my way back, but they were gone.
For months I trailed their faint scent.
Finally, just when I was about to give up, I tracked them to this neighborhood.
I ran the last few yards to the house, but in my excitement I failed to notice **the car**.
The driver read my tags, reeking of beer. Afraid that he'd **killed his new** neighbor's dog, he panicked and buried me in his yard.
But I wasn't dead yet. I awoke in the dark, where I've been all these years...
...waiting for someone to answer my cry for help. Thank you, all of you. Now I'm free to rejoin my family at last. It won't be hard to find them this time...

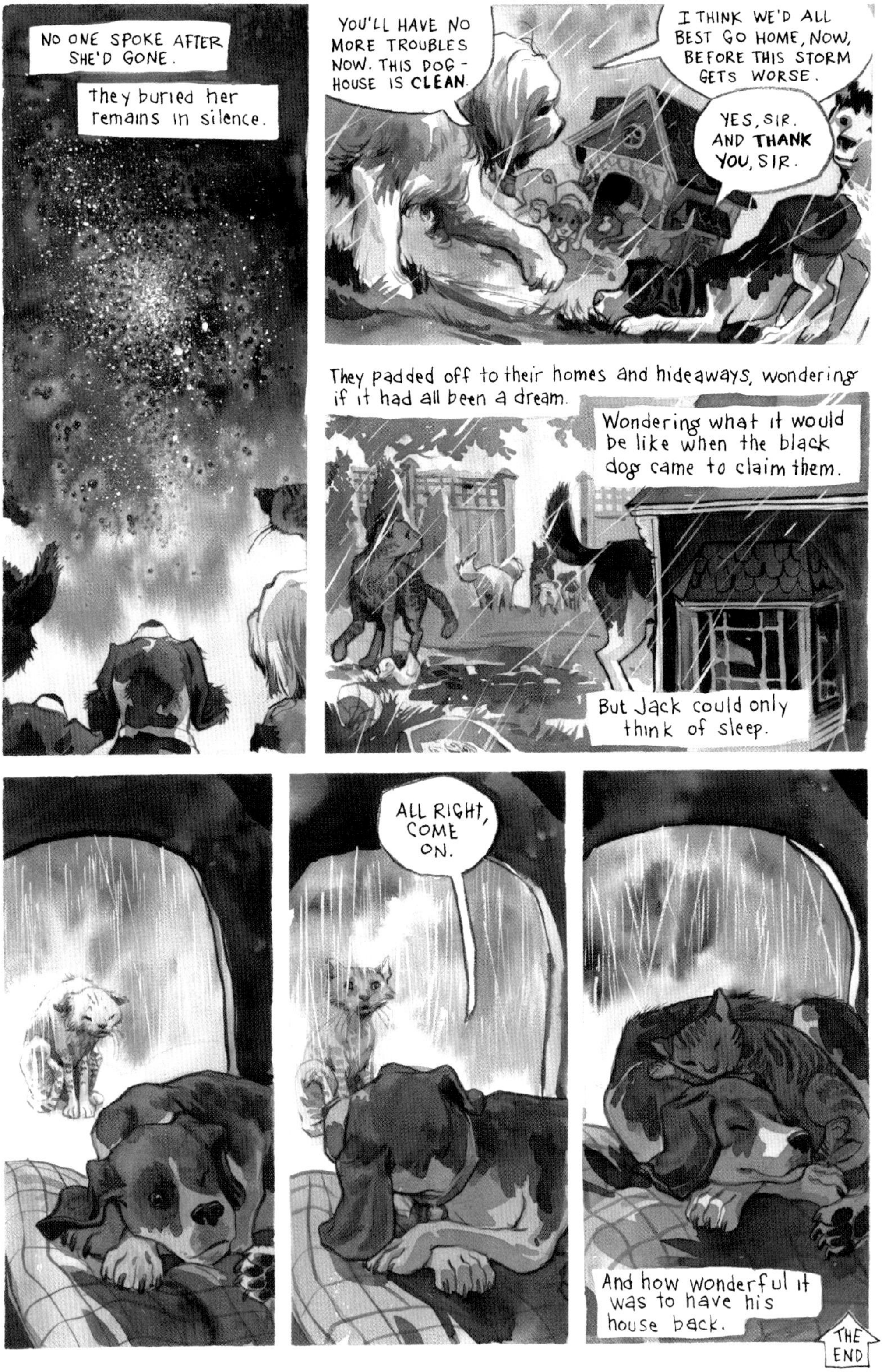
NO ONE SPOKE AFTER SHE'D GONE.
they buried her remains in silence.
YOU'LL HAVE NO MORE TROUBLES NOW. THIS DOG-HOUSE IS **CLEAN**.
I THINK WE'D ALL BEST GO HOME, NOW, BEFORE THIS STORM GETS WORSE.
YES, SIR. AND **THANK** YOU, SIR.
They padded off to their homes and hideaways, wondering if it had all been a dream.
Wondering what it would be like when the black dog came to claim them.
But Jack could only think of sleep.
ALL RIGHT, COME ON.
And how wonderful it was to have his house back.
THE END

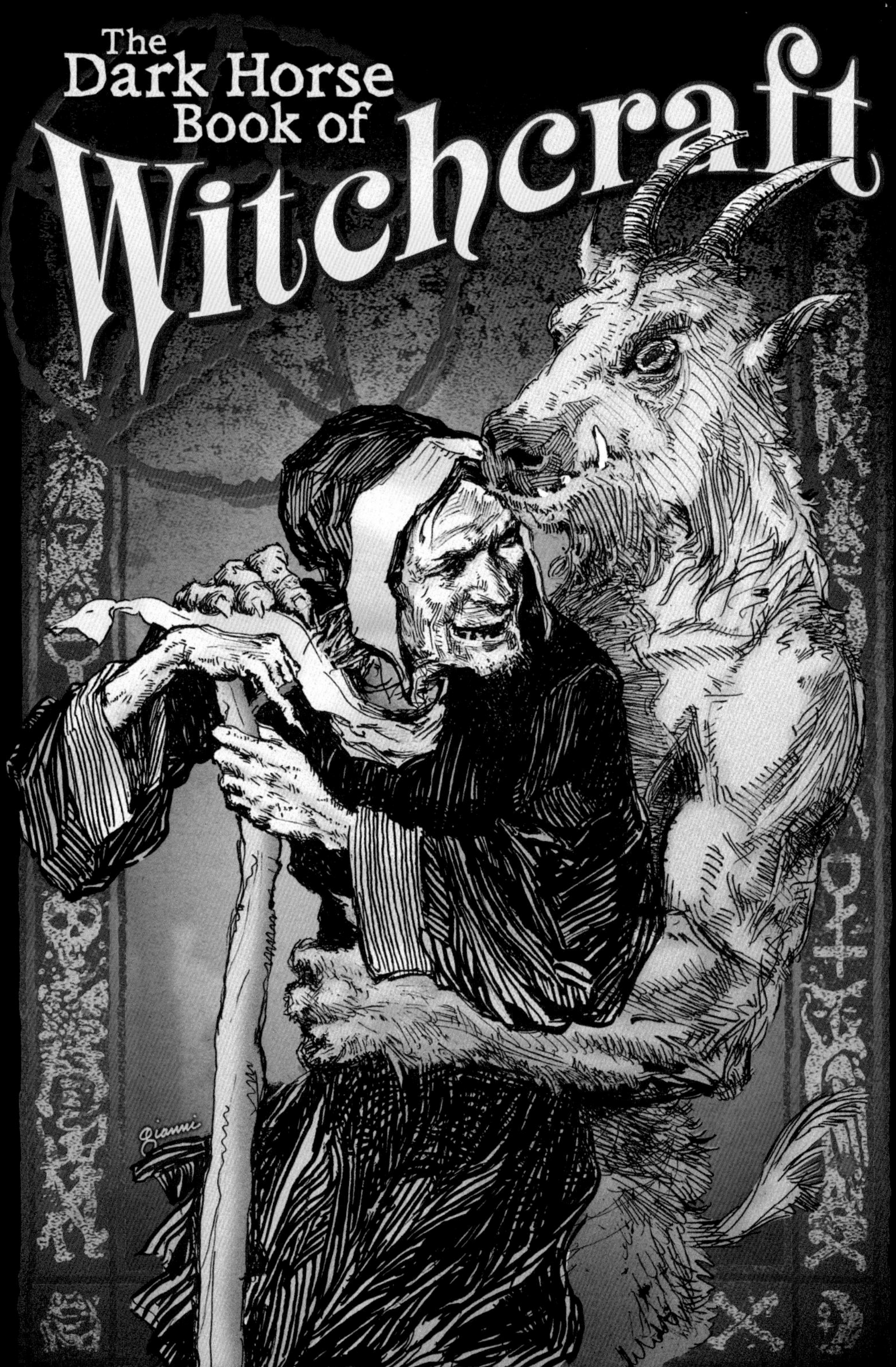
The Dark Horse Book of
Witchcraft
gianni

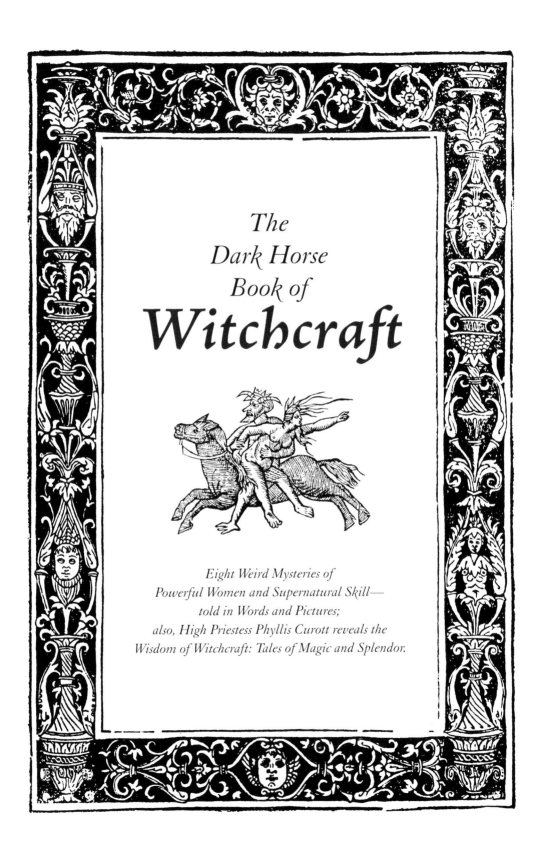

The
Dark Horse
Book of
Witchcraft

Eight Weird Mysteries of
Powerful Women and Supernatural Skill—
told in Words and Pictures;
also, High Priestess Phyllis Curott reveals the
Wisdom of Witchcraft: Tales of Magic and Splendor.

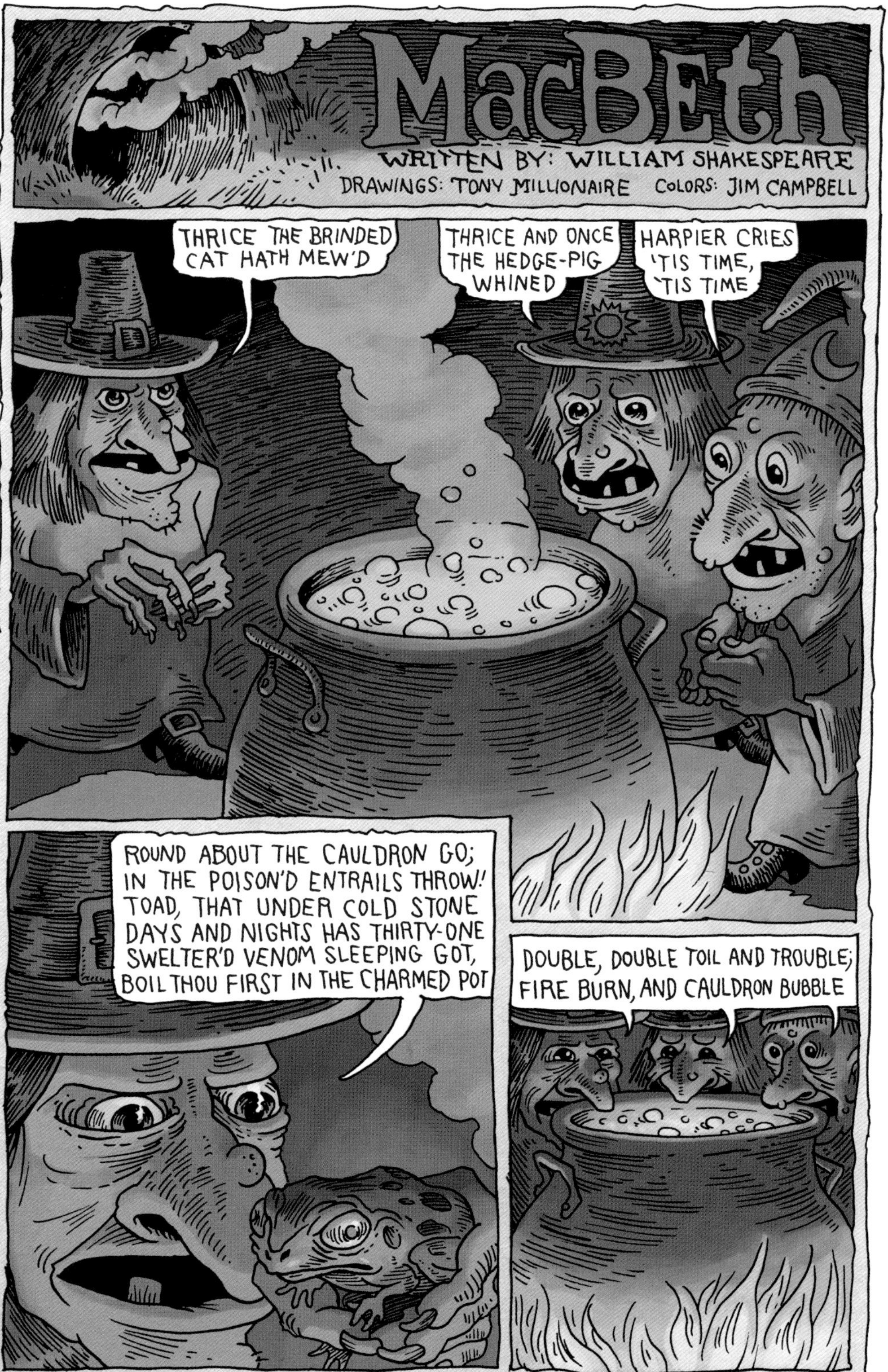
MacBeth
WRITTEN BY: WILLIAM SHAKESPEARE
DRAWINGS: TONY MILLIONAIRE COLORS: JIM CAMPBELL
THRICE THE BRINDED CAT HATH MEW'D
THRICE AND ONCE THE HEDGE-PIG WHINED
HARPIER CRIES 'TIS TIME, 'TIS TIME
ROUND ABOUT THE CAULDRON GO; IN THE POISON'D ENTRAILS THROW! TOAD, THAT UNDER COLD STONE DAYS AND NIGHTS HAS THIRTY-ONE SWELTER'D VENOM SLEEPING GOT, BOIL THOU FIRST IN THE CHARMED POT
DOUBLE, DOUBLE TOIL AND TROUBLE; FIRE BURN, AND CAULDRON BUBBLE

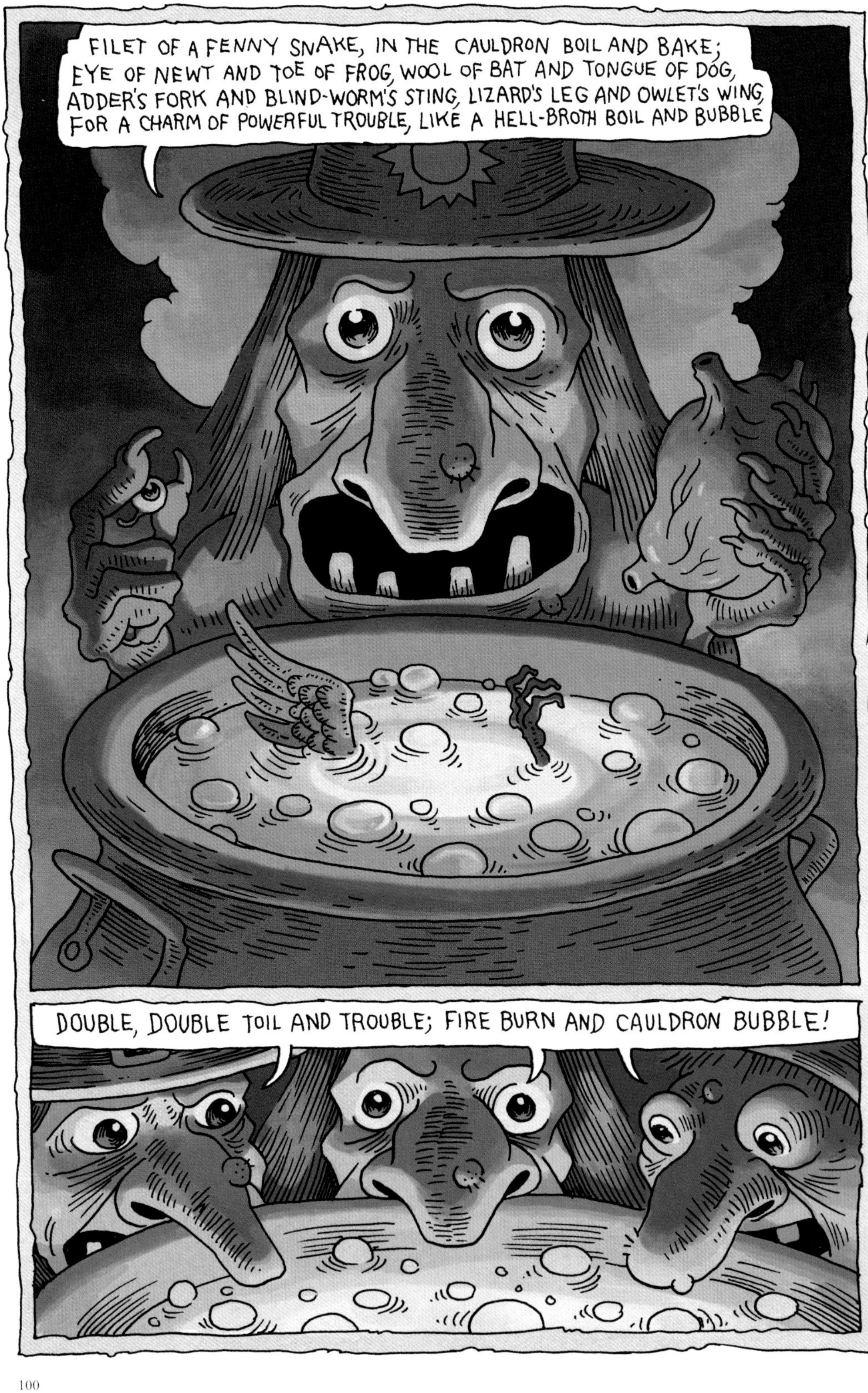
FILET OF A FENNY SNAKE, IN THE CAULDRON BOIL AND BAKE; EYE OF NEWT AND TOE OF FROG, WOOL OF BAT AND TONGUE OF DOG, ADDER'S FORK AND BLIND-WORM'S STING, LIZARD'S LEG AND OWLET'S WING, FOR A CHARM OF POWERFUL TROUBLE, LIKE A HELL-BROTH BOIL AND BUBBLE
DOUBLE, DOUBLE TOIL AND TROUBLE; FIRE BURN AND CAULDRON BUBBLE!

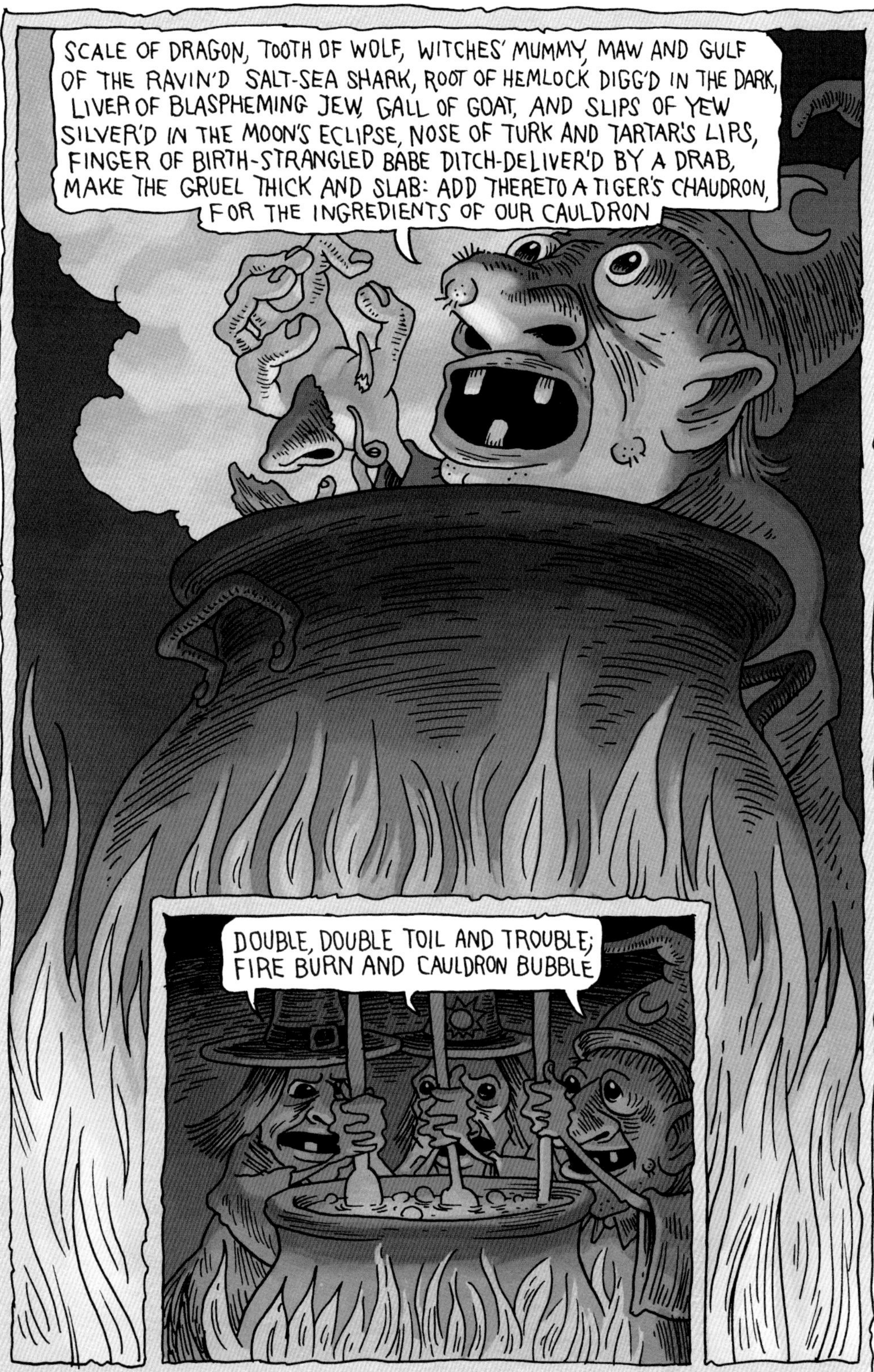
SCALE OF DRAGON, TOOTH OF WOLF, WITCHES' MUMMY, MAW AND GULF OF THE RAVIN'D SALT-SEA SHARK, ROOT OF HEMLOCK DIGG'D IN THE DARK, LIVER OF BLASPHEMING JEW, GALL OF GOAT, AND SLIPS OF YEW SILVER'D IN THE MOON'S ECLIPSE, NOSE OF TURK AND TARTAR'S LIPS, FINGER OF BIRTH-STRANGLED BABE DITCH-DELIVER'D BY A DRAB, MAKE THE GRUEL THICK AND SLAB: ADD THERETO A TIGER'S CHAUDRON, FOR THE INGREDIENTS OF OUR CAULDRON
DOUBLE, DOUBLE TOIL AND TROUBLE; FIRE BURN AND CAULDRON BUBBLE

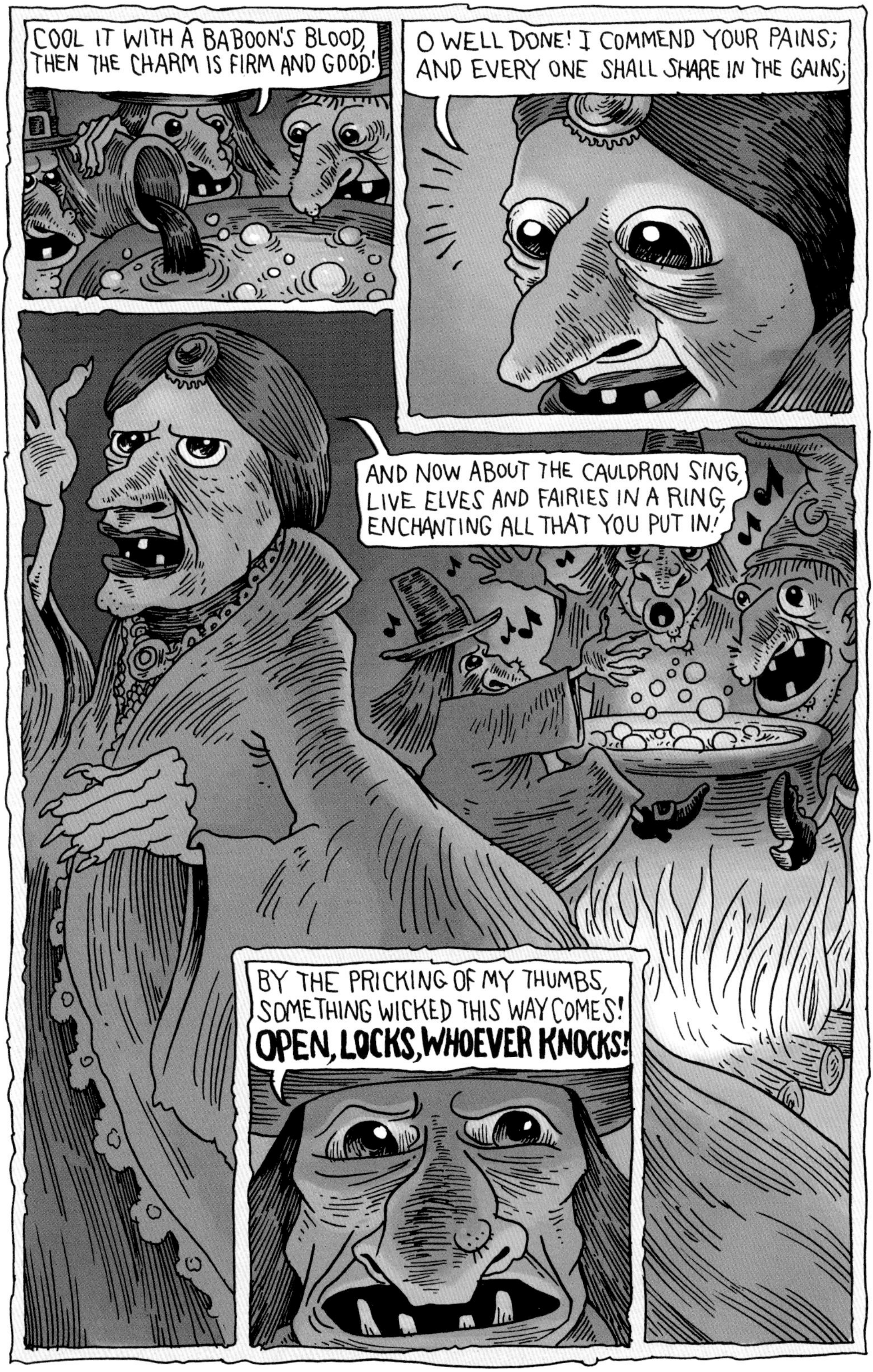
COOL IT WITH A BABOON'S BLOOD, THEN THE CHARM IS FIRM AND GOOD!
O WELL DONE! I COMMEND YOUR PAINS; AND EVERY ONE SHALL SHARE IN THE GAINS;
AND NOW ABOUT THE CAULDRON SING, LIVE ELVES AND FAIRIES IN A RING, ENCHANTING ALL THAT YOU PUT IN!
BY THE PRICKING OF MY THUMBS, SOMETHING WICKED THIS WAY COMES!
OPEN, LOCKS, WHOEVER KNOCKS!

The Troll-witch

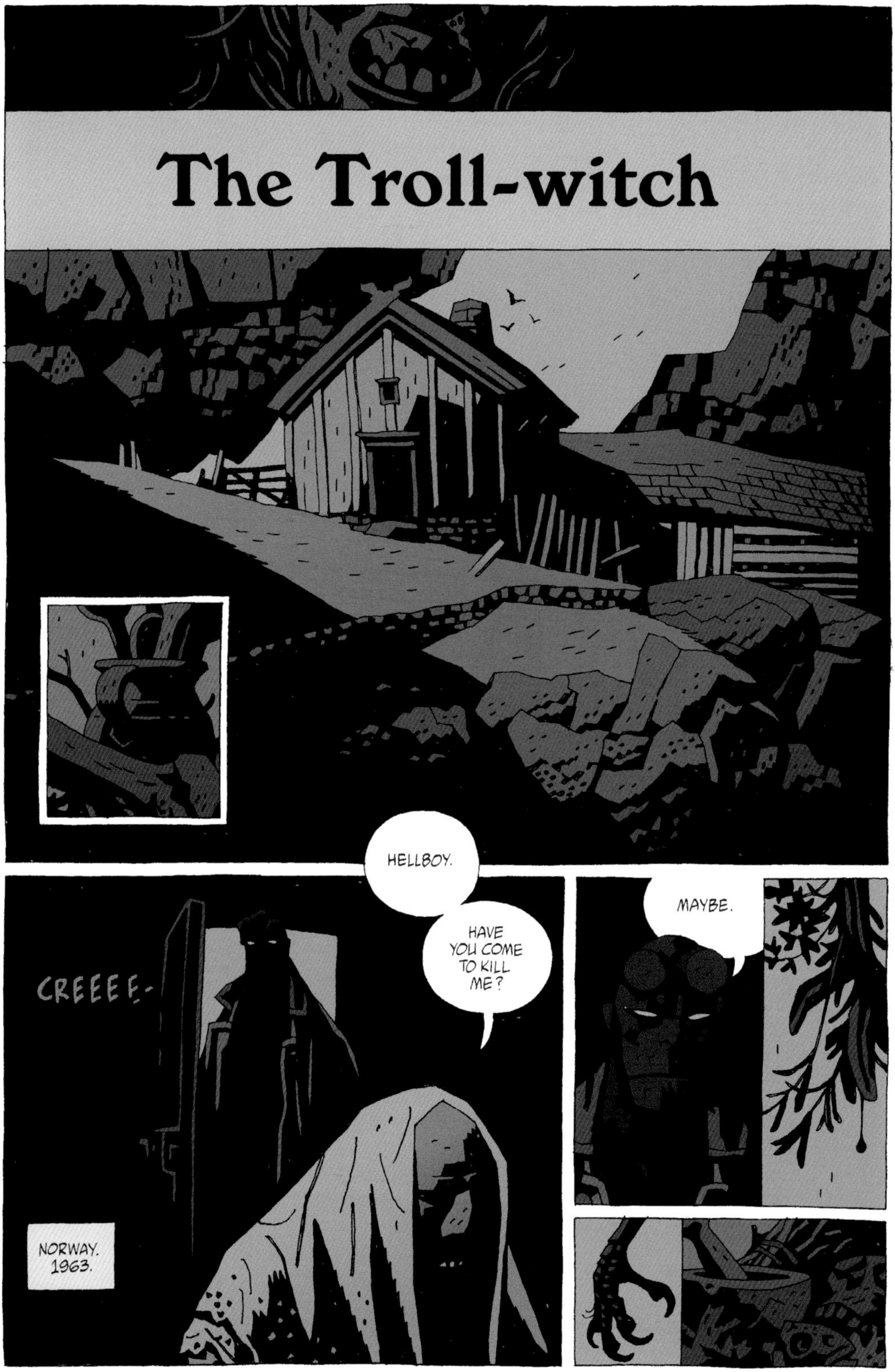
CREEEE-
HELLBOY.
HAVE YOU COME TO KILL ME?
MAYBE.
NORWAY. 1963.

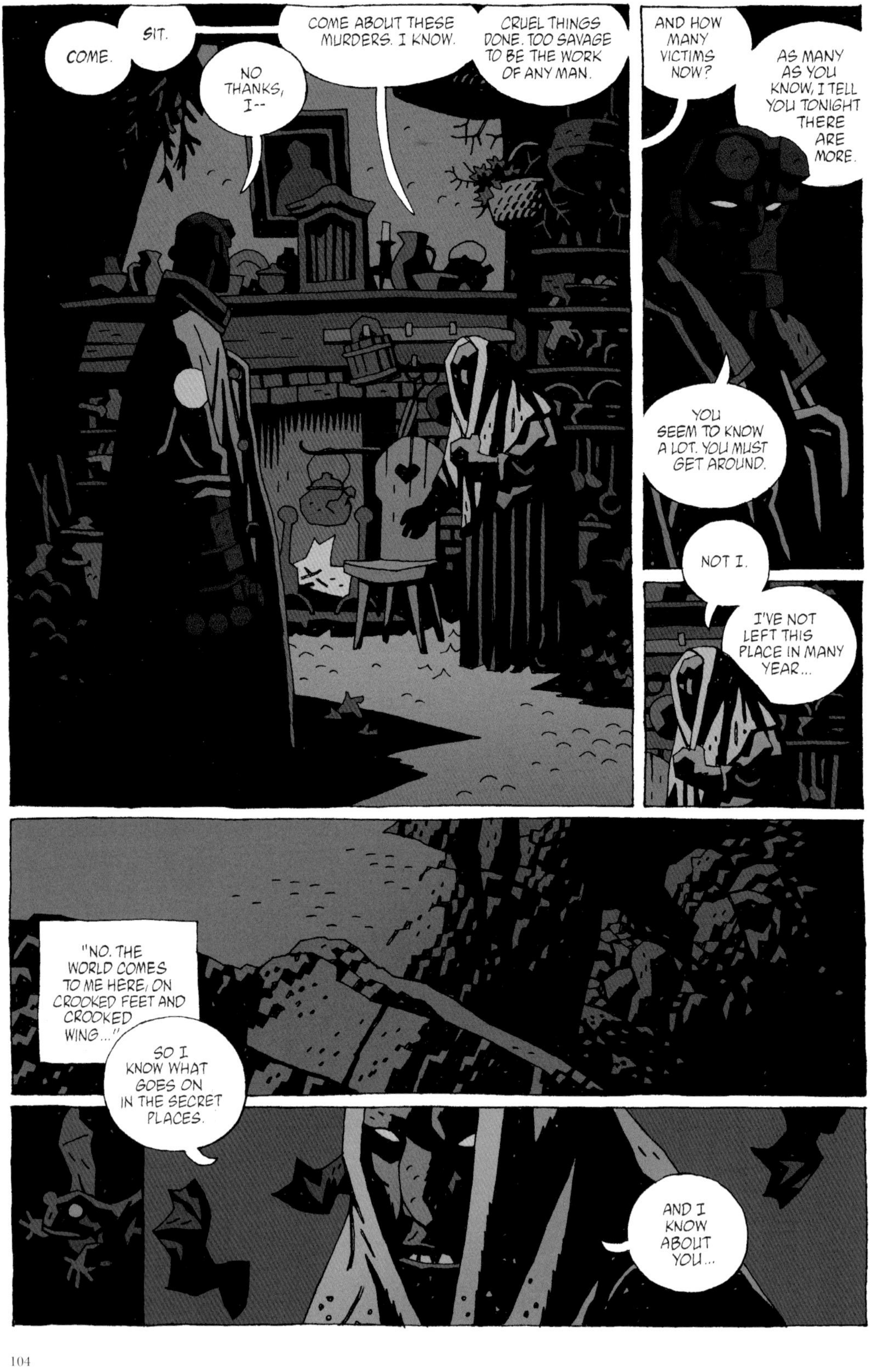
COME.
SIT.
NO THANKS, I--
COME ABOUT THESE MURDERS. I KNOW.
CRUEL THINGS DONE. TOO SAVAGE TO BE THE WORK OF ANY MAN.
AND HOW MANY VICTIMS NOW?
AS MANY AS YOU KNOW, I TELL YOU TONIGHT THERE ARE MORE.
YOU SEEM TO KNOW A LOT. YOU MUST GET AROUND.
NOT I.
I'VE NOT LEFT THIS PLACE IN MANY YEAR...
"NO. THE WORLD COMES TO ME HERE, ON CROOKED FEET AND CROOKED WING..."
SO I KNOW WHAT GOES ON IN THE SECRET PLACES.
AND I KNOW ABOUT YOU...

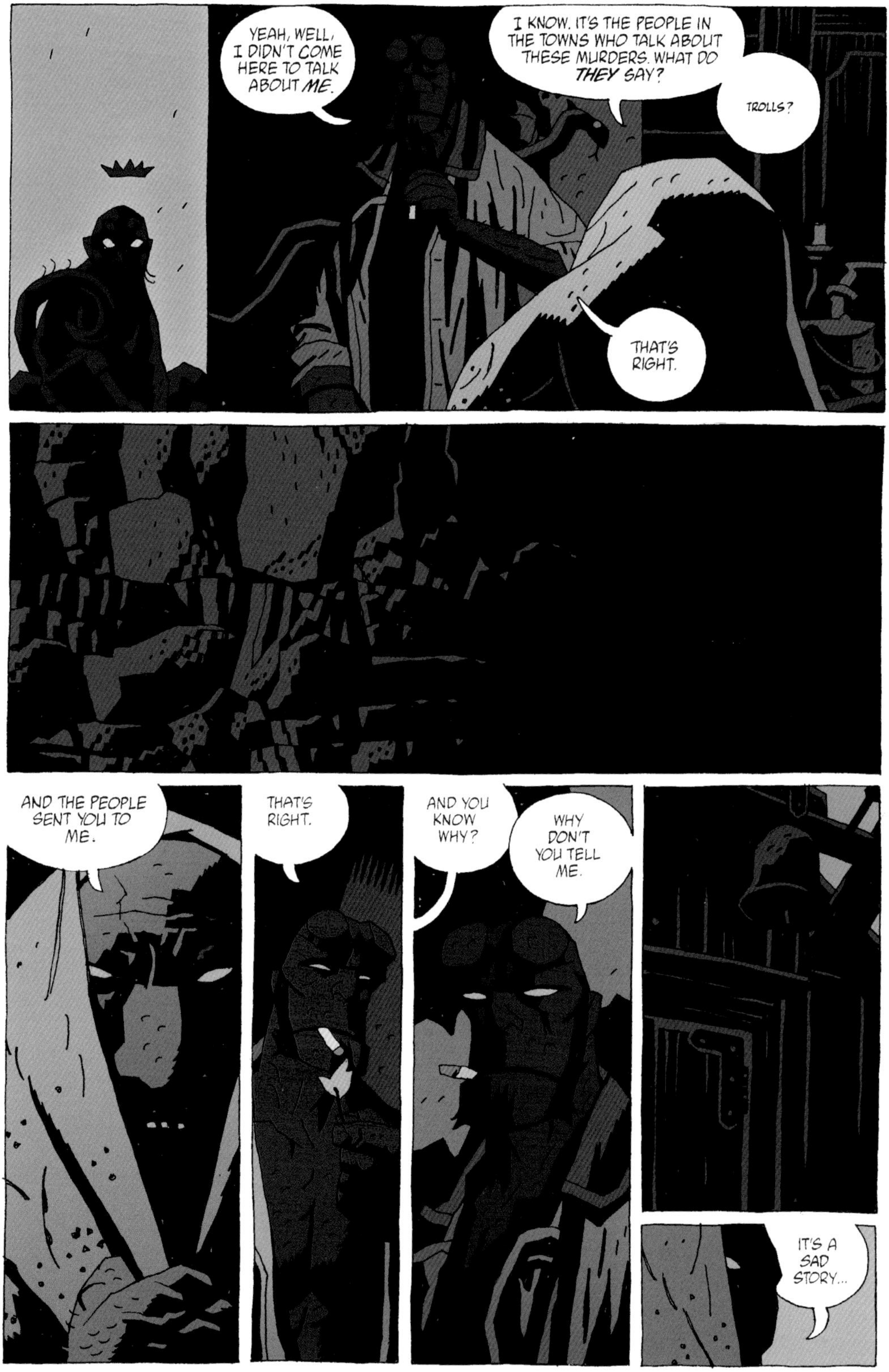
YEAH, WELL, I DIDN'T COME HERE TO TALK ABOUT ME.
I KNOW. IT'S THE PEOPLE IN THE TOWNS WHO TALK ABOUT THESE MURDERS. WHAT DO THEY SAY?
TROLLS?
THAT'S RIGHT.
AND THE PEOPLE SENT YOU TO ME.
THAT'S RIGHT.
AND YOU KNOW WHY?
WHY DON'T YOU TELL ME.
IT'S A SAD STORY...

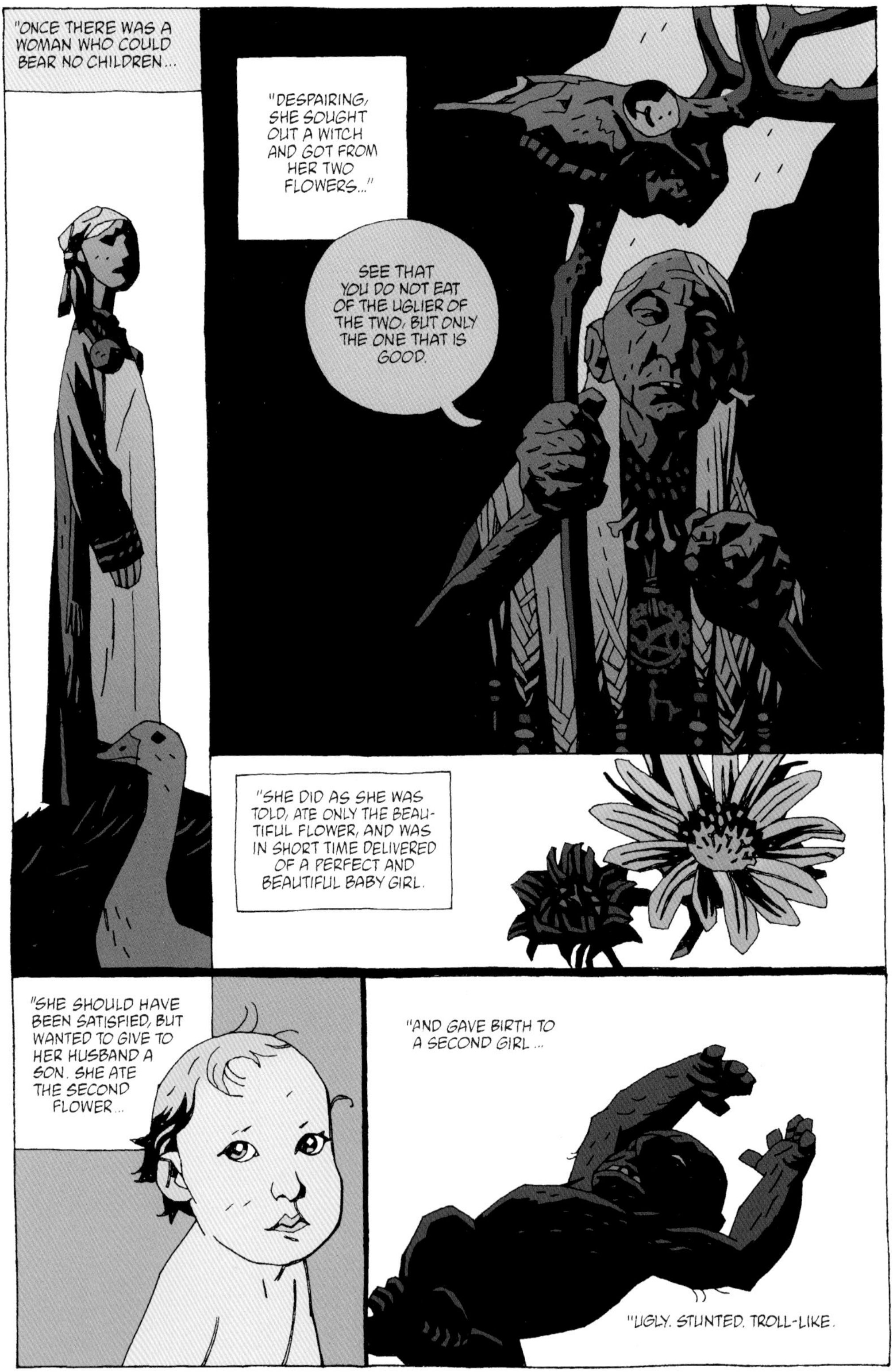
"ONCE THERE WAS A WOMAN WHO COULD BEAR NO CHILDREN...
"DESPAIRING, SHE SOUGHT OUT A WITCH AND GOT FROM HER TWO FLOWERS..."
SEE THAT YOU DO NOT EAT OF THE UGLIER OF THE TWO, BUT ONLY THE ONE THAT IS GOOD.
"SHE DID AS SHE WAS TOLD, ATE ONLY THE BEAUTIFUL FLOWER, AND WAS IN SHORT TIME DELIVERED OF A PERFECT AND BEAUTIFUL BABY GIRL.
"SHE SHOULD HAVE BEEN SATISFIED, BUT WANTED TO GIVE TO HER HUSBAND A SON. SHE ATE THE SECOND FLOWER...
"AND GAVE BIRTH TO A SECOND GIRL...
"UGLY. STUNTED. TROLL-LIKE.

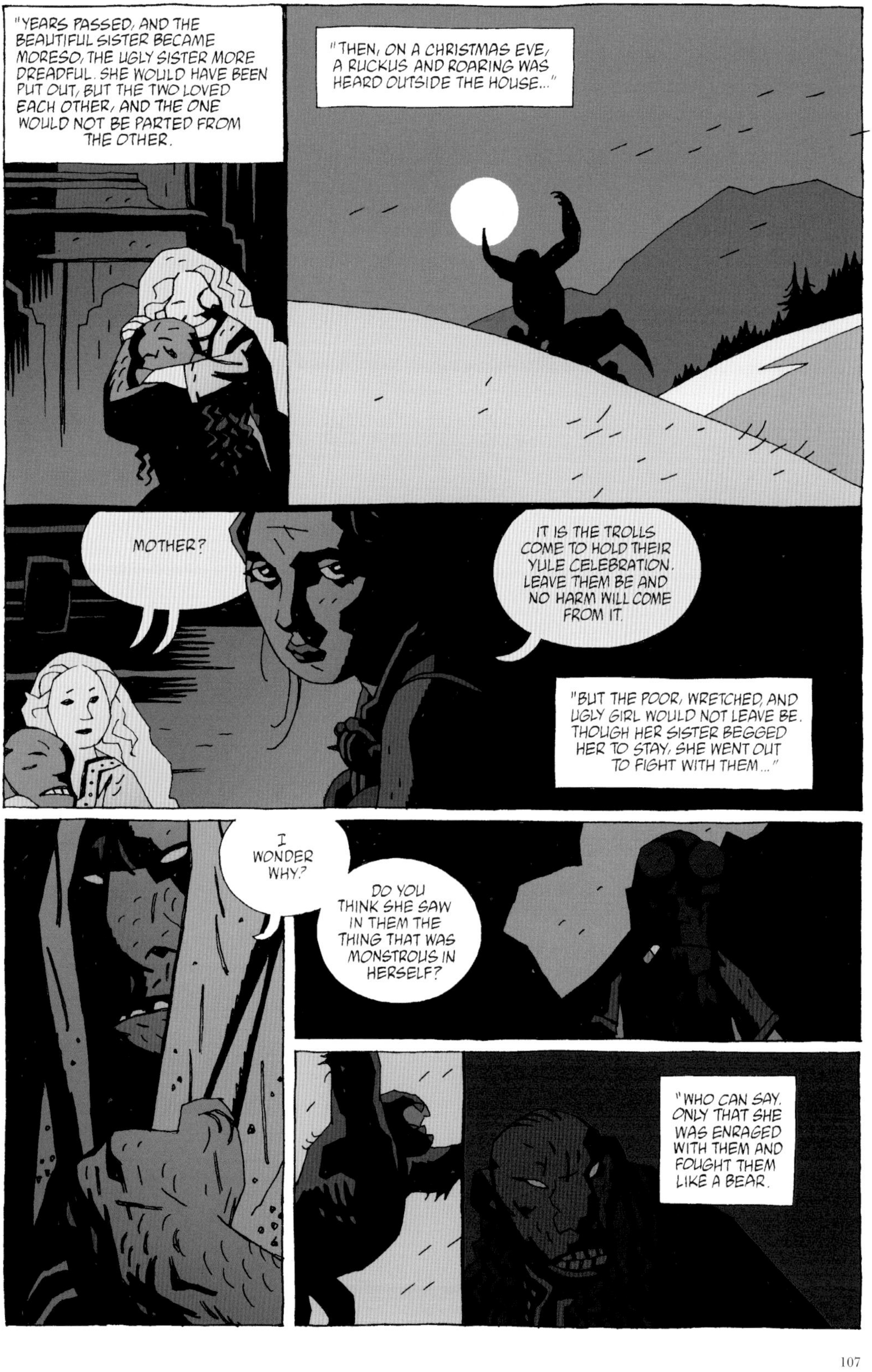
"YEARS PASSED, AND THE BEAUTIFUL SISTER BECAME MORESO, THE UGLY SISTER MORE DREADFUL. SHE WOULD HAVE BEEN PUT OUT, BUT THE TWO LOVED EACH OTHER, AND THE ONE WOULD NOT BE PARTED FROM THE OTHER.
"THEN, ON A CHRISTMAS EVE, A RUCKUS AND ROARING WAS HEARD OUTSIDE THE HOUSE..."
MOTHER?
IT IS THE TROLLS COME TO HOLD THEIR YULE CELEBRATION. LEAVE THEM BE AND NO HARM WILL COME FROM IT.
"BUT THE POOR, WRETCHED, AND UGLY GIRL WOULD NOT LEAVE BE. THOUGH HER SISTER BEGGED HER TO STAY, SHE WENT OUT TO FIGHT WITH THEM..."
I WONDER WHY?
DO YOU THINK SHE SAW IN THEM THE THING THAT WAS MONSTROUS IN HERSELF?
"WHO CAN SAY. ONLY THAT SHE WAS ENRAGED WITH THEM AND FOUGHT THEM LIKE A BEAR.

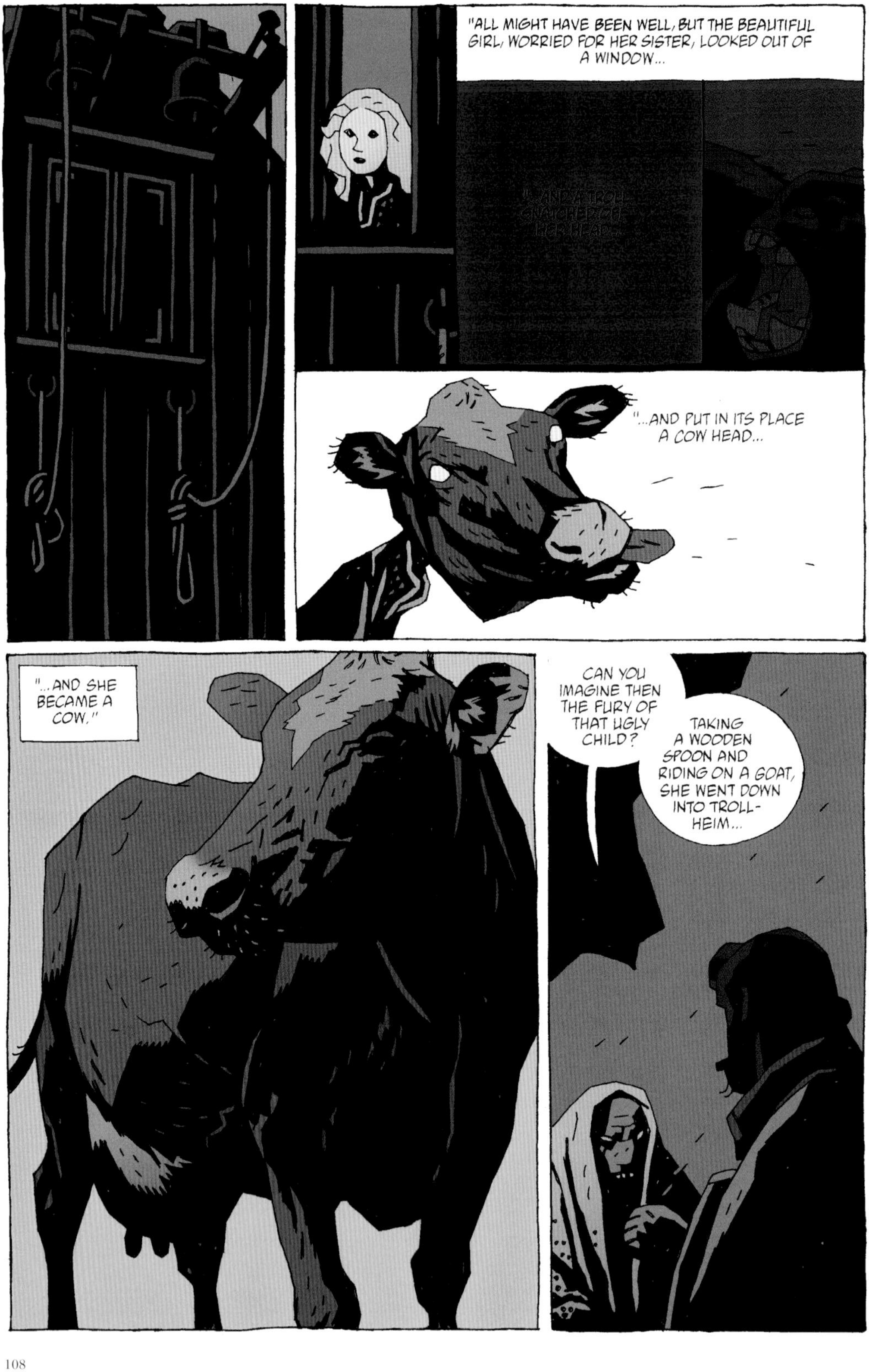
"ALL MIGHT HAVE BEEN WELL, BUT THE BEAUTIFUL GIRL, WORRIED FOR HER SISTER, LOOKED OUT OF A WINDOW...
"...AND A TROLL SNATCHED OFF HER HEAD...
"...AND PUT IN ITS PLACE A COW HEAD...
"...AND SHE BECAME A COW."
CAN YOU IMAGINE THEN THE FURY OF THAT UGLY CHILD?
TAKING A WOODEN SPOON AND RIDING ON A GOAT, SHE WENT DOWN INTO TROLL-HEIM...

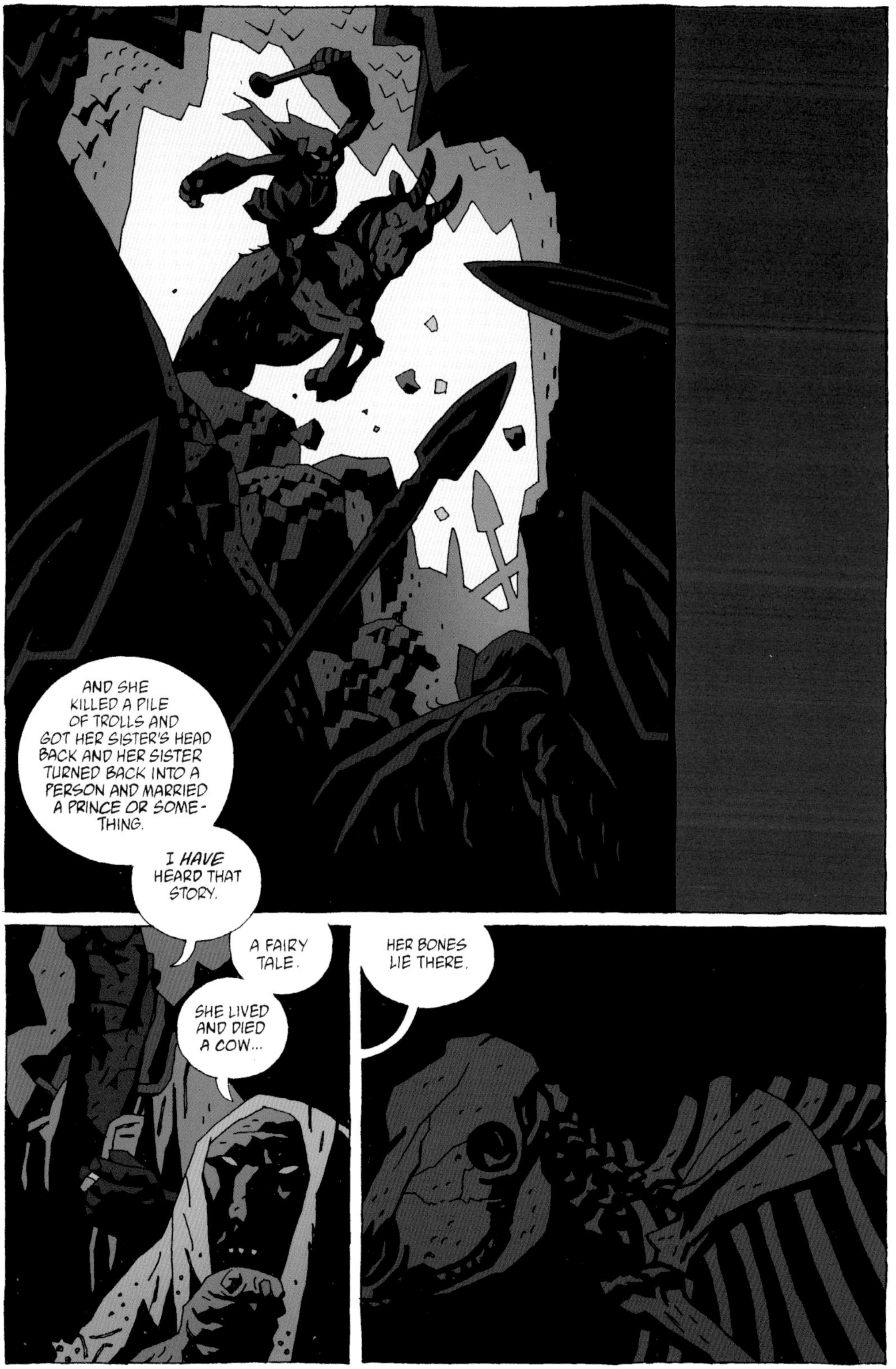
AND SHE KILLED A PILE OF TROLLS AND GOT HER SISTER'S HEAD BACK AND HER SISTER TURNED BACK INTO A PERSON AND MARRIED A PRINCE OR SOME-THING.
I *HAVE* HEARD THAT STORY.
A FAIRY TALE.
SHE LIVED AND DIED A COW...
HER BONES LIE THERE.

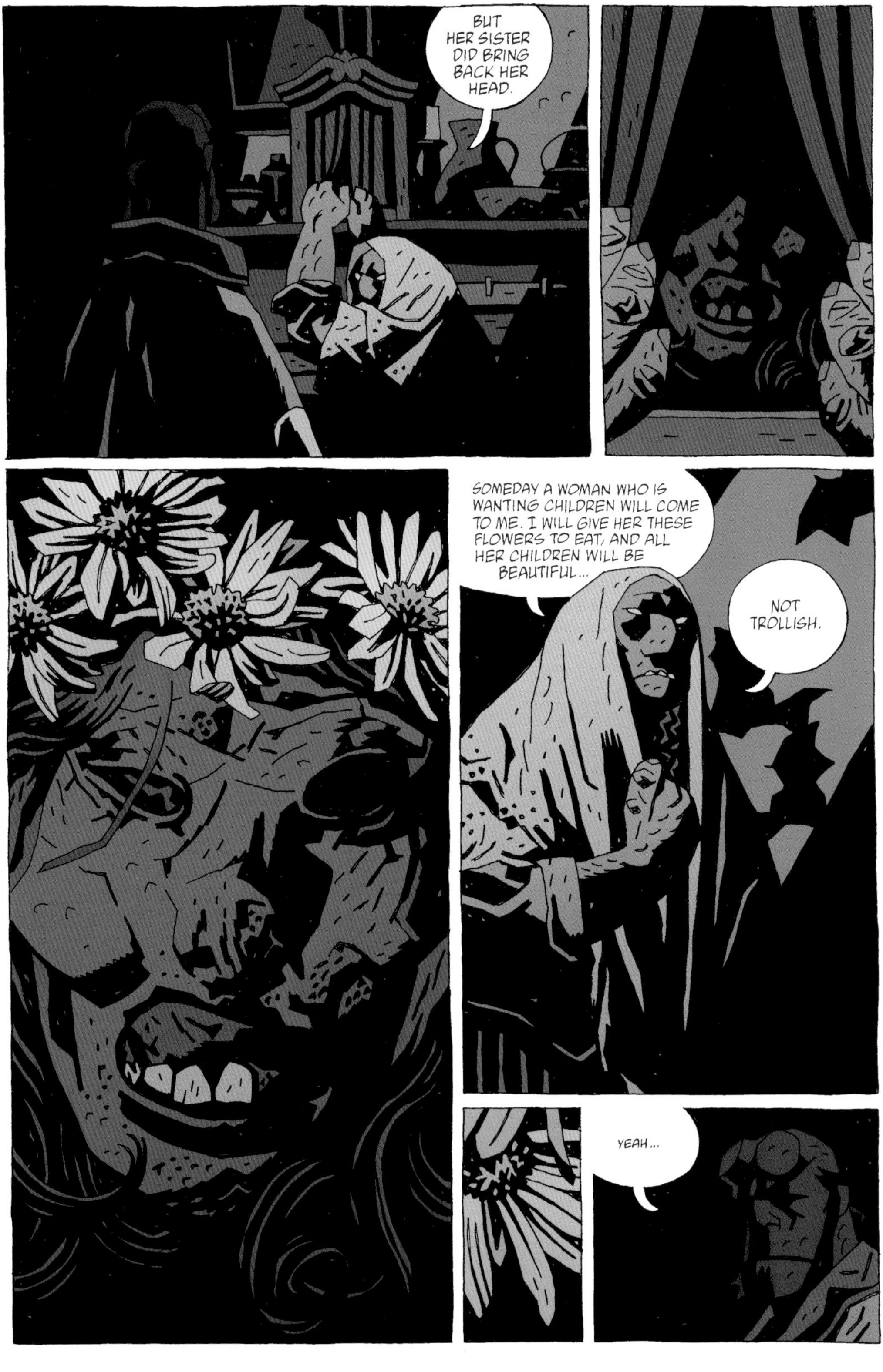
BUT HER SISTER DID BRING BACK HER HEAD.
SOMEDAY A WOMAN WHO IS WANTING CHILDREN WILL COME TO ME. I WILL GIVE HER THESE FLOWERS TO EAT, AND ALL HER CHILDREN WILL BE BEAUTIFUL...
NOT TROLLISH.
YEAH...

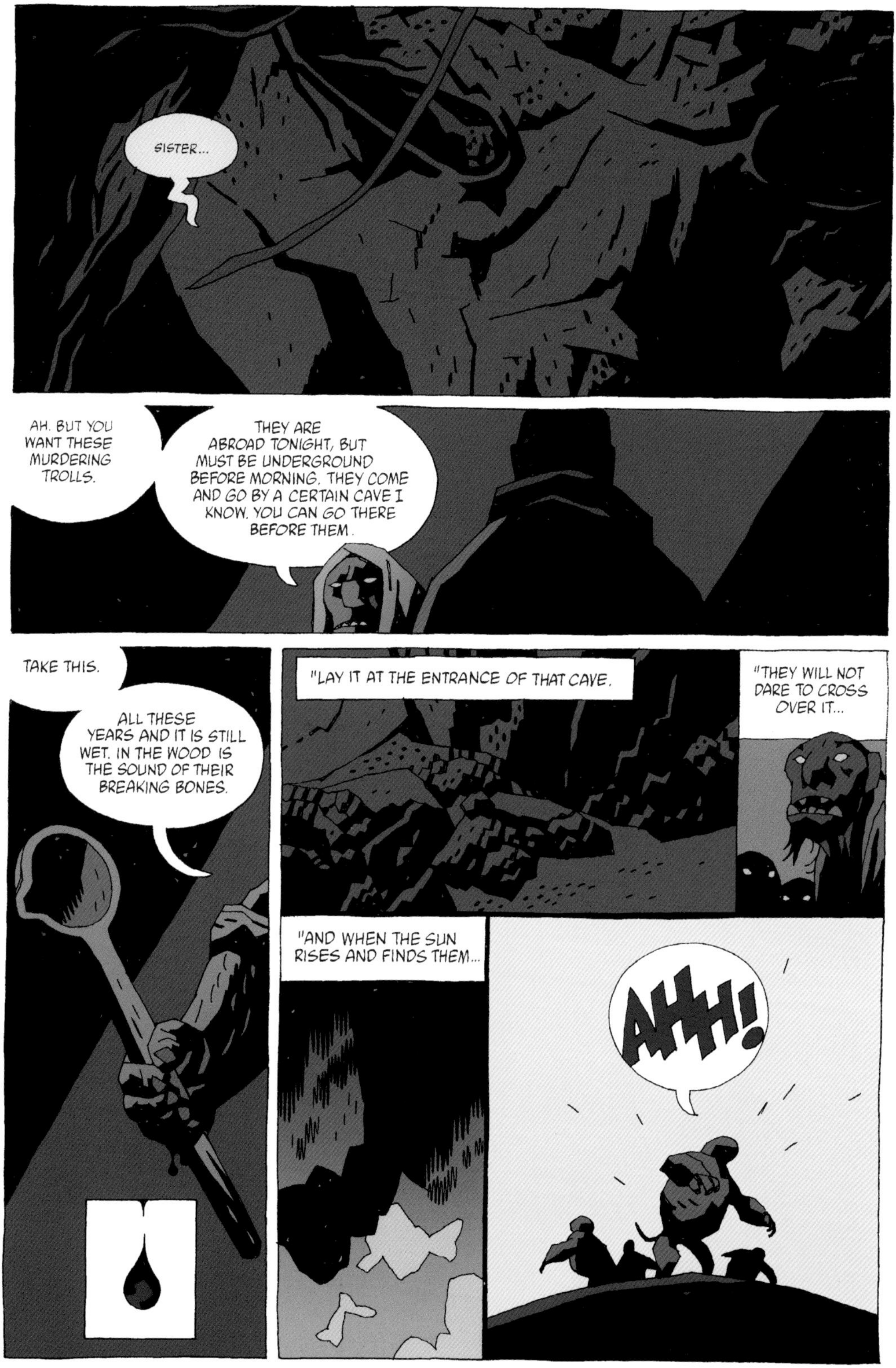
SISTER...
AH. BUT YOU WANT THESE MURDERING TROLLS.
THEY ARE ABROAD TONIGHT, BUT MUST BE UNDERGROUND BEFORE MORNING. THEY COME AND GO BY A CERTAIN CAVE I KNOW. YOU CAN GO THERE BEFORE THEM.
TAKE THIS.
ALL THESE YEARS AND IT IS STILL WET. IN THE WOOD IS THE SOUND OF THEIR BREAKING BONES.
"LAY IT AT THE ENTRANCE OF THAT CAVE.
"THEY WILL NOT DARE TO CROSS OVER IT...
"AND WHEN THE SUN RISES AND FINDS THEM...
AHH!

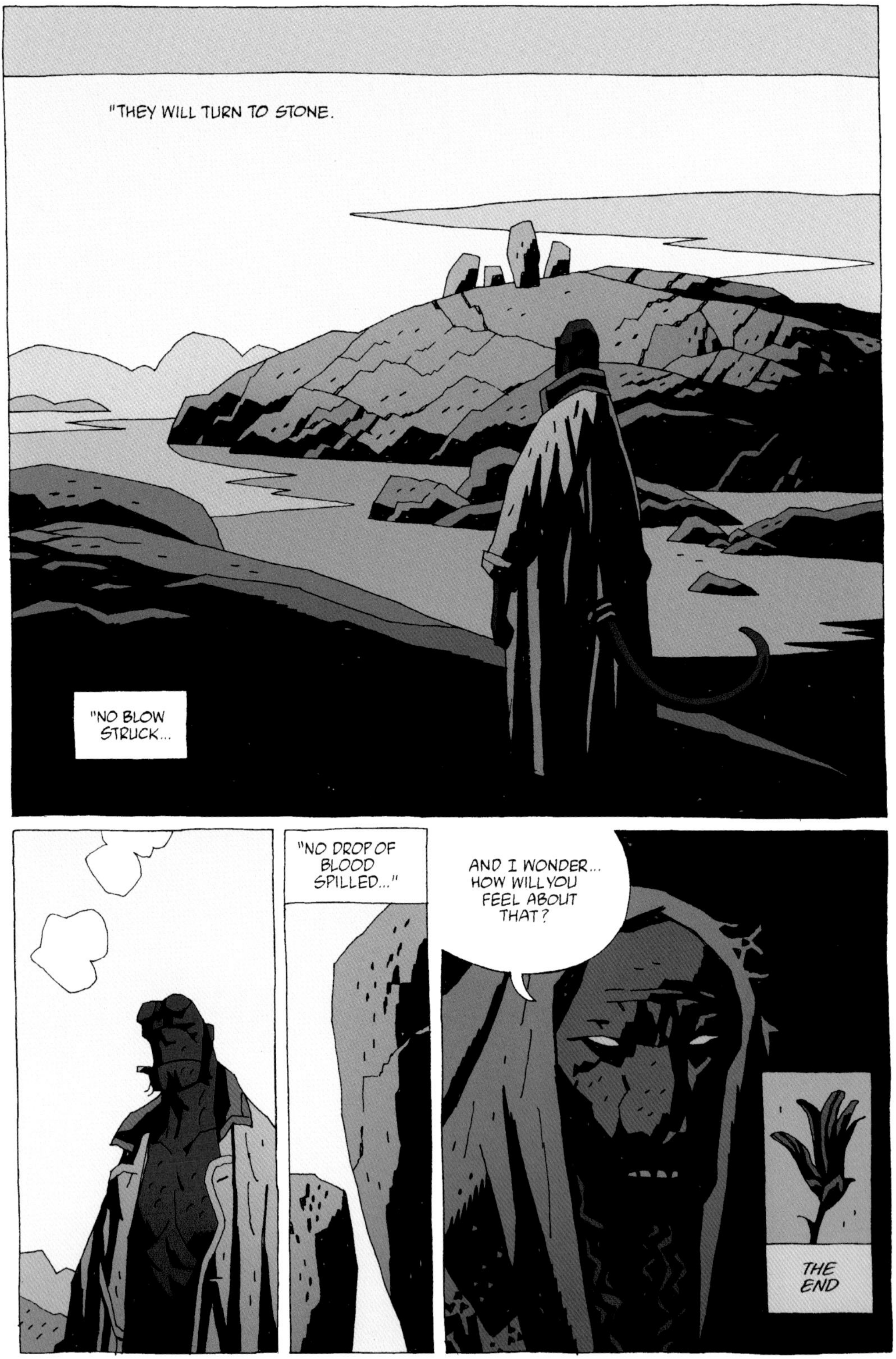
"THEY WILL TURN TO STONE.
"NO BLOW STRUCK...
"NO DROP OF BLOOD SPILLED..."
AND I WONDER... HOW WILL YOU FEEL ABOUT THAT?
THE END

Mother of Toads

by CLARK ASHTON SMITH

ILLUSTRATIONS by GARY GIANNI

W hy must you always hurry away, my little one?"

The voice of Mére Antoinette, the witch, was an amorous croaking. She ogled Pierre, the apothecary's young apprentice, with eyes full-orbed and unblinking as those of a toad. The folds beneath her chin swelled like the throat of some great batrachian. Her huge breasts, pale as frog-bellies, bulged from her torn gown as she leaned toward him.

Pierre Baudin, as usual, gave no answer; and she came closer, till he saw in the hollow of those breasts a moisture glistening like the dew of marshes ... like the slime of some amphibian ... a moisture that seemed always to linger there.

Her voice, raucously coaxing, persisted. "Stay a while tonight, my pretty orphan. No one will miss you in the village. And your master will not mind." She pressed against him with shuddering folds of fat. With her short flat fingers, which gave almost the appearance of being webbed, she seized his hand and drew it to her bosom.

Pierre wrenched the hand away and drew back discreetly. Repelled, rather than abashed, he averted his eyes. The witch was more than twice his age, and her charms were too uncouth and unsavory to tempt him for an instant. Also, her repute was such as to have nullified the attractions of even a younger and fairer sorceress. Her witchcraft had made her feared among the peasantry of that remote province, where belief in spells and philters was still common. The people of Averoigne called her La Mére des Crapauds, The Mother of Toads, a name given for more than one reason. Toads swarmed innumerably about her hut; they were said to be her familiars, and dark tales were told concerning their relationship to the sorceress, and the duties they performed at her bidding. Such tales were all the more readily believed because of those batrachian features that had always been remarked in her aspect.

The youth disliked her, even as he disliked the sluggish, abnormally large toads on which he had sometimes trodden in the dusk, upon the path between her hut and the village of Les Hiboux. He could hear some of these creatures croaking now; and it seemed, weirdly, that they uttered half-articulate echoes of the witch's words.

It would be dark soon, he reflected. The path along the marshes was not pleasant by night, and he felt doubly anxious to depart. Still without replying to Mére Antoinette's invitation, he reached for the black triangular vial she had set before him on her greasy table. The vial contained a philter of curious potency which his master, Alain le Dindon, had sent him to procure. Le Dindon, the village apothecary, was wont to deal surreptitiously in certain dubious medicaments supplied by the witch, and Pierre had often gone on such errands to her osier-hidden hut.

The old apothecary, whose humor was rough and ribald, had sometimes rallied Pierre concerning Mére Antoinette's preference for him. "Some night, my lad, you will remain with her," he had said. "Be careful, or the big toad will crush you." Remembering this gibe, the boy flushed angrily as he turned to go.

"Stay," insisted Mére Antoinette. "The fog is cold on the marshes; and it thickens apace. I knew that you were coming, and I have mulled for you a goodly measure of the red wine of Ximes."

She removed the lid from an earthen pitcher and poured its steaming contents into a large cup. The purplish-red wine creamed delectably, and an odor of hot, delicious spices filled the hut, overpowering the less agreeable odors from the simmering cauldron, the half-dried newts, vipers, bat wings, and evil, nauseous herbs hanging on the walls, and the reek of the black candles of pitch and corpse-tallow that burned always, by noon or night, in that murky interior.

"I'll drink it," said Pierre, a little grudgingly. "That is, if it contains nothing of your own concoction."

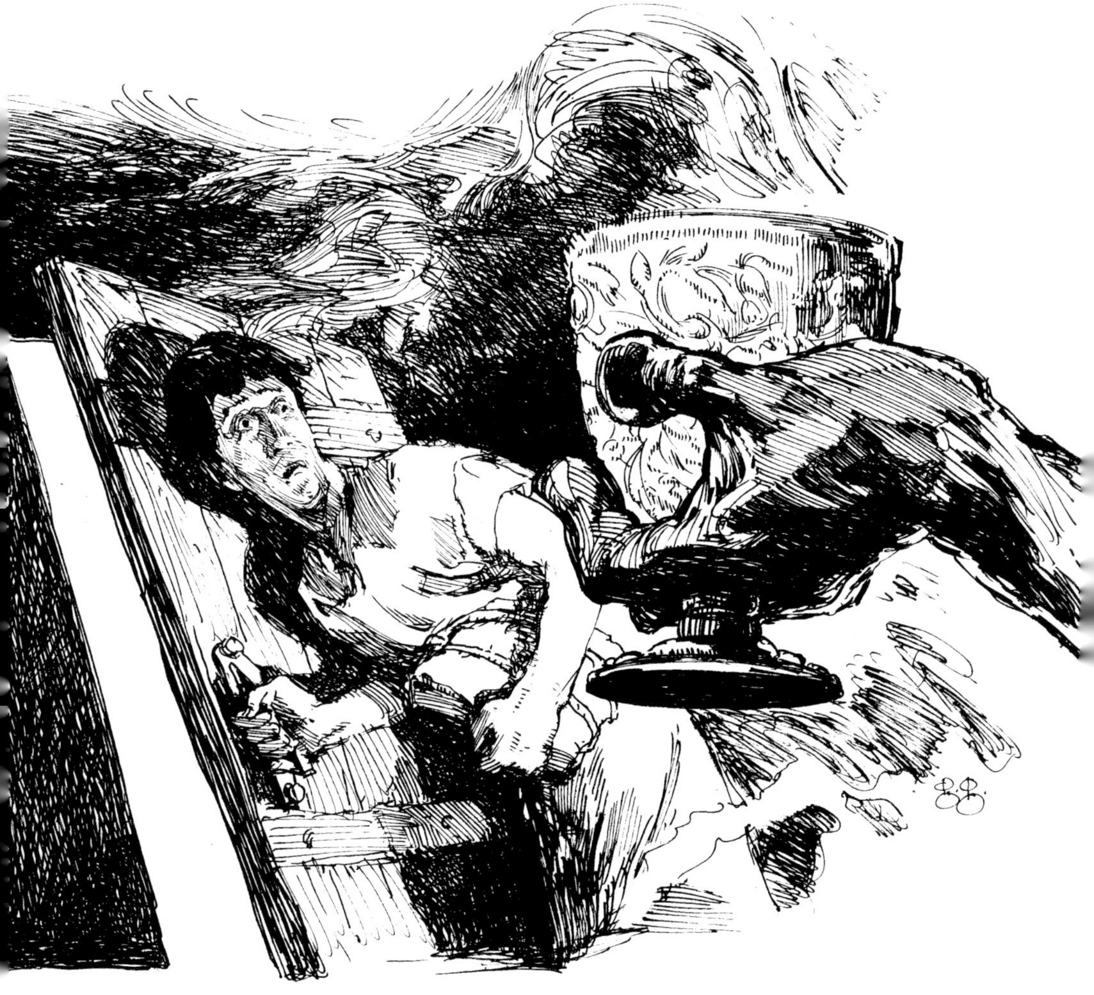

"'Tis naught but sound wine, four seasons old, with spices of Arabia," the sorceress croaked ingratiatingly. "'Twill warm your stomach and ..." She added something inaudible as Pierre accepted the cup.

Before drinking, he inhaled the fumes of the beverage with some caution but was reassured by its pleasant smell. Surely it was innocent of any drug, any philter brewed by the witch, for, to his knowledge, her preparations were all evil-smelling.

Still, as if warned by some premonition, he hesitated. Then he remembered that the sunset air was indeed chill, that mists had gathered furtively behind him as he came to Mére Antoinette's dwelling. The wine would fortify him for the dismal return walk to Les Hiboux. He quaffed it quickly and set down the cup.

"Truly, it is good wine," he declared. "But I must go now."

Even as he spoke, he felt in his stomach and veins the spreading warmth of the alcohol, of the spices ... of something more ardent than these. It seemed that his voice was unreal and strange, falling as if from a height above him. The warmth grew, mounting within him like a golden flame fed by magic oils. His blood, a seething torrent, poured tumultuously and more tumultuously through his members.

There was a deep soft thundering in his ears, a rosy dazzlement in his eyes. Somehow the hut appeared to expand, to change luminously about him. He hardly recognized its squalid furnishings, its litter of baleful oddments, on which a torrid splendor was shed by the black candles, tipped with ruddy fire, that towered and swelled gigantically into the soft gloom. His blood burned as with the throbbing flame of the candles.

It came to him, for an instant, that all this was a questionable enchantment, a glamour wrought by the witch's wine. Fear was upon him and he wished to flee. Then, close beside him, he saw Mére Antoinette.

Briefly he marveled at the change that had befallen her. Then fear and wonder were alike forgotten, together with his old repulsion. He knew why the magic warmth mounted ever higher and hotter within him; why his flesh glowed like the ruddy tapers.

The soiled skirt she had worn lay at her feet, and she stood naked as Lilith, the first witch. The lumpish limbs and body had grown voluptuous; the pale, thick-lipped mouth enticed him with a promise of ampler kisses than other mouths could yield. The pits of her short round arms, the concave of her ponderously drooping breasts, the heavy creases and swollen rondures of flanks and thighs, all were fraught with luxurious allurement.

"Do you like me now, my little one?" she questioned.

This time he did not draw away but met her with hot, questing hands when she pressed heavily against him. Her limbs were cool and moist; her

breasts yielded like the turf-mounds above a bog. Her body was white and wholly hairless, but here and there he found curious roughnesses ... like those on the skin of a toad ... that somehow sharpened his desire instead of repelling it.

She was so huge that his fingers barely joined behind her. His two hands, together, were equal only to the cupping of a single breast. But the wine had filled his blood with a philterous ardor.

She led him to her couch beside the hearth where a great cauldron boiled mysteriously, sending up its fumes in strange-twining coils that suggested vague and obscene figures. The couch was rude and bare. But the flesh of the sorceress was like deep, luxurious cushions ...

Pierre awoke in the ashy dawn, when the tall black tapers had dwindled down and had melted limply in their sockets. Sick and confused, he sought vainly to remember where he was or what he had done. Then, turning a little, he saw beside him on the couch a thing that was like some impossible monster of ill dreams: a toadlike form, large as a fat woman. Its limbs were somehow like a woman's arms and legs. Its pale, warty body pressed and bulged against him, and he felt the rounded softness of something that resembled a breast.

Nausea rose within him as memory of that delirious night returned. Most foully he had been beguiled by the witch, and had succumbed to her evil enchantments.

It seemed that an incubus smothered him, weighing upon all his limbs and body. He shut his eyes, that he might no longer behold the loathsome thing that was Mére Antoinette in her true semblance. Slowly, with prodigious effort, he drew himself away from the crushing nightmare shape. It did not stir or appear to waken, and he slid quickly from the couch.

Again, compelled by a noisome fascination, he peered at the thing on the couch—and saw only the gross form of Mére Antoinette. Perhaps his impression of a great toad beside him had been but an illusion, a half-dream that lingered after slumber. He lost something of his nightmarish horror, but his gorge still rose in a sick disgust, remembering the lewdness to which he had yielded.

Fearing that the witch might awaken at any moment and seek to detain him, he stole noiselessly from the hut. It was broad daylight, but a cold, hueless mist lay everywhere, shrouding the reedy marshes, and hanging like a ghostly curtain on the path he must follow to Les Hiboux. Moving and seething always, the mist seemed to reach toward him with intercepting fingers as he started homeward. He shivered at its touch, he bowed his head and drew his cloak closer around him.

Thicker and thicker the mist swirled, coiling, writhing endlessly, as if to bar Pierre's progress. He could discern the twisting, narrow path for only a few paces in advance. It was hard to find the familiar landmarks, hard to recognize the osiers and willows that loomed suddenly before him like gray phantoms and faded again into the white nothingness as he went onward. Never had he seen such fog: it was like the blinding, stifling fumes of a thousand witch-stirred cauldrons.

Though he was not altogether sure of his surroundings, Pierre thought that he had covered half the distance to the village. Then, all at once, he began to meet the toads. They were hidden by the mist till he came close upon them. Misshapen, unnaturally big and bloated, they squatted in his way on the little footpath or hopped sluggishly from the pallid gloom on either hand.

Several struck against his feet with a horrible and heavy flopping. He stepped unaware upon one of them, and slipped in the squashy putrescence it had made, barely saving himself from a headlong fall on the bog's rim. Black, miry water gloomed close beside him as he staggered there.

Turning to regain his path, he crushed others of the toads to an abhorrent pulp under his feet. The marshy soil was alive with them. They

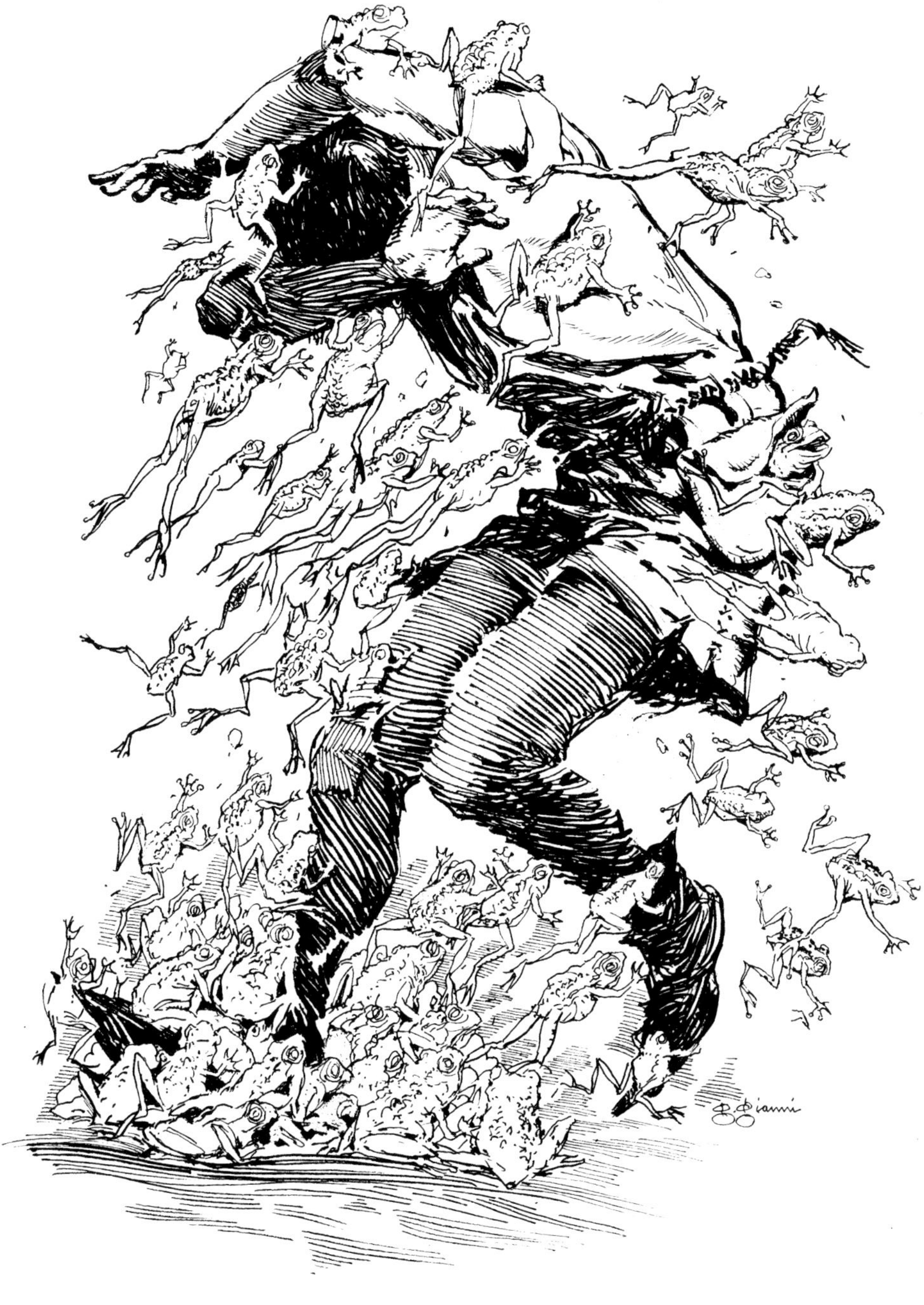

flopped against him from the mist, striking his legs, his bosom, his very face with their clammy bodies. They rose up by scores like a devil-driven legion. It seemed that there was a malignance, an evil purpose in their movements, in the buffeting of their violent impact. He could make no progress on the swarming path, but lurched to and fro, slipping blindly, and shielding his face with lifted hands. He felt an eerie consternation, an eldritch horror. It was as if the nightmare of his awakening in the witch's hut had somehow returned upon him.

The toads came always from the direction of Les Hiboux, as if to drive him back toward Mére Antoinette's dwelling. They bounded against him, like a monstrous hail, like missiles flung by unseen demons. The ground was covered by them; the air was filled with their hurtling bodies. Once, he nearly went down beneath them.

Their number seemed to increase, they pelted him in a noxious storm. He gave way before them, his courage broke, and he started to run at random, without knowing that he had left the safe path. Losing all thought of direction in his frantic desire to escape from those impossible myriads, he plunged on amid the dim reeds and sedges, over ground that quivered gelatinously beneath him. Always at his heels he heard the soft, heavy

flopping of the toads; and sometimes they rose up like a sudden wall to bar his way and turn him aside. More than once, they drove him back from the verge of hidden quagmires into which he would otherwise have fallen. It was as if they were herding him deliberately and concertedly to a destined goal.

Now, like the lifting of a dense curtain, the mist rolled away, and Pierre saw before him in a golden dazzle of morning sunshine the green, thick-growing osiers that surrounded Mére Antoinette's hut. The toads had all disappeared, though he could have sworn that hundreds of them were hopping close about him an instant previously. With a feeling of helpless fright and panic, he knew that he was still within the witch's toils; that the toads were indeed her familiars, as so many people believed them to be. They had prevented his escape, and had brought him back to the foul creature ... whether woman, batrachian, or both ... who was known as The Mother of Toads.

Pierre's sensations were those of one who sinks momently deeper into some black and bottomless quicksand. He saw the witch emerge from the hut and come toward him. Her thick fingers, with pale folds of skin between them like the beginnings of a web, were stretched and flattened on the steaming cup that she carried. A sudden gust of wind arose as if from nowhere, lifting the scanty skirts of Mére Antoinette about her fat thighs, and bearing to Pierre's nostrils the hot, familiar spices of the drugged wine. "Why did you leave so hastily, my little one?" There was an amorous wheedling in the very tone of the witch's question. "I should not have let you go without another cup of the good red wine, mulled and spiced for the warming of your stomach … See, I have prepared it for you … knowing that you would return."

She came very close to him as she spoke, leering and sidling, and held the cup toward his lips. Pierre grew dizzy with the strange fumes and turned his head away. It seemed that a paralyzing spell had seized his muscles, for the simple movement required an immense effort.

His mind, however, was still clear, and the sick revulsion of that nightmare dawn returned upon him. He saw again the great toad that had lain at his side when he awakened.

"I will not drink your wine," he said firmly. "You are a foul witch, and I loathe you. Let me go."

"Why do you loathe me?" croaked Mére Antoinette. "You loved me yesternight. I can give you all that other women give … and more."

"You are not a woman," said Pierre. "You are a big toad. I saw you in your true shape this morning. I'd rather drown in the marsh waters than sleep with you again."

An indescribable change came upon the sorceress before Pierre had finished speaking. The leer slid from her thick and pallid features, leaving them blankly inhuman for an instant. Then her eyes bulged and goggled horribly, and her whole body appeared to swell as if inflated with venom.

"Go, then!" she spat with a guttural virulence. "But you will soon wish that you had stayed …"

The queer paralysis had lifted from Pierre's muscles. It was as if the injunction of the angry witch had served to revoke an insidious, half-woven spell. With no parting glance or word, Pierre turned from her and fled with long, hasty steps, almost running, on the path to Les Hiboux.

He had gone little more than a hundred paces when the fog began to return. It coiled shoreward in vast volumes from the marshes, it poured like smoke from the very ground at his feet. Almost instantly, the sun dimmed to a wan silver disk and disappeared. The blue heavens were lost in the pale and seething voidness overhead. The path before Pierre was blotted out till he seemed to walk on the sheer rim of a white abyss that moved with him as he went.

Like the clammy arms of specters, with death-chill fingers that clutched and caressed, the weird mists drew closer still about Pierre. They thickened in his nostrils and throat, they dripped in a heavy dew from his garments.

They choked him with the fetor of rank waters and putrescent ooze ... and a stench as of liquefying corpses that had risen somewhere to the surface amid the fen.

Then, from the blank whiteness, the toads assailed Pierre in a surging, solid wave that towered above his head and swept him from the dim path with the force of failing seas as it descended. He went down, splashing and floundering, into water that swarmed with the numberless batrachians. Thick slime was in his mouth and nose as he struggled to regain his footing. The water, however, was only knee-deep, and the bottom, though slippery and oozy, supported him with little yielding when he stood erect.

He discerned indistinctly through the mist the nearby margin from which he had fallen. But his steps were weirdly and horribly hampered by the toad-seething waters when he strove to reach it. Inch by inch, with a hopeless panic deepening upon him, he fought toward the solid shore. The toads leaped and tumbled about him with a dizzying eddylike motion. They swirled like a viscid undertow around his feet and shins. They swept and swelled in great loathsome undulations against his retarded knees.

However, he made slow and painful progress, till his outstretched fingers could almost grasp the wiry sedges that trailed from the low bank. Then, from that mist-bound shore, there fell and broke upon him a second deluge of those demoniac toads; and Pierre was borne helplessly backward into the filthy waters.

Held down by the piling and crawling masses, and drowning in nauseous darkness at the thick-oozed bottom, he clawed feebly at his assailants. For a moment, ere oblivion

came, his fingers found among them the outlines of a monstrous form that was somehow toadlike ... but large and heavy as a fat woman. At the last, it seemed to him that two enormous breasts were crushed closely down upon his face.

The End

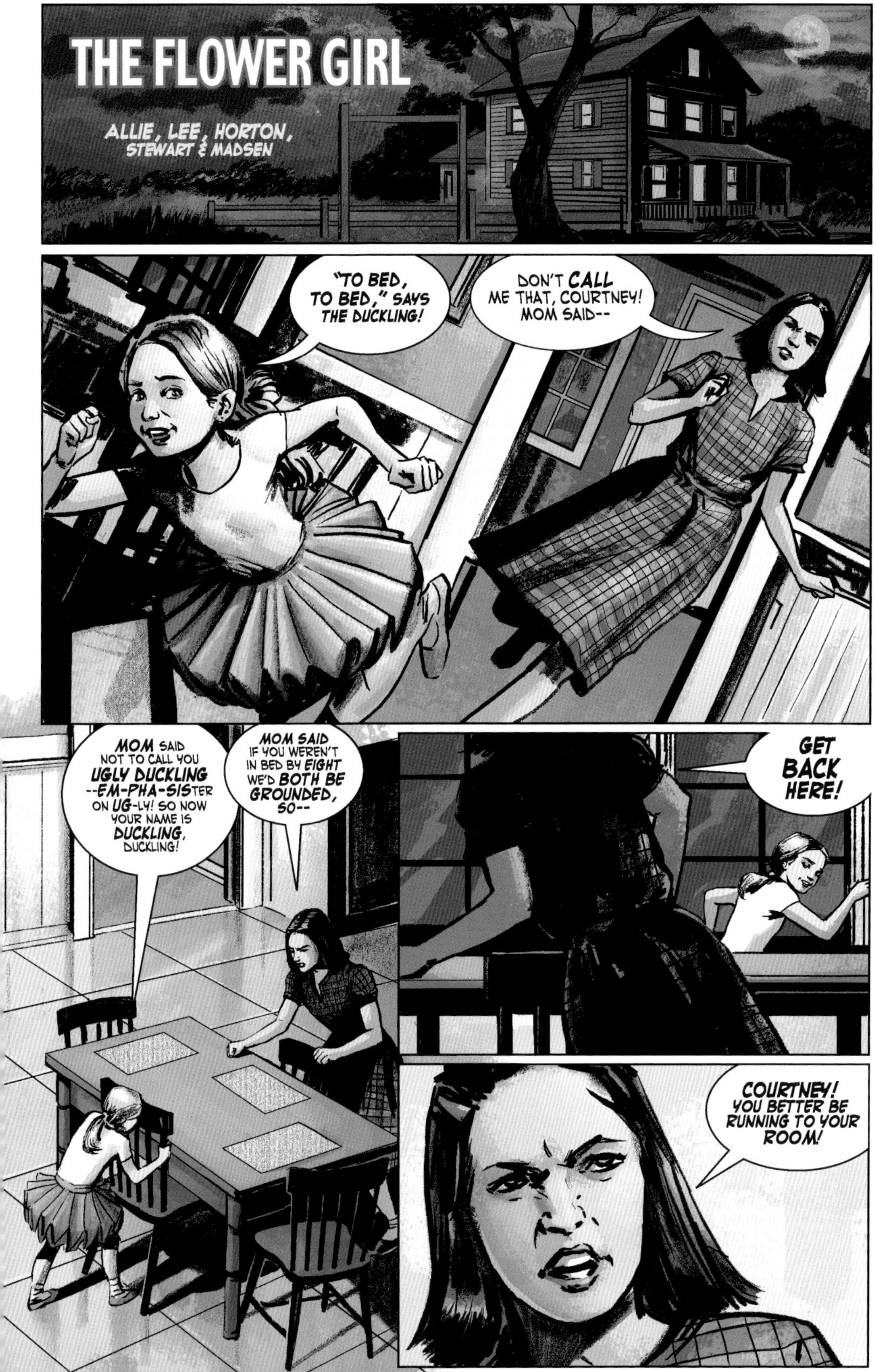
THE FLOWER GIRL
ALLIE, LEE, HORTON, STEWART & MADSEN
"TO BED, TO BED," SAYS THE DUCKLING!
DON'T CALL ME THAT, COURTNEY! MOM SAID--
MOM SAID NOT TO CALL YOU UGLY DUCKLING --EM-PHA-SIS-TER ON UG-LY! SO NOW YOUR NAME IS DUCKLING, DUCKLING!
MOM SAID IF YOU WEREN'T IN BED BY EIGHT WE'D BOTH BE GROUNDED, SO--
GET BACK HERE!
COURTNEY! YOU BETTER BE RUNNING TO YOUR ROOM!

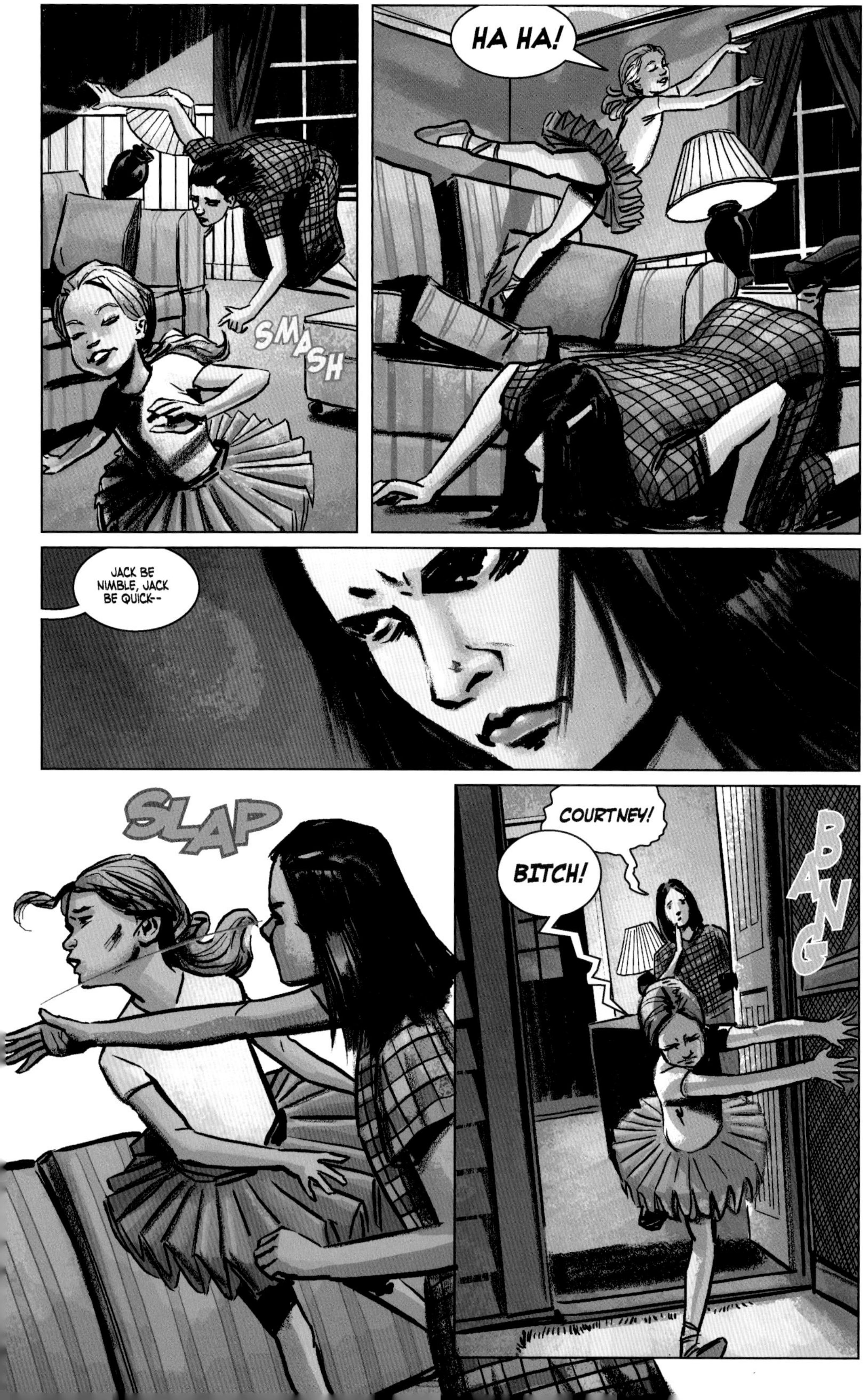
SMASH
HA HA!
JACK BE NIMBLE, JACK BE QUICK--
SLAP
COURTNEY!
BITCH!
BANG

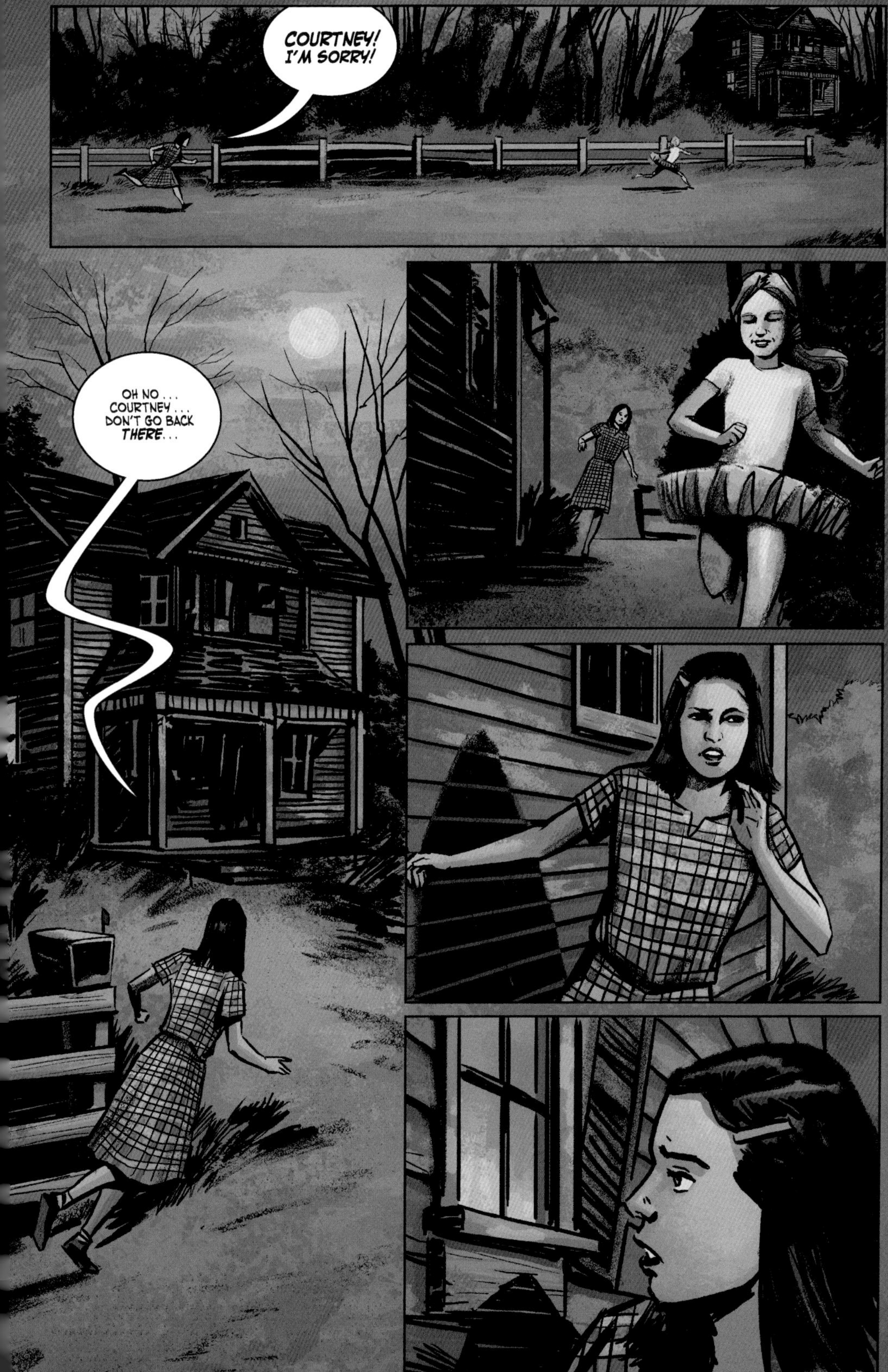
COURTNEY! I'M SORRY!
OH NO . . . COURTNEY . . . DON'T GO BACK THERE . . .

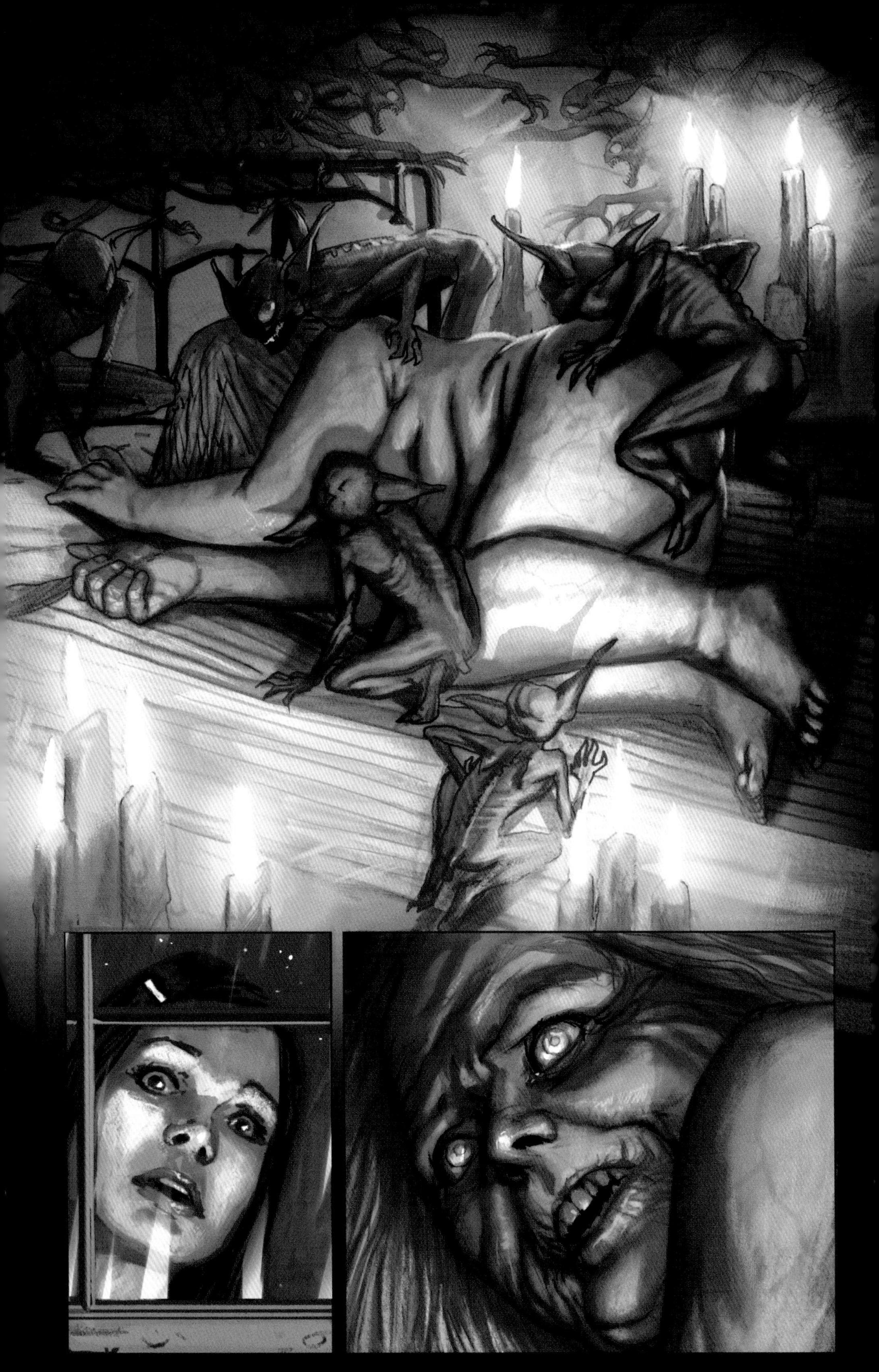

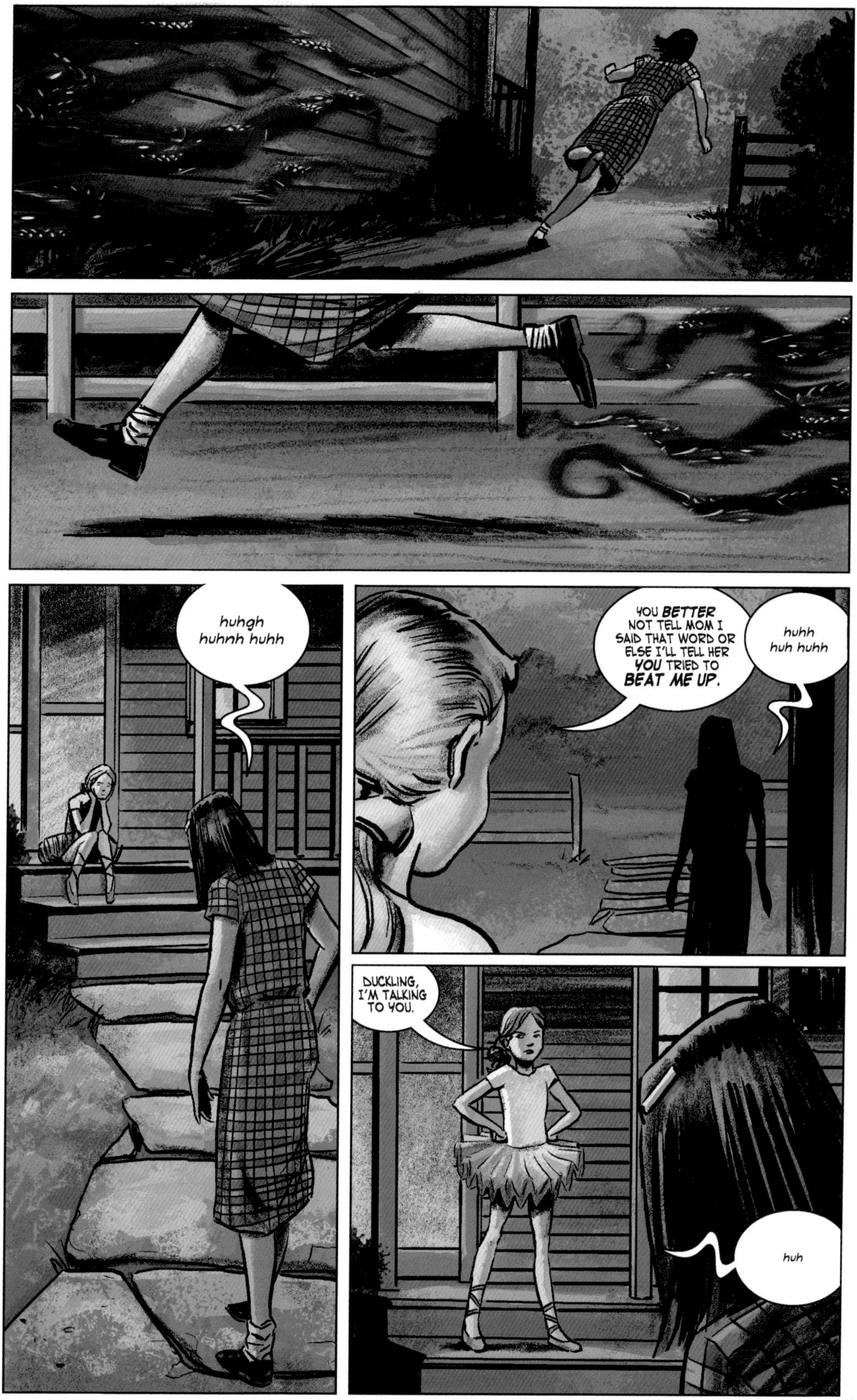
huhgh huhnh huhh
YOU BETTER NOT TELL MOM I SAID THAT WORD OR ELSE I'LL TELL HER YOU TRIED TO BEAT ME UP.
huhh huh huhh
DUCKLING, I'M TALKING TO YOU.
huh

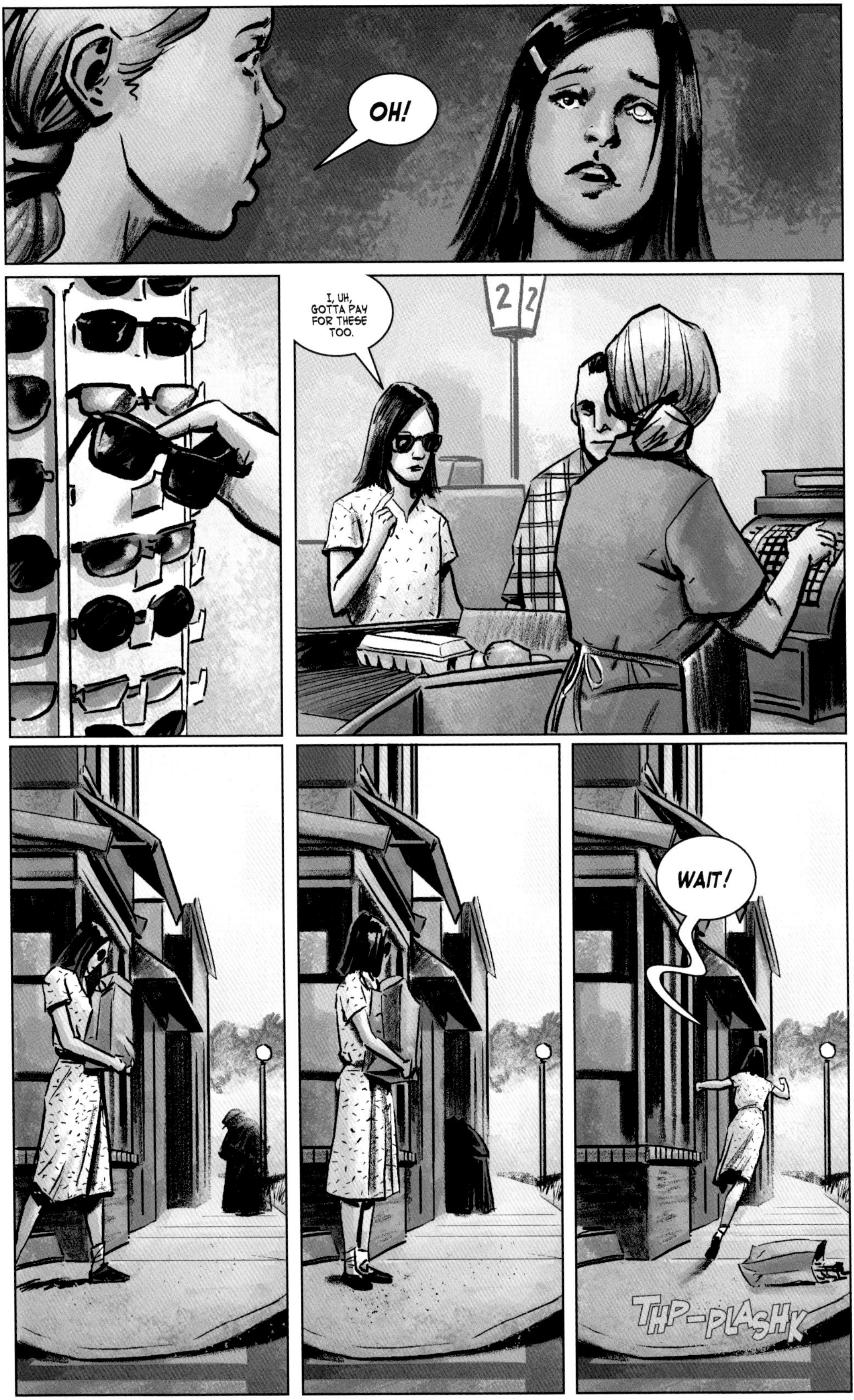
OH!
I, UH, GOTTA PAY FOR THESE TOO.
WAIT!
THP-PLASHK

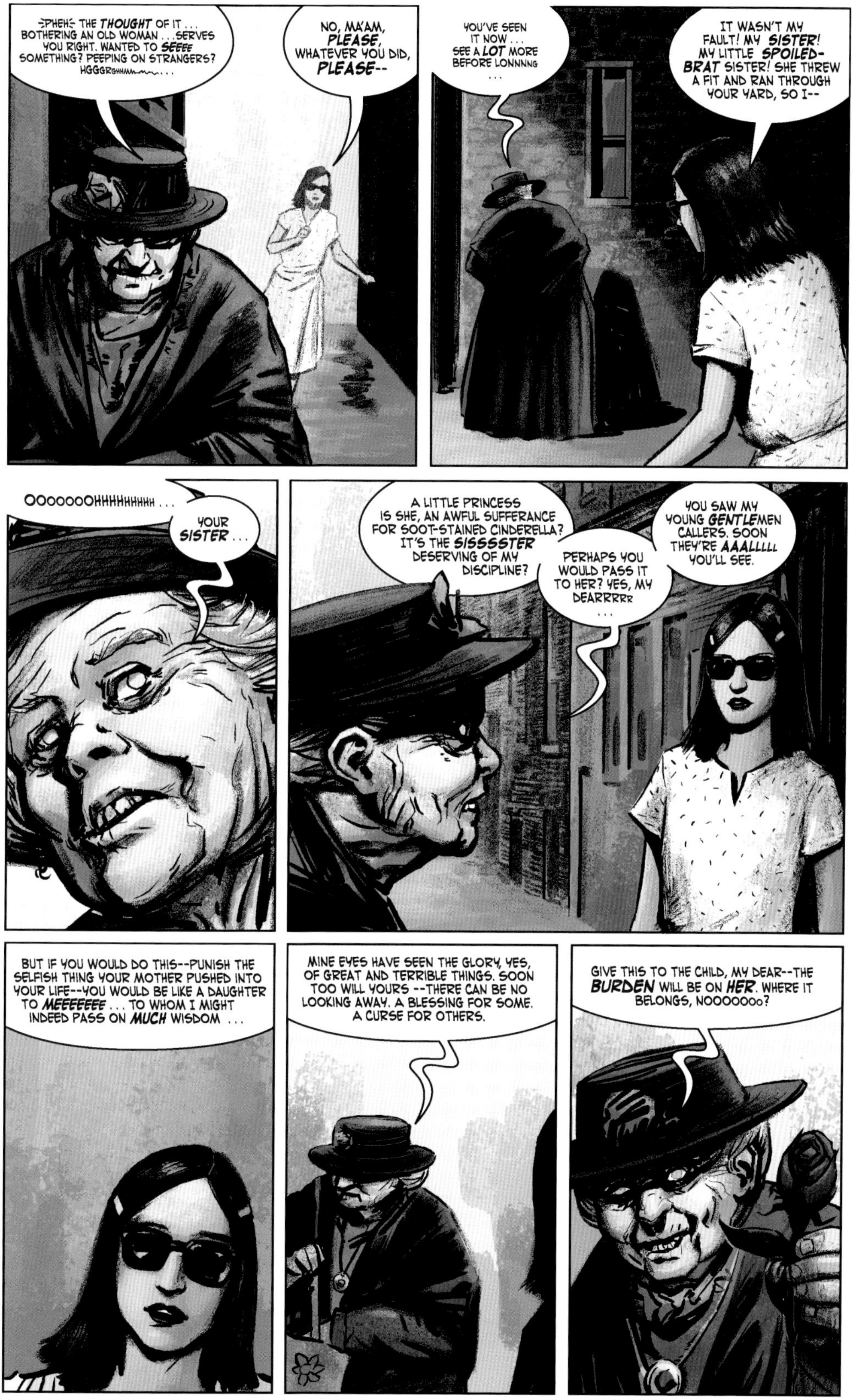
PHEH THE THOUGHT OF IT . . . BOTHERING AN OLD WOMAN . . . SERVES YOU RIGHT. WANTED TO SEEEE SOMETHING? PEEPING ON STRANGERS? HGGGRGHHMM . . .
NO, MA'AM, PLEASE, WHATEVER YOU DID, PLEASE--
YOU'VE SEEN IT NOW . . . SEE A LOT MORE BEFORE LONNNNG . . .
IT WASN'T MY FAULT! MY SISTER! MY LITTLE SPOILED-BRAT SISTER! SHE THREW A FIT AND RAN THROUGH YOUR YARD, SO I--
OOOOOOOHHHHHHHHH . . .
YOUR SISTER . . .
A LITTLE PRINCESS IS SHE, AN AWFUL SUFFERANCE FOR SOOT-STAINED CINDERELLA? IT'S THE SISSSSTER DESERVING OF MY DISCIPLINE?
YOU SAW MY YOUNG GENTLEMEN CALLERS. SOON THEY'RE AAALLLLL YOU'LL SEE.
PERHAPS YOU WOULD PASS IT TO HER? YES, MY DEARRRRR . . .
BUT IF YOU WOULD DO THIS--PUNISH THE SELFISH THING YOUR MOTHER PUSHED INTO YOUR LIFE--YOU WOULD BE LIKE A DAUGHTER TO MEEEEEEE . . . TO WHOM I MIGHT INDEED PASS ON MUCH WISDOM . . .
MINE EYES HAVE SEEN THE GLORY, YES, OF GREAT AND TERRIBLE THINGS. SOON TOO WILL YOURS --THERE CAN BE NO LOOKING AWAY. A BLESSING FOR SOME. A CURSE FOR OTHERS.
GIVE THIS TO THE CHILD, MY DEAR--THE BURDEN WILL BE ON HER. WHERE IT BELONGS, NOOOOOOo?

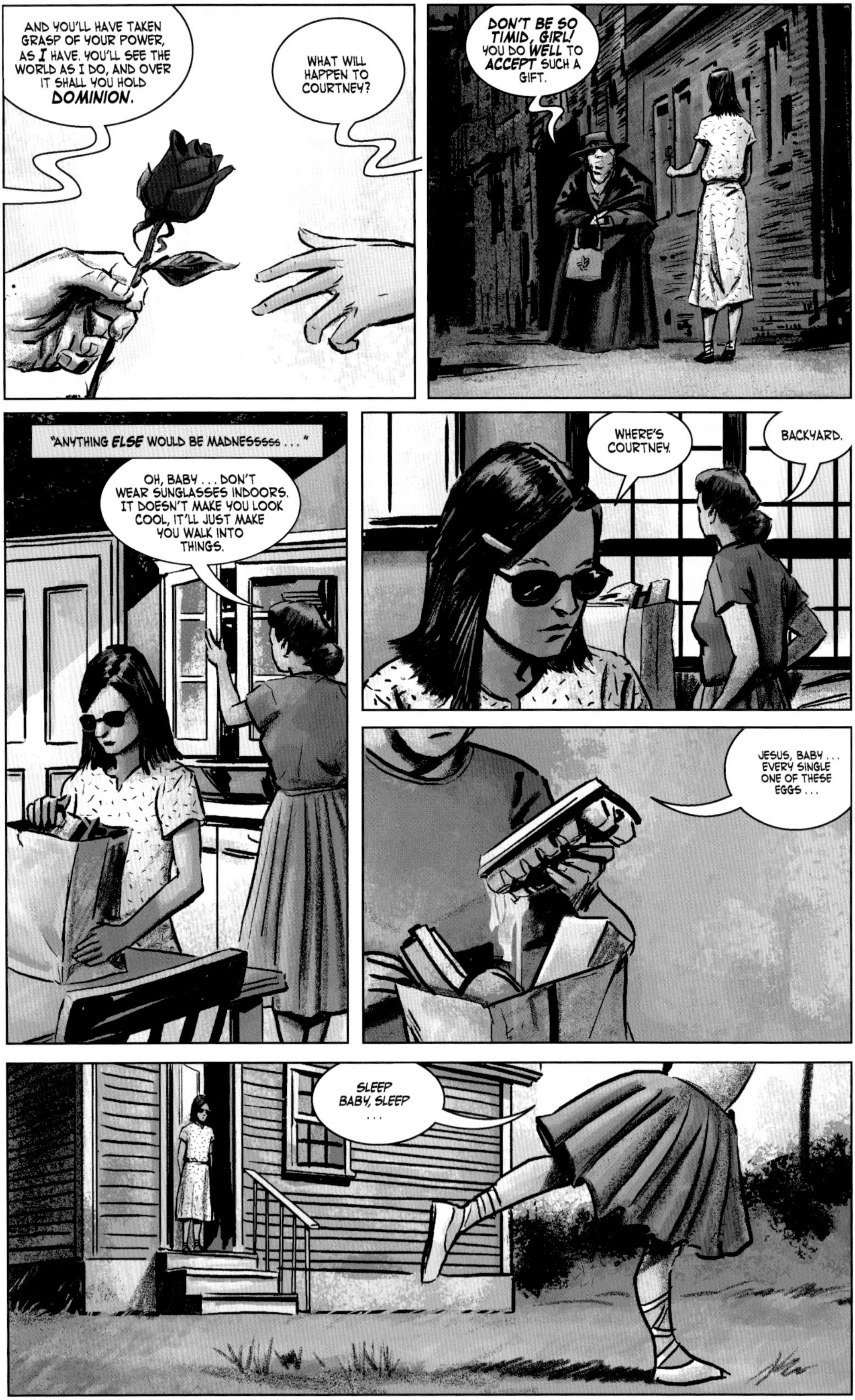
AND YOU'LL HAVE TAKEN GRASP OF YOUR POWER, AS I HAVE. YOU'LL SEE THE WORLD AS I DO, AND OVER IT SHALL YOU HOLD DOMINION.
WHAT WILL HAPPEN TO COURTNEY?
DON'T BE SO TIMID, GIRL! YOU DO WELL TO ACCEPT SUCH A GIFT.
"ANYTHING ELSE WOULD BE MADNESSSSS . . ."
OH, BABY . . . DON'T WEAR SUNGLASSES INDOORS. IT DOESN'T MAKE YOU LOOK COOL, IT'LL JUST MAKE YOU WALK INTO THINGS.
WHERE'S COURTNEY.
BACKYARD.
JESUS, BABY . . . EVERY SINGLE ONE OF THESE EGGS . . .
SLEEP BABY, SLEEP . . .

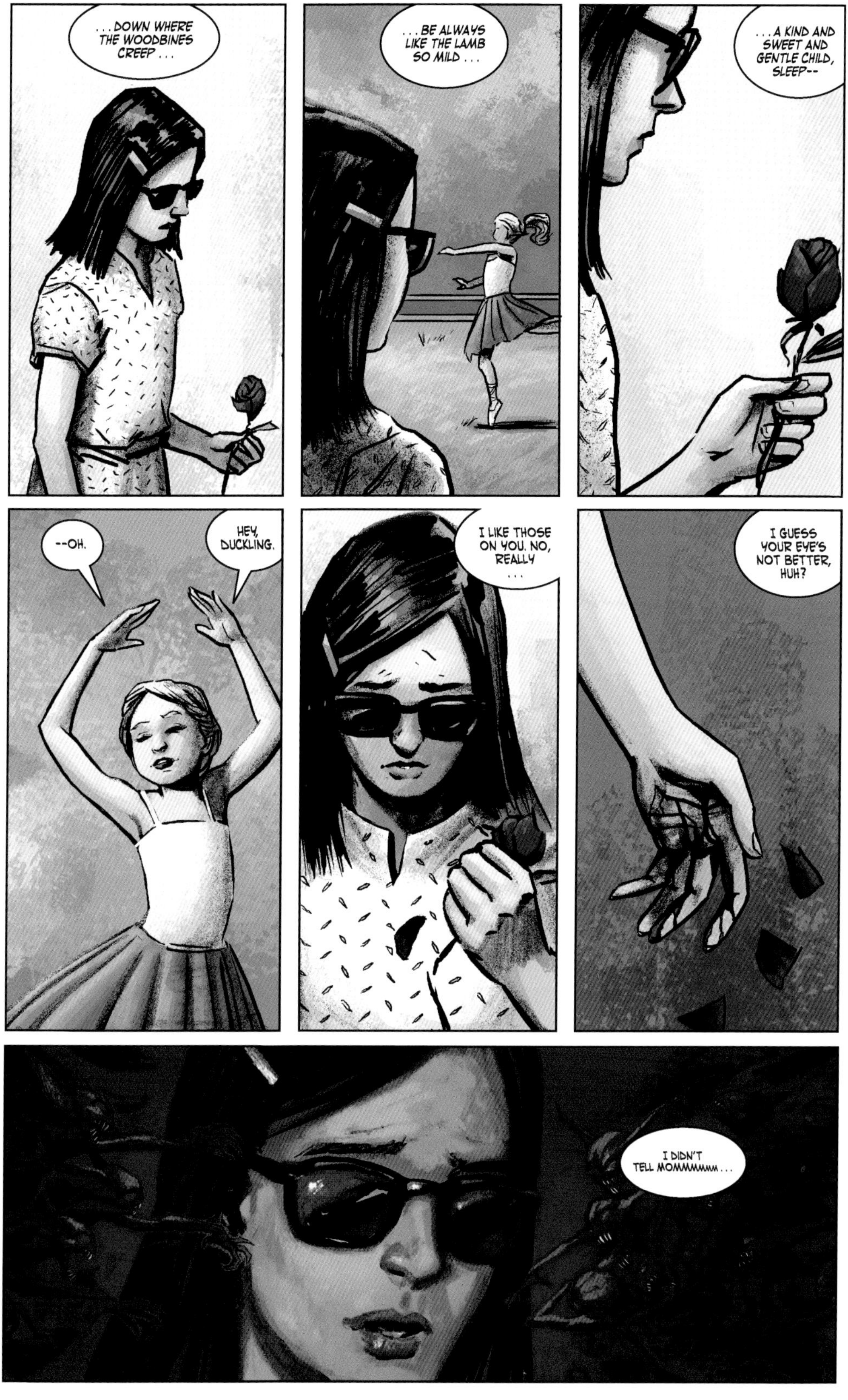
. . . DOWN WHERE THE WOODBINES CREEP . . .
. . . BE ALWAYS LIKE THE LAMB SO MILD . . .
. . . A KIND AND SWEET AND GENTLE CHILD, SLEEP--
--OH.
HEY, DUCKLING.
I LIKE THOSE ON YOU. NO, REALLY . . .
I GUESS YOUR EYE'S NOT BETTER, HUH?
I DIDN'T TELL MOMMMMMM . . .

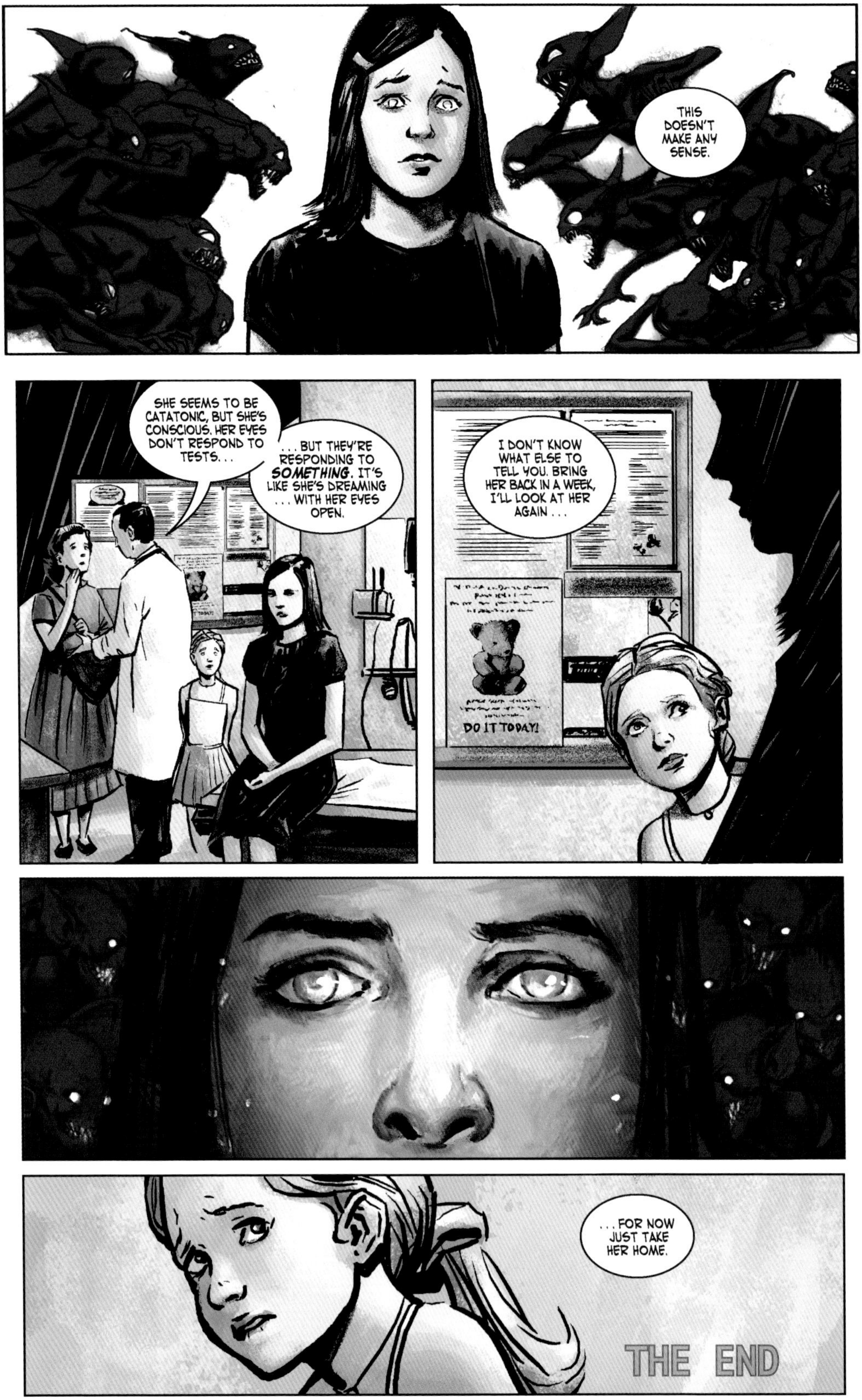
THIS DOESN'T MAKE ANY SENSE.
SHE SEEMS TO BE CATATONIC, BUT SHE'S CONSCIOUS. HER EYES DON'T RESPOND TO TESTS. . .
. . . BUT THEY'RE RESPONDING TO *SOMETHING*. IT'S LIKE SHE'S DREAMING . . . WITH HER EYES OPEN.
I DON'T KNOW WHAT ELSE TO TELL YOU. BRING HER BACK IN A WEEK, I'LL LOOK AT HER AGAIN . . .
DO IT TODAY!
. . . FOR NOW JUST TAKE HER HOME.
THE END

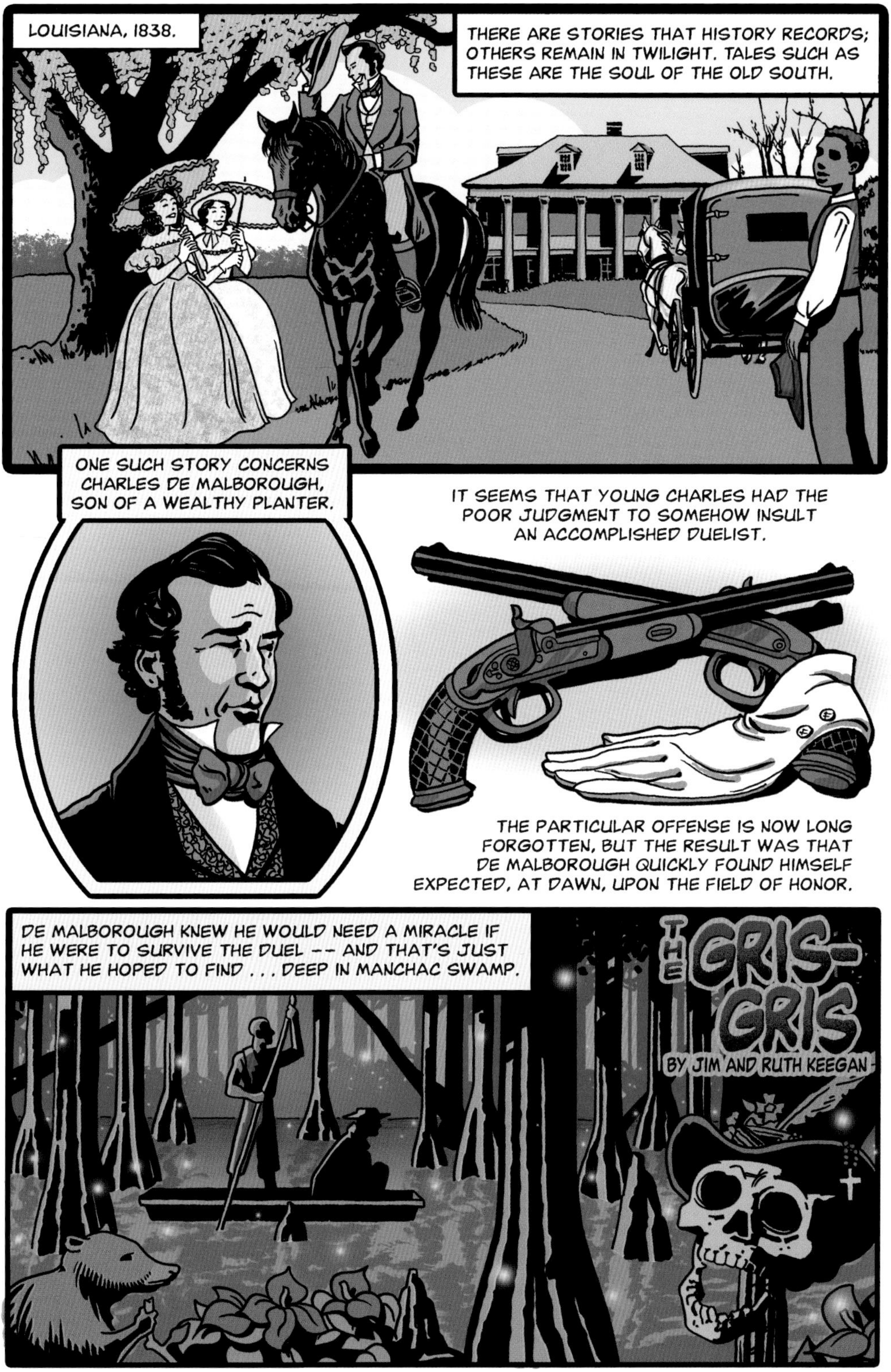

LOUISIANA, 1838.
THERE ARE STORIES THAT HISTORY RECORDS; OTHERS REMAIN IN TWILIGHT. TALES SUCH AS THESE ARE THE SOUL OF THE OLD SOUTH.
ONE SUCH STORY CONCERNS CHARLES DE MALBOROUGH, SON OF A WEALTHY PLANTER.
IT SEEMS THAT YOUNG CHARLES HAD THE POOR JUDGMENT TO SOMEHOW INSULT AN ACCOMPLISHED DUELIST.
THE PARTICULAR OFFENSE IS NOW LONG FORGOTTEN, BUT THE RESULT WAS THAT DE MALBOROUGH QUICKLY FOUND HIMSELF EXPECTED, AT DAWN, UPON THE FIELD OF HONOR.
DE MALBOROUGH KNEW HE WOULD NEED A MIRACLE IF HE WERE TO SURVIVE THE DUEL -- AND THAT'S JUST WHAT HE HOPED TO FIND . . . DEEP IN MANCHAC SWAMP.
THE GRIS-GRIS
BY JIM AND RUTH KEEGAN

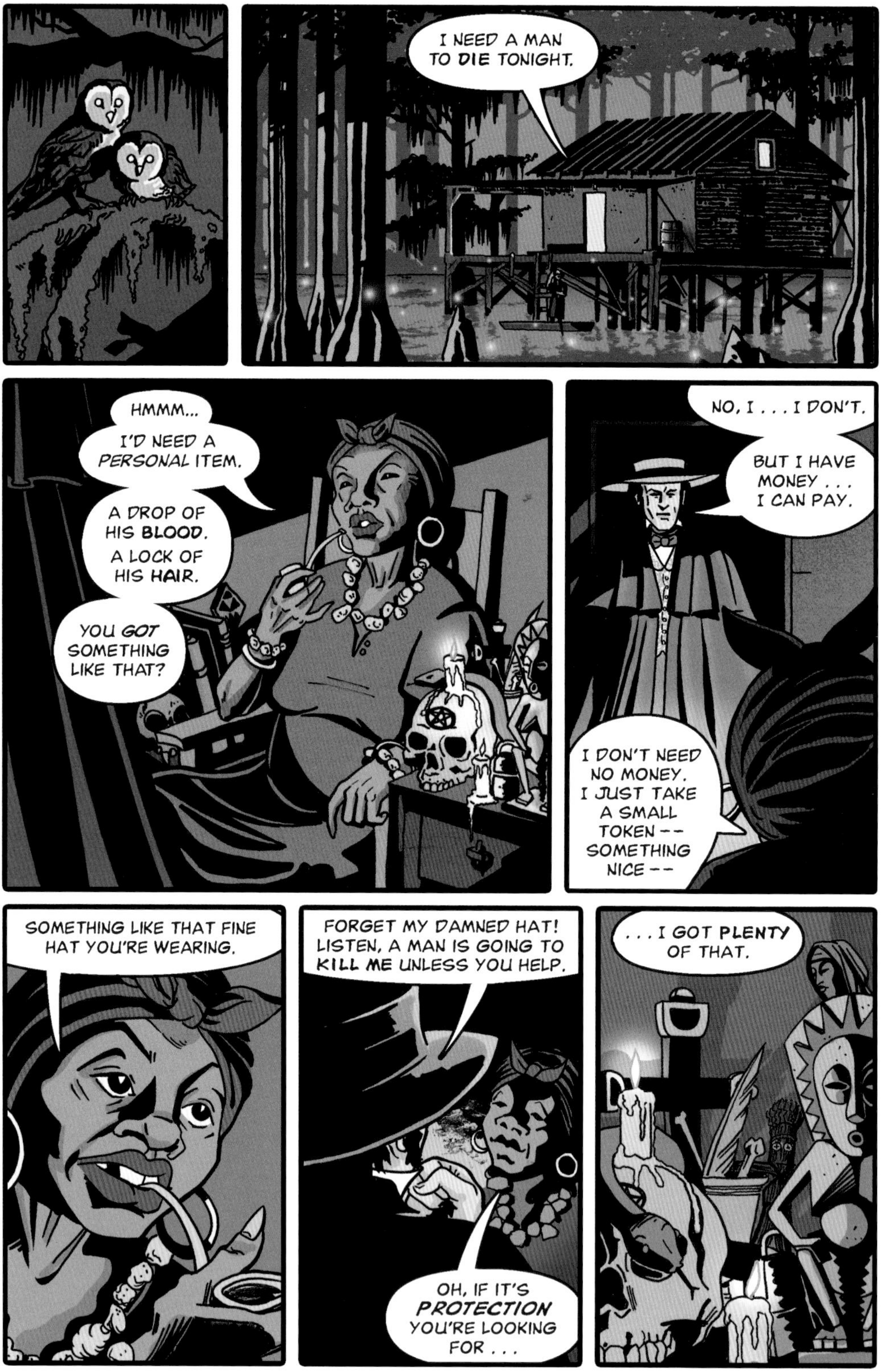
I NEED A MAN TO DIE TONIGHT.
HMMM...
I'D NEED A PERSONAL ITEM.
A DROP OF HIS BLOOD.
A LOCK OF HIS HAIR.
YOU GOT SOMETHING LIKE THAT?
NO, I . . . I DON'T.
BUT I HAVE MONEY . . . I CAN PAY.
I DON'T NEED NO MONEY. I JUST TAKE A SMALL TOKEN -- SOMETHING NICE --
SOMETHING LIKE THAT FINE HAT YOU'RE WEARING.
FORGET MY DAMNED HAT! LISTEN, A MAN IS GOING TO KILL ME UNLESS YOU HELP.
OH, IF IT'S PROTECTION YOU'RE LOOKING FOR . . .
. . . I GOT PLENTY OF THAT.

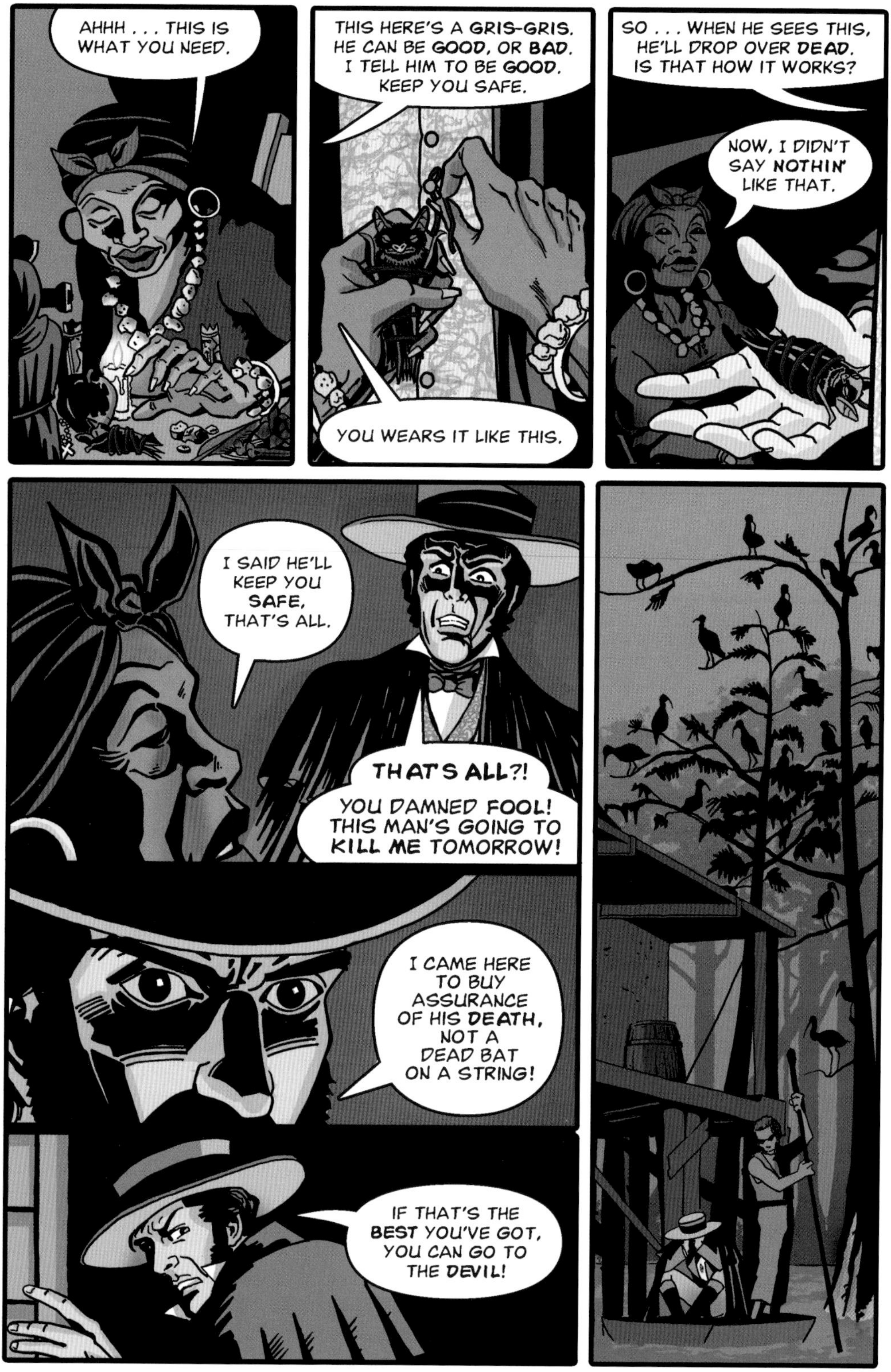
AHHH . . . THIS IS WHAT YOU NEED.
THIS HERE'S A GRIS-GRIS. HE CAN BE GOOD, OR BAD. I TELL HIM TO BE GOOD. KEEP YOU SAFE.
YOU WEARS IT LIKE THIS.
SO . . . WHEN HE SEES THIS, HE'LL DROP OVER DEAD. IS THAT HOW IT WORKS?
NOW, I DIDN'T SAY NOTHIN' LIKE THAT.
I SAID HE'LL KEEP YOU SAFE, THAT'S ALL.
THAT'S ALL?! YOU DAMNED FOOL! THIS MAN'S GOING TO KILL ME TOMORROW!
I CAME HERE TO BUY ASSURANCE OF HIS DEATH, NOT A DEAD BAT ON A STRING!
IF THAT'S THE BEST YOU'VE GOT, YOU CAN GO TO THE DEVIL!

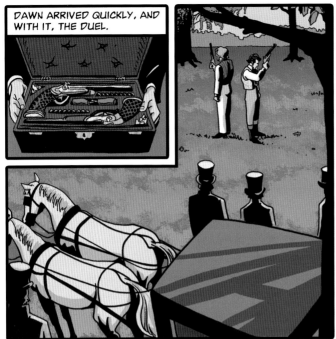

DAWN ARRIVED QUICKLY, AND WITH IT, THE DUEL.

EIGHT . . .

NINE . . .

TEN.

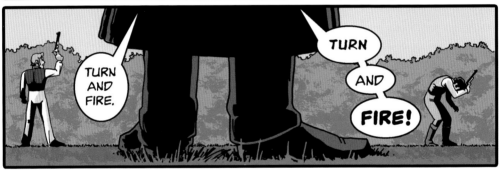

TURN AND FIRE.

TURN AND FIRE!

SIR, YOU *MUST* TURN!

MY GOD, YOU'RE NOT EVEN A *MAN.*

YOU'RE NOT **WORTHY** OF MY BULLET!

BLAM!

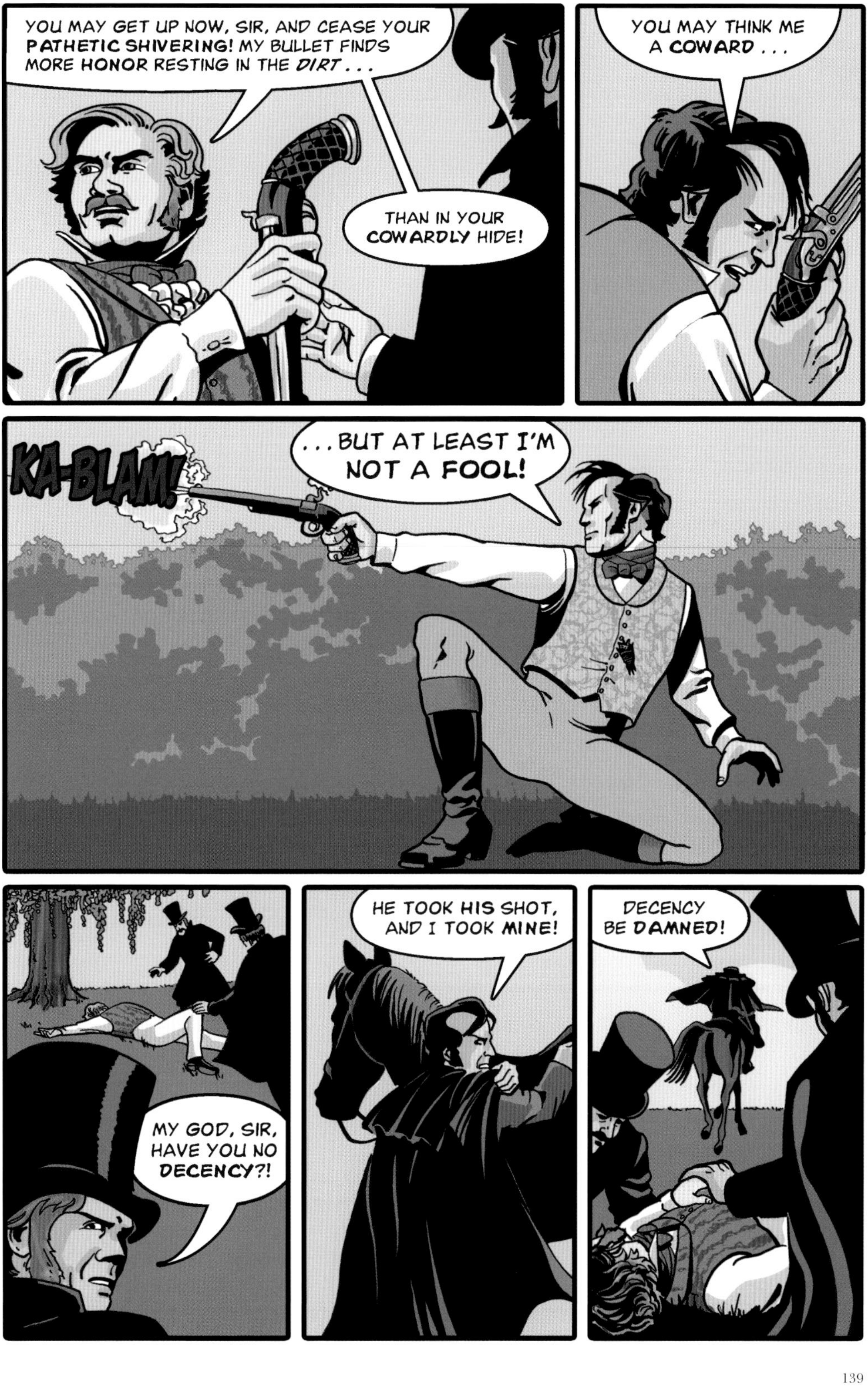
YOU MAY GET UP NOW, SIR, AND CEASE YOUR **PATHETIC SHIVERING!** MY BULLET FINDS MORE **HONOR** RESTING IN THE *DIRT* . . .
THAN IN YOUR **COWARDLY** HIDE!
YOU MAY THINK ME A **COWARD** . . .
KA-BLAM!
. . . BUT AT LEAST I'M **NOT A FOOL!**
MY GOD, SIR, HAVE YOU NO **DECENCY**?!
HE TOOK **HIS** SHOT, AND I TOOK **MINE!**
DECENCY BE **DAMNED!**

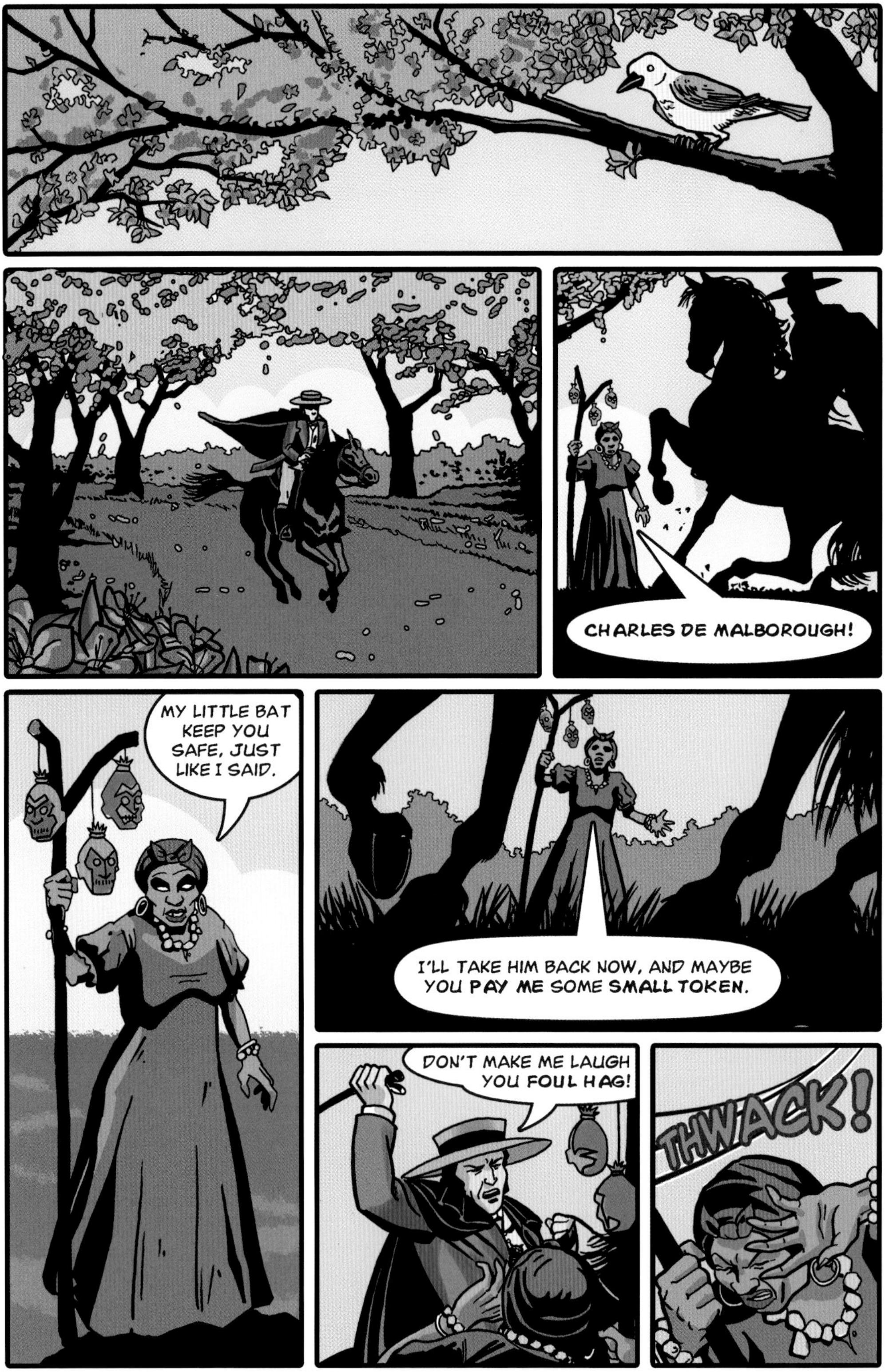

CHARLES DE MALBOROUGH!
MY LITTLE BAT KEEP YOU SAFE, JUST LIKE I SAID.
I'LL TAKE HIM BACK NOW, AND MAYBE YOU PAY ME SOME SMALL TOKEN.
DON'T MAKE ME LAUGH YOU FOUL HAG!
THWACK!

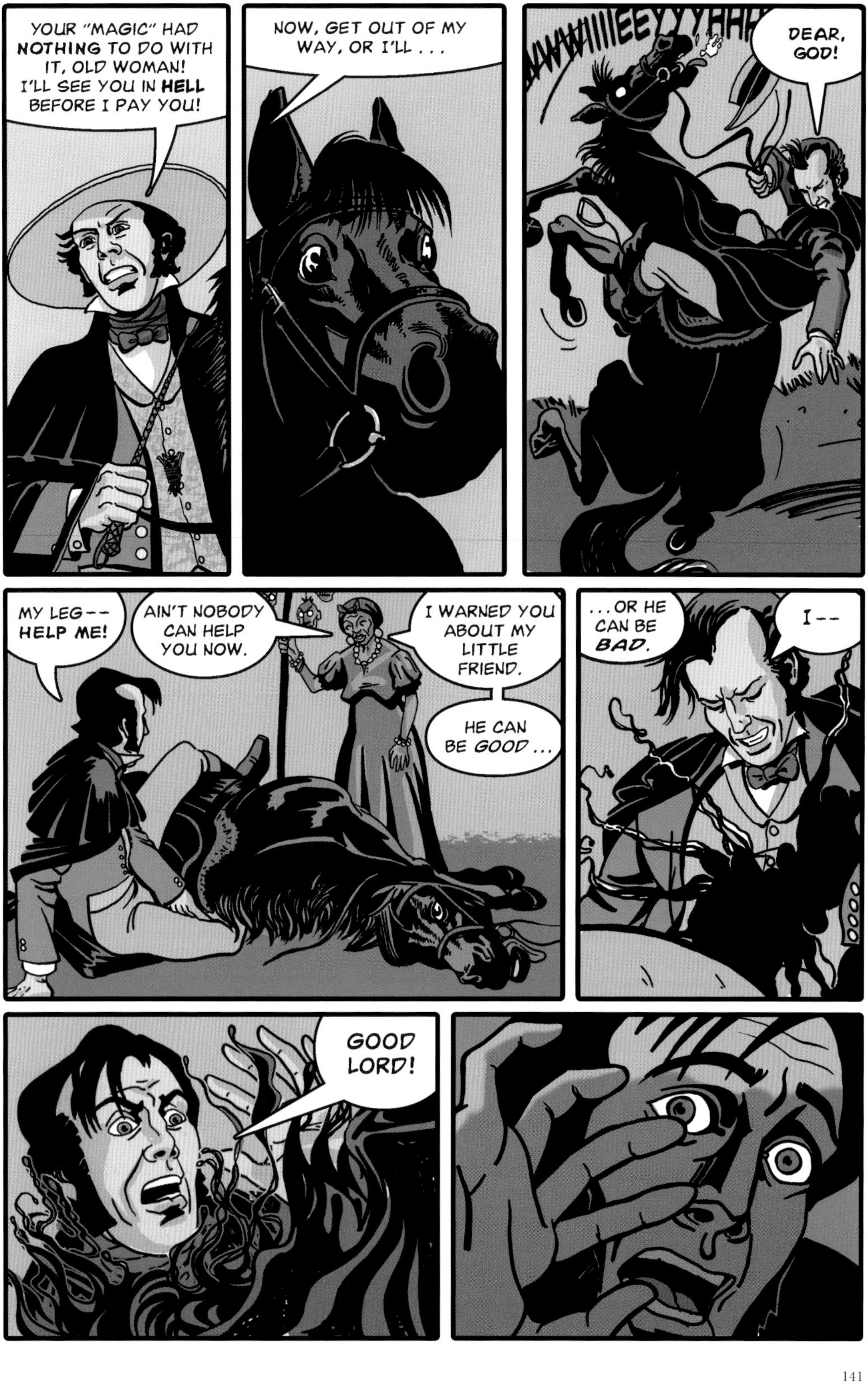
YOUR "MAGIC" HAD NOTHING TO DO WITH IT, OLD WOMAN! I'LL SEE YOU IN HELL BEFORE I PAY YOU!
NOW, GET OUT OF MY WAY, OR I'LL . . .
DEAR, GOD!
MY LEG-- HELP ME!
AIN'T NOBODY CAN HELP YOU NOW.
I WARNED YOU ABOUT MY LITTLE FRIEND.
HE CAN BE GOOD . . .
. . .OR HE CAN BE BAD.
I--
GOOD LORD!

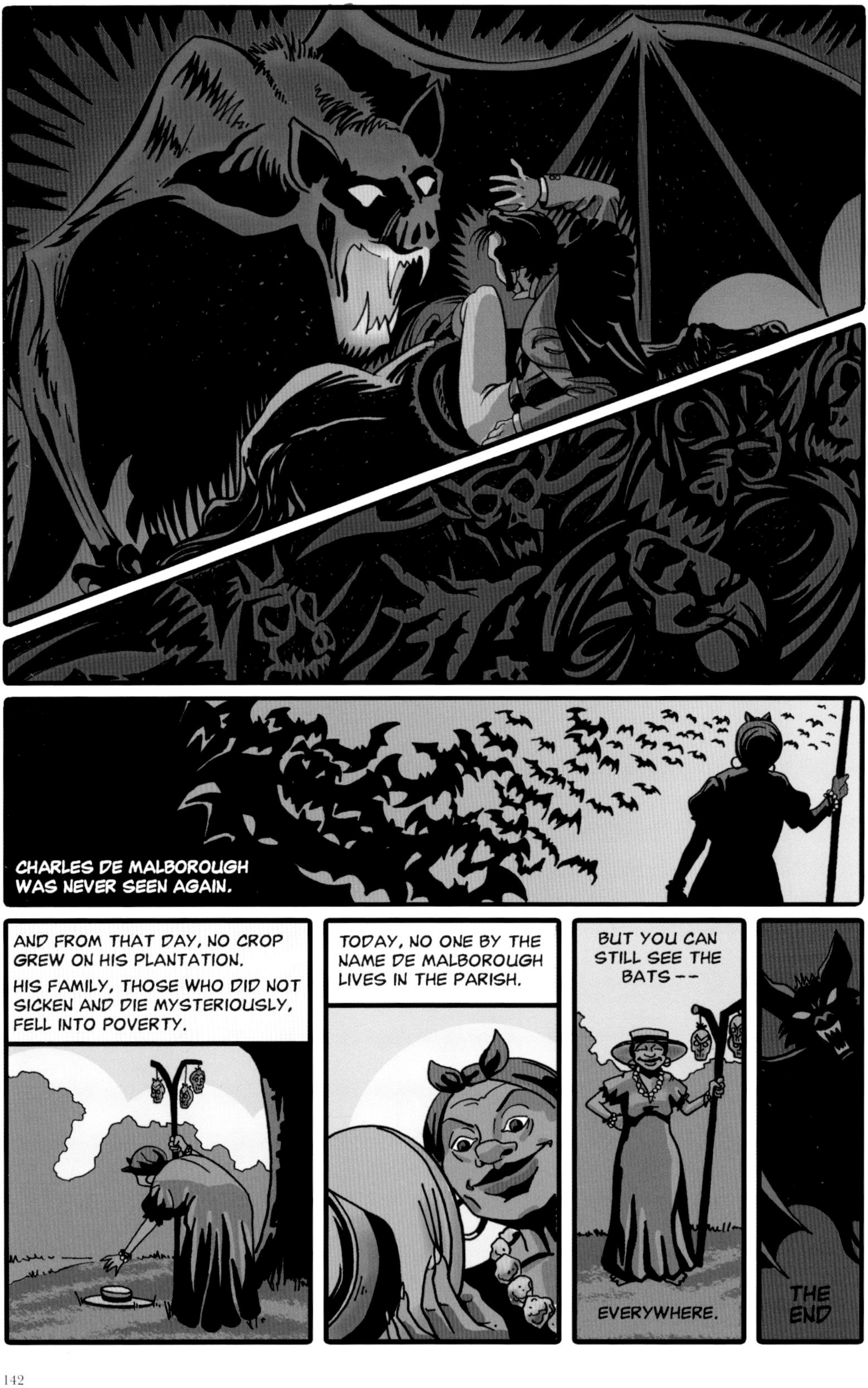
CHARLES DE MALBOROUGH
WAS NEVER SEEN AGAIN.
AND FROM THAT DAY, NO CROP GREW ON HIS PLANTATION.
HIS FAMILY, THOSE WHO DID NOT SICKEN AND DIE MYSTERIOUSLY, FELL INTO POVERTY.
TODAY, NO ONE BY THE NAME DE MALBOROUGH LIVES IN THE PARISH.
BUT YOU CAN STILL SEE THE BATS --
EVERYWHERE.
THE END

Golden Calf Blues

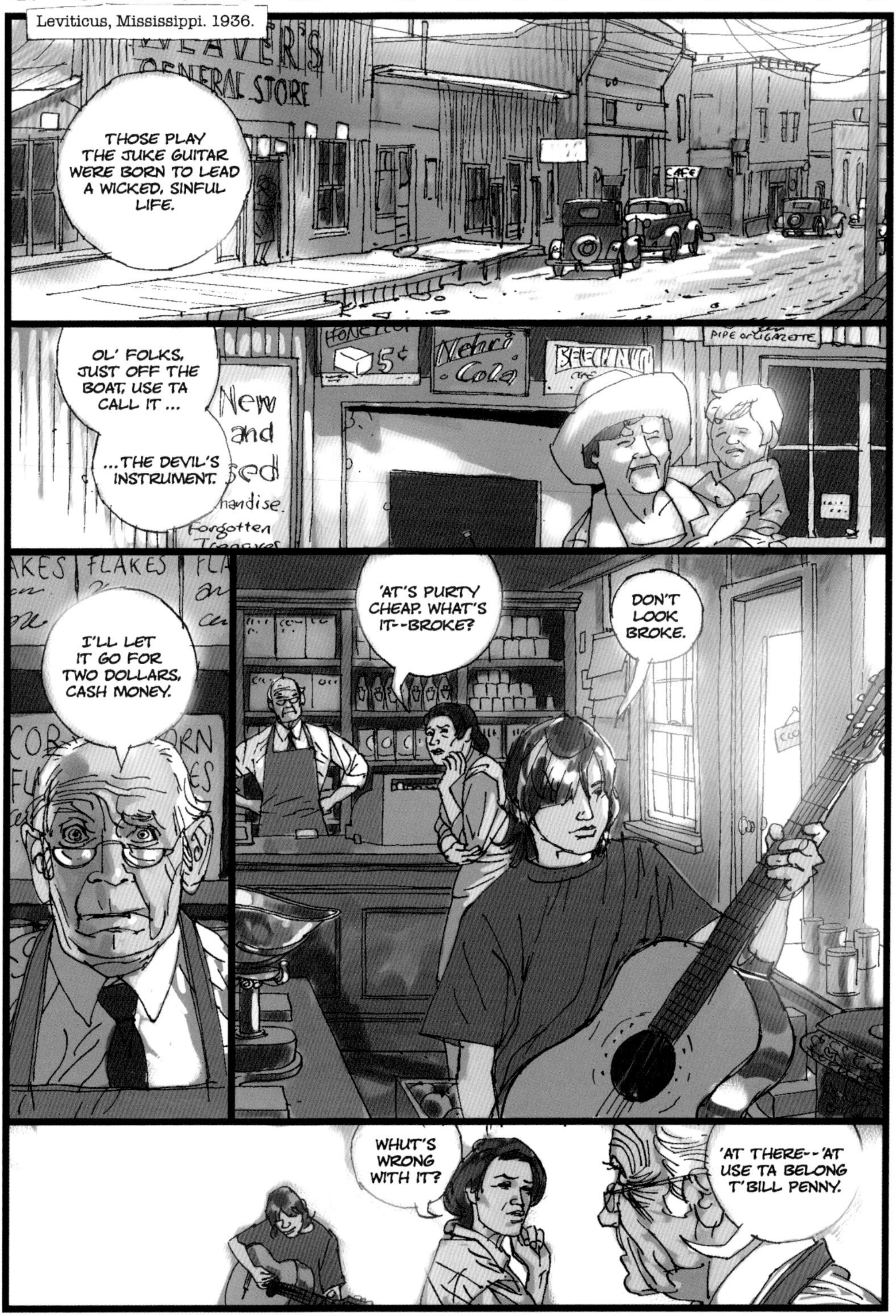

Leviticus, Mississippi. 1936.
GENERAL STORE
THOSE PLAY THE JUKE GUITAR WERE BORN TO LEAD A WICKED, SINFUL LIFE.
CAFE
5¢
Nehi Cola
PIPE or CIGARETTE
OL' FOLKS, JUST OFF THE BOAT, USE TA CALL IT ...
...THE DEVIL'S INSTRUMENT.
FLAKES
I'LL LET IT GO FOR TWO DOLLARS, CASH MONEY.
'AT'S PURTY CHEAP. WHAT'S IT--BROKE?
DON'T LOOK BROKE.
WHUT'S WRONG WITH IT?
'AT THERE--'AT USE TA BELONG T'BILL PENNY.

By Mark Ricketts & Sean Phillips

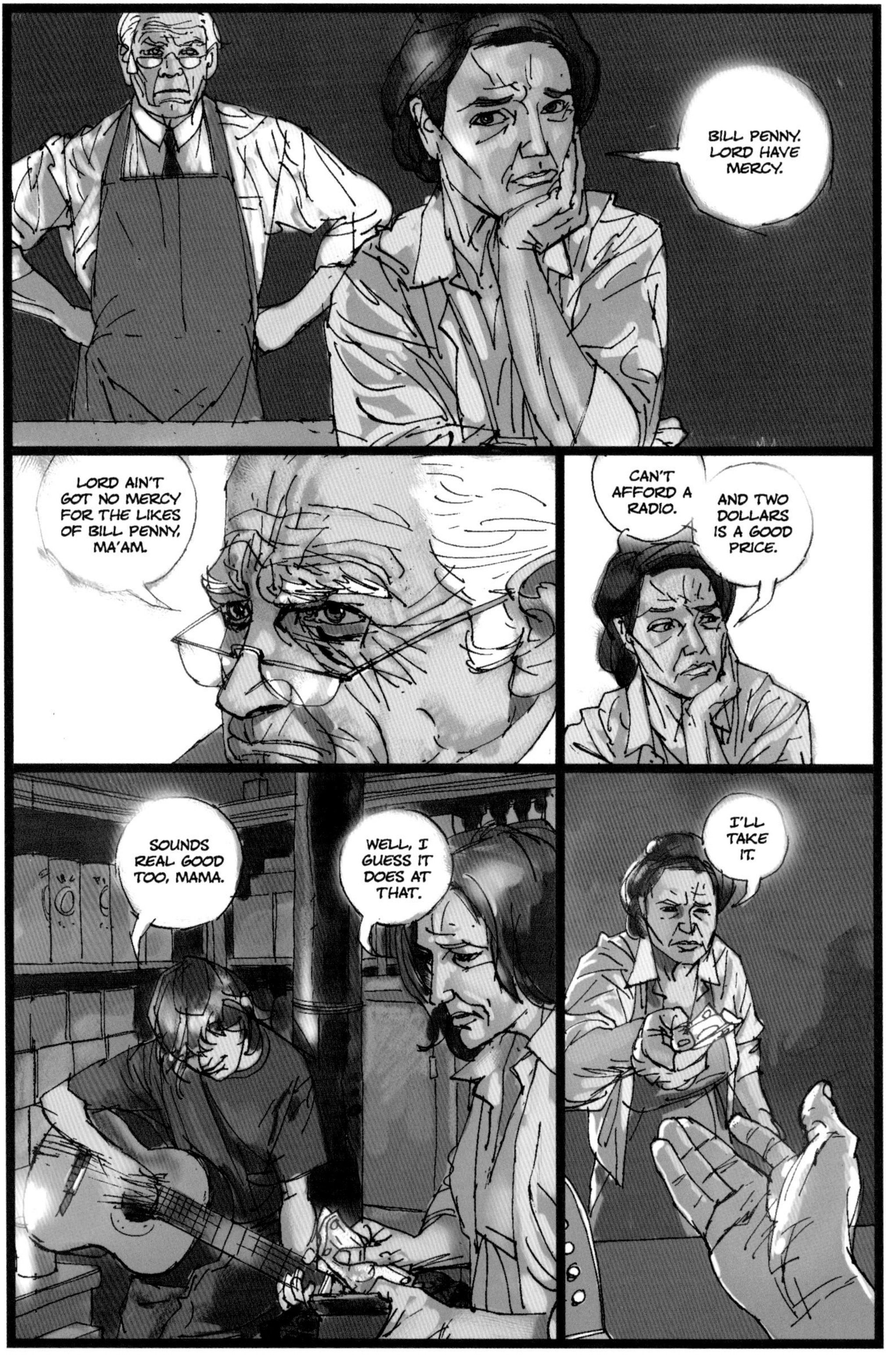
BILL PENNY. LORD HAVE MERCY.
LORD AIN'T GOT NO MERCY FOR THE LIKES OF BILL PENNY, MA'AM.
CAN'T AFFORD A RADIO.
AND TWO DOLLARS IS A GOOD PRICE.
SOUNDS REAL GOOD TOO, MAMA.
WELL, I GUESS IT DOES AT THAT.
I'LL TAKE IT.

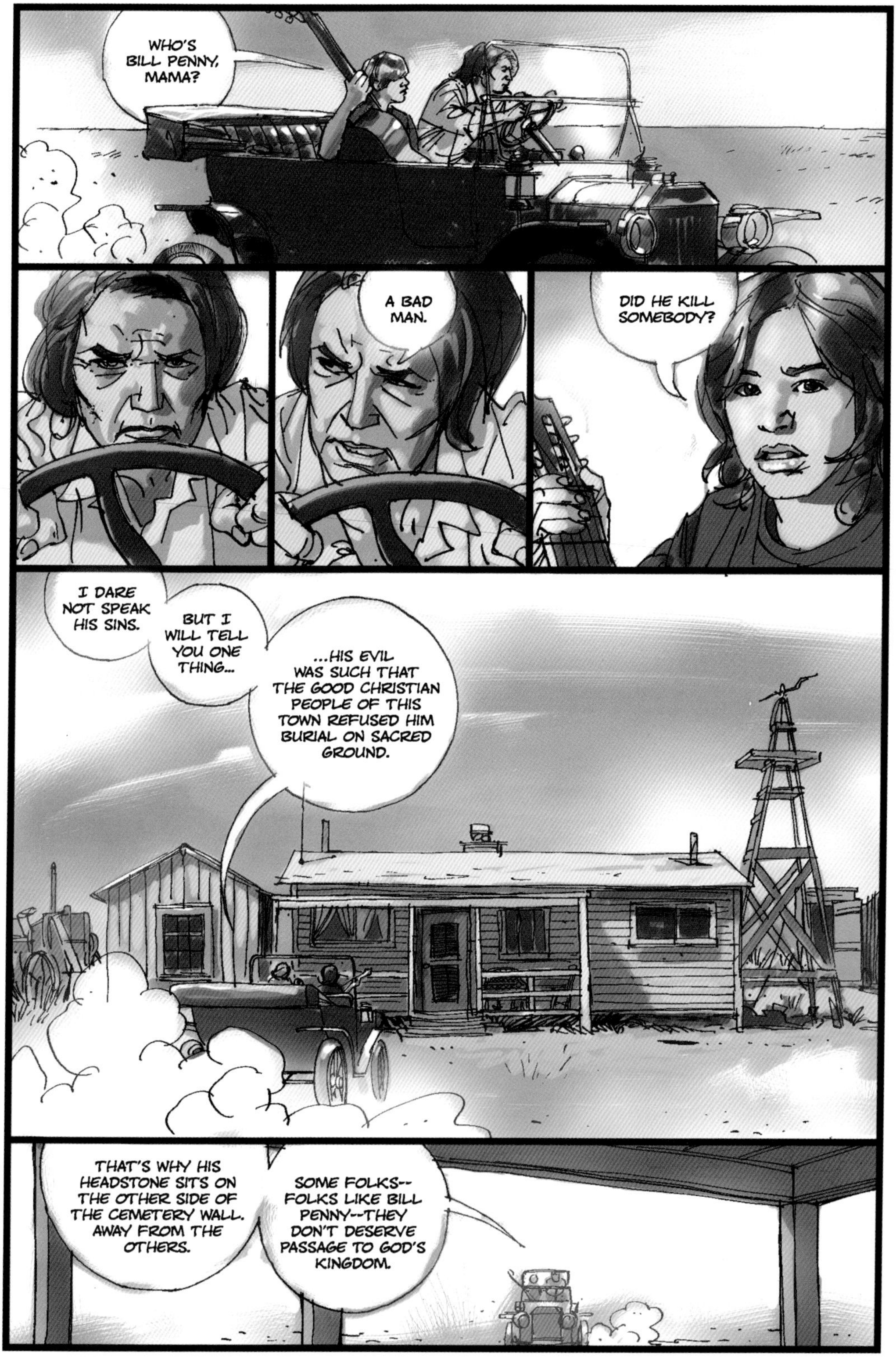
WHO'S BILL PENNY, MAMA?
A BAD MAN.
DID HE KILL SOMEBODY?
I DARE NOT SPEAK HIS SINS.
BUT I WILL TELL YOU ONE THING...
...HIS EVIL WAS SUCH THAT THE GOOD CHRISTIAN PEOPLE OF THIS TOWN REFUSED HIM BURIAL ON SACRED GROUND.
THAT'S WHY HIS HEADSTONE SITS ON THE OTHER SIDE OF THE CEMETERY WALL. AWAY FROM THE OTHERS.
SOME FOLKS--FOLKS LIKE BILL PENNY--THEY DON'T DESERVE PASSAGE TO GOD'S KINGDOM.

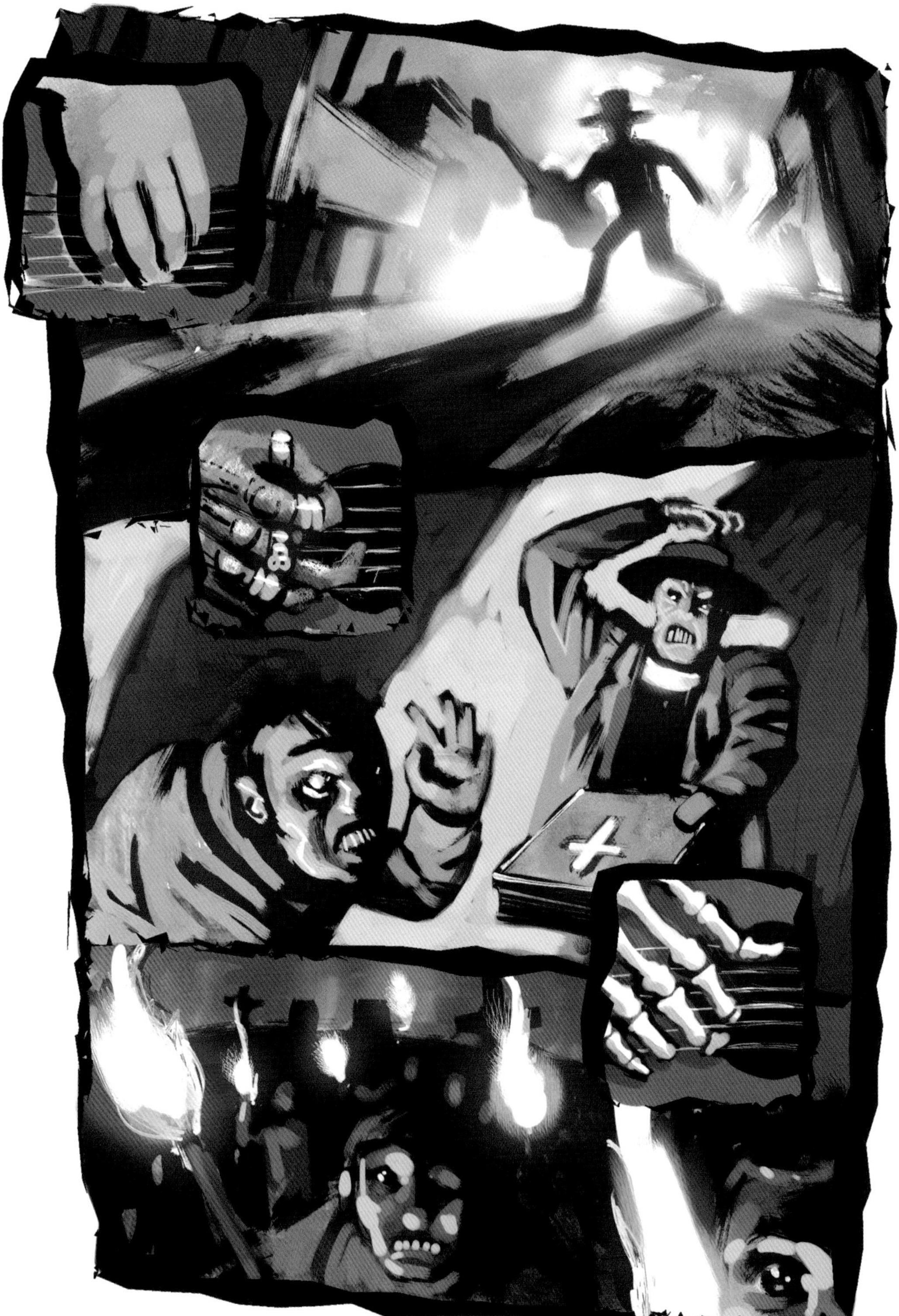

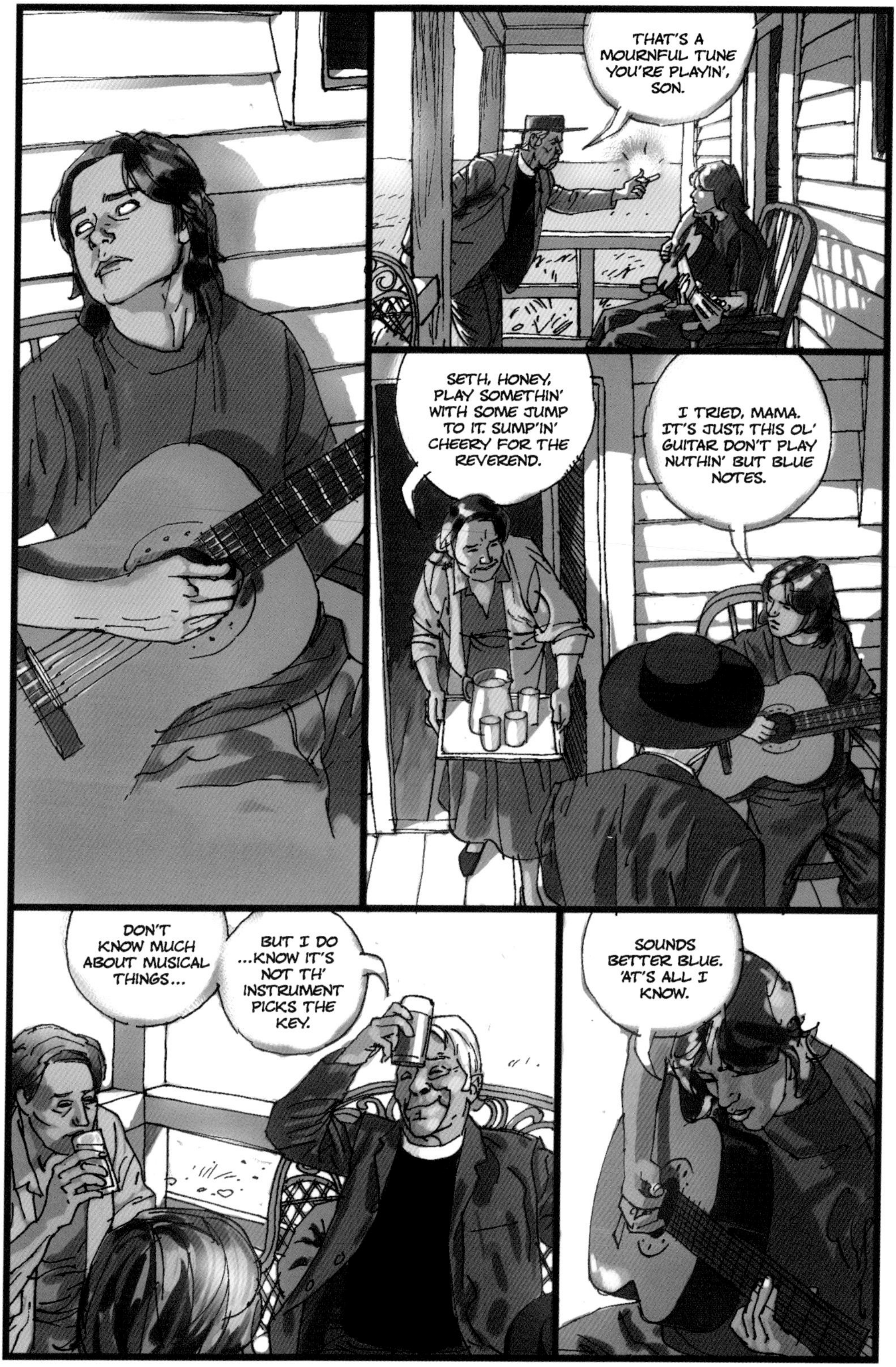
THAT'S A MOURNFUL TUNE YOU'RE PLAYIN', SON.
SETH, HONEY, PLAY SOMETHIN' WITH SOME JUMP TO IT. SUMP'IN' CHEERY FOR THE REVEREND.
I TRIED, MAMA. IT'S JUST, THIS OL' GUITAR DON'T PLAY NUTHIN' BUT BLUE NOTES.
DON'T KNOW MUCH ABOUT MUSICAL THINGS...
BUT I DO ...KNOW IT'S NOT TH' INSTRUMENT PICKS THE KEY.
SOUNDS BETTER BLUE. 'AT'S ALL I KNOW.

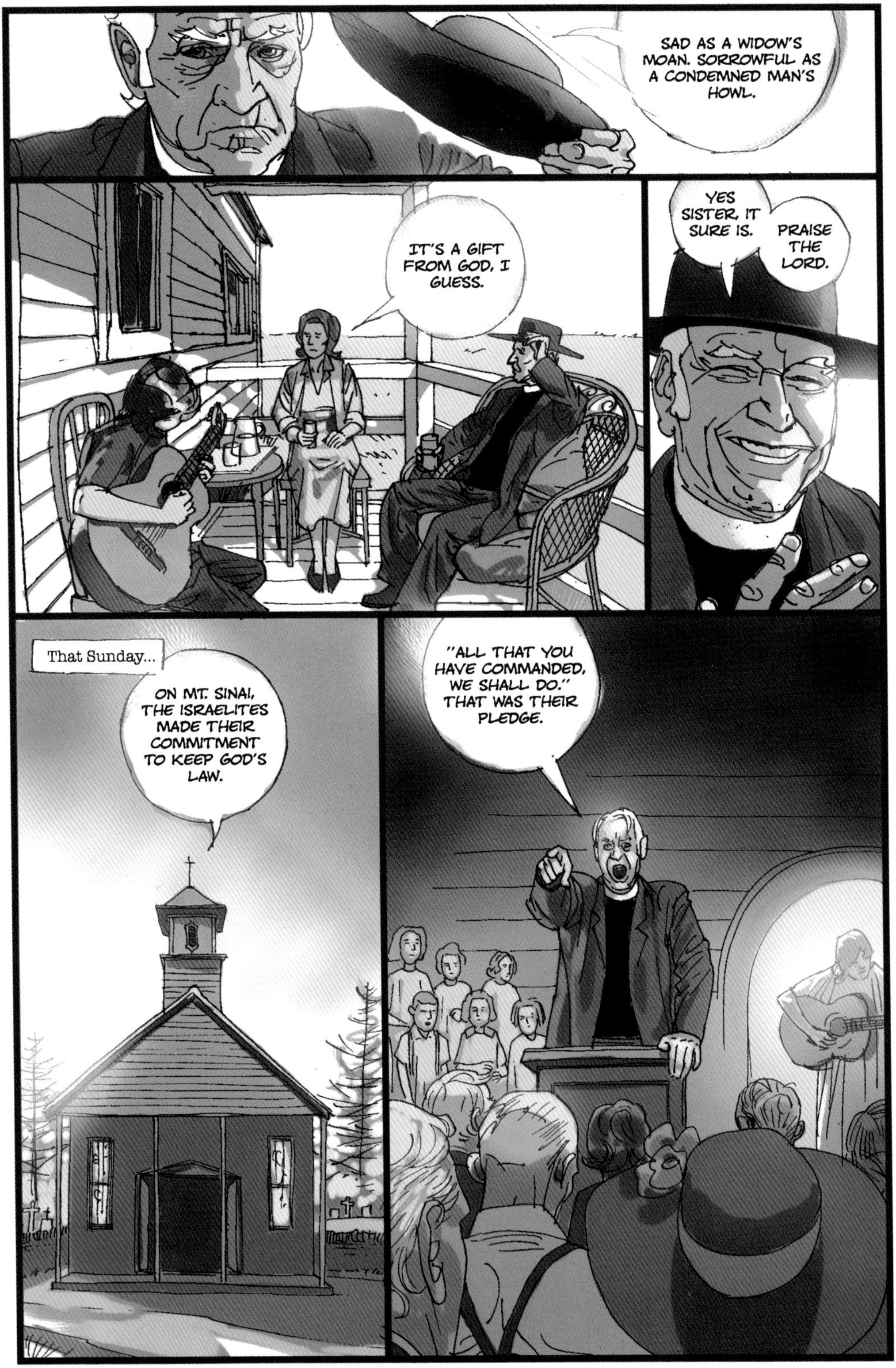
SAD AS A WIDOW'S MOAN. SORROWFUL AS A CONDEMNED MAN'S HOWL.
IT'S A GIFT FROM GOD, I GUESS.
YES SISTER, IT SURE IS.
PRAISE THE LORD.
That Sunday...
ON MT. SINAI, THE ISRAELITES MADE THEIR COMMITMENT TO KEEP GOD'S LAW.
"ALL THAT YOU HAVE COMMANDED, WE SHALL DO." THAT WAS THEIR PLEDGE.

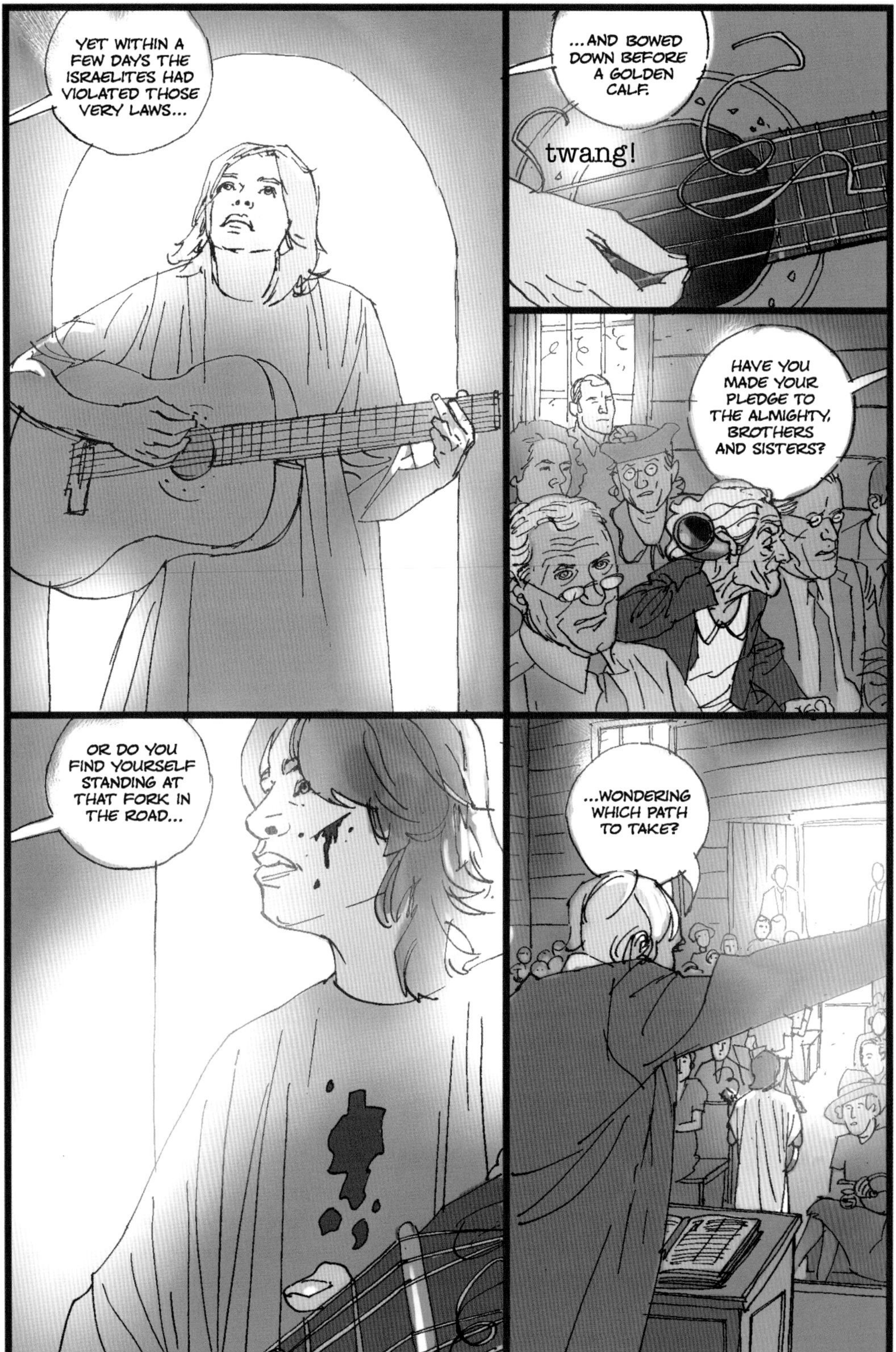
YET WITHIN A FEW DAYS THE ISRAELITES HAD VIOLATED THOSE VERY LAWS...
...AND BOWED DOWN BEFORE A GOLDEN CALF.
twang!
HAVE YOU MADE YOUR PLEDGE TO THE ALMIGHTY, BROTHERS AND SISTERS?
OR DO YOU FIND YOURSELF STANDING AT THAT FORK IN THE ROAD...
...WONDERING WHICH PATH TO TAKE?

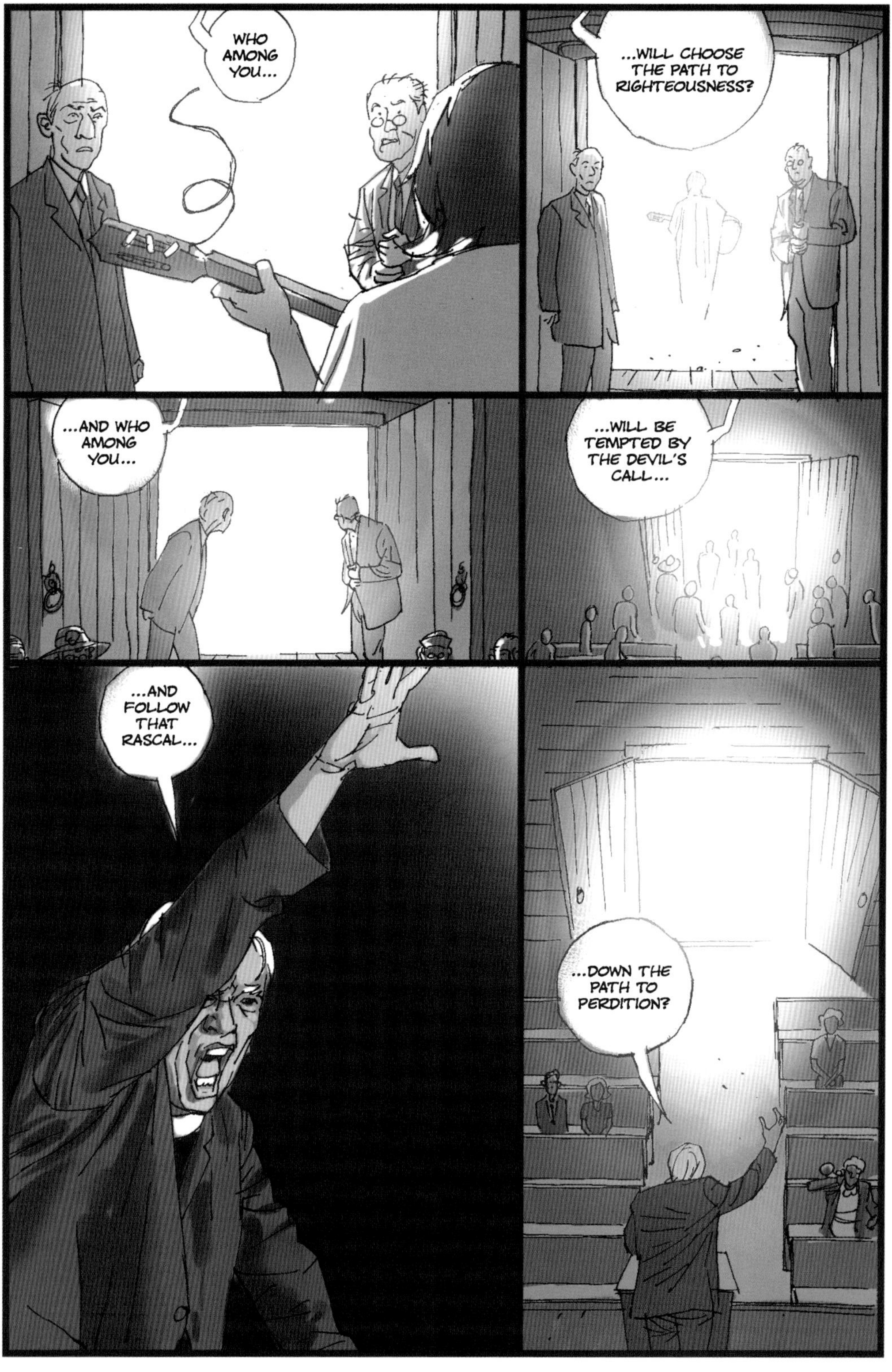
WHO AMONG YOU...
...WILL CHOOSE THE PATH TO RIGHTEOUSNESS?
...AND WHO AMONG YOU...
...WILL BE TEMPTED BY THE DEVIL'S CALL...
...AND FOLLOW THAT RASCAL...
...DOWN THE PATH TO PERDITION?

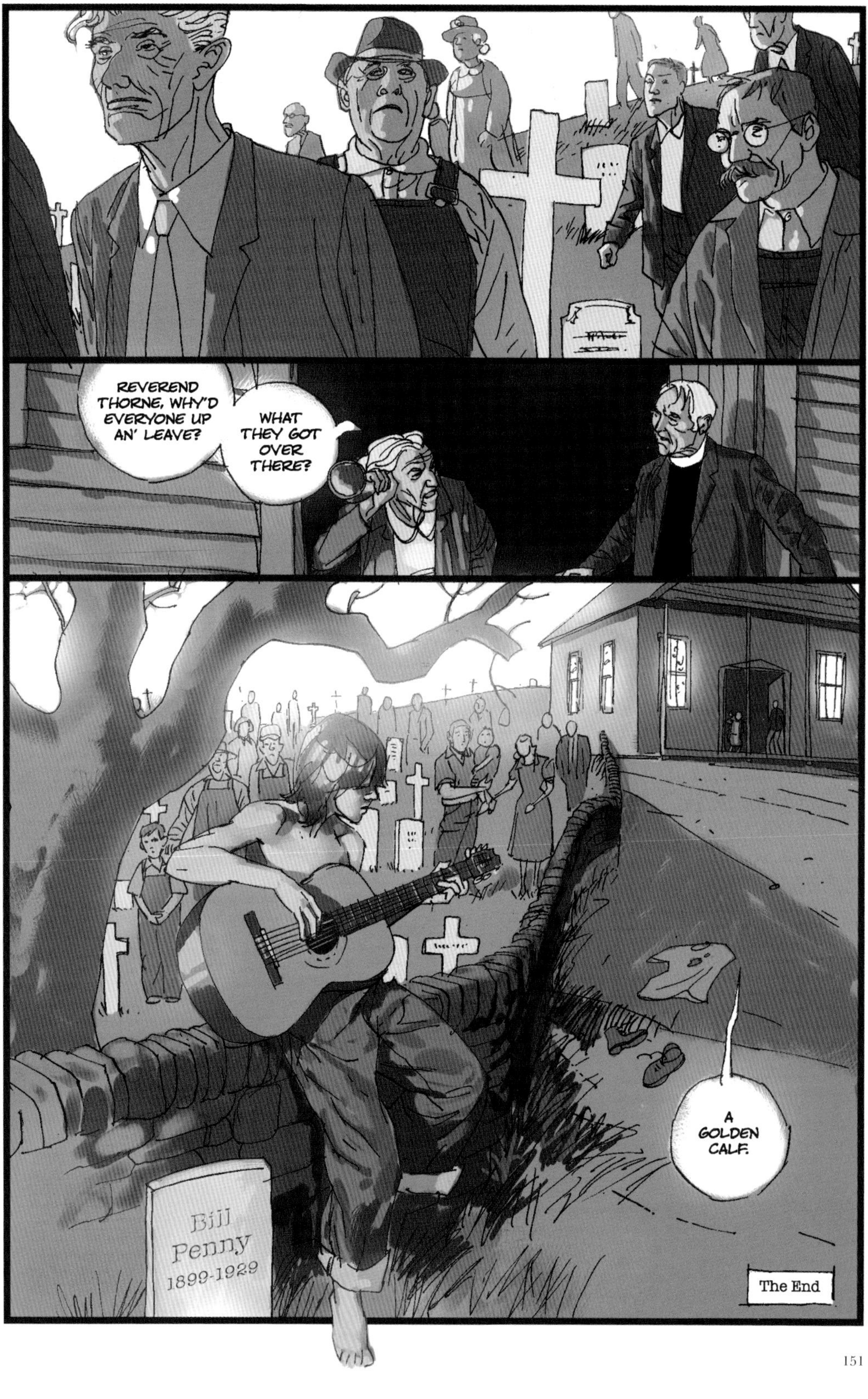
REVEREND THORNE, WHY'D EVERYONE UP AN' LEAVE?
WHAT THEY GOT OVER THERE?
A GOLDEN CALF.
Bill Penny 1899-1929
The End

The Truth about Witchcraft

An interview with High Priestess PHYLLIS CUROTT

by SCOTT ALLIE

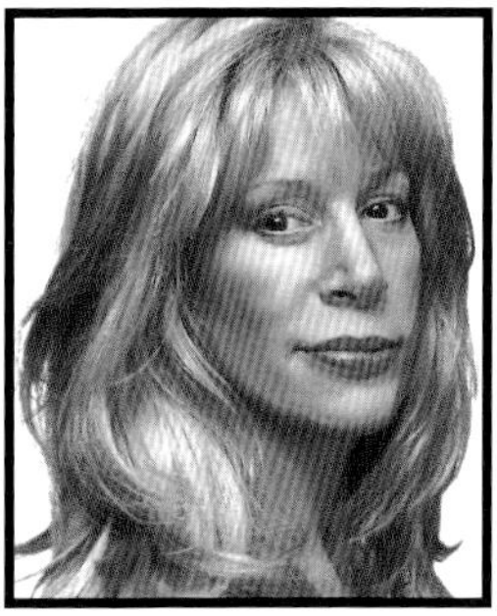

Photo © Bruce Fields

HPs. Phyllis Curott, J.D., was named alongside Hillary Clinton as one of the Ten Gutsiest Women of the Year by Jane Magazine *and described by* New York Magazine *as one of NYC's most intellectually cutting-edge speakers. As an attorney, she has successfully won the right of Wiccan clergy to perform marriages in New York City, and has been a pro bono consultant on numerous religious liberties cases. She was a member of the United Nations' Committee on the Status of Women, and is the Wiccan representative to the Harvard University's Consultation on Religious Discrimination and Accommodation. She serves on the Association for Union Democracy, opposing corruption in trade unions. She began her legal career as the Legal Director for PROD/Teamsters for a Democratic Union, fighting organized crime within the Teamsters union. Ms. Curott studied filmmaking at NYU, producing several independent features, including* New Year's Day, *which competed in the Venice Film Festival, as well as several short films screened at the Cannes and Sundance Film Festivals. She received her B.A. in philosophy from Brown University, and her Juris Doctor from New York University School of Law. She continues to practice law in New York City and is at work on her third book.*

ALLIE: How did a New York lawyer become involved in Witchcraft?

CUROTT: It began with a summoning from a presence I call the daemon. Socrates talked about his daemon; a divine figure that lives within you, like a muse. During my last year in law school, he laid down a trail of breadcrumbs in the form of synchronicities. I think these things happen to almost everyone. The difference was that I was very receptive, because there was an objective component. I'm a rationalist. I needed proof, and the universe kept proving itself. Pan piped and I followed. At the time you couldn't find Witchcraft. It was extremely difficult to pry that door open. And it was flung open for me.

Did being a philosophy student at Brown help open the door?

No, my specialty was ethics and political philosophy. I was very pragmatic. And I wasn't raised in a religious household. When I asked my parents, "What religion are we?" they said, "You are half Viking and half Maccabee, and when you grow up you can look for yourself as to whether God exists." I never intended to do that, but they were looking for me. And it wasn't just God. It was the Goddess, and something beyond gender. The door between the worlds opened. It was hardly where I expected to find myself, but I was sent a sign I couldn't argue with. I'd had a repeating dream of a woman. She was seated and bare breasted, wearing a triangular crown. At her throat she had a star like a little blazing light, and a book in her hand. The star would flare and the dream would go white. Then my daemon led me into a friendship with a woman managing a rock band—and she was a Witch. She was great, so I decided to ignore that particular idiosyncrasy. One day she took me to have my cards read at the Magical Child, an occult bookstore in New York. The reading was astonishing, and I was invited to this coven. I thanked the priestess and left, and had no intention of going back. But my friend said, "It's almost impossible to get into a coven. You shouldn't blow it off." I wasn't sure. But a few days later I went to the Metropolitan Museum of Art, a very powerful, sacred space for me. I wandered into a new section, a garden filled with statuary, and right in front of me was a statue of the woman in my dream. Precisely. The room bleached out. I got lightheaded. I spent the whole afternoon staring at her. She was called The Libyan Sibyl. I went home and pulled out my dictionary and looked up the word *sibyl*. It said, "An ancient prophetess, a Witch." The next week I went back. There were about seventy-five women. Every week I was invited to come back as they whittled down that seventy-five to eight women, who became the Mother Grove of the Minoan tradition. At first it all seemed preposterous to me—real mumbo jumbo, but I wanted that quality of magic that had come to me, so I stayed.

In your second book, Witchcrafting, *you use the words* Wicca *and* Witch *interchangeably. Are you dismissing other magical practices?*

No. Wicca is a specific method of practicing within the broader movement of Witchcraft. Almost twenty years ago, the people who first went public in the United States, like Margot Adler and myself, used the term *Wicca* because that was our background. The word was used synonymously with *Witchcraft* by the media and the early movement, although it blurs distinctions. Mainstream media isn't interested in the distinctions the way we are. Some of us practice Stregheria, or Asatru—there's a long list now. The movement has become more diverse in the various ethnic traditions. I use the term *Wicca* when I deal with mainstream culture because I want people to be able to practice this religion in peace and in freedom. Every time you say *Witchcraft*, the person listening is seeing and hearing through the filter of this toxic stereotype. Using the word *Wicca* makes it easier for mainstream culture to see what this is really about. Even if the practices never make their way into mainstream culture, the core values of this spirituality are critical to the survival of the species and the planet. That's my priority. I don't like labels—they limit engagement rather than expanding it.

You talk about a process of un-naming when dealing with the natural world. Is that the same thing?

One of the things I do is look at the influences on our beliefs and practices. This is the rebirth of an ancient religion, but it's also very modern. We are creating it every time we do something. It is very personal, innovative, and creative. There are influences from ceremonial traditions which unfortunately carry biblical, patriarchal perspectives. The biblical model views God as transcendent, not present in the world. The power's out *there* somewhere. But the core experience in Witchcraft is that the divine is in us and the world and is the source of magic. But a lot of our language and practices are the opposite. One of the best examples is the ceremonial notion that by naming something you have power over it. It's a cognitive principle—if you can identify something, you are empowered. That is also a very profound magical principle. In the Bible, God and man name things; that gives them power over what's named. But when we tell ourselves we control something, we distance ourselves from it. We establish a position of power over what we've named, instead of opening ourselves to learning from it. My work is not about the projection of will, which is the old ceremonial model of magic, but about opening yourself to the divine, letting it transform and teach you. Instead of naming, like, *Oak tree*, you pay attention to it, and describe it without that term: home for birds, maker of oxygen, giver of life. And you begin to recognize connections. That's what a Witch is. Someone who pays attention to the divine. When you un-name, you engage the living divinity of the natural world. Instead of naming and having power *over*, it's un-naming and opening yourself to the power *of*.

Did Gerald Gardner create Wicca?

Without him, contemporary Wicca would not exist. Something would exist, but this movement would not. He was a link in a fascinating chain of influences and made important contributions and brought it to the public eye. For me Wicca is a dynamic spirituality—it's something we are all creating everytime we practice. I think Uncle Gerry would approve.

Gardner worked with Aleister Crowley, and Crowley died in 1947. When did Gardner popularize Wicca?

In the early fifties, when the Witchcraft laws were repealed in England. His books were published in England in the fifties, and he was interviewed on radio and in newspapers. His motivation was to keep the religion from dying out, and he did his job, far better than I think he expected.

He created the initiatory part of Wicca, right?

Well, he borrowed from various sources to create certain rituals. But there were initiations going back to Eleusis. In all indigenous religions there is an initiation, a death and rebirth experience. He borrowed a little here, a little there. Most importantly he evoked the underlying archetypal energies of initiations as a transformative spiritual experience.

You said there was a new level of public activism for Wiccans twenty years ago. What's the difference between that and Gardner going public in the fifties? I thought Wicca became known to mainstream America in the sixties.

Both points were historical breakthroughs that required activists with personal courage. But in the sixties, mainstream America, if they paid any attention, knew Sybil Leek, and my friend Hans Holzer, because they went on television. And they knew Elizabeth Montgomery from *Bewitched*.

What do you think of the stereotype put forward by Bewitched?

Adorable. I love that dress, those heels. Every ten years or so, since the thirties, Hollywood has managed to generate a positive image of the Witch. Dorothy in *The Wizard of Oz* is the epitome of the Witch. She makes the journey and finds she had the power all along. Veronica Lake in *I Married a Witch. Bell, Book, and Candle*, ten years later, Kim Novak. Mischievous, sexy, smart—she went to Vassar. And then Elizabeth Montgomery. She turned the suburban status quo on its ear. That's what Witches do. We are Dionysian. We dance naked around bonfires under the moon. We do think sex is fabulous. We are sexy. So they captured the truth there. Spending the last twenty years trying to banish the negative stereotype in the media, my perspective is that anything that shows the Witch in a positive light is a step forward. The first step is to educate people that Witches don't kill babies, we don't worship Satan. All these images that present Witches as good and attractive help rebut that stereotype. Aside from the green-faced hag, the other big misconception is that Witches have this supernatural power, to cast spells on people. Witches do cast spells, but we don't work with supernatural power. For us, the natural world is full of divine energy. It's natural and it's accessible to us. That's the energy we work with. A spell is like a prayer, except in patriarchal religions, where God is not present in the world, people pray to this father figure to intervene on their behalf. When we cast a spell, we invoke the aid of divinity, and also go into the well of our own innate, divine power, and draw it up, and pour it out into the world. And the most powerful spells are not borrowed from somebody else's book. They are created by you. There are things that have to be learned— practices, techniques, vocabulary, and symbols. It requires devotion and study.

But it's also an innate wisdom, and comes from the heart. So just as you would never pray to harm another person, you would never cast a spell to harm or manipulate another person.

But people do both, I'm sure.

Maybe. I don't run into them practicing Wicca, though. If everything that exists is a manifestation of divine energy, it is logically and spiritually impossible to use that energy to harm. You can use your ego, your misguided self-destructiveness. But those things are the result of not working in harmony with the divine. And it usually backfires. Magic is the way we co-create reality with the sacred. It is not about controlling or manipulating. Shamanism is about ecstasy, the bliss that comes from being connected to the sacred. You can get that by breathing, walking in the country, or making love. Once the veil comes off, your life becomes very magical. In *The Love Spell*—

The book you're writing now?

Right. Love spells can be the trickiest magic there is. Things that we are not aware of influence who we find attractive at a certain point and why. But whether it lasts forever, or you grow apart, it's okay—it's part of the journey to real love. When you make a love spell you're setting the forces in motion so love can manifest. A lot of magic is that capacity to know what the right thing is. We have a preoccupation with manipulation in magical traditions. In most indigenous cultures, ninety percent of what they do is to say, "Thank you. This is good. If you could help us with a little rain, that would be great." It's a posture of asking as opposed to demanding. Prayer is the opening of the heart, an act of optimism that renders a kind of peacefulness, an immediate benefit. That's one reason I love divination. It's a way of engaging in a dialogue with the sacred. Where else can you get that? The mind has phenomenal powers to affect reality—the integrated self working in harmony with the laws of nature, of physics. Quantum laws. We are not defying the laws of nature, but working with them.

In doing so, the religion acknowledges a whole pantheon of Gods and Goddesses. To what level do you interact with them?

To some extent it's a matter of choice, and of their decision to tap you on the shoulder. People ask, "Are the gods psychological forces that dwell within, or do they exist in the outside world?" And my answer is, "Yes."

As a Wiccan, do you tap into Celtic and British tradition?

There are people that do, but I don't focus there. For whatever reason I'm drawn to Italy. If it works, work it. I advocate working with spirits of place, because if the divine is in the world, it is going to express itself very specifically. I don't think it was an accident that the beginning of my Wiccan training corresponded with the beginning of my core shamanic training.

What's "core shamanic"?

The techniques that Michael Harner refined from his work with the Jivarro and other indigenous people. Core practices found in indigenous cultures all over the world, including our ancestors, whether they were Celtic, Greek, African, Native American, or Chinese. These practices alter consciousness, get you out of beta brain waves, which is what we are in right now. The analytical, survival consciousness. There are practices that indigenous cultures and mystical traditions share, to alter the consciousness from beta into alpha, theta, delta—deeper, longer brain waves. In those modes, one is able to apprehend the "magical" nature of reality, and work with those connections. Wherever you find shamanic cultures there is the creation of sacred space, working in a circle, addressing the four directions, invocation, use of prayer, and ecstatic techniques—dancing, fasting, chanting, sleep deprivation, journeying—my favorite is steady percussive rhythm. The priestesses in Egypt used sistrums—rattles. In Greece they used drums. Celtic, Inuit, Japanese, Korean, Siberian, African, and Native American shamans all use drums. It shifts you into an altered state, into non-ordinary reality, where we experience magic and communion with the divine.

In the book you make a pretty definitive statement about not using drugs, but there are traditions that incorporate hallucinogens.

I don't have a moral objection. It's an ancient and appropriate form of shifting consciousness and engaging in Dionysian ecstasy. My problem is the legality. I'm an activist. It was important to me to get these values into the dominant culture, and using drugs might make me vulnerable to arrest. And it's not necessary. There are lots of other techniques to alter consciousness.

How long after you got into that first coven did you start your own?

I trained with my first coven for three years, and about a year later I started my own. There were so few covens that I was pressed into it by people who wanted to study.

Is your original coven around today?

Yes, but with new people. I have relationships with people from way back, but now I'm also working on teaching in new ways with groups all over the world.

You call it the Ara coven. Where does the name come from?

I visited the temple at Paestum in Italy, which is in really marvelous condition compared to other ancient sites. While I was there, I asked for guidance. I was told to "build my temples." I was like, "I live in New York City! Do you have any concept of the cost?" I was stymied, but the seed had been planted. I was tilling the soil and trying to figure out how to make it grow. Part of magic is perceiving the patterns as they manifest in your life. And if you pay attention, that pattern will tell you your purpose, and how to make magic. That's magic, and most people don't realize it. I tell people, "You want to discover a living universe, you want to make magic? Pay attention to synchronicity, to dreams, and find a method of divination that works. And you are making magic right away. The whole world is going to shift."

So where does the name Ara come from?

I came back from Italy and started paying attention. I came across this ancient shamanic idea that each of us is the place where heaven and earth combine, where the world and the sacred are unified. Each of us is an altar within the temple of our lives. Then I had my astrological chart done, and was told that at the moment I was born, on the horizon was the constellation of Ara within the Zodiacal sign of Scorpio. *Ara* means the *altar*. I was born on the altar. That cinched it. I realized the way to build the temples was by teaching people how to practice so they could become the altars within the temples of their lives.

The way you talk about Italy I assumed you'd taken the name from Aradia.

That was another part of it. I'd been drawn to the story of Aradia. She seems to be a real person who was then mythologized. I expect she was a practitioner of the old religion and a sort of female Robin Hood. She was born around 1313. The 1300s was a period of tremendous volatility in the politics and religion of Europe, and very much so in Italy. The church was beginning to consolidate power. The pressure was on the old religion. Aradia was supposedly raised in Voltaria, outside Florence. She was holding a meeting in Nemi in the Alban hills outside of Rome when there was an attack by the Church's troops. She escaped and disappeared. One story is that in that meeting Aradia's teachings were inscribed on scrolls. They spread these teachings about the divinity of nature and the sacredness of sexuality, and working with the power of the earth. The story goes that the scrolls were seized. There were nine of them, and they were sent to the Pope. But we can't get into the Vatican library, so it's a mystery. Would she have written things down? I doubt it. The shamanic message was always an oral tradition, certainly since the burning of the library in Alexandria.

Charles Leland did a lot of the research into the history of Italian magic, right?

He was an anthropologist before that existed as an academic study. He was American, lived in England, lived in Italy. There's controversy about the material he retrieved. There's a lot of Christian overlay—but that's how it would've evolved. You see that in Santeria, you see it in Voudou. A blending goes on. It makes sense that that would happen. To me, Italy is the lap of the Goddess. There's a powerful move to practice shamanic Wicca over there. I have a hundred people every time I do in these workshops. Whenever I go, I ask them, "Tell me the stories. Tell me what your grandma knew."

Wiccans in current fiction are usually portrayed as following an ancient and unbroken tradition, but you don't claim that. In general, do modern Wiccans believe that?

Oh, some do. But I don't need to be able to point to a continuous initiatory tradition to legitimize what we do. It's the fastest-growing spirituality, not just in the U.S., but in Britain, Canada, and Australia, and the rest of Europe. And it wouldn't be if it didn't bring people into a very intimate and powerful connection to the magic of the divine.

You said the stereotype of the wart-covered hag arose six hundred years ago, during the Inquisition against the Jews. But the crone is a part of every tradition. Different portrayals of Hecate have her as a crone.

Yeah, in contemporary cosmologies. In fact, if you go back far enough, she is depicted as a maiden figure. I was stunned when I explored early Greek mythology. She was not identified with the crone. She has come to be, and I have a theory as to why. The story was that Apollo came to Hecate's priestess, one of the twelve Sibyls, in Cumae on the bay of Naples in Italy, and said, "I will grant you one wish." She scooped up a handful of sand and said, "I want to live as long as there are grains of sand in my hand," but she didn't ask to remain youthful. So she got old. The Sibyl at Cumae was probably a very ancient site. The function of the priestess at Hecate's temple was to take the pilgrim into the underworld and across the River Styx to meet with a deceased relative. She is a very shamanic Goddess—the only one in the Greek pantheon who can move from the underworld to the mortal realm, to the upper, Olympian world. She is actually a surviving Titan, from the previous generation of divinity. In that sense, she is very old. I think over time she came to be depicted as a crone because of that combination of the myth of aging and the actual age of the site going back to Magna Graecia [Great Greece]. The crone is part of the cosmology of the Goddess—the maiden, the mother, and the crone—three phases of womanhood, three phases of the moon. They don't have green faces, and they don't have warts. They don't ride broomsticks in the middle of the night, and they don't eat babies. That stereotype—the way you've got them portrayed on the cover of the book—comes out of the Witch craze. It precisely matches the propaganda against the Jews in the Inquisition. It was an extension of those persecutions. The Witch craze began as the Inquisition was ending. The Inquisition had been very successful and the Church didn't want to give up the wealth and power it provided.

What do you think happened in Salem?

Salem was a Pilgrim community, and the persecutions of Witches in Europe were still going on in the 1600s, so it was part of the climate. When you go back and look at the politics and economics, it was much more driven by greed. If you look at the history of the persecutions of the old religion, some of the earliest persecutions were in the 1300s in Italy, and there is no mention of Satan whatsoever, only the mention of the worship of the Goddess Diana.

There were Roman Witch hunts going back to the fourth century.

There were persecutions going back to 3000 B.C. I'm talking about the origins of this stereotype. If you look at the early persecutions, it's only in the late 1400s that the Church links the old religion to Satan. That was not their position initially, because there's no Satan in the old religion, and they knew it. He belongs to the Bible. He's their personification of their own shadow. They need to deal with it instead of projecting it onto other people and then murdering them.

If you go far enough back it's hard to distinguish folklore from fiction. These ideas survived through writers who kept it alive and on the printed page.

In both books I pointed out the continuous subterranean current in western culture, composed of these practices rooted in divine magic. They have different cultural manifestations, but that current is there. You find the romantic poets, the transcendentalists, Goethe, Coleridge, and Wordsworth. Walt Whitman. The progressives of their era. There is always a certain energy, a life force that runs through history and culture.

A life force that wills for change?

The sacred energy. The divine seeking expression in the world, to open our consciousness, so we can realize that we're gods wearing the masks of humans. Scary thoughts to fundamentalists. Scary thoughts to most of us. It's an overwhelming responsibility, but that's the deal. You are a little piece of it. If you don't embrace that, you're cheating yourself of so much fun.

One of America's first public Wiccan Priestesses, Phyllis Currott is an attorney and an outspoken advocate of religious minorities. Phyllis was the first Wiccan Trustee of the Council for the Parliament of the World's Religions, the oldest and largest international interfaith organization. Phyllis is the best selling author of Book of Shadows *(Broadway Books) and* The Love Spell *(Gotham/Penguin). She has been profiled in the* New York Times, L.A. Times, Washington Post, The Nation, Marie Claire, Harper's Bazaar, CNN & Company, *and many others.*

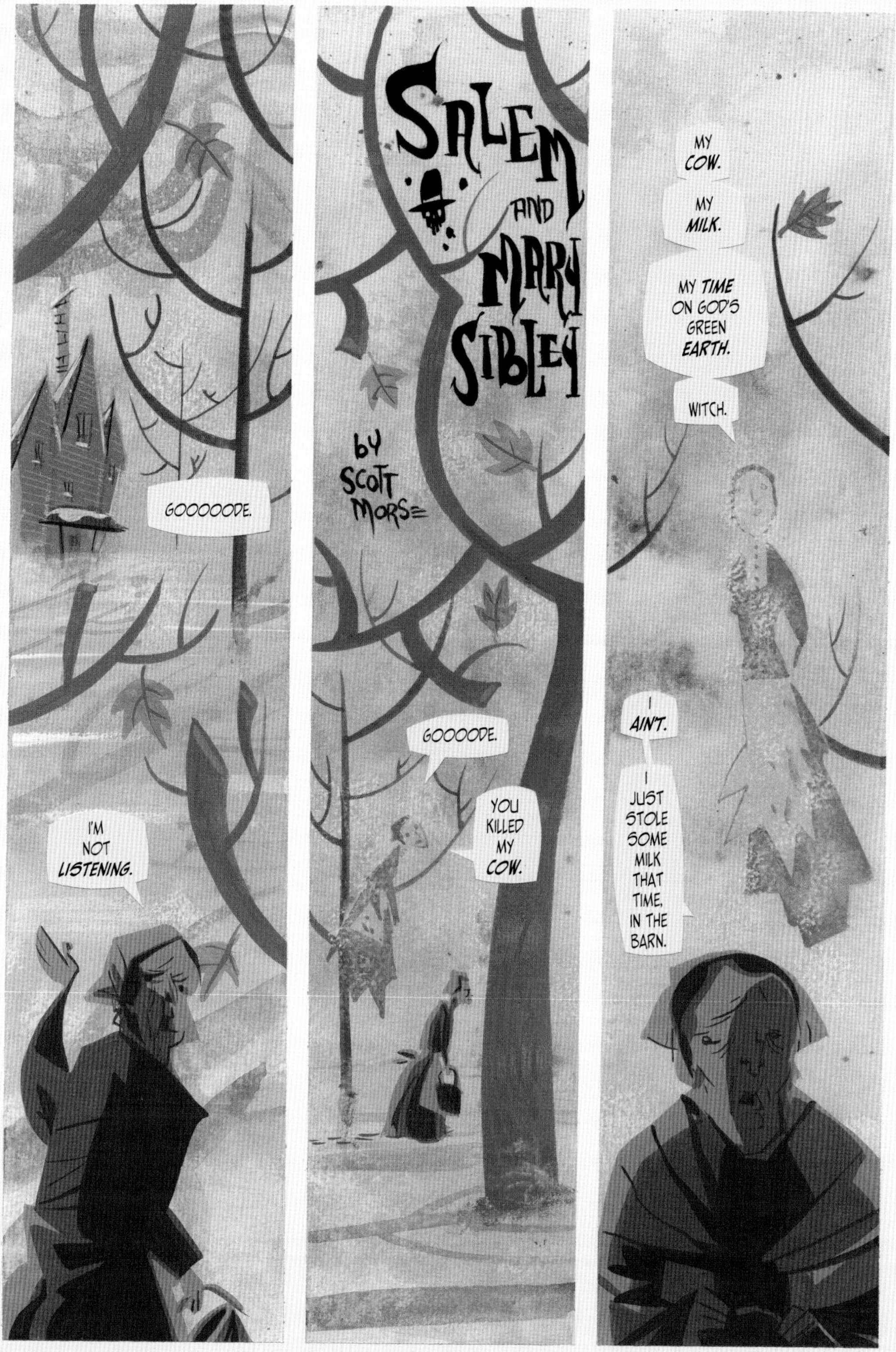
Salem and Mary Sibley
by Scott Morse
GOOOOODE.
I'M NOT LISTENING.
GOOOODE.
YOU KILLED MY COW.
MY COW.
MY MILK.
MY TIME ON GOD'S GREEN EARTH.
WITCH.
I AIN'T.
I JUST STOLE SOME MILK THAT TIME, IN THE BARN.

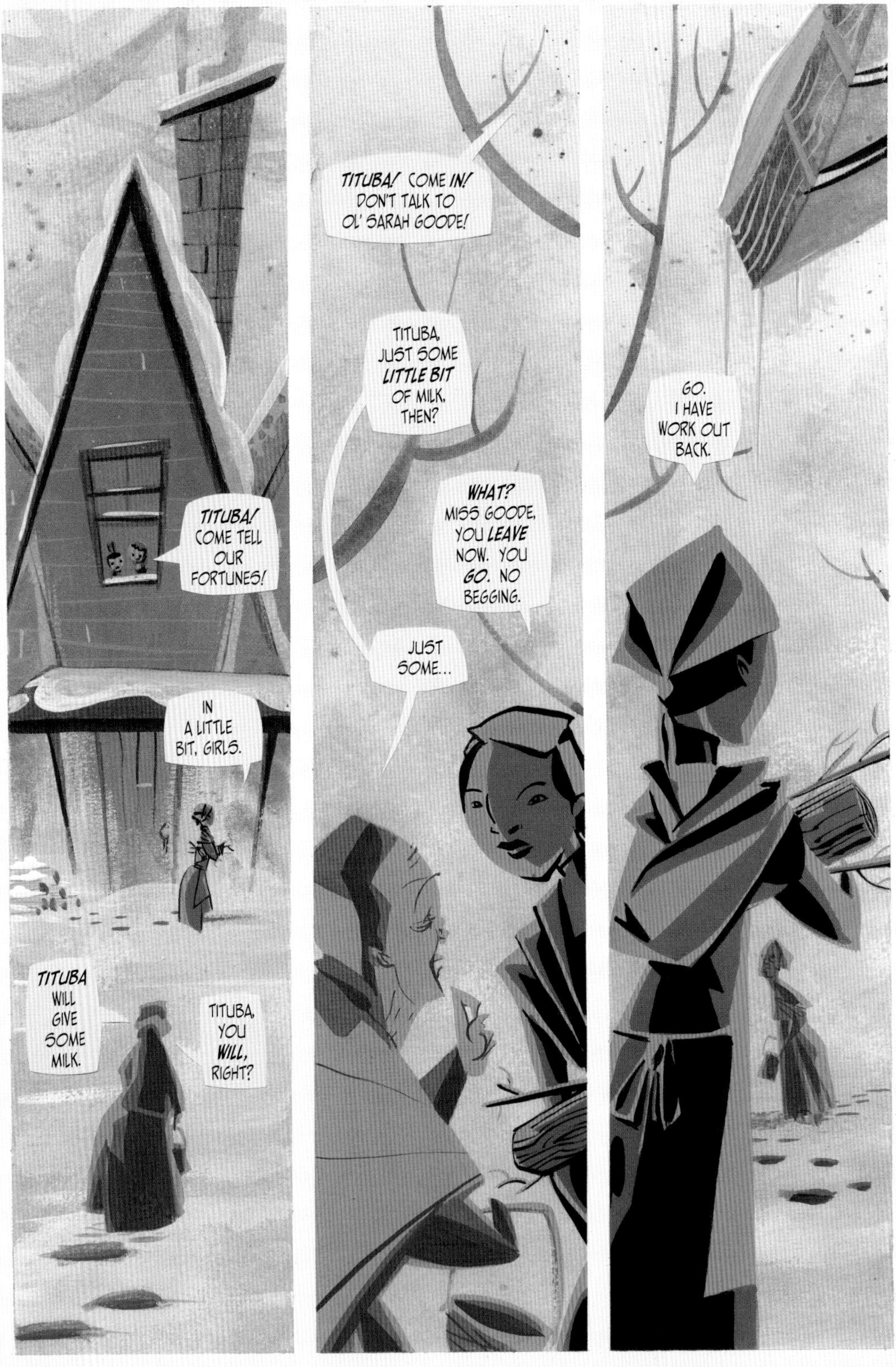

TITUBA! COME TELL OUR FORTUNES!
IN A LITTLE BIT, GIRLS.
TITUBA WILL GIVE SOME MILK.
TITUBA, YOU WILL, RIGHT?
TITUBA! COME IN! DON'T TALK TO OL' SARAH GOODE!
TITUBA, JUST SOME LITTLE BIT OF MILK, THEN?
WHAT? MISS GOODE, YOU LEAVE NOW. YOU GO. NO BEGGING.
JUST SOME...
GO. I HAVE WORK OUT BACK.

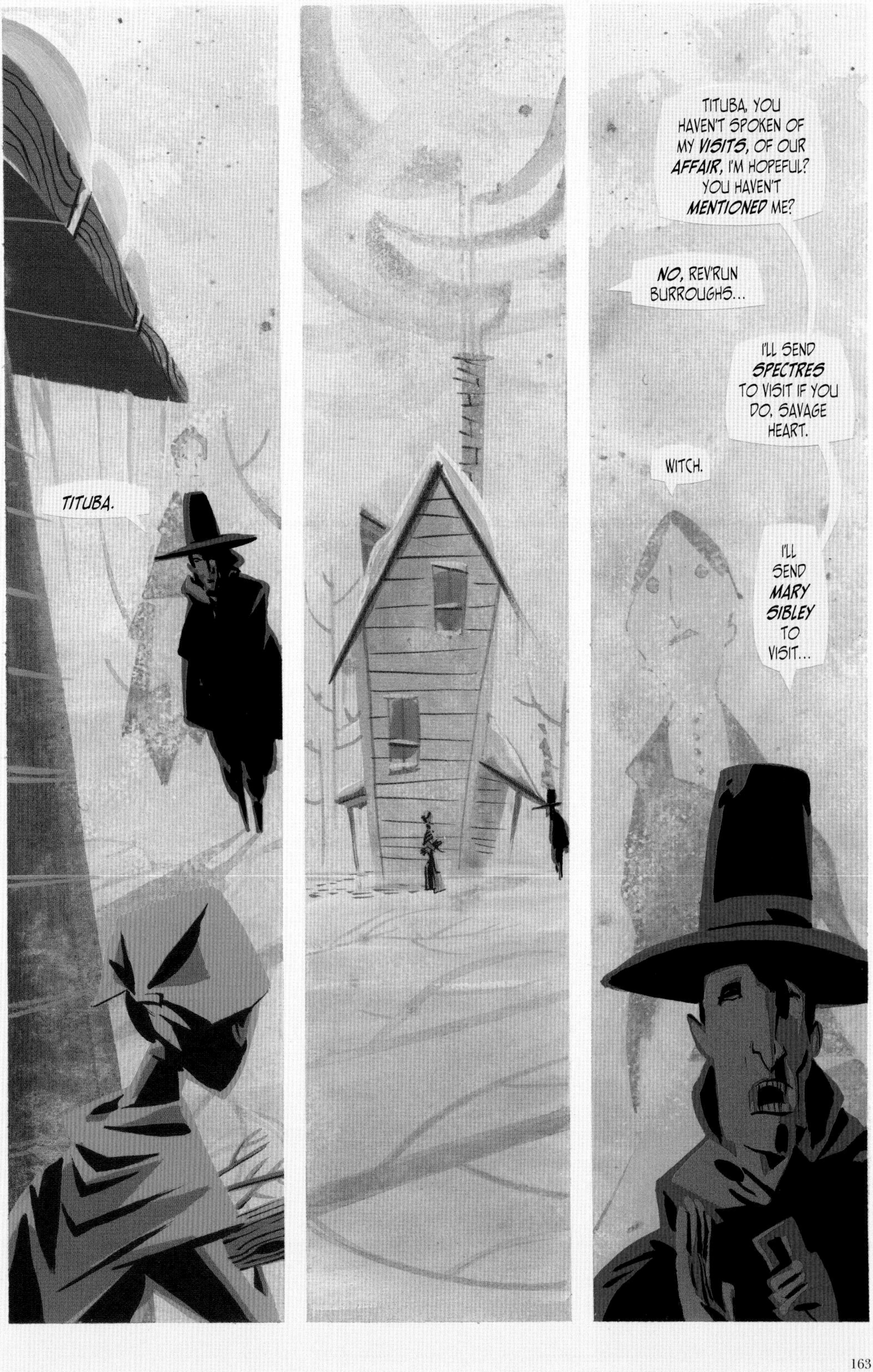
TITUBA.
TITUBA, YOU HAVEN'T SPOKEN OF MY VISITS, OF OUR AFFAIR, I'M HOPEFUL? YOU HAVEN'T MENTIONED ME?
NO, REV'RUN BURROUGHS...
I'LL SEND SPECTRES TO VISIT IF YOU DO, SAVAGE HEART.
WITCH.
I'LL SEND MARY SIBLEY TO VISIT...

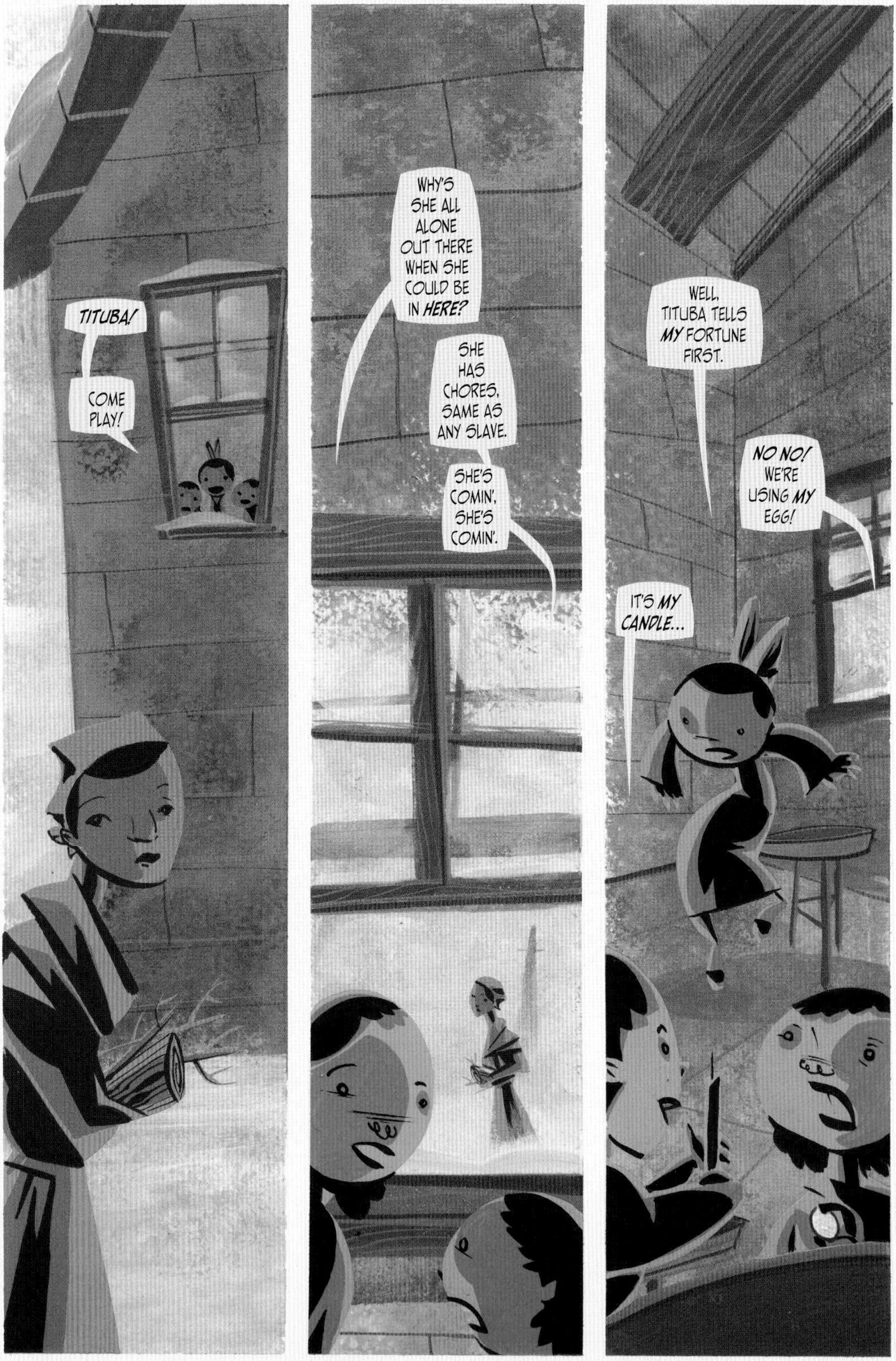
TITUBA!
COME PLAY!
WHY'S SHE ALL ALONE OUT THERE WHEN SHE COULD BE IN HERE?
SHE HAS CHORES, SAME AS ANY SLAVE.
SHE'S COMIN', SHE'S COMIN'.
WELL, TITUBA TELLS MY FORTUNE FIRST.
NO NO! WE'RE USING MY EGG!
IT'S MY CANDLE...

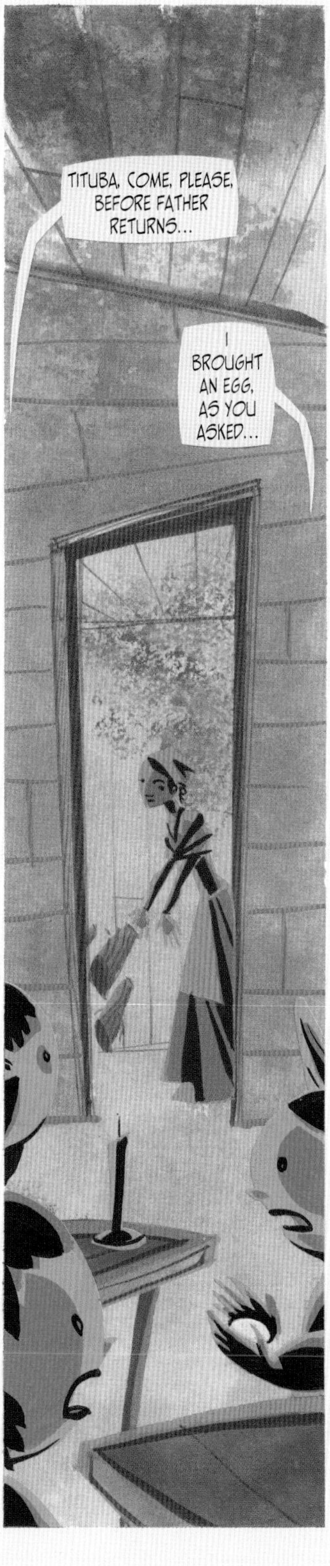
TITUBA, COME, PLEASE, BEFORE FATHER RETURNS...
I BROUGHT AN EGG, AS YOU ASKED...

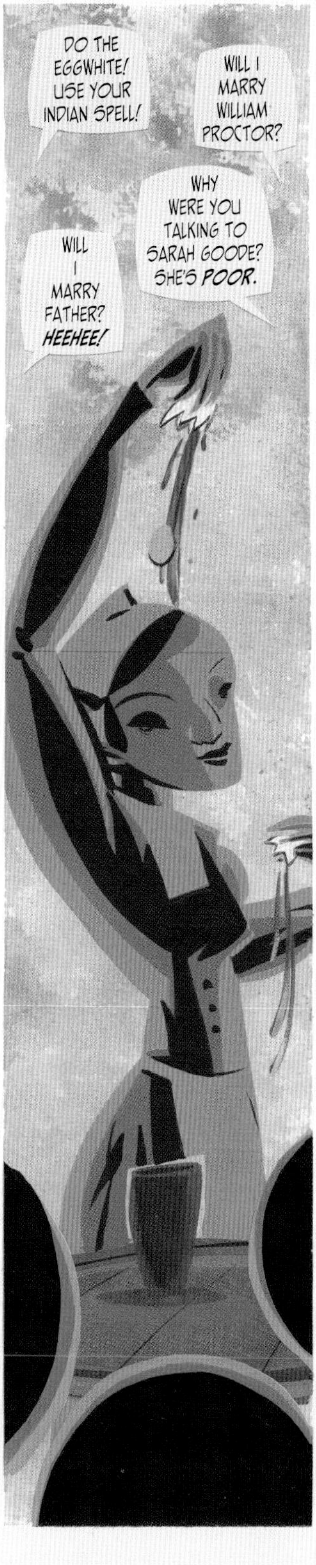
DO THE EGGWHITE! USE YOUR INDIAN SPELL!
WILL I MARRY WILLIAM PROCTOR?
WHY WERE YOU TALKING TO SARAH GOODE? SHE'S POOR.
WILL I MARRY FATHER? HEEHEE!

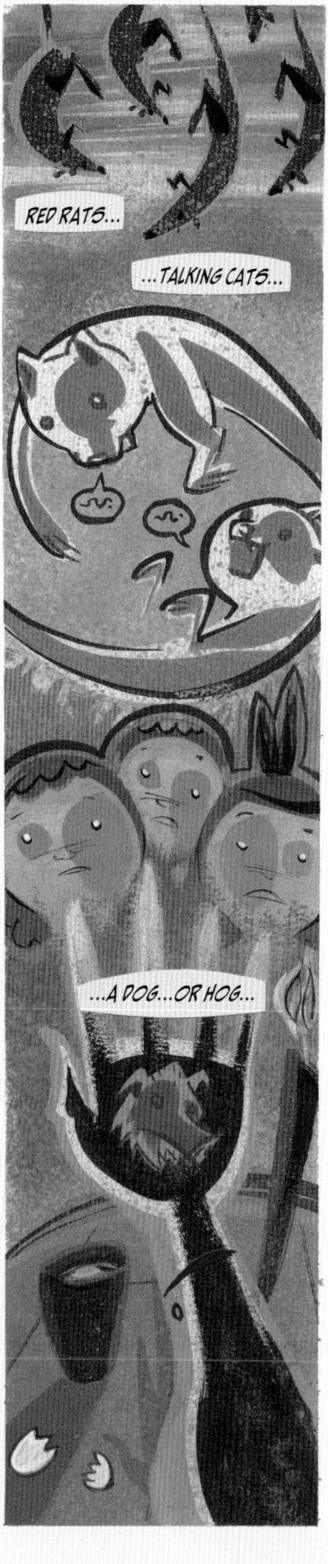
RED RATS...
...TALKING CATS...
...A DOG...OR HOG...

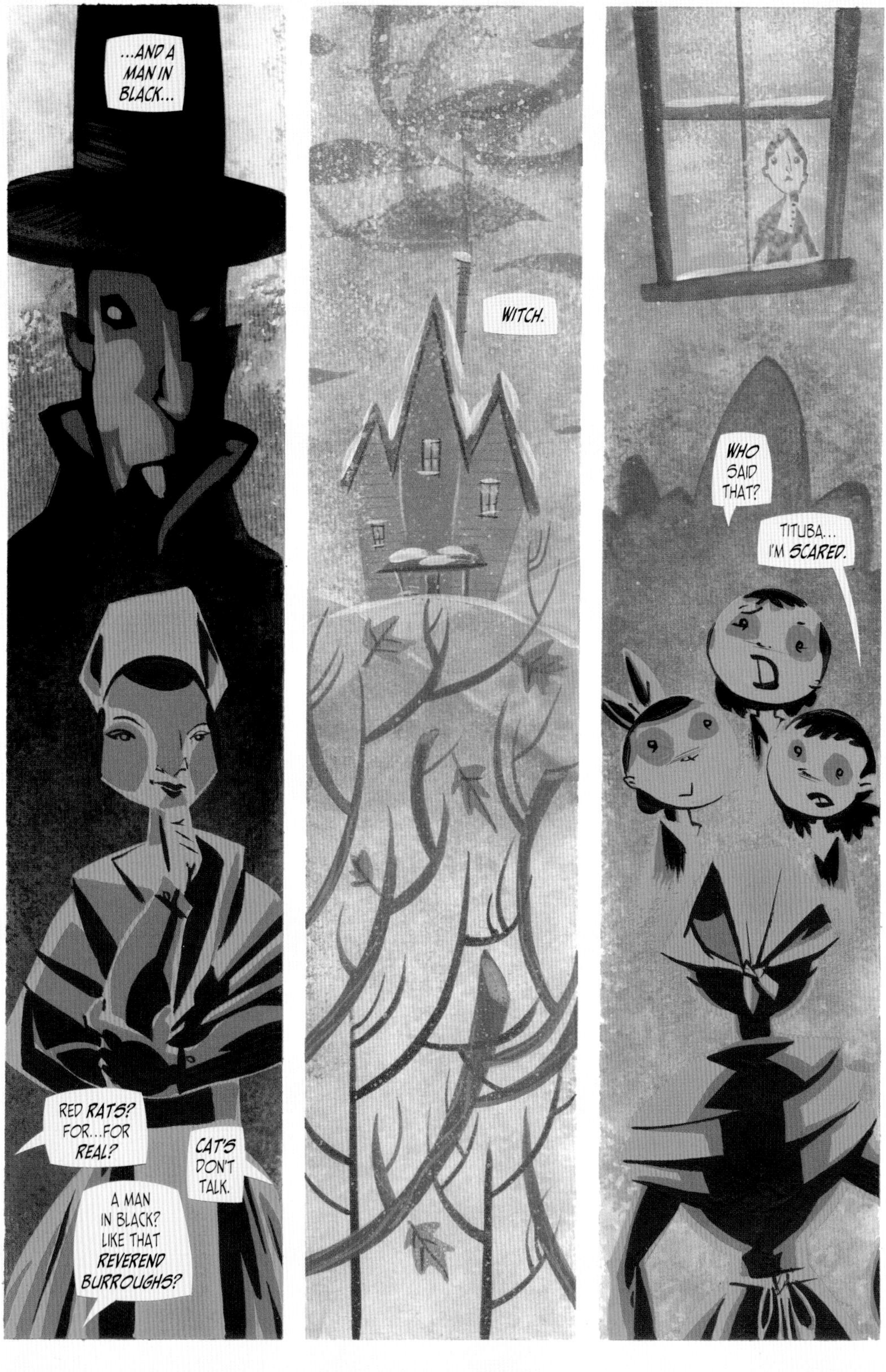
...AND A MAN IN BLACK...
RED RATS? FOR...FOR REAL?
CAT'S DON'T TALK.
A MAN IN BLACK? LIKE THAT REVEREND BURROUGHS?
WITCH.
WHO SAID THAT?
TITUBA... I'M SCARED.

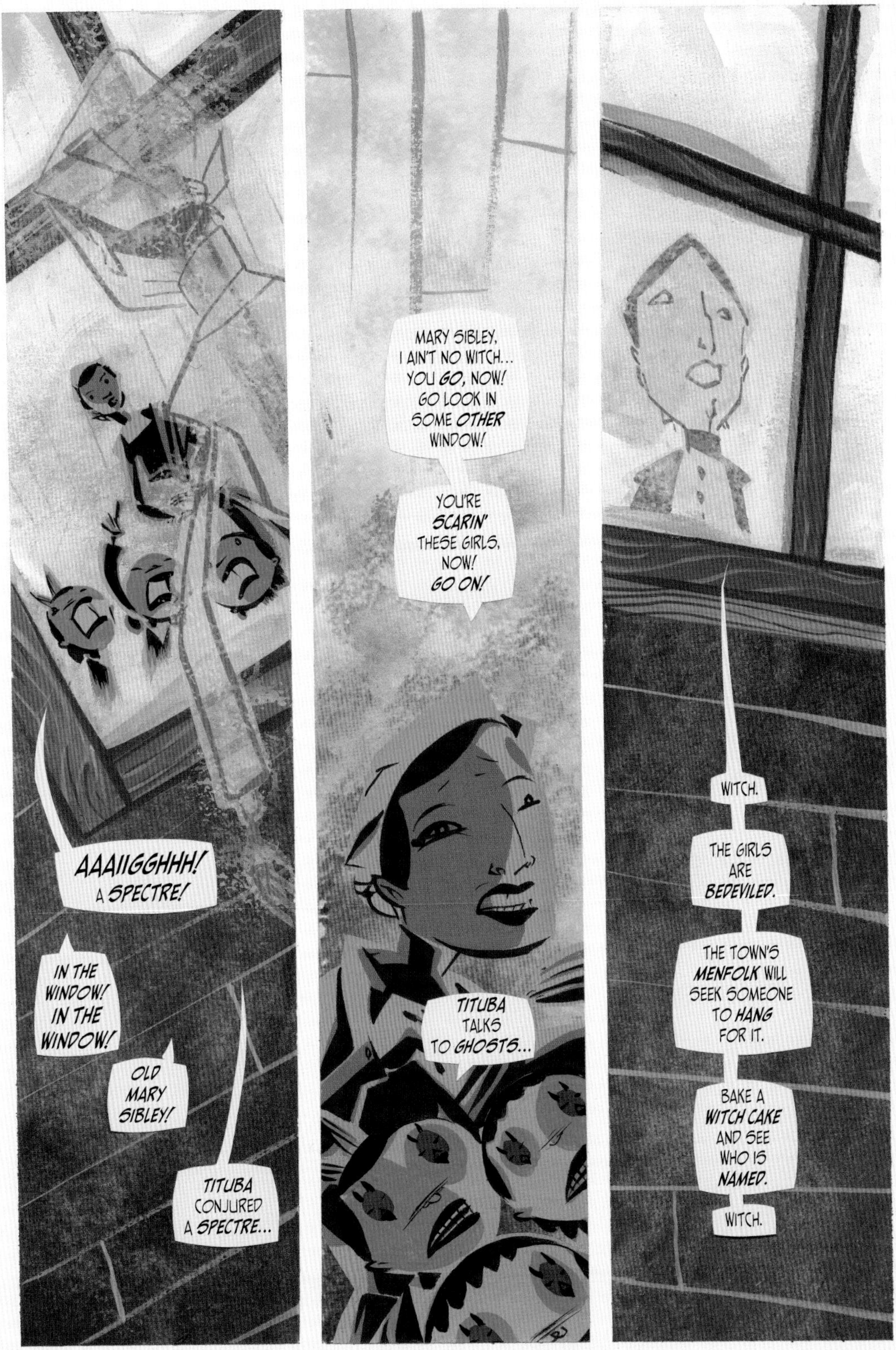
AAAIIGGHHH! A SPECTRE!
IN THE WINDOW! IN THE WINDOW!
OLD MARY SIBLEY!
TITUBA CONJURED A SPECTRE...
MARY SIBLEY, I AIN'T NO WITCH... YOU GO, NOW! GO LOOK IN SOME OTHER WINDOW!
YOU'RE SCARIN' THESE GIRLS, NOW! GO ON!
TITUBA TALKS TO GHOSTS...
WITCH.
THE GIRLS ARE BEDEVILED.
THE TOWN'S MENFOLK WILL SEEK SOMEONE TO HANG FOR IT.
BAKE A WITCH CAKE AND SEE WHO IS NAMED.
WITCH.

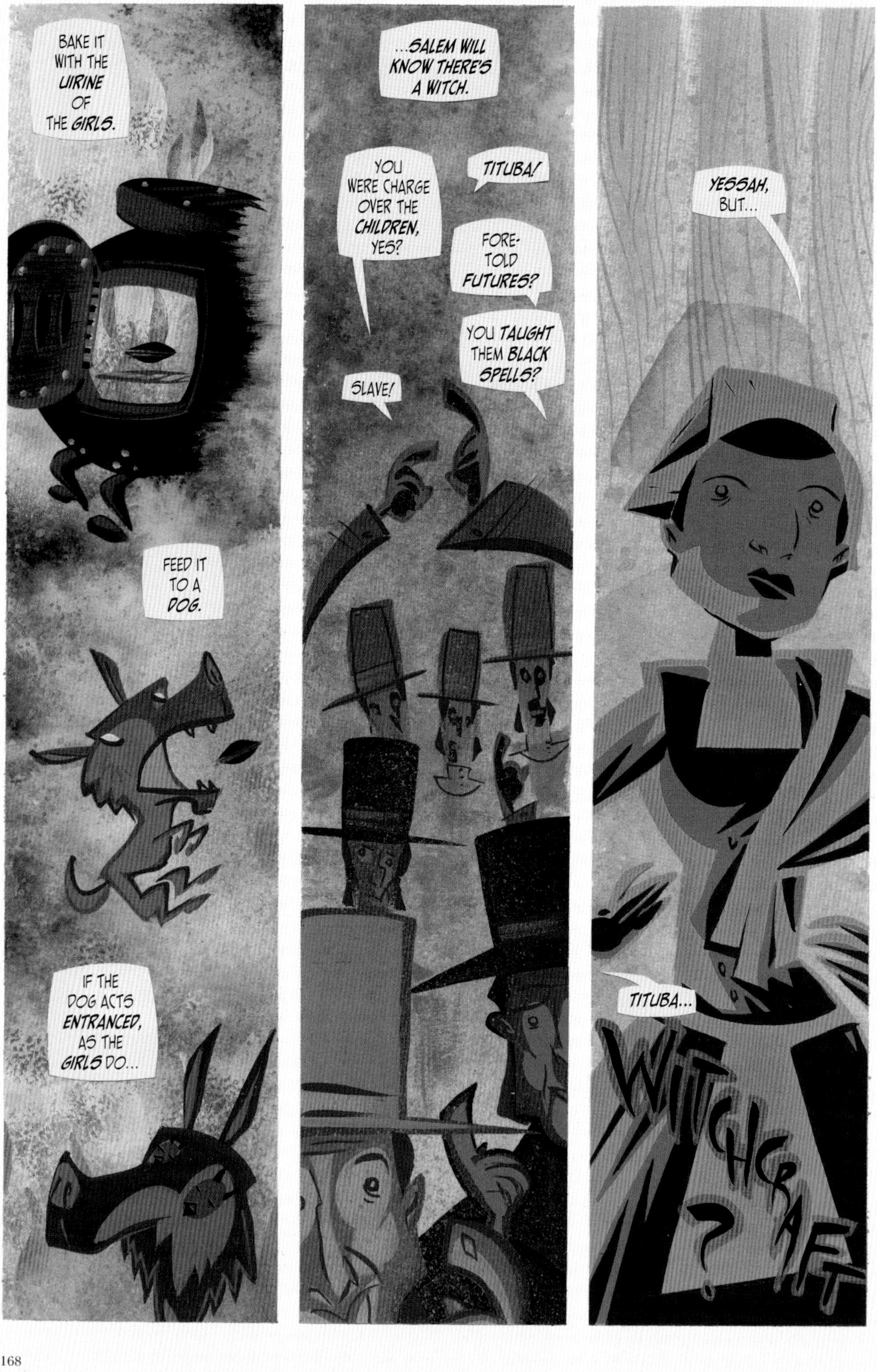
BAKE IT WITH THE URINE OF THE GIRLS.
FEED IT TO A DOG.
IF THE DOG ACTS ENTRANCED, AS THE GIRLS DO...
...SALEM WILL KNOW THERE'S A WITCH.
YOU WERE CHARGE OVER THE CHILDREN, YES?
TITUBA!
FORE-TOLD FUTURES?
YOU TAUGHT THEM BLACK SPELLS?
SLAVE!
YESSAH, BUT...
TITUBA...
WITCHCRAFT?

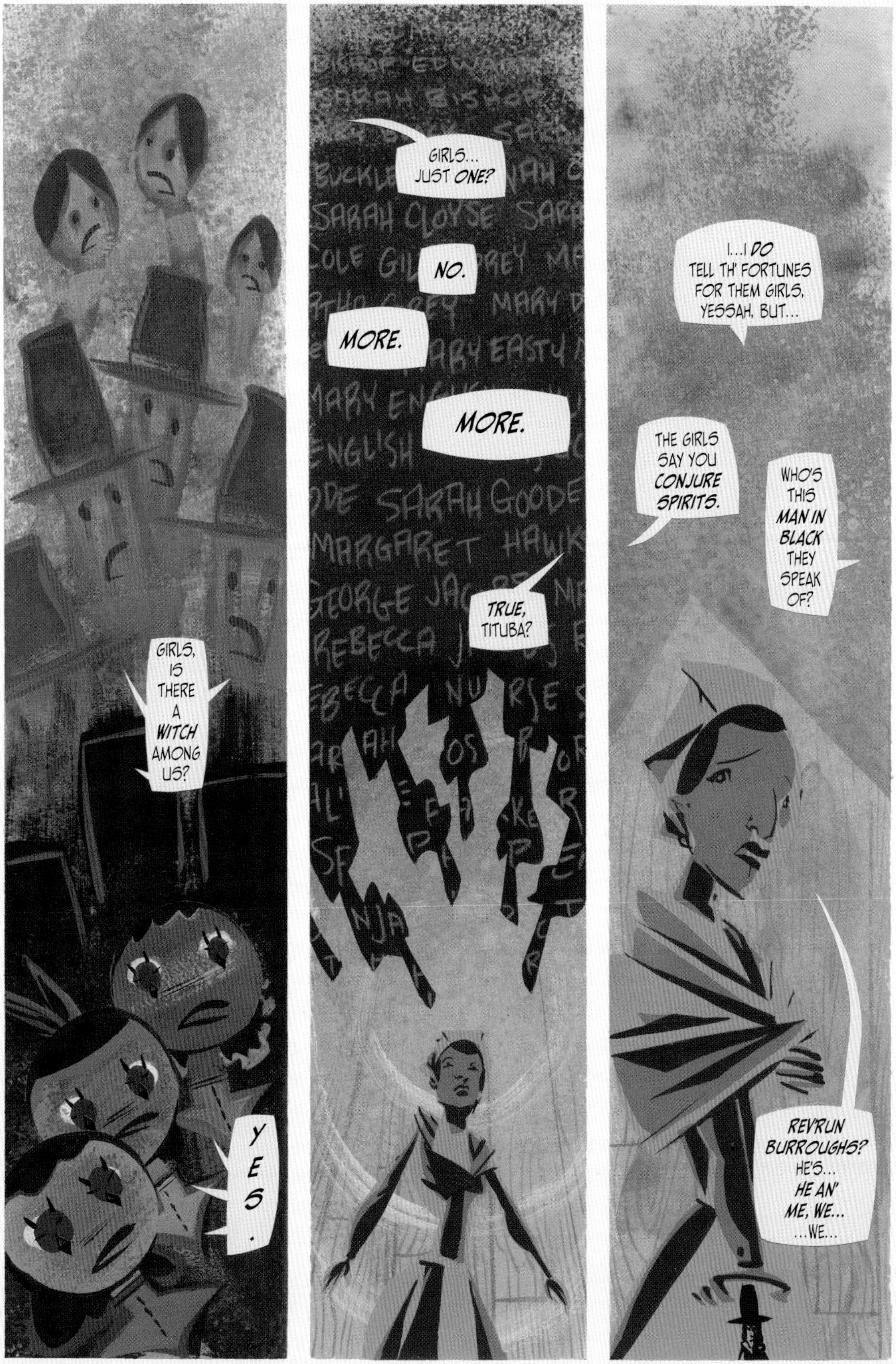
GIRLS, IS THERE A WITCH AMONG US?
YES.
GIRLS... JUST ONE?
NO.
MORE.
MORE.
SARAH CLOYSE
SARAH GOODE
TRUE, TITUBA?
I...I DO TELL TH' FORTUNES FOR THEM GIRLS, YESSAH, BUT...
THE GIRLS SAY YOU CONJURE SPIRITS.
WHO'S THIS MAN IN BLACK THEY SPEAK OF?
REV'RUN BURROUGHS? HE'S... HE AN' ME, WE... ...WE...

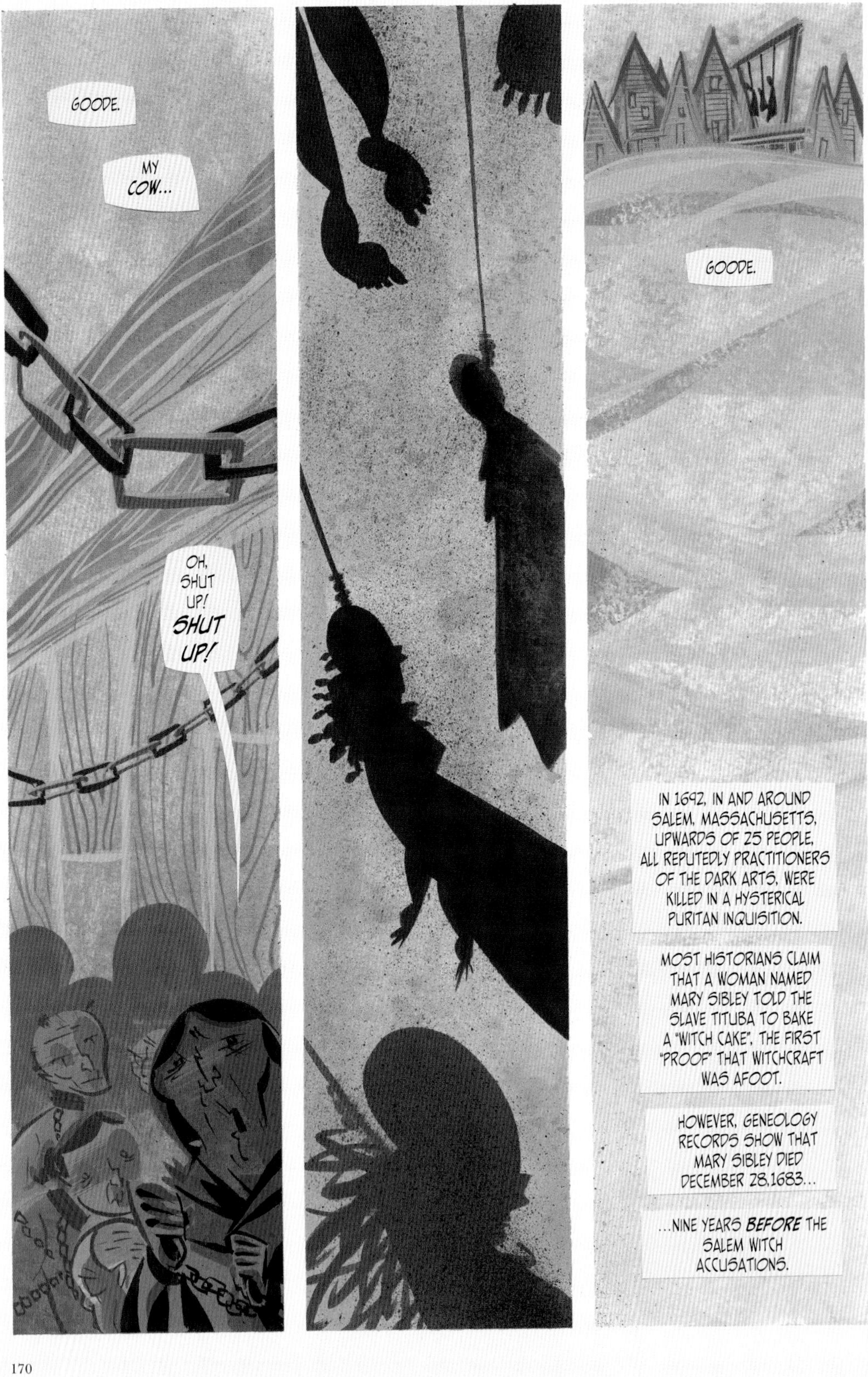
GOODE.
MY COW...
OH, SHUT UP! SHUT UP!
GOODE.
IN 1692, IN AND AROUND SALEM, MASSACHUSETTS, UPWARDS OF 25 PEOPLE, ALL REPUTEDLY PRACTITIONERS OF THE DARK ARTS, WERE KILLED IN A HYSTERICAL PURITAN INQUISITION.
MOST HISTORIANS CLAIM THAT A WOMAN NAMED MARY SIBLEY TOLD THE SLAVE TITUBA TO BAKE A "WITCH CAKE", THE FIRST "PROOF" THAT WITCHCRAFT WAS AFOOT.
HOWEVER, GENEOLOGY RECORDS SHOW THAT MARY SIBLEY DIED DECEMBER 28,1683...
...NINE YEARS BEFORE THE SALEM WITCH ACCUSATIONS.

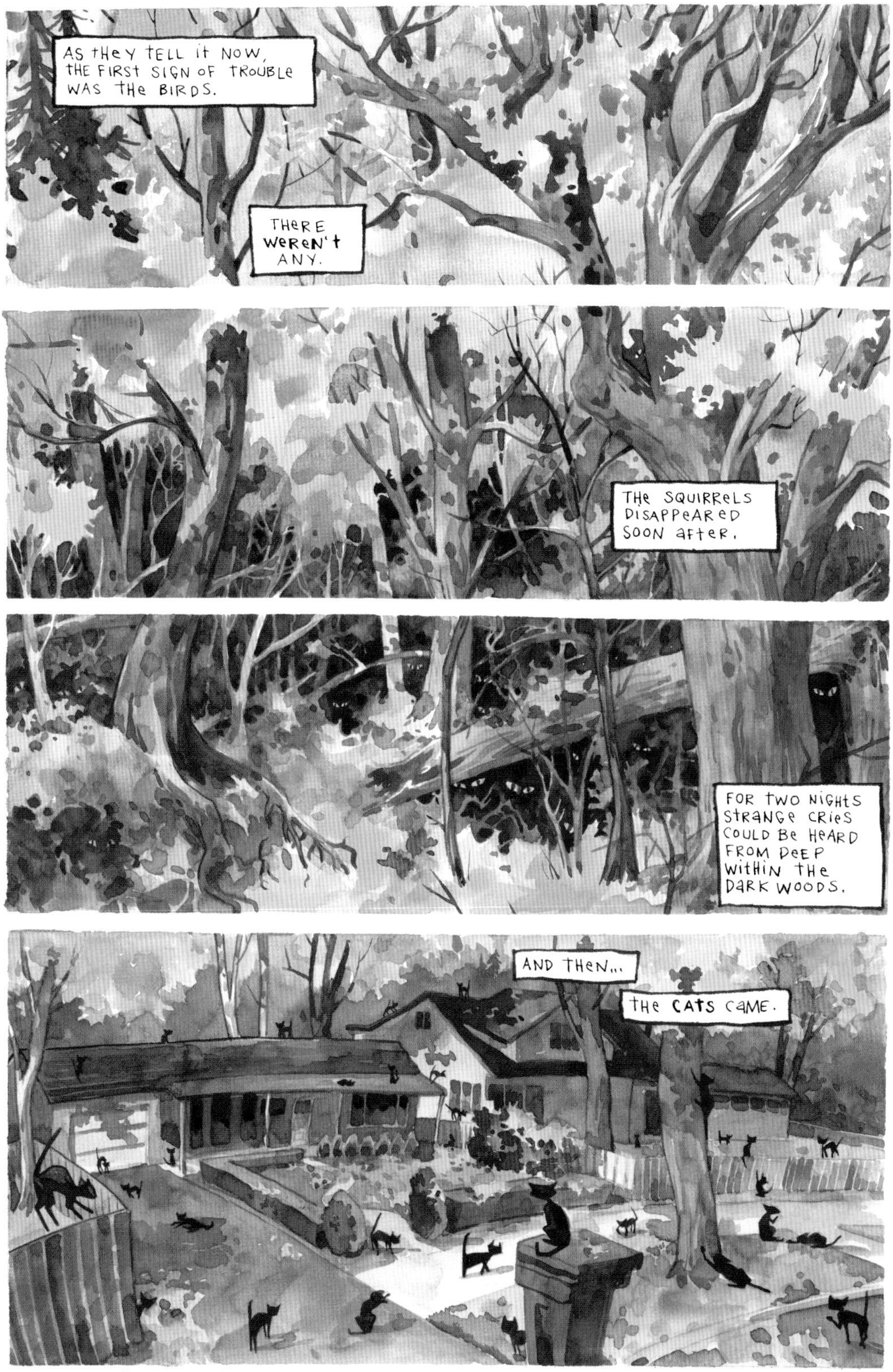
AS THEY TELL IT NOW, THE FIRST SIGN OF TROUBLE WAS THE BIRDS.
THERE WEREN'T ANY.
THE SQUIRRELS DISAPPEARED SOON AFTER.
FOR TWO NIGHTS STRANGE CRIES COULD BE HEARD FROM DEEP WITHIN THE DARK WOODS.
AND THEN...
THE CATS CAME.

the Unfamiliar by Evan Dorkin and Jill Thompson 2004

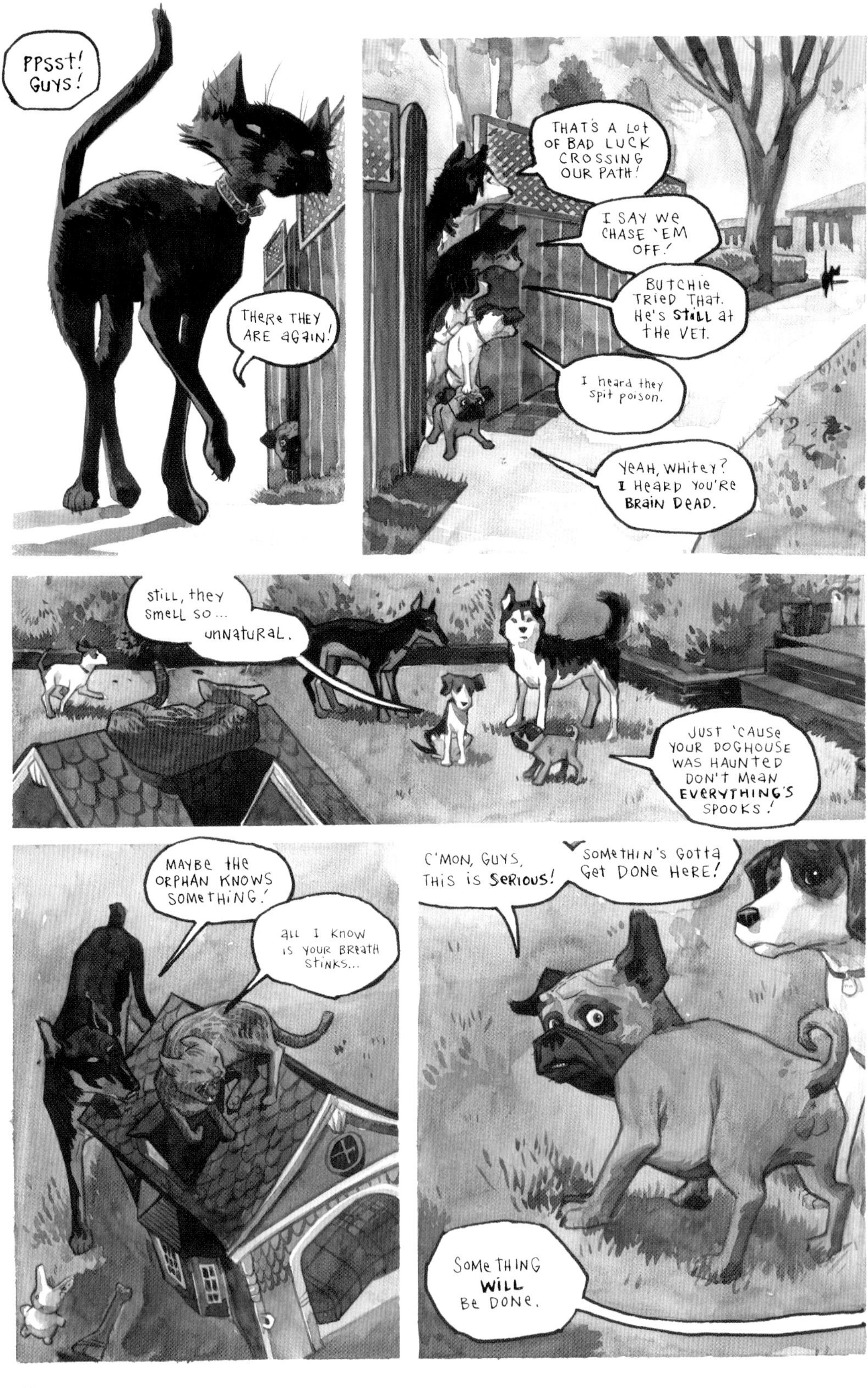
PPSST! GUYS!
THERE THEY ARE AGAIN!
THAT'S A LOT OF BAD LUCK CROSSING OUR PATH!
I SAY WE CHASE 'EM OFF!
BUTCHIE TRIED THAT. HE'S STILL AT THE VET.
I heard they spit poison.
YEAH, WHITEY? I HEARD YOU'RE BRAIN DEAD.
STILL, THEY SMELL SO... UNNATURAL.
JUST 'CAUSE YOUR DOGHOUSE WAS HAUNTED DON'T MEAN EVERYTHING'S SPOOKS!
MAYBE THE ORPHAN KNOWS SOMETHING!
ALL I KNOW IS YOUR BREATH STINKS...
C'MON, GUYS, THIS IS SERIOUS!
SOMETHIN'S GOTTA GET DONE HERE!
SOMETHING WILL BE DONE.

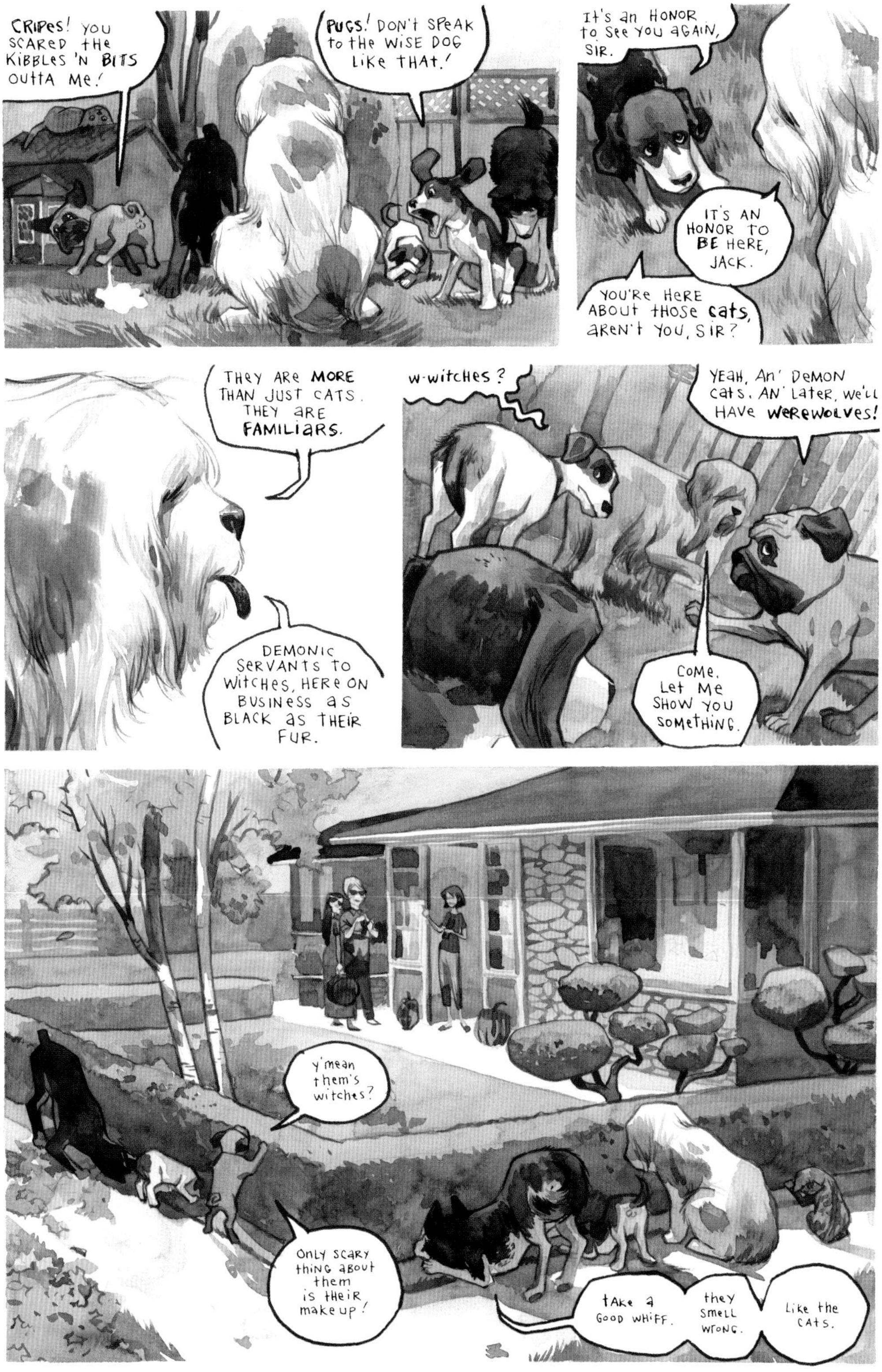

CRIPES! YOU SCARED THE KIBBLES 'N BITS OUTTA ME!
PUGS! DON'T SPEAK TO THE WISE DOG LIKE THAT!
IT'S AN HONOR TO SEE YOU AGAIN, SIR.
IT'S AN HONOR TO BE HERE, JACK.
YOU'RE HERE ABOUT THOSE CATS, AREN'T YOU, SIR?
THEY ARE MORE THAN JUST CATS. THEY ARE FAMILIARS.
DEMONIC SERVANTS TO WITCHES, HERE ON BUSINESS AS BLACK AS THEIR FUR.
W-WITCHES?
YEAH, AN' DEMON CATS. AN' LATER, WE'LL HAVE WEREWOLVES!
COME. LET ME SHOW YOU SOMETHING.
Y'MEAN THEM'S WITCHES?
ONLY SCARY THING ABOUT THEM IS THEIR MAKEUP!
TAKE A GOOD WHIFF.
THEY SMELL WRONG.
LIKE THE CATS.

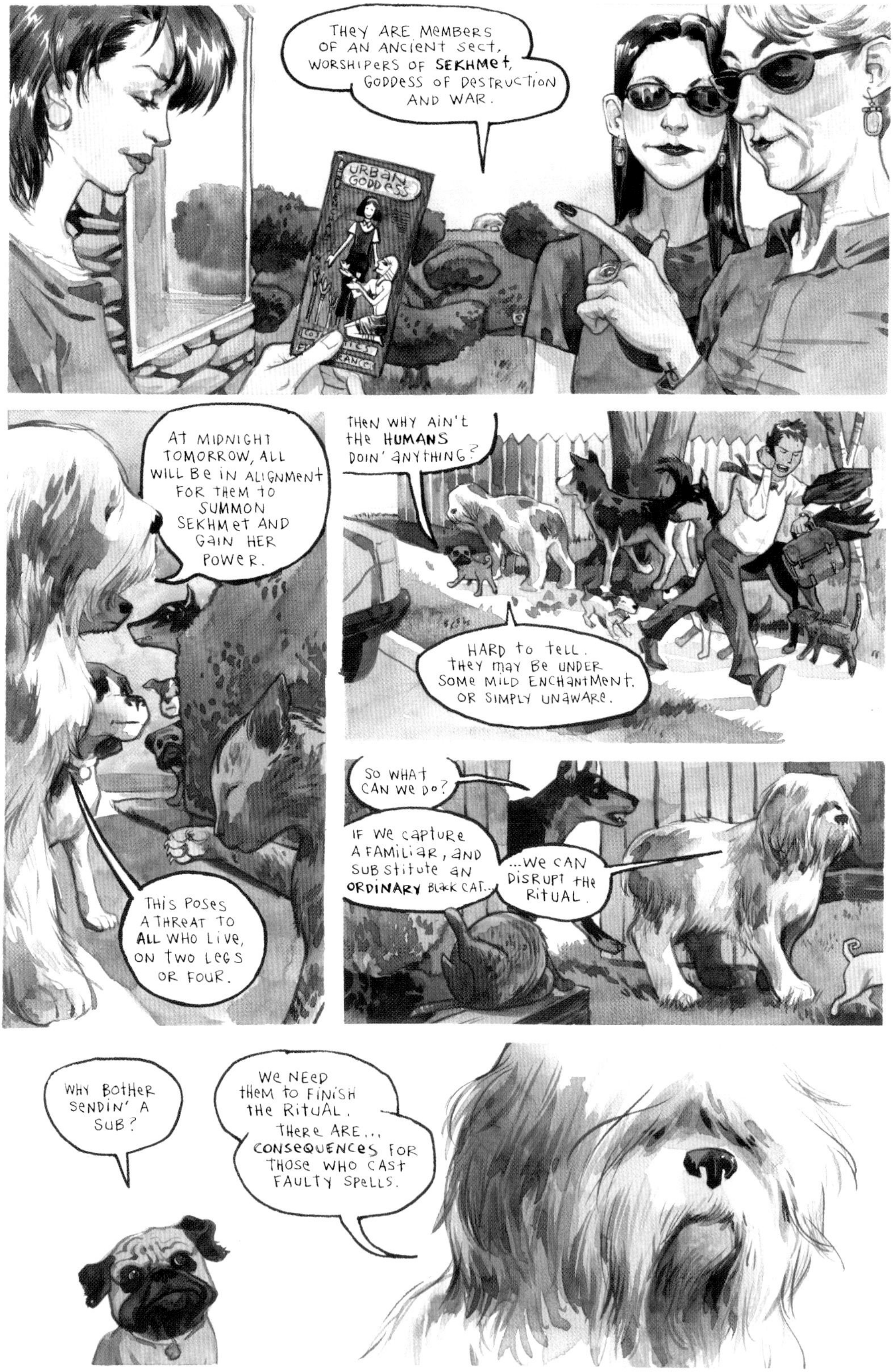
THEY ARE MEMBERS OF AN ANCIENT SECT, WORSHIPERS OF **SEKHMET**, GODDESS OF DESTRUCTION AND WAR.
URBAN GODDESS
AT MIDNIGHT TOMORROW, ALL WILL BE IN ALIGNMENT FOR THEM TO SUMMON SEKHMET AND GAIN HER POWER.
THIS POSES A THREAT TO **ALL** WHO LIVE, ON TWO LEGS OR FOUR.
THEN WHY AIN'T THE **HUMANS** DOIN' ANYTHING?
HARD TO TELL. THEY MAY BE UNDER SOME MILD ENCHANTMENT. OR SIMPLY UNAWARE.
SO WHAT CAN WE DO?
IF WE CAPTURE A FAMILIAR, AND SUBSTITUTE AN **ORDINARY** BLACK CAT...
...WE CAN DISRUPT THE RITUAL.
WHY BOTHER SENDIN' A SUB?
WE NEED THEM TO FINISH THE RITUAL. THERE ARE... **CONSEQUENCES** FOR THOSE WHO CAST FAULTY SPELLS.

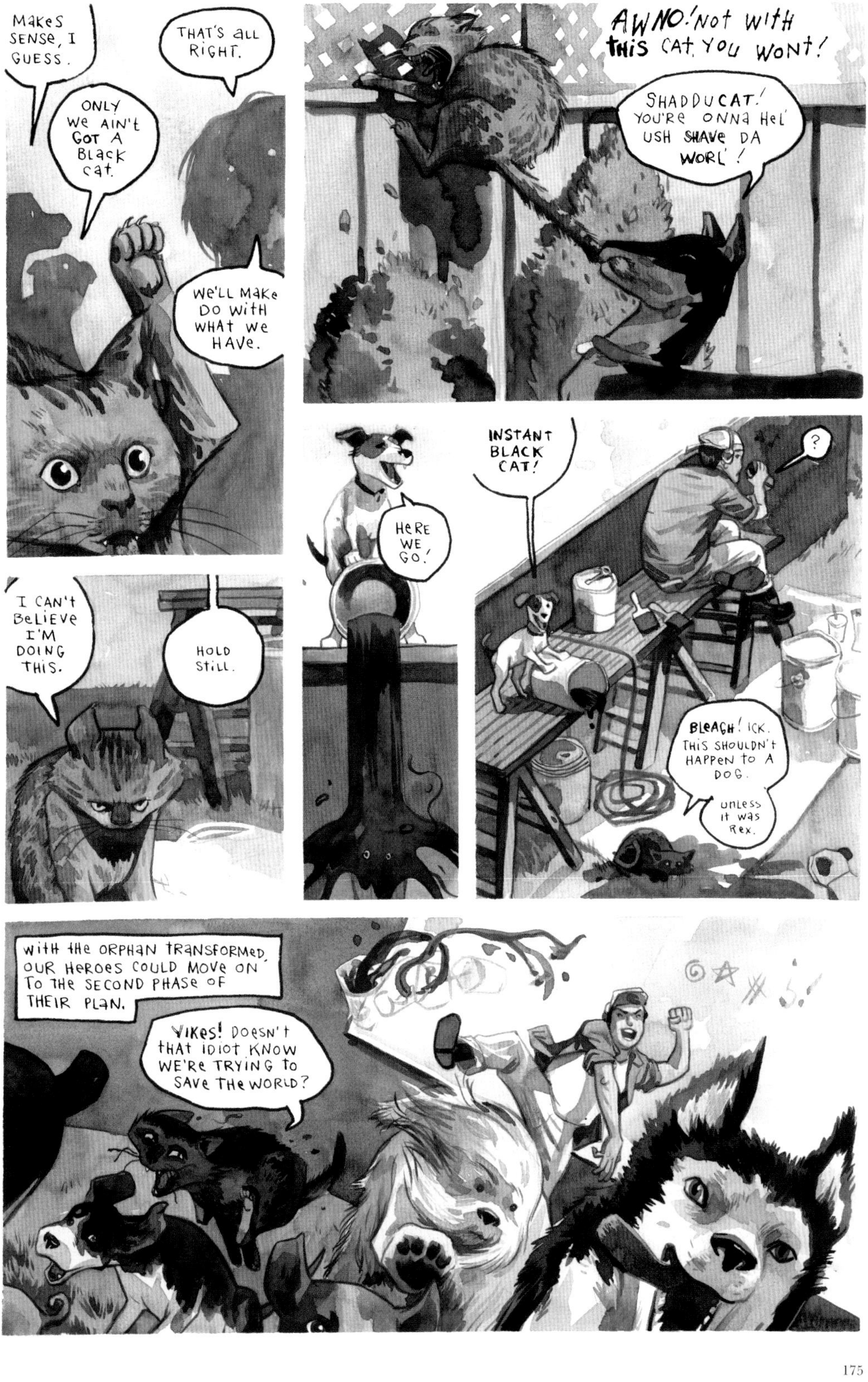

Makes sense, I guess.
That's all right.
Only we ain't got a black cat.
We'll make do with what we have.
AW NO! Not with this cat, you wont!
Shadducat! You're onna hel' ush shave da worl'!
Here we go!
Instant black cat!
?
I can't believe I'm doing this.
Hold still.
Bleagh! Ick. This shouldn't happen to a dog.
Unless it was Rex.
With the orphan transformed, our heroes could move on to the second phase of their plan.
Yikes! Doesn't that idiot know we're trying to save the world?

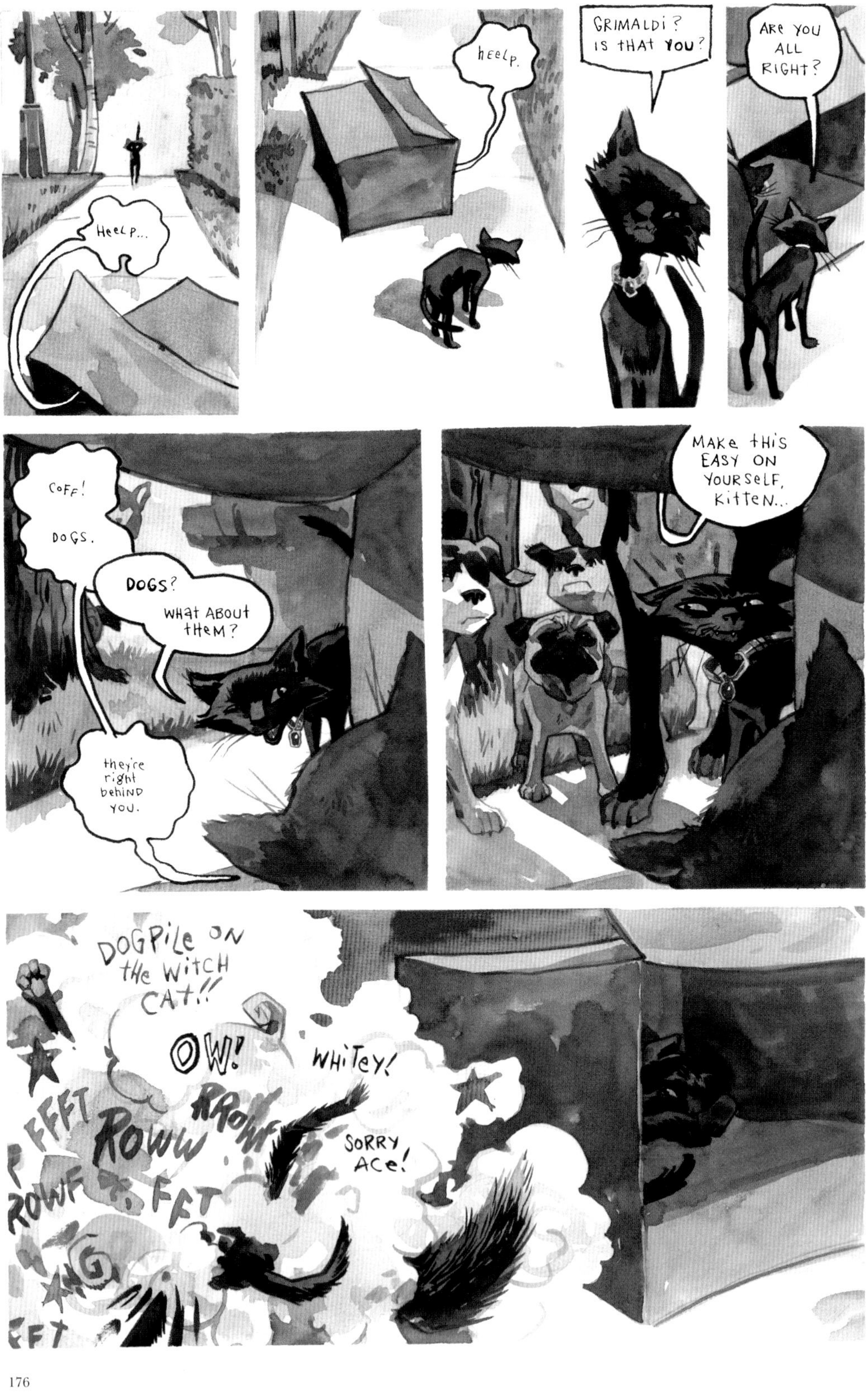
Heelp...
heelp.
GRIMALDI? IS THAT YOU?
Are YOU ALL RIGHT?
COFF!
DOGS.
DOGS? WHAT ABOUT THEM?
they're right behind YOU.
MAKE THIS EASY ON YOURSELF, KITTEN...
DOGPILE ON THE WITCH CAT!!
OW!
WHITEY!
SORRY ACE!
FFFT
ROWW
RROWF
ROWF
FFT

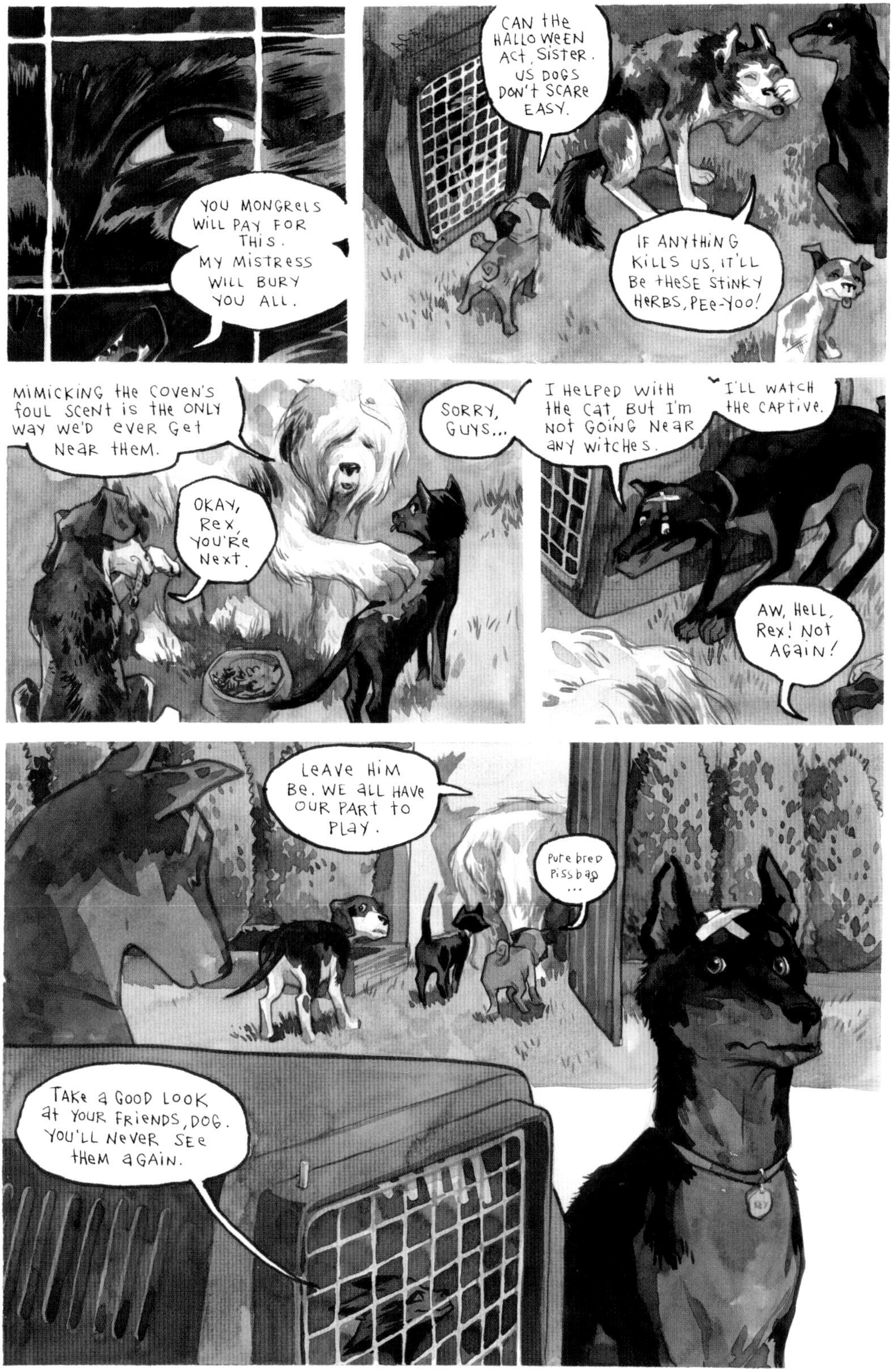
YOU MONGRELS WILL PAY FOR THIS. MY MISTRESS WILL BURY YOU ALL.
CAN THE HALLOWEEN ACT, SISTER. US DOGS DON'T SCARE EASY.
IF ANYTHING KILLS US, IT'LL BE THESE STINKY HERBS, PEE-YOO!
MIMICKING THE COVEN'S FOUL SCENT IS THE ONLY WAY WE'D EVER GET NEAR THEM.
OKAY, REX, YOU'RE NEXT.
SORRY, GUYS...
I HELPED WITH THE CAT, BUT I'M NOT GOING NEAR ANY WITCHES.
I'LL WATCH THE CAPTIVE.
AW, HELL, REX! NOT AGAIN!
LEAVE HIM BE. WE ALL HAVE OUR PART TO PLAY.
PURE BRED PISSBAG...
TAKE A GOOD LOOK AT YOUR FRIENDS, DOG. YOU'LL NEVER SEE THEM AGAIN.

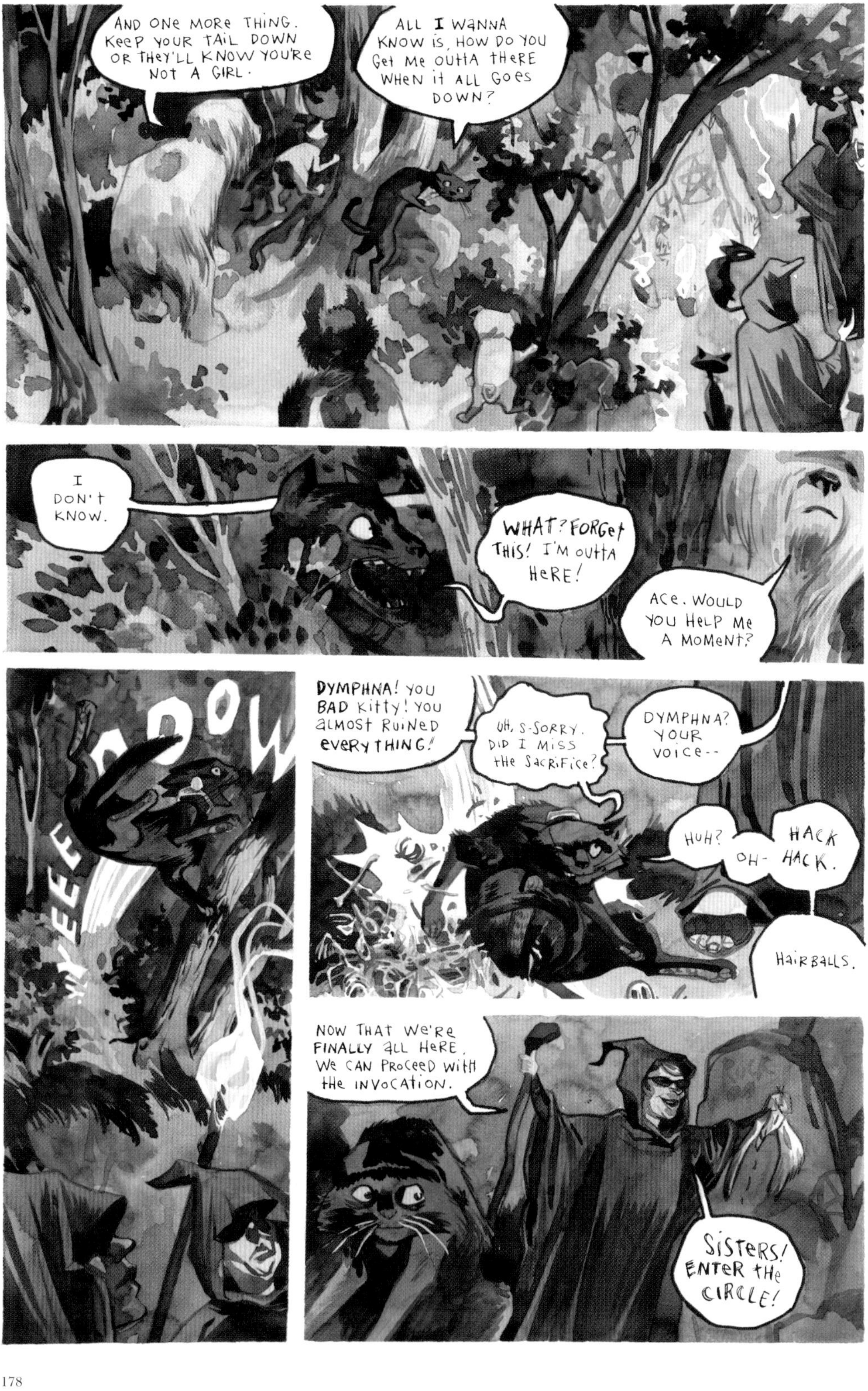
AND ONE MORE THING. KEEP YOUR TAIL DOWN OR THEY'LL KNOW YOU'RE NOT A GIRL.
ALL I WANNA KNOW IS, HOW DO YOU GET ME OUTTA THERE WHEN IT ALL GOES DOWN?
I DON'T KNOW.
WHAT? FORGET THIS! I'M OUTTA HERE!
ACE. WOULD YOU HELP ME A MOMENT?
DYMPHNA! YOU BAD KITTY! YOU ALMOST RUINED EVERYTHING!
UH, S-SORRY. DID I MISS THE SACRIFICE?
DYMPHNA? YOUR VOICE--
HUH?
OH-
HACK HACK.
HAIRBALLS.
NOW THAT WE'RE FINALLY ALL HERE, WE CAN PROCEED WITH THE INVOCATION.
SISTERS! ENTER THE CIRCLE!

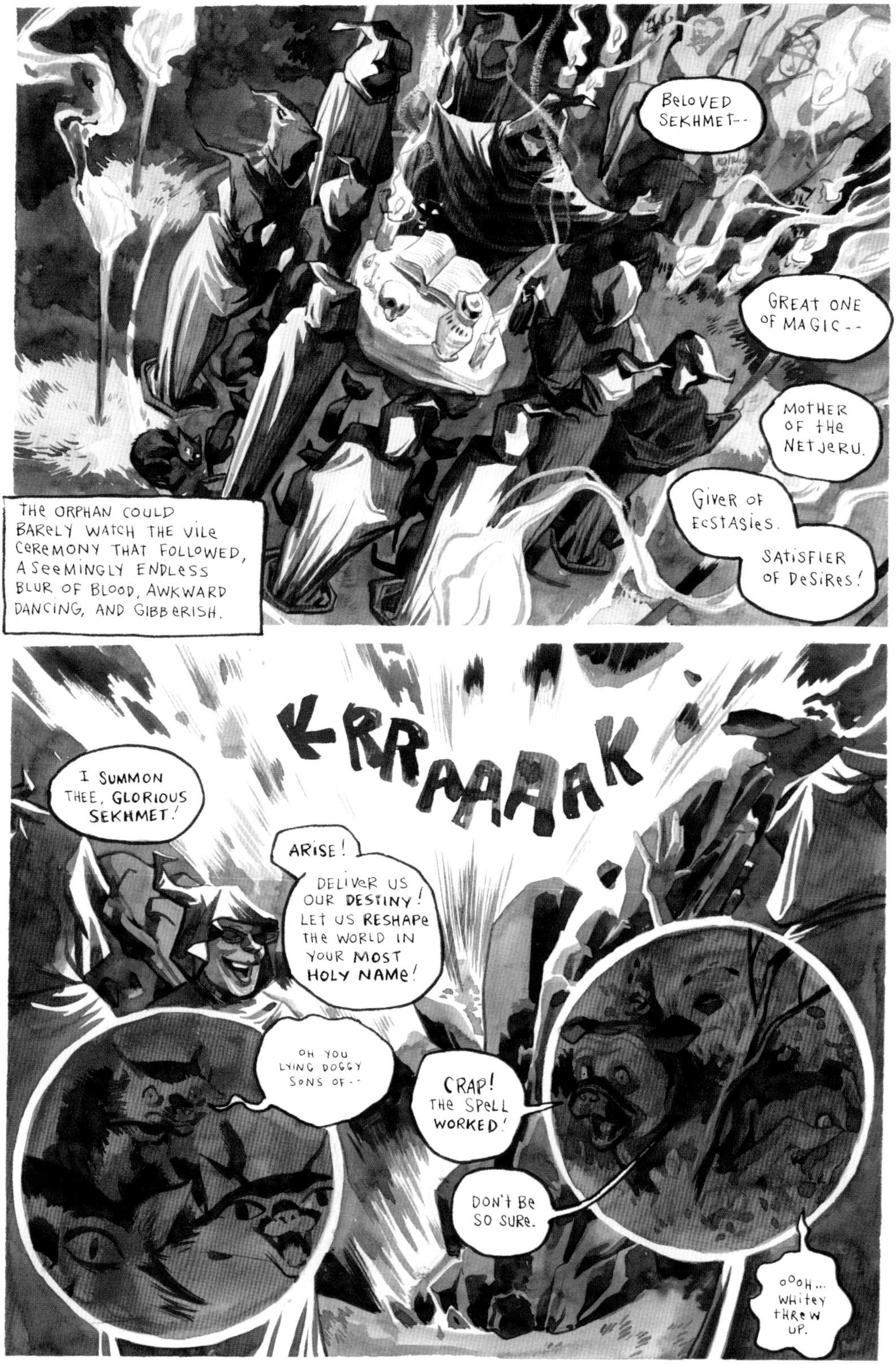
BELOVED SEKHMET--
GREAT ONE OF MAGIC--
MOTHER OF THE NETJERU.
THE ORPHAN COULD BARELY WATCH THE VILE CEREMONY THAT FOLLOWED, A SEEMINGLY ENDLESS BLUR OF BLOOD, AWKWARD DANCING, AND GIBBERISH.
GIVER OF ECSTASIES.
SATISFIER OF DESIRES!
KRRAAAAK
I SUMMON THEE, GLORIOUS SEKHMET!
ARISE!
DELIVER US OUR DESTINY! LET US RESHAPE THE WORLD IN YOUR MOST HOLY NAME!
OH YOU LYING DOGGY SONS OF--
CRAP! THE SPELL WORKED!
DON'T BE SO SURE.
OOOH... WHITEY THREW UP.

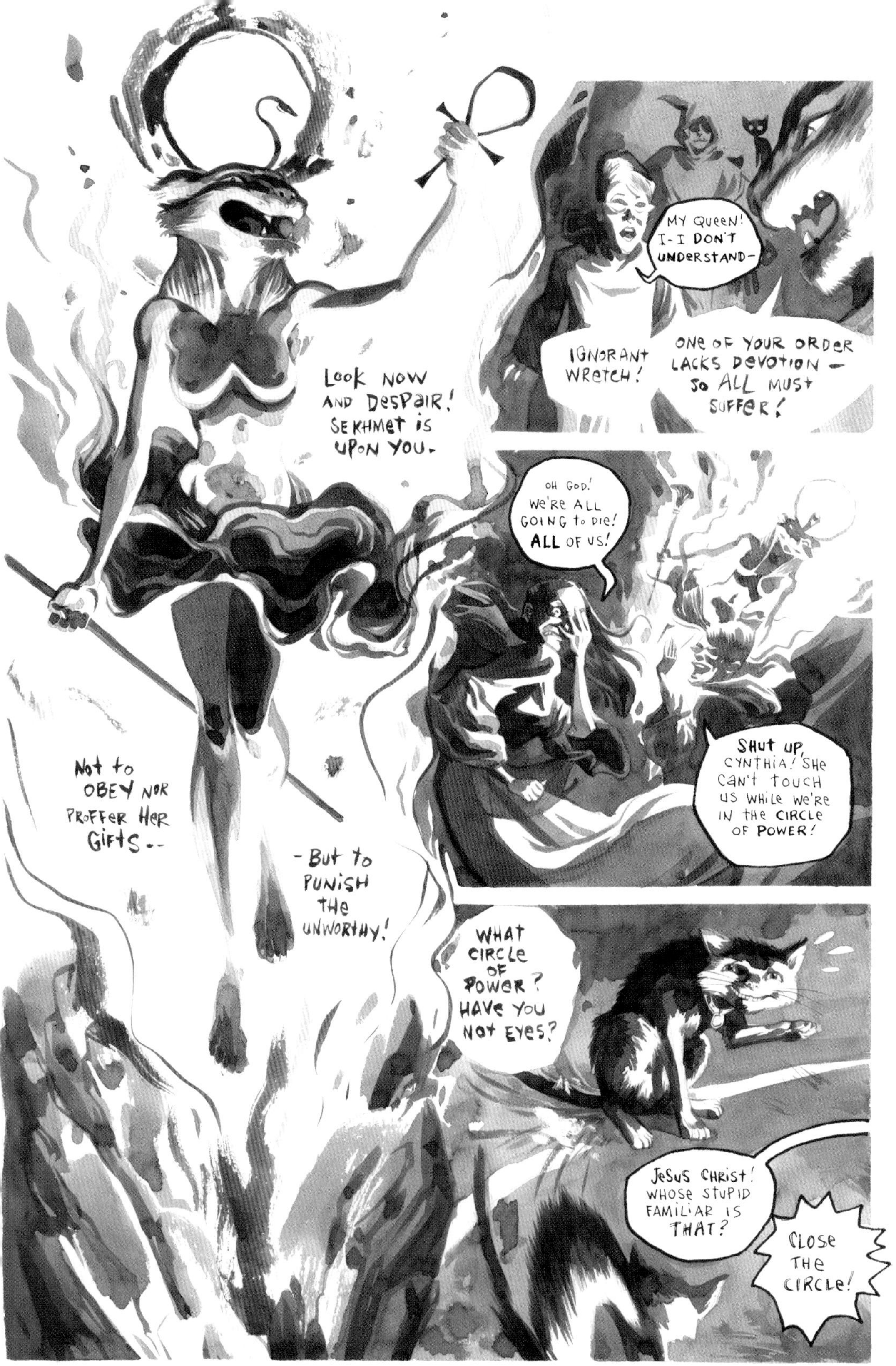
LOOK NOW AND DESPAIR! SEKHMET IS UPON YOU.
MY QUEEN! I-I DON'T UNDERSTAND-
IGNORANT WRETCH!
ONE OF YOUR ORDER LACKS DEVOTION - SO ALL MUST SUFFER!
OH GOD! WE'RE ALL GOING TO DIE! ALL OF US!
SHUT UP, CYNTHIA! SHE CAN'T TOUCH US WHILE WE'RE IN THE CIRCLE OF POWER!
NOT TO OBEY NOR PROFFER HER GIFTS--
-BUT TO PUNISH THE UNWORTHY!
WHAT CIRCLE OF POWER? HAVE YOU NOT EYES?
JESUS CHRIST! WHOSE STUPID FAMILIAR IS THAT?
CLOSE THE CIRCLE!

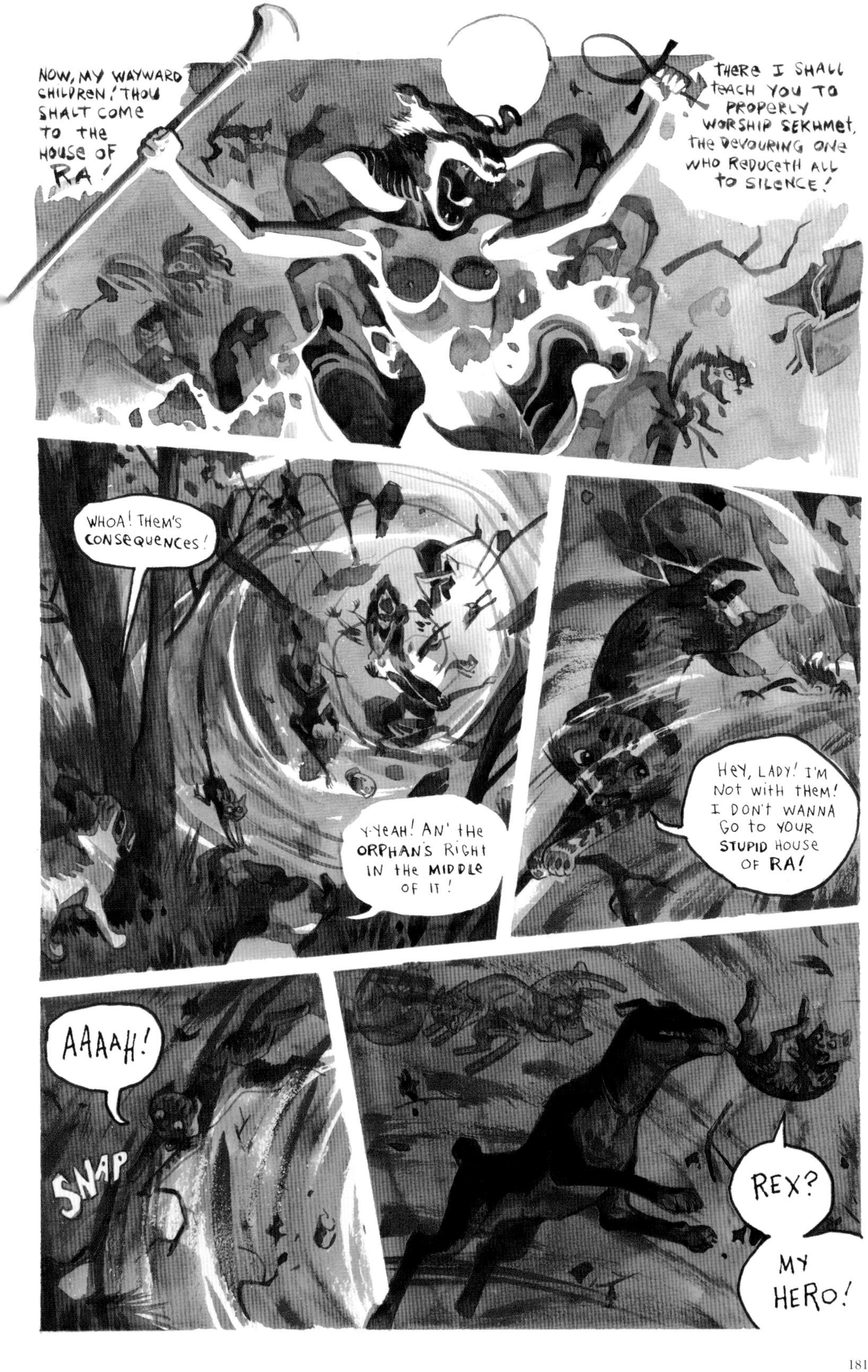
NOW, MY WAYWARD CHILDREN! THOU SHALT COME TO THE HOUSE OF RA!
THERE I SHALL TEACH YOU TO PROPERLY WORSHIP SEKHMET, THE DEVOURING ONE WHO REDUCETH ALL TO SILENCE!
WHOA! THEM'S CONSEQUENCES!
Y-YEAH! AN' THE ORPHAN'S RIGHT IN THE MIDDLE OF IT!
HEY, LADY! I'M NOT WITH THEM! I DON'T WANNA GO TO YOUR STUPID HOUSE OF RA!
AAAAH!
SNAP
REX?
MY HERO!

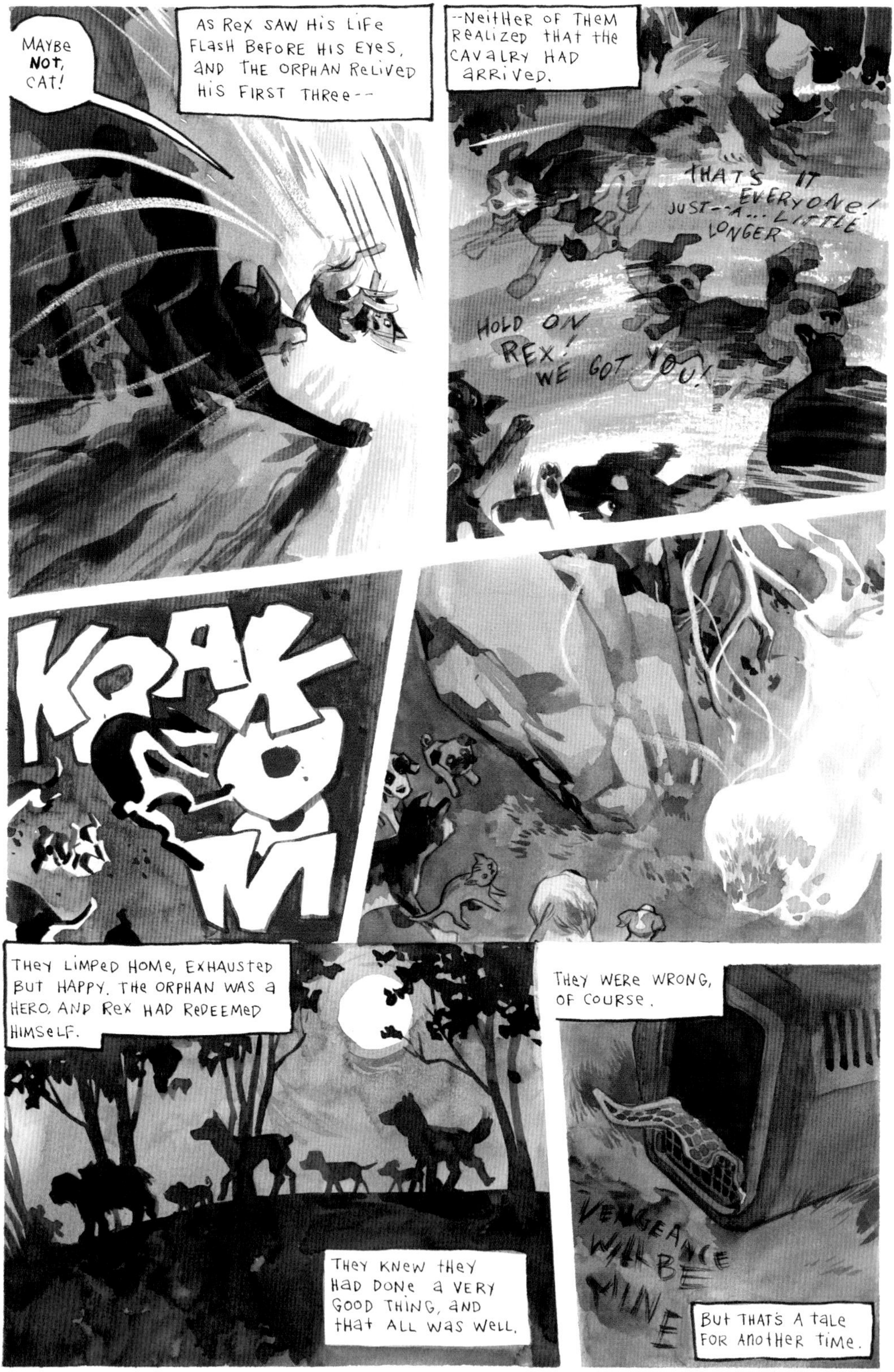
MAYBE NOT, CAT!
AS REX SAW HIS LIFE FLASH BEFORE HIS EYES, AND THE ORPHAN RELIVED HIS FIRST THREE--
--NEITHER OF THEM REALIZED THAT THE CAVALRY HAD ARRIVED.
THAT'S IT EVERYONE! JUST--A...LITTLE LONGER
HOLD ON REX! WE GOT YOU!
THEY LIMPED HOME, EXHAUSTED BUT HAPPY. THE ORPHAN WAS A HERO, AND REX HAD REDEEMED HIMSELF.
THEY KNEW THEY HAD DONE A VERY GOOD THING, AND THAT ALL WAS WELL.
THEY WERE WRONG, OF COURSE.
VENGEANCE WILL BE MINE
BUT THAT'S A TALE FOR ANOTHER TIME.

THE END

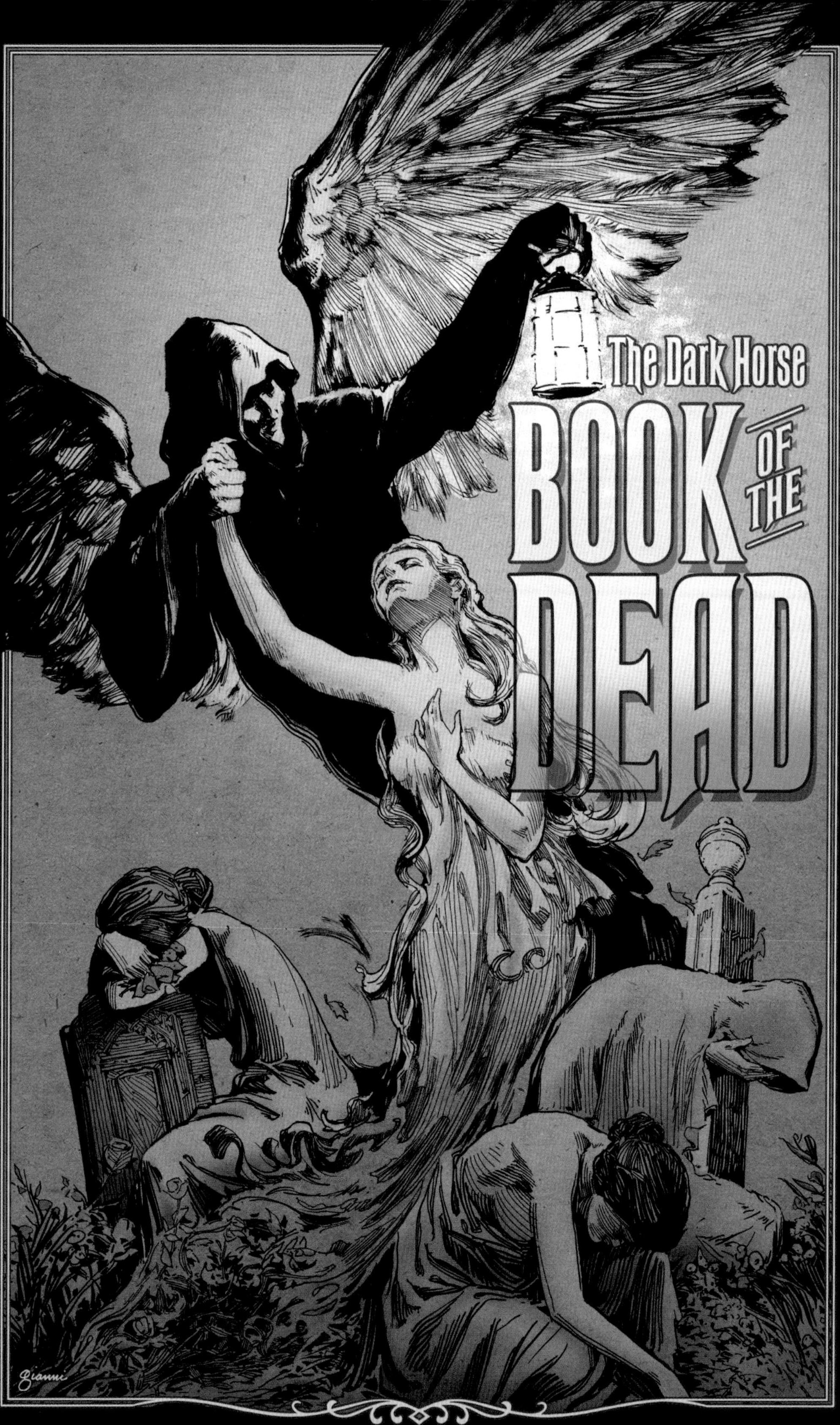
The Dark Horse
BOOK OF THE DEAD
Gianni

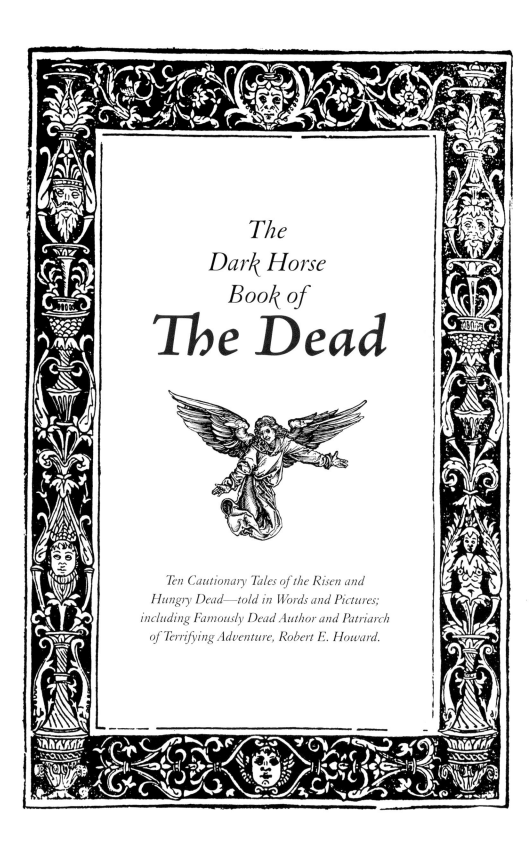

The
Dark Horse
Book of

The Dead

Ten Cautionary Tales of the Risen and
Hungry Dead—told in Words and Pictures;
including Famously Dead Author and Patriarch
of Terrifying Adventure, Robert E. Howard.

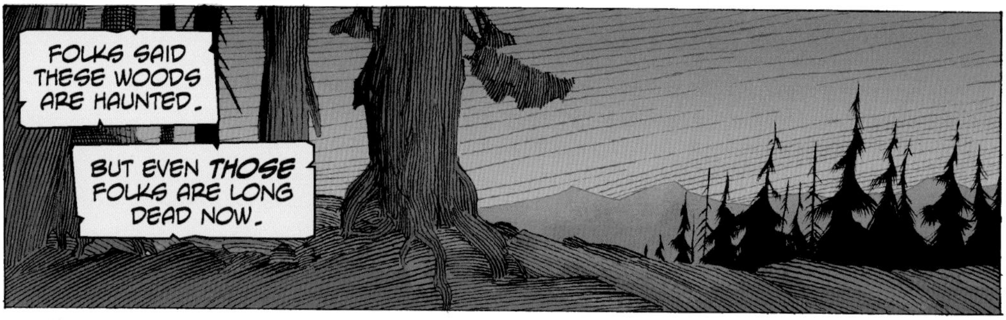
FOLKS SAID THESE WOODS ARE HAUNTED.
BUT EVEN THOSE FOLKS ARE LONG DEAD NOW.

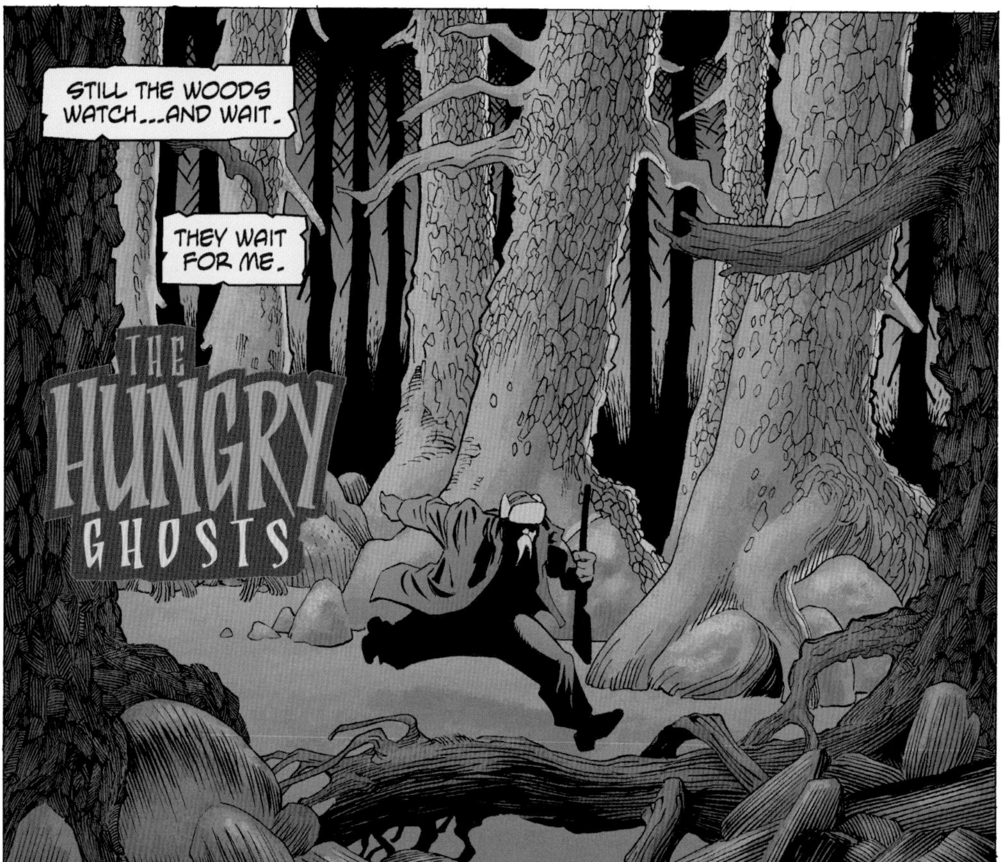
STILL THE WOODS WATCH...AND WAIT.
THEY WAIT FOR ME.
THE HUNGRY GHOSTS

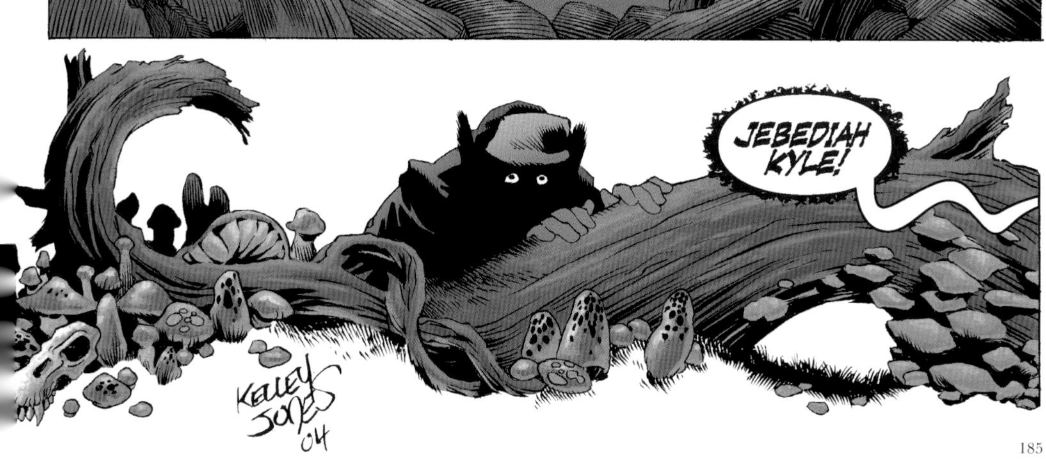
JEBEDIAH KYLE!
KELLEY JONES '04

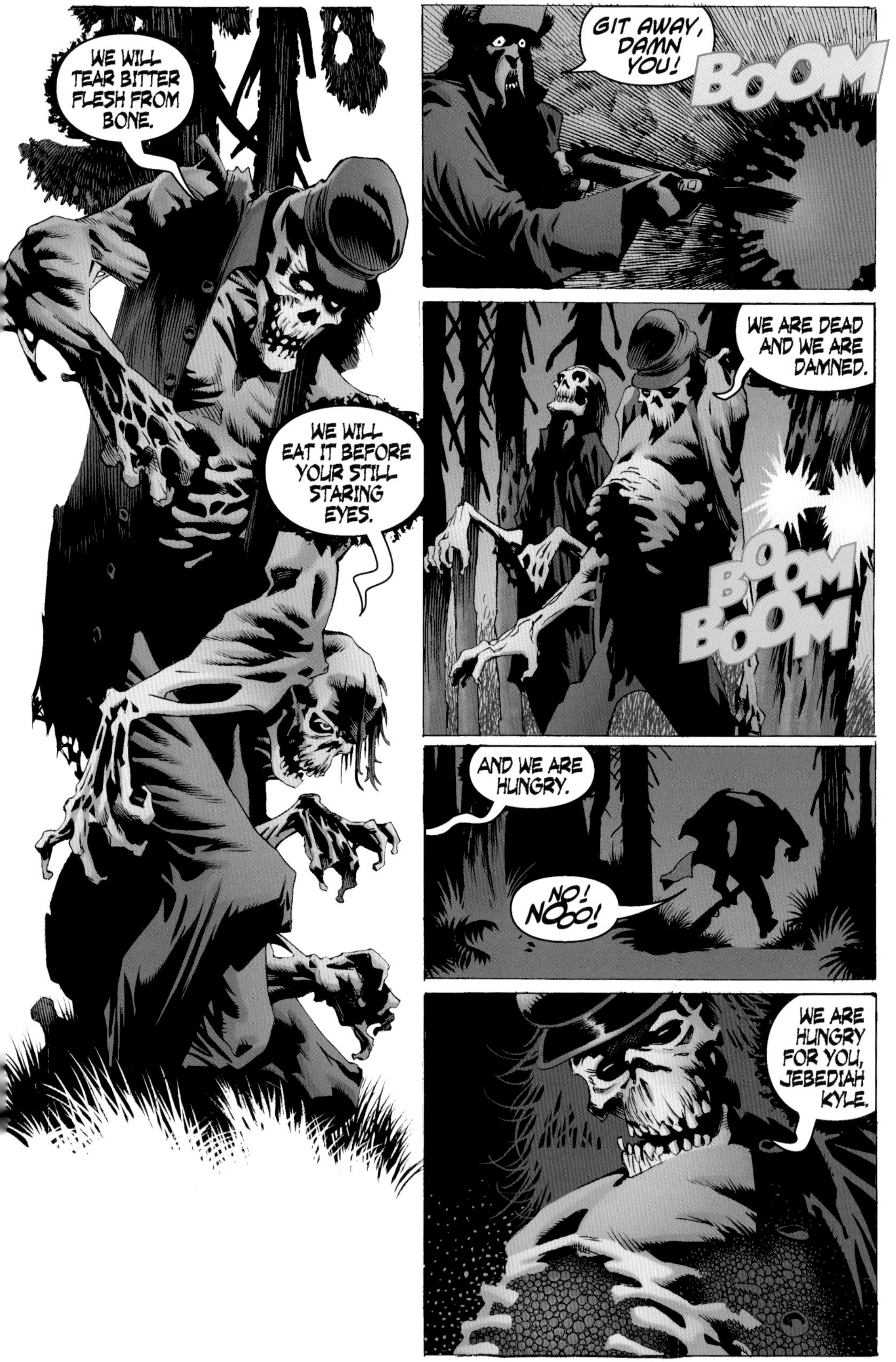
WE WILL TEAR BITTER FLESH FROM BONE.
WE WILL EAT IT BEFORE YOUR STILL STARING EYES.
GIT AWAY, DAMN YOU!
BOOM
WE ARE DEAD AND WE ARE DAMNED.
BOOM
BOOM
AND WE ARE HUNGRY.
NO! NOOO!
WE ARE HUNGRY FOR YOU, JEBEDIAH KYLE.

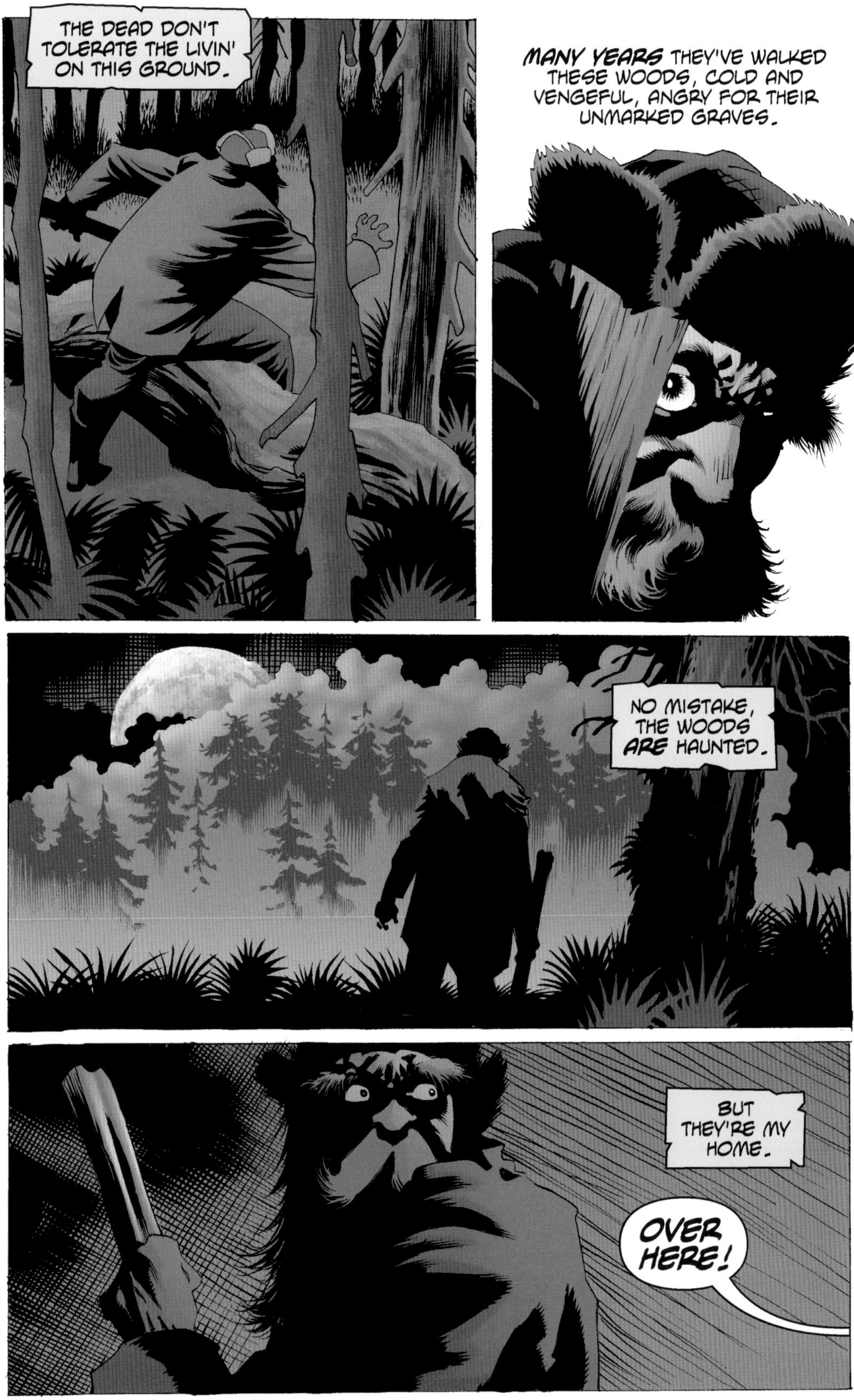
THE DEAD DON'T TOLERATE THE LIVIN' ON THIS GROUND.
MANY YEARS THEY'VE WALKED THESE WOODS, COLD AND VENGEFUL, ANGRY FOR THEIR UNMARKED GRAVES.
NO MISTAKE, THE WOODS ARE HAUNTED.
BUT THEY'RE MY HOME.
OVER HERE!

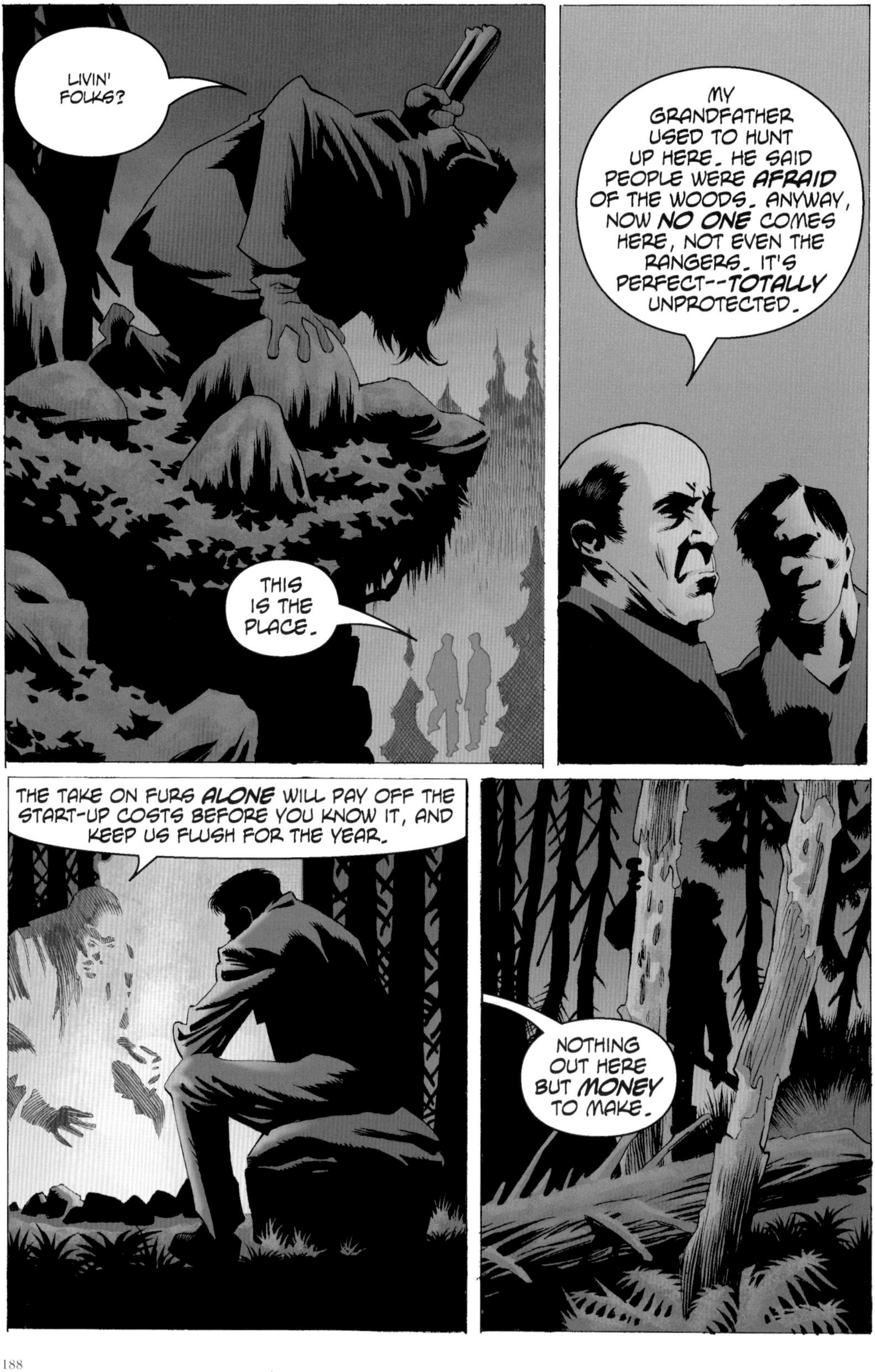
LIVIN' FOLKS?
THIS IS THE PLACE.
MY GRANDFATHER USED TO HUNT UP HERE. HE SAID PEOPLE WERE AFRAID OF THE WOODS. ANYWAY, NOW NO ONE COMES HERE, NOT EVEN THE RANGERS. IT'S PERFECT--TOTALLY UNPROTECTED.
THE TAKE ON FURS ALONE WILL PAY OFF THE START-UP COSTS BEFORE YOU KNOW IT, AND KEEP US FLUSH FOR THE YEAR.
NOTHING OUT HERE BUT MONEY TO MAKE.

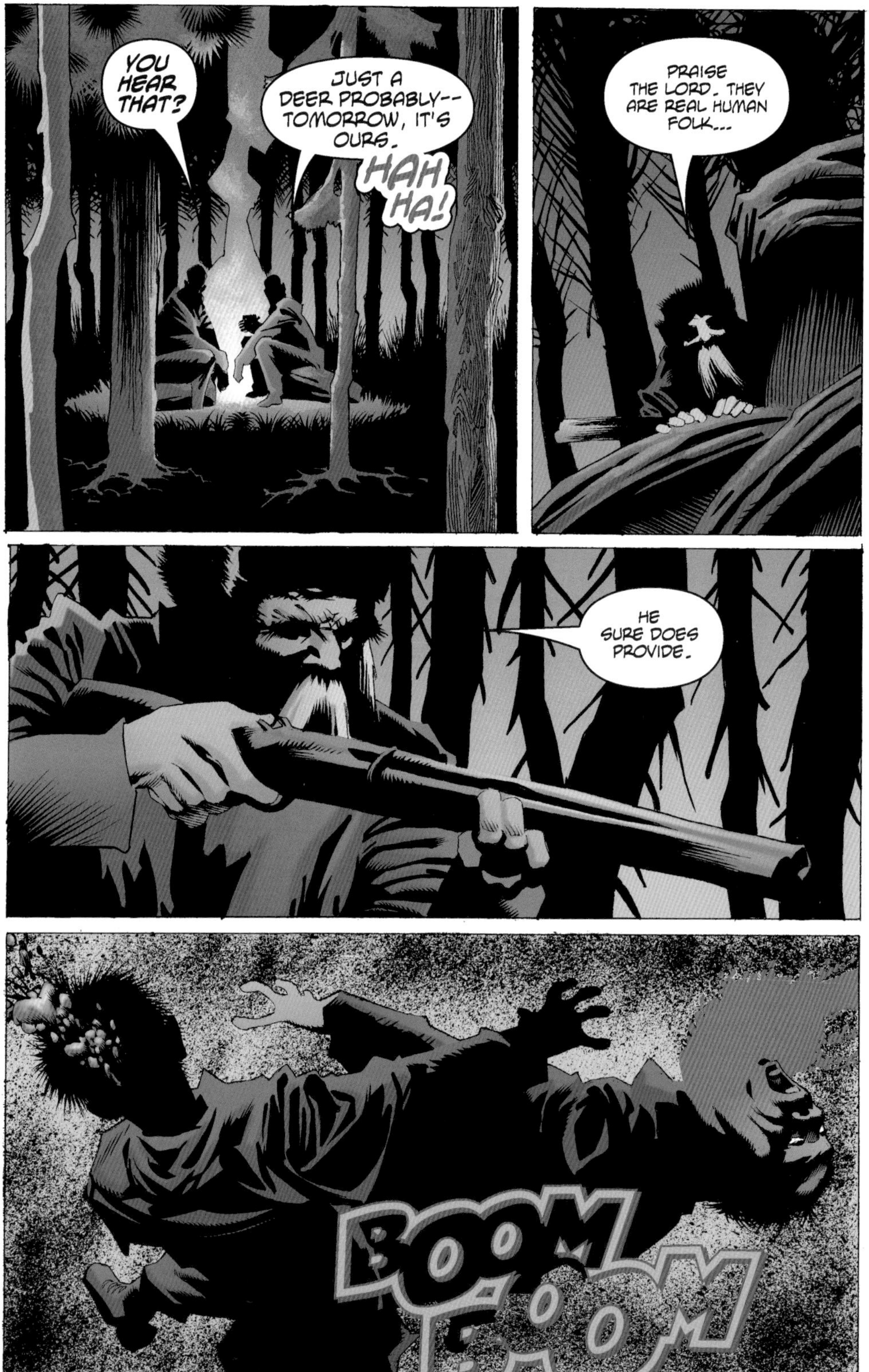
YOU HEAR THAT?
JUST A DEER PROBABLY-- TOMORROW, IT'S OURS.
HAH HA!
PRAISE THE LORD. THEY ARE REAL HUMAN FOLK...
HE SURE DOES PROVIDE.
BOOM
BOOM

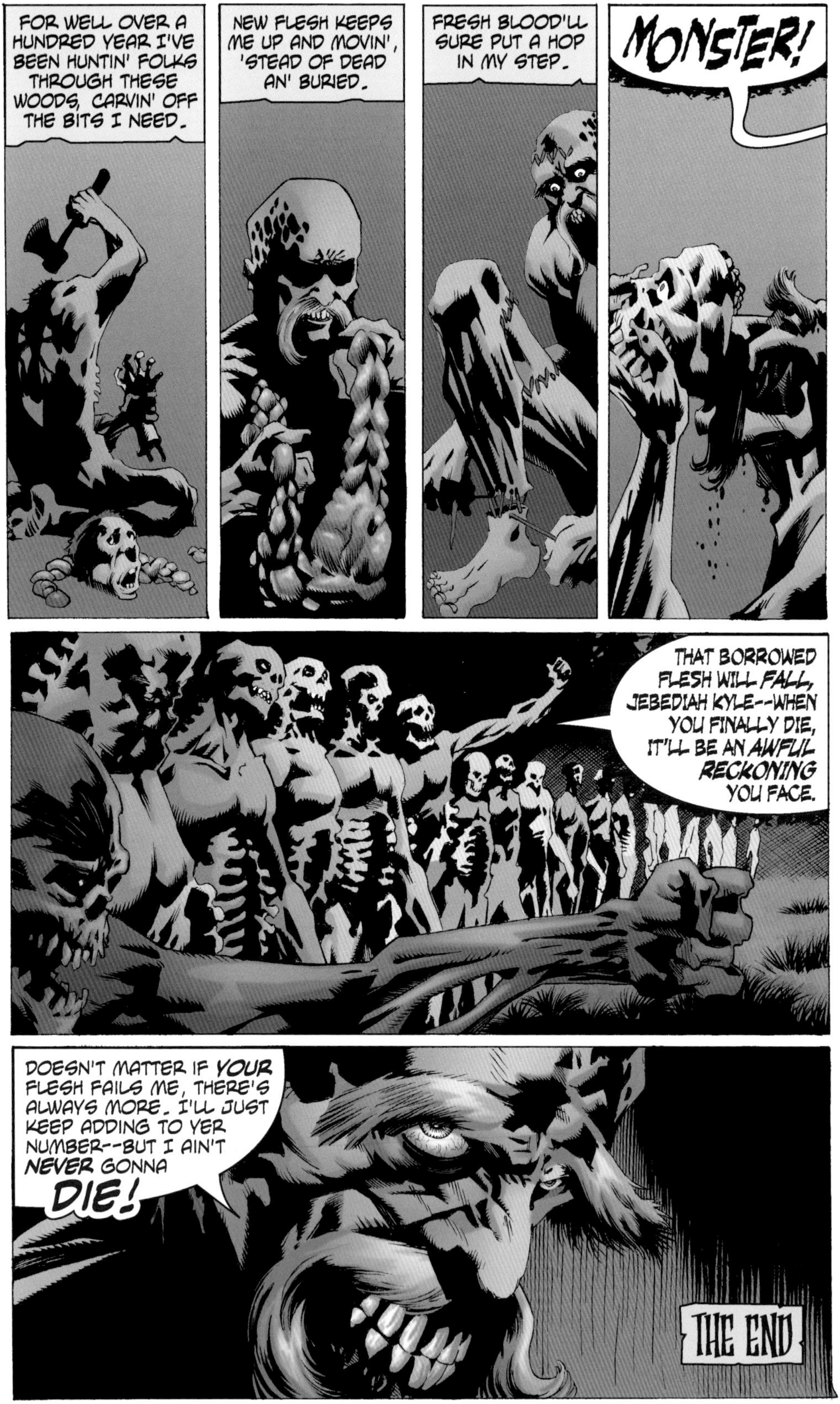
FOR WELL OVER A HUNDRED YEAR I'VE BEEN HUNTIN' FOLKS THROUGH THESE WOODS, CARVIN' OFF THE BITS I NEED.
NEW FLESH KEEPS ME UP AND MOVIN', 'STEAD OF DEAD AN' BURIED.
FRESH BLOOD'LL SURE PUT A HOP IN MY STEP.
MONSTER!
THAT BORROWED FLESH WILL FALL, JEBEDIAH KYLE--WHEN YOU FINALLY DIE, IT'LL BE AN AWFUL RECKONING YOU FACE.
DOESN'T MATTER IF YOUR FLESH FAILS ME, THERE'S ALWAYS MORE. I'LL JUST KEEP ADDING TO YER NUMBER--BUT I AIN'T NEVER GONNA DIE!
THE END

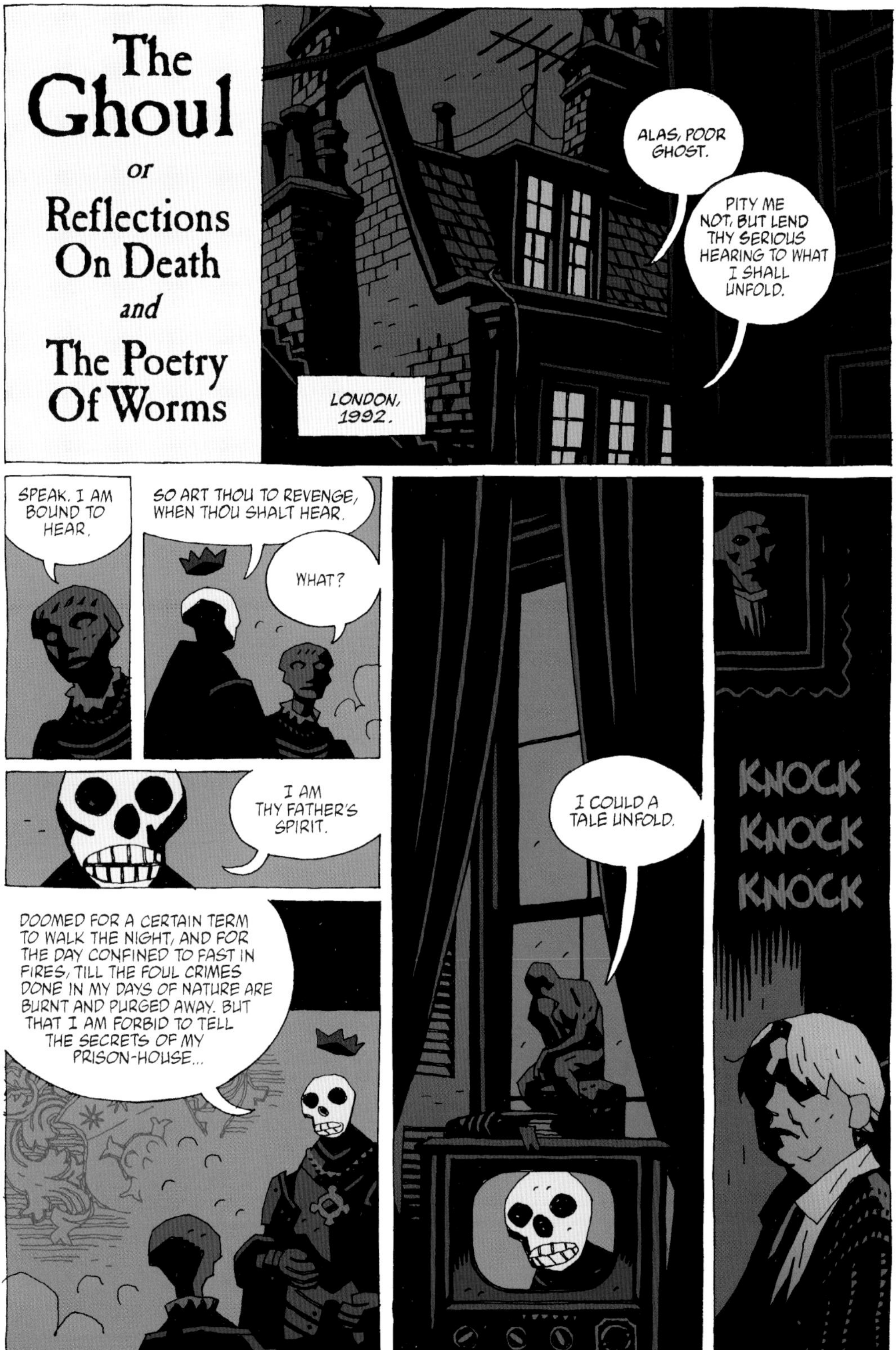
The Ghoul or Reflections On Death and The Poetry Of Worms
LONDON, 1992.
ALAS, POOR GHOST.
PITY ME NOT, BUT LEND THY SERIOUS HEARING TO WHAT I SHALL UNFOLD.
SPEAK. I AM BOUND TO HEAR.
SO ART THOU TO REVENGE, WHEN THOU SHALT HEAR.
WHAT?
I AM THY FATHER'S SPIRIT.
DOOMED FOR A CERTAIN TERM TO WALK THE NIGHT, AND FOR THE DAY CONFINED TO FAST IN FIRES, TILL THE FOUL CRIMES DONE IN MY DAYS OF NATURE ARE BURNT AND PURGED AWAY. BUT THAT I AM FORBID TO TELL THE SECRETS OF MY PRISON-HOUSE...
I COULD A TALE UNFOLD.
KNOCK KNOCK KNOCK

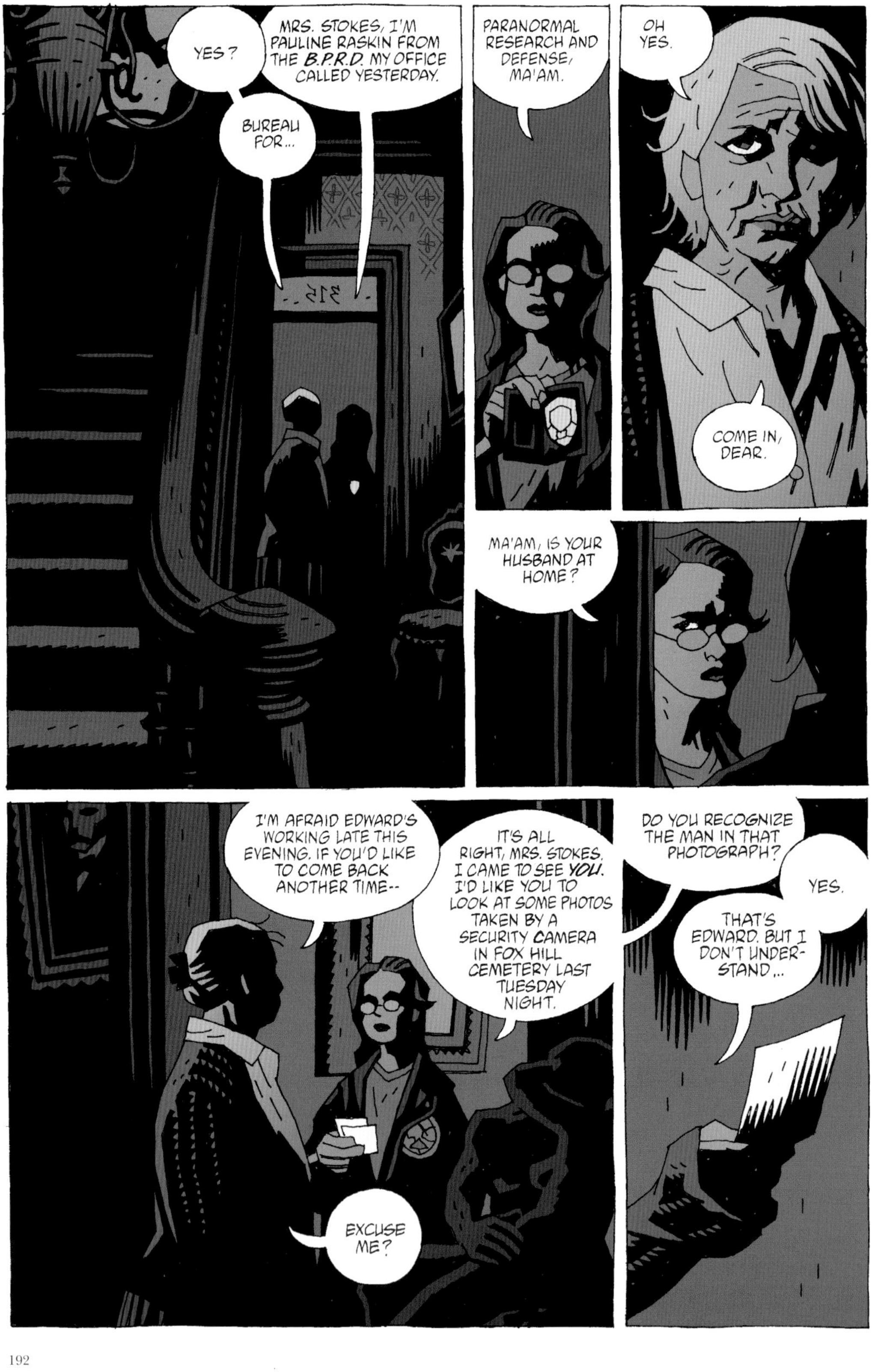
YES?
MRS. STOKES, I'M PAULINE RASKIN FROM THE B.P.R.D. MY OFFICE CALLED YESTERDAY.
BUREAU FOR...
PARANORMAL RESEARCH AND DEFENSE, MA'AM.
OH YES.
COME IN, DEAR.
MA'AM, IS YOUR HUSBAND AT HOME?
I'M AFRAID EDWARD'S WORKING LATE THIS EVENING. IF YOU'D LIKE TO COME BACK ANOTHER TIME--
IT'S ALL RIGHT, MRS. STOKES. I CAME TO SEE YOU. I'D LIKE YOU TO LOOK AT SOME PHOTOS TAKEN BY A SECURITY CAMERA IN FOX HILL CEMETERY LAST TUESDAY NIGHT.
EXCUSE ME?
DO YOU RECOGNIZE THE MAN IN THAT PHOTOGRAPH?
YES.
THAT'S EDWARD. BUT I DON'T UNDER-STAND...

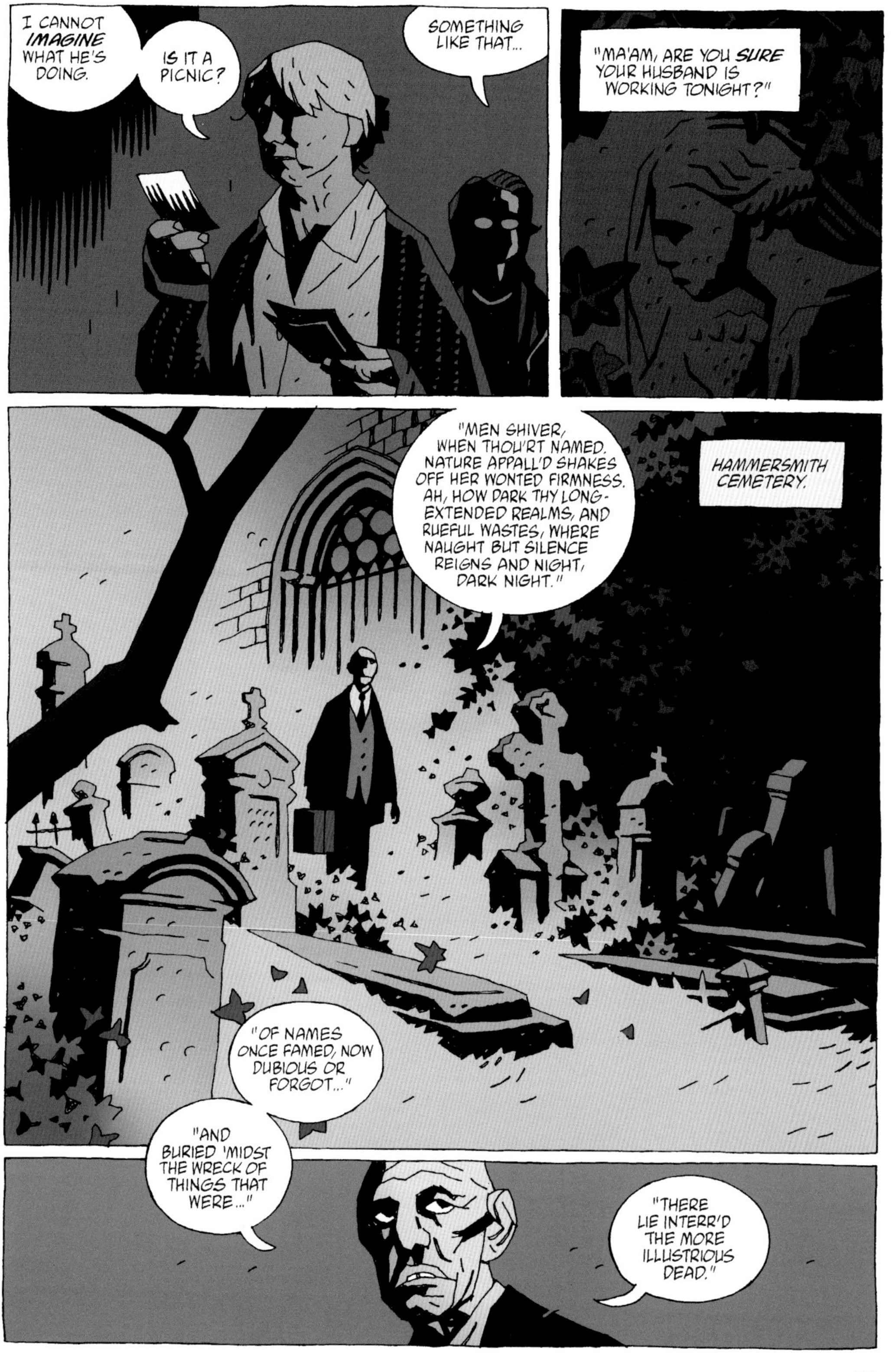
I CANNOT IMAGINE WHAT HE'S DOING.
IS IT A PICNIC?
SOMETHING LIKE THAT...
"MA'AM, ARE YOU SURE YOUR HUSBAND IS WORKING TONIGHT?"
"MEN SHIVER, WHEN THOU'RT NAMED. NATURE APPALL'D SHAKES OFF HER WONTED FIRMNESS. AH, HOW DARK THY LONG-EXTENDED REALMS, AND RUEFUL WASTES, WHERE NAUGHT BUT SILENCE REIGNS AND NIGHT, DARK NIGHT."
HAMMERSMITH CEMETERY.
"OF NAMES ONCE FAMED, NOW DUBIOUS OR FORGOT..."
"AND BURIED 'MIDST THE WRECK OF THINGS THAT WERE..."
"THERE LIE INTERR'D THE MORE ILLUSTRIOUS DEAD."

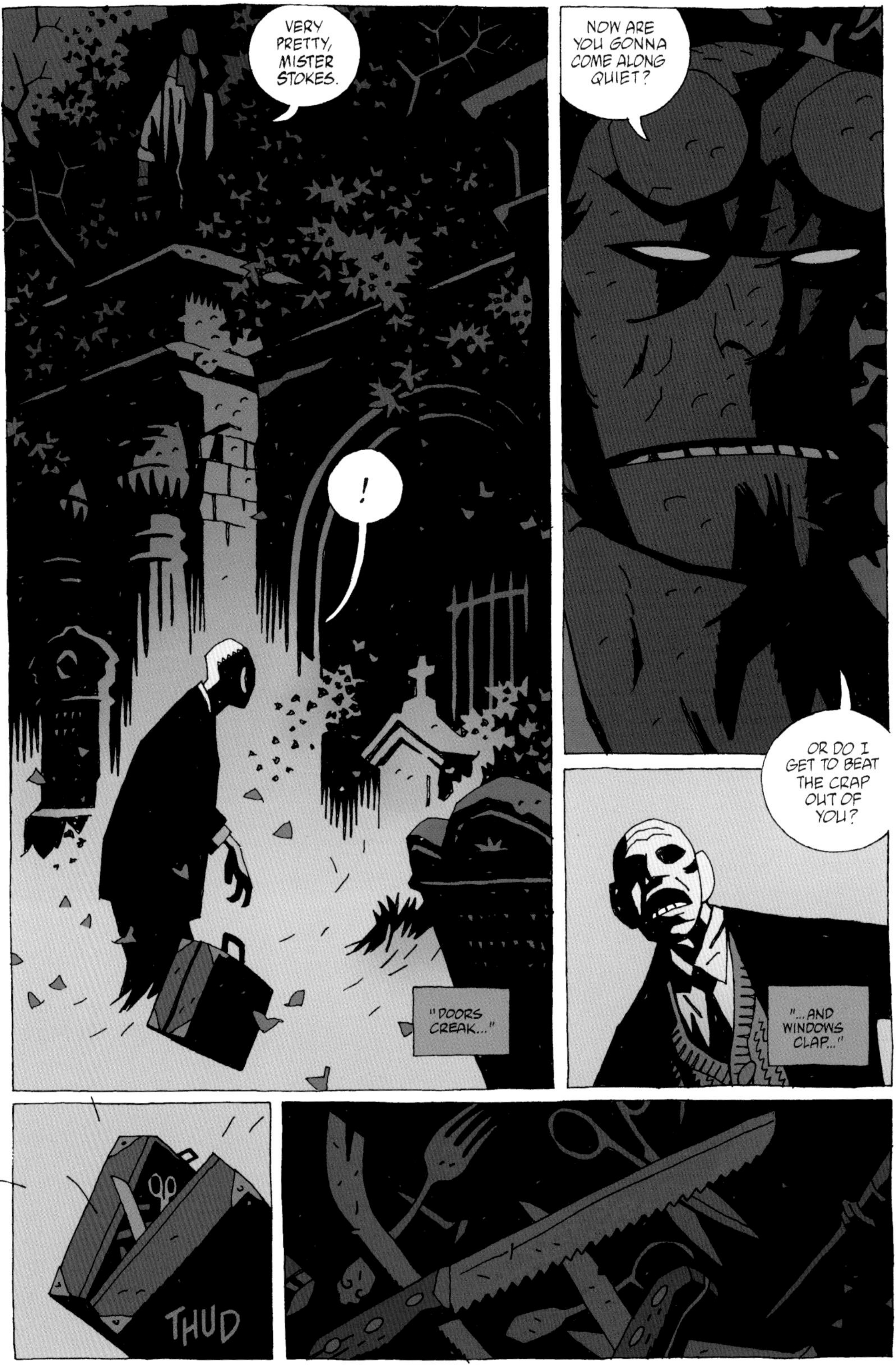
VERY PRETTY, MISTER STOKES.
!
"DOORS CREAK..."
NOW ARE YOU GONNA COME ALONG QUIET?
OR DO I GET TO BEAT THE CRAP OUT OF YOU?
"...AND WINDOWS CLAP..."
THUD

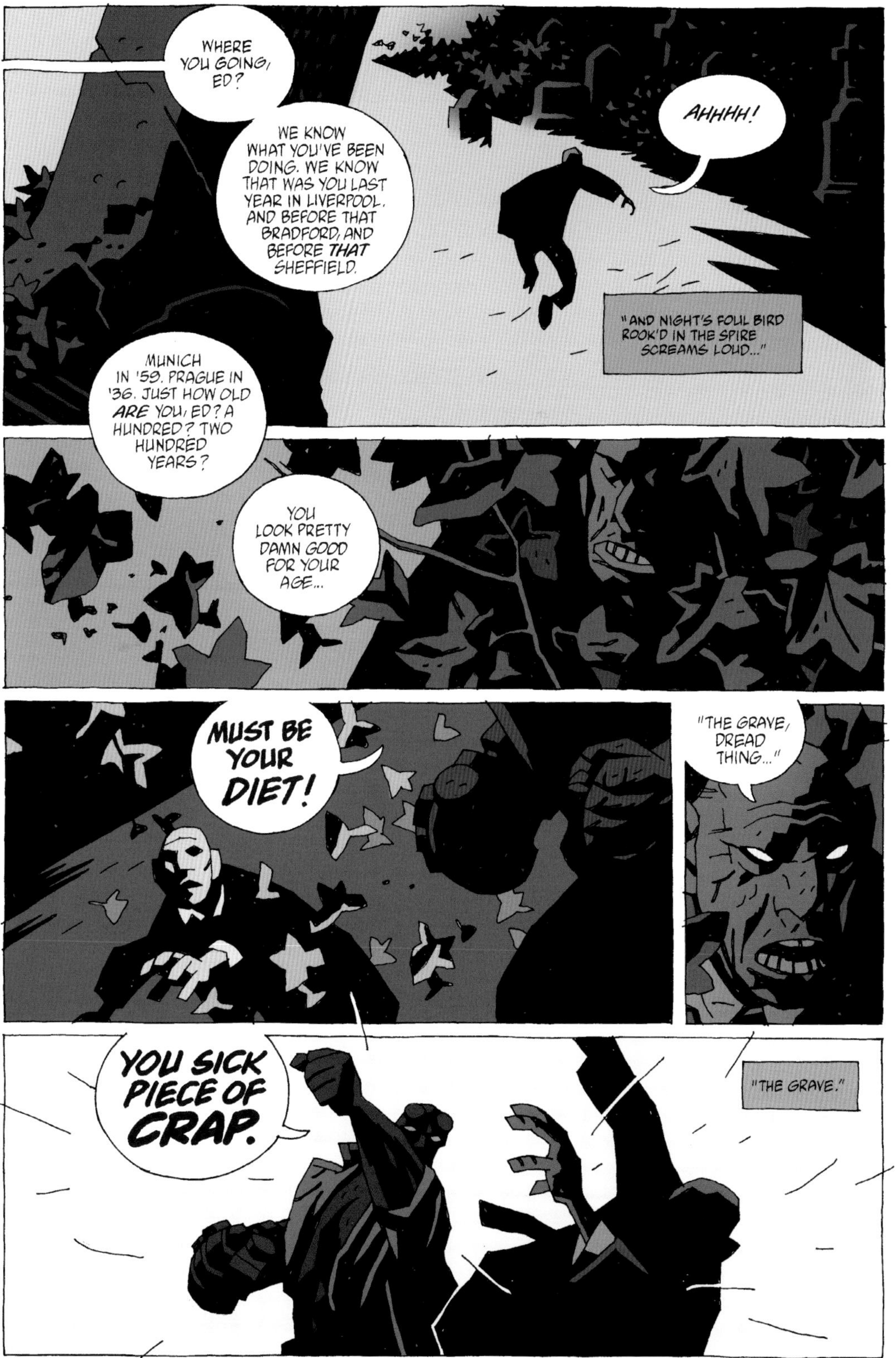
WHERE YOU GOING, ED?
WE KNOW WHAT YOU'VE BEEN DOING. WE KNOW THAT WAS YOU LAST YEAR IN LIVERPOOL. AND BEFORE THAT BRADFORD, AND BEFORE THAT SHEFFIELD.
AHHHH!
"AND NIGHT'S FOUL BIRD ROOK'D IN THE SPIRE SCREAMS LOUD..."
MUNICH IN '59. PRAGUE IN '36. JUST HOW OLD ARE YOU, ED? A HUNDRED? TWO HUNDRED YEARS?
YOU LOOK PRETTY DAMN GOOD FOR YOUR AGE...
MUST BE YOUR DIET!
"THE GRAVE, DREAD THING..."
YOU SICK PIECE OF CRAP.
"THE GRAVE."

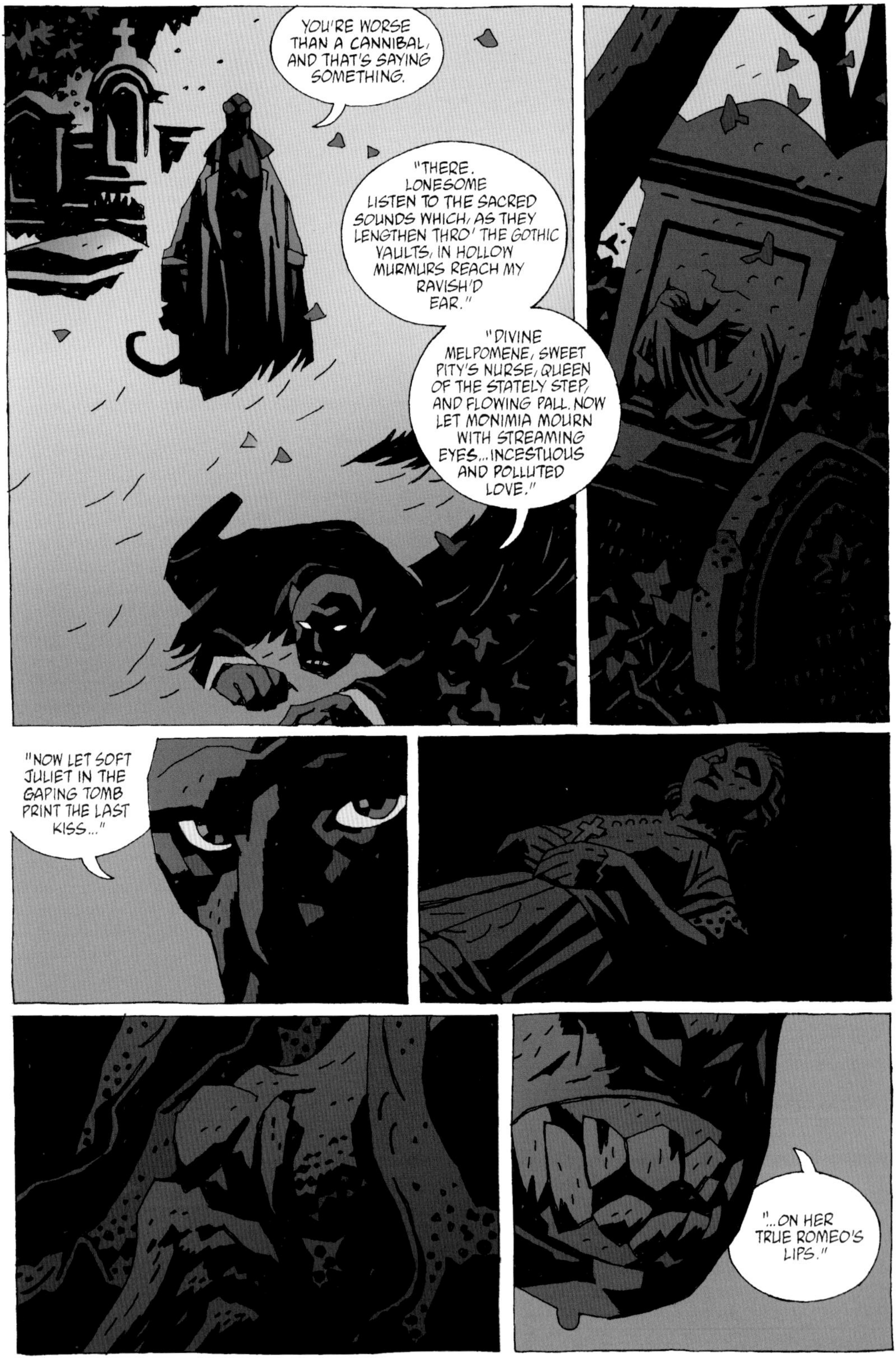
YOU'RE WORSE THAN A CANNIBAL, AND THAT'S SAYING SOMETHING.
"THERE. LONESOME LISTEN TO THE SACRED SOUNDS WHICH, AS THEY LENGTHEN THRO' THE GOTHIC VAULTS, IN HOLLOW MURMURS REACH MY RAVISH'D EAR."
"DIVINE MELPOMENE, SWEET PITY'S NURSE, QUEEN OF THE STATELY STEP, AND FLOWING PALL. NOW LET MONIMIA MOURN WITH STREAMING EYES...INCESTUOUS AND POLLUTED LOVE."
"NOW LET SOFT JULIET IN THE GAPING TOMB PRINT THE LAST KISS..."
"...ON HER TRUE ROMEO'S LIPS."

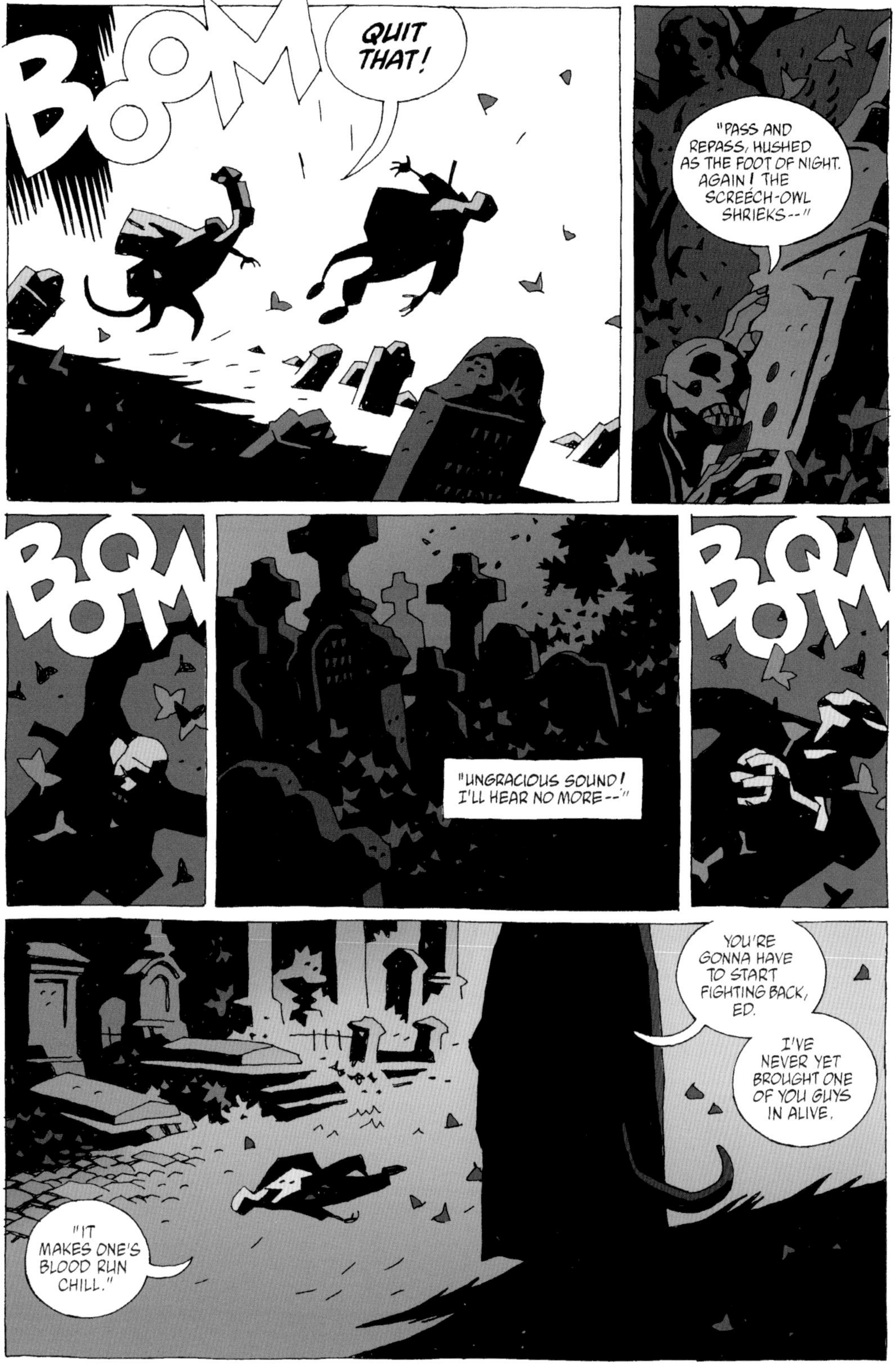
BOOM
QUIT THAT!
"PASS AND REPASS, HUSHED AS THE FOOT OF NIGHT. AGAIN! THE SCREECH-OWL SHRIEKS--"
BOOM
"UNGRACIOUS SOUND! I'LL HEAR NO MORE--"
BOOM
YOU'RE GONNA HAVE TO START FIGHTING BACK, ED.
I'VE NEVER YET BROUGHT ONE OF YOU GUYS IN ALIVE.
"IT MAKES ONE'S BLOOD RUN CHILL."

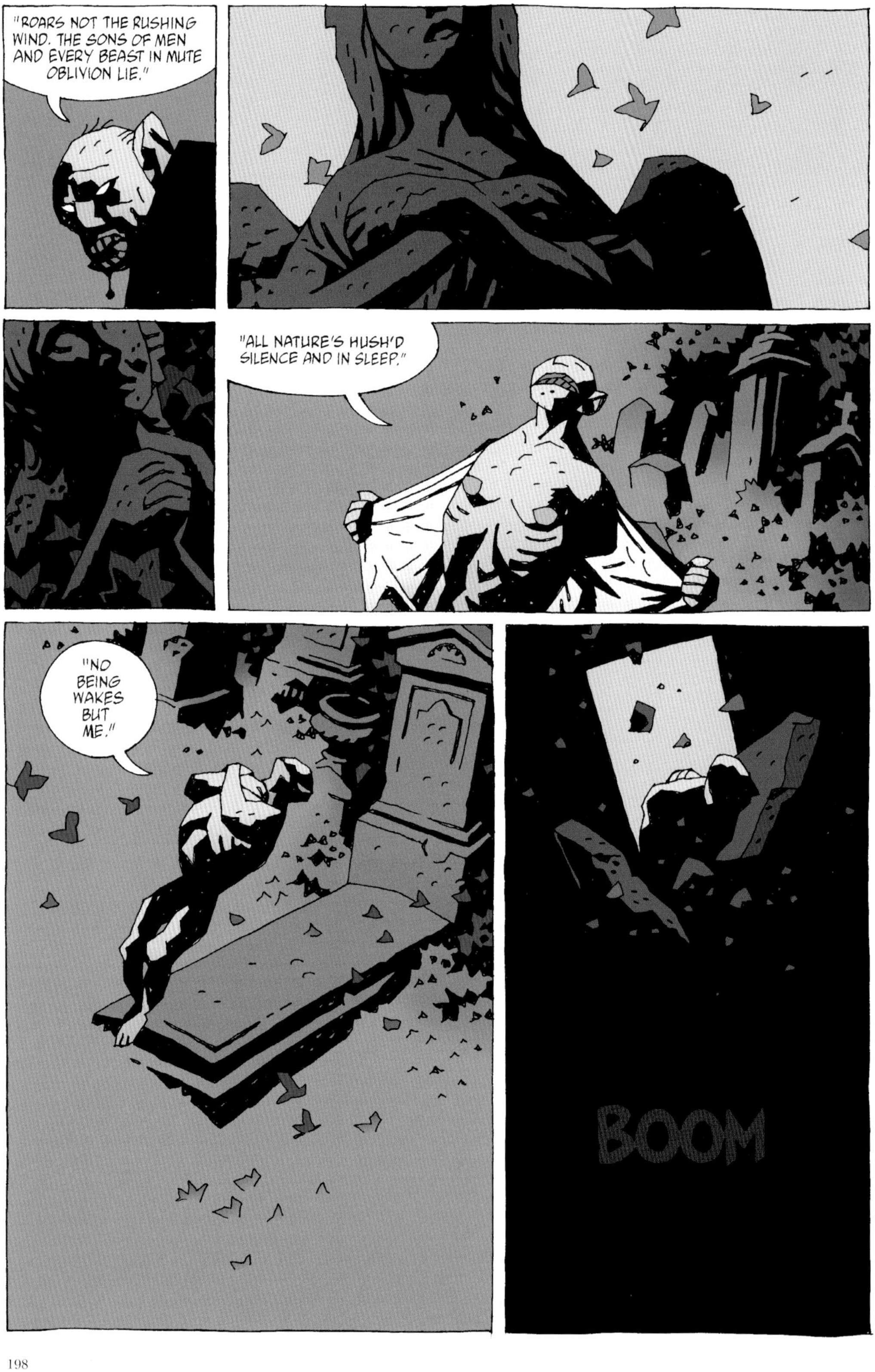
"ROARS NOT THE RUSHING WIND. THE SONS OF MEN AND EVERY BEAST IN MUTE OBLIVION LIE."
"ALL NATURE'S HUSH'D SILENCE AND IN SLEEP."
"NO BEING WAKES BUT ME."
BOOM

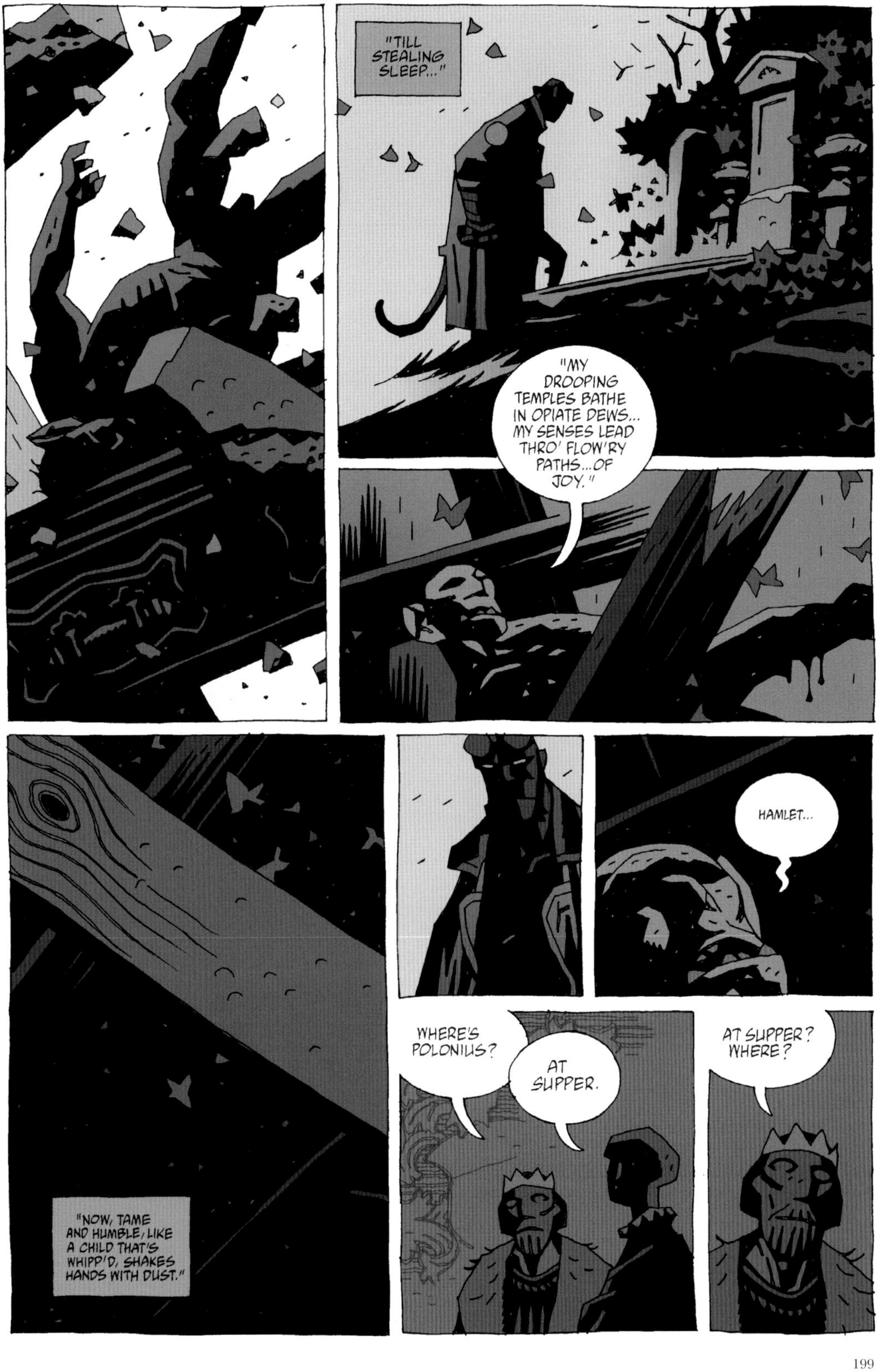
"TILL STEALING SLEEP..."
"MY DROOPING TEMPLES BATHE IN OPIATE DEWS... MY SENSES LEAD THRO' FLOW'RY PATHS...OF JOY."
HAMLET...
"NOW, TAME AND HUMBLE, LIKE A CHILD THAT'S WHIPP'D, SHAKES HANDS WITH DUST."
WHERE'S POLONIUS?
AT SUPPER.
AT SUPPER? WHERE?

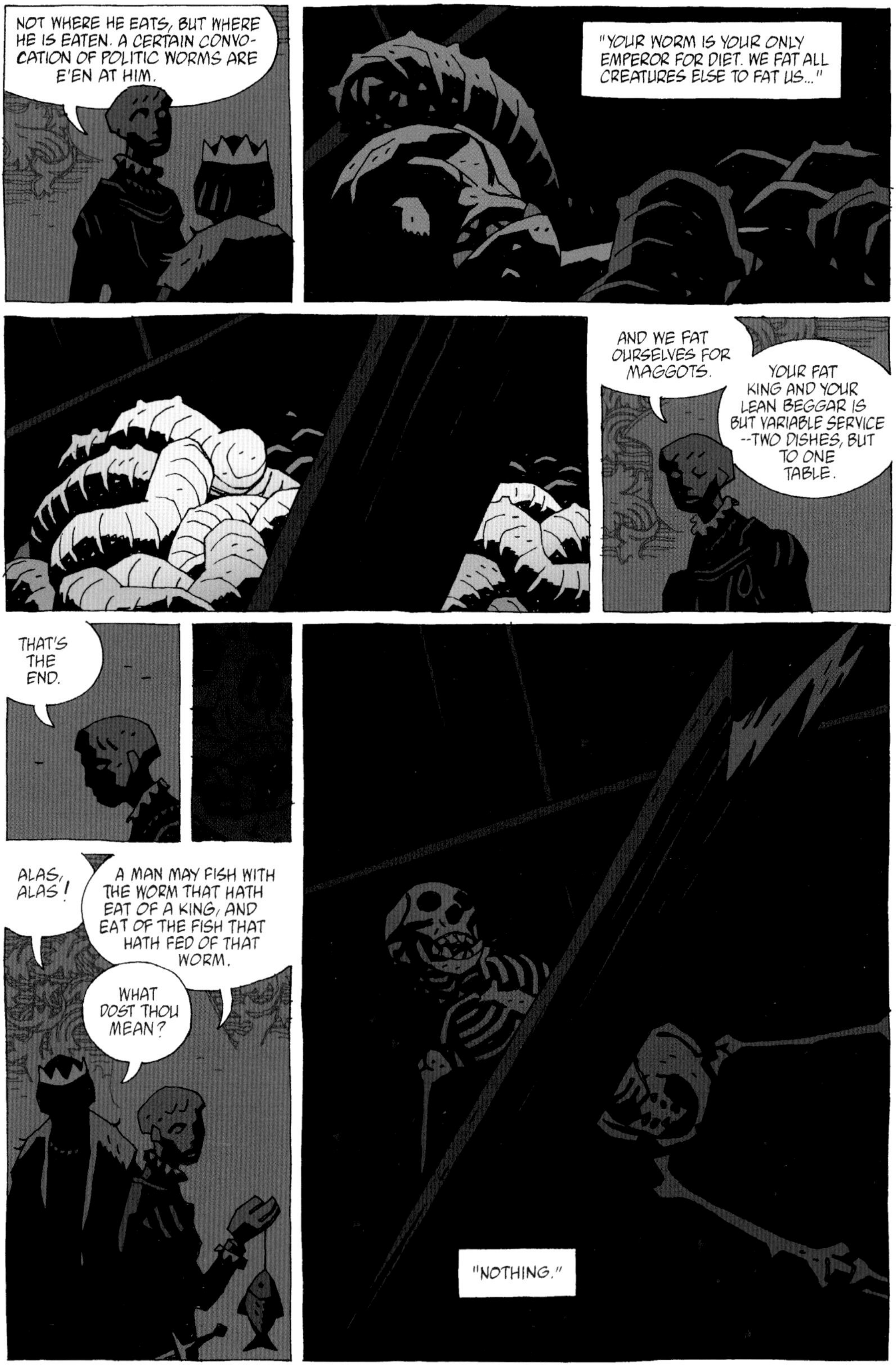
NOT WHERE HE EATS, BUT WHERE HE IS EATEN. A CERTAIN CONVOCATION OF POLITIC WORMS ARE E'EN AT HIM.
"YOUR WORM IS YOUR ONLY EMPEROR FOR DIET. WE FAT ALL CREATURES ELSE TO FAT US..."
AND WE FAT OURSELVES FOR MAGGOTS.
YOUR FAT KING AND YOUR LEAN BEGGAR IS BUT VARIABLE SERVICE --TWO DISHES, BUT TO ONE TABLE.
THAT'S THE END.
ALAS, ALAS!
A MAN MAY FISH WITH THE WORM THAT HATH EAT OF A KING, AND EAT OF THE FISH THAT HATH FED OF THAT WORM.
WHAT DOST THOU MEAN?
"NOTHING."

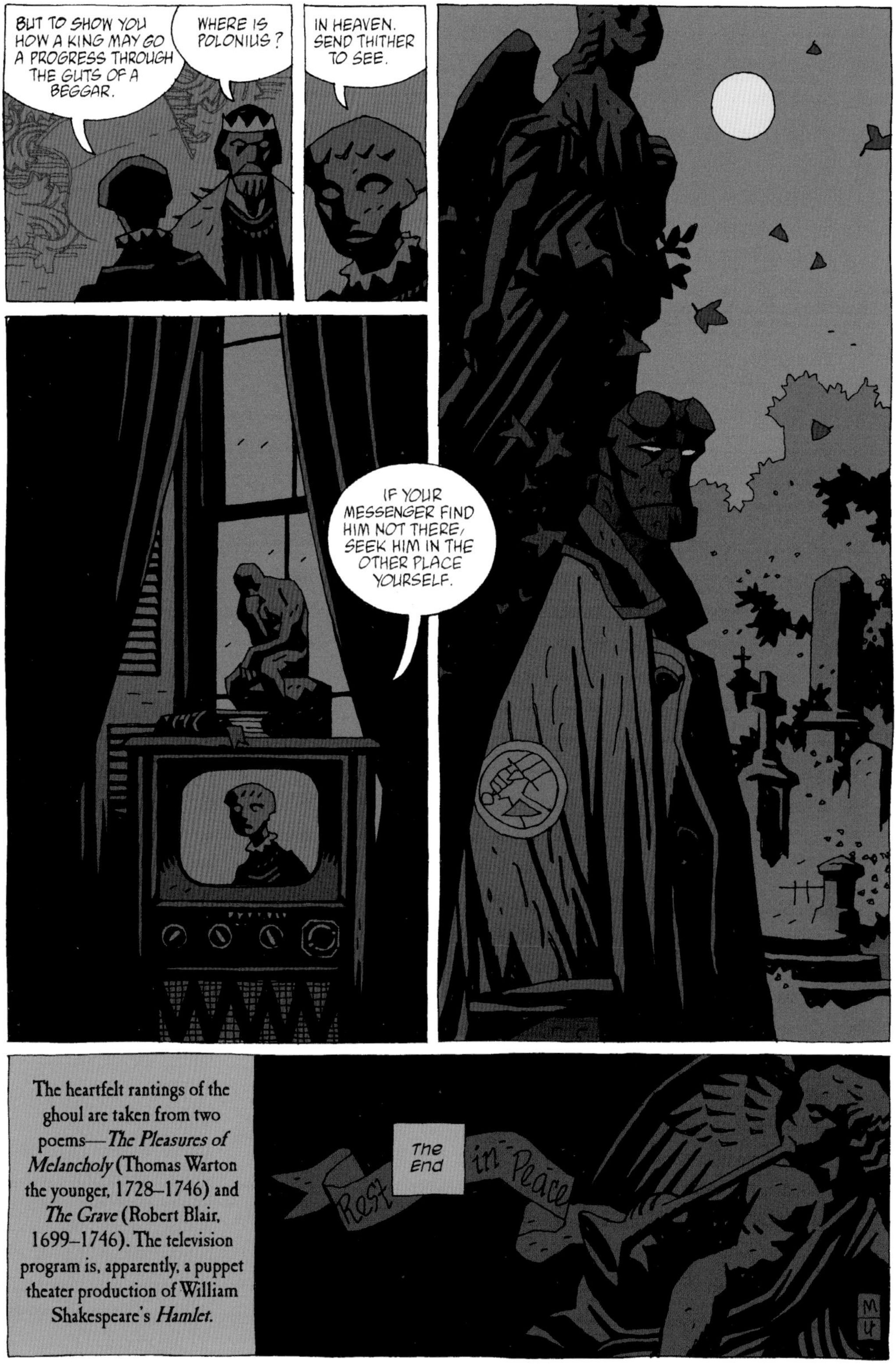
BUT TO SHOW YOU HOW A KING MAY GO A PROGRESS THROUGH THE GUTS OF A BEGGAR.
WHERE IS POLONIUS?
IN HEAVEN. SEND THITHER TO SEE.
IF YOUR MESSENGER FIND HIM NOT THERE, SEEK HIM IN THE OTHER PLACE YOURSELF.
The heartfelt rantings of the ghoul are taken from two poems—*The Pleasures of Melancholy* (Thomas Warton the younger, 1728–1746) and *The Grave* (Robert Blair, 1699–1746). The television program is, apparently, a puppet theater production of William Shakespeare's *Hamlet.*
The End
Rest in Peace

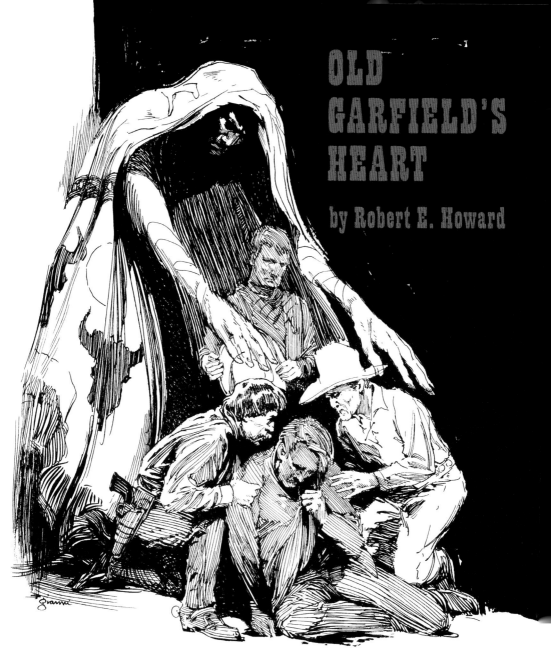

OLD GARFIELD'S HEART

by Robert E. Howard

ILLUSTRATIONS *by* GARY GIANNI

I was sitting on the porch when my grandfather hobbled out and sank
down on his favorite chair with the cushioned seat, and began to stuff
tobacco in his old corncob pipe.

"I thought you'd be goin' to the dance," he said.

"I'm waiting for Doc Blaine," I answered. "I'm going over to old man
Garfield's with him."

My grandfather sucked at his pipe awhile before he spoke again.

"Old Jim purty bad off?"

"Doc says he hasn't a chance."

"Who's takin' care of him?"

"Joe Braxton—against Garfield's wishes. But somebody had to stay with him."

My grandfather sucked his pipe noisily, and watched the heat lightning playing away off up in the hills; then he said: "You think old Jim's the biggest liar in this county, don't you?"

"He tells some pretty tall tales," I admitted. "Some of the things he claimed he took part in, must have happened before he was born."

"I came from Tennessee to Texas in 1870," my grandfather said abruptly. "I saw this town of Lost Knob grow up from nothin'. There wasn't even a log-hut store here when I came. But old Jim Garfield was here, livin' in the same place he lives now, only then it was a log cabin. He didn't look a day older now than he did the first time I saw him."

"You never mentioned that before," I said in some surprise.

"I knew you'd put it down to an old man's maunderin's," he answered. "Old Jim was the first white man to settle in this country. He built his cabin a good fifty miles west of the frontier. God knows how he done it, for these hills swarmed with Comanches then.

"I remember the first time I ever saw him. Even then everybody called him 'old Jim.'

"I remember him tellin' me the same tales he's told you—how he was at the battle of San Jacinto when he was a youngster, and how he'd rode with Ewen Cameron and Jack Hayes. Only I believe him, and you don't."

"That was so long ago—" I protested.

"The last Indian raid through this country was in 1874," said my grandfather, engrossed in his own reminiscences. "I was in on that fight, and so was old Jim. I saw him knock old Yellow Tail off his mustang at seven hundred yards with a buffalo rifle.

"But before that I was with him in a fight up near the head of Locust Creek. A band of Comanches came down Mesquital, lootin' and burnin', rode through the hills and started back up Locust Creek, and a scout of us were hot on their heels. We ran on to them just at sundown in a mesquite flat. We killed seven of them, and the rest skinned out through the brush on foot. But three of our boys were killed, and Jim Garfield got a thrust in the breast with a lance.

"It was an awful wound. He lay like a dead man, and it seemed sure nobody could live after a wound like that. But an old Indian came out of the brush, and when we aimed our guns at him, he made the peace sign and spoke to us in Spanish. I don't know why the boys didn't shoot him in his tracks, because our blood was heated with the fightin' and killin', but

somethin' about him made us hold our fire. He said he wasn't a Comanche, but was an old friend of Garfield's, and wanted to help him. He asked us to carry Jim into a clump of mesquite, and leave him alone with him, and to this day I don't know why we did, but we did. It was an awful time—the wounded moanin' and callin' for water, the starin' corpses strewn about the camp, night comin' on, and no way of knowin' that the Indians wouldn't return when dark fell.

"We made camp right there, because the horses were fagged out, and we watched all night, but the Comanches didn't come back. I don't know what went on out in the mesquite where Jim Garfield's body lay, because I never saw that strange Indian again, but durin' the night I kept hearin' a weird moanin' that wasn't made by the dyin' men, and an owl hooted from midnight till dawn.

"And at sunrise Jim Garfield came walkin' out of the mesquite, pale and haggard, but alive, and already the wound in his breast had closed and begun to heal. And since then he's never mentioned that wound, nor that fight, nor the strange Indian who came and went so mysteriously. And he hasn't aged a bit; he looks now just like he did then—a man of about fifty."

In the silence that followed, a car began to purr down the road, and twin shafts of light cut through the dusk.

"That's Doc Blaine," I said. "When I come back I'll tell you how Garfield is."

Doc Blaine was prompt with his predictions as we drove the three miles of post oak-covered hills that lay between Lost Knob and the Garfield farm.

"I'll be surprised to find him alive," he said, "smashed up like he is. A man his age ought to have more sense than to try to break a young horse."

"He doesn't look so old," I remarked.

"I'll be fifty, my next birthday," answered Doc Blaine. "I've known him all my life, and he must have been at least fifty the first time I ever saw him. His looks are deceiving."

Old Garfield's dwelling place was reminiscent of the past. The boards of the low, squat house had never known paint. Orchard fence and corrals were built of rails.

Old Jim lay on his rude bed, tended crudely but efficiently by the man Doc Blaine had hired over the old man's protests. As I looked at him, I was impressed anew by his evident vitality. His frame was stooped but unwithered, his limbs rounded out with springy muscles. In his corded neck and in his face, drawn though it was with suffering, was apparent an innate virility. His eyes, though partly glazed with pain, burned with the same unquenchable element.

"He's been ravin'," said Joe Braxton stolidly.

"First white man in this country," muttered old Jim, becoming intelligible. "Hills no white man ever set foot in before. Gettin' too old. Have to settle down. Can't move on like I used to. Settle down here. Good country before it filled up with cow-men and squatters. Wish Ewen Cameron could see this country. The Mexicans shot him. Damn 'em!"

Doc Blaine shook his head. "He's all smashed up inside. He won't live till daylight."

Garfield unexpectedly lifted his head and looked at us with clear eyes.

"Wrong, Doc," he wheezed, his breath whistling with pain. "I'll live. What's broken bones and twisted guts? Nothin'! It's the heart that counts. Long as the heart keeps pumpin', a man can't die. My heart's sound. Listen to it! Feel of it!"

He groped painfully for Doc Blaine's wrist, dragged his hand to his bosom and held it there, staring up into the doctor's face with avid intensity.

"Regular dynamo, ain't it?" he gasped. "Stronger'n a gasoline engine!"

Blaine beckoned me. "Lay your hand here," he said, placing my hand on the old man's bare breast. "He does have a remarkable heart action."

I noted, in the light of the coal-oil lamp, a great livid scar as might be made by a flint-headed spear. I laid my hand directly on this scar, and an exclamation escaped my lips.

Under my hand old Jim Garfield's heart pulsed, but its throb was like no other heart action I have ever observed. Its power was astounding; his ribs vibrated to its steady throb. It felt more like the vibrating of a dynamo than the action of a human organ. I could feel its amazing vitality radiating from his breast, stealing up into my hand and up my arm, until my own heart seemed to speed up in response.

"I can't die," old Jim gasped. "Not so long as my heart's in my breast. Only a bullet through the brain can kill me. And even then I wouldn't be rightly dead, as long as my heart beats in my breast. Yet it ain't rightly mine, either. It belongs to Ghost Man, the Lipan chief. It was the heart of a god the Lipans worshipped before the Comanches drove 'em out of their native hills.

"I knew Ghost Man down on the Rio Grande, when I was with Ewen Cameron. I saved his life from the Mexicans once. He tied the string of ghost wampum between him and me—the wampum no man but me and him can see or feel. He came when he knowed I needed him, in that fight up on the headwaters of Locust Creek, when I got this scar.

"I was dead as a man can be. My heart was sliced in two, like the heart of a butchered beef steer.

"All night Ghost Man did magic, callin' my ghost back from spirit-land. I remember that flight, a little. It was dark, and gray-like, and I drifted through gray mists and heard the dead wailin' past me in the mist. But Ghost Man brought me back.

"He took out what was left of my mortal heart, and put the heart of the god in my bosom. But it's his, and when I'm through with it, he'll come for it. It's kept me alive and strong for the lifetime of a man. Age can't touch me. What do I care if these fools around here call me an old liar? What I know, I know. But hark'ee!"

His fingers became claws, clamping fiercely on Doc Blaine's wrist. His old eyes, old yet strangely young, burned fierce as those of an eagle under his bushy brows.

"If by some mischance I *should* die, now or later, promise me this! Cut into my bosom and take out the heart Ghost Man lent me so long ago! It's his. And as long as it beats in my body, my spirit'll be tied to that body, though my head be crushed like an egg underfoot! A livin' thing in a rottin' body! Promise!"

"All right, I promise," replied Doc Blaine, to humor him, and old Jim Garfield sank back with a whistling sigh of relief.

He did not die that night, nor the next, nor the next. I well remember the next day, because it was that day that I had the fight with Jack Kirby.

People will take a good deal from a bully, rather than to spill blood. Because nobody had gone to the trouble of killing him, Kirby thought the whole countryside was afraid of him.

He had bought a steer from my father, and when my father went to collect for it, Kirby told him that he had paid the money to me—which was a lie. I went looking for Kirby, and came upon him in a bootleg joint, boasting of his toughness, and telling the crowd that he was going to beat me up and

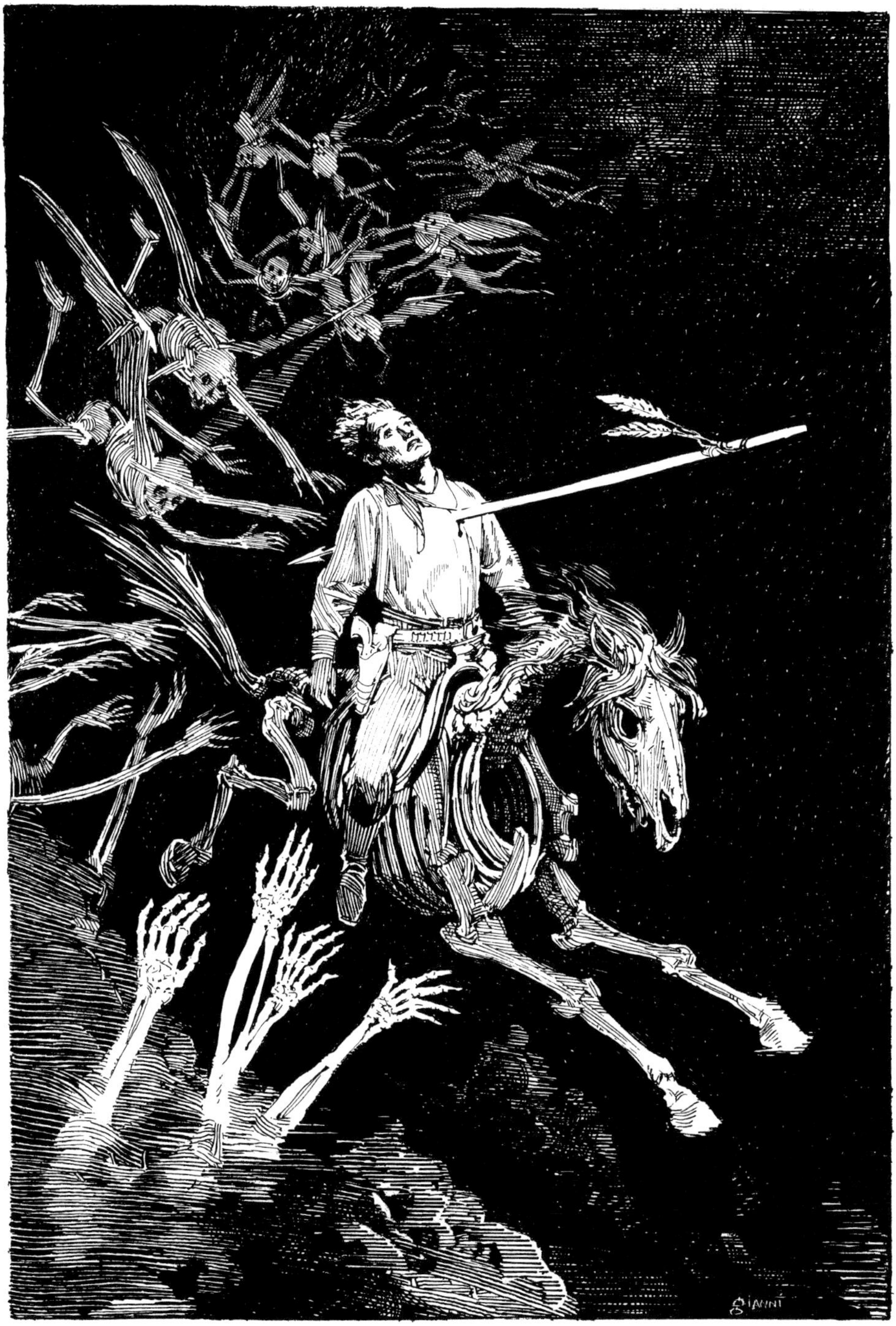
GIANNI

make me say that he had paid me the money, and that I had stuck it into my own pocket. When I heard him say that, I saw red, and ran in on him with a stockman's knife, and cut him across the face, and in the neck, side, breast and belly, and the only thing that saved his life was the fact that the crowd pulled me off.

There was a preliminary hearing, and I was indicted on a charge of assault, and my trial was set for the following term of court. Kirby was as tough-fibered as a post-oak, country bully ought to be, and he recovered, swearing vengeance, for he was vain of his looks, though God knows why, and I had permanently impaired them.

And while Jack Kirby was recovering, old man Garfield recovered, too, to the amazement of everybody, especially Doc Blaine.

I well remember the night Doc Blaine took me again out to old Jim Garfield's farm. I was in Shifty Corlan's joint, trying to drink enough of the slop he called beer to get a kick out of it, when Doc Blaine came in and persuaded me to go with him.

As we drove along the winding old road in Doc's car, I asked: "Why are you insistent that I go with you this particular night? This isn't a professional call, is it?"

"No," he said. "You couldn't kill old Jim with a post-oak maul. He's completely recovered from injuries that ought to have killed an ox. To tell you the truth, Jack Kirby is in Lost Knob, swearing he'll shoot you on sight."

"Well, for God's sake!" I exclaimed angrily. "Now everybody'll think I left town because I was afraid of him. Turn around and take me back, damn it!"

"Be reasonable," said Doc. "Everybody knows you're not afraid of Kirby. Nobody's afraid of him now. His bluff's broken, and that's why he's so wild against you. But you can't afford to have any more trouble with him now, and your trial only a short time off."

I laughed and said: "Well, if he's looking for me hard enough, he can find me as easily at old Garfield's as in town, because Shifty Corlan heard you say where we were going. And Shifty's hated me ever since I skinned him in that horse swap last fall. He'll tell Kirby where I went."

"I never thought of that," said Doc Blaine, worried.

"Hell, forget it," I advised. "Kirby hasn't got guts enough to do anything but blow."

But I was mistaken. Puncture a bully's vanity and you touch his one vital spot.

Old Jim had not gone to bed when we got there. He was sitting in the room opening on to his sagging porch, the room which was at once living room and bedroom, smoking his old cob pipe and trying to read a newspaper by the light of his coal-oil lamp. All the windows and doors were wide open for the coolness, and the insects which swarmed in and fluttered around the lamp didn't seem to bother him.

We sat down and discussed the weather—which isn't so inane as one might suppose, in a country where a man's livelihood depends on sun and rain, and is at the mercy of wind and drouth. The talk drifted into the other kindred channels, and after some time, Doc Blaine bluntly spoke of something that hung in his mind.

"Jim," he said, "that night I thought you were dying, you babbled a lot of stuff about your heart, and an Indian who lent you his. How much of that was delirium?"

"None, Doc," said Garfield, pulling at his pipe. "It was gospel truth. Ghost Man, the Lipan priest of the Gods of Night, replaced my dead, torn heart with one from somethin' he worshipped. I ain't sure myself just what that somethin' is—somethin' from a way back and a long way off, he said. But bein' a god, it can do without a heart for a while. But when I die—if I ever get my head smashed so my consciousness is destroyed—the heart must be given back to Ghost Man."

"You mean you were in earnest about the cutting out your heart?" demanded Doc Blaine.

"It has to be," answered old Garfield. "A livin' thing in a dead thing is opposed to nat'er. That's what Ghost Man said."

"Who the devil was Ghost Man?"

"I told you. A witch-doctor of the Lipans, who dwelt in this country before the Comanches came down from the Staked Plains and drove 'em south across the Rio Grande. I was a friend to 'em. I reckon Ghost Man is the only one left alive."

"Alive? Now?"

"I dunno," confessed old Jim. "I dunno whether he's alive or dead. I dunno whether he was alive when he came to me after the fight on Locust Creek, or even if he was alive when I knowed him in the southern country. Alive as we understand life, I mean."

"What balderdash is this?" demanded Doc Blaine uneasily, and I felt a slight stirring in my hair. Outside was stillness, and the stars, and the black shadows of the post-oak woods. The lamp cast old Garfield's shadow grotesquely on the wall, so that it did not at all resemble that of a human, and his words were strange as words heard in a nightmare.

"I knowed you wouldn't understand," said old Jim. "I don't understand myself, and I ain't got the words to explain them things I feel and know without understandin'. The Lipans were kin to the Apaches, and the Apaches learnt curious things from the Pueblos. Ghost Man *was*. That's all I can say—alive or dead, I don't know, but he *was*. What's more, he *is*."

"Is it you or me that's crazy?" asked Doc Blaine.

"Well," said old Jim, "I'll tell you this much—Ghost Man knew Coronado."

"Crazy as a loon!" murmured Doc Blaine. Then he lifted his head. "What's that?"

"Horse turning in from the road," I said. "Sounds like it stopped."

I stepped to the door, like a fool, and stood etched in the light behind me. I got a glimpse of a shadowy bulk I knew to be a man on a horse; then Doc Blaine yelled: "Look out!" and threw himself against me, knocking us both sprawling. At the same instant I heard the smashing report of a rifle, and old Garfield grunted and fell heavily.

"Jack Kirby!" screamed Doc Blaine. "He's killed Jim!"

I scrambled up, hearing the clatter of retreating hoofs, snatched old Jim's shotgun from the wall, rushed recklessly out on to the sagging porch and let go both barrels at the fleeing shape, dim in the starlight. The charge was too light to kill at that range, but the bird-shot stung the horse and maddened him. He swerved, crashed headlong through a rail fence and charged across the orchard, and a peach tree limb knocked his rider out of the saddle. He never moved after he hit the ground. I ran out there and looked down at him. It was Jack Kirby, right enough, and his neck was broken like a rotten branch.

I let him lie, and ran back to the house. Doc Blaine had stretched old Garfield out on a bench he'd dragged in from the porch, and Doc's face was whiter than I'd ever seen it. Old Jim was a ghastly sight; he had been shot with an old-fashioned .45-70, and at that range the heavy ball had literally torn off the top of his head. His features were masked with blood and brains. He had been directly behind me, poor old devil, and he had stopped the slug meant for me.

Doc Blaine was trembling, though he was anything but a stranger to such sights.

"Would you pronounce him dead?" he asked.

"That's for you to say," I answered. "But even a fool could tell that he's dead."

"He *is* dead," said Doc Blaine in a strained unnatural voice. "Rigor mortis is already setting in. But feel his heart!"

I did, and cried out. The flesh was already cold and clammy; but beneath it that mysterious heart still hammered steadily away, like a dynamo in a deserted house. No blood coursed through those veins; yet the heart pounded, pounded, pounded, like the pulse of Eternity.

"A living thing in a dead thing," whispered Doc Blaine, cold sweat on his face. "This is opposed to nature. I am going to keep the promise I made him. I'll assume full responsibility. This is too monstrous to ignore."

Our implements were a butcher-knife and a hack-saw. Outside only the still stars looked down on the black post-oak shadows and the dead man that lay in the orchard. Inside, the oil lamp flickered, making strange shadows move and shiver and cringe in the corners, and glistened on the blood on the floor, and the red-dabbled figure on the bench. The only sound inside was the crunch of the saw-edge in bone; outside an owl began to hoot weirdly.

Doc Blaine thrust a red-stained hand into the aperture he had made, and drew out a red, pulsing object that caught the lamplight. With a choked cry he recoiled, and the thing slipped from his fingers and fell on the table. And I, too, cried out involuntarily. For it did not fall with a soft meaty thud, as a piece of flesh should fall. It *thumped* hard on the table.

Impelled by an irresistible urge, I bent and gingerly picked up old Garfield's heart. The feel of it was brittle, unyielding, like steel or stone, but smoother than either. In size and shape it was the duplicate of a human heart, but it was slick and smooth, and its crimson surface reflected the lamplight like a jewel more lambent than any ruby; and in my hand it still throbbed mightily, sending vibratory radiations of energy up my arm until my own heart seemed swelling and bursting in response. It was cosmic *power*, beyond my comprehension, concentrated into the likeness of a human heart.

The thought came to me that here was a dynamo of life, the nearest approach to immortality that is possible for the destructible human body, the materialization of a cosmic secret more wonderful than the fabulous fountain sought for by Ponce de Leon. My soul was drawn into that unterrestrial gleam, and I suddenly wished passionately that it hammered and thundered in my own bosom in place of my paltry heart of tissue and muscle.

Doc Blaine ejaculated incoherently. I wheeled.

The noise of his coming had been no greater than the whispering of a night wind through the corn. There in the doorway he stood, tall, dark, inscrutable—an Indian warrior, in the paint, war bonnet, breech-clout and moccasins of an elder age. His dark eyes burned like fires gleaming deep under fathomless black lakes. Silently he extended his hand, and I dropped Jim Garfield's heart into it. Then without a word he turned and stalked into the night. But when Doc Blaine and I rushed out into the yard an instant later, there was no sign of any human being. He had vanished like a phantom of the night, and only something that looked like an owl was flying, dwindling from sight, into the rising moon.

The End

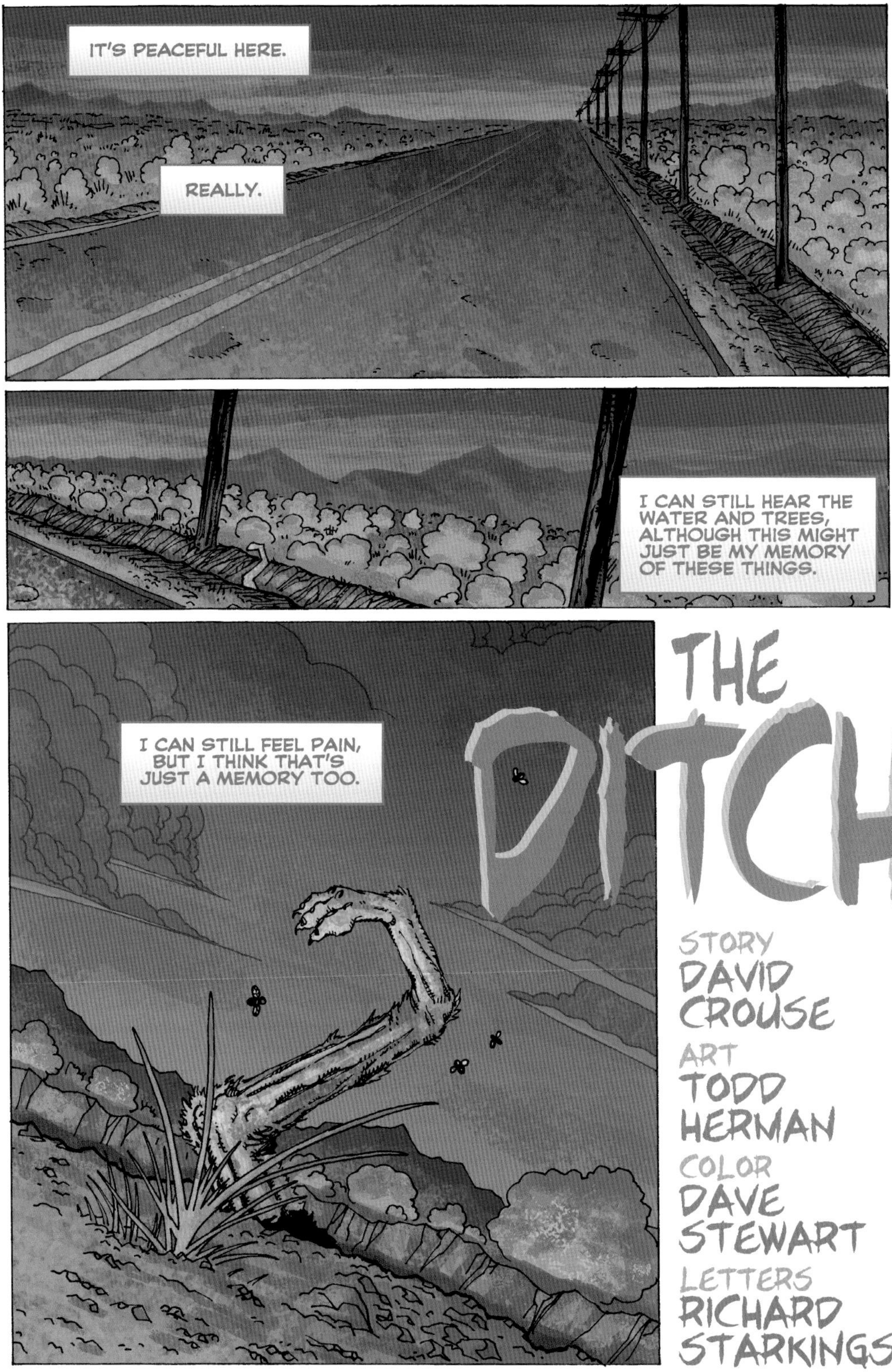
IT'S PEACEFUL HERE.
REALLY.
I CAN STILL HEAR THE WATER AND TREES, ALTHOUGH THIS MIGHT JUST BE MY MEMORY OF THESE THINGS.
I CAN STILL FEEL PAIN, BUT I THINK THAT'S JUST A MEMORY TOO.

THE DITCH

STORY
DAVID CROUSE
ART
TODD HERMAN
COLOR
DAVE STEWART
LETTERS
RICHARD STARKINGS

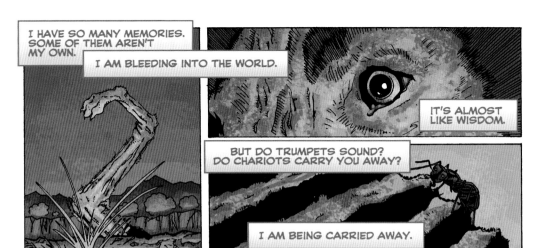

I HAVE SO MANY MEMORIES. SOME OF THEM AREN'T MY OWN.

I AM BLEEDING INTO THE WORLD.

IT'S ALMOST LIKE WISDOM.

BUT DO TRUMPETS SOUND? DO CHARIOTS CARRY YOU AWAY?

I AM BEING CARRIED AWAY.

I REMEMBER THE HEADLIGHTS. THE SMELL OF GASOLINE.

THE PAIN.

BUT I REMEMBER THE SONG ON THE RADIO TOO. THE TASTE OF MAYONNAISE ON THE DRIVER'S TONGUE. THE NUMBER ON THE SPEEDOMETER.

SEVENTY-NINE.

HE DECIDED IT WAS AN OPOSSUM.

HALF A MILE LATER HE WAS TRYING TO REMEMBER HOW TO SPELL THE WORD.

OPOSSUM. SEVEN LETTERS. ONE P. OR WAS IT TWO?

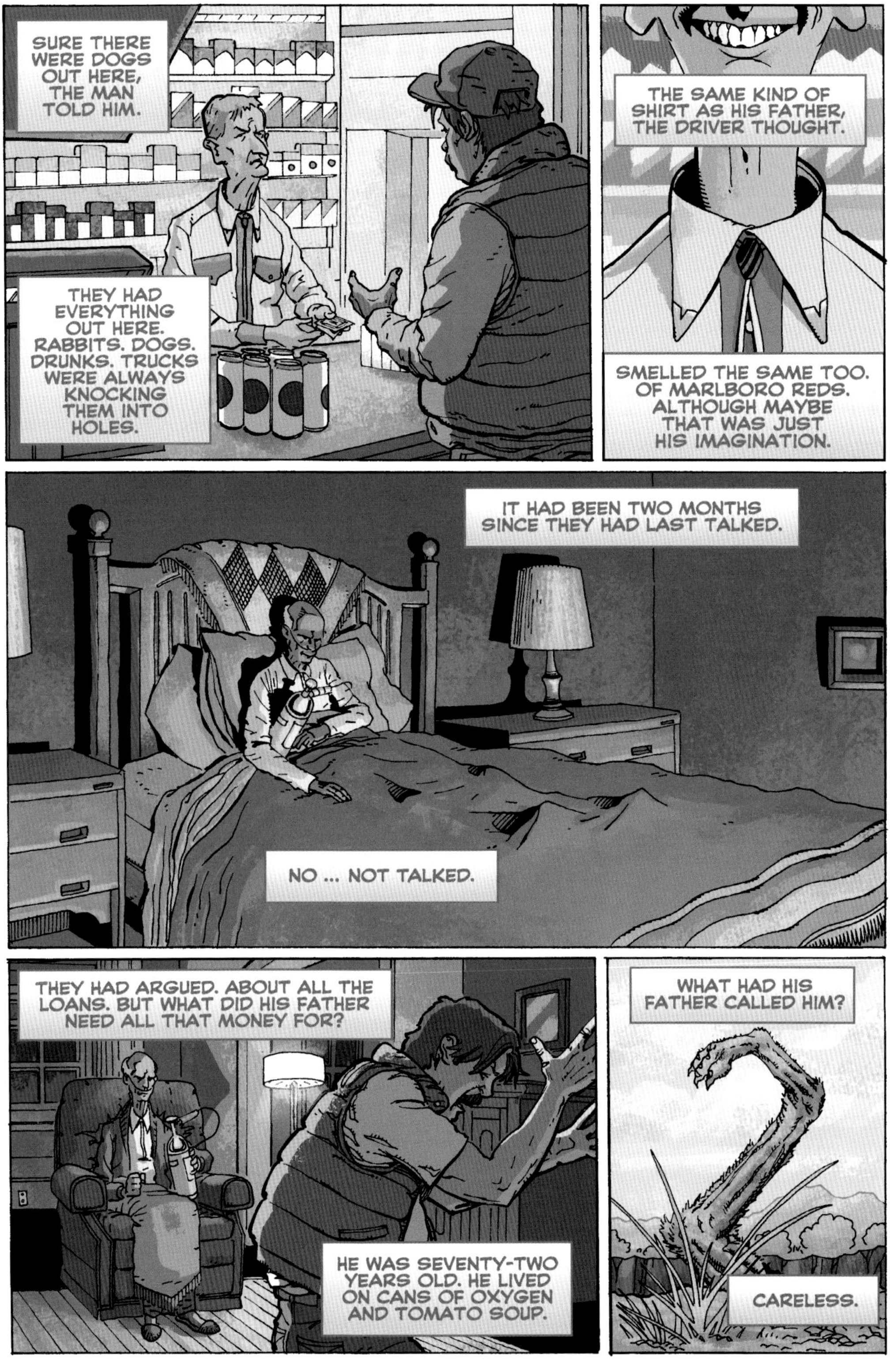
SURE THERE WERE DOGS OUT HERE, THE MAN TOLD HIM.
THEY HAD EVERYTHING OUT HERE. RABBITS. DOGS. DRUNKS. TRUCKS WERE ALWAYS KNOCKING THEM INTO HOLES.
THE SAME KIND OF SHIRT AS HIS FATHER, THE DRIVER THOUGHT.
SMELLED THE SAME TOO. OF MARLBORO REDS. ALTHOUGH MAYBE THAT WAS JUST HIS IMAGINATION.
IT HAD BEEN TWO MONTHS SINCE THEY HAD LAST TALKED.
NO ... NOT TALKED.
THEY HAD ARGUED. ABOUT ALL THE LOANS. BUT WHAT DID HIS FATHER NEED ALL THAT MONEY FOR?
HE WAS SEVENTY-TWO YEARS OLD. HE LIVED ON CANS OF OXYGEN AND TOMATO SOUP.
WHAT HAD HIS FATHER CALLED HIM?
CARELESS.

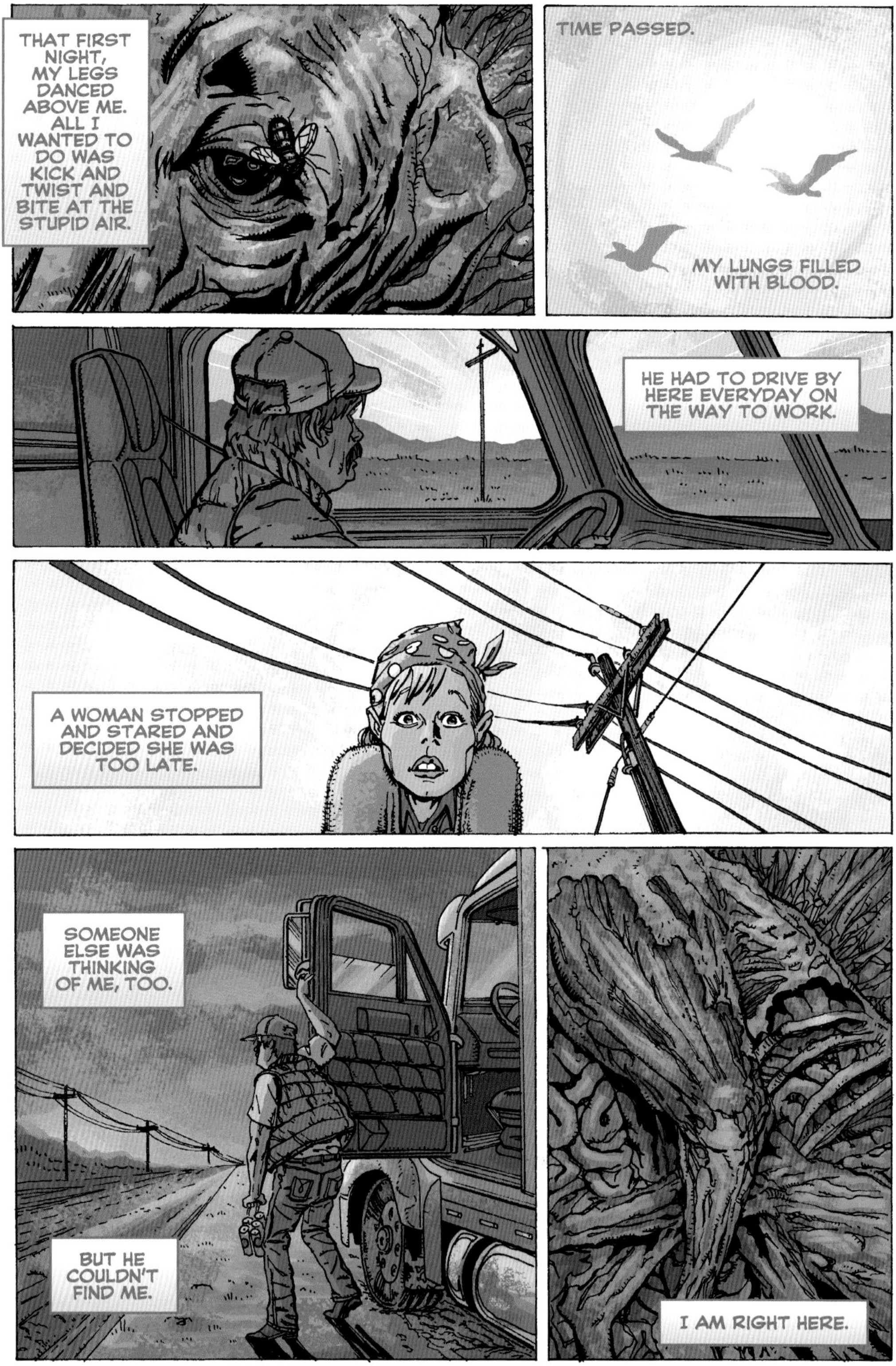
THAT FIRST NIGHT, MY LEGS DANCED ABOVE ME. ALL I WANTED TO DO WAS KICK AND TWIST AND BITE AT THE STUPID AIR.
TIME PASSED.
MY LUNGS FILLED WITH BLOOD.
HE HAD TO DRIVE BY HERE EVERYDAY ON THE WAY TO WORK.
A WOMAN STOPPED AND STARED AND DECIDED SHE WAS TOO LATE.
SOMEONE ELSE WAS THINKING OF ME, TOO.
BUT HE COULDN'T FIND ME.
I AM RIGHT HERE.

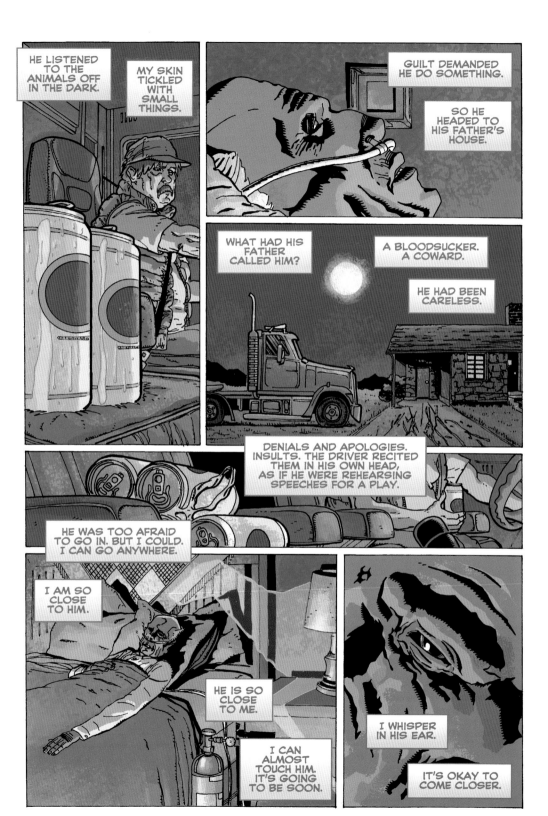

HE LISTENED TO THE ANIMALS OFF IN THE DARK.

MY SKIN TICKLED WITH SMALL THINGS.

GUILT DEMANDED HE DO SOMETHING.

SO HE HEADED TO HIS FATHER'S HOUSE.

WHAT HAD HIS FATHER CALLED HIM?

A BLOODSUCKER. A COWARD.

HE HAD BEEN CARELESS.

DENIALS AND APOLOGIES. INSULTS. THE DRIVER RECITED THEM IN HIS OWN HEAD, AS IF HE WERE REHEARSING SPEECHES FOR A PLAY.

HE WAS TOO AFRAID TO GO IN. BUT I COULD. I CAN GO ANYWHERE.

I AM SO CLOSE TO HIM.

HE IS SO CLOSE TO ME.

I CAN ALMOST TOUCH HIM. IT'S GOING TO BE SOON.

I WHISPER IN HIS EAR.

IT'S OKAY TO COME CLOSER.

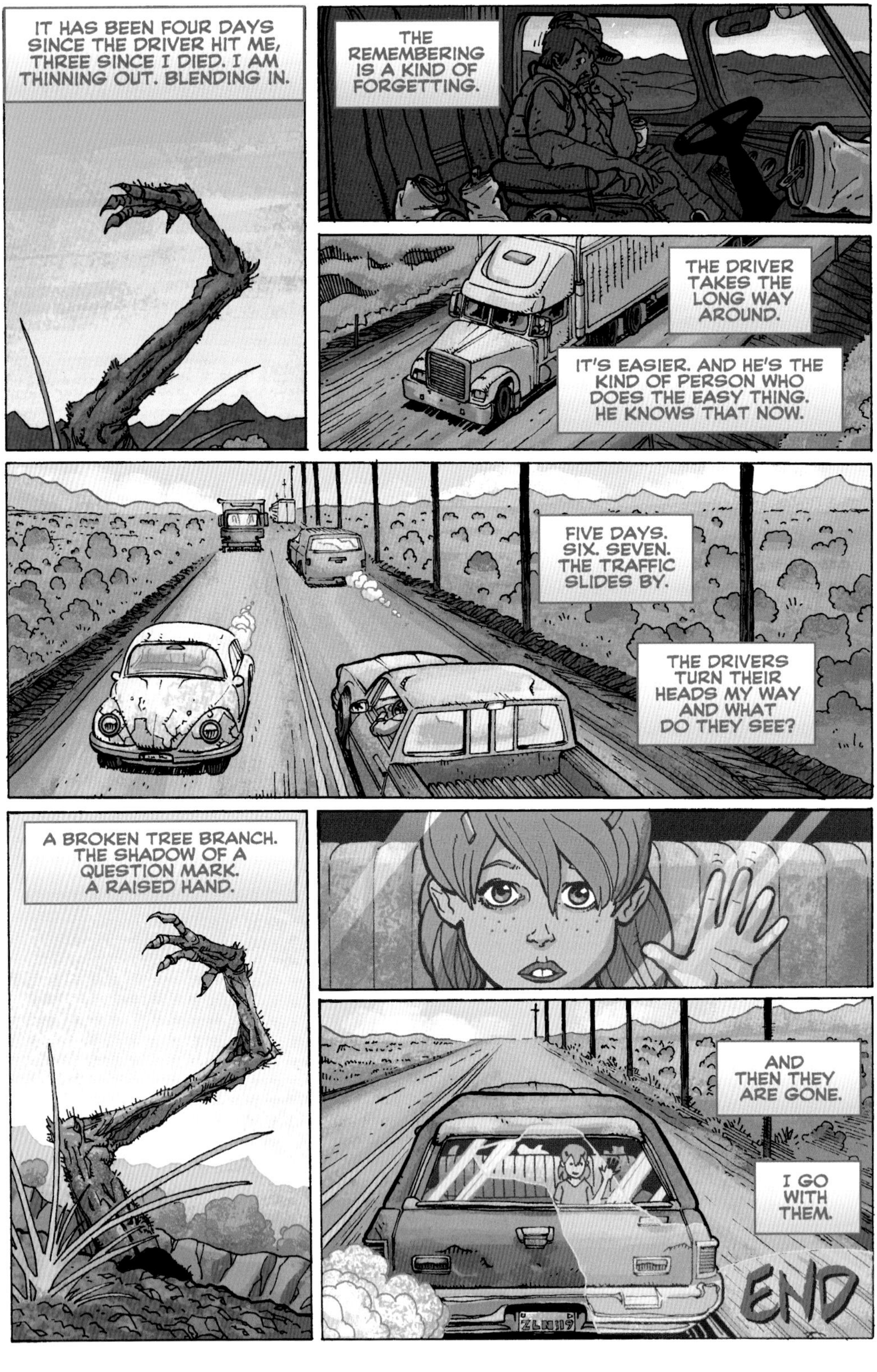
IT HAS BEEN FOUR DAYS SINCE THE DRIVER HIT ME, THREE SINCE I DIED. I AM THINNING OUT. BLENDING IN.
THE REMEMBERING IS A KIND OF FORGETTING.
THE DRIVER TAKES THE LONG WAY AROUND.
IT'S EASIER. AND HE'S THE KIND OF PERSON WHO DOES THE EASY THING. HE KNOWS THAT NOW.
FIVE DAYS. SIX. SEVEN. THE TRAFFIC SLIDES BY.
THE DRIVERS TURN THEIR HEADS MY WAY AND WHAT DO THEY SEE?
A BROKEN TREE BRANCH. THE SHADOW OF A QUESTION MARK. A RAISED HAND.
AND THEN THEY ARE GONE.
I GO WITH THEM.
END

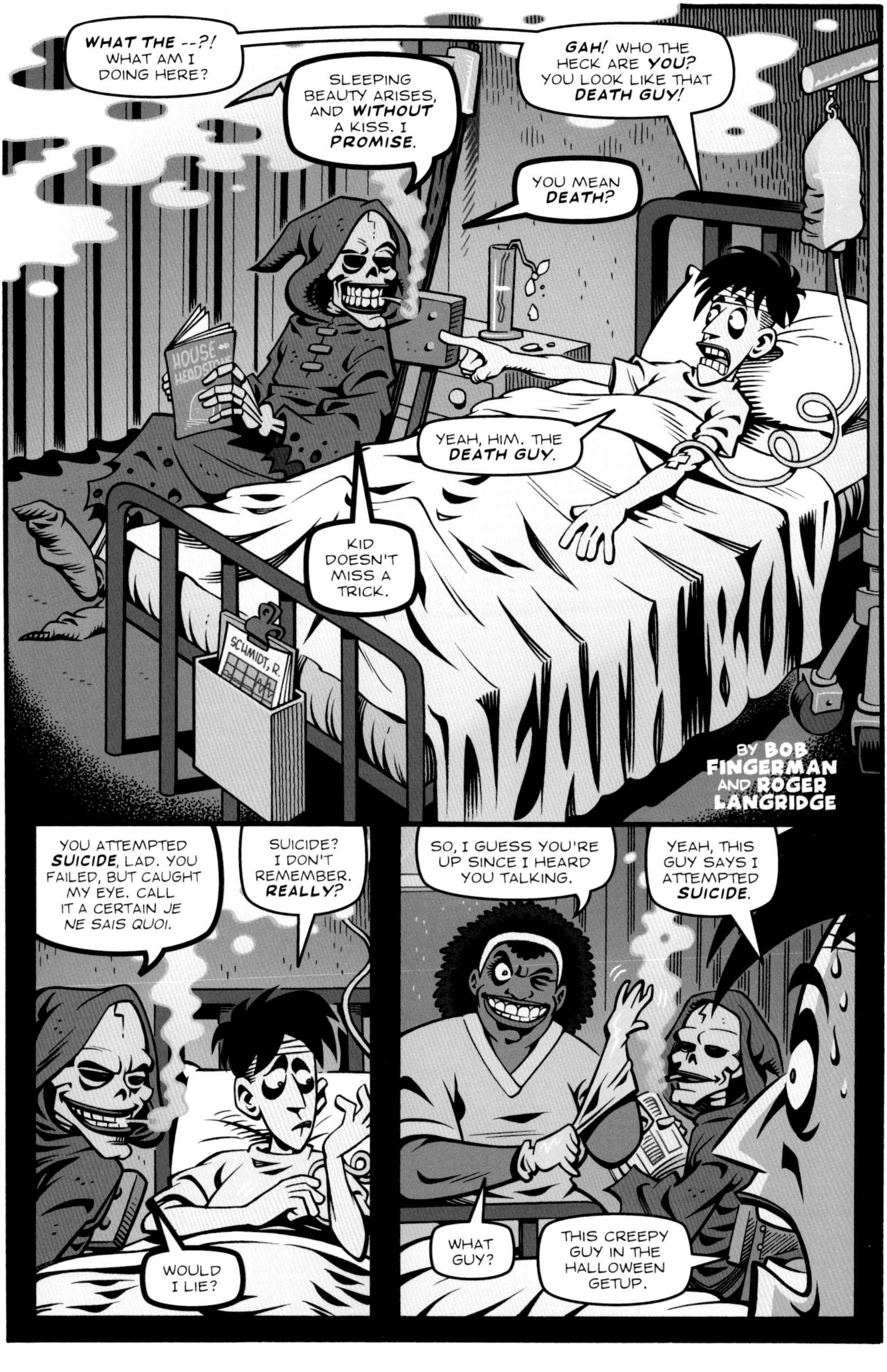
WHAT THE --?! WHAT AM I DOING HERE?
SLEEPING BEAUTY ARISES, AND WITHOUT A KISS. I PROMISE.
GAH! WHO THE HECK ARE YOU? YOU LOOK LIKE THAT DEATH GUY!
YOU MEAN DEATH?
HOUSE AND HEADSTONE
YEAH, HIM. THE DEATH GUY.
KID DOESN'T MISS A TRICK.
SCHMIDT, R.
DEATH BOY
BY BOB FINGERMAN AND ROGER LANGRIDGE
YOU ATTEMPTED SUICIDE, LAD. YOU FAILED, BUT CAUGHT MY EYE. CALL IT A CERTAIN JE NE SAIS QUOI.
SUICIDE? I DON'T REMEMBER. REALLY?
WOULD I LIE?
SO, I GUESS YOU'RE UP SINCE I HEARD YOU TALKING.
YEAH, THIS GUY SAYS I ATTEMPTED SUICIDE.
WHAT GUY?
THIS CREEPY GUY IN THE HALLOWEEN GETUP.

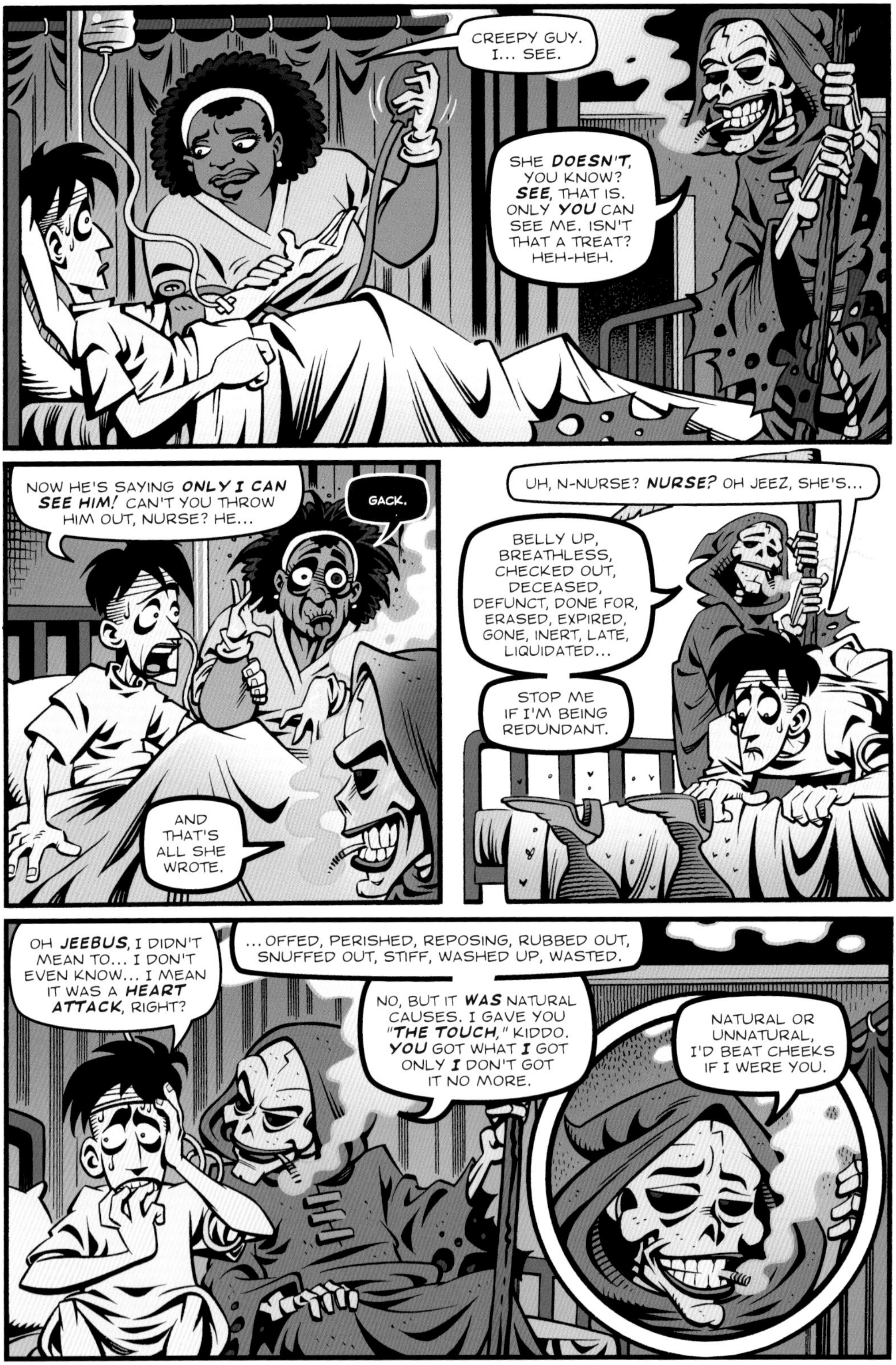
CREEPY GUY. I... SEE.
SHE DOESN'T, YOU KNOW? SEE, THAT IS. ONLY YOU CAN SEE ME. ISN'T THAT A TREAT? HEH-HEH.
NOW HE'S SAYING ONLY I CAN SEE HIM! CAN'T YOU THROW HIM OUT, NURSE? HE...
GACK.
AND THAT'S ALL SHE WROTE.
UH, N-NURSE? NURSE? OH JEEZ, SHE'S...
BELLY UP, BREATHLESS, CHECKED OUT, DECEASED, DEFUNCT, DONE FOR, ERASED, EXPIRED, GONE, INERT, LATE, LIQUIDATED...
STOP ME IF I'M BEING REDUNDANT.
OH JEEBUS, I DIDN'T MEAN TO... I DON'T EVEN KNOW... I MEAN IT WAS A HEART ATTACK, RIGHT?
...OFFED, PERISHED, REPOSING, RUBBED OUT, SNUFFED OUT, STIFF, WASHED UP, WASTED.
NO, BUT IT WAS NATURAL CAUSES. I GAVE YOU "THE TOUCH," KIDDO. YOU GOT WHAT I GOT ONLY I DON'T GOT IT NO MORE.
NATURAL OR UNNATURAL, I'D BEAT CHEEKS IF I WERE YOU.

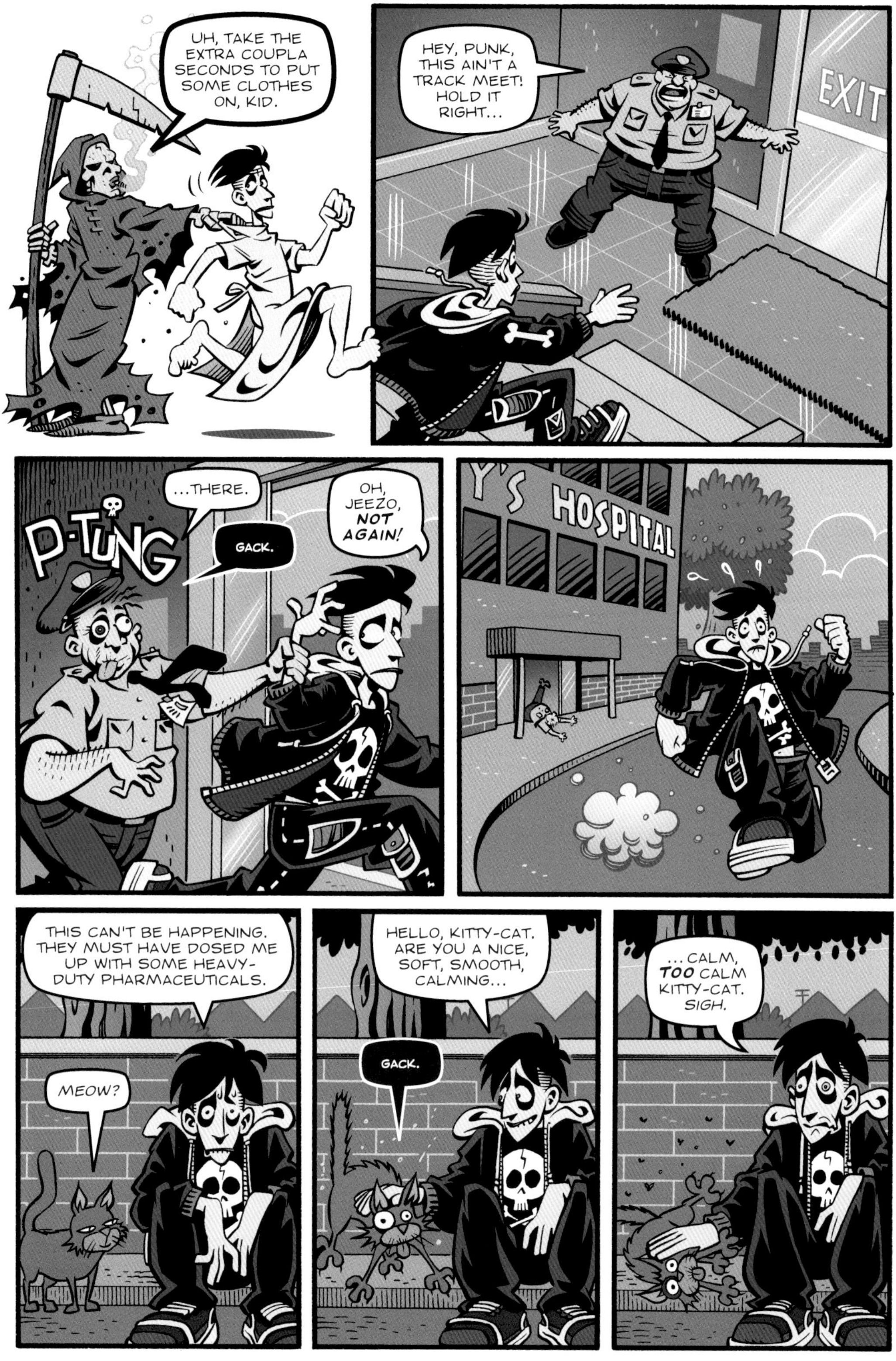
UH, TAKE THE EXTRA COUPLA SECONDS TO PUT SOME CLOTHES ON, KID.
HEY, PUNK, THIS AIN'T A TRACK MEET! HOLD IT RIGHT...
EXIT
...THERE.
P-TUNG
GACK.
OH, JEEZO, **NOT AGAIN!**
Y'S HOSPITAL
THIS CAN'T BE HAPPENING. THEY MUST HAVE DOSED ME UP WITH SOME HEAVY-DUTY PHARMACEUTICALS.
MEOW?
HELLO, KITTY-CAT. ARE YOU A NICE, SOFT, SMOOTH, CALMING...
GACK.
...CALM, **TOO** CALM KITTY-CAT. SIGH.

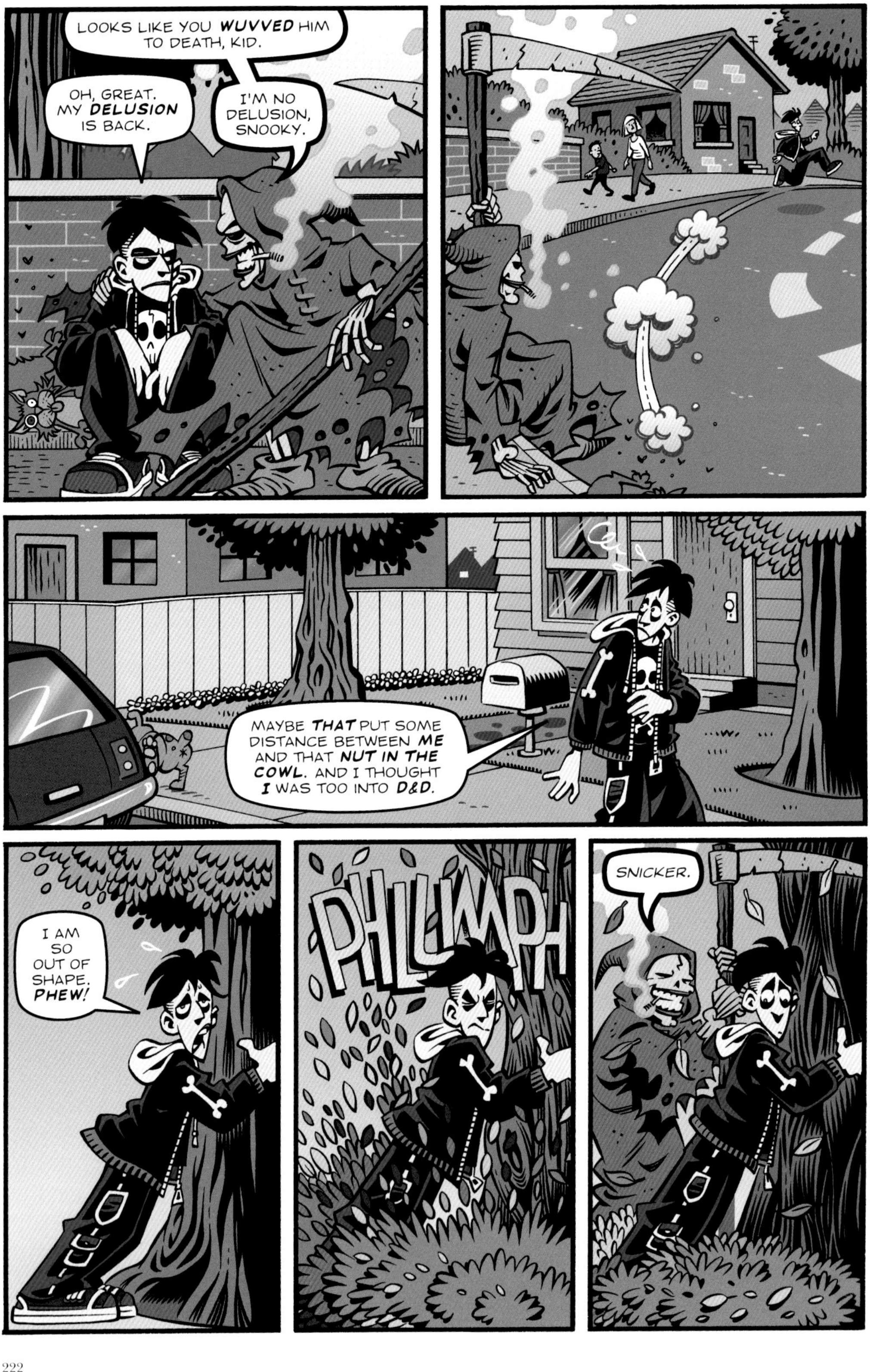
LOOKS LIKE YOU WUVVED HIM TO DEATH, KID.
OH, GREAT. MY DELUSION IS BACK.
I'M NO DELUSION, SNOOKY.
MAYBE THAT PUT SOME DISTANCE BETWEEN ME AND THAT NUT IN THE COWL. AND I THOUGHT I WAS TOO INTO D&D.
I AM SO OUT OF SHAPE. PHEW!
PHLUMPH
SNICKER.

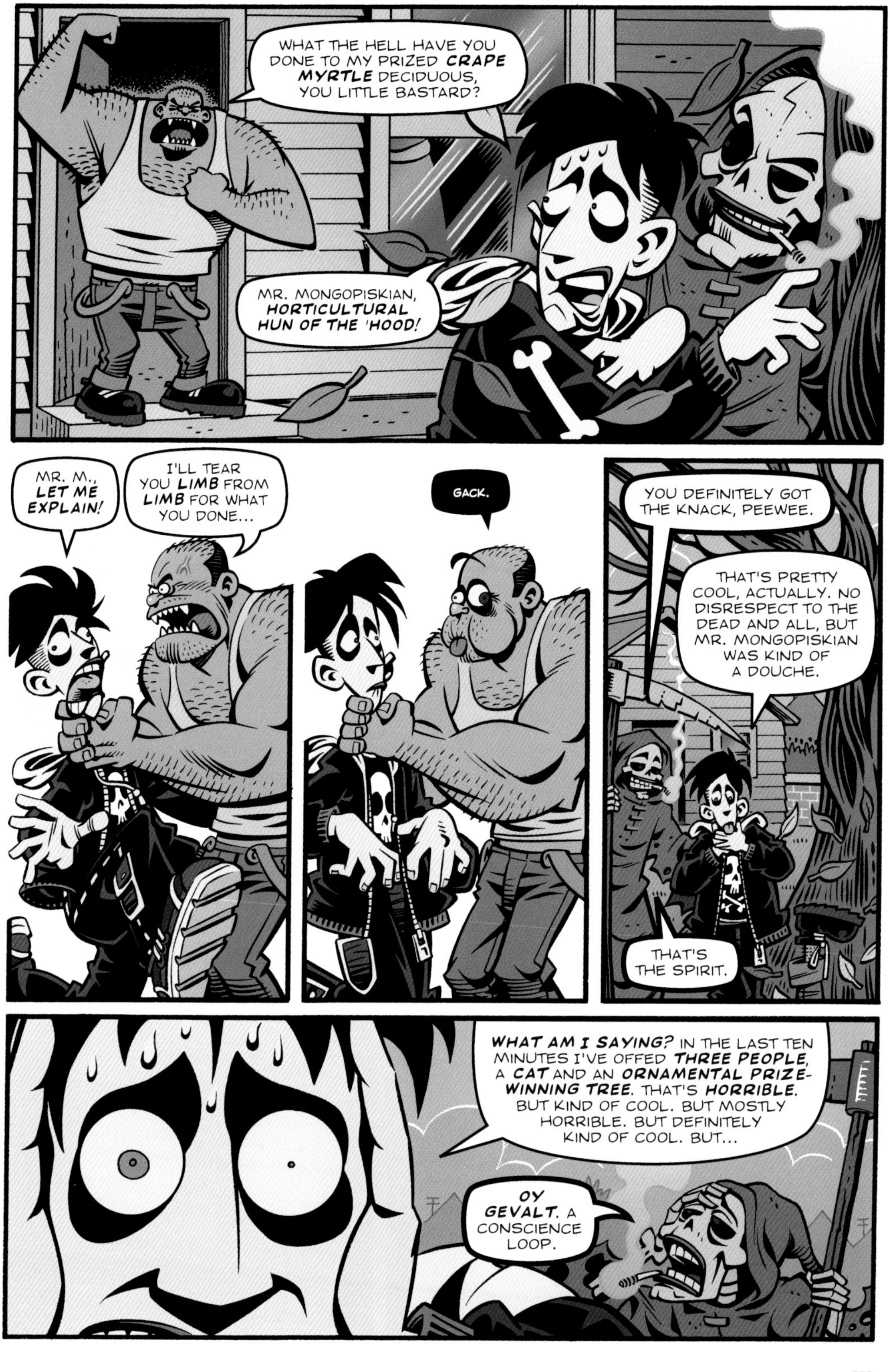
WHAT THE HELL HAVE YOU DONE TO MY PRIZED CRAPE MYRTLE DECIDUOUS, YOU LITTLE BASTARD?
MR. MONGOPISKIAN, HORTICULTURAL HUN OF THE 'HOOD!
MR. M., LET ME EXPLAIN!
I'LL TEAR YOU LIMB FROM LIMB FOR WHAT YOU DONE...
GACK.
YOU DEFINITELY GOT THE KNACK, PEEWEE.
THAT'S PRETTY COOL, ACTUALLY. NO DISRESPECT TO THE DEAD AND ALL, BUT MR. MONGOPISKIAN WAS KIND OF A DOUCHE.
THAT'S THE SPIRIT.
WHAT AM I SAYING? IN THE LAST TEN MINUTES I'VE OFFED THREE PEOPLE, A CAT AND AN ORNAMENTAL PRIZE-WINNING TREE. THAT'S HORRIBLE. BUT KIND OF COOL. BUT MOSTLY HORRIBLE. BUT DEFINITELY KIND OF COOL. BUT...
OY GEVALT. A CONSCIENCE LOOP.

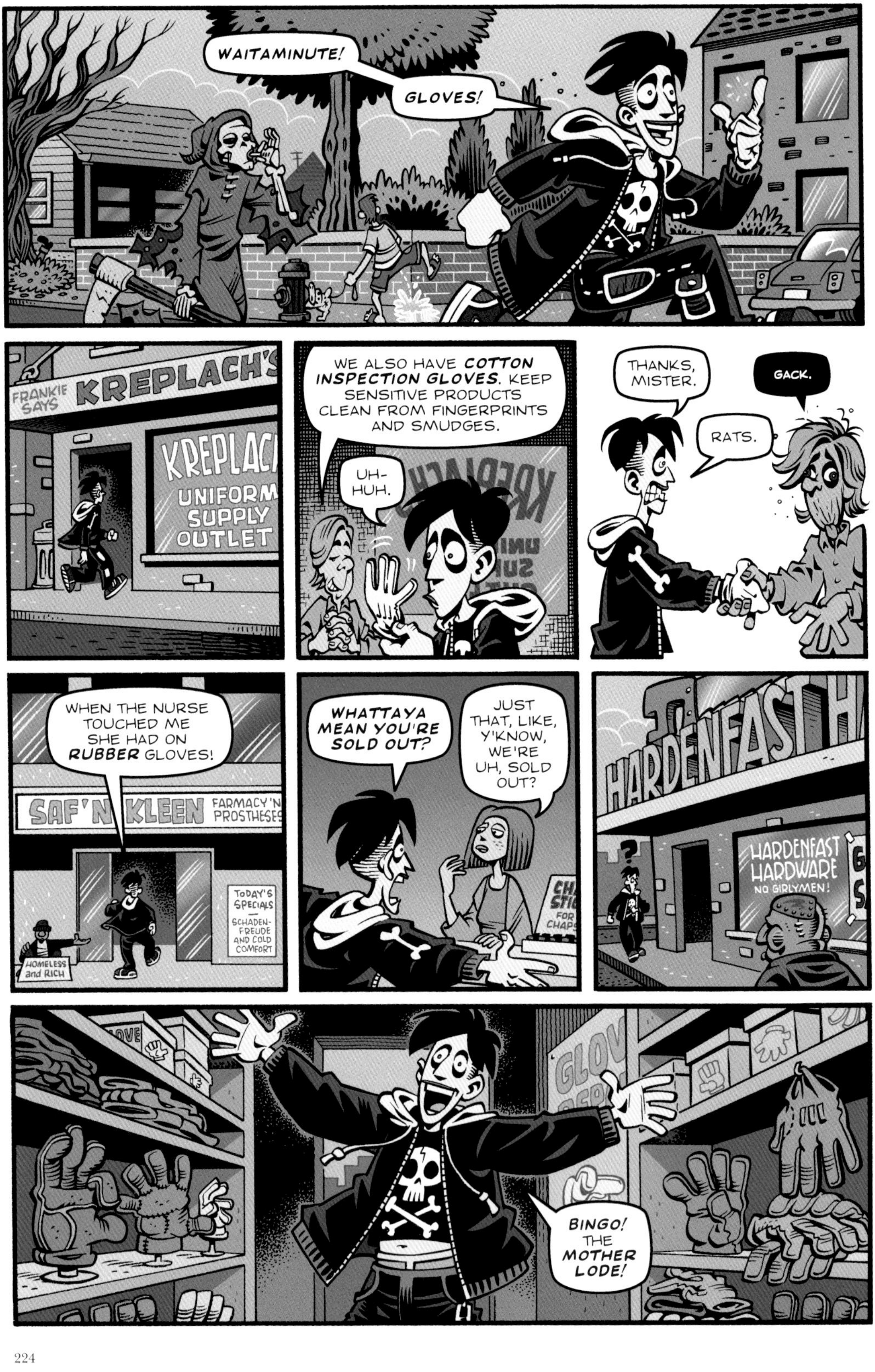
WAITAMINUTE!
GLOVES!
FRANKIE SAYS
KREPLACH'S
KREPLACH UNIFORM SUPPLY OUTLET
WE ALSO HAVE COTTON INSPECTION GLOVES. KEEP SENSITIVE PRODUCTS CLEAN FROM FINGERPRINTS AND SMUDGES.
UH-HUH.
THANKS, MISTER.
GACK.
RATS.
WHEN THE NURSE TOUCHED ME SHE HAD ON RUBBER GLOVES!
SAF'N KLEEN
FARMACY'N PROSTHESES
TODAY'S SPECIALS
SCHADEN-FREUDE AND COLD COMFORT
HOMELESS and RICH
WHATTAYA MEAN YOU'RE SOLD OUT?
JUST THAT, LIKE, Y'KNOW, WE'RE UH, SOLD OUT?
HARDENFAST
HARDENFAST HARDWARE
NO GIRLYMEN!
?
BINGO! THE MOTHER LODE!

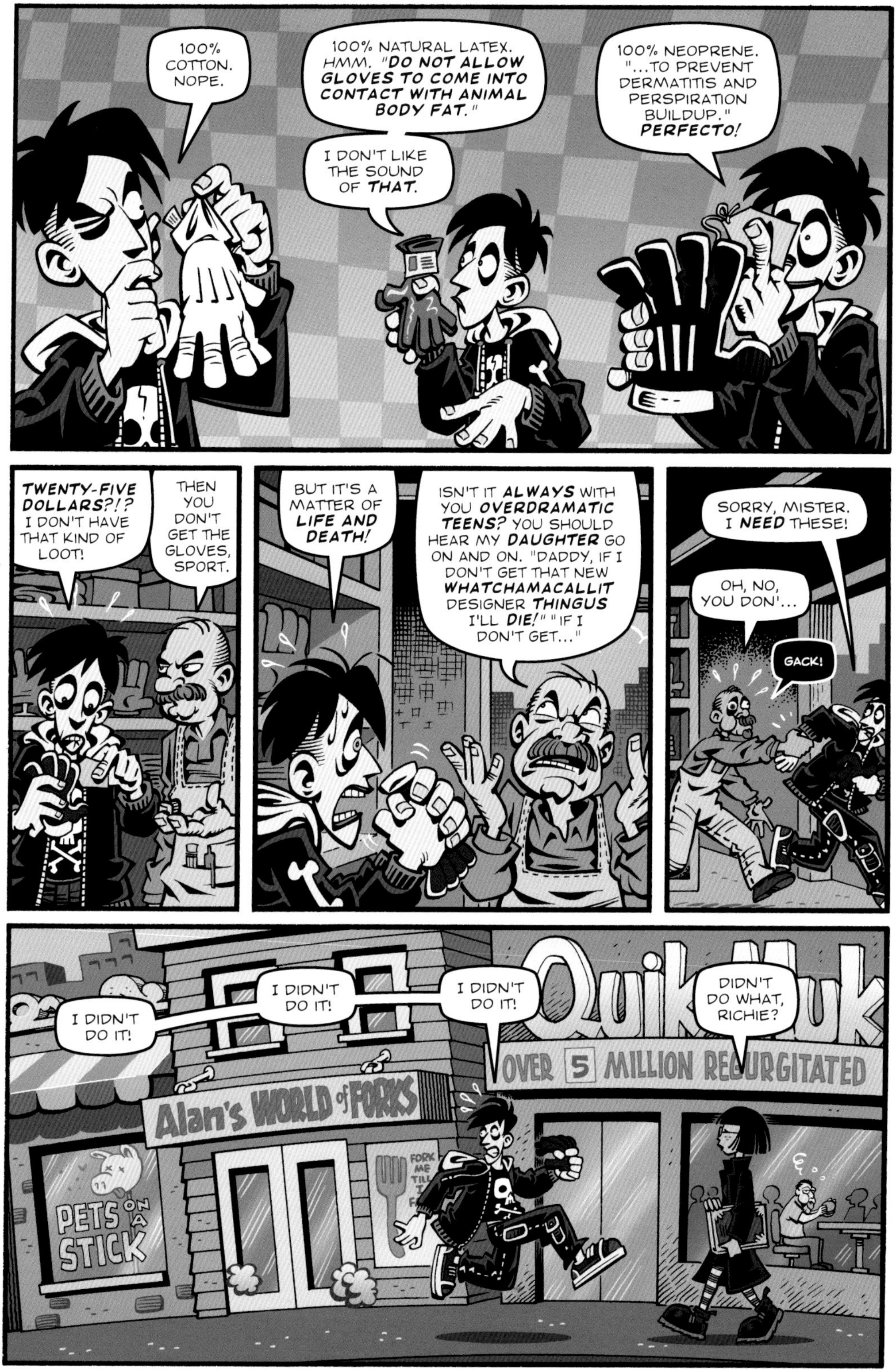
100% COTTON. NOPE.
100% NATURAL LATEX. HMM. "DO NOT ALLOW GLOVES TO COME INTO CONTACT WITH ANIMAL BODY FAT."
I DON'T LIKE THE SOUND OF THAT.
100% NEOPRENE. "...TO PREVENT DERMATITIS AND PERSPIRATION BUILDUP." PERFECTO!
TWENTY-FIVE DOLLARS?!? I DON'T HAVE THAT KIND OF LOOT!
THEN YOU DON'T GET THE GLOVES, SPORT.
BUT IT'S A MATTER OF LIFE AND DEATH!
ISN'T IT ALWAYS WITH YOU OVERDRAMATIC TEENS? YOU SHOULD HEAR MY DAUGHTER GO ON AND ON. "DADDY, IF I DON'T GET THAT NEW WHATCHAMACALLIT DESIGNER THINGUS I'LL DIE!" "IF I DON'T GET..."
SORRY, MISTER. I NEED THESE!
OH, NO, YOU DON'...
GACK!
I DIDN'T DO IT!
I DIDN'T DO IT!
I DIDN'T DO IT!
DIDN'T DO WHAT, RICHIE?
OVER 5 MILLION REGURGITATED
Alan's WORLD of FORKS
PETS ON A STICK
FORK ME TILL I F

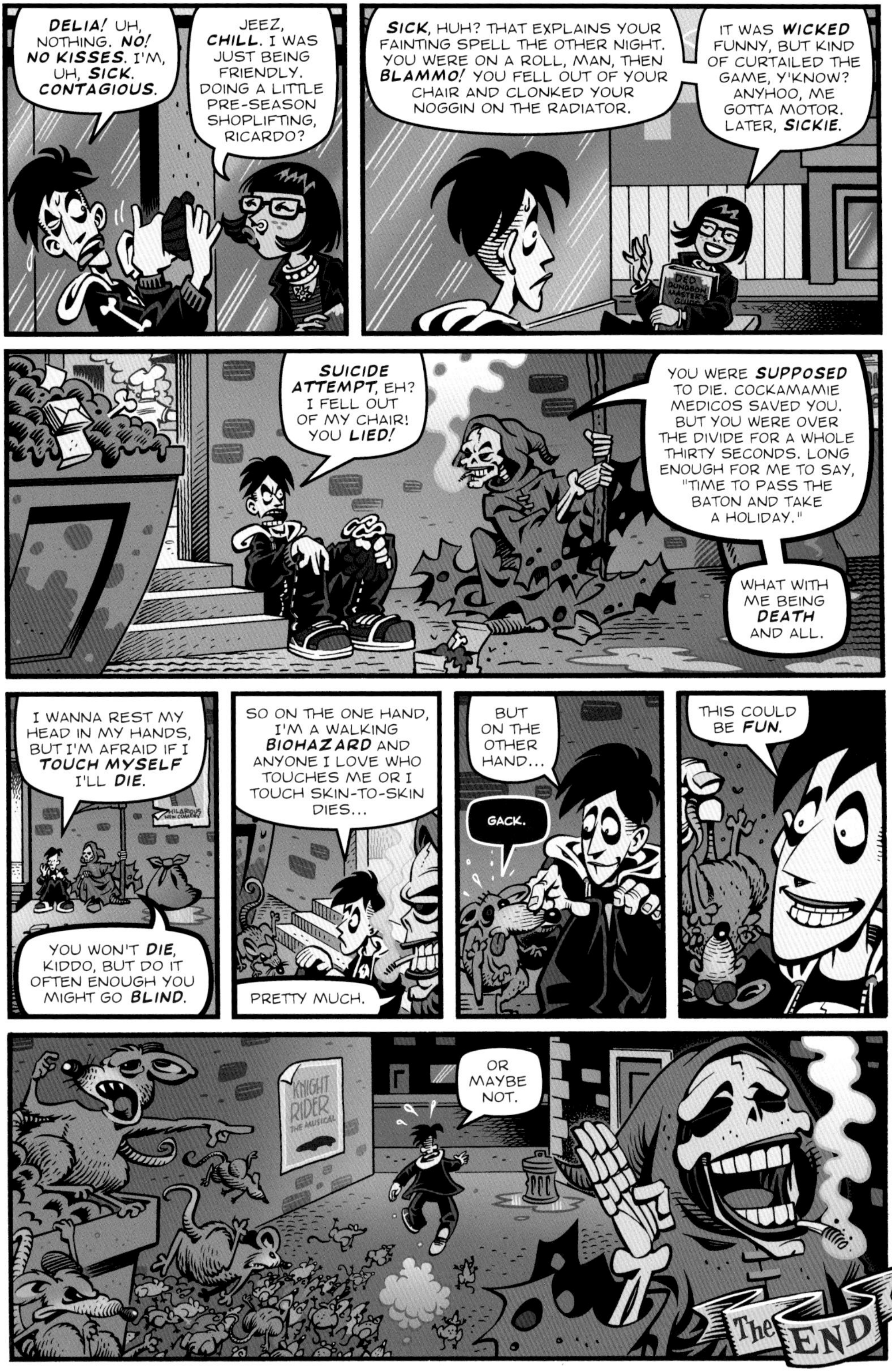
DELIA! UH, NOTHING. NO! NO KISSES. I'M, UH, SICK. CONTAGIOUS.
JEEZ, CHILL. I WAS JUST BEING FRIENDLY. DOING A LITTLE PRE-SEASON SHOPLIFTING, RICARDO?
SICK, HUH? THAT EXPLAINS YOUR FAINTING SPELL THE OTHER NIGHT. YOU WERE ON A ROLL, MAN, THEN BLAMMO! YOU FELL OUT OF YOUR CHAIR AND CLONKED YOUR NOGGIN ON THE RADIATOR.
IT WAS WICKED FUNNY, BUT KIND OF CURTAILED THE GAME, Y'KNOW? ANYHOO, ME GOTTA MOTOR. LATER, SICKIE.
DED DUNGEON MASTER'S GUIDE
SUICIDE ATTEMPT, EH? I FELL OUT OF MY CHAIR! YOU LIED!
YOU WERE SUPPOSED TO DIE. COCKAMAMIE MEDICOS SAVED YOU. BUT YOU WERE OVER THE DIVIDE FOR A WHOLE THIRTY SECONDS. LONG ENOUGH FOR ME TO SAY, "TIME TO PASS THE BATON AND TAKE A HOLIDAY."
WHAT WITH ME BEING DEATH AND ALL.
I WANNA REST MY HEAD IN MY HANDS, BUT I'M AFRAID IF I TOUCH MYSELF I'LL DIE.
HILARIOUS NEW COMEDY
YOU WON'T DIE, KIDDO, BUT DO IT OFTEN ENOUGH YOU MIGHT GO BLIND.
SO ON THE ONE HAND, I'M A WALKING BIOHAZARD AND ANYONE I LOVE WHO TOUCHES ME OR I TOUCH SKIN-TO-SKIN DIES...
PRETTY MUCH.
BUT ON THE OTHER HAND...
GACK.
THIS COULD BE FUN.
KNIGHT RIDER THE MUSICAL
OR MAYBE NOT.
The END

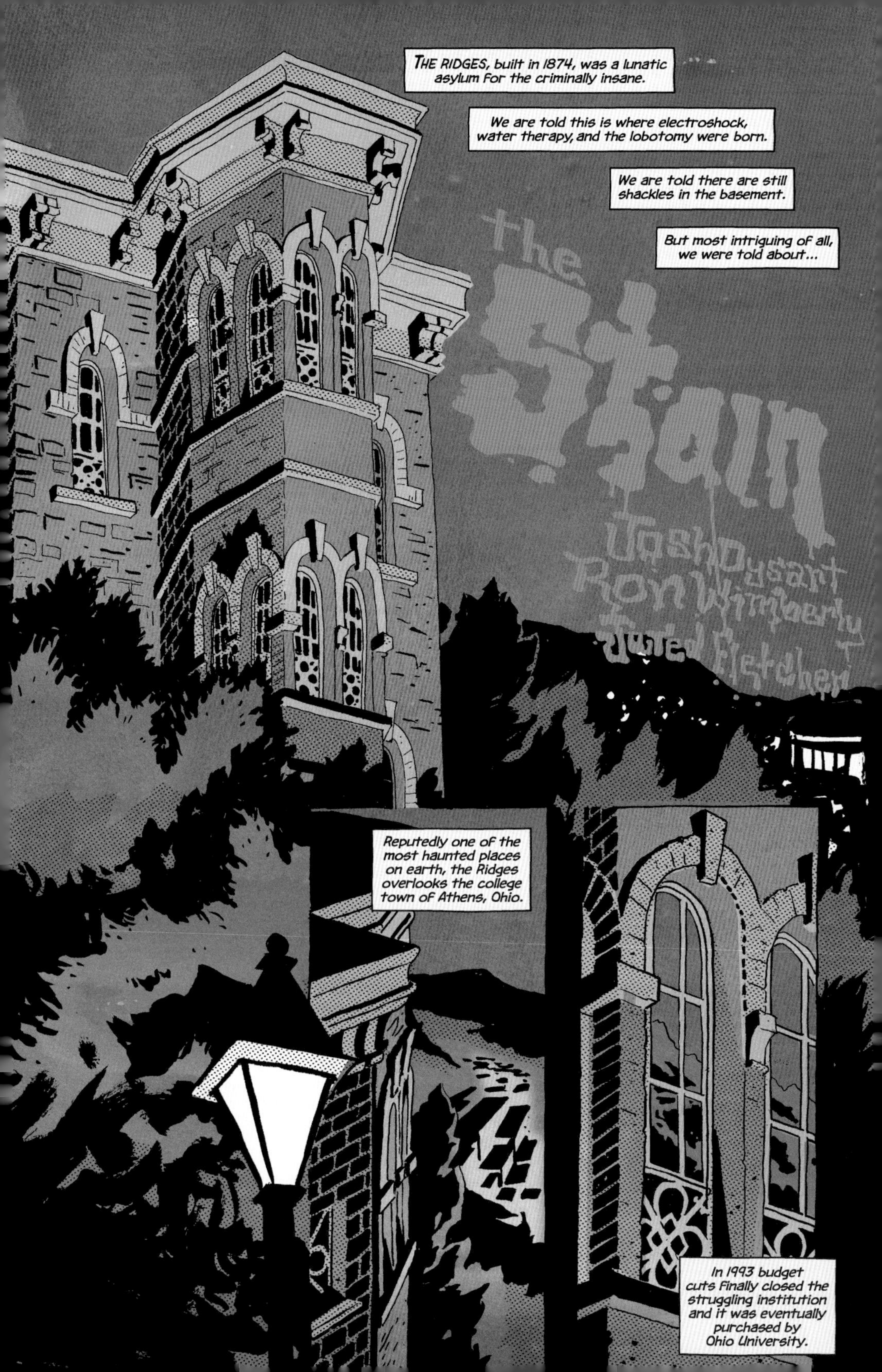
THE RIDGES, built in 1874, was a lunatic asylum for the criminally insane.
We are told this is where electroshock, water therapy, and the lobotomy were born.
We are told there are still shackles in the basement.
But most intriguing of all, we were told about...
The Stain
Josh Dysart
Ron Wimberly
Jared Fletcher
Reputedly one of the most haunted places on earth, the Ridges overlooks the college town of Athens, Ohio.
In 1993 budget cuts finally closed the struggling institution and it was eventually purchased by Ohio University.

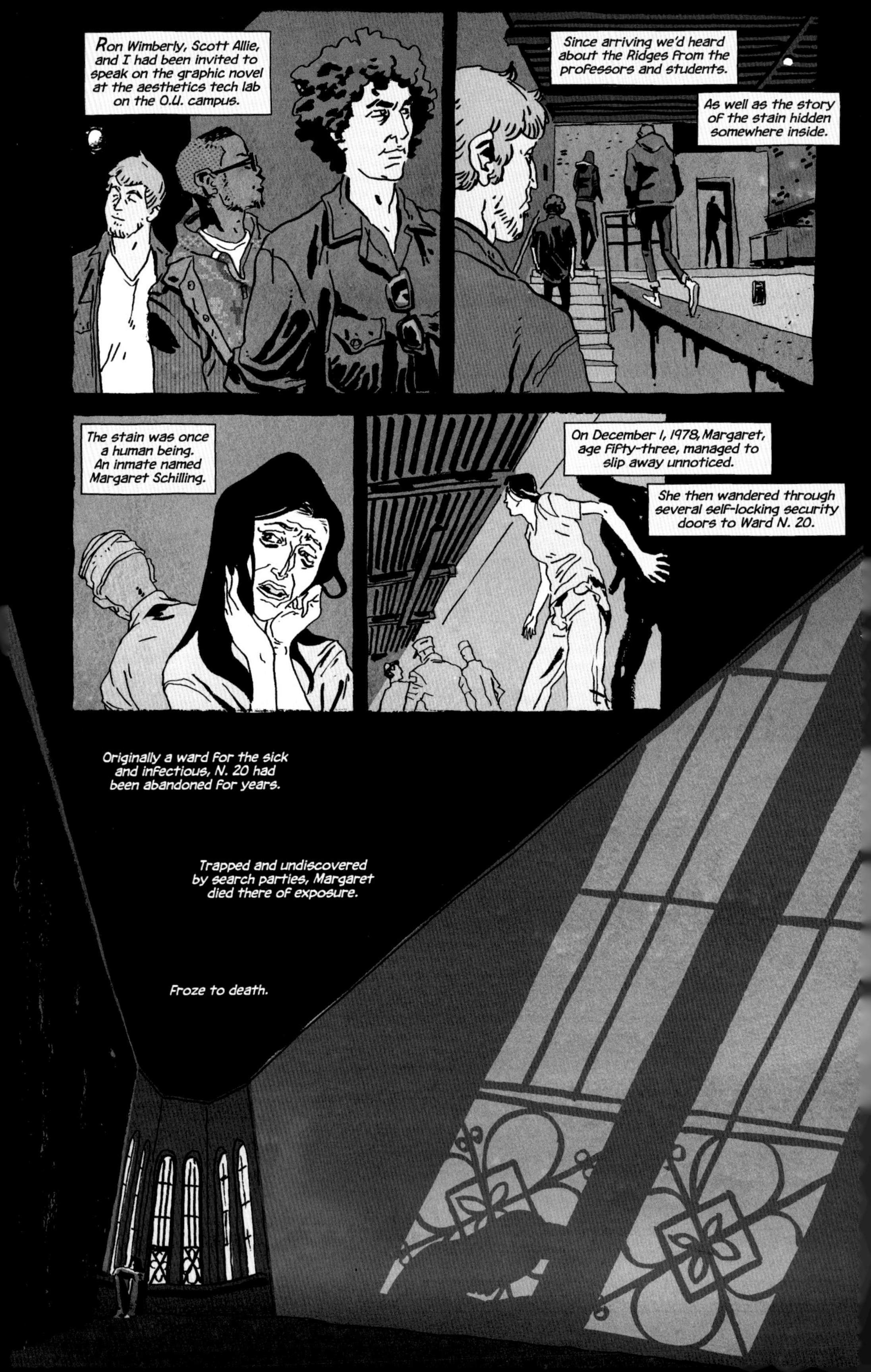
Ron Wimberly, Scott Allie, and I had been invited to speak on the graphic novel at the aesthetics tech lab on the O.U. campus.
Since arriving we'd heard about the Ridges from the professors and students.
As well as the story of the stain hidden somewhere inside.
The stain was once a human being. An inmate named Margaret Schilling.
On December 1, 1978, Margaret, age fifty-three, managed to slip away unnoticed.
She then wandered through several self-locking security doors to Ward N. 20.
Originally a ward for the sick and infectious, N. 20 had been abandoned for years.
Trapped and undiscovered by search parties, Margaret died there of exposure.
Froze to death.

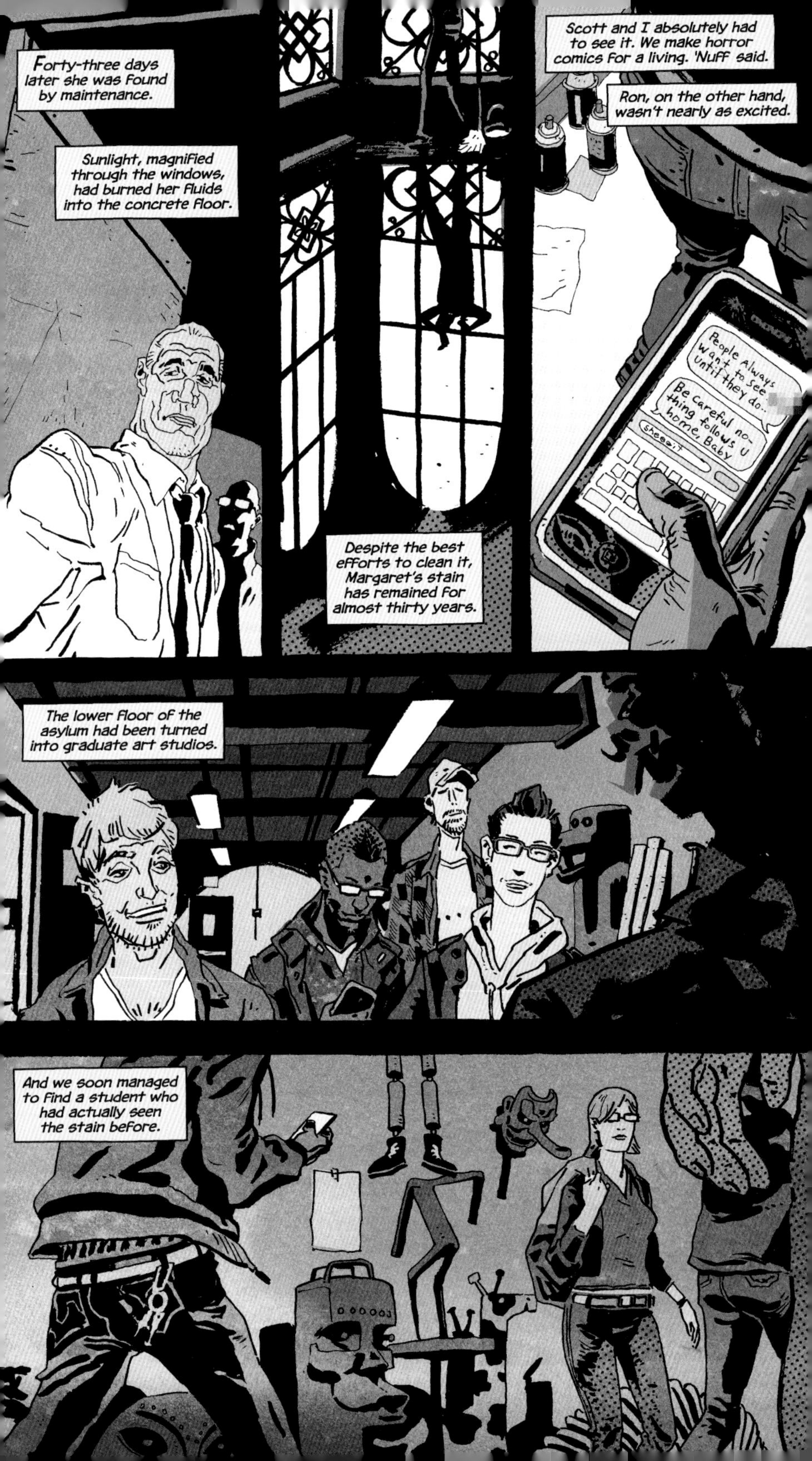
Forty-three days later she was found by maintenance.
Sunlight, magnified through the windows, had burned her fluids into the concrete floor.
Despite the best efforts to clean it, Margaret's stain has remained for almost thirty years.
Scott and I absolutely had to see it. We make horror comics for a living. 'Nuff said.
Ron, on the other hand, wasn't nearly as excited.
People Always want to see. Until they do..
Be careful nothing follows U home, Baby
sheeeit
The lower floor of the asylum had been turned into graduate art studios.
And we soon managed to find a student who had actually seen the stain before.

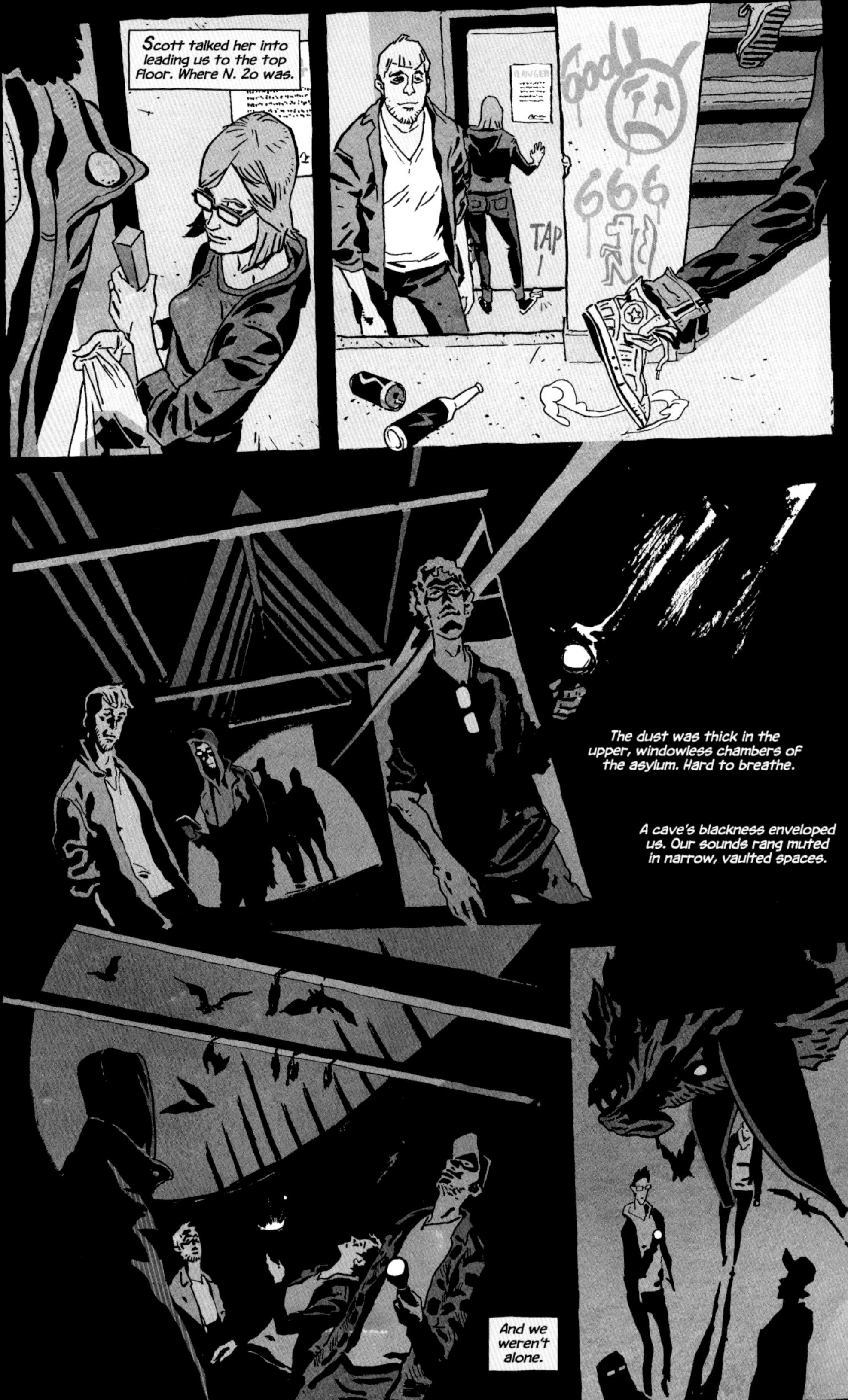
Scott talked her into leading us to the top floor. Where N. 2o was.
DANGER
God
666
TAP
The dust was thick in the upper, windowless chambers of the asylum. Hard to breathe.
A cave's blackness enveloped us. Our sounds rang muted in narrow, vaulted spaces.
And we weren't alone.

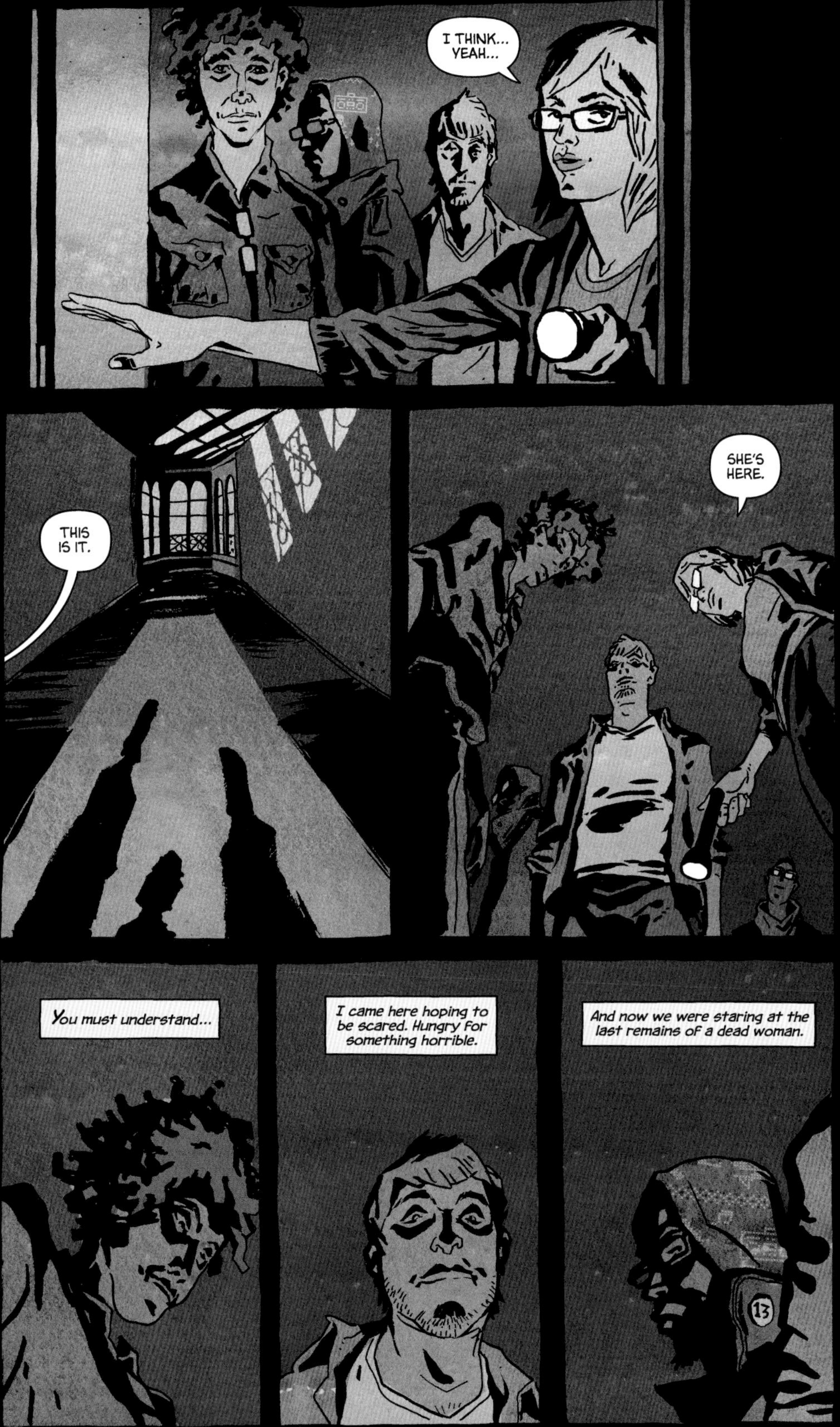
I THINK... YEAH...
THIS IS IT.
SHE'S HERE.
You must understand...
I came here hoping to be scared. Hungry for something horrible.
And now we were staring at the last remains of a dead woman.

Perfectly etched.

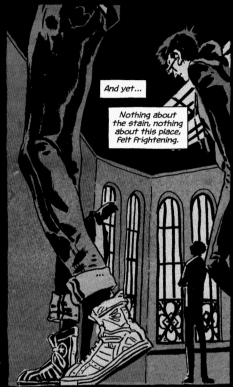

And yet...

Nothing about the stain, nothing about this place, felt frightening.

The whole asylum reeked of tranquility. Serenity.

Later I discovered that Margaret had taken off her clothes, Folded them neatly next to her, then laid down to die.

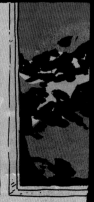

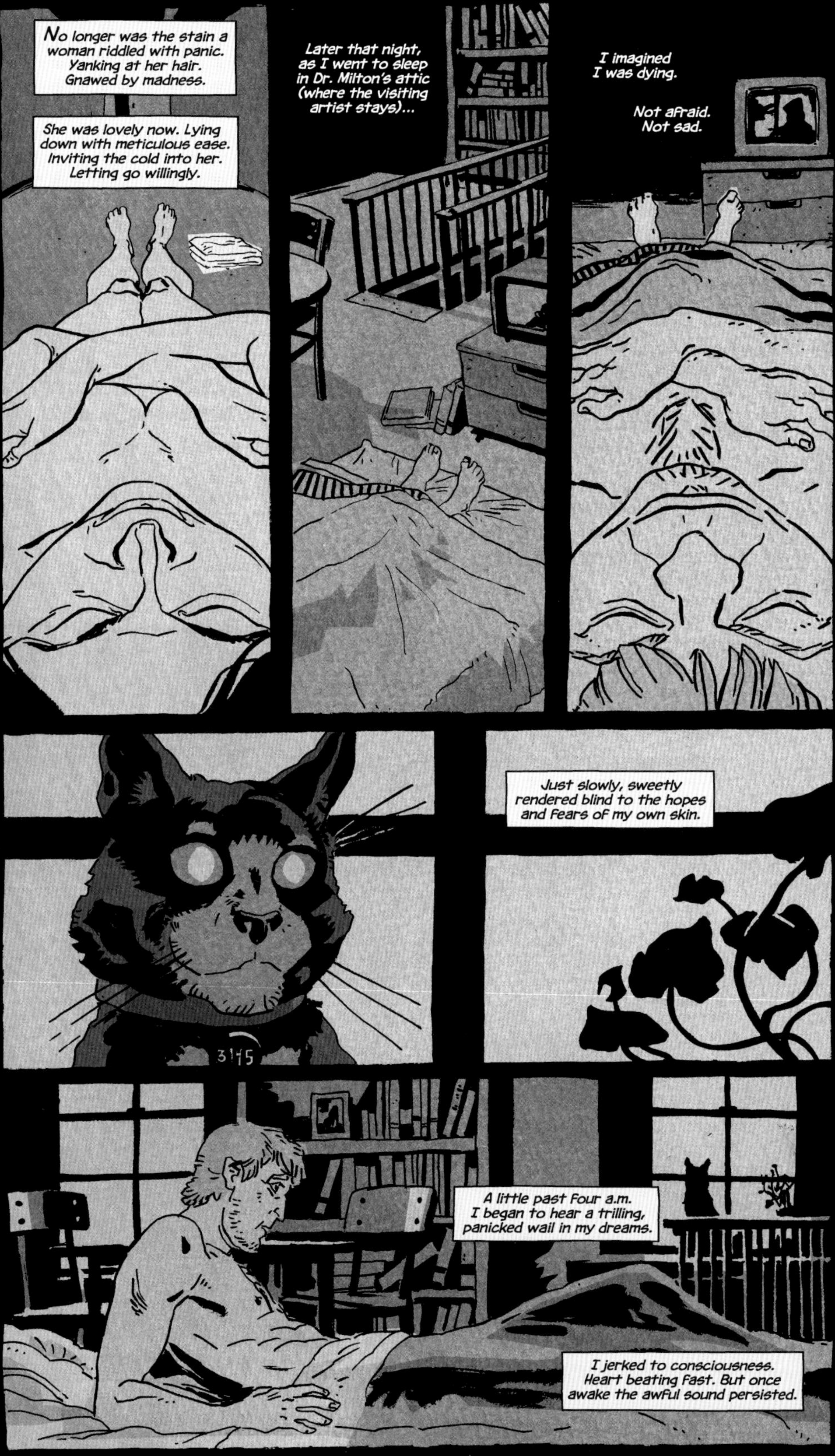
No longer was the stain a woman riddled with panic. Yanking at her hair. Gnawed by madness.
She was lovely now. Lying down with meticulous ease. Inviting the cold into her. Letting go willingly.
Later that night, as I went to sleep in Dr. Milton's attic (where the visiting artist stays)...
I imagined I was dying.
Not afraid. Not sad.
3:45
Just slowly, sweetly rendered blind to the hopes and fears of my own skin.
A little past four a.m. I began to hear a trilling, panicked wail in my dreams.
I jerked to consciousness. Heart beating fast. But once awake the awful sound persisted.

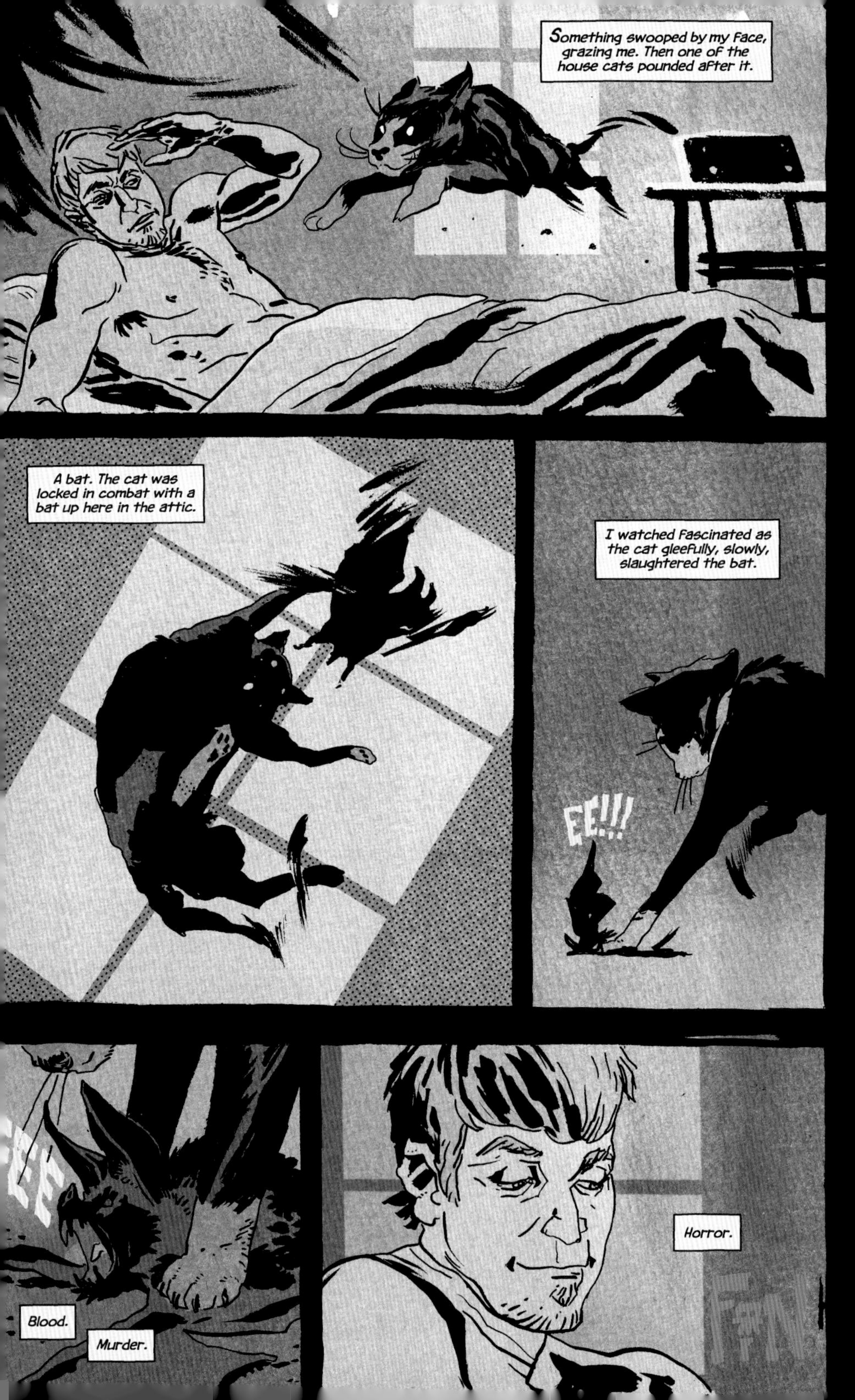
Something swooped by my face, grazing me. Then one of the house cats pounded after it.
A bat. The cat was locked in combat with a bat up here in the attic.
I watched fascinated as the cat gleefully, slowly, slaughtered the bat.
EE!!!
Blood.
Murder.
Horror.

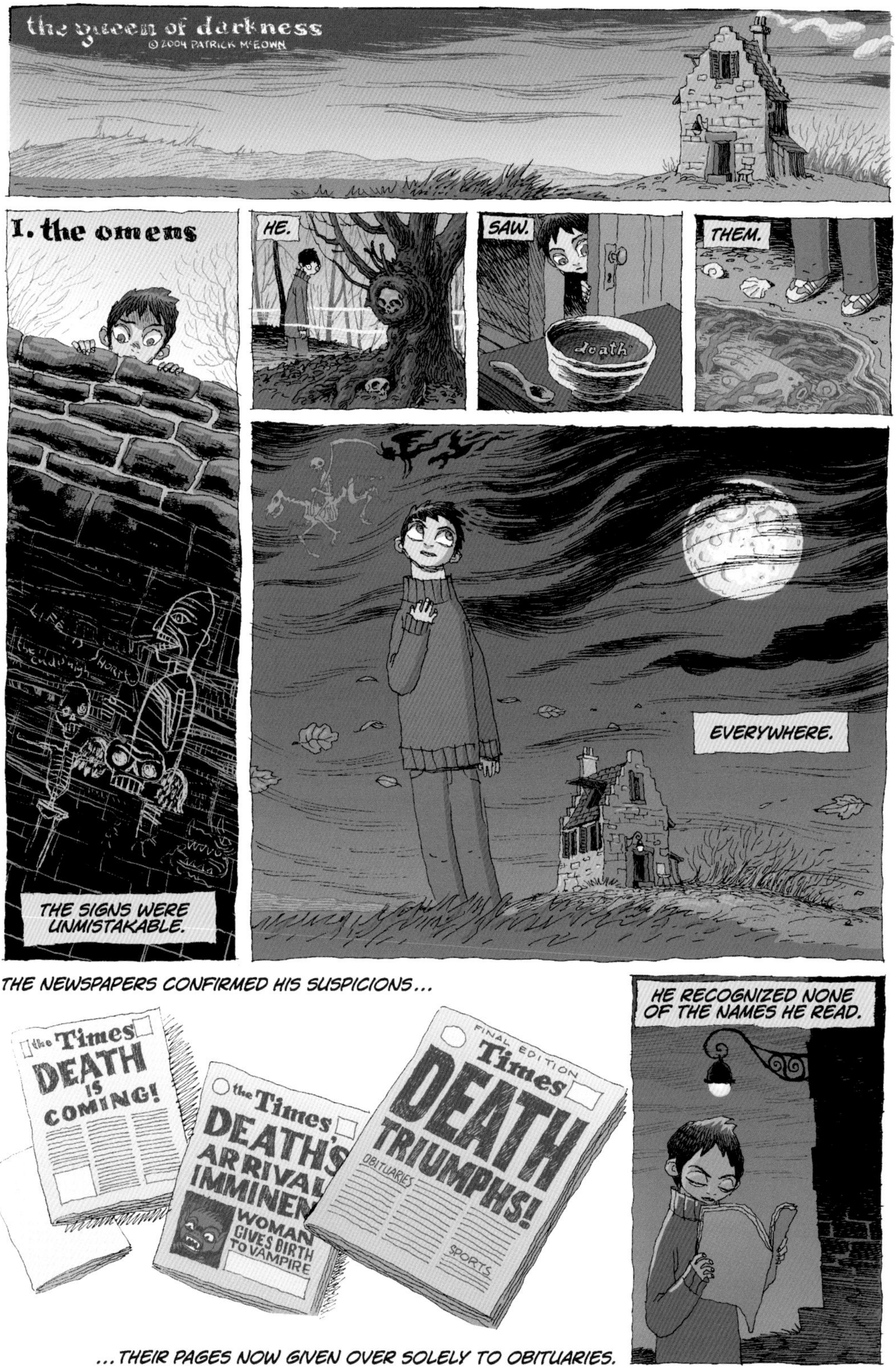
the queen of darkness
©2004 PATRICK McEOWN
I. the omens
HE.
SAW.
THEM.
death
THE SIGNS WERE UNMISTAKABLE.
EVERYWHERE.
THE NEWSPAPERS CONFIRMED HIS SUSPICIONS…
the Times
DEATH IS COMING!
the Times
DEATH'S ARRIVAL IMMINEN
WOMAN GIVES BIRTH TO VAMPIRE
FINAL EDITION
Times
DEATH TRIUMPHS!
OBITUARIES
SPORTS
…THEIR PAGES NOW GIVEN OVER SOLELY TO OBITUARIES.
HE RECOGNIZED NONE OF THE NAMES HE READ.

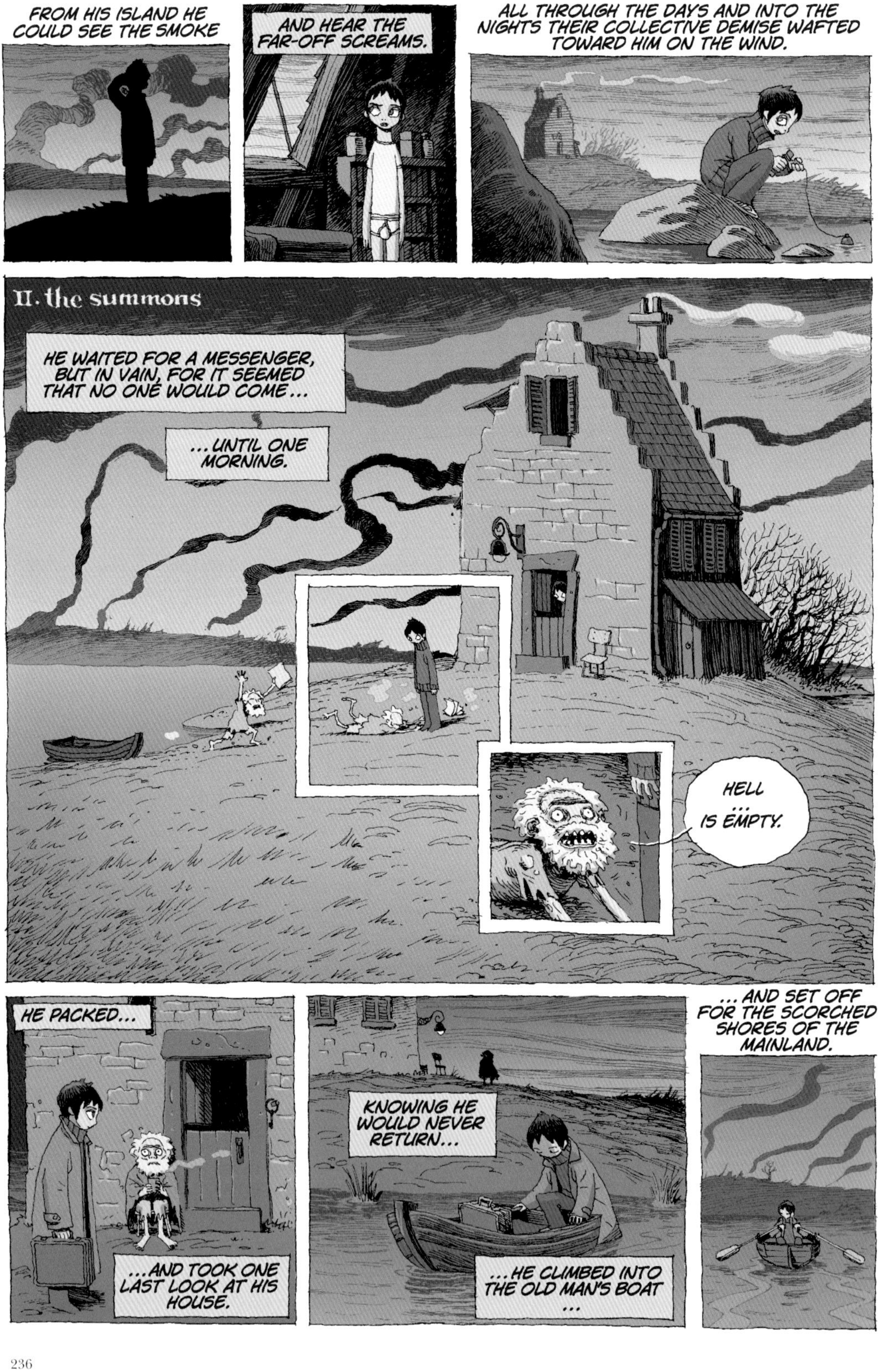
FROM HIS ISLAND HE COULD SEE THE SMOKE
AND HEAR THE FAR-OFF SCREAMS.
ALL THROUGH THE DAYS AND INTO THE NIGHTS THEIR COLLECTIVE DEMISE WAFTED TOWARD HIM ON THE WIND.
II. the summons
HE WAITED FOR A MESSENGER, BUT IN VAIN, FOR IT SEEMED THAT NO ONE WOULD COME...
...UNTIL ONE MORNING.
HELL ... IS EMPTY.
HE PACKED...
...AND TOOK ONE LAST LOOK AT HIS HOUSE.
KNOWING HE WOULD NEVER RETURN...
...HE CLIMBED INTO THE OLD MAN'S BOAT ...
...AND SET OFF FOR THE SCORCHED SHORES OF THE MAINLAND.

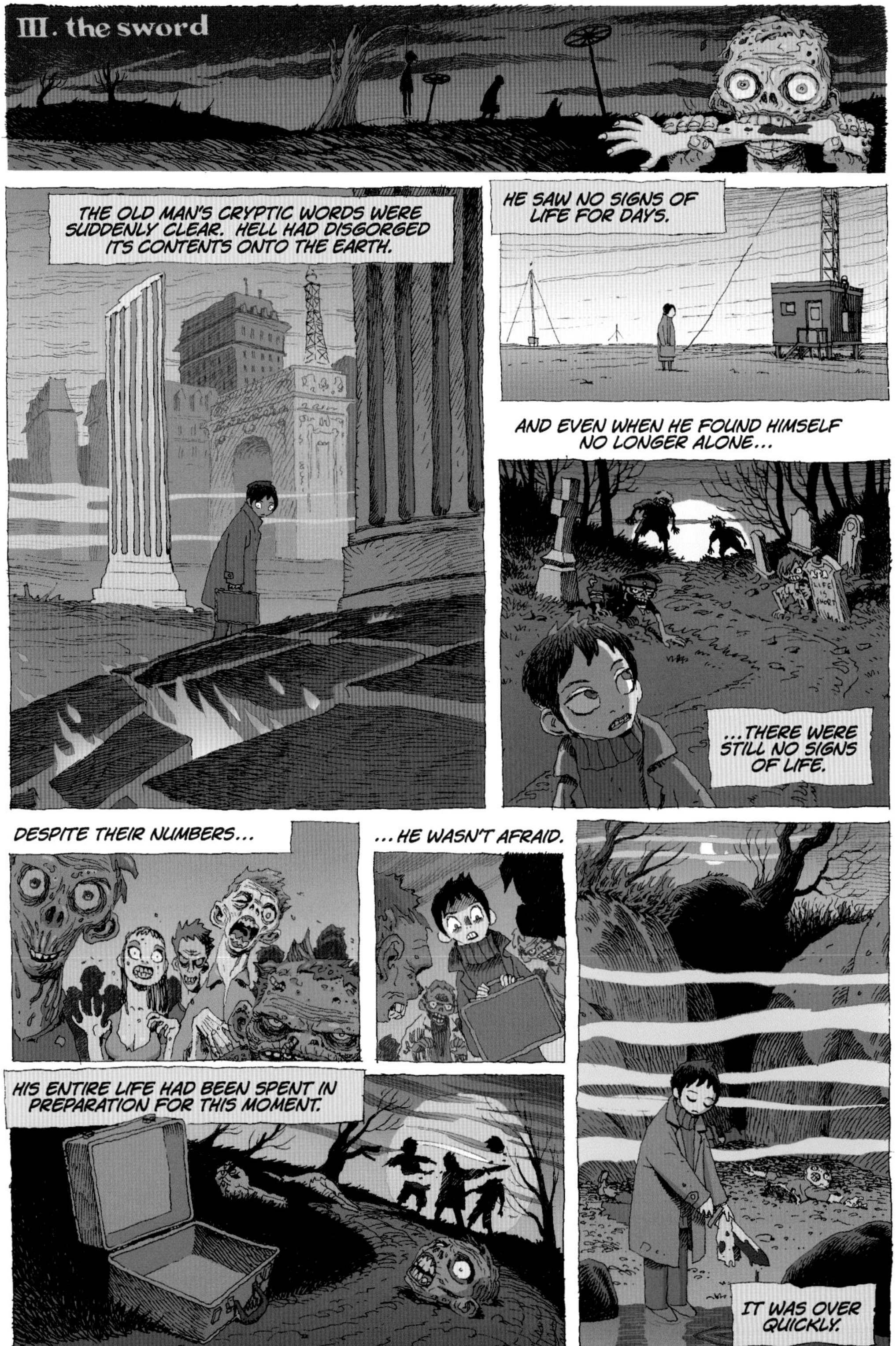
III. the sword
THE OLD MAN'S CRYPTIC WORDS WERE SUDDENLY CLEAR. HELL HAD DISGORGED ITS CONTENTS ONTO THE EARTH.
HE SAW NO SIGNS OF LIFE FOR DAYS.
AND EVEN WHEN HE FOUND HIMSELF NO LONGER ALONE...
LIFE IS SHORT
...THERE WERE STILL NO SIGNS OF LIFE.
DESPITE THEIR NUMBERS...
...HE WASN'T AFRAID.
HIS ENTIRE LIFE HAD BEEN SPENT IN PREPARATION FOR THIS MOMENT.
IT WAS OVER QUICKLY.

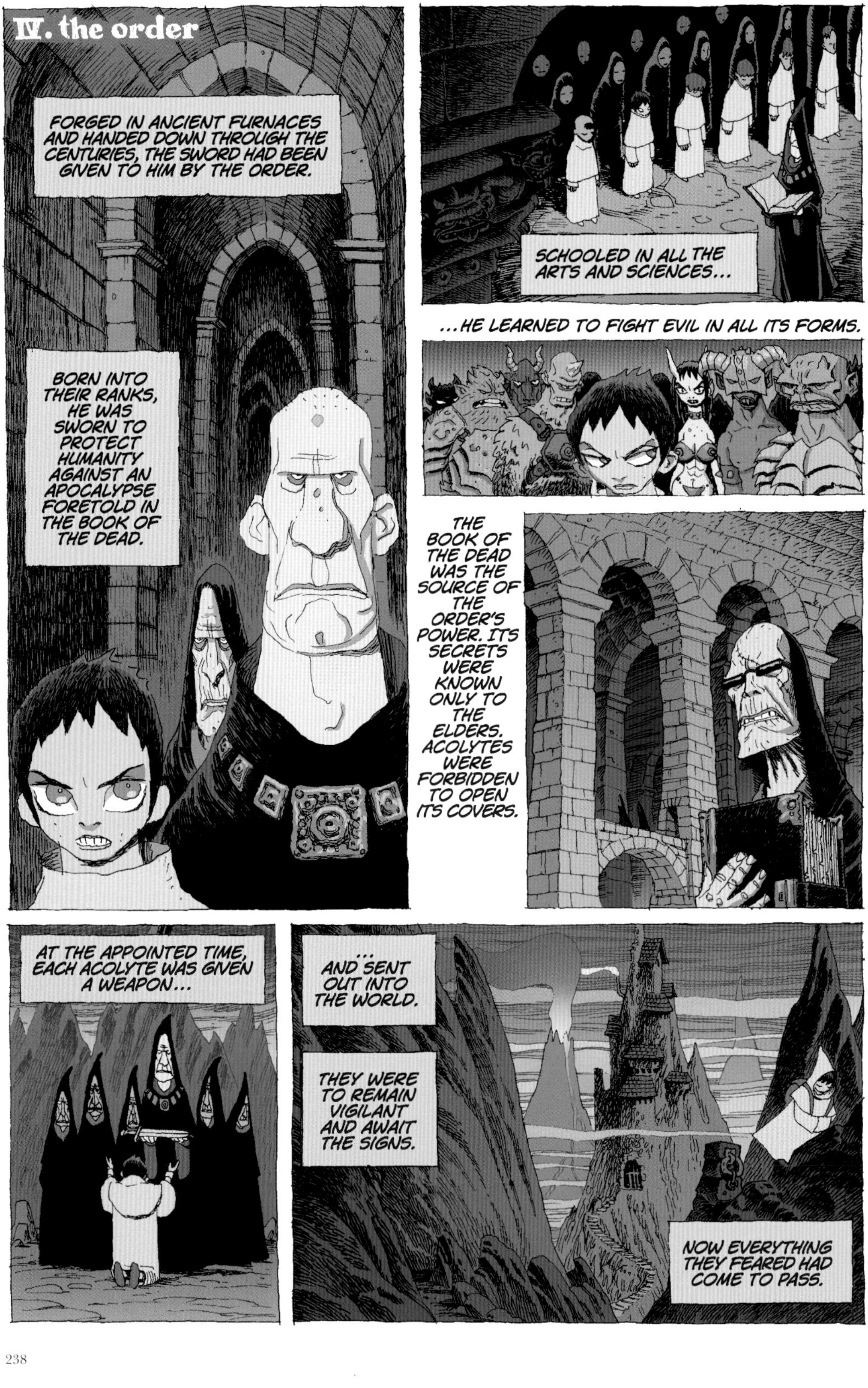
IV. the order
FORGED IN ANCIENT FURNACES AND HANDED DOWN THROUGH THE CENTURIES, THE SWORD HAD BEEN GIVEN TO HIM BY THE ORDER.
BORN INTO THEIR RANKS, HE WAS SWORN TO PROTECT HUMANITY AGAINST AN APOCALYPSE FORETOLD IN THE BOOK OF THE DEAD.
SCHOOLED IN ALL THE ARTS AND SCIENCES...
...HE LEARNED TO FIGHT EVIL IN ALL ITS FORMS.
THE BOOK OF THE DEAD WAS THE SOURCE OF THE ORDER'S POWER. ITS SECRETS WERE KNOWN ONLY TO THE ELDERS. ACOLYTES WERE FORBIDDEN TO OPEN ITS COVERS.
AT THE APPOINTED TIME, EACH ACOLYTE WAS GIVEN A WEAPON...
... AND SENT OUT INTO THE WORLD.
THEY WERE TO REMAIN VIGILANT AND AWAIT THE SIGNS.
NOW EVERYTHING THEY FEARED HAD COME TO PASS.

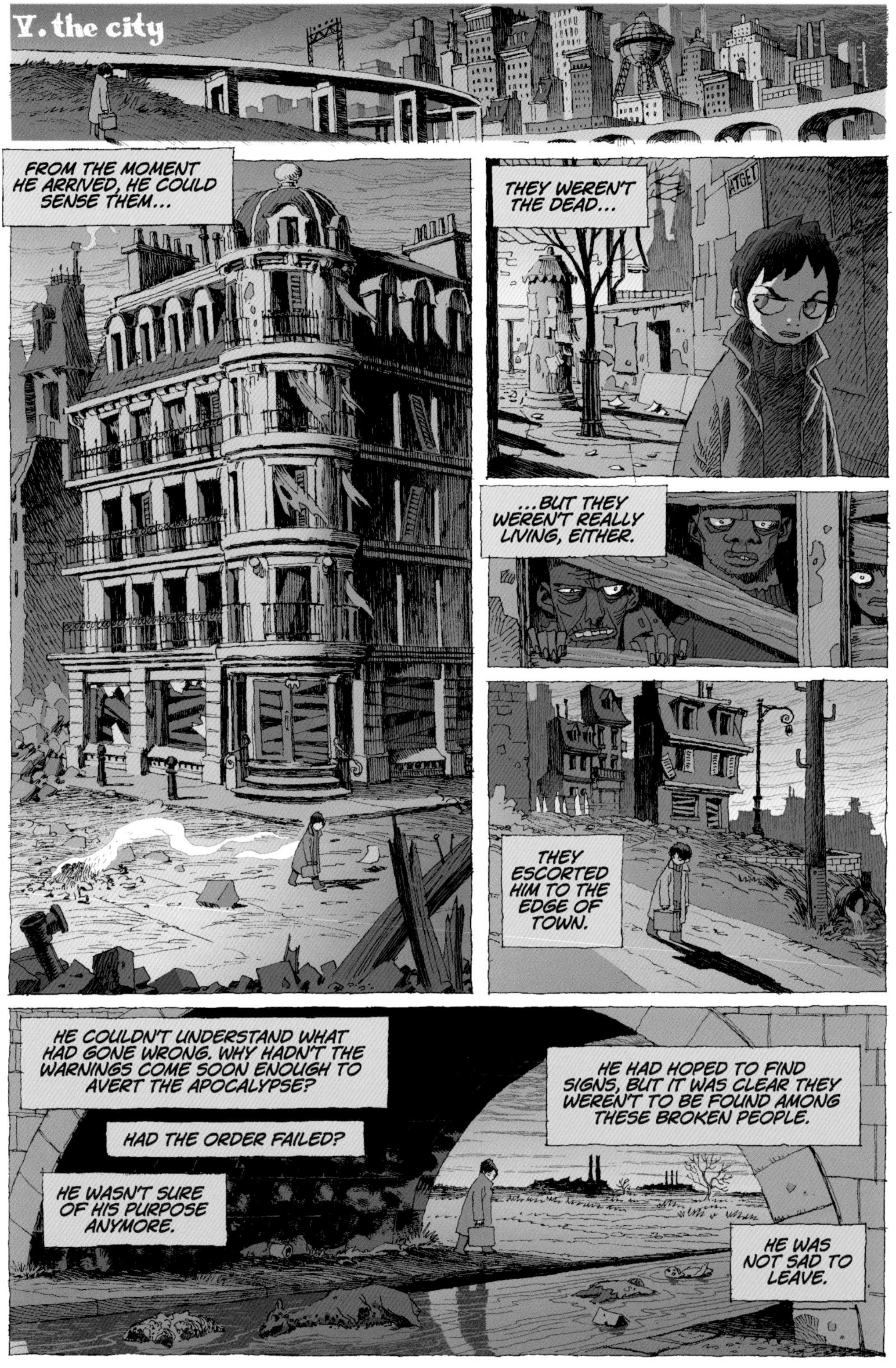
V. the city
FROM THE MOMENT HE ARRIVED, HE COULD SENSE THEM...
THEY WEREN'T THE DEAD...
ATGET
...BUT THEY WEREN'T REALLY LIVING, EITHER.
THEY ESCORTED HIM TO THE EDGE OF TOWN.
HE COULDN'T UNDERSTAND WHAT HAD GONE WRONG. WHY HADN'T THE WARNINGS COME SOON ENOUGH TO AVERT THE APOCALYPSE?
HAD THE ORDER FAILED?
HE WASN'T SURE OF HIS PURPOSE ANYMORE.
HE HAD HOPED TO FIND SIGNS, BUT IT WAS CLEAR THEY WEREN'T TO BE FOUND AMONG THESE BROKEN PEOPLE.
HE WAS NOT SAD TO LEAVE.

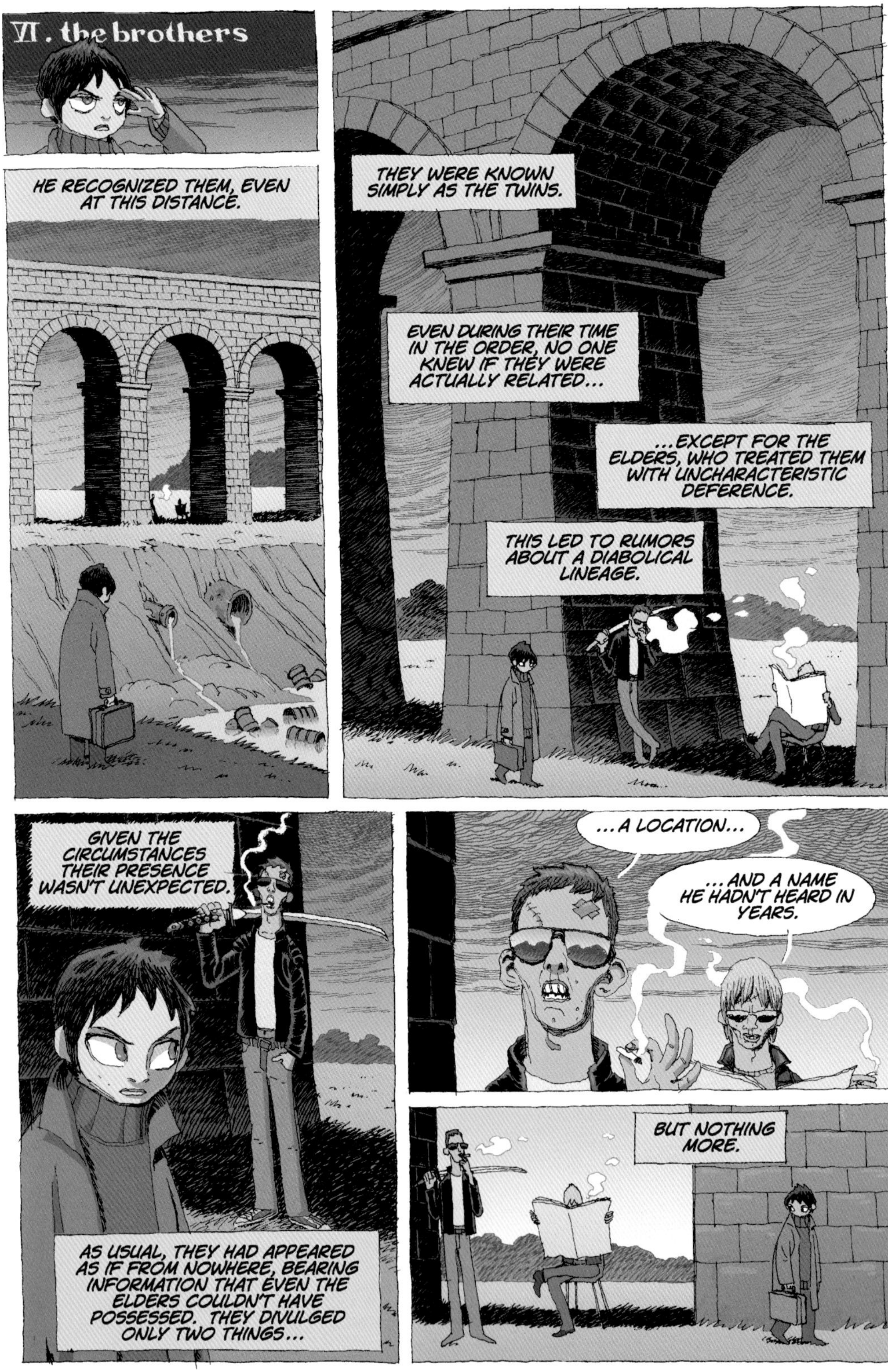
VI. the brothers
HE RECOGNIZED THEM, EVEN AT THIS DISTANCE.
THEY WERE KNOWN SIMPLY AS THE TWINS.
EVEN DURING THEIR TIME IN THE ORDER, NO ONE KNEW IF THEY WERE ACTUALLY RELATED...
...EXCEPT FOR THE ELDERS, WHO TREATED THEM WITH UNCHARACTERISTIC DEFERENCE.
THIS LED TO RUMORS ABOUT A DIABOLICAL LINEAGE.
GIVEN THE CIRCUMSTANCES THEIR PRESENCE WASN'T UNEXPECTED.
AS USUAL, THEY HAD APPEARED AS IF FROM NOWHERE, BEARING INFORMATION THAT EVEN THE ELDERS COULDN'T HAVE POSSESSED. THEY DIVULGED ONLY TWO THINGS...
...A LOCATION...
...AND A NAME HE HADN'T HEARD IN YEARS.
BUT NOTHING MORE.

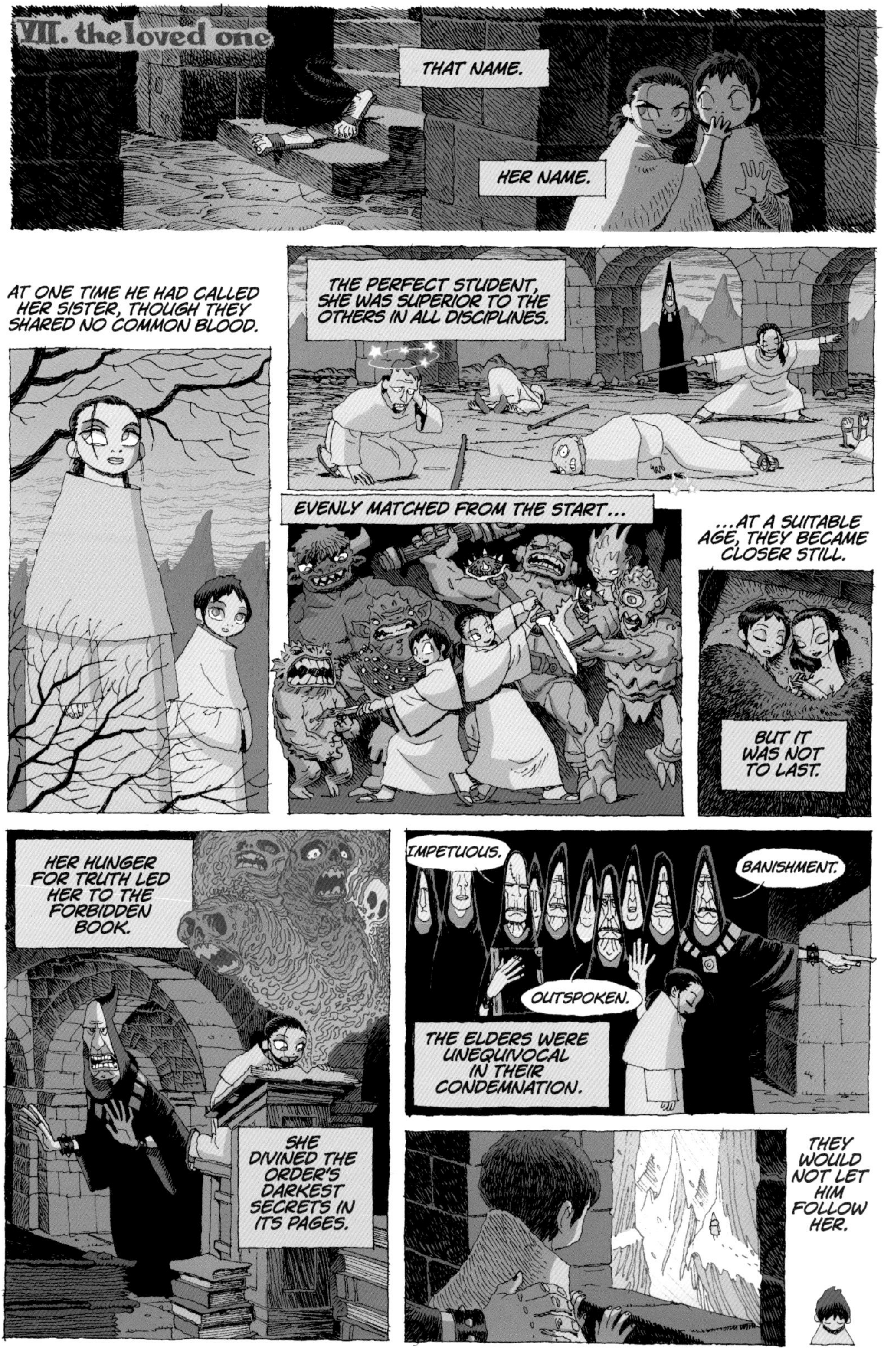
VII. the loved one
THAT NAME.
HER NAME.
AT ONE TIME HE HAD CALLED HER SISTER, THOUGH THEY SHARED NO COMMON BLOOD.
THE PERFECT STUDENT, SHE WAS SUPERIOR TO THE OTHERS IN ALL DISCIPLINES.
EVENLY MATCHED FROM THE START...
...AT A SUITABLE AGE, THEY BECAME CLOSER STILL.
BUT IT WAS NOT TO LAST.
HER HUNGER FOR TRUTH LED HER TO THE FORBIDDEN BOOK.
SHE DIVINED THE ORDER'S DARKEST SECRETS IN ITS PAGES.
IMPETUOUS.
BANISHMENT.
OUTSPOKEN.
THE ELDERS WERE UNEQUIVOCAL IN THEIR CONDEMNATION.
THEY WOULD NOT LET HIM FOLLOW HER.

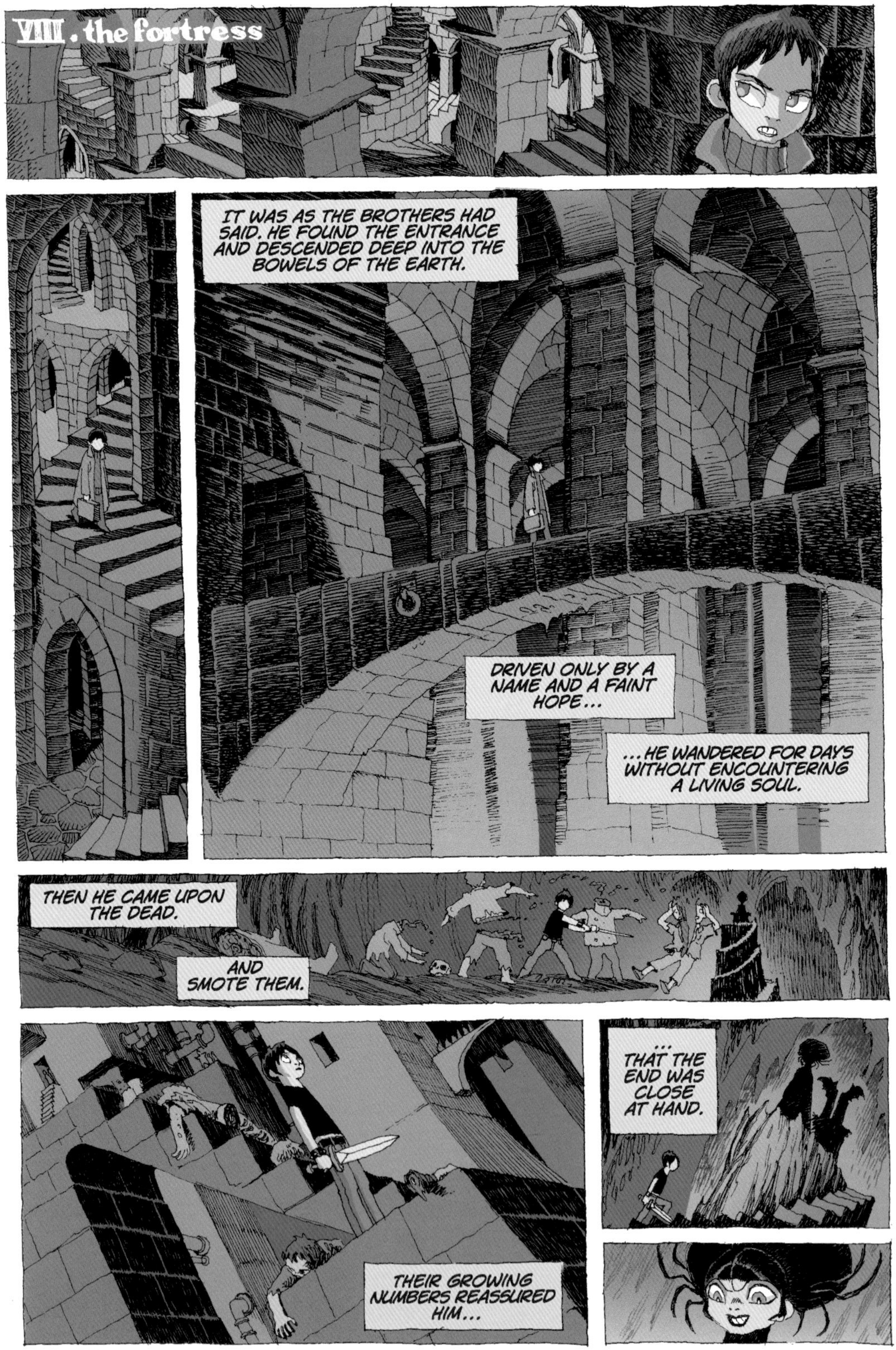
VIII. the fortress
IT WAS AS THE BROTHERS HAD SAID. HE FOUND THE ENTRANCE AND DESCENDED DEEP INTO THE BOWELS OF THE EARTH.
DRIVEN ONLY BY A NAME AND A FAINT HOPE...
...HE WANDERED FOR DAYS WITHOUT ENCOUNTERING A LIVING SOUL.
THEN HE CAME UPON THE DEAD.
AND SMOTE THEM.
THEIR GROWING NUMBERS REASSURED HIM...
...THAT THE END WAS CLOSE AT HAND.

IT WAS SHE WHOM HE HAD LOST...

...BUT NOT AS HE EXPECTED TO FIND HER.

YOU CAUSED ALL THIS...?

NO.

NOT ME.

THEY BROUGHT IT UPON THEMSELVES.

THE BOOK OF THE DEAD FORETOLD THIS.

BUT THE ORDER ...?

...KNEW IT WOULD COME TO PASS.

THEY WERE POWERLESS TO STOP HUMAN-KIND'S SELF-DESTRUCTION.

THEY HONED US ALL, KNOWING ONLY ONE WOULD SUCCEED TO USHER IN A NEW AGE.

THEY ALSO FORESAW OUR REUNION, AND THE DECISION YOU WOULD FACE.

THE FATE OF THE WORLD RESTS IN YOUR HANDS.

BUT KNOW THIS--

DESTROYING ME WILL NOT RESTORE THE LIVING.

YOUR BRETHREN HAVE PROVEN NO MATCH FOR ME.

WOULD YOU SUCCEED WHERE THEY HAVE FAILED?

"I OFFER YOU A LOVE THAT STILL BURNS IN THE ASHES OF A RUINED WORLD...

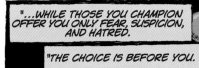

"...WHILE THOSE YOU CHAMPION OFFER YOU ONLY FEAR, SUSPICION, AND HATRED.

"THE CHOICE IS BEFORE YOU.

"YOU MUST DECIDE..."

end.

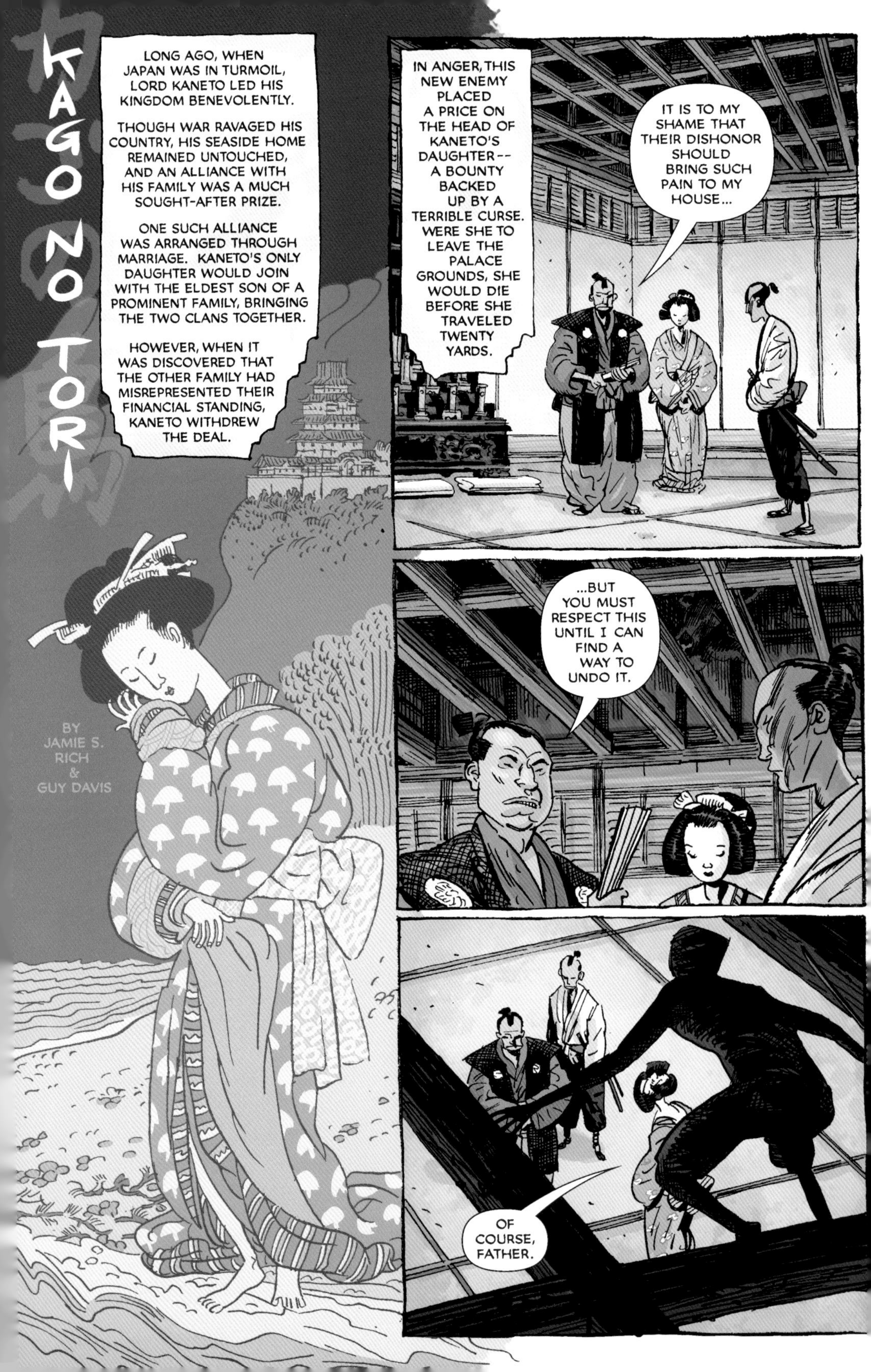

KAGO NO TORI
LONG AGO, WHEN JAPAN WAS IN TURMOIL, LORD KANETO LED HIS KINGDOM BENEVOLENTLY.
THOUGH WAR RAVAGED HIS COUNTRY, HIS SEASIDE HOME REMAINED UNTOUCHED, AND AN ALLIANCE WITH HIS FAMILY WAS A MUCH SOUGHT-AFTER PRIZE.
ONE SUCH ALLIANCE WAS ARRANGED THROUGH MARRIAGE. KANETO'S ONLY DAUGHTER WOULD JOIN WITH THE ELDEST SON OF A PROMINENT FAMILY, BRINGING THE TWO CLANS TOGETHER.
HOWEVER, WHEN IT WAS DISCOVERED THAT THE OTHER FAMILY HAD MISREPRESENTED THEIR FINANCIAL STANDING, KANETO WITHDREW THE DEAL.
BY JAMIE S. RICH & GUY DAVIS
IN ANGER, THIS NEW ENEMY PLACED A PRICE ON THE HEAD OF KANETO'S DAUGHTER-- A BOUNTY BACKED UP BY A TERRIBLE CURSE. WERE SHE TO LEAVE THE PALACE GROUNDS, SHE WOULD DIE BEFORE SHE TRAVELED TWENTY YARDS.
IT IS TO MY SHAME THAT THEIR DISHONOR SHOULD BRING SUCH PAIN TO MY HOUSE...
...BUT YOU MUST RESPECT THIS UNTIL I CAN FIND A WAY TO UNDO IT.
OF COURSE, FATHER.

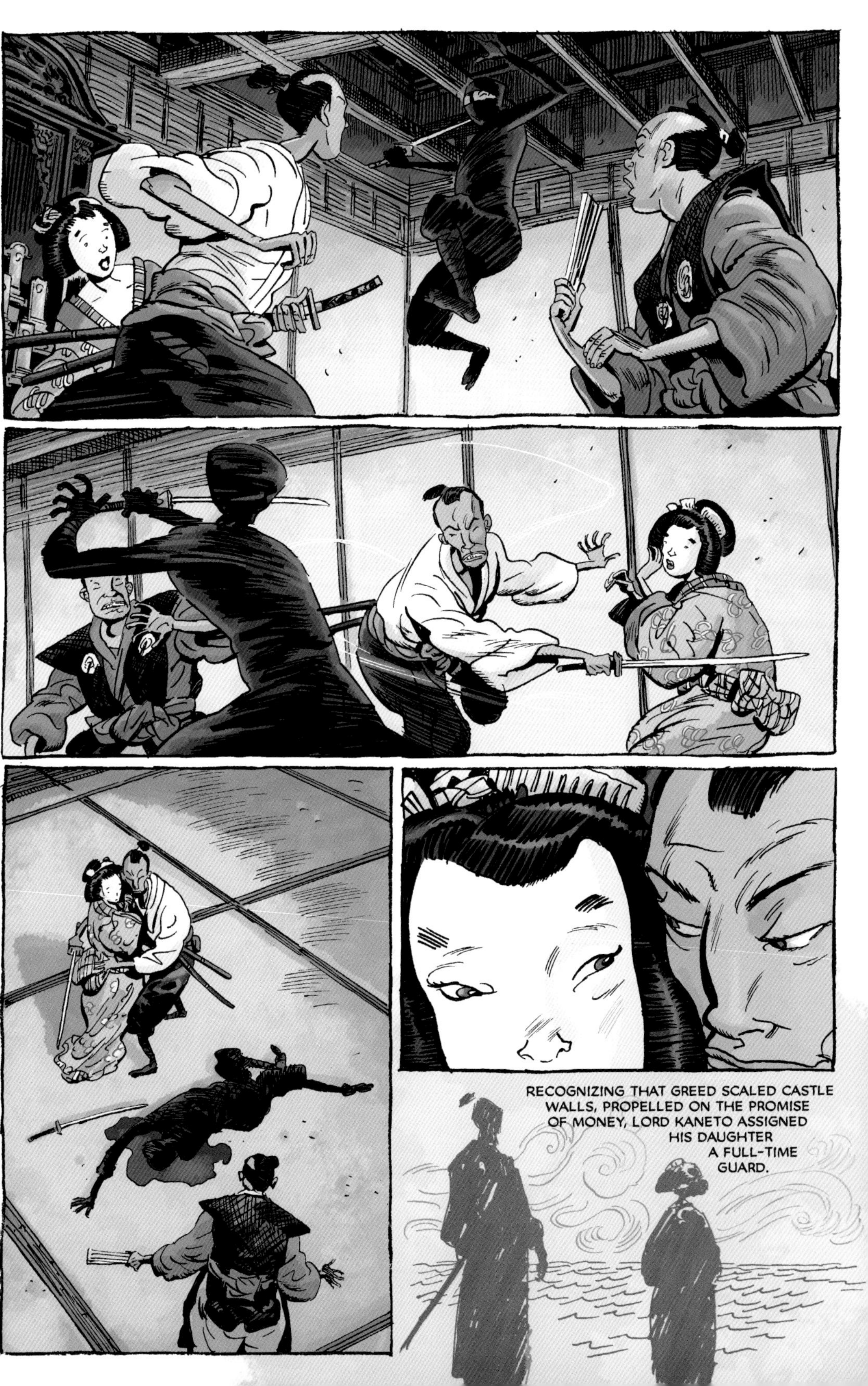
RECOGNIZING THAT GREED SCALED CASTLE WALLS, PROPELLED ON THE PROMISE OF MONEY, LORD KANETO ASSIGNED HIS DAUGHTER A FULL-TIME GUARD.

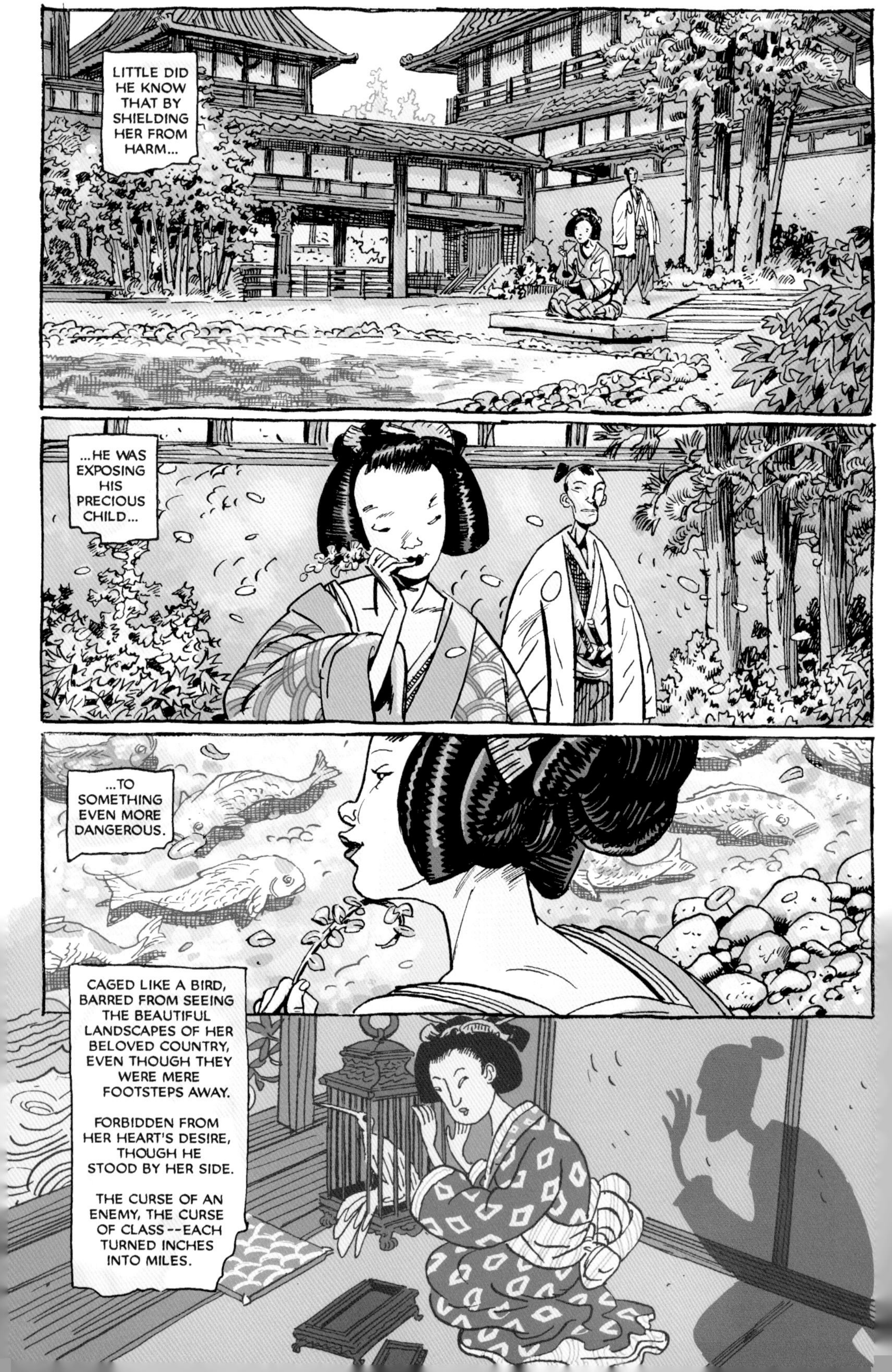
LITTLE DID HE KNOW THAT BY SHIELDING HER FROM HARM...
...HE WAS EXPOSING HIS PRECIOUS CHILD...
...TO SOMETHING EVEN MORE DANGEROUS.
CAGED LIKE A BIRD, BARRED FROM SEEING THE BEAUTIFUL LANDSCAPES OF HER BELOVED COUNTRY, EVEN THOUGH THEY WERE MERE FOOTSTEPS AWAY.
FORBIDDEN FROM HER HEART'S DESIRE, THOUGH HE STOOD BY HER SIDE.
THE CURSE OF AN ENEMY, THE CURSE OF CLASS--EACH TURNED INCHES INTO MILES.

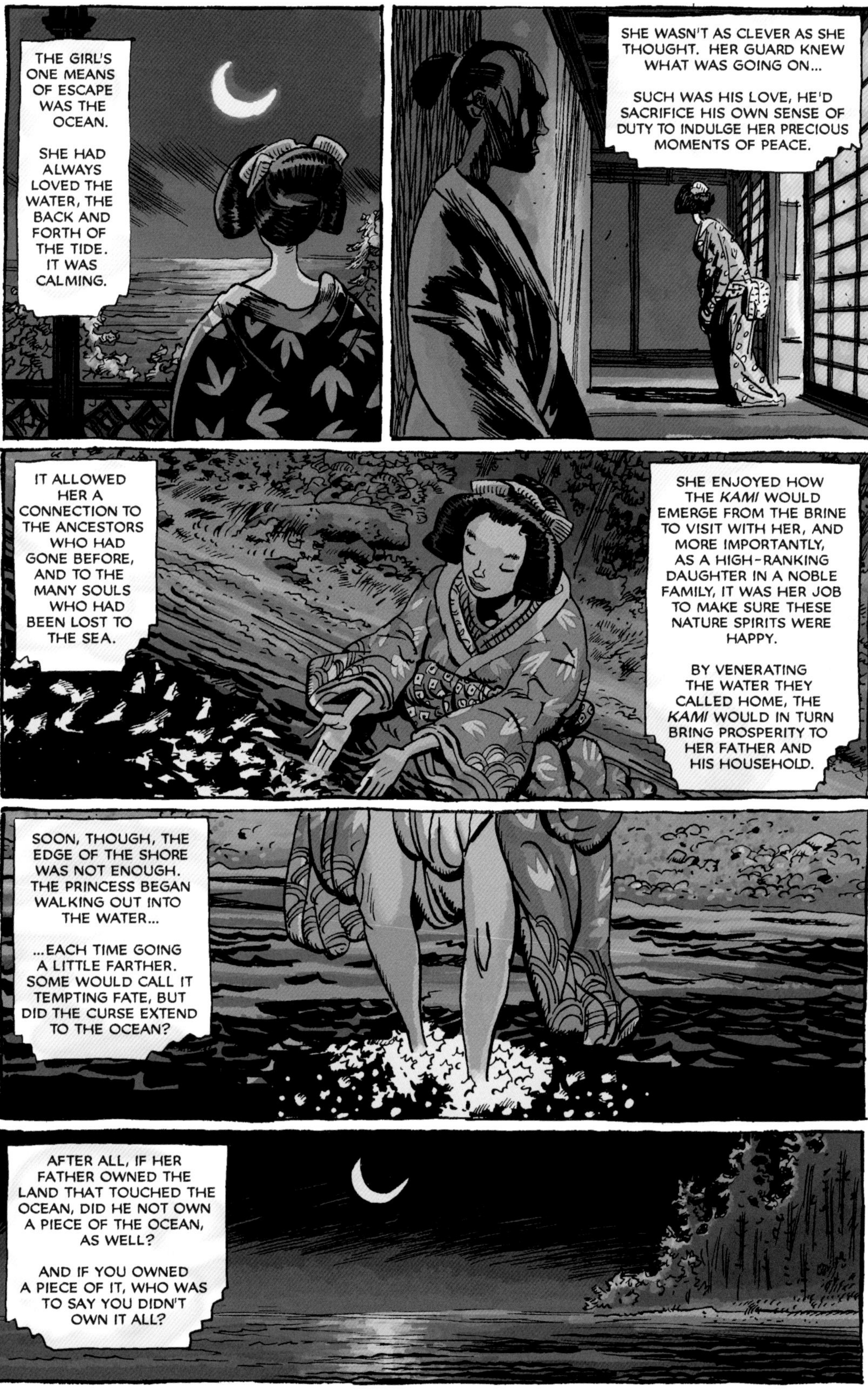
THE GIRL'S ONE MEANS OF ESCAPE WAS THE OCEAN.
SHE HAD ALWAYS LOVED THE WATER, THE BACK AND FORTH OF THE TIDE. IT WAS CALMING.
SHE WASN'T AS CLEVER AS SHE THOUGHT. HER GUARD KNEW WHAT WAS GOING ON...
SUCH WAS HIS LOVE, HE'D SACRIFICE HIS OWN SENSE OF DUTY TO INDULGE HER PRECIOUS MOMENTS OF PEACE.
IT ALLOWED HER A CONNECTION TO THE ANCESTORS WHO HAD GONE BEFORE, AND TO THE MANY SOULS WHO HAD BEEN LOST TO THE SEA.
SHE ENJOYED HOW THE *KAMI* WOULD EMERGE FROM THE BRINE TO VISIT WITH HER, AND MORE IMPORTANTLY, AS A HIGH-RANKING DAUGHTER IN A NOBLE FAMILY, IT WAS HER JOB TO MAKE SURE THESE NATURE SPIRITS WERE HAPPY.
BY VENERATING THE WATER THEY CALLED HOME, THE *KAMI* WOULD IN TURN BRING PROSPERITY TO HER FATHER AND HIS HOUSEHOLD.
SOON, THOUGH, THE EDGE OF THE SHORE WAS NOT ENOUGH. THE PRINCESS BEGAN WALKING OUT INTO THE WATER...
...EACH TIME GOING A LITTLE FARTHER. SOME WOULD CALL IT TEMPTING FATE, BUT DID THE CURSE EXTEND TO THE OCEAN?
AFTER ALL, IF HER FATHER OWNED THE LAND THAT TOUCHED THE OCEAN, DID HE NOT OWN A PIECE OF THE OCEAN, AS WELL?
AND IF YOU OWNED A PIECE OF IT, WHO WAS TO SAY YOU DIDN'T OWN IT ALL?

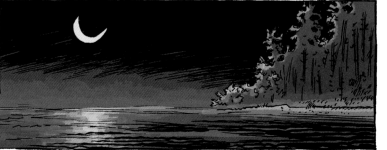

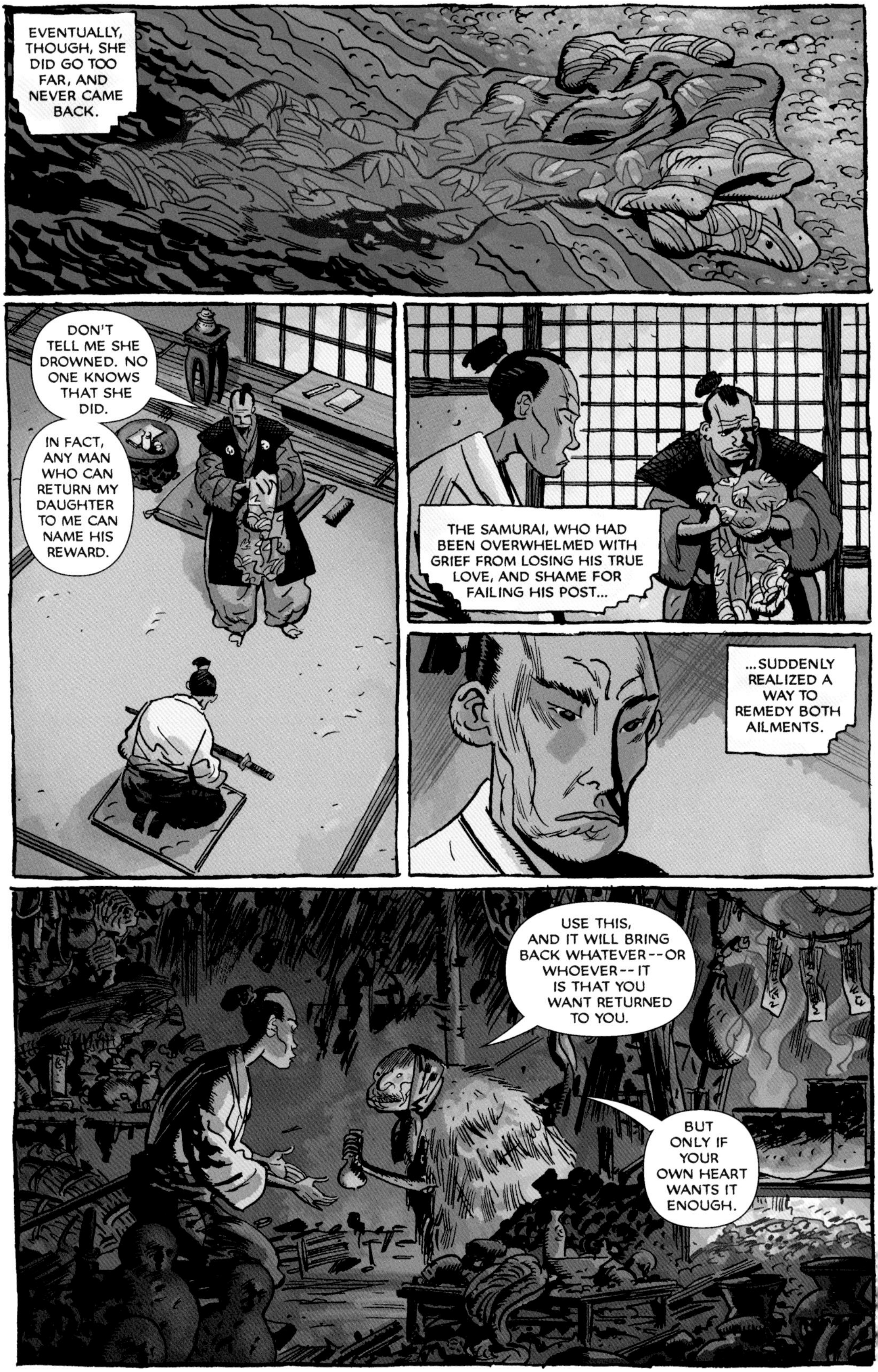
EVENTUALLY, THOUGH, SHE DID GO TOO FAR, AND NEVER CAME BACK.
DON'T TELL ME SHE DROWNED. NO ONE KNOWS THAT SHE DID.
IN FACT, ANY MAN WHO CAN RETURN MY DAUGHTER TO ME CAN NAME HIS REWARD.
THE SAMURAI, WHO HAD BEEN OVERWHELMED WITH GRIEF FROM LOSING HIS TRUE LOVE, AND SHAME FOR FAILING HIS POST...
...SUDDENLY REALIZED A WAY TO REMEDY BOTH AILMENTS.
USE THIS, AND IT WILL BRING BACK WHATEVER--OR WHOEVER--IT IS THAT YOU WANT RETURNED TO YOU.
BUT ONLY IF YOUR OWN HEART WANTS IT ENOUGH.

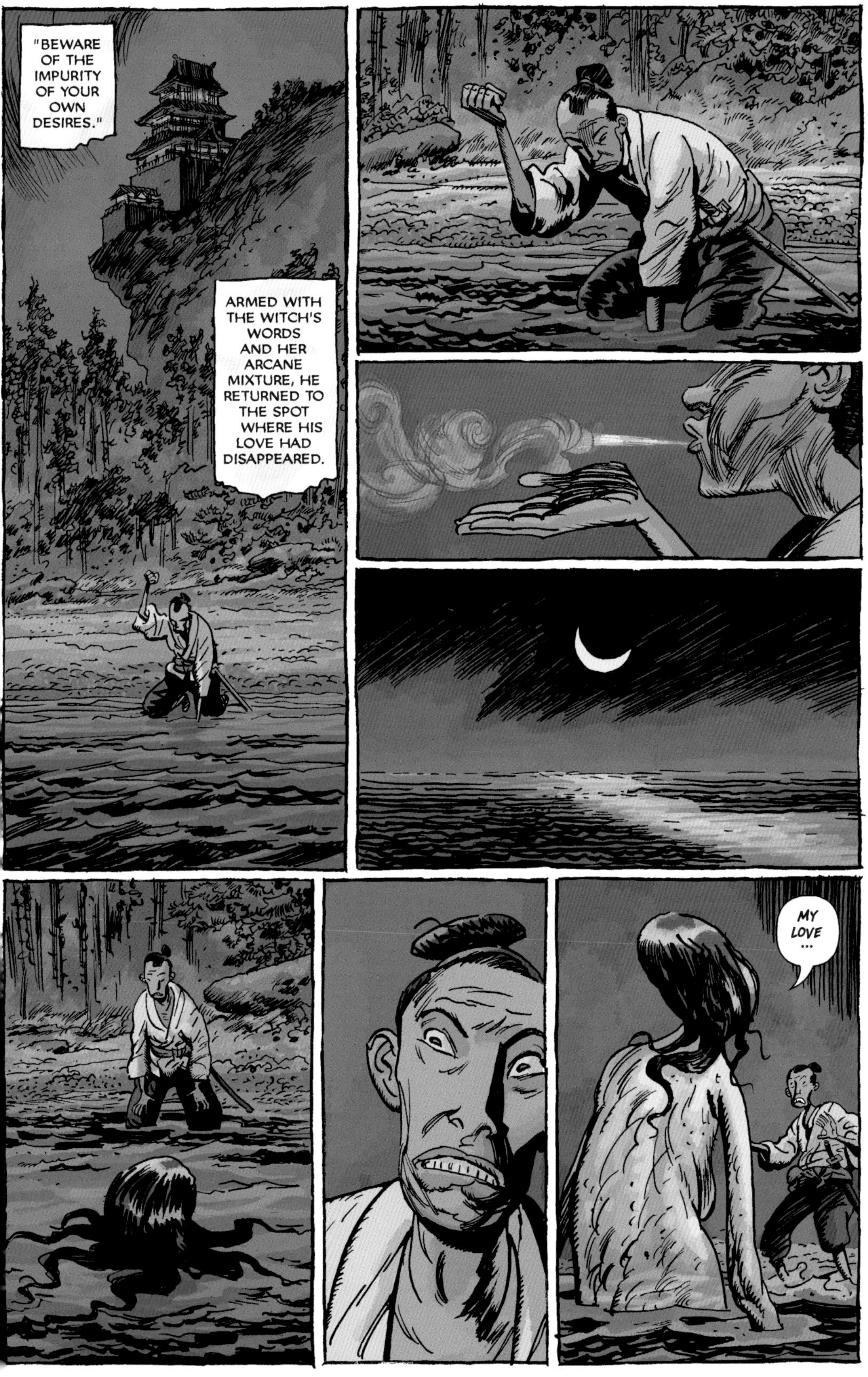
"BEWARE OF THE IMPURITY OF YOUR OWN DESIRES."
ARMED WITH THE WITCH'S WORDS AND HER ARCANE MIXTURE, HE RETURNED TO THE SPOT WHERE HIS LOVE HAD DISAPPEARED.
MY LOVE ...

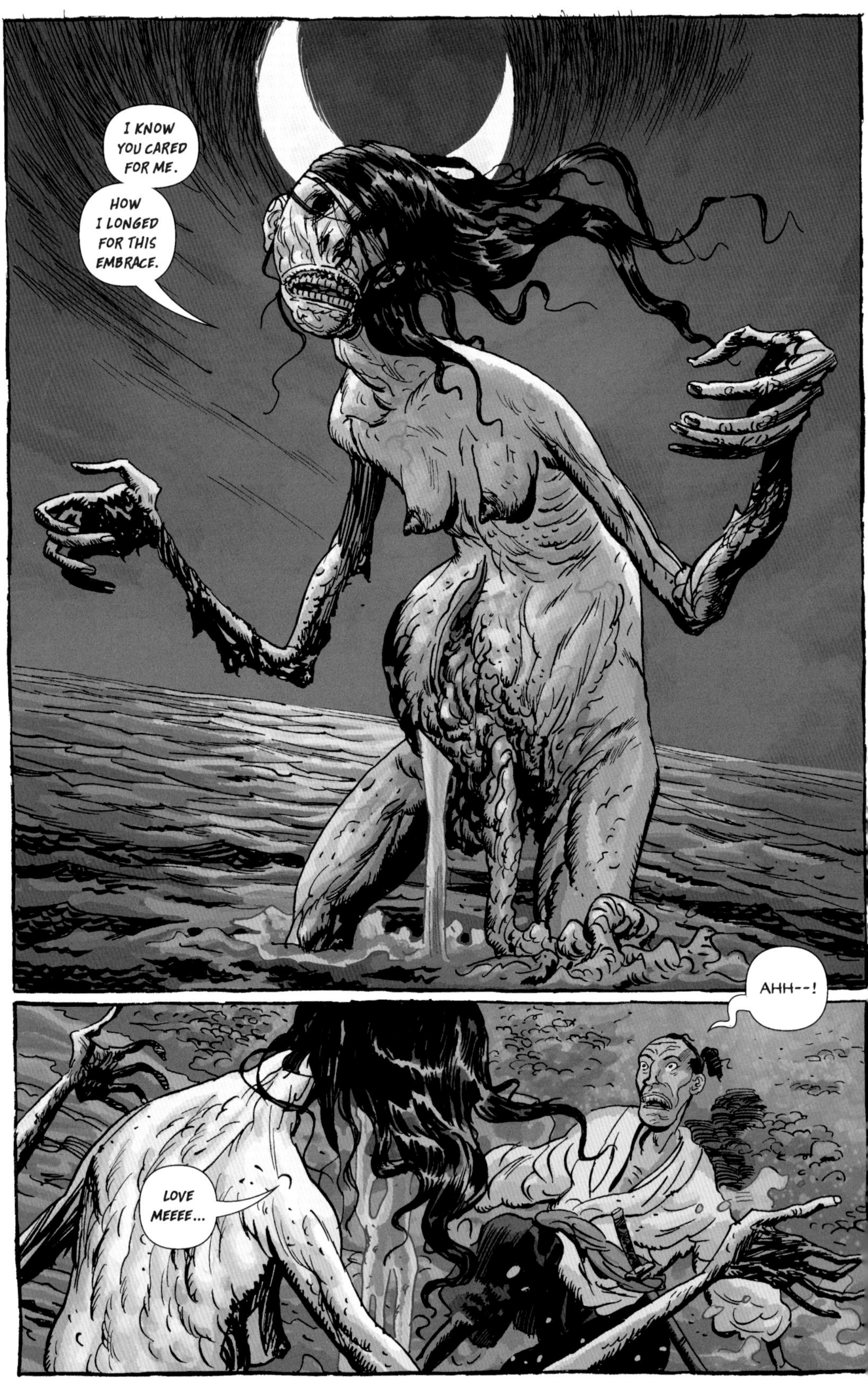
I KNOW YOU CARED FOR ME.
HOW I LONGED FOR THIS EMBRACE.
AHH--!
LOVE MEEEE...

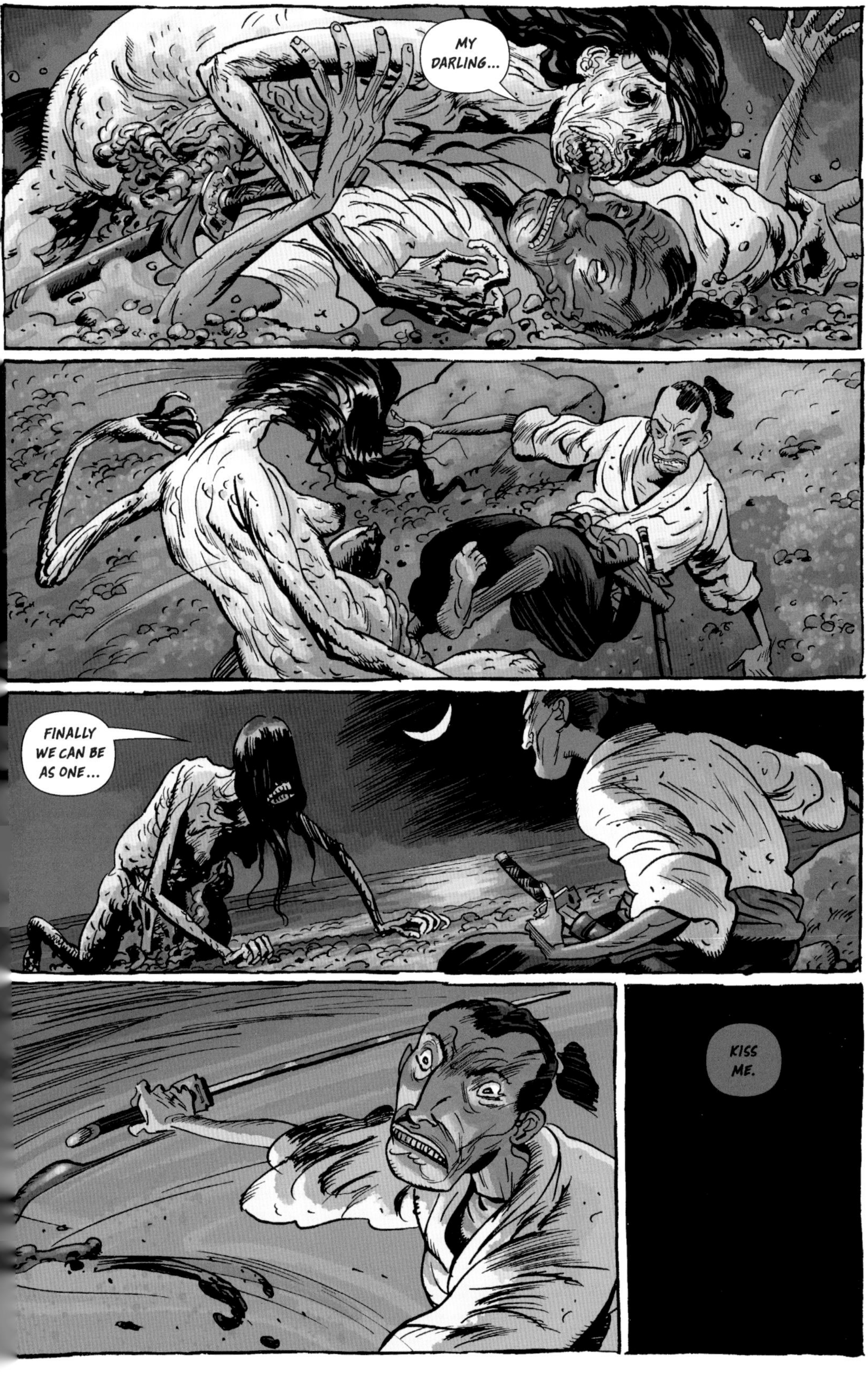
MY DARLING...
FINALLY WE CAN BE AS ONE...
KISS ME.

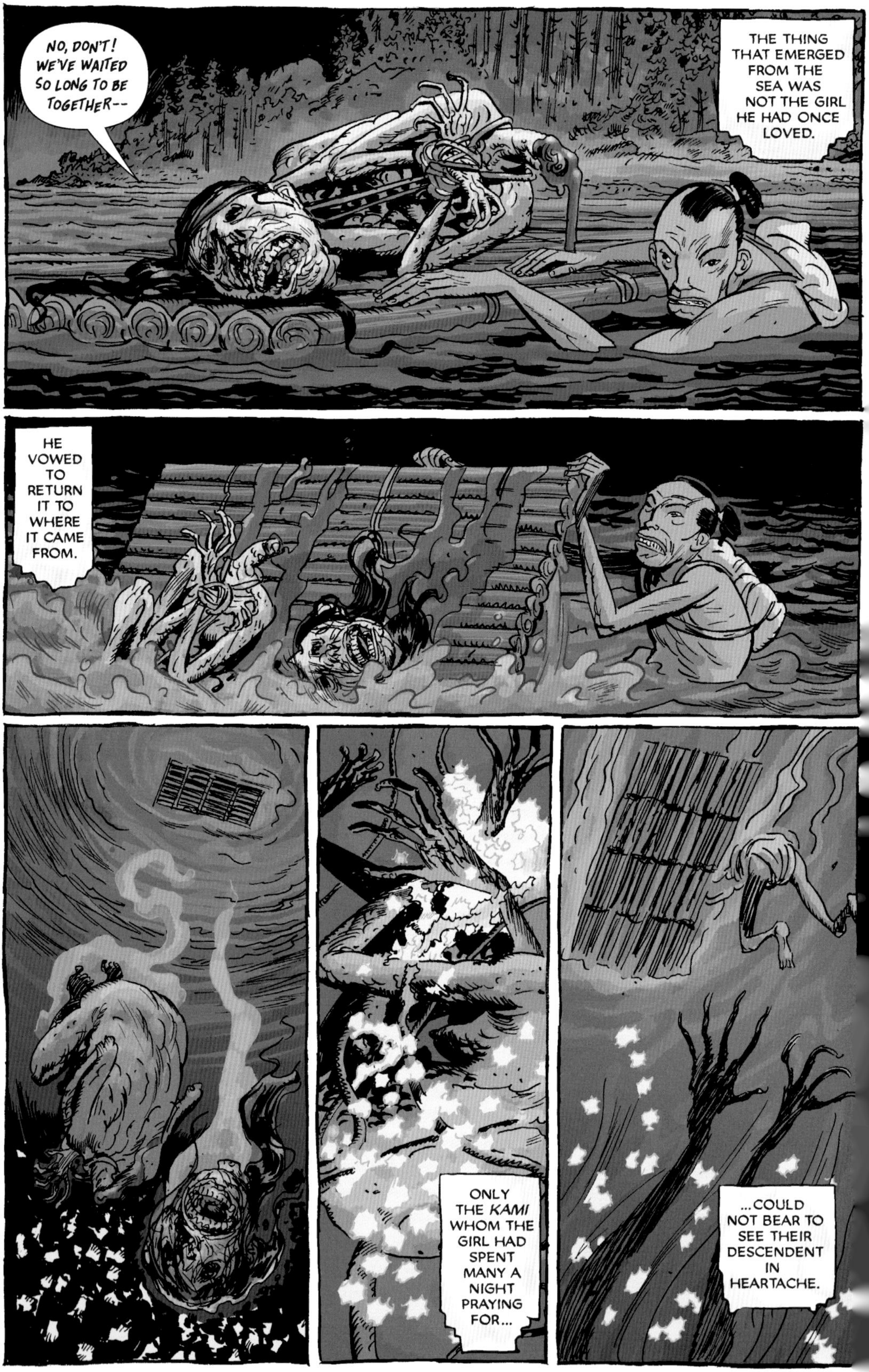
NO, DON'T! WE'VE WAITED SO LONG TO BE TOGETHER--
THE THING THAT EMERGED FROM THE SEA WAS NOT THE GIRL HE HAD ONCE LOVED.
HE VOWED TO RETURN IT TO WHERE IT CAME FROM.
ONLY THE *KAMI* WHOM THE GIRL HAD SPENT MANY A NIGHT PRAYING FOR...
...COULD NOT BEAR TO SEE THEIR DESCENDENT IN HEARTACHE.

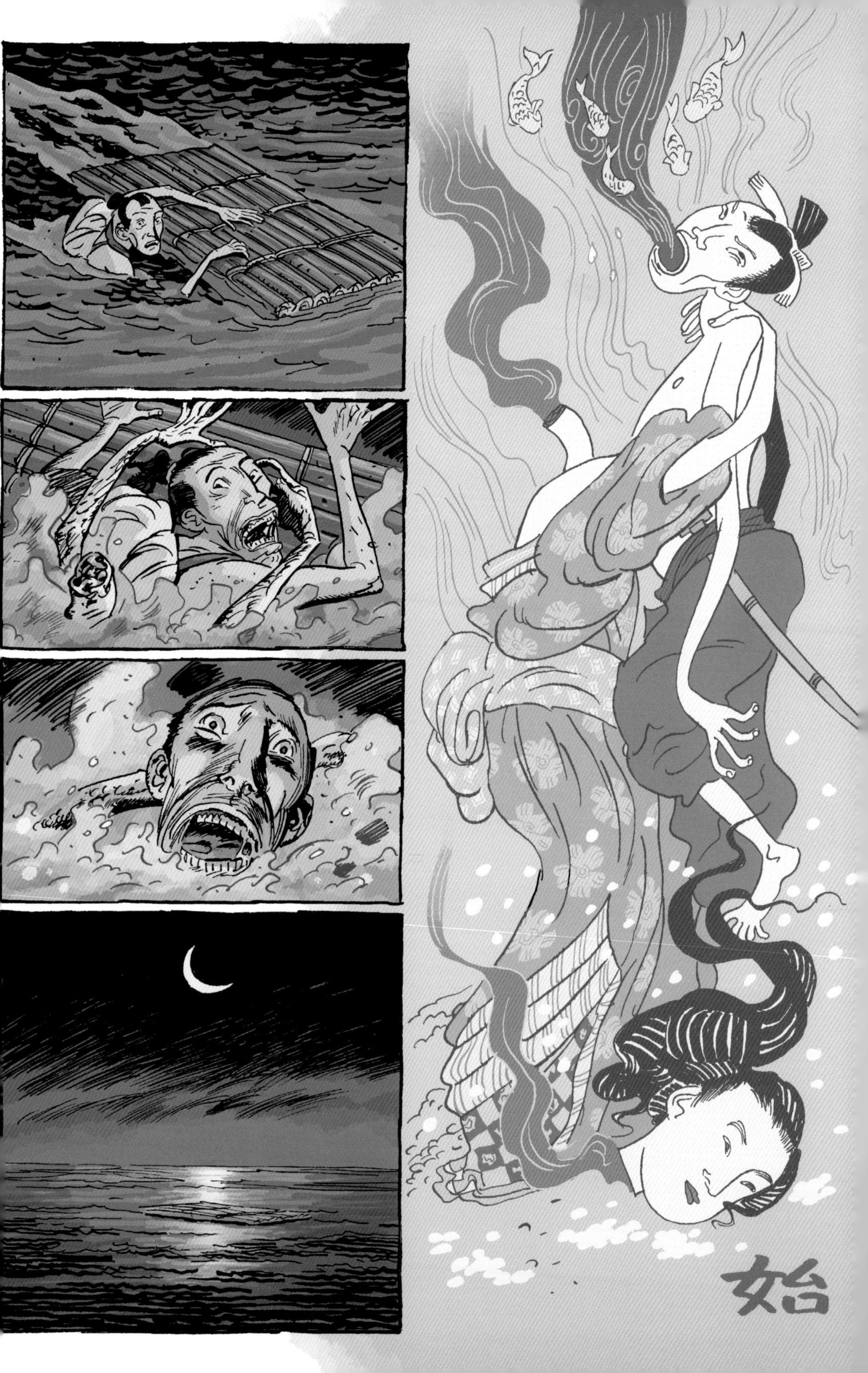
始

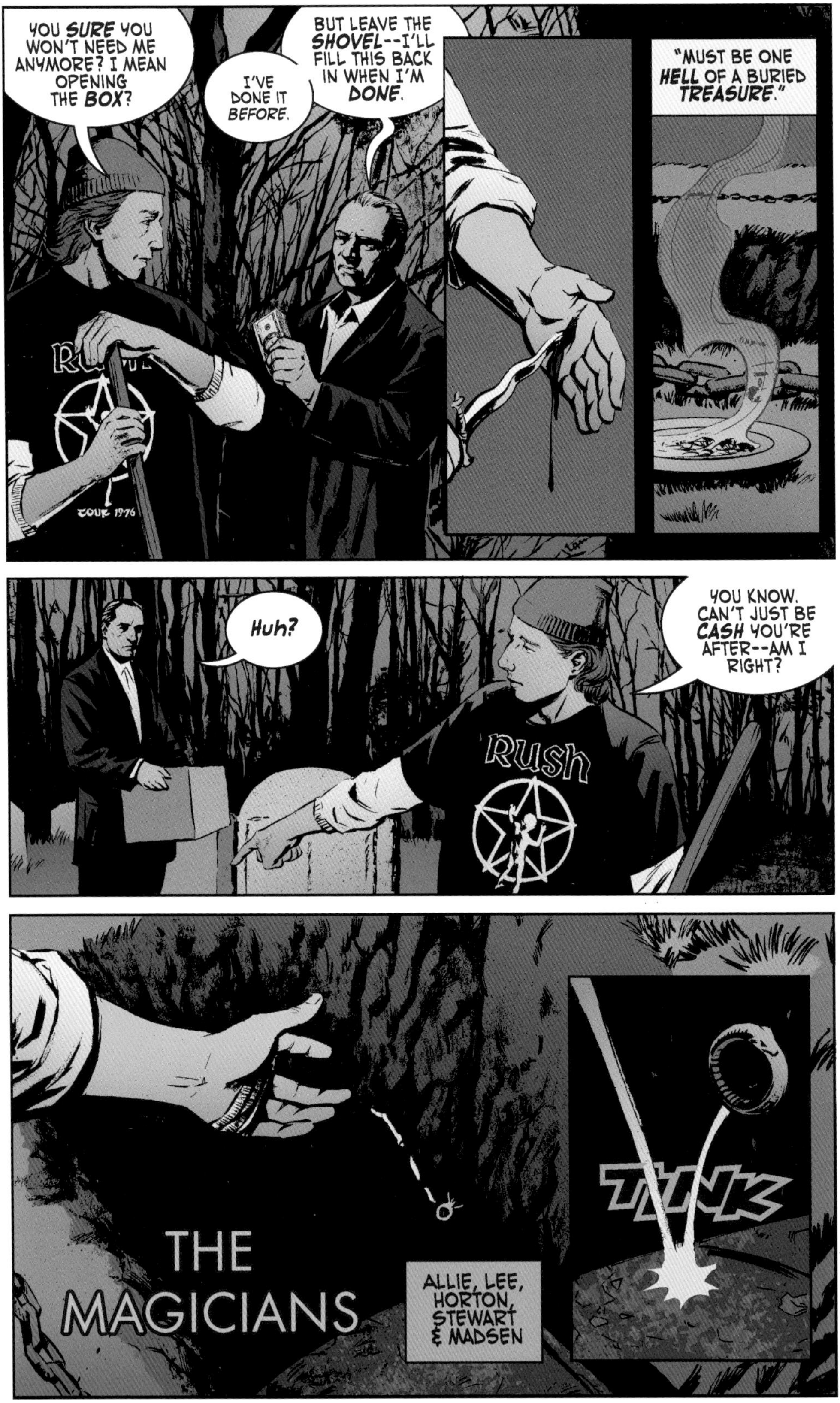
YOU SURE YOU WON'T NEED ME ANYMORE? I MEAN OPENING THE BOX?
I'VE DONE IT BEFORE.
BUT LEAVE THE SHOVEL--I'LL FILL THIS BACK IN WHEN I'M DONE.
"MUST BE ONE HELL OF A BURIED TREASURE."
Huh?
YOU KNOW. CAN'T JUST BE CASH YOU'RE AFTER--AM I RIGHT?
RUSH
TINK
THE MAGICIANS
ALLIE, LEE, HORTON, STEWART & MADSEN

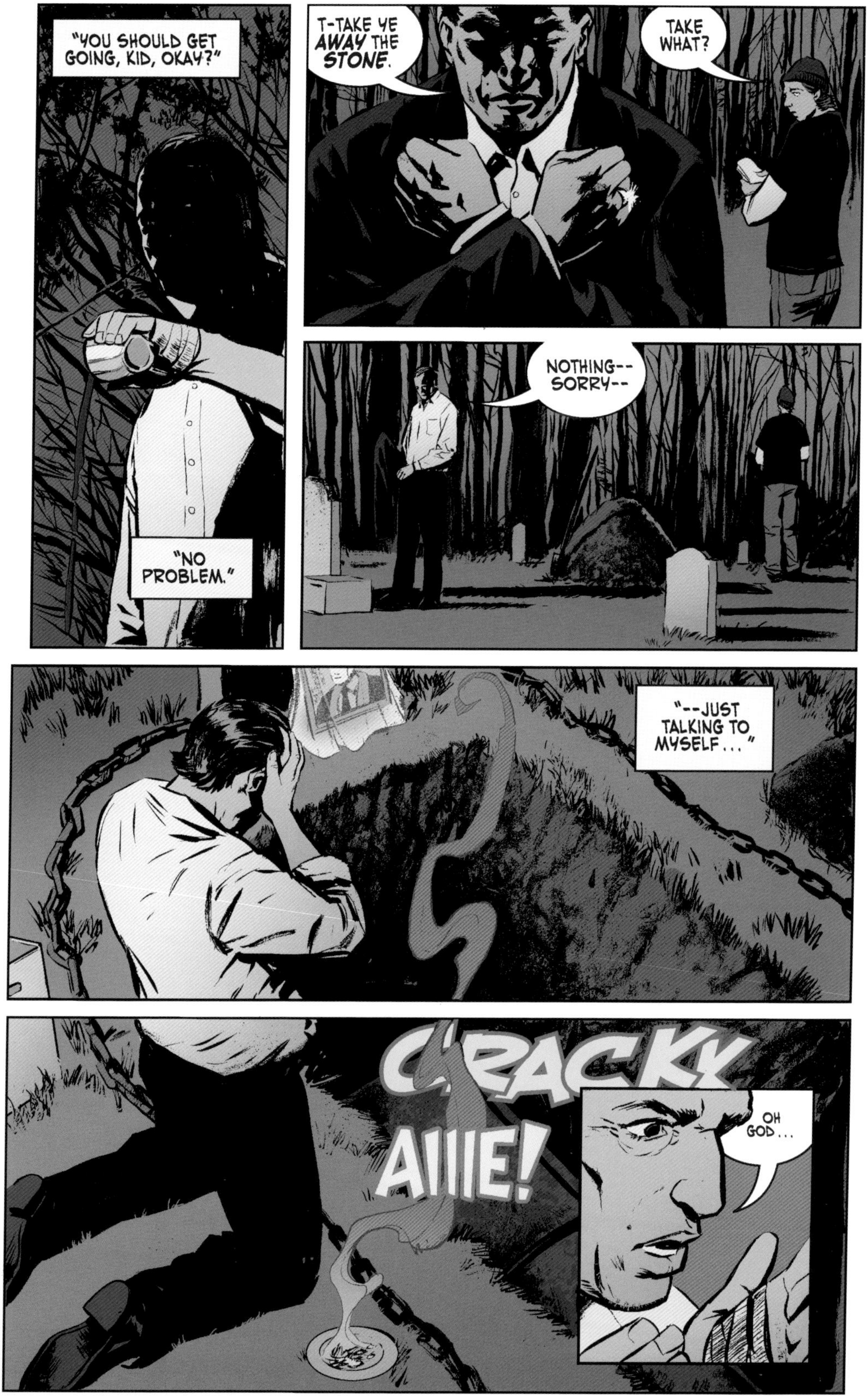
"YOU SHOULD GET GOING, KID, OKAY?"
"NO PROBLEM."
T-TAKE YE AWAY THE STONE.
TAKE WHAT?
NOTHING-- SORRY--
"--JUST TALKING TO MYSELF..."
CRACK!
AIIIE!
OH GOD...

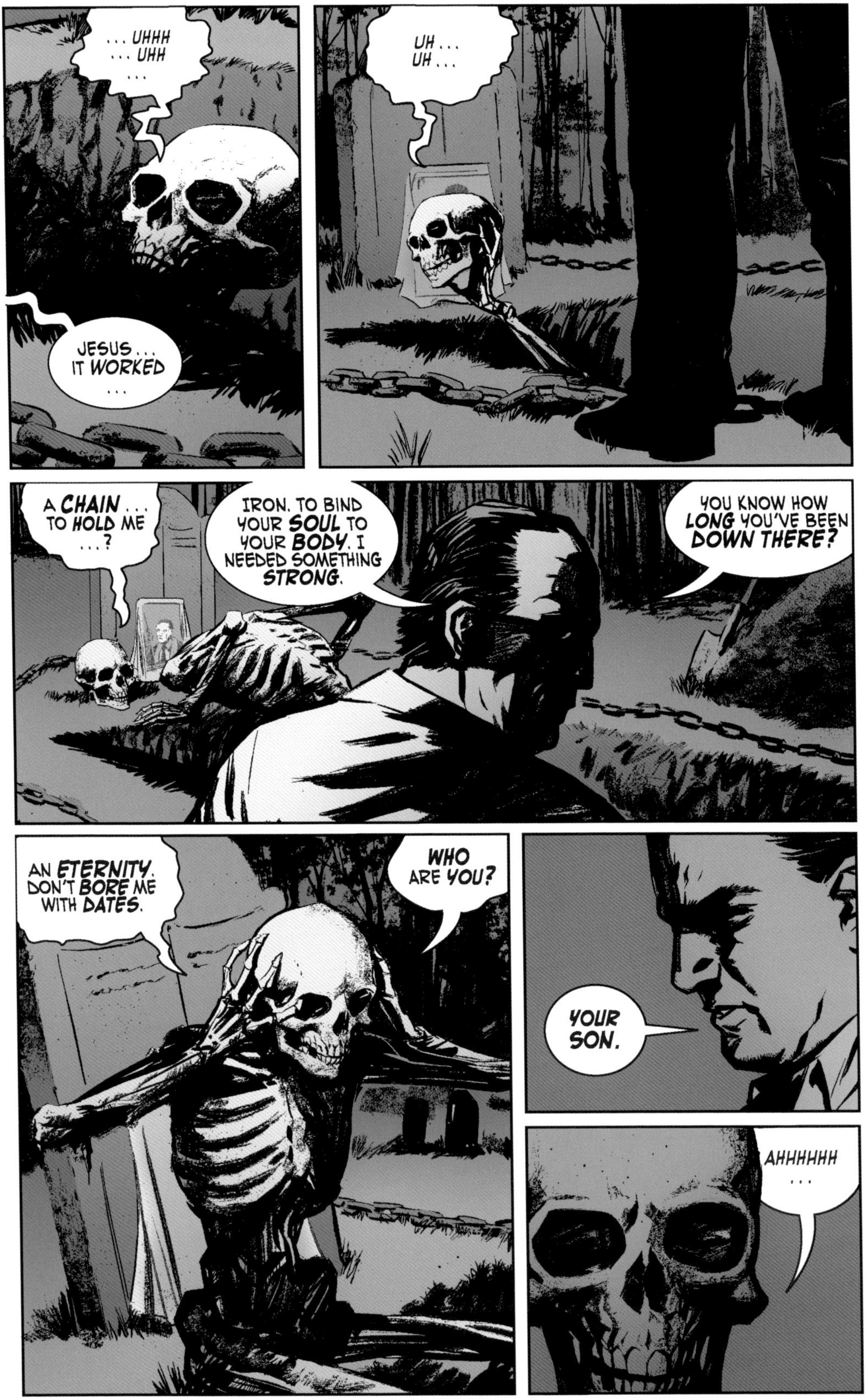
. . . UHHH . . . UHH . . .
JESUS . . . IT WORKED . . .
UH . . . UH . . .
A CHAIN . . . TO HOLD ME . . . ?
IRON. TO BIND YOUR SOUL TO YOUR BODY. I NEEDED SOMETHING STRONG.
YOU KNOW HOW LONG YOU'VE BEEN DOWN THERE?
AN ETERNITY. DON'T BORE ME WITH DATES.
WHO ARE YOU?
YOUR SON.
AHHHHHH . . .

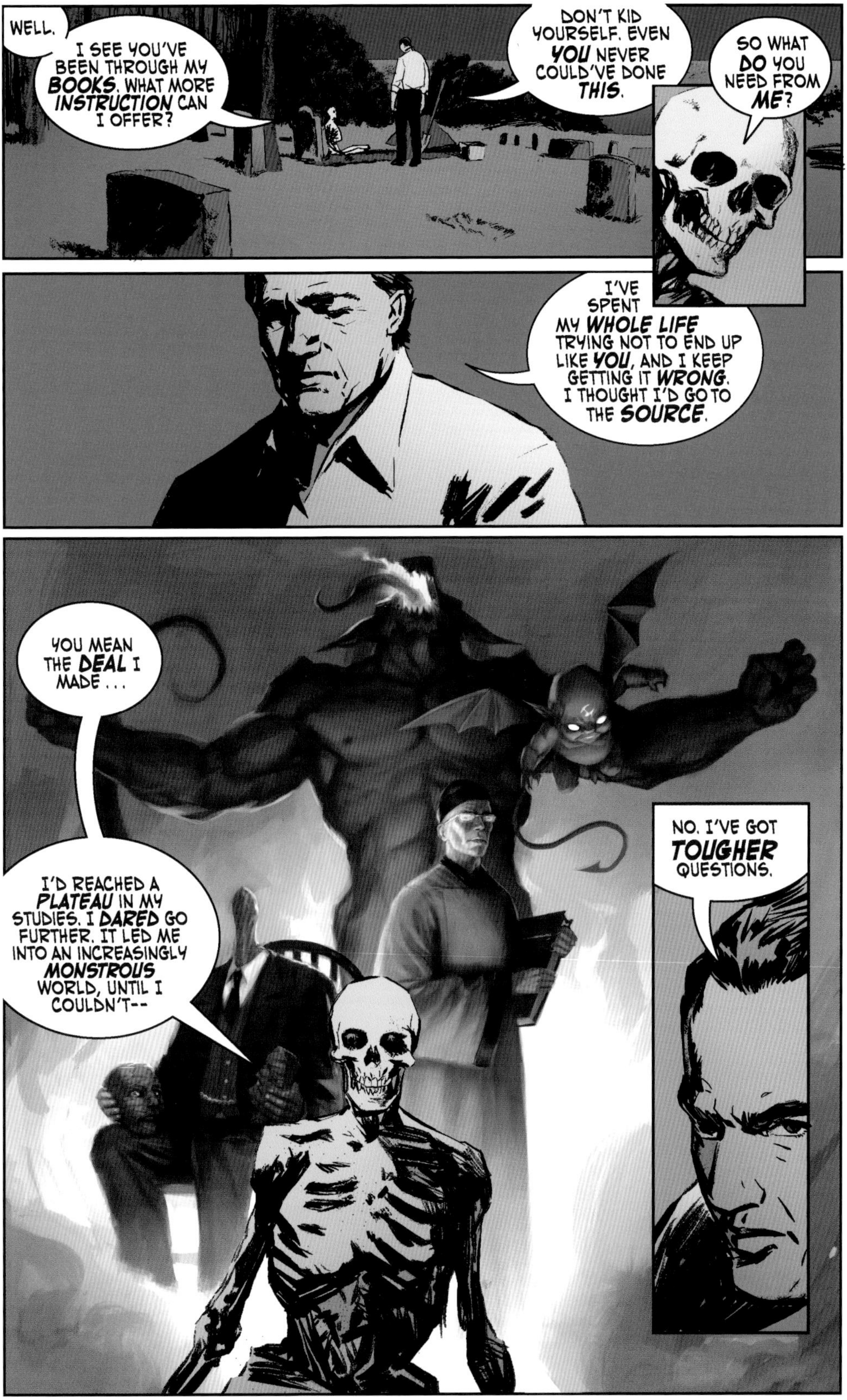
WELL.
I SEE YOU'VE BEEN THROUGH MY BOOKS. WHAT MORE INSTRUCTION CAN I OFFER?
DON'T KID YOURSELF. EVEN YOU NEVER COULD'VE DONE THIS.
SO WHAT DO YOU NEED FROM ME?
I'VE SPENT MY WHOLE LIFE TRYING NOT TO END UP LIKE YOU, AND I KEEP GETTING IT WRONG. I THOUGHT I'D GO TO THE SOURCE.
YOU MEAN THE DEAL I MADE . . .
I'D REACHED A PLATEAU IN MY STUDIES. I DARED GO FURTHER. IT LED ME INTO AN INCREASINGLY MONSTROUS WORLD, UNTIL I COULDN'T--
NO. I'VE GOT TOUGHER QUESTIONS.

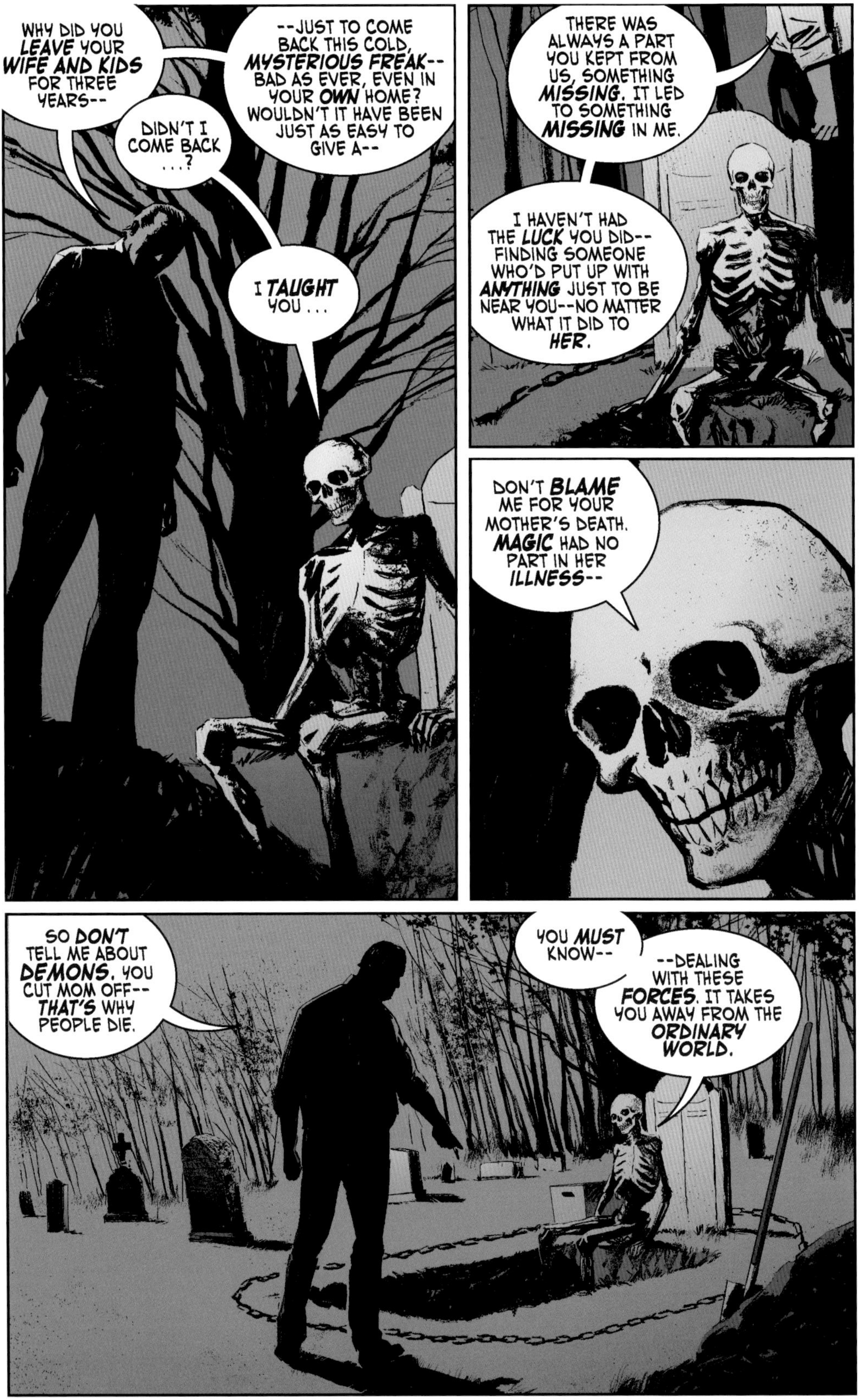
WHY DID YOU LEAVE YOUR WIFE AND KIDS FOR THREE YEARS--
--JUST TO COME BACK THIS COLD, MYSTERIOUS FREAK-- BAD AS EVER, EVEN IN YOUR OWN HOME? WOULDN'T IT HAVE BEEN JUST AS EASY TO GIVE A--
DIDN'T I COME BACK ...?
I TAUGHT YOU ...
THERE WAS ALWAYS A PART YOU KEPT FROM US, SOMETHING MISSING. IT LED TO SOMETHING MISSING IN ME.
I HAVEN'T HAD THE LUCK YOU DID-- FINDING SOMEONE WHO'D PUT UP WITH ANYTHING JUST TO BE NEAR YOU--NO MATTER WHAT IT DID TO HER.
DON'T BLAME ME FOR YOUR MOTHER'S DEATH. MAGIC HAD NO PART IN HER ILLNESS--
SO DON'T TELL ME ABOUT DEMONS. YOU CUT MOM OFF-- THAT'S WHY PEOPLE DIE.
YOU MUST KNOW--
--DEALING WITH THESE FORCES. IT TAKES YOU AWAY FROM THE ORDINARY WORLD.

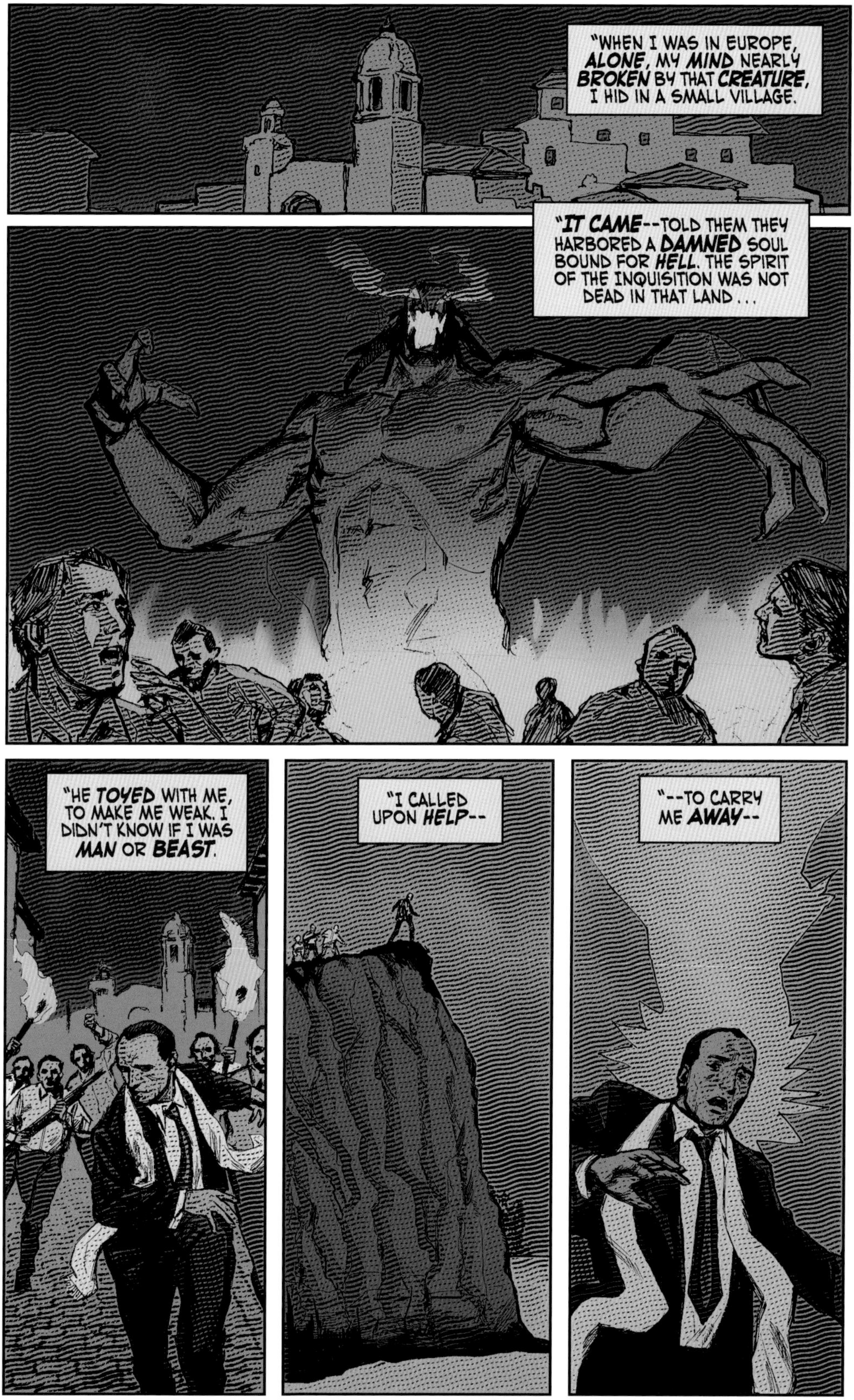
"WHEN I WAS IN EUROPE, ALONE, MY MIND NEARLY BROKEN BY THAT CREATURE, I HID IN A SMALL VILLAGE.
"IT CAME--TOLD THEM THEY HARBORED A DAMNED SOUL BOUND FOR HELL. THE SPIRIT OF THE INQUISITION WAS NOT DEAD IN THAT LAND . . .
"HE TOYED WITH ME, TO MAKE ME WEAK. I DIDN'T KNOW IF I WAS MAN OR BEAST.
"I CALLED UPON HELP--
"--TO CARRY ME AWAY--

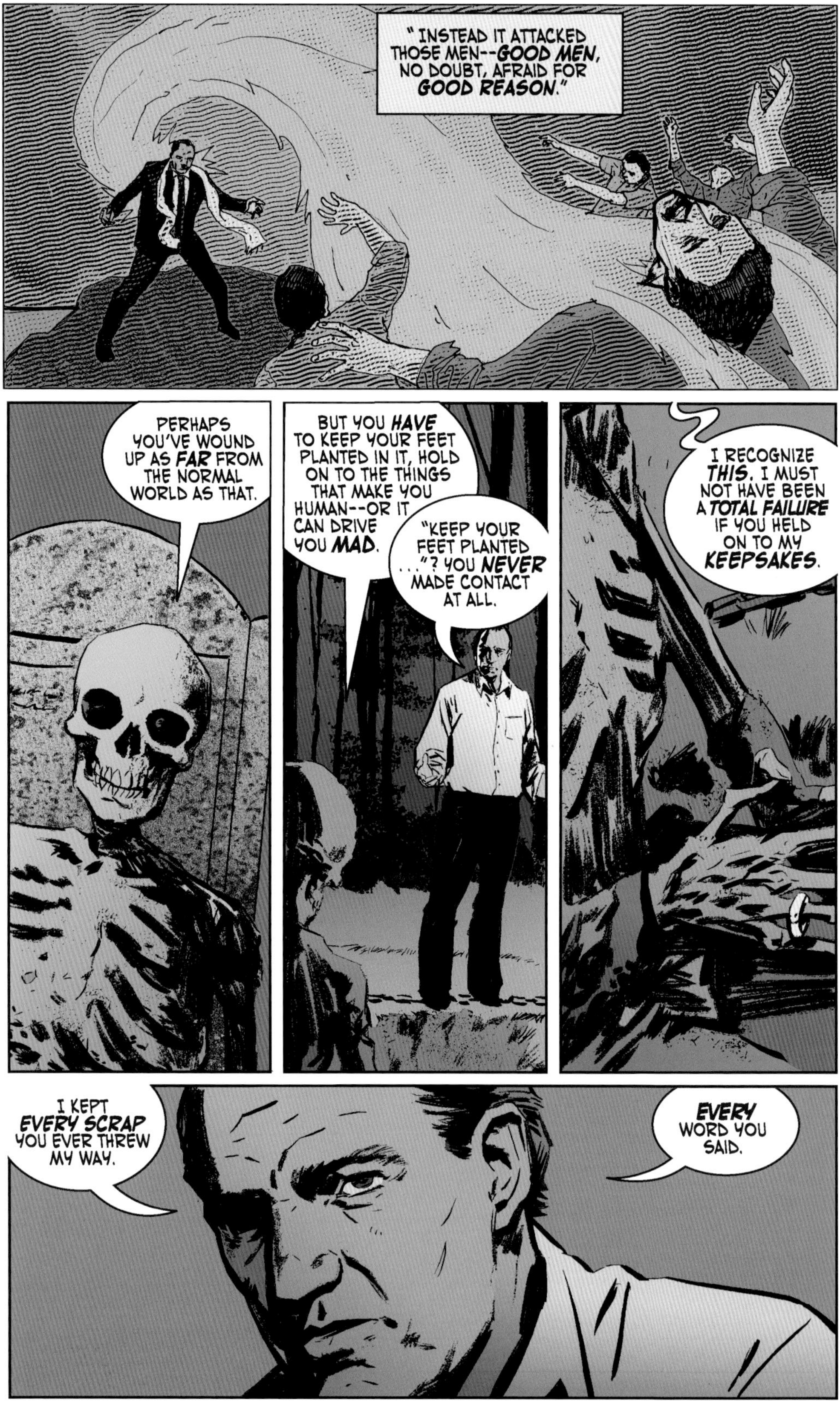
"INSTEAD IT ATTACKED THOSE MEN--GOOD MEN, NO DOUBT, AFRAID FOR GOOD REASON."
PERHAPS YOU'VE WOUND UP AS FAR FROM THE NORMAL WORLD AS THAT.
BUT YOU HAVE TO KEEP YOUR FEET PLANTED IN IT, HOLD ON TO THE THINGS THAT MAKE YOU HUMAN--OR IT CAN DRIVE YOU MAD.
"KEEP YOUR FEET PLANTED ..."? YOU NEVER MADE CONTACT AT ALL.
I RECOGNIZE THIS. I MUST NOT HAVE BEEN A TOTAL FAILURE IF YOU HELD ON TO MY KEEPSAKES.
I KEPT EVERY SCRAP YOU EVER THREW MY WAY.
EVERY WORD YOU SAID.

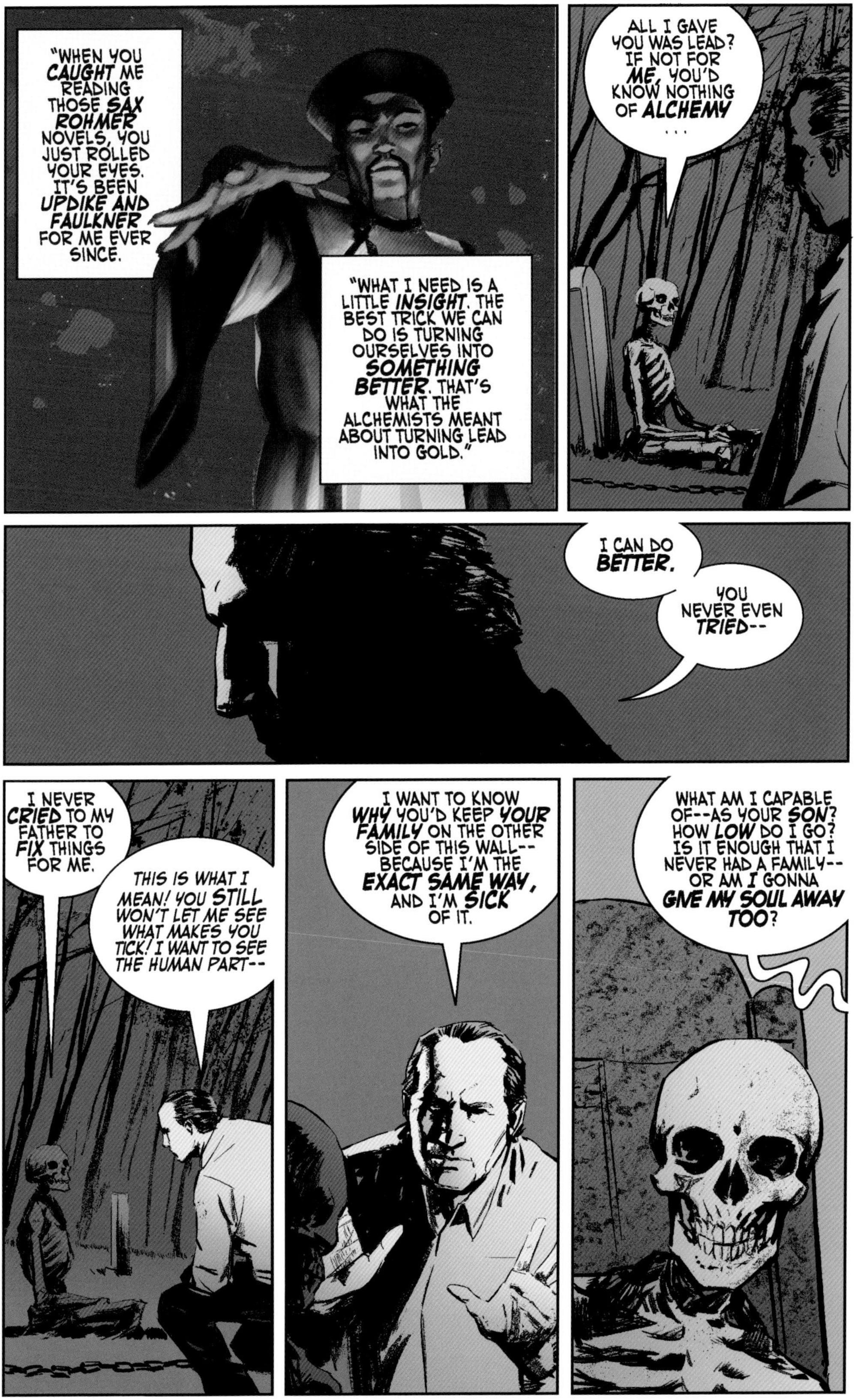
"WHEN YOU CAUGHT ME READING THOSE SAX ROHMER NOVELS, YOU JUST ROLLED YOUR EYES. IT'S BEEN UPDIKE AND FAULKNER FOR ME EVER SINCE.
"WHAT I NEED IS A LITTLE INSIGHT. THE BEST TRICK WE CAN DO IS TURNING OURSELVES INTO SOMETHING BETTER. THAT'S WHAT THE ALCHEMISTS MEANT ABOUT TURNING LEAD INTO GOLD."
ALL I GAVE YOU WAS LEAD? IF NOT FOR ME, YOU'D KNOW NOTHING OF ALCHEMY . . .
I CAN DO BETTER.
YOU NEVER EVEN TRIED--
I NEVER CRIED TO MY FATHER TO FIX THINGS FOR ME.
THIS IS WHAT I MEAN! YOU STILL WON'T LET ME SEE WHAT MAKES YOU TICK! I WANT TO SEE THE HUMAN PART--
I WANT TO KNOW WHY YOU'D KEEP YOUR FAMILY ON THE OTHER SIDE OF THIS WALL--BECAUSE I'M THE EXACT SAME WAY, AND I'M SICK OF IT.
WHAT AM I CAPABLE OF--AS YOUR SON? HOW LOW DO I GO? IS IT ENOUGH THAT I NEVER HAD A FAMILY--OR AM I GONNA GIVE MY SOUL AWAY TOO?

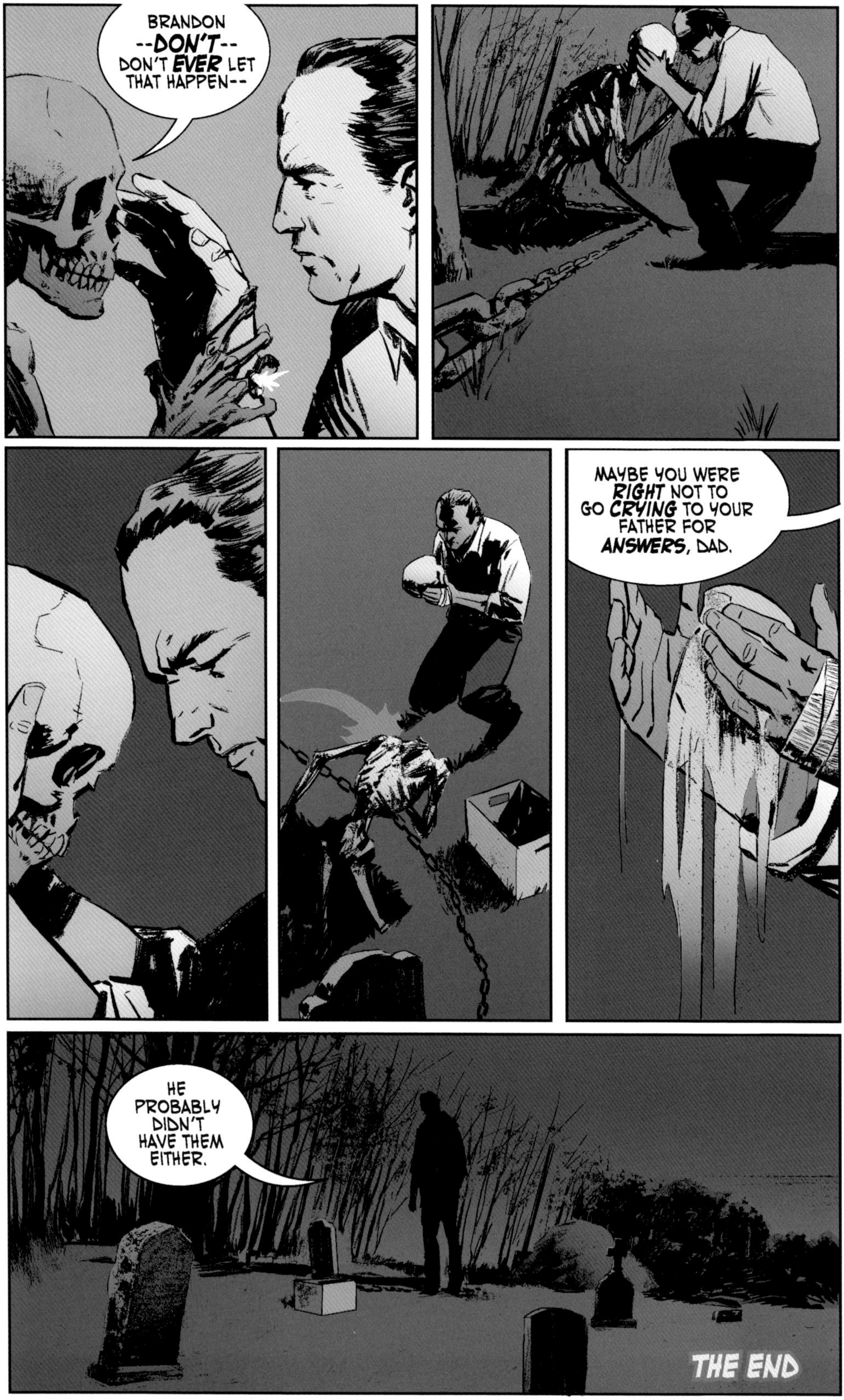
BRANDON --DON'T-- DON'T EVER LET THAT HAPPEN--
MAYBE YOU WERE RIGHT NOT TO GO CRYING TO YOUR FATHER FOR ANSWERS, DAD.
HE PROBABLY DIDN'T HAVE THEM EITHER.
THE END

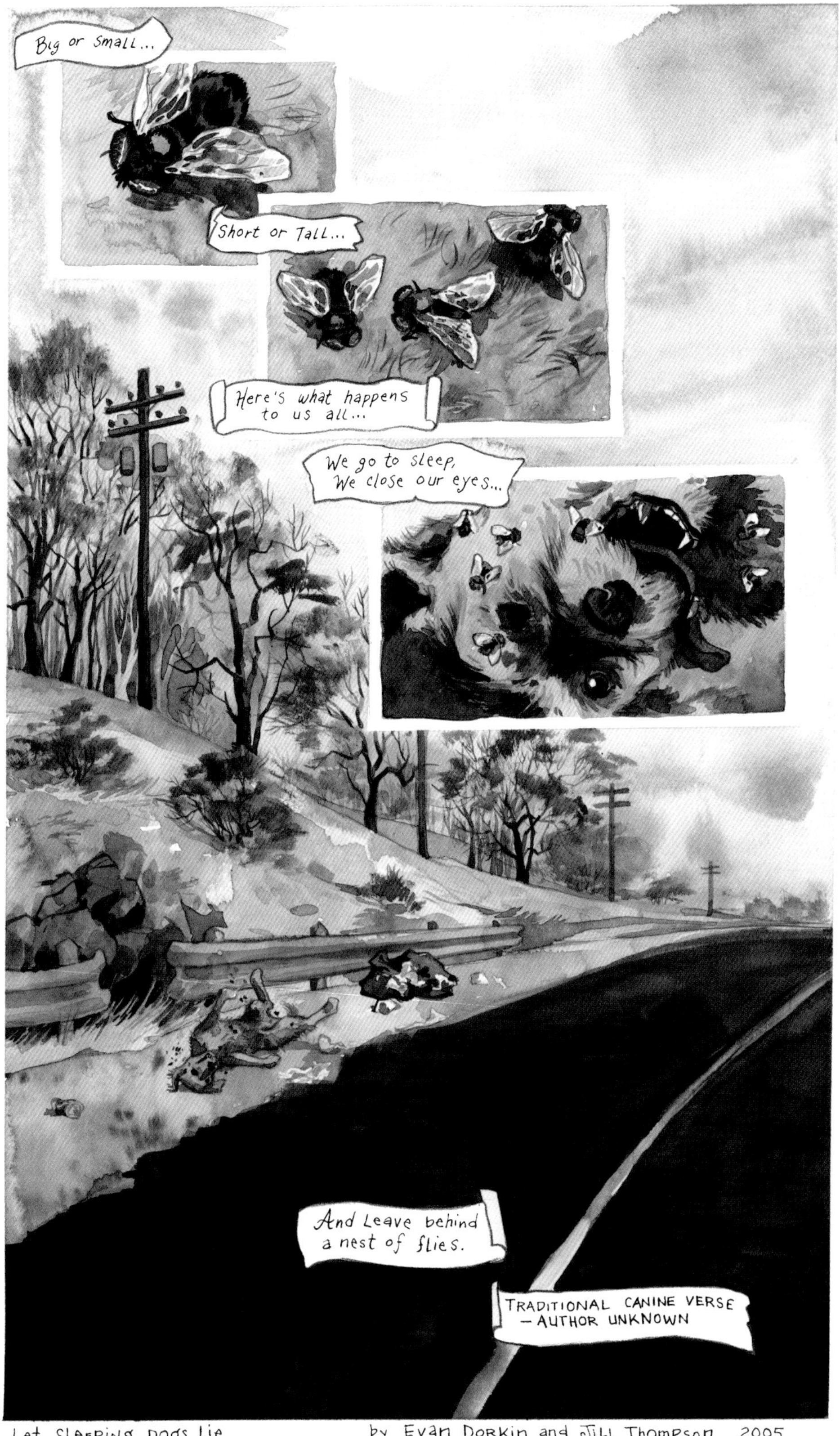
Big or small...
Short or Tall...
Here's what happens to us all...
We go to sleep, We close our eyes...
And Leave behind a nest of flies.
TRADITIONAL CANINE VERSE — AUTHOR UNKNOWN

Let Sleeping Dogs Lie by Evan Dorkin and Jill Thompson 2005

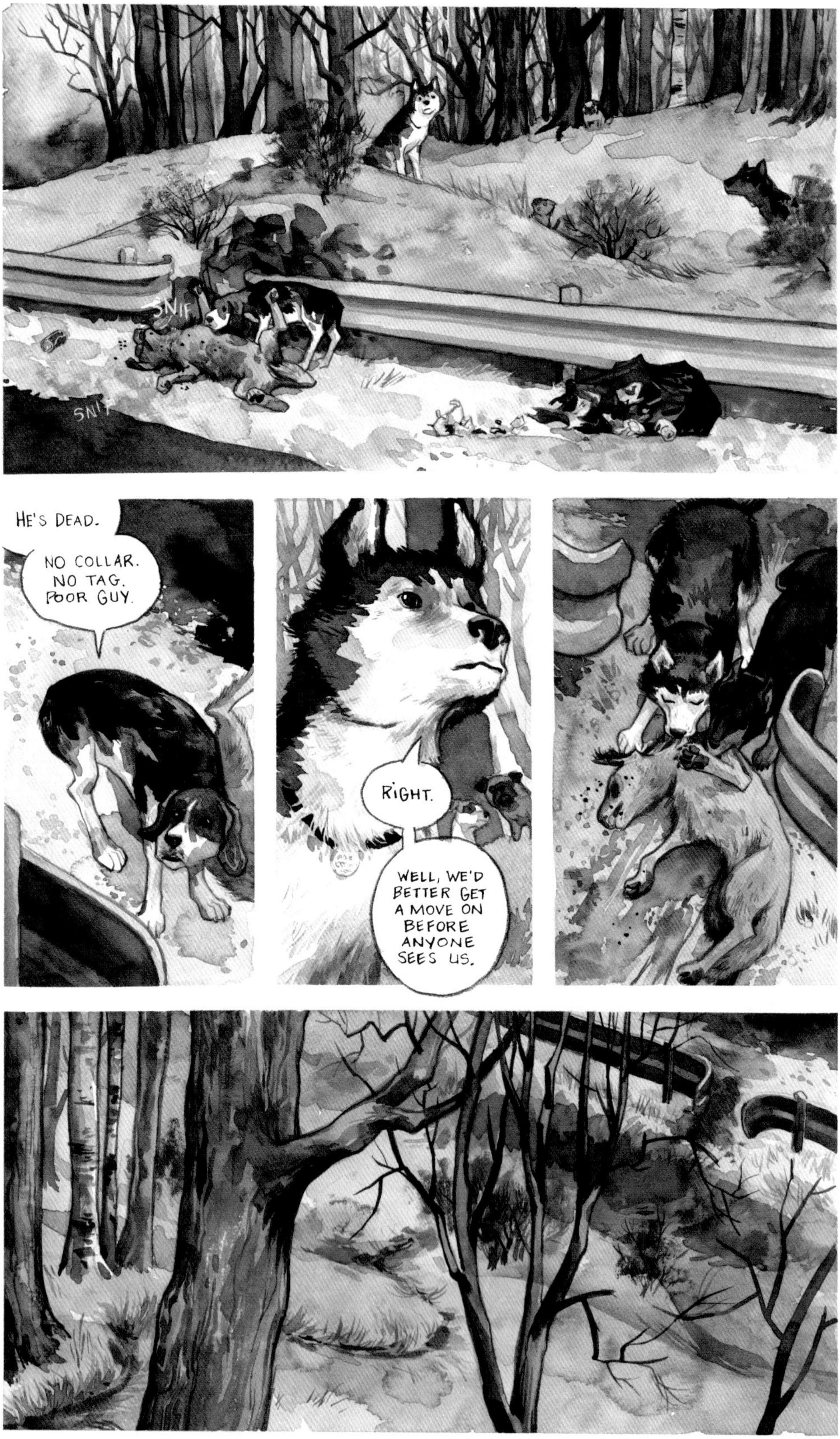
SNIF
SNIF
HE'S DEAD.
NO COLLAR. NO TAG. POOR GUY.
RIGHT.
WELL, WE'D BETTER GET A MOVE ON BEFORE ANYONE SEES US.

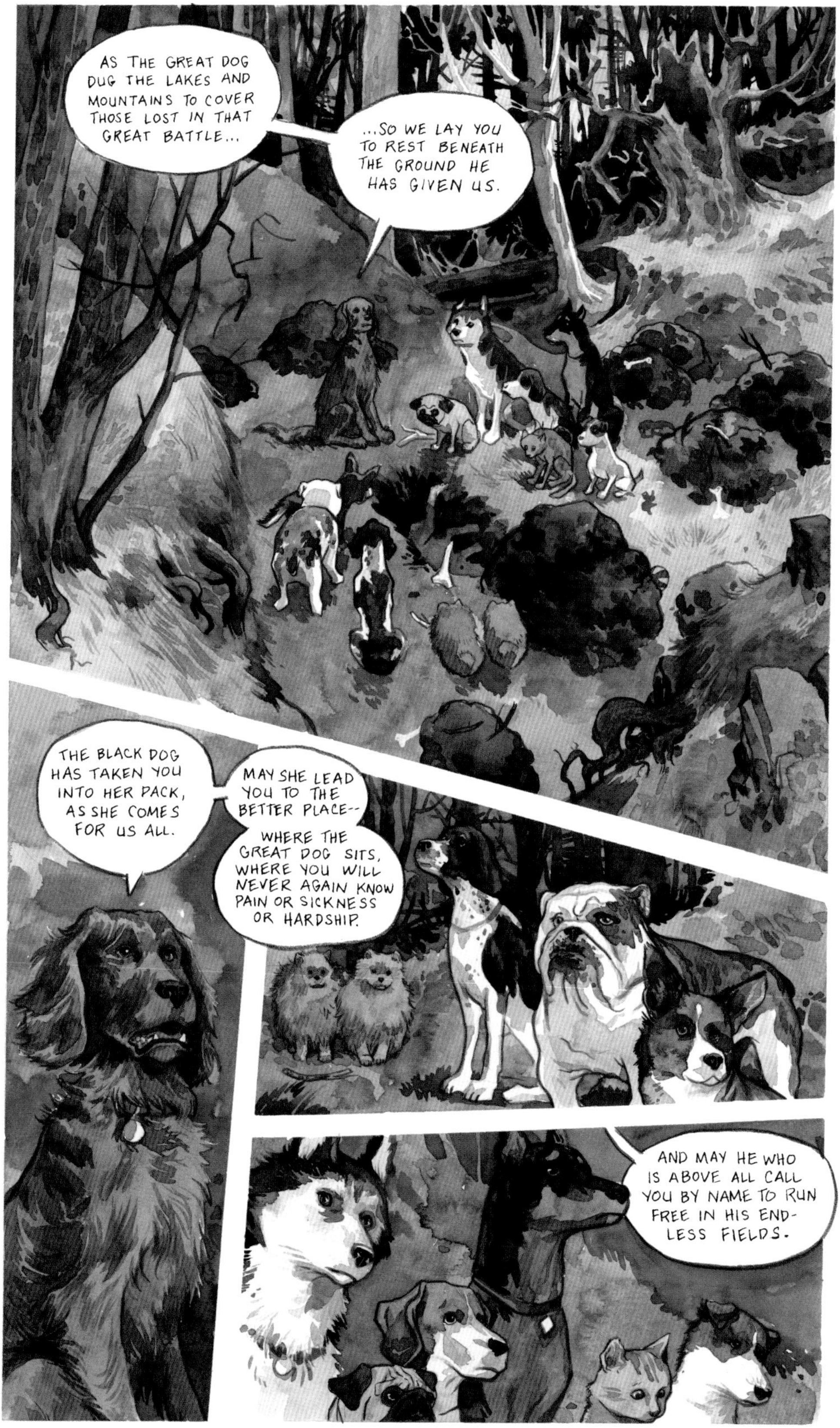
AS THE GREAT DOG DUG THE LAKES AND MOUNTAINS TO COVER THOSE LOST IN THAT GREAT BATTLE...
...SO WE LAY YOU TO REST BENEATH THE GROUND HE HAS GIVEN US.
THE BLACK DOG HAS TAKEN YOU INTO HER PACK, AS SHE COMES FOR US ALL.
MAY SHE LEAD YOU TO THE BETTER PLACE--
WHERE THE GREAT DOG SITS, WHERE YOU WILL NEVER AGAIN KNOW PAIN OR SICKNESS OR HARDSHIP.
AND MAY HE WHO IS ABOVE ALL CALL YOU BY NAME TO RUN FREE IN HIS END-LESS FIELDS.

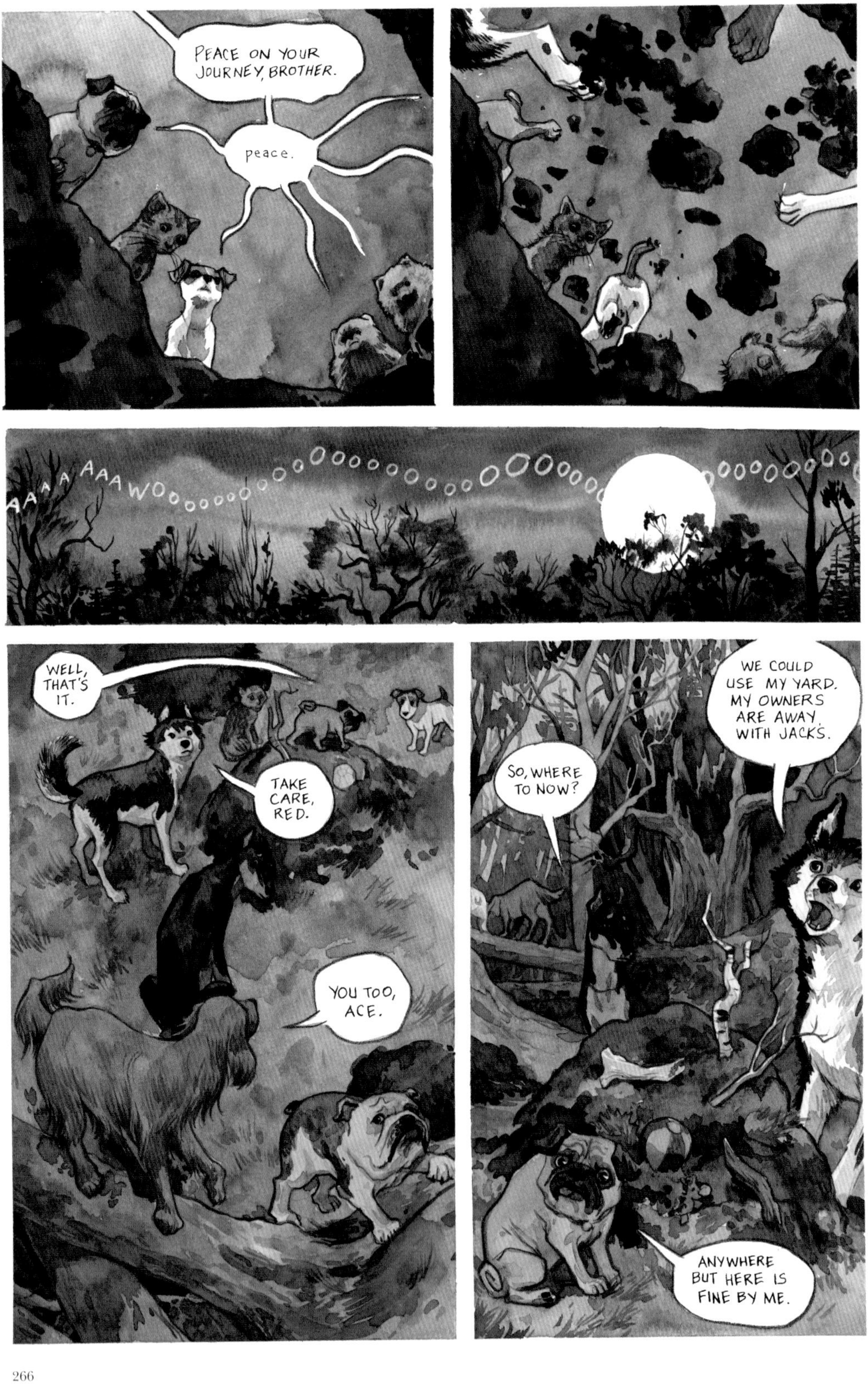
PEACE ON YOUR JOURNEY, BROTHER.
peace.
AAAAAAAWOoooooooooOOOOooooooooOOOOooooooooooOOOOOOO
WELL, THAT'S IT.
TAKE CARE, RED.
YOU TOO, ACE.
SO, WHERE TO NOW?
WE COULD USE MY YARD. MY OWNERS ARE AWAY WITH JACK'S.
ANYWHERE BUT HERE IS FINE BY ME.

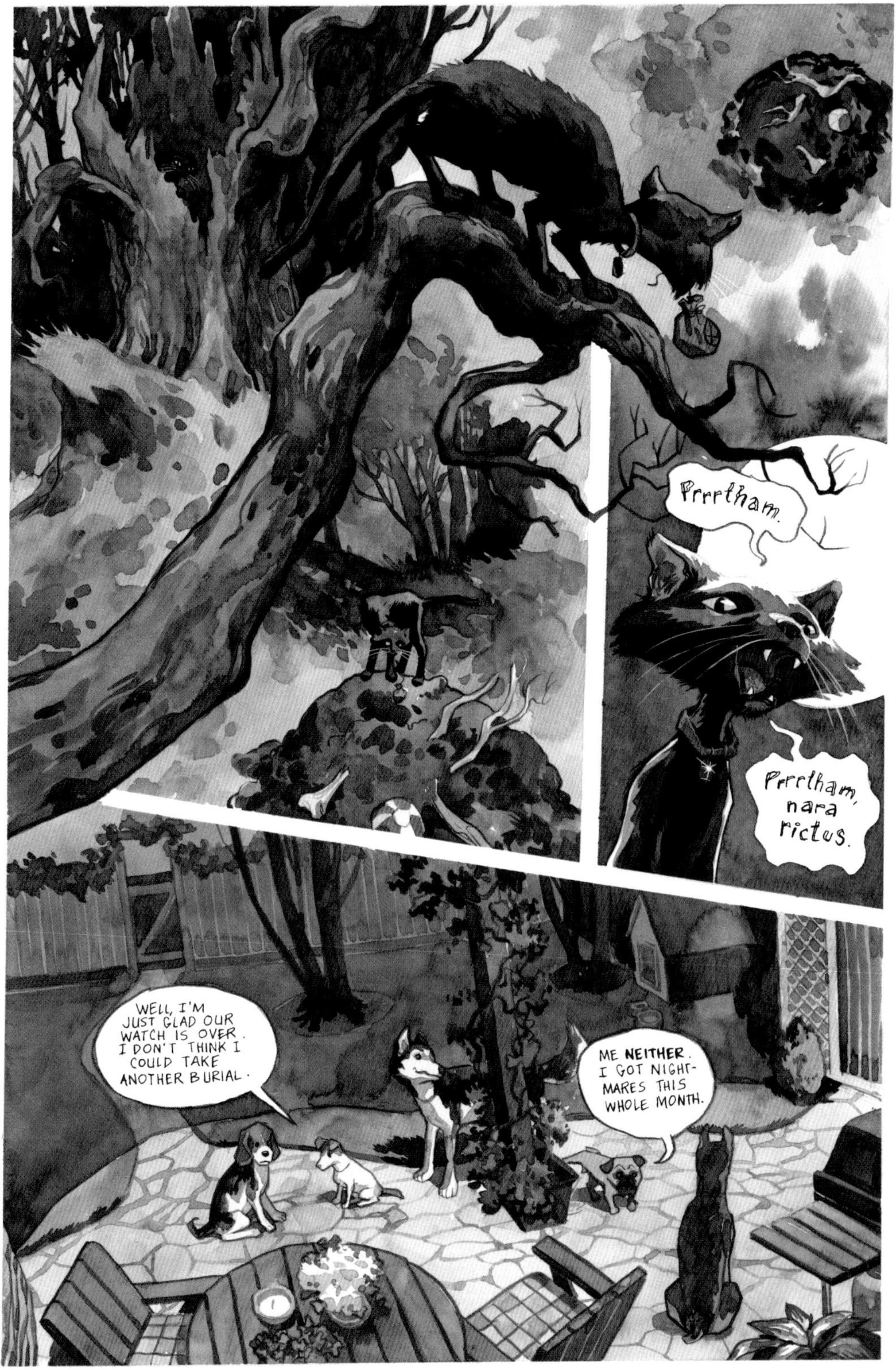
Prrrtham.
Prrrtham, nara rictus.
WELL, I'M JUST GLAD OUR WATCH IS OVER. I DON'T THINK I COULD TAKE ANOTHER BURIAL.
ME NEITHER. I GOT NIGHT-MARES THIS WHOLE MONTH.

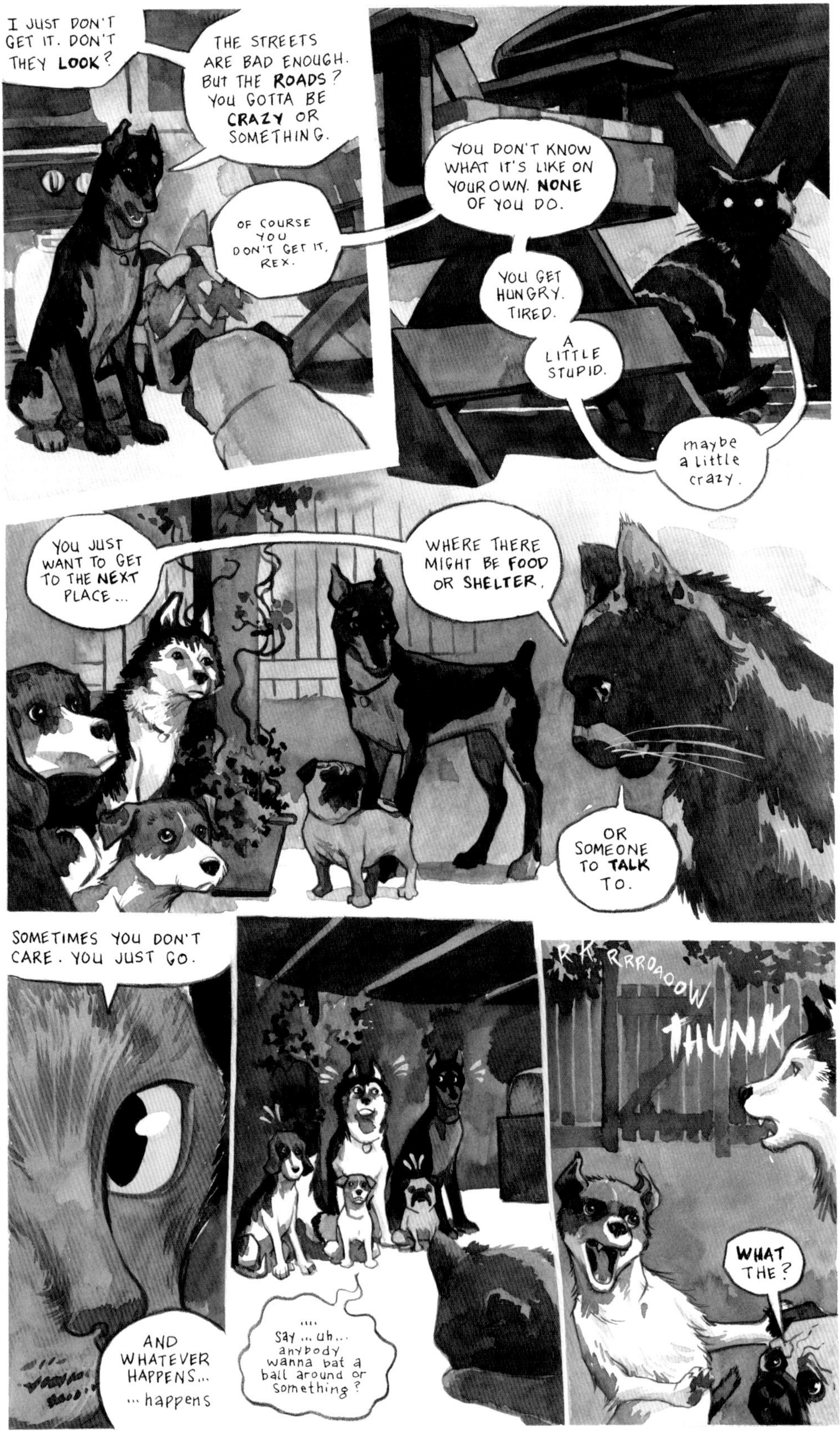
I JUST DON'T GET IT. DON'T THEY LOOK?
THE STREETS ARE BAD ENOUGH. BUT THE ROADS? YOU GOTTA BE CRAZY OR SOMETHING.
OF COURSE YOU DON'T GET IT, REX.
YOU DON'T KNOW WHAT IT'S LIKE ON YOUR OWN. NONE OF YOU DO.
YOU GET HUNGRY. TIRED.
A LITTLE STUPID.
maybe a little crazy.
YOU JUST WANT TO GET TO THE NEXT PLACE...
WHERE THERE MIGHT BE FOOD OR SHELTER,
OR SOMEONE TO TALK TO.
SOMETIMES YOU DON'T CARE. YOU JUST GO.
AND WHATEVER HAPPENS...
...happens
.... say ... uh... anybody wanna bat a ball around or something?
R R RRROAOOW
THUNK
WHAT THE?

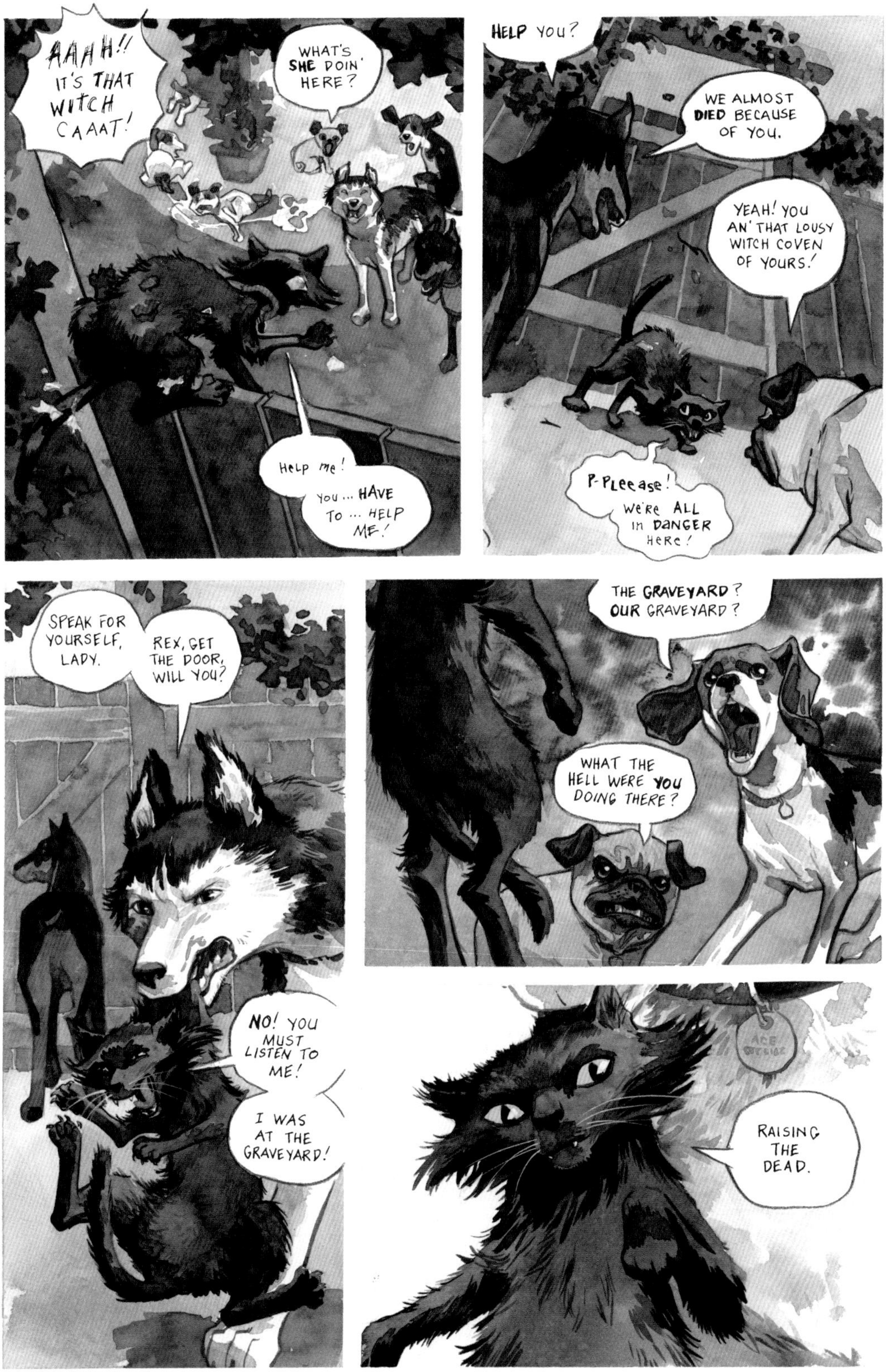

AAAH!! IT'S THAT WITCH CAAAT!
WHAT'S SHE DOIN' HERE?
Help me!
You... HAVE TO... HELP ME!
HELP YOU?
WE ALMOST DIED BECAUSE OF YOU.
YEAH! YOU AN' THAT LOUSY WITCH COVEN OF YOURS!
P-Pleease!
We're ALL in DANGER here!
SPEAK FOR YOURSELF, LADY.
REX, GET THE DOOR, WILL YOU?
NO! YOU MUST LISTEN TO ME!
I WAS AT THE GRAVEYARD!
THE GRAVEYARD? OUR GRAVEYARD?
WHAT THE HELL WERE YOU DOING THERE?
RAISING THE DEAD.

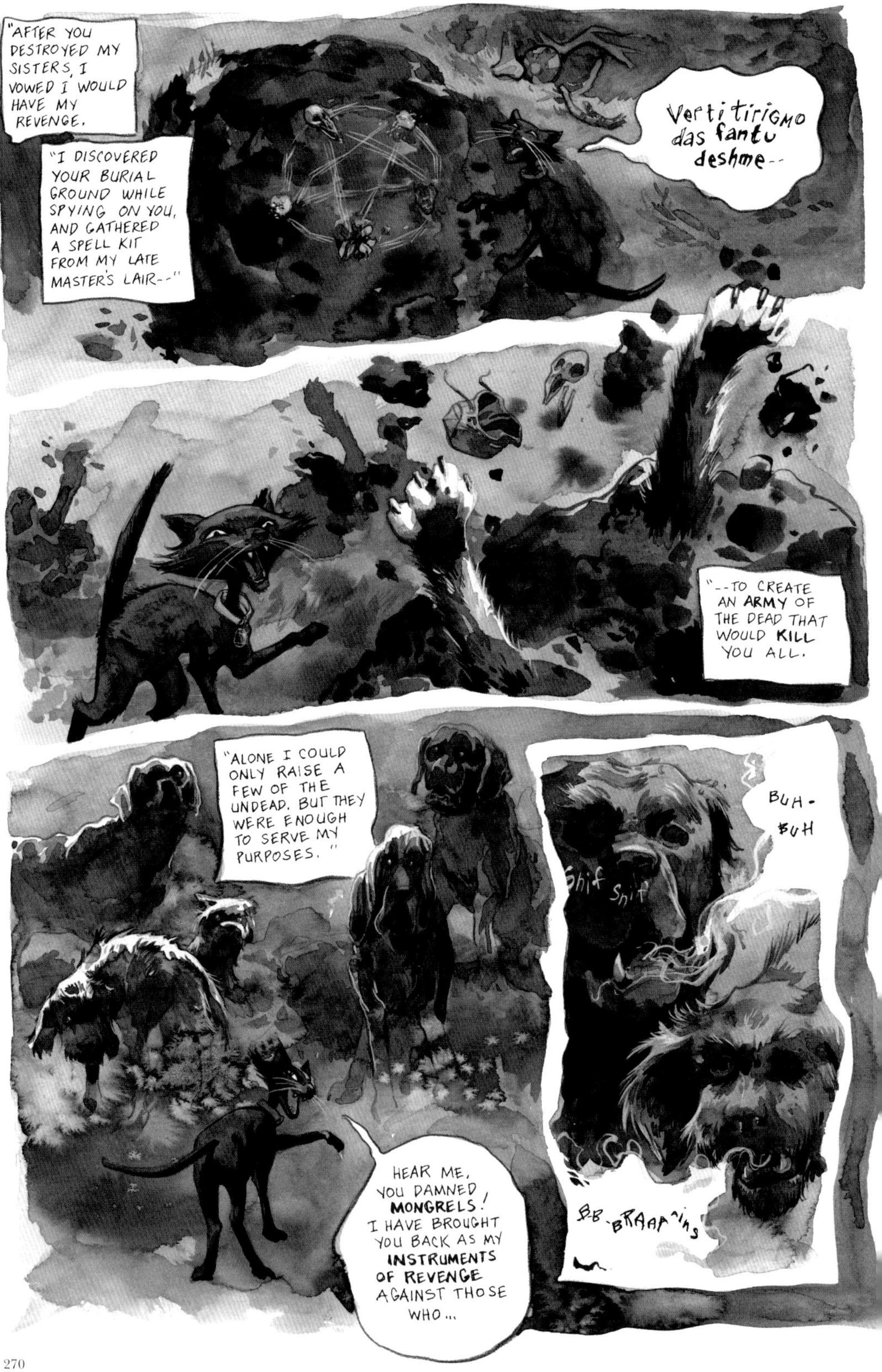
"AFTER YOU DESTROYED MY SISTERS, I VOWED I WOULD HAVE MY REVENGE.
"I DISCOVERED YOUR BURIAL GROUND WHILE SPYING ON YOU, AND GATHERED A SPELL KIT FROM MY LATE MASTER'S LAIR--"
Vertitirigmo das fantu deshme--
"--TO CREATE AN ARMY OF THE DEAD THAT WOULD KILL YOU ALL.
"ALONE I COULD ONLY RAISE A FEW OF THE UNDEAD. BUT THEY WERE ENOUGH TO SERVE MY PURPOSES."
HEAR ME, YOU DAMNED MONGRELS! I HAVE BROUGHT YOU BACK AS MY INSTRUMENTS OF REVENGE AGAINST THOSE WHO...
BUH-BUH
Shif Shif
B-B-BRAAAins

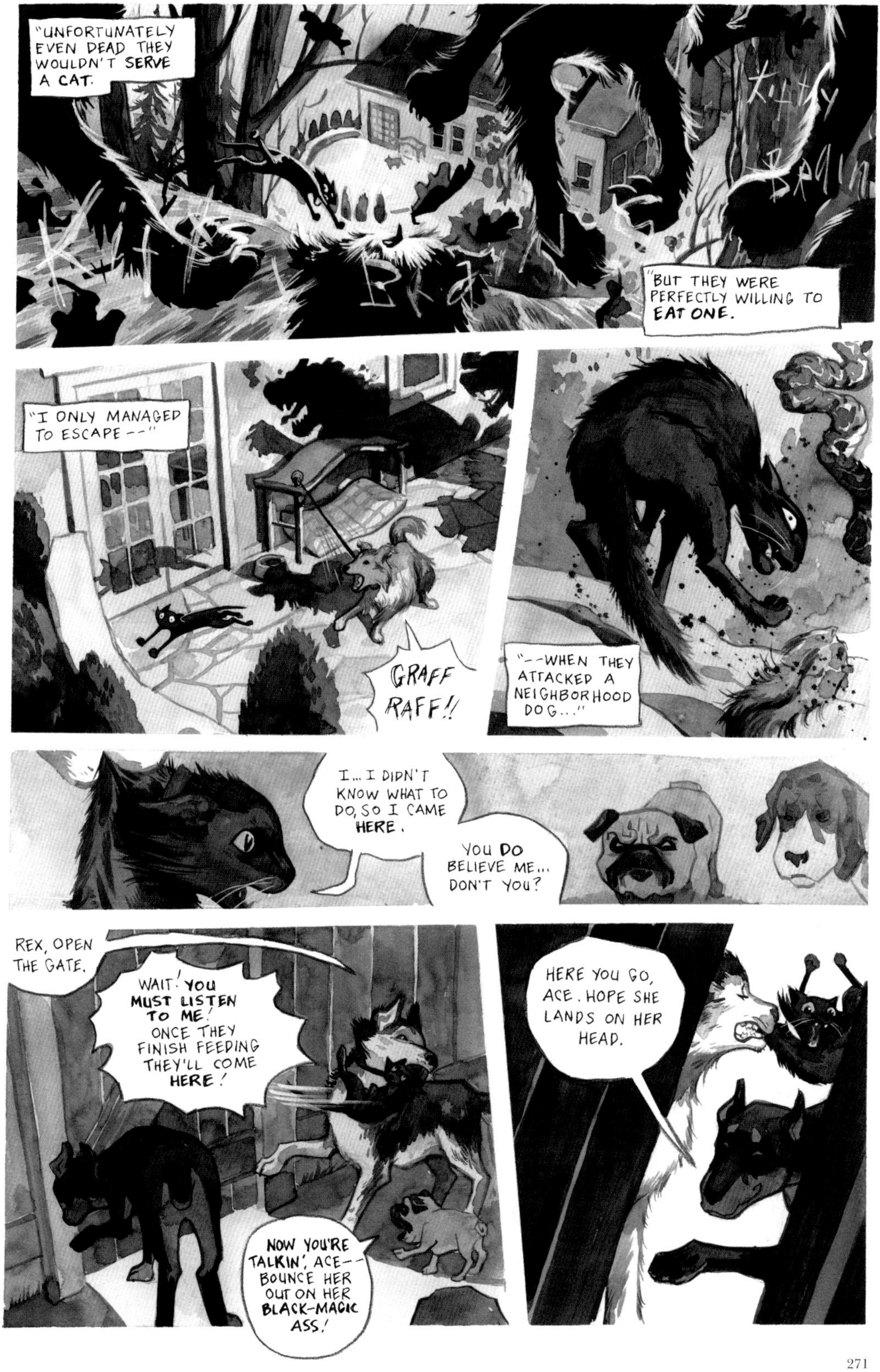

"UNFORTUNATELY EVEN DEAD THEY WOULDN'T SERVE A CAT.
"BUT THEY WERE PERFECTLY WILLING TO EAT ONE.
"I ONLY MANAGED TO ESCAPE --"
GRAFF RAFF!!
"--WHEN THEY ATTACKED A NEIGHBORHOOD DOG..."
I... I DIDN'T KNOW WHAT TO DO, SO I CAME HERE.
YOU DO BELIEVE ME... DON'T YOU?
REX, OPEN THE GATE.
WAIT! YOU MUST LISTEN TO ME! ONCE THEY FINISH FEEDING THEY'LL COME HERE!
NOW YOU'RE TALKIN', ACE-- BOUNCE HER OUT ON HER BLACK-MAGIC ASS!
HERE YOU GO, ACE. HOPE SHE LANDS ON HER HEAD.

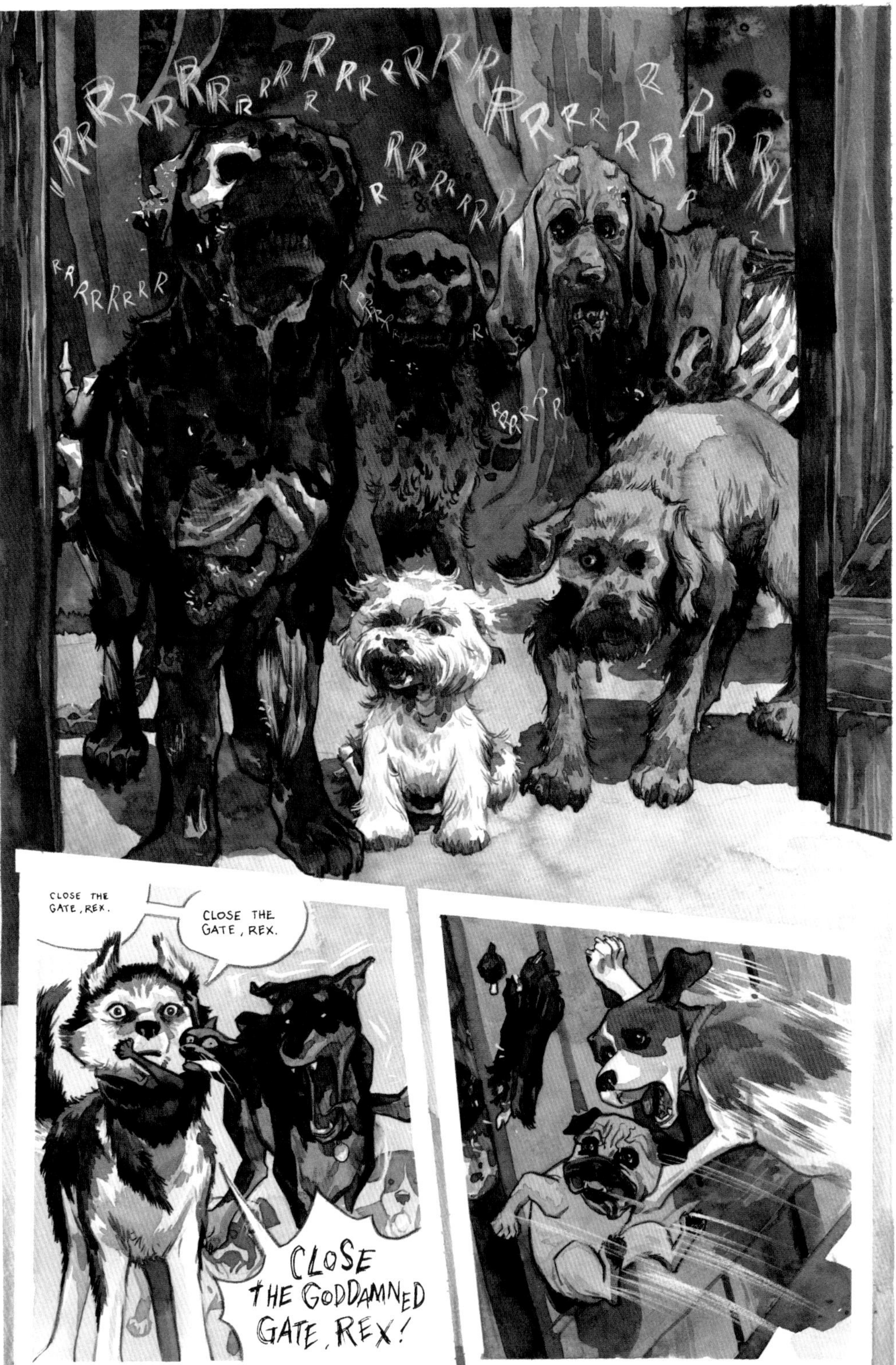
CLOSE THE GATE, REX.
CLOSE THE GATE, REX.
CLOSE THE GODDAMNED GATE, REX!

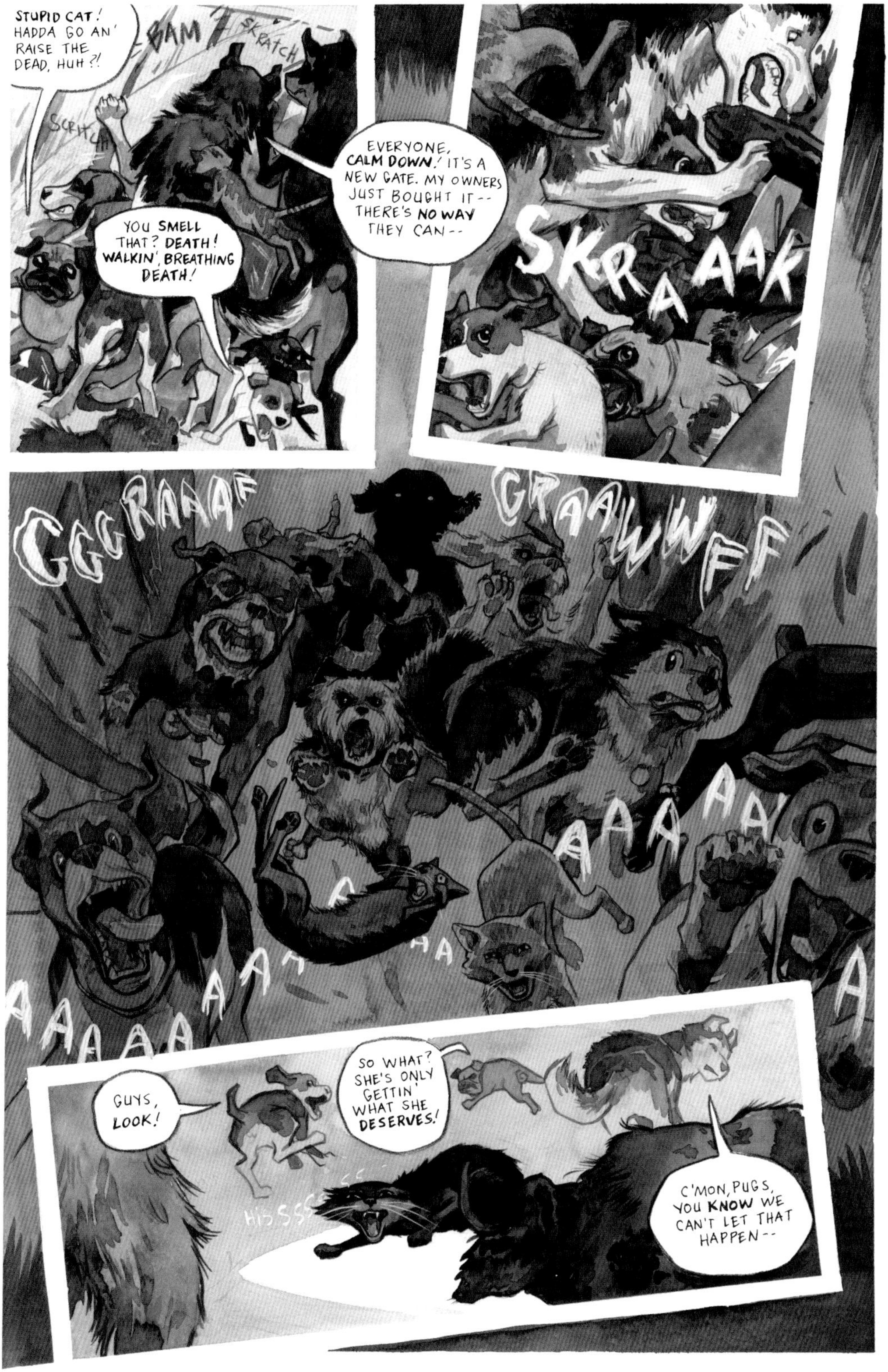
STUPID CAT! HADDA GO AN' RAISE THE DEAD, HUH?!
BAM
SKRATCH
SCRITCH
YOU SMELL THAT? DEATH! WALKIN', BREATHING DEATH!
EVERYONE, CALM DOWN! IT'S A NEW GATE. MY OWNERS JUST BOUGHT IT-- THERE'S NO WAY THEY CAN--
SKRAAAK
GGGRAAAF
GRAAWWFF
AAAAAAAA
GUYS, LOOK!
SO WHAT? SHE'S ONLY GETTIN' WHAT SHE DESERVES!
HISSSS
C'MON, PUGS, YOU KNOW WE CAN'T LET THAT HAPPEN--

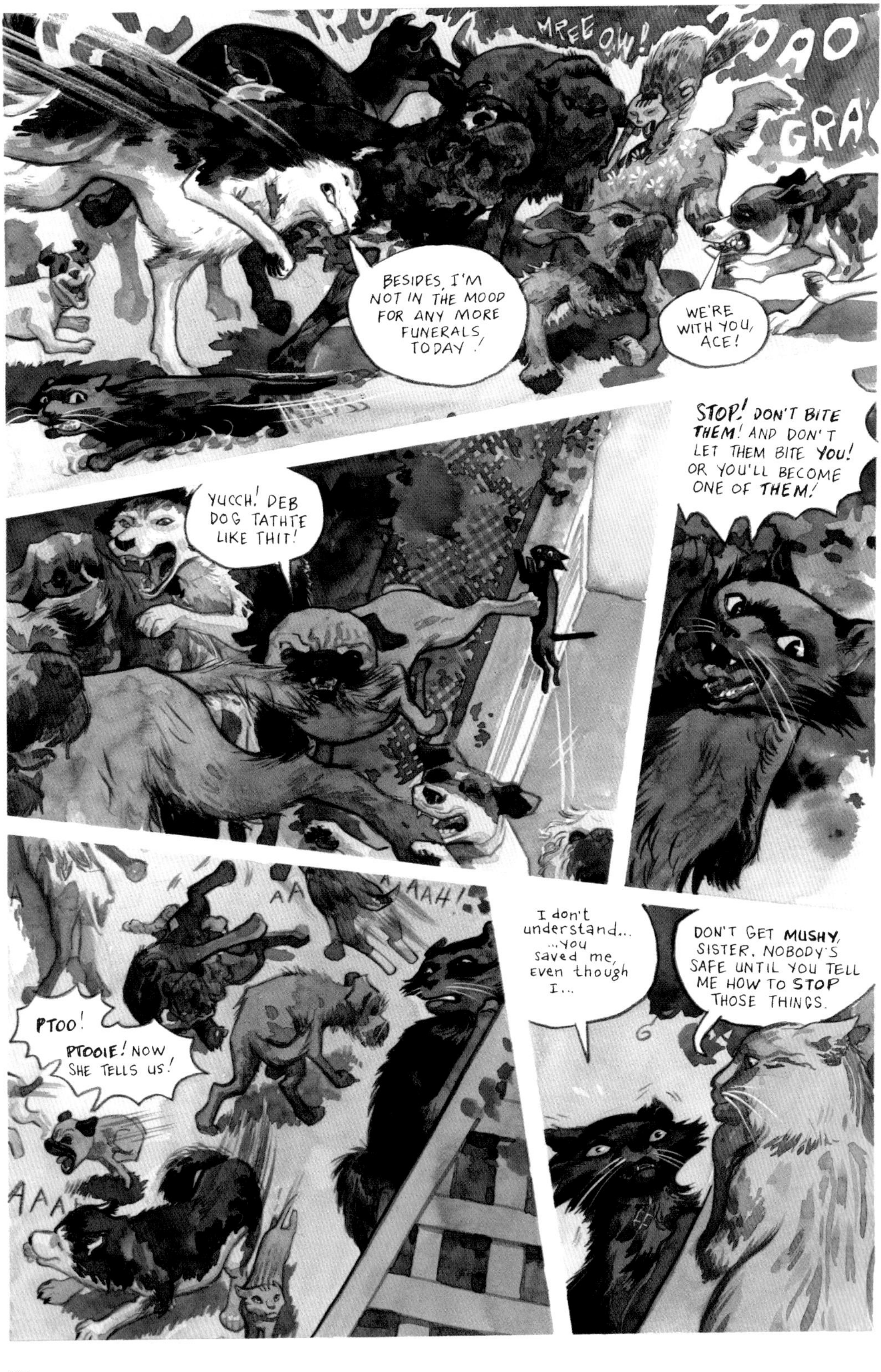
MREEOW!
BESIDES, I'M NOT IN THE MOOD FOR ANY MORE FUNERALS TODAY!
WE'RE WITH YOU, ACE!
STOP! DON'T BITE THEM! AND DON'T LET THEM BITE YOU! OR YOU'LL BECOME ONE OF THEM!
YUCCH! DEB DOG TATHTE LIKE THIT!
AAAH!
PTOO! PTOOIE! NOW SHE TELLS US!
I don't understand... ...you saved me, even though I...
DON'T GET MUSHY, SISTER. NOBODY'S SAFE UNTIL YOU TELL ME HOW TO STOP THOSE THINGS.

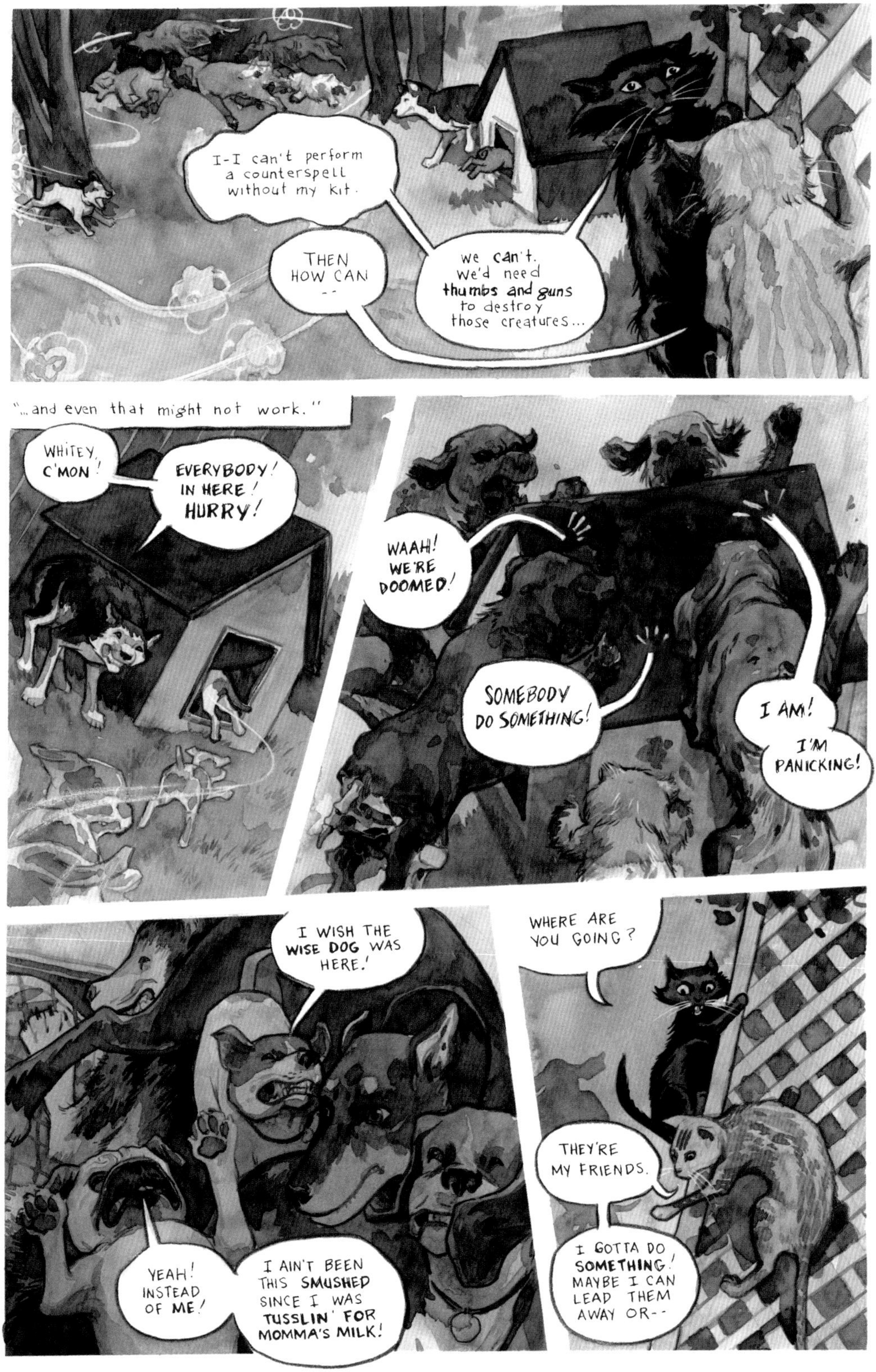
I-I can't perform a counterspell without my kit.
THEN HOW CAN --
We can't. We'd need **thumbs and guns** to destroy those creatures...
"...and even that might not work."
WHITEY, C'MON!
EVERYBODY! IN HERE! HURRY!
WAAH! WE'RE DOOMED!
SOMEBODY DO SOMETHING!
I AM! I'M PANICKING!
I WISH THE **WISE DOG** WAS HERE!
YEAH! INSTEAD OF **ME**!
I AIN'T BEEN THIS **SMUSHED** SINCE I WAS **TUSSLIN' FOR MOMMA'S MILK**!
WHERE ARE YOU GOING?
THEY'RE MY FRIENDS.
I GOTTA DO **SOMETHING**! MAYBE I CAN LEAD THEM AWAY OR--

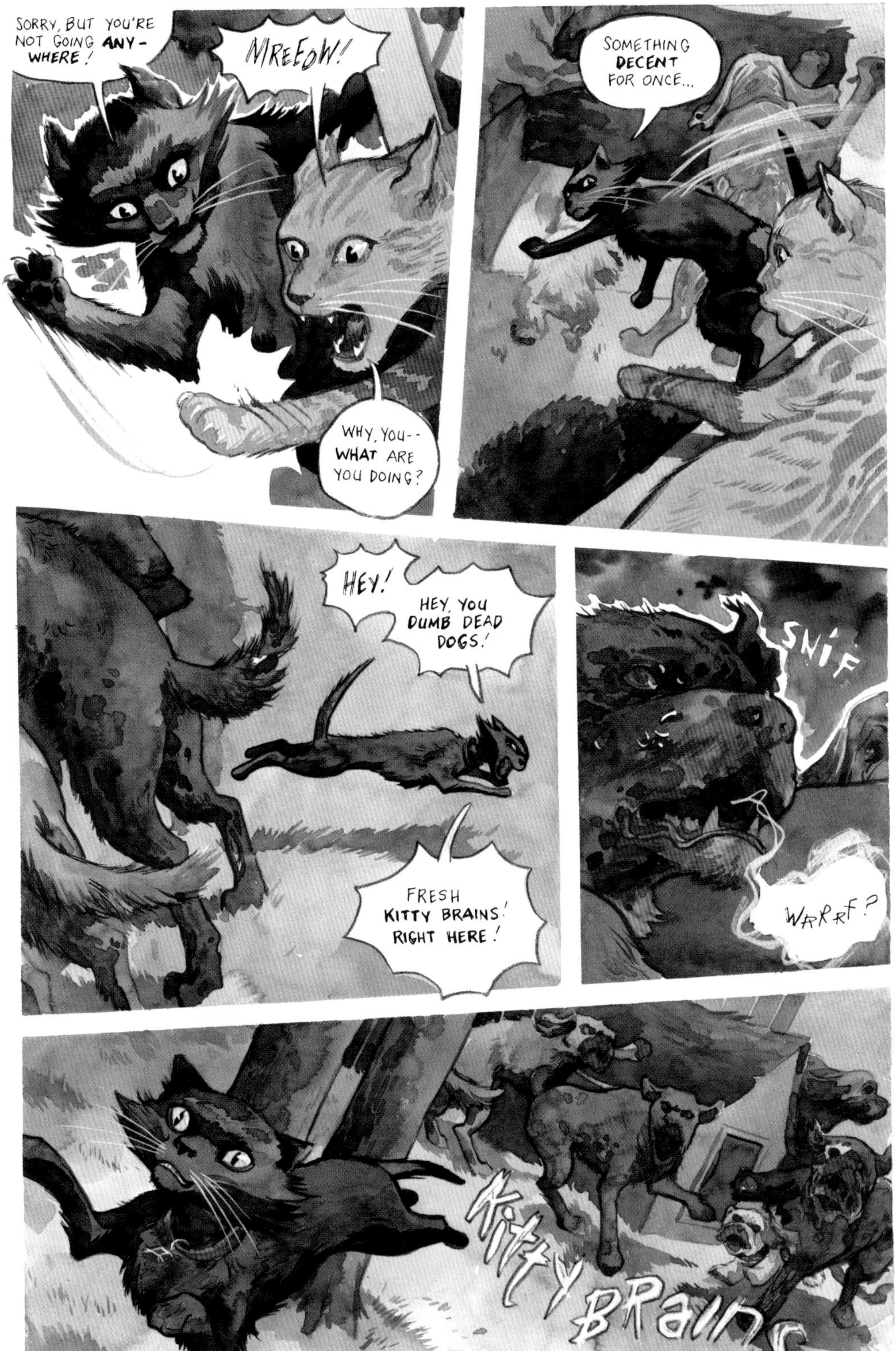
SORRY, BUT YOU'RE NOT GOING ANY-WHERE!
MREEOW!
WHY, YOU-- WHAT ARE YOU DOING?
SOMETHING DECENT FOR ONCE...
HEY!
HEY, YOU DUMB DEAD DOGS!
FRESH KITTY BRAINS! RIGHT HERE!
SNIF
WARRF?
Kitty Brains

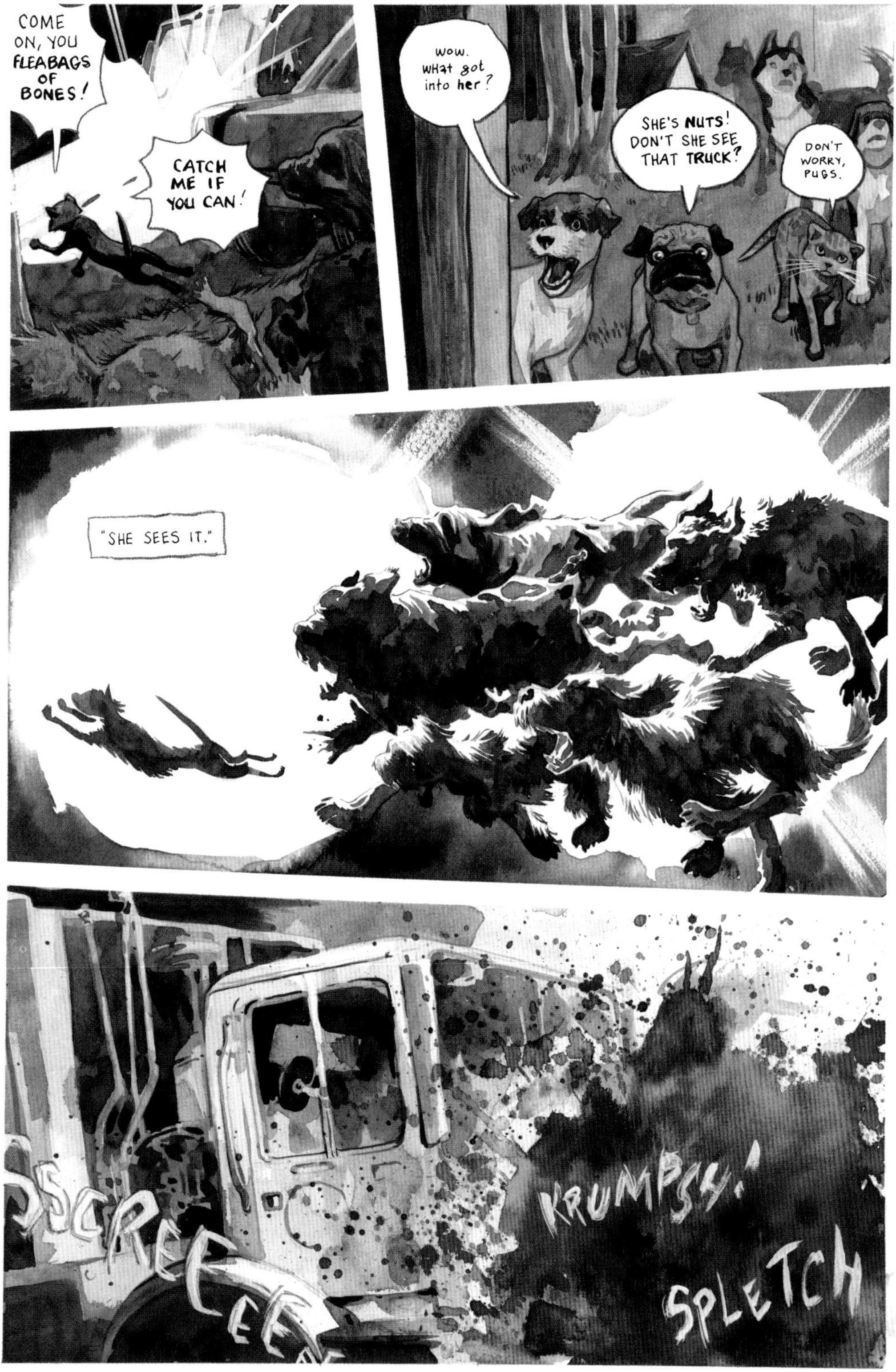
COME ON, YOU FLEABAGS OF BONES!
CATCH ME IF YOU CAN!
WOW. WHAT GOT INTO HER?
SHE'S NUTS! DON'T SHE SEE THAT TRUCK?
DON'T WORRY, PUGS.
"SHE SEES IT."
SSCREEEEE
KRUMPSH!
SPLETCH

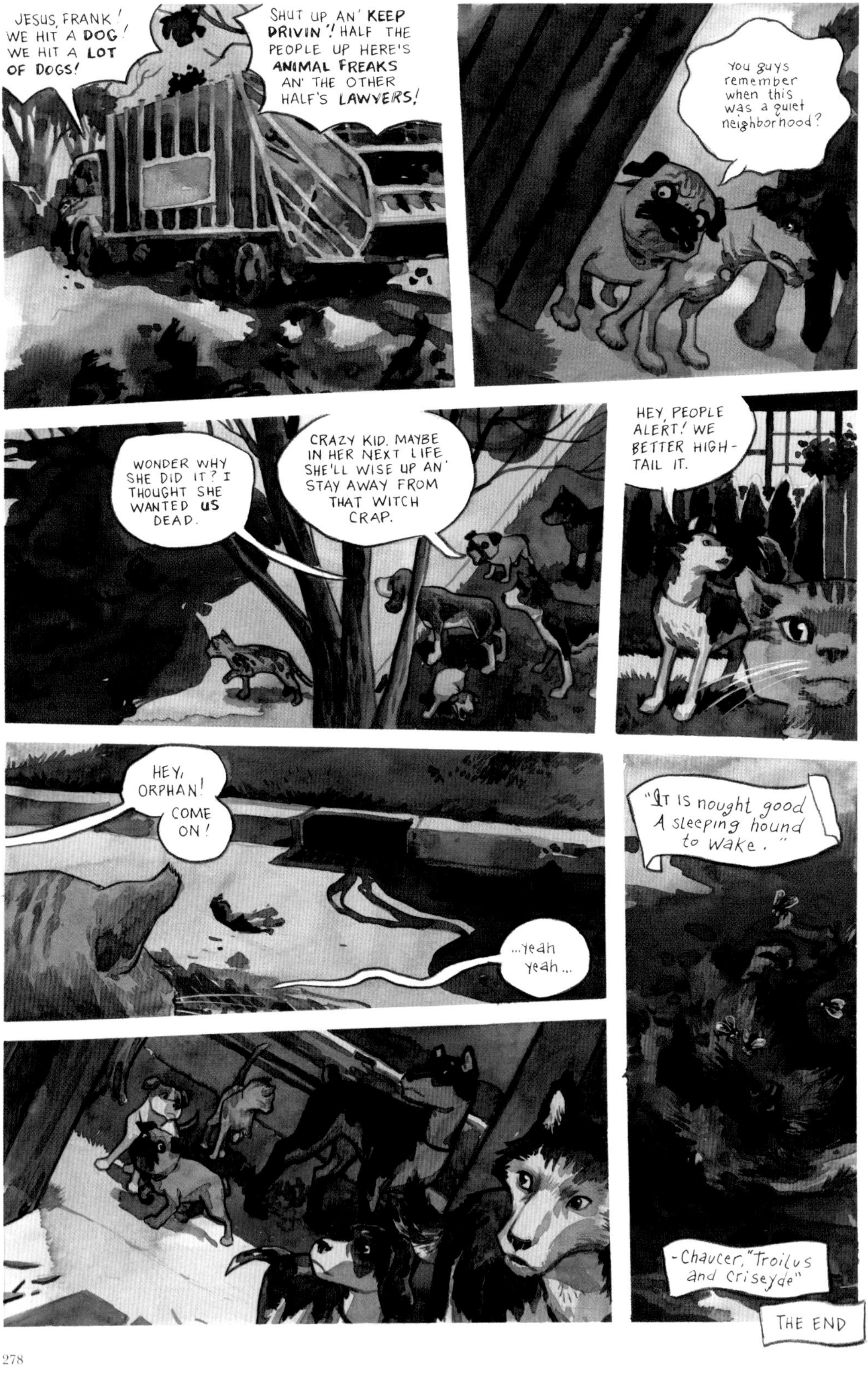
JESUS, FRANK! WE HIT A DOG! WE HIT A LOT OF DOGS!
SHUT UP AN' KEEP DRIVIN'! HALF THE PEOPLE UP HERE'S ANIMAL FREAKS AN' THE OTHER HALF'S LAWYERS!
You guys remember when this was a quiet neighborhood?
WONDER WHY SHE DID IT? I THOUGHT SHE WANTED US DEAD.
CRAZY KID. MAYBE IN HER NEXT LIFE SHE'LL WISE UP AN' STAY AWAY FROM THAT WITCH CRAP.
HEY, PEOPLE ALERT! WE BETTER HIGH-TAIL IT.
HEY, ORPHAN!
COME ON!
...yeah yeah...
"It is nought good A sleeping hound to wake."
-Chaucer, "Troilus and Criseyde"
THE END

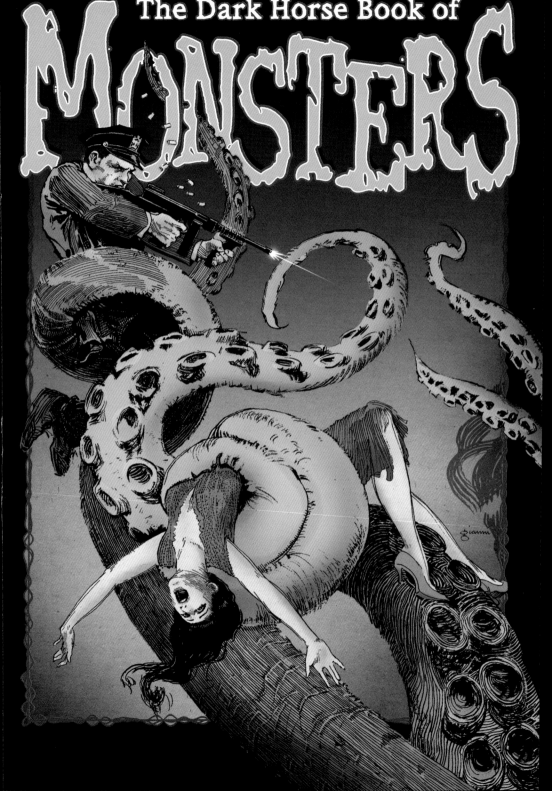

The Dark Horse Book of MONSTERS

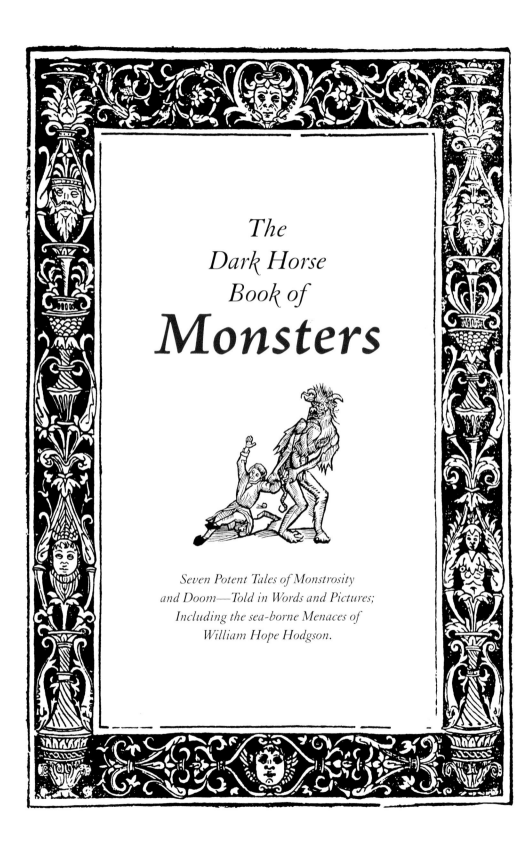

The
Dark Horse
Book of
Monsters

*Seven Potent Tales of Monstrosity
and Doom—Told in Words and Pictures;
Including the sea-borne Menaces of
William Hope Hodgson.*

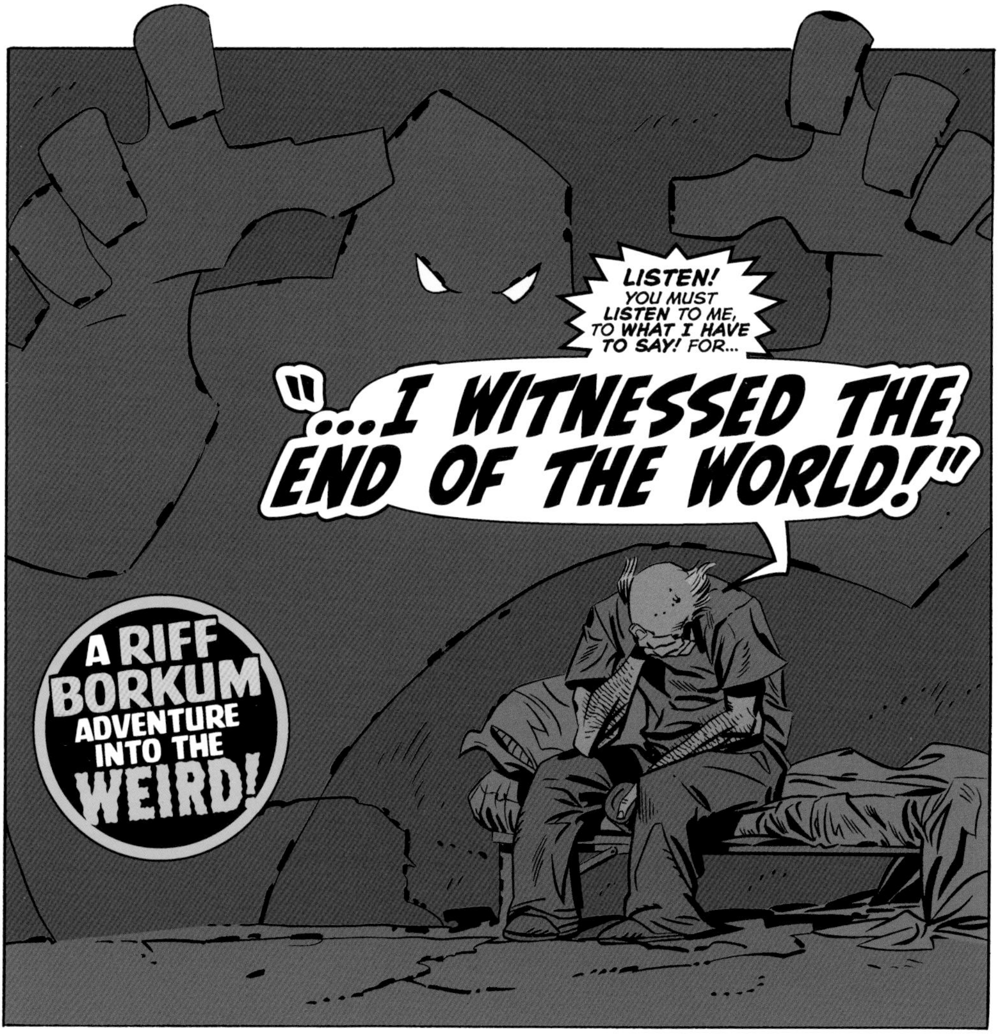
LISTEN! YOU MUST LISTEN TO ME, TO WHAT I HAVE TO SAY! FOR...
"...I WITNESSED THE END OF THE WORLD!"
A RIFF BORKUM ADVENTURE INTO THE WEIRD!

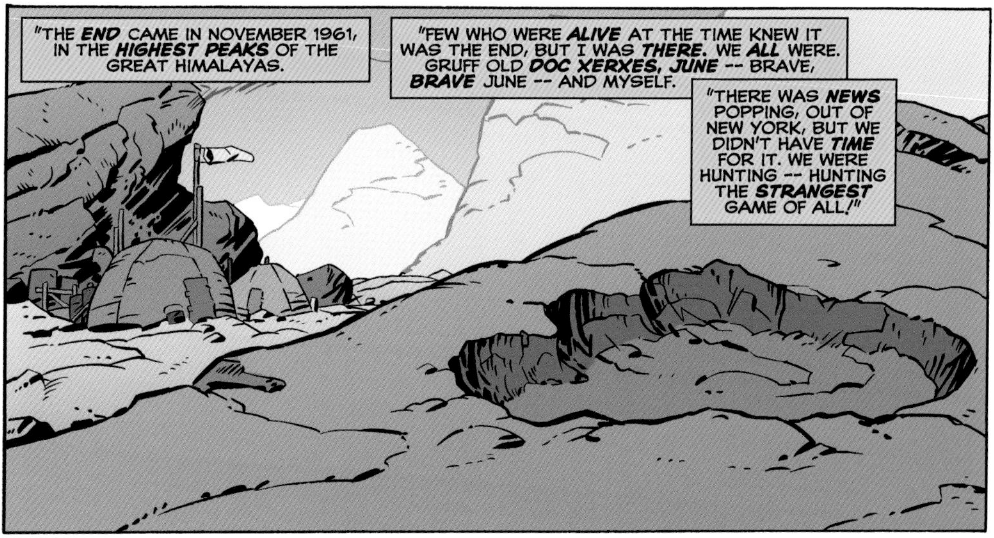
"THE END CAME IN NOVEMBER 1961, IN THE HIGHEST PEAKS OF THE GREAT HIMALAYAS.
"FEW WHO WERE ALIVE AT THE TIME KNEW IT WAS THE END, BUT I WAS THERE. WE ALL WERE. GRUFF OLD DOC XERXES, JUNE -- BRAVE, BRAVE JUNE -- AND MYSELF.
"THERE WAS NEWS POPPING, OUT OF NEW YORK, BUT WE DIDN'T HAVE TIME FOR IT. WE WERE HUNTING -- HUNTING THE STRANGEST GAME OF ALL!"

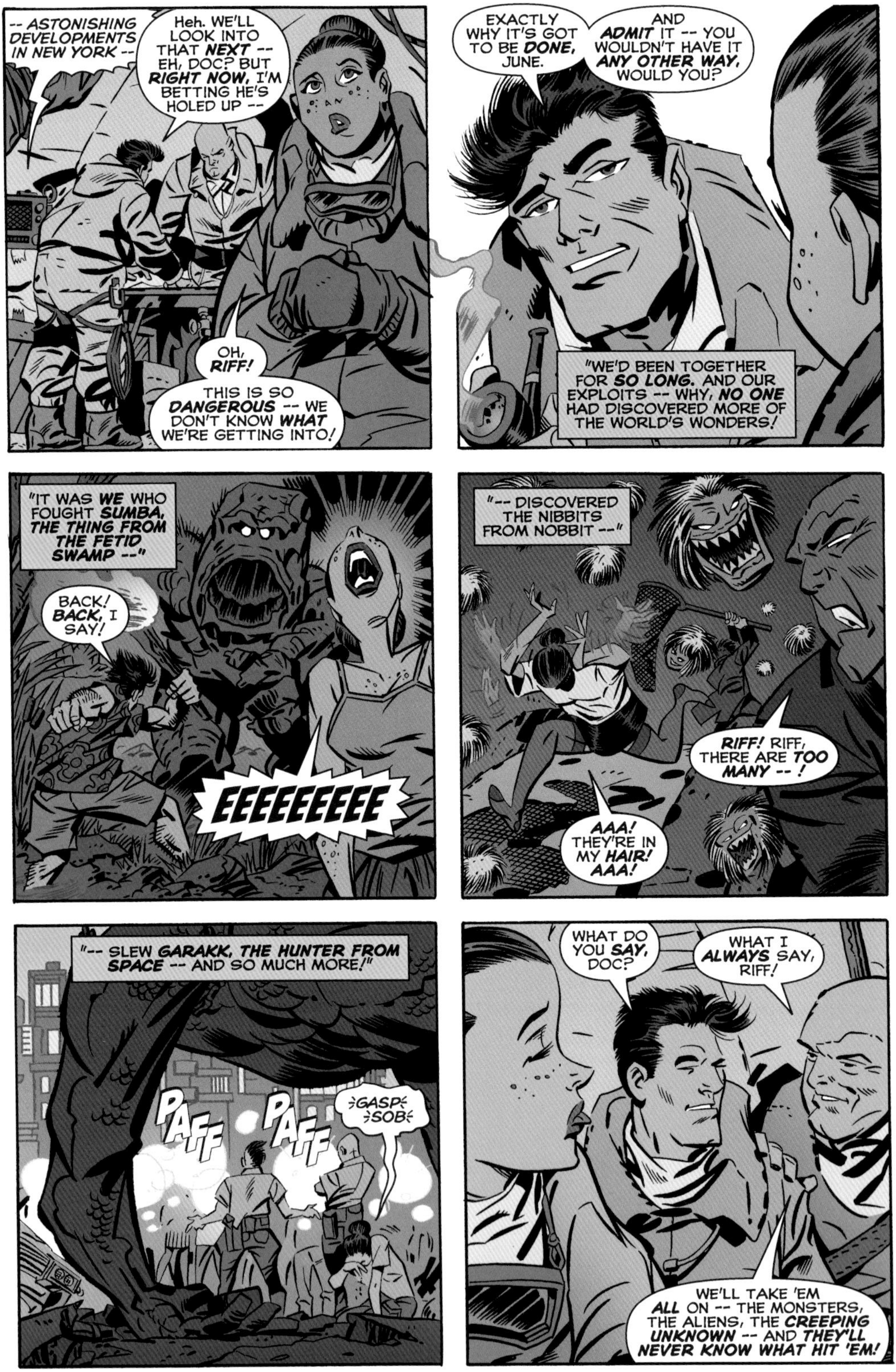
-- ASTONISHING DEVELOPMENTS IN NEW YORK --
Heh. WE'LL LOOK INTO THAT NEXT -- EH, DOC? BUT RIGHT NOW, I'M BETTING HE'S HOLED UP --
OH, RIFF!
THIS IS SO DANGEROUS -- WE DON'T KNOW WHAT WE'RE GETTING INTO!
EXACTLY WHY IT'S GOT TO BE DONE, JUNE.
AND ADMIT IT -- YOU WOULDN'T HAVE IT ANY OTHER WAY, WOULD YOU?
"WE'D BEEN TOGETHER FOR SO LONG. AND OUR EXPLOITS -- WHY, NO ONE HAD DISCOVERED MORE OF THE WORLD'S WONDERS!
"IT WAS WE WHO FOUGHT SUMBA, THE THING FROM THE FETID SWAMP --"
BACK! BACK, I SAY!
EEEEEEEEE
"-- DISCOVERED THE NIBBITS FROM NOBBIT --"
RIFF! RIFF, THERE ARE TOO MANY -- !
AAA! THEY'RE IN MY HAIR! AAA!
"-- SLEW GARAKK, THE HUNTER FROM SPACE -- AND SO MUCH MORE!"
PAFF
PAFF
GASP SOB
WHAT DO YOU SAY, DOC?
WHAT I ALWAYS SAY, RIFF!
WE'LL TAKE 'EM ALL ON -- THE MONSTERS, THE ALIENS, THE CREEPING UNKNOWN -- AND THEY'LL NEVER KNOW WHAT HIT 'EM!

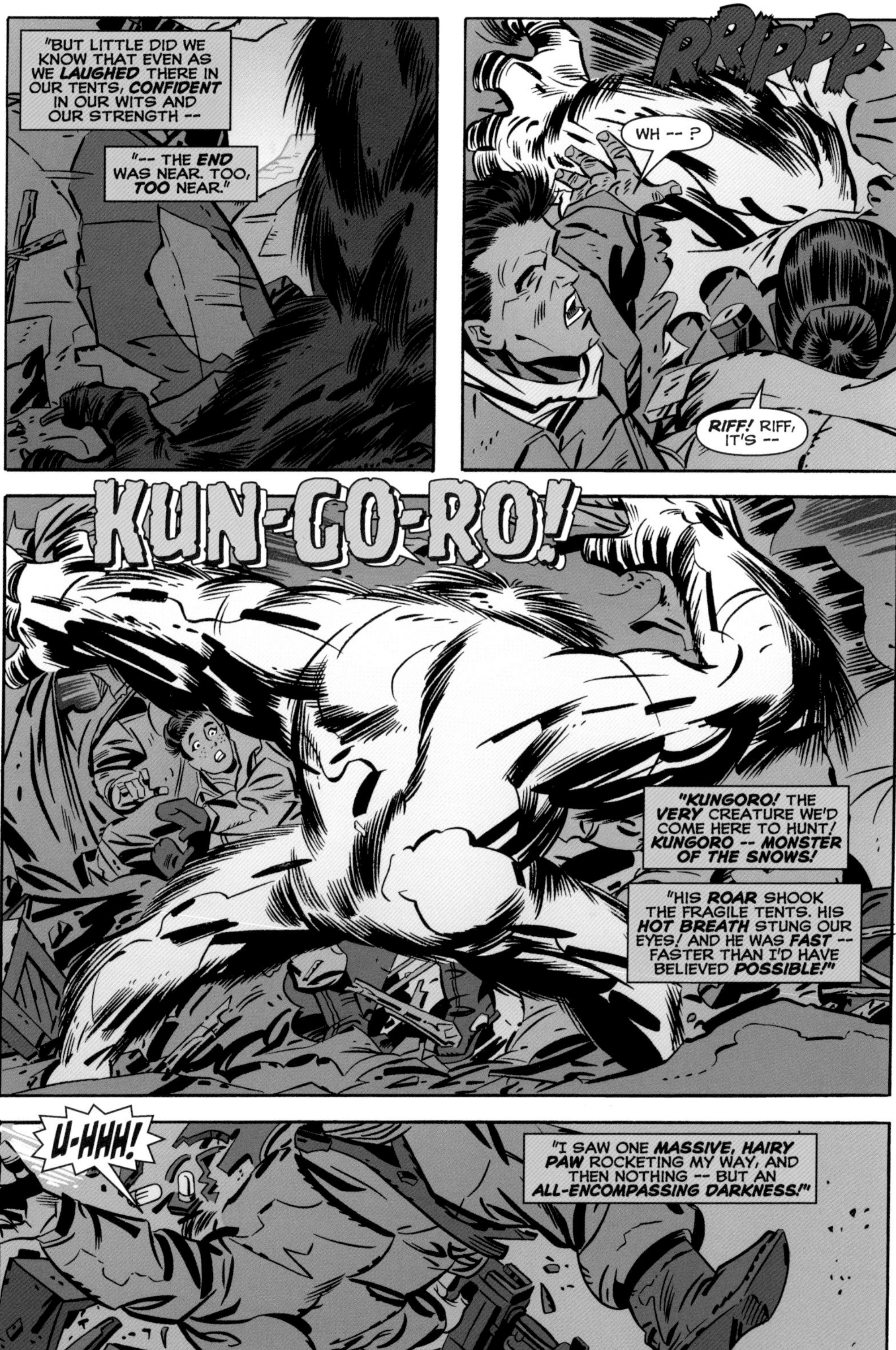
"BUT LITTLE DID WE KNOW THAT EVEN AS WE LAUGHED THERE IN OUR TENTS, CONFIDENT IN OUR WITS AND OUR STRENGTH --
"-- THE END WAS NEAR. TOO, TOO NEAR."
RRIPPP
WH -- ?
RIFF! RIFF, IT'S --
KUN-GO-RO!
"KUNGORO! THE VERY CREATURE WE'D COME HERE TO HUNT! KUNGORO -- MONSTER OF THE SNOWS!
"HIS ROAR SHOOK THE FRAGILE TENTS. HIS HOT BREATH STUNG OUR EYES! AND HE WAS FAST -- FASTER THAN I'D HAVE BELIEVED POSSIBLE!"
U-HHH!
"I SAW ONE MASSIVE, HAIRY PAW ROCKETING MY WAY, AND THEN NOTHING -- BUT AN ALL-ENCOMPASSING DARKNESS!"

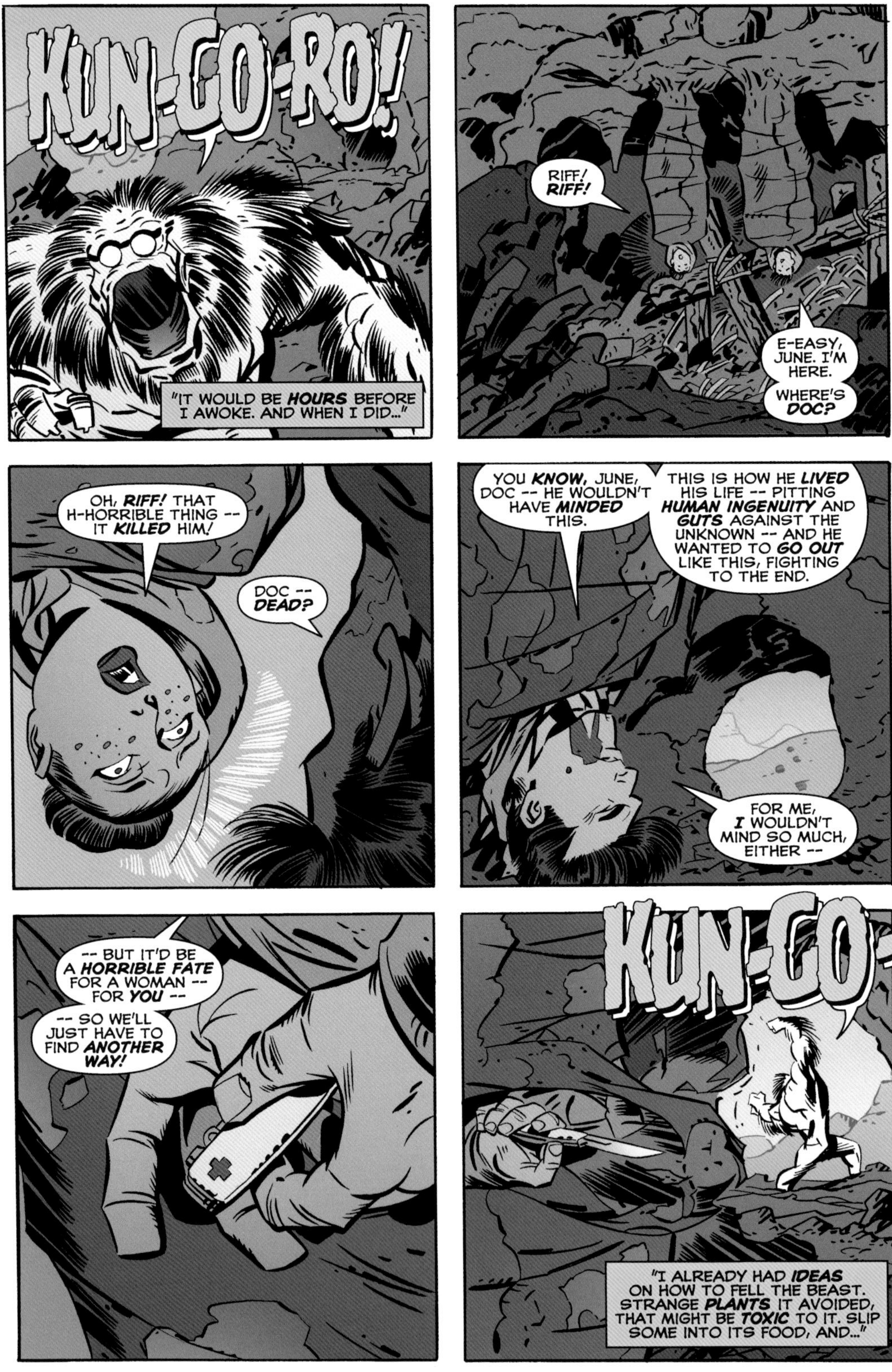
KUN-GO-RO!
"IT WOULD BE HOURS BEFORE I AWOKE. AND WHEN I DID..."
RIFF! RIFF!
E-EASY, JUNE. I'M HERE.
WHERE'S DOC?
OH, RIFF! THAT H-HORRIBLE THING -- IT KILLED HIM!
DOC -- DEAD?
YOU KNOW, JUNE, DOC -- HE WOULDN'T HAVE MINDED THIS.
THIS IS HOW HE LIVED HIS LIFE -- PITTING HUMAN INGENUITY AND GUTS AGAINST THE UNKNOWN -- AND HE WANTED TO GO OUT LIKE THIS, FIGHTING TO THE END.
FOR ME, I WOULDN'T MIND SO MUCH, EITHER --
-- BUT IT'D BE A HORRIBLE FATE FOR A WOMAN -- FOR YOU --
-- SO WE'LL JUST HAVE TO FIND ANOTHER WAY!
KUN-GO-
"I ALREADY HAD IDEAS ON HOW TO FELL THE BEAST. STRANGE PLANTS IT AVOIDED, THAT MIGHT BE TOXIC TO IT. SLIP SOME INTO ITS FOOD, AND..."

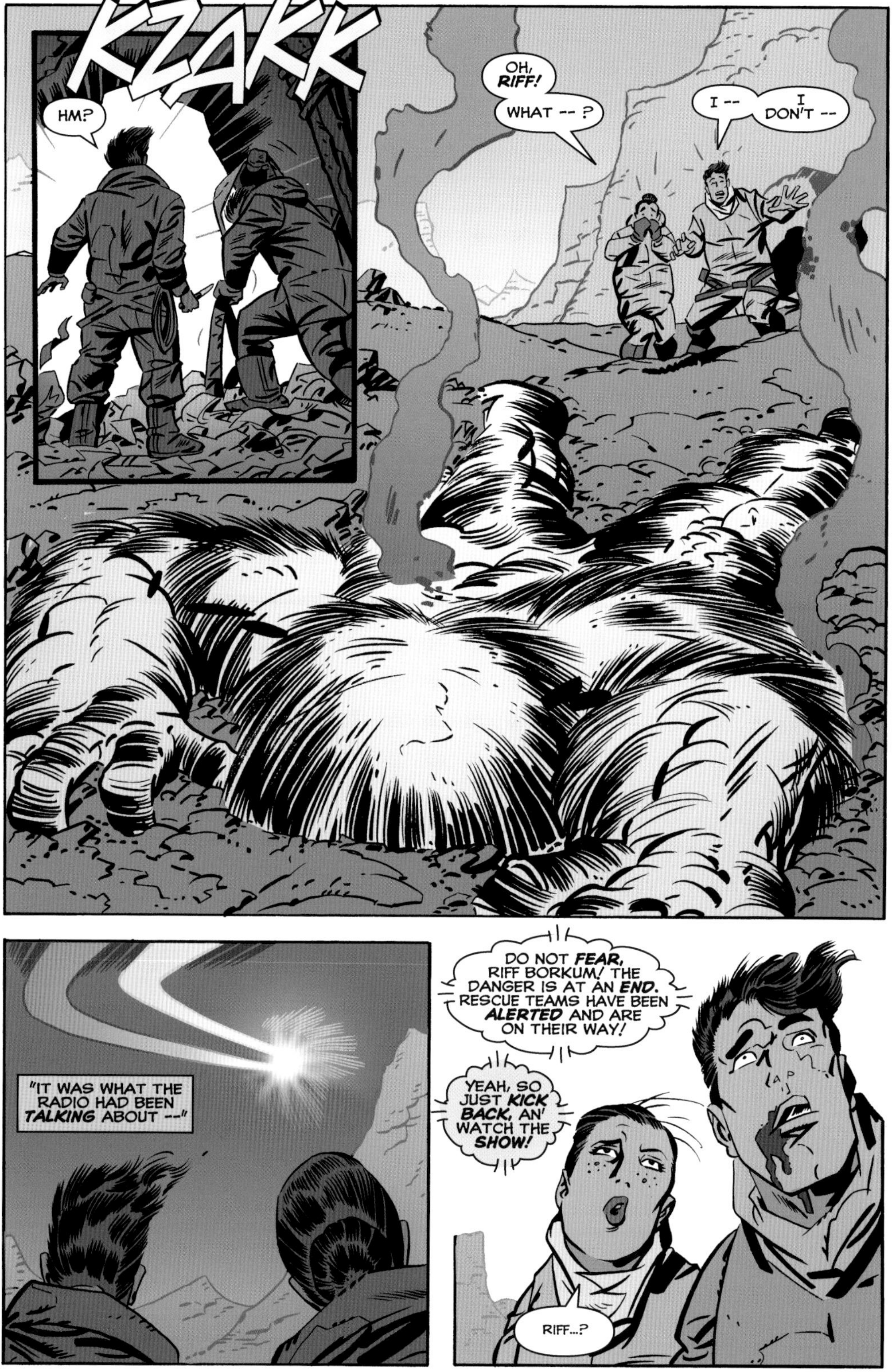
KZAKK
HM?
OH, RIFF!
WHAT -- ?
I --
I DON'T --
"IT WAS WHAT THE RADIO HAD BEEN TALKING ABOUT --"
DO NOT FEAR, RIFF BORKUM! THE DANGER IS AT AN END. RESCUE TEAMS HAVE BEEN ALERTED AND ARE ON THEIR WAY!
YEAH, SO JUST KICK BACK, AN' WATCH THE SHOW!
RIFF...?

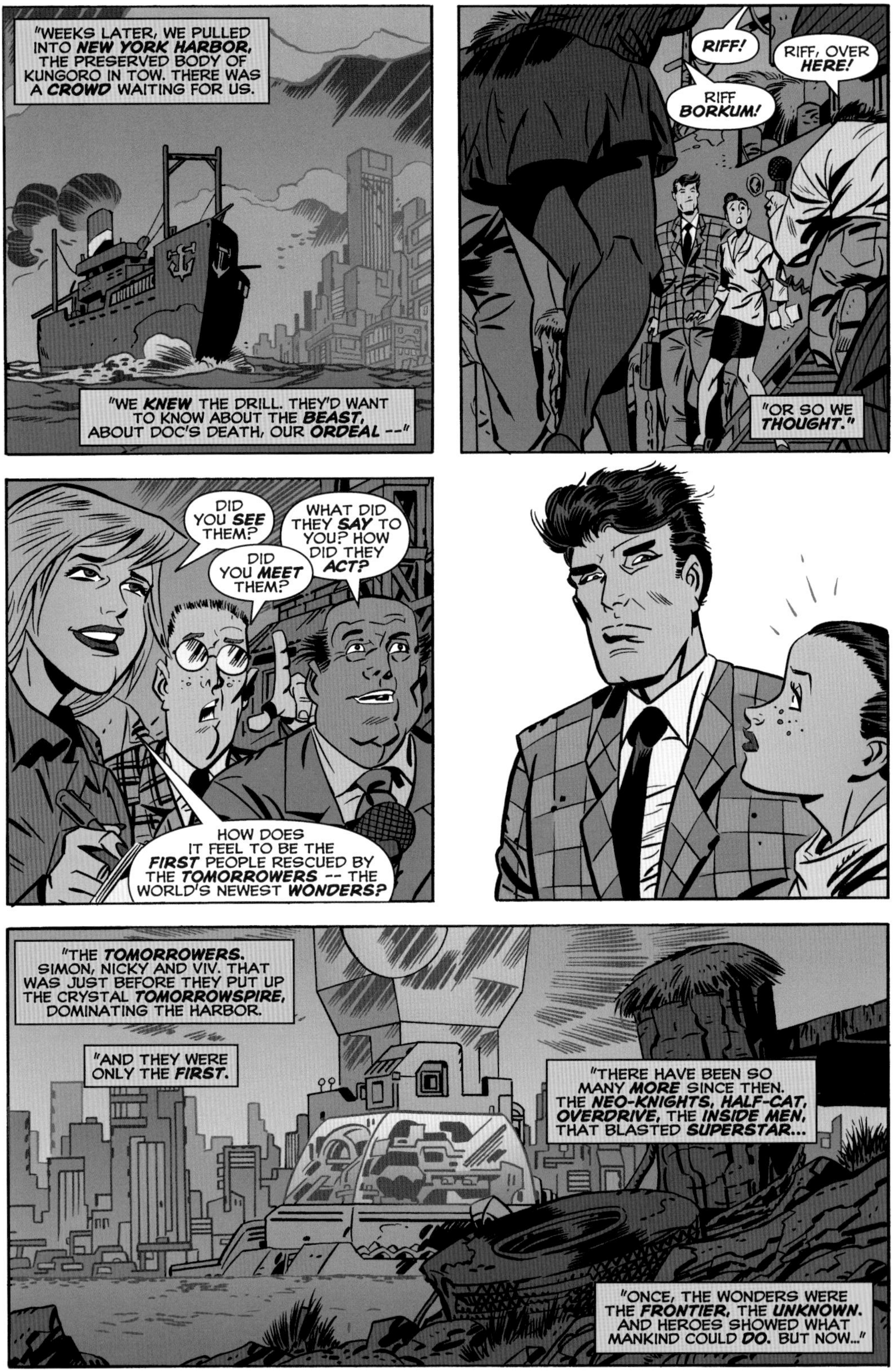

"WEEKS LATER, WE PULLED INTO NEW YORK HARBOR, THE PRESERVED BODY OF KUNGORO IN TOW. THERE WAS A CROWD WAITING FOR US.
"WE KNEW THE DRILL. THEY'D WANT TO KNOW ABOUT THE BEAST, ABOUT DOC'S DEATH, OUR ORDEAL --"
RIFF!
RIFF BORKUM!
RIFF, OVER HERE!
"OR SO WE THOUGHT."
DID YOU SEE THEM?
DID YOU MEET THEM?
WHAT DID THEY SAY TO YOU? HOW DID THEY ACT?
HOW DOES IT FEEL TO BE THE FIRST PEOPLE RESCUED BY THE TOMORROWERS -- THE WORLD'S NEWEST WONDERS?
"THE TOMORROWERS. SIMON, NICKY AND VIV. THAT WAS JUST BEFORE THEY PUT UP THE CRYSTAL TOMORROWSPIRE, DOMINATING THE HARBOR.
"AND THEY WERE ONLY THE FIRST.
"THERE HAVE BEEN SO MANY MORE SINCE THEN. THE NEO-KNIGHTS, HALF-CAT, OVERDRIVE, THE INSIDE MEN, THAT BLASTED SUPERSTAR...
"ONCE, THE WONDERS WERE THE FRONTIER, THE UNKNOWN. AND HEROES SHOWED WHAT MANKIND COULD DO. BUT NOW..."

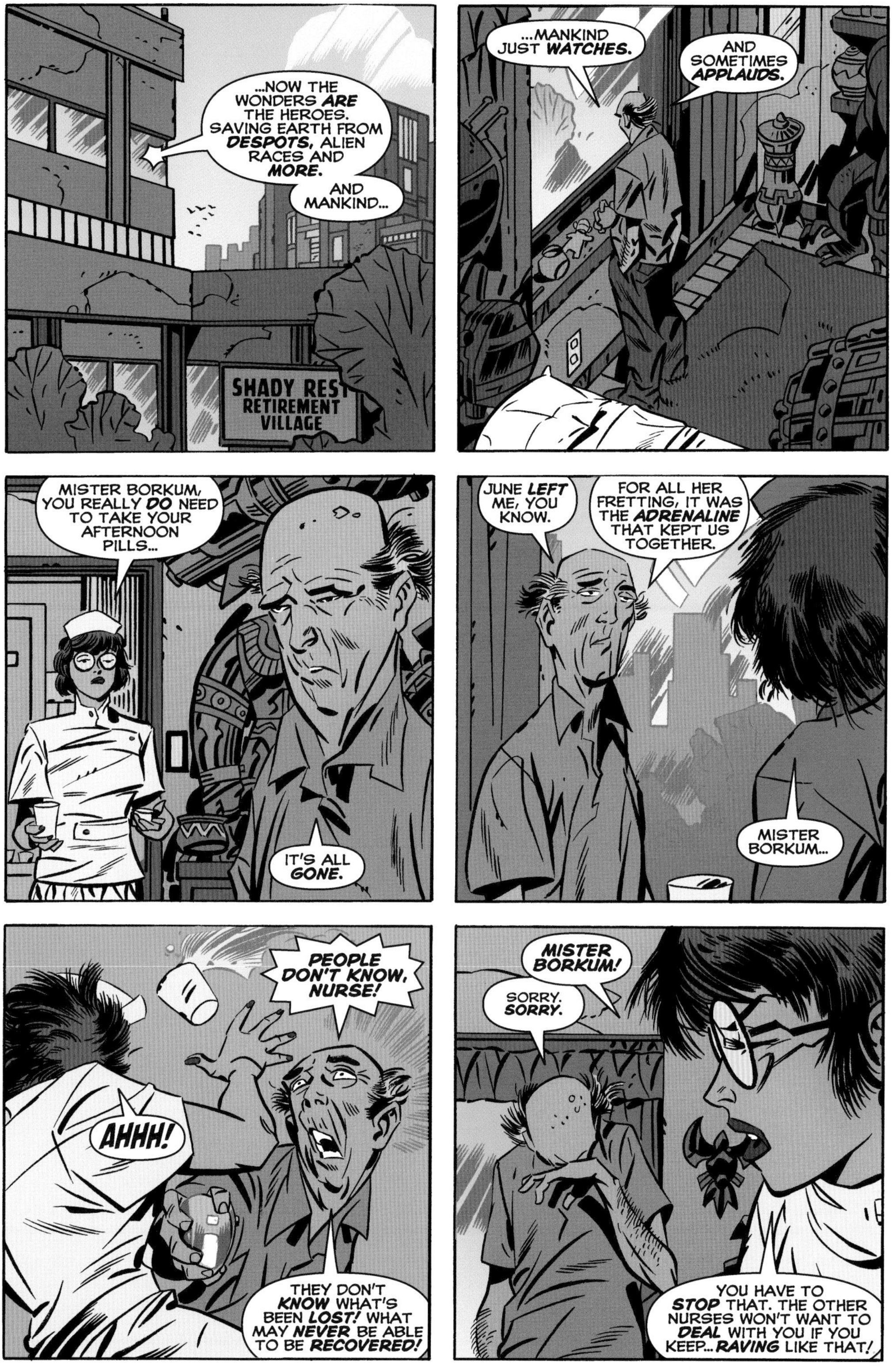
...NOW THE WONDERS ARE THE HEROES. SAVING EARTH FROM DESPOTS, ALIEN RACES AND MORE.
AND MANKIND...
SHADY REST RETIREMENT VILLAGE
...MANKIND JUST WATCHES.
AND SOMETIMES APPLAUDS.
MISTER BORKUM, YOU REALLY DO NEED TO TAKE YOUR AFTERNOON PILLS...
IT'S ALL GONE.
JUNE LEFT ME, YOU KNOW.
FOR ALL HER FRETTING, IT WAS THE ADRENALINE THAT KEPT US TOGETHER.
MISTER BORKUM...
PEOPLE DON'T KNOW, NURSE!
AHHH!
THEY DON'T KNOW WHAT'S BEEN LOST! WHAT MAY NEVER BE ABLE TO BE RECOVERED!
MISTER BORKUM!
SORRY. SORRY.
YOU HAVE TO STOP THAT. THE OTHER NURSES WON'T WANT TO DEAL WITH YOU IF YOU KEEP... RAVING LIKE THAT!

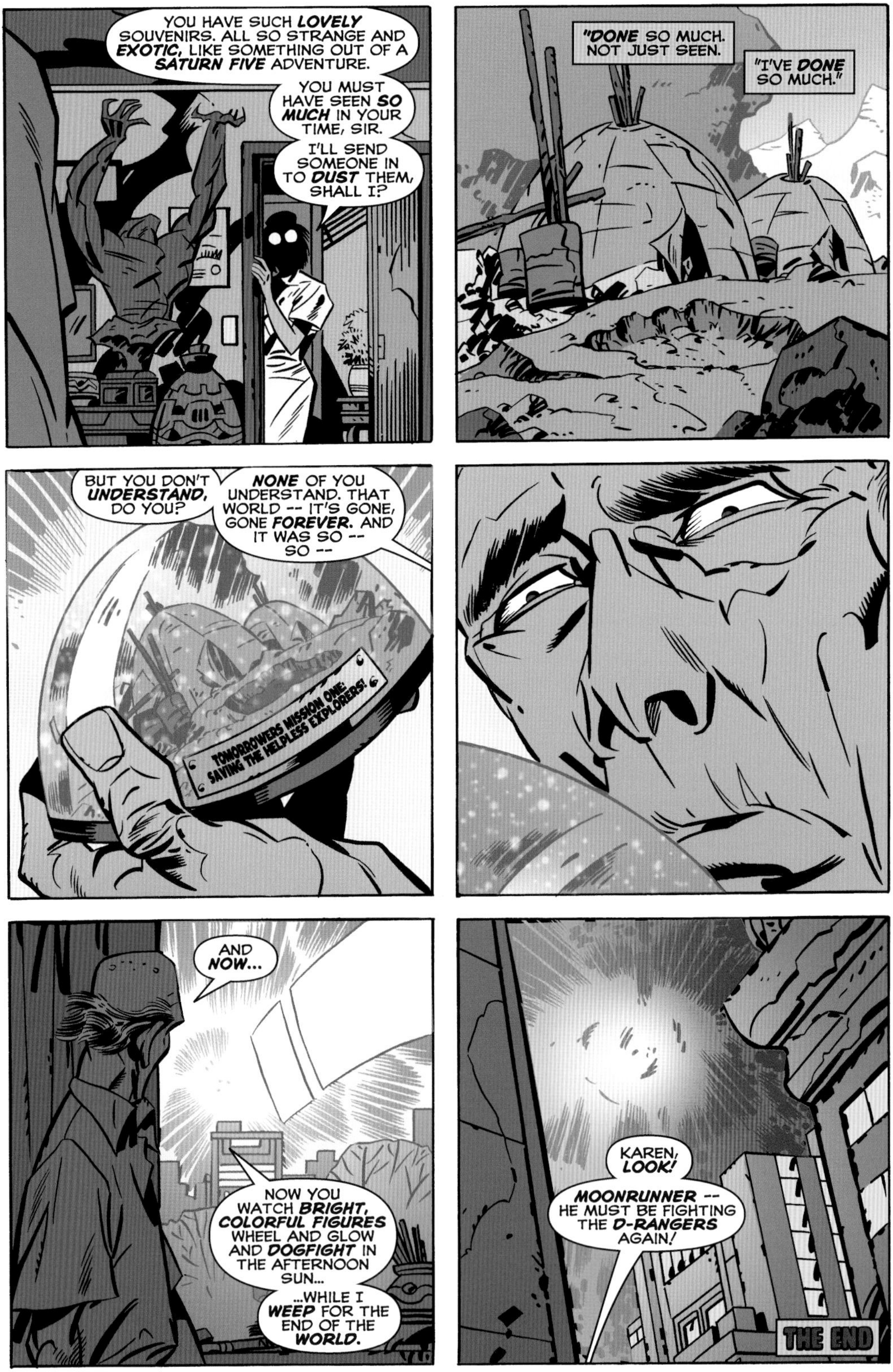
YOU HAVE SUCH LOVELY SOUVENIRS. ALL SO STRANGE AND EXOTIC, LIKE SOMETHING OUT OF A SATURN FIVE ADVENTURE.
YOU MUST HAVE SEEN SO MUCH IN YOUR TIME, SIR.
I'LL SEND SOMEONE IN TO DUST THEM, SHALL I?
"DONE SO MUCH. NOT JUST SEEN.
"I'VE DONE SO MUCH."
BUT YOU DON'T UNDERSTAND, DO YOU?
NONE OF YOU UNDERSTAND. THAT WORLD -- IT'S GONE, GONE FOREVER. AND IT WAS SO -- SO --
TOMORROWERS MISSION ONE: SAVING THE HELPLESS EXPLORERS!
AND NOW...
NOW YOU WATCH BRIGHT, COLORFUL FIGURES WHEEL AND GLOW AND DOGFIGHT IN THE AFTERNOON SUN...
...WHILE I WEEP FOR THE END OF THE WORLD.
KAREN, LOOK!
MOONRUNNER -- HE MUST BE FIGHTING THE D-RANGERS AGAIN!
THE END

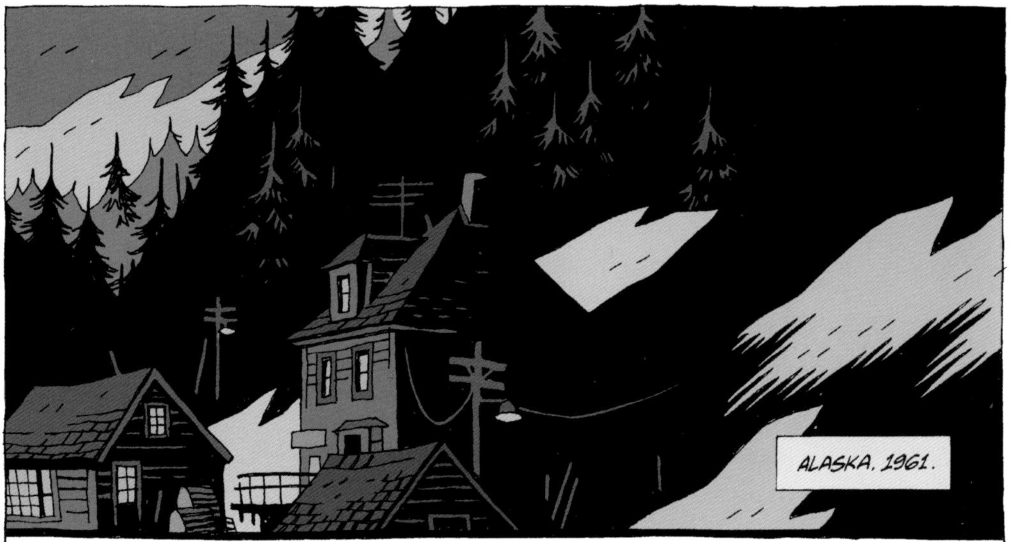
ALASKA, 1961.

The Hydra and the Lion

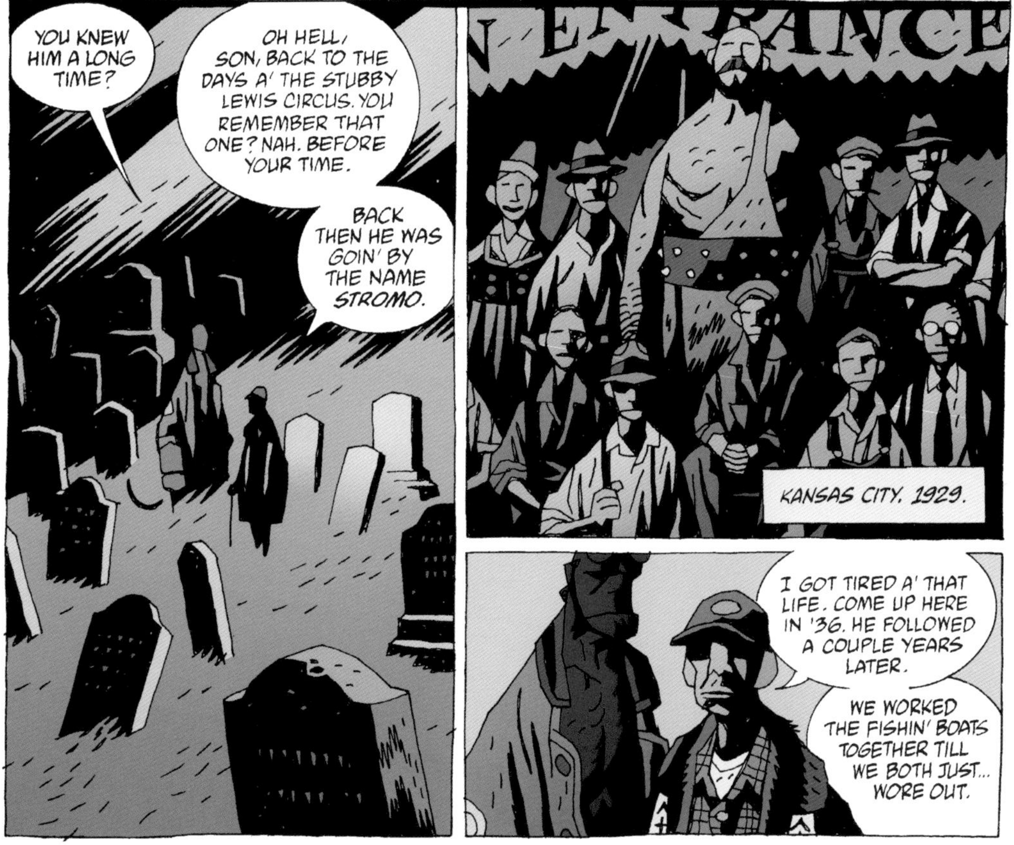
YOU KNEW HIM A LONG TIME?
OH HELL, SON, BACK TO THE DAYS A' THE STUBBY LEWIS CIRCUS. YOU REMEMBER THAT ONE? NAH. BEFORE YOUR TIME.
BACK THEN HE WAS GOIN' BY THE NAME STROMO.
KANSAS CITY, 1929.
I GOT TIRED A' THAT LIFE. COME UP HERE IN '36. HE FOLLOWED A COUPLE YEARS LATER.
WE WORKED THE FISHIN' BOATS TOGETHER TILL WE BOTH JUST... WORE OUT.

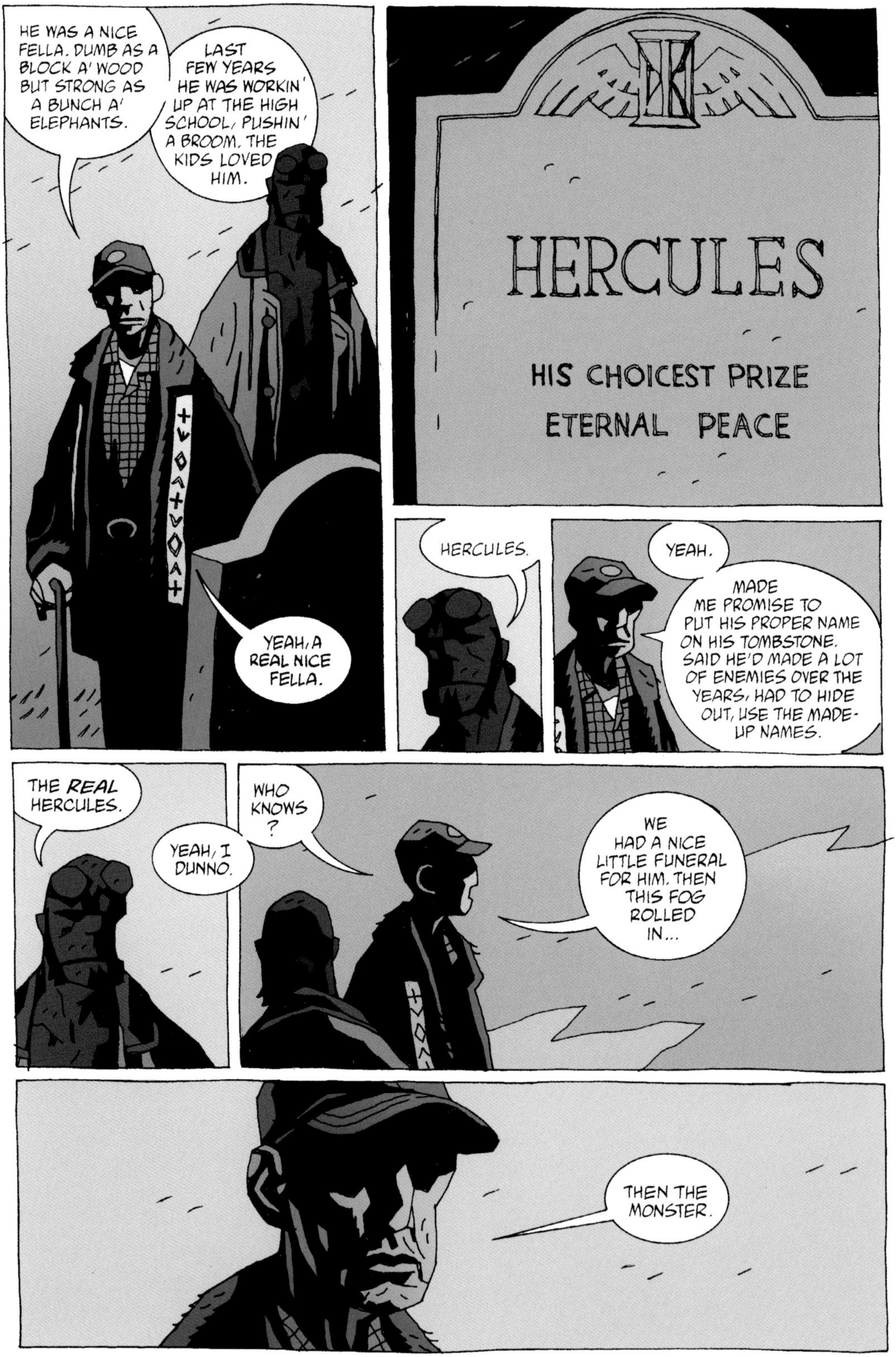
HE WAS A NICE FELLA. DUMB AS A BLOCK A' WOOD BUT STRONG AS A BUNCH A' ELEPHANTS.
LAST FEW YEARS HE WAS WORKIN' UP AT THE HIGH SCHOOL, PUSHIN' A BROOM. THE KIDS LOVED HIM.
YEAH, A REAL NICE FELLA.
HERCULES
HIS CHOICEST PRIZE
ETERNAL PEACE
HERCULES.
YEAH.
MADE ME PROMISE TO PUT HIS PROPER NAME ON HIS TOMBSTONE. SAID HE'D MADE A LOT OF ENEMIES OVER THE YEARS, HAD TO HIDE OUT, USE THE MADE-UP NAMES.
THE *REAL* HERCULES.
YEAH, I DUNNO.
WHO KNOWS?
WE HAD A NICE LITTLE FUNERAL FOR HIM. THEN THIS FOG ROLLED IN...
THEN THE MONSTER.

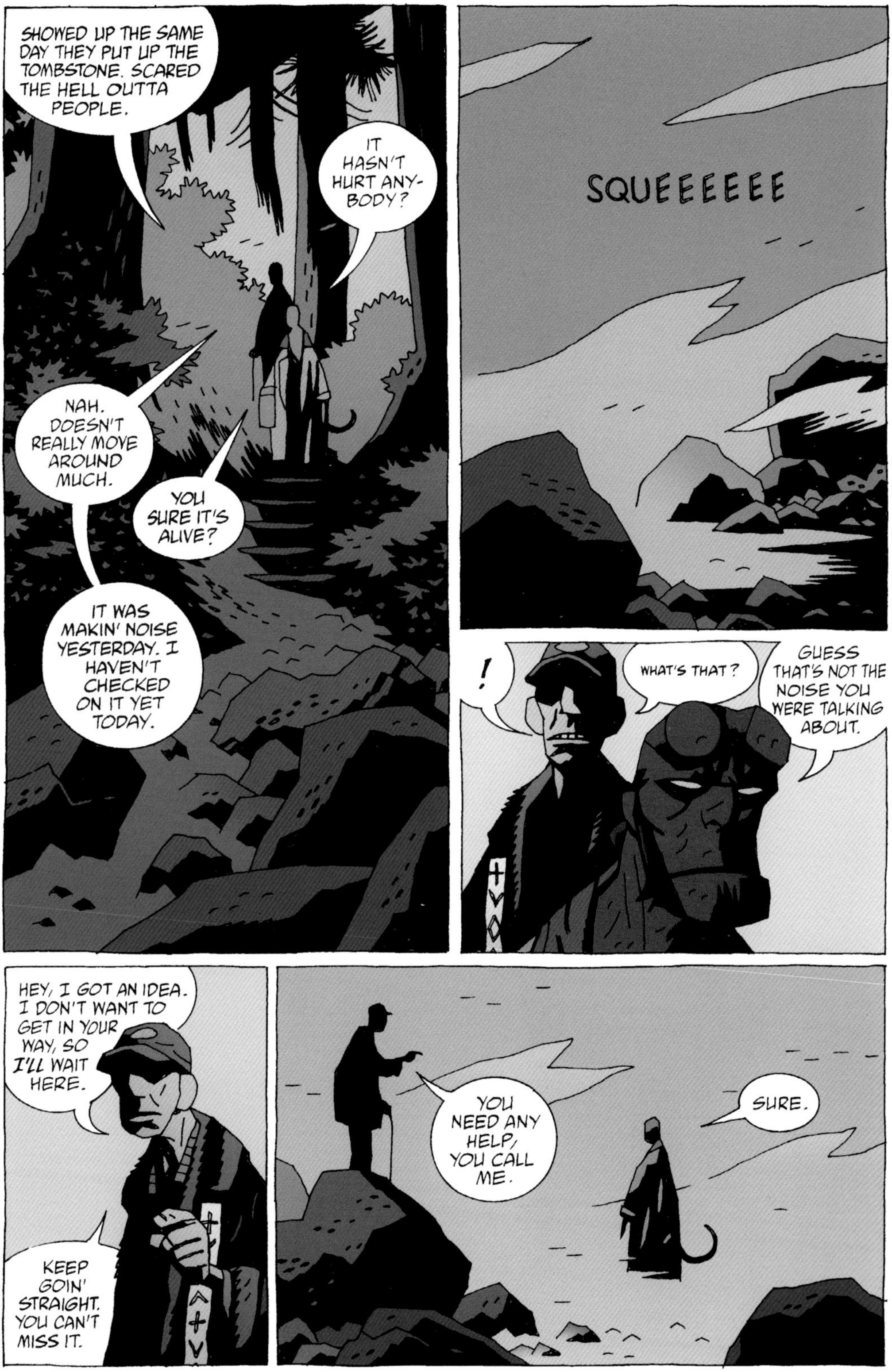

SHOWED UP THE SAME DAY THEY PUT UP THE TOMBSTONE. SCARED THE HELL OUTTA PEOPLE.
IT HASN'T HURT ANYBODY?
NAH. DOESN'T REALLY MOVE AROUND MUCH.
YOU SURE IT'S ALIVE?
IT WAS MAKIN' NOISE YESTERDAY. I HAVEN'T CHECKED ON IT YET TODAY.
SQUEEEEEEE
!
WHAT'S THAT?
GUESS THAT'S NOT THE NOISE YOU WERE TALKING ABOUT.
HEY, I GOT AN IDEA. I DON'T WANT TO GET IN YOUR WAY, SO I'LL WAIT HERE.
KEEP GOIN' STRAIGHT. YOU CAN'T MISS IT.
YOU NEED ANY HELP, YOU CALL ME.
SURE.

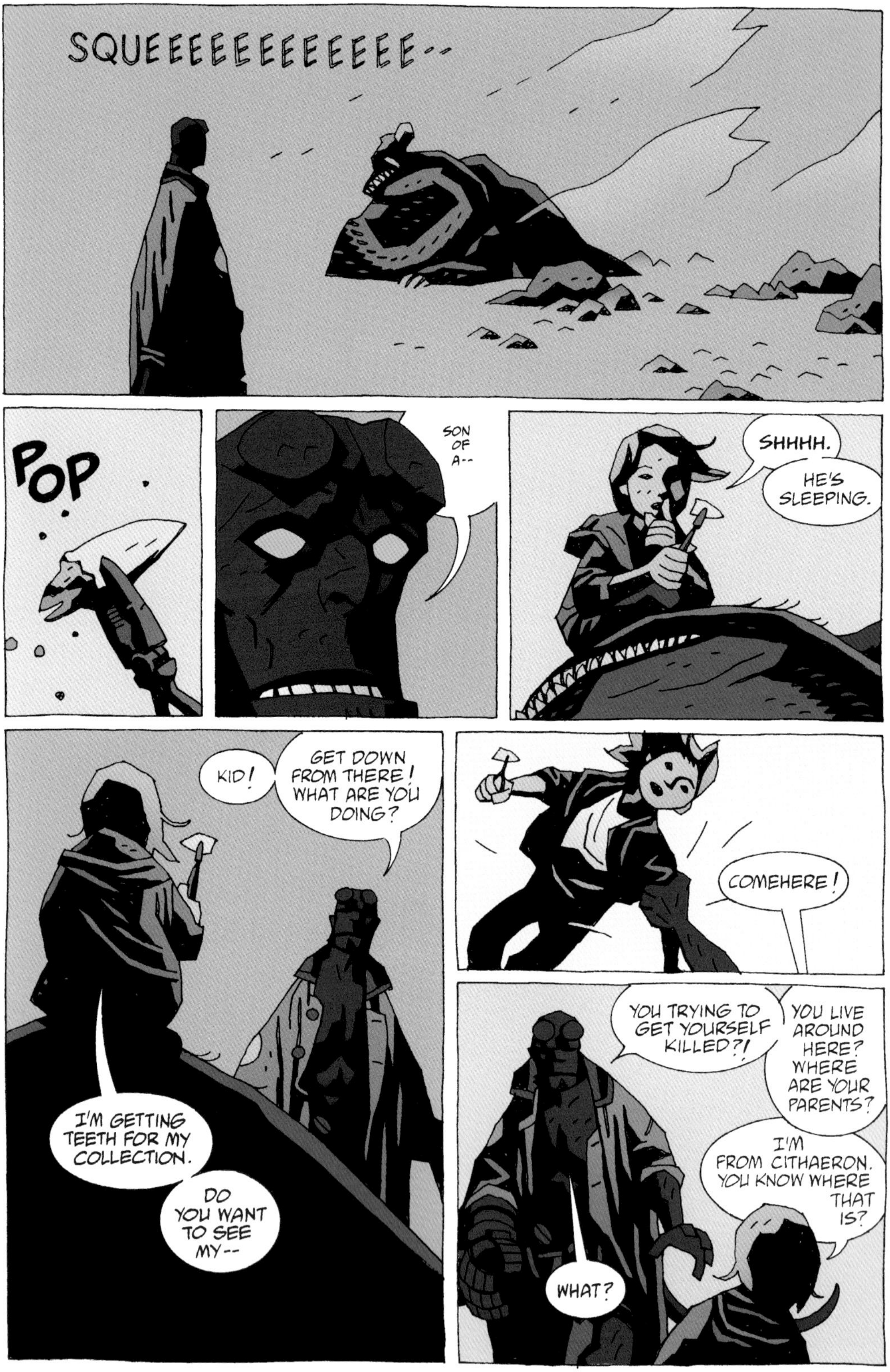
SQUEEEEEEEEEEEE--
POP
SON OF A--
SHHHH.
HE'S SLEEPING.
KID!
GET DOWN FROM THERE! WHAT ARE YOU DOING?
I'M GETTING TEETH FOR MY COLLECTION.
DO YOU WANT TO SEE MY--
COMEHERE!
YOU TRYING TO GET YOURSELF KILLED?!
YOU LIVE AROUND HERE? WHERE ARE YOUR PARENTS?
I'M FROM CITHAERON. YOU KNOW WHERE THAT IS?
WHAT?

YOU WANT TO SEE MY COLLECTION?

KID--

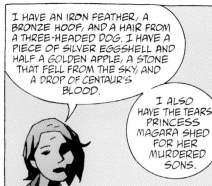

I HAVE AN IRON FEATHER, A BRONZE HOOF, AND A HAIR FROM A THREE-HEADED DOG. I HAVE A PIECE OF SILVER EGGSHELL AND HALF A GOLDEN APPLE, A STONE THAT FELL FROM THE SKY, AND A DROP OF CENTAUR'S BLOOD.

I ALSO HAVE THE TEARS PRINCESS MAGARA SHED FOR HER MURDERED SONS.

?

GO HOME.

DON'T WORRY ABOUT ME, I'M HALF LION.

THAT'S GREAT, NOW GET--

I CAN PROVE IT!

GRRRRRRRR

RNARR NARR

JEEZ, KID! WHAT ARE YOU TRYING TO--

AH CRAP.

YOU SAID A BAD WORD.

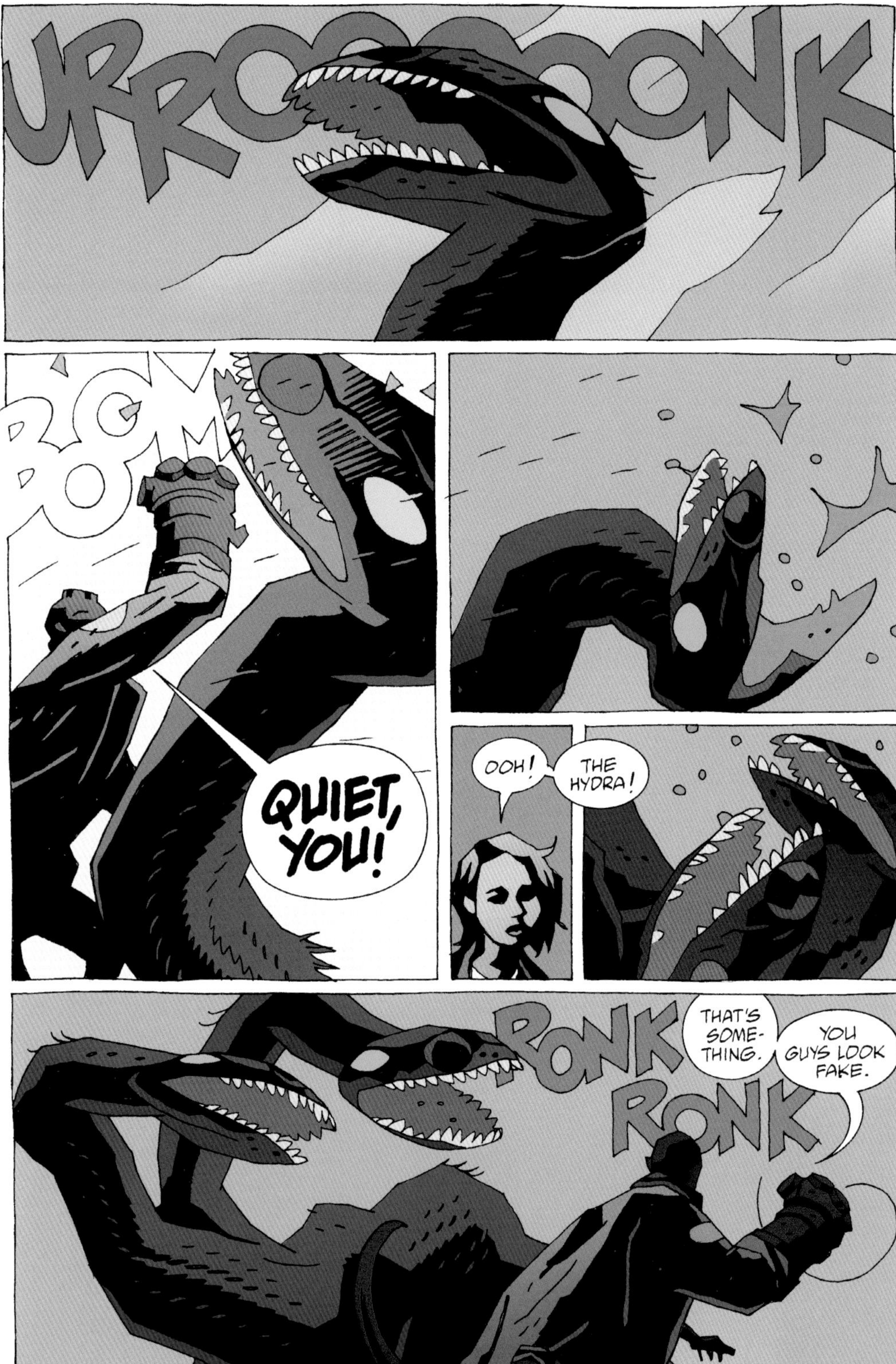
UROOOOOONK
BOOM
QUIET, YOU!
OOH!
THE HYDRA!
RONK RONK
THAT'S SOME-THING.
YOU GUYS LOOK FAKE.

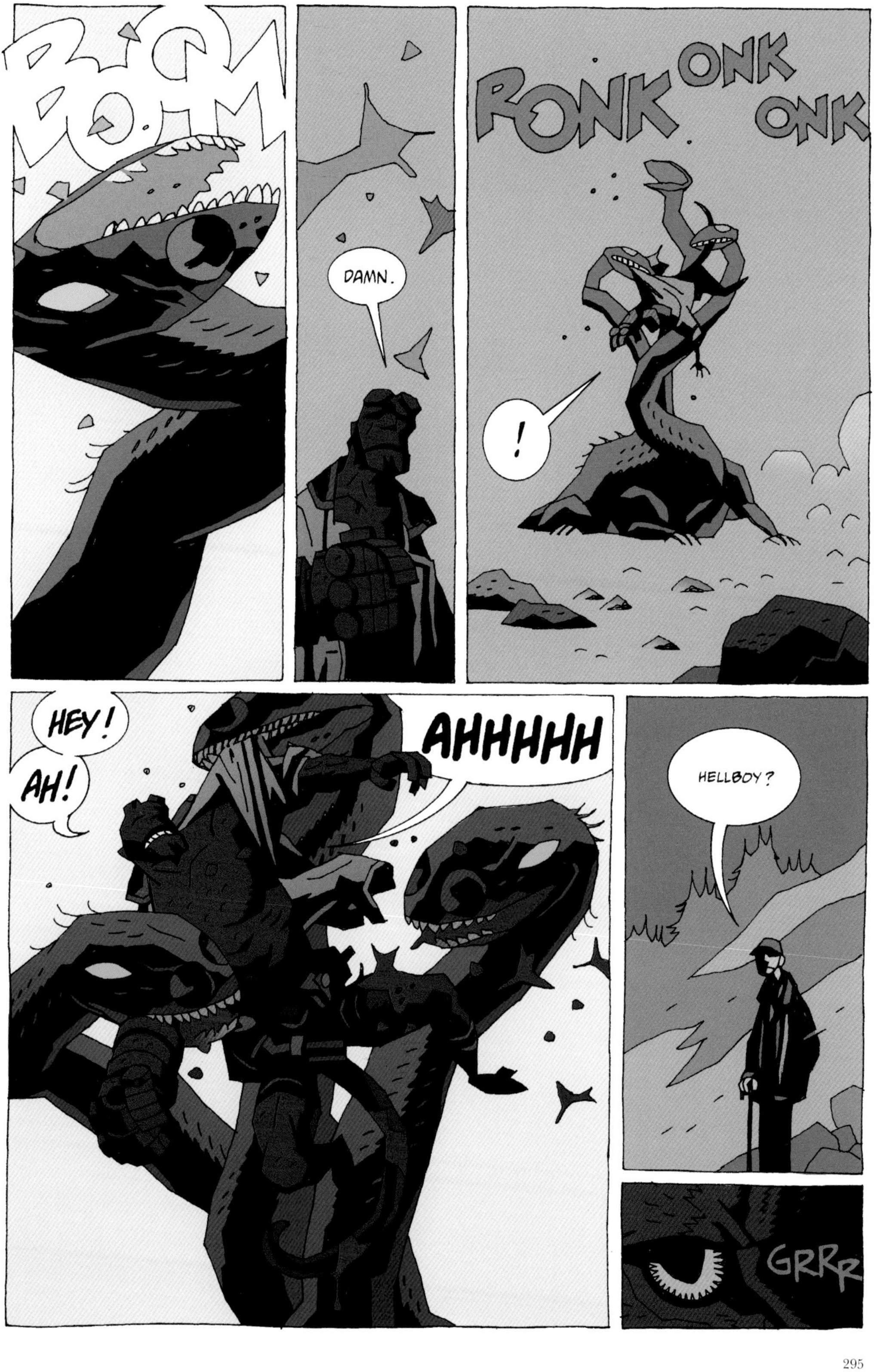
BOOM
DAMN.
RONK ONK ONK ONK
!
HEY!
AH!
AHHHHH
HELLBOY?
GRRR

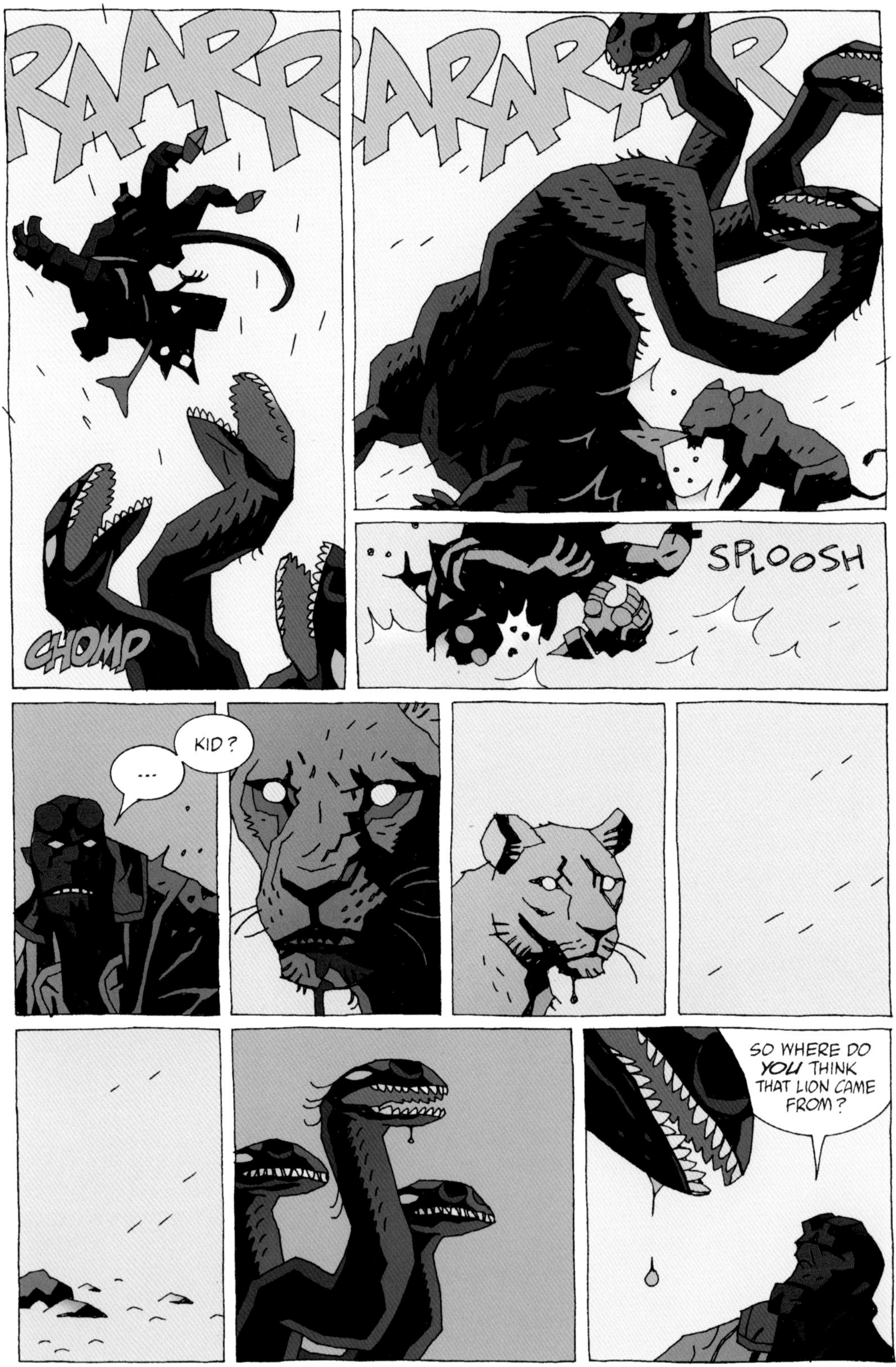
RAARRR
RARARRR
CHOMP
SPLOOSH
...
KID?
SO WHERE DO YOU THINK THAT LION CAME FROM?

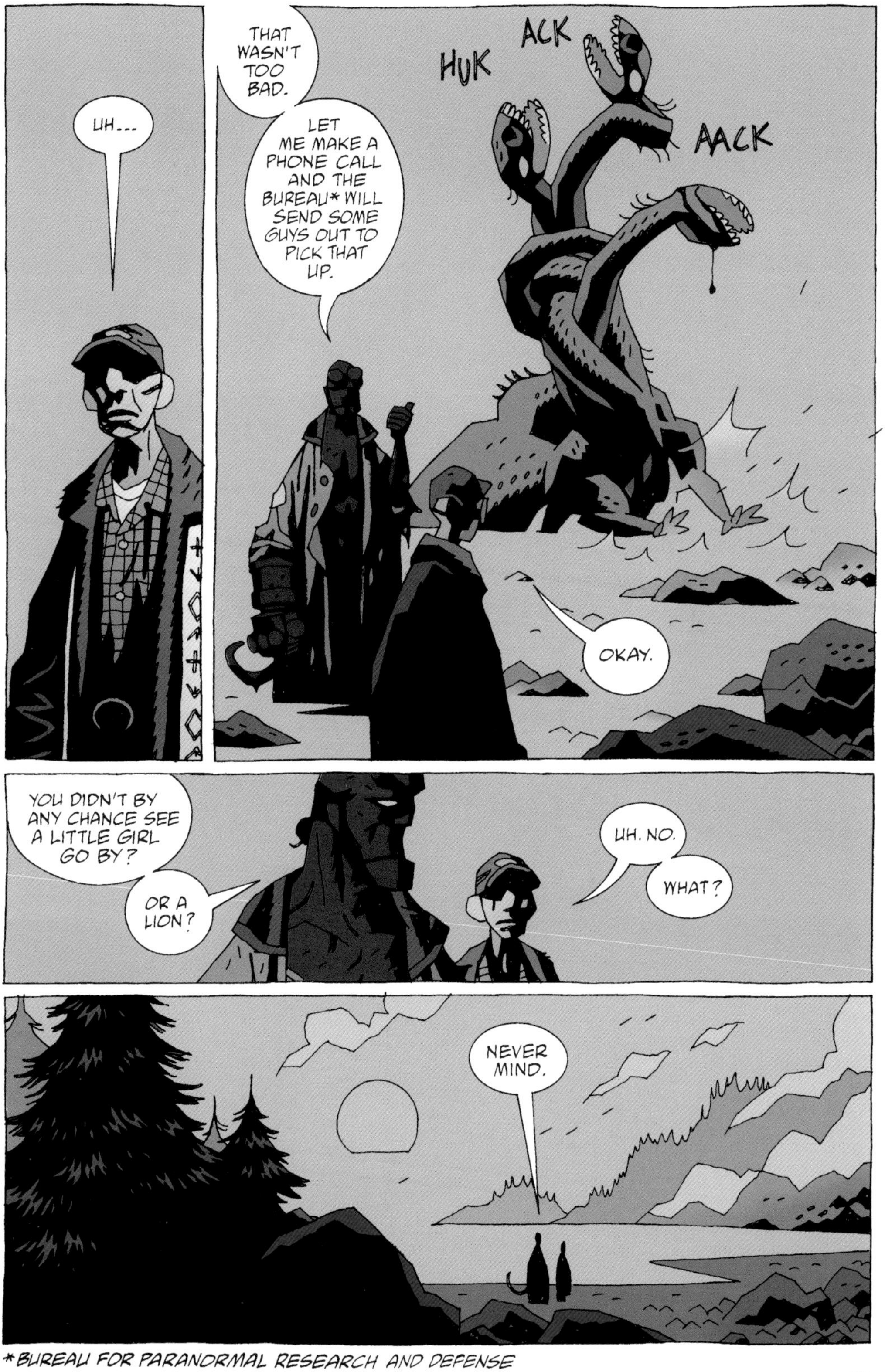
UH...
THAT WASN'T TOO BAD.
LET ME MAKE A PHONE CALL AND THE BUREAU* WILL SEND SOME GUYS OUT TO PICK THAT UP.
HUK
ACK
AACK
OKAY.
YOU DIDN'T BY ANY CHANCE SEE A LITTLE GIRL GO BY?
OR A LION?
UH. NO.
WHAT?
NEVER MIND.

*BUREAU FOR PARANORMAL RESEARCH AND DEFENSE

SIXTEEN HOURS LATER. *B.P.R.D.* HEADQUARTERS, FAIRFIELD, CT.

FASCINATING. THE GIRL SAID SHE WAS FROM CITHAERON...

"ACCORDING TO LEGEND, HERCULES, AT EIGHTEEN, WENT ALONE INTO THE WOODS OF CITHAERON AND KILLED THE THESPIAN LION..."

AND FOR THE REST OF HIS LIFE, HE WORE ITS SKIN.

YOU THINK THE LITTLE GIRL WAS THE GHOST OF HIS PANTS?

CLOAK, HELLBOY. HE WORE THE SKIN AS A CLOAK.

STILL...

IT'S A GOOD THEORY, PROFESSOR, BUT IF I MIGHT SUGGEST SOMETHING...

SHE REFERRED TO MAGARA, WHO WAS HERCULES' WIFE. HERCULES KILLED HIS WIFE AND SONS WHILE DRIVEN MAD BY HERA. THE FEATHERS, APPLES, AND HOOVES REFER TO THE LABORS OF HERCULES, BUT HIS *FIRST* LABOR, UNDERTAKEN TO ATONE FOR THOSE MURDERS, WAS TO SLAY THE *NEMEAN* LION.

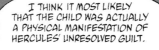

I THINK IT MOST LIKELY THAT THE CHILD WAS ACTUALLY A PHYSICAL MANIFESTATION OF HERCULES' UNRESOLVED GUILT.

OY!

HERCULES

THE END

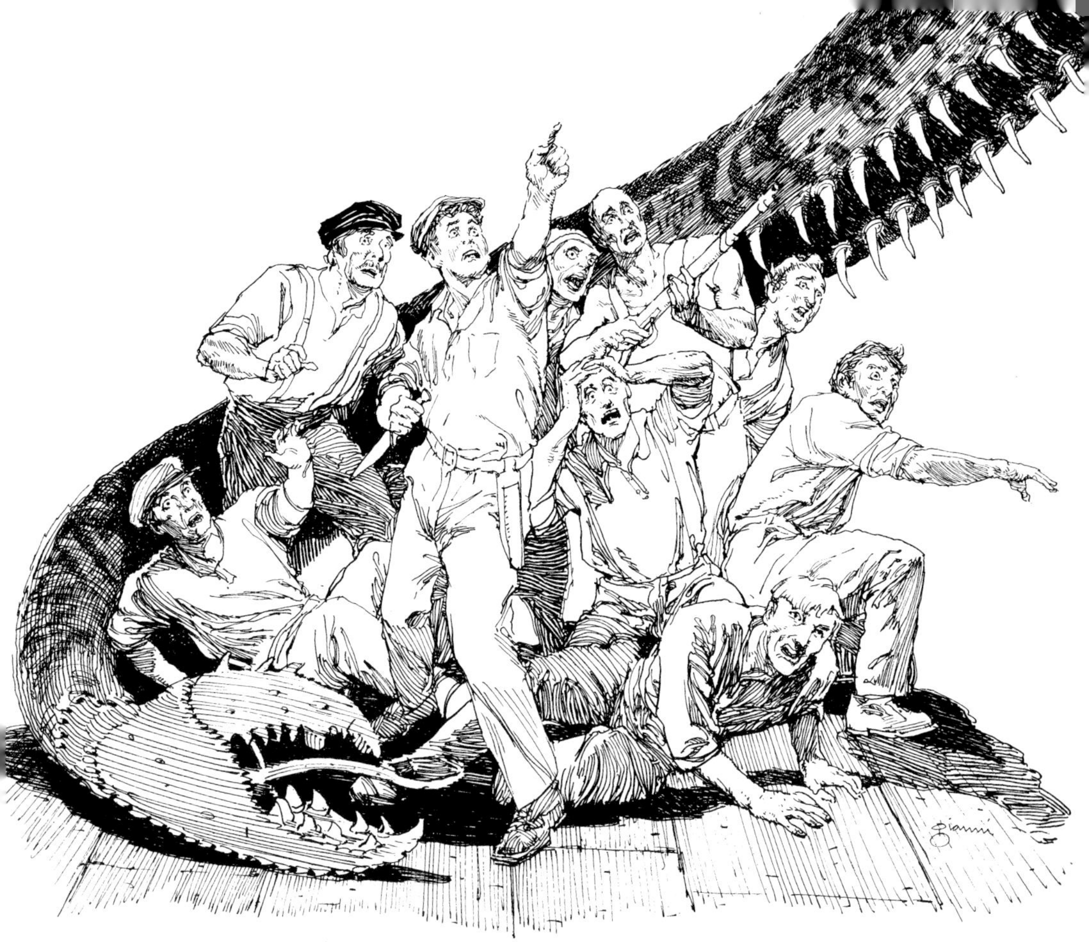

A Tropical Horror

by WILLIAM HOPE HODGSON

ILLUSTRATIONS *by* GARY GIANNI

We are a hundred and thirty days out from Melbourne, and for three weeks we have lain in this sweltering calm.

It is midnight, and our watch on deck until four a.m. I go out and sit on the hatch. A minute later, Joky, our youngest 'prentice, joins me for a chatter. Many are the hours we have sat thus and talked in the night watches; though, to be sure, it is Joky who does the talking. I am content to smoke and listen, giving an occasional grunt at seasons to show that I am attentive.

Joky has been silent for some time, his head bent in meditation. Suddenly he looks up, evidently with the intention of making some remark. As he does so, I see his face stiffen with a nameless horror. He crouches back, his eyes staring past me at some unseen fear. Then his mouth opens. He gives forth a

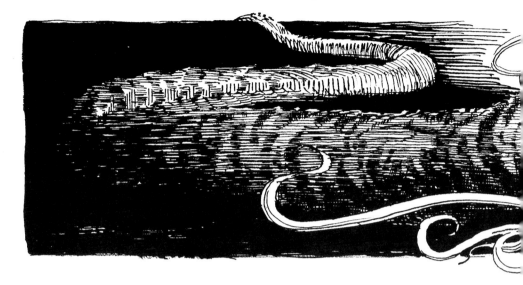

stranglulated cry and topples backward off the hatch, striking his head against the deck. Fearing I know not what, I turn to look.

Great Heavens! Rising above the bulwarks, seen plainly in the bright moonlight, is a vast slobbering mouth a fathom across. From the huge dripping lips hang great tentacles. As I look the Thing comes further over the rail. It is rising, rising, higher and higher. There are no eyes visible; only that fearful slobbering mouth set on the tremendous trunk-like neck; which, even as I watch, is curling inboard with the stealthy celerity of an enormous eel. Over it comes in vast heaving folds. Will it never end? The ship gives a slow, sullen roll to starboard as she feels the weight. Then the tail, a broad, flat-shaped mass, slips over the teak rail and falls with a loud slump on to the deck.

For a few seconds the hideous creature lies heaped in writhing, slimy coils. Then, with quick, darting movements, the monstrous head travels along the deck. Close by the main-mast stand the harness casks, and alongside of these a freshly opened cask of salt beef with the top loosely replaced. The smell of the meat seems to attract the monster, and I can hear it sniffing with a vast indrawing breath. Then those lips open, displaying four huge fangs; there is a quick forward motion of the head, a sudden crashing, crunching sound, and beef and barrel have disappeared. The noise brings one of the ordinary seamen out of the fo'cas'le. Coming into the night, he can see nothing for a moment. Then, as he gets further aft, he sees, and with horrified cries rushes forward. Too late! From the mouth of the Thing there flashes forth a long, broad blade of glistening white, set with fierce teeth. I avert my eyes, but cannot shut out the sickening "Glut! Glut!" that follows.

The man on the look-out, attracted by the disturbance, has witnessed the tragedy, and flies for refuge into the fo'cas'le, flinging to the heavy iron door after him.

The carpenter and sailmaker come running out from the halfdeck in their drawers. Seeing the awful Thing, they rush aft to the cabins with shouts of fear. The Second Mate, after one glance over the break of the poop, runs down the companion-way with the Helmsman after him. I can hear them barring the scuttle, and abruptly I realise that I am on the main-deck alone.

So far I have forgotten my own danger. The past few minutes seem like a portion of an awful dream. Now, however, I comprehend my position and, shaking off the horror that has held me, turn to seek safety. As I do so my eyes fall upon Joky, lying huddled and senseless with fright where he has fallen. I cannot leave him there. Close by stands the empty half-deck—a little steel-built house with iron doors. The lee one is hooked open. Once inside I am safe.

Up to the present the Thing has seemed to be unconsious of my presence. Now, however, the huge barrel-like head sways in my direction; then comes a muffled bellow, and the great tongue flickers in and out as the brute turns and swirls aft to meet me. I know there is not a moment to lose, and, picking up the helpless lad, I make a run for the open door. It is only distant a few yards, but that awful shape is coming down the deck to me in great wreathing coils. I reach the house and tumble in with my burden; then out on deck again to unhook and close the door. Even as I do so something white curls around the end of the house. With a bound I am inside and the door is shut and bolted. Through the thick glass of the ports I see the Thing sweep round the house, in vain search for me.

Joky has not moved yet; so, kneeling down, I loosen his shirt collar and sprinkle some water from the breaker over his face. While I am doing this I hear Morgan shout something; then comes a great shriek of terror, and again that sickening "Glut! Glut!" Joky stirs uneasily, rubs his eyes, and sits up suddenly.

"Was that Morgan shouting—?" He breaks off with a cry. "Where are we? I have had such awful dreams!"

At this instant that is a sound of running footsteps on the deck and I hear Morgan's voice at the door.

"Tom, open—!"

He stops abruptly and gives an awful cry of despair. Then I hear him rush forward. Through the porthole, I see him spring into the fore rigging and scramble madly aloft. Something steals up after him. It shows white in the moonlight. It wraps itself around his right ankle. Morgan stops dead, plucks out his sheath-knife, and hacks fiercely at the fiendish thing. It lets go, and in a second he is over the top and running for dear life up the t'gallant rigging.

A time of quietness follows, and presently I see that the day is breaking. Not a sound can be heard save the heavy gasping breathing of the Thing. As the sun rises higher the creature stretches itself out along the deck and seems to enjoy the warmth. Still no sound, either from the men forward or the officers aft. I can only suppose that they are afraid of attracting its attention. Yet, a little later, I hear the report of a pistol away aft, and looking out I see the serpent raise its huge head as though listening. As it does so I get a good view of the fore part, and in the daylight see what the night has hidden.

There, right about the mouth, is a pair of little pig-eyes, that seem to twinkle with a diabolical intelligence. It is swaying its head slowly from side to side; then, without any warning, it turns quickly and looks right through the port. I dodge out of sight; but not soon enough. It has seen me, and it brings its great mouth up against the glass.

I hold my breath. My God! If it breaks the glass! I cower, horrified. From the direction of the port there comes a loud, harsh, scraping sound. I shiver. Then I remember that there are little iron doors to shut over the ports in bad weather. Without a moment's waste of time I rise to my feet and slam to the door over the port. Then I go round to the others and do the same. We are now in darkness, and I tell Joky in a whisper to light the lamp, which, after some fumbling, he does.

About an hour before midnight I fall asleep. I am awakened suddenly some hours later by a scream of agony and the rattle of a water-dipper. There

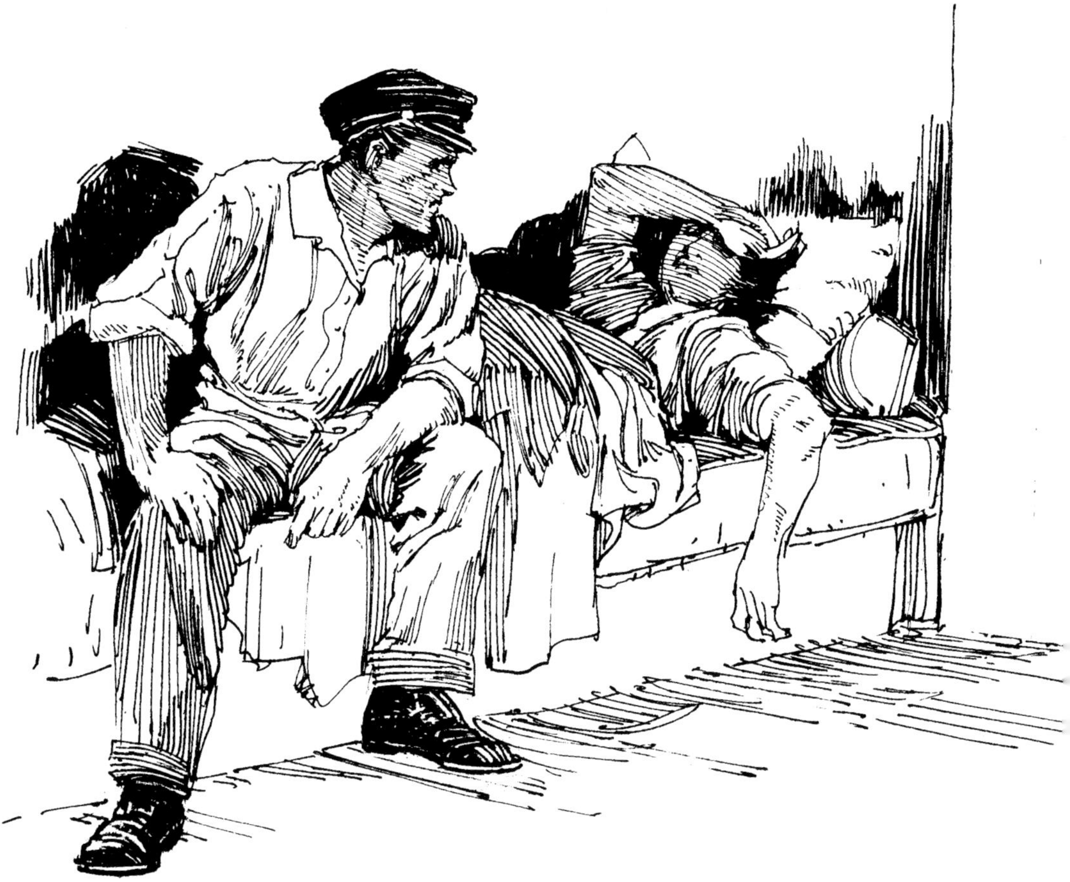

is a slight scuffling sound; then that soul-revolting "Glut!Glut!"

I guess what has happened. One of the men forrad has slipped out of the fo'cas'le to try and get a little water. Evidently he has trusted to the darkness to hide his movements. Poor beggar! He has paid for his attempt with his life!

After this I cannot sleep, though the rest of the night passes quietly enough. Towards morning I doze a bit, but wake every few minutes with a start. Joky is sleeping peacefully; indeed, he seems worn out with the terrible strain of the past twenty-four hours. About eight a.m. I call him, and we make a light breakfast off the dry ship's biscuit and water. Of the latter happily we have a good supply. Joky seems more himself, and starts to talk a little—possibly somewhat louder than what is safe; for, as he chatters on, wondering how it will end, there comes a tremendous blow against the side of the house, making it ring again. After this Joky is very silent. As we sit there I cannot but wonder what all the rest are doing, and how the poor beggars forrad are faring, cooped up without water, as the tragedy of the night has proved.

Towards noon, I hear a loud bang, followed by a terrific bellowing. Then comes a great smashing of woodwork, and the cries of men in pain. Vainly I ask myself what has happened. I begin to reason. By the sound of the report it was evidently something much heavier than a rifle or pistol, and judging from the mad roaring of the Thing, the shot must have done some execution. On thinking it over further, I become convinced that, by some means, those aft have got hold of the small signal cannon we carry, and though I know that some have been hurt, perhaps killed, yet a feeling of exhultation seizes me as I listen to the roars of the Thing, and realise that it is badly wounded, perhaps mortally. After a while, however, the bellowing dies away, and only an occasional roar, denoting more of anger than aught else, is heard.

Presently I become aware, by the ship's canting over to starboard, that the creature has gone over to that side, and a great hope springs up within me that possibly it has had enough of us and is going over the rail into the sea. For a time all is silent and my hope grows stronger. I lean across and nudge Joky, who is sleeping with his head on the table. He starts up sharply with a loud cry.

"Hush!" I whisper hoarsely. "I'm not certain, but I do believe it's gone."

Joky's face brightens wonderfully, and he questions me eagerly. We wait another hour or so, with hope ever rising. Our confidence is returning fast. Not a sound can we hear, not even the breathing of the Beast. I get out some biscuits, and Joky, after rummaging in the locker, produces a small piece of pork and a bottle of ship's vinegar. We fall to with a relish. After our long abstinence from food the meal acts on us like wine, and what must Joky do but insist on opening the door, to make sure the Thing has gone. This I will not allow, telling him that at least it will be safer to open the iron port-covers first and have a look out. Joky argues, but I am immovable. He becomes excited. I believe the youngster is light-headed. Then, as I turn to unscrew one of the

after-covers, Joky makes a dash at the door. Before he can undo the bolts I have him, and after a short struggle lead him back to the table. Even as I endeavour to quieten him there comes at the starboard door—the door that Joky has tried to open—a sharp, loud sniff, sniff, followed immediately by a thunderous grunting howl and a foul stench of putrid breath sweeps in under the door. A great trembling takes me, and were it not for the Carpenter's tool-chest I should fall. Joky turns very white and is violently sick, after which he is seized by a hopeless fit of sobbing.

Hour after hour passes, and, weary to death, I lie down on the chest upon which I have been sitting, and try to rest.

It must be about half-past two in the morning, after a somewhat longer doze, that I am awakened by a most tremendous uproar away forrad—men's voices shrieking, cursing, praying; but in spite of the terror expressed, so weak and feeble; while in the midst, and at times broken off short with that hellishly suggestive "Glut! Glut!" is the unearthly bellowing of the Thing. Fear incarnate seizes me, and I can only fall on my knees and pray. Too well I know what is happening.

Joky has slept through it all, and I am thankful.

Presently, under the door there steals a narrow ribbon of light, and I know that the day has broken on the second morning of our imprisonment. I let Joky sleep on. I will let him have peace while he may. Time passes, but I take little notice. The Thing is quiet, probably sleeping. About midday I eat a little biscuit and drink some of the water. Joky still sleeps. It is best so.

A sound breaks the stillness. The ship gives a slight heave, and I know that once more the Thing is awake. Round the deck it moves, causing the ship to roll perceptibly. Once it goes forrad—I fancy to again explore the fo'cas'le. Evidently it finds nothing, for it returns almost immediately. It pauses a moment at the house, then goes on further aft. Up aloft, somewhere in the fore-rigging, there rings out a peal of wild laughter, though sounding very faint and far away. The Horror stops suddenly. I listen intently, but hear nothing save a sharp creaking beyond the after end of the house, as though a strain had come upon the rigging.

A minute later I hear a cry aloft, followed almost instantly by a loud crash on deck that seems to shake the ship. I wait in anxious fear. What is happening? The minutes pass slowly. Then comes another frightened shout. It ceases suddenly. The suspense has become terrible, and I am no longer able to bear it. Very cautiously I open one of the after port-covers, and peep out to see a fearful sight. There, with its tail upon the deck and its vast body curled round the main-mast, is the monster, its head above the top-sail yard, and its great claw-armed tentacle waving in the air. It is the first proper sight that I have had of the Thing. Good Heavens! It must weigh a hundred tons!

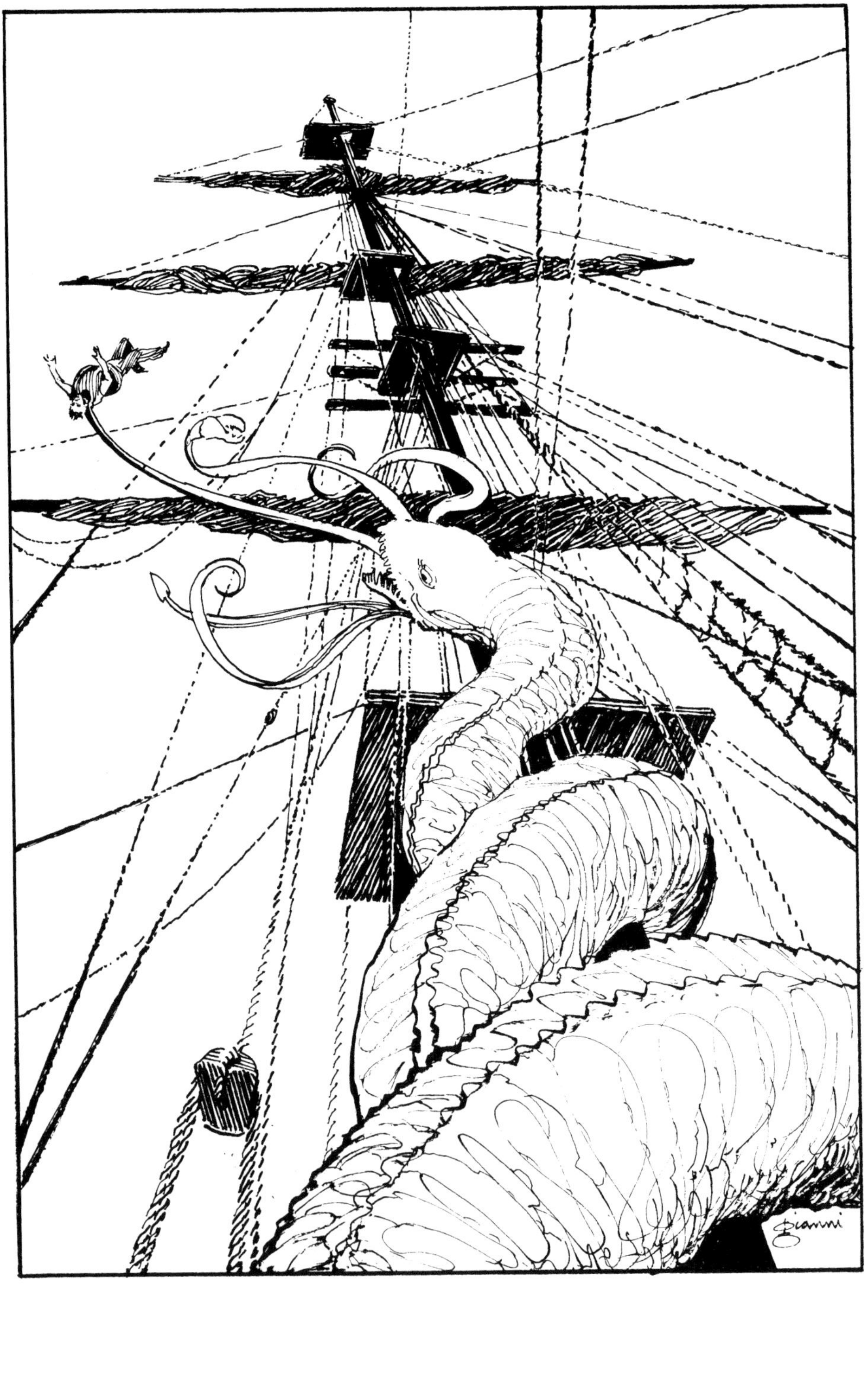

Knowing that I shall have time, I open the port itself then crane my head out and look up. There on the extreme end of the lower top-sail yard I see one of the able seamen. Even down here I note the staring horror of his face. At this moment he sees me and gives a weak, hoarse cry for help. I can do nothing for him. As I look the great tongue shoots out and licks him off the yard, much as might a dog a fly off the window-pane.

Higher still, but happily out of reach, are two more of the men. As far as I can judge they are lashed to the mast above the royal yard. The Thing attempts to reach them, but after a futile effort it ceases, and starts to slide down, coil on coil, to the deck. While doing this I notice a great gaping wound on its body some twenty feet above the tail.

I drop my gaze from aloft and look aft. The cabin door is torn from its hinges, and the bulkhead—which, unlike the half-deck, is of teak wood—is partly broken down. With a shudder I realise the cause of those cries after the cannon-shot. Turning I screw my head round and try to see the foremast, but cannot. The sun, I notice, is low, and the night is near. Then I draw in my head and fasten up both port and cover.

How will it end? Oh! how will it end?

After a while Joky wakes up. He is very restless, yet though he has eaten nothing during the day I cannot get him to touch anything.

Night draws on. We are too weary—too dispirited to talk. I lie down, but not to sleep . . . Time passes.

A ventilator rattles violently somewhere on the main-deck, and there sounds constantly that slurring, gritty noise. Later I hear a cat's agonised howl, and then again all is quiet. Some time after comes a great splash alongside. Then, for some hours all is silent as the grave. Occasionally I sit up on the chest and listen, yet never a whisper of noise comes to me. There is an absolute silence, even the monotonous creak of the gear has died away entirely, and at last a real hope is springing up within me. That splash, this silence—surely I am justified in hoping. I do not wake Joky this time. I will prove first for myself that all is safe. Still I wait. I will run no unnecessary risks. After a time I creep to the after-port and will listen; but there is no sound. I put up my hand and feel at the screw, then again I hesitate, yet not for long. Noiselessly I begin to unscrew the fastening of the heavy shield. It swings loose on its hinge, and I pull it back and peer out. Perhaps the moon has gone behind a cloud. Suddenly a beam of moonlight enters through the port, and goes as quickly. I stare out. Something moves. Again the light streams in, and now I seem to be looking into a great cavern, at the bottom of which quivers and curls something palely white.

My heart seems to stand still! It is the Horror! I start back and seize the iron port-flap to slam it to. As I do so, something strikes the glass like a steam

ram, shatters it to atoms, and flicks past me into the berth. I scream and spring away. The port is quite filled with it. The lamp shows it dimly. It is curling and twisting here and there. It is as thick as a tree and covered with a smooth slimy skin. At the end is a great claw, like a lobster's, only a thousand times larger. I cower down into the farthest corner . . . It has broken the tool-chest to pieces with one click of those frightful mandibles. Joky has crawled under a bunk. The Thing sweeps round in my direction. I feel a drop of sweat trickle slowly down my face—it tastes salty. Nearer comes that awful death . . . Crash! I roll over backwards. It has crushed the water breaker against which I leant, and I am rolling in the water across the floor. The claw drives up, then down, with a quick uncertain movement, striking the deck a dull, heavy blow, a foot from my head. Joky gives a little gasp of horror. Slowly the Thing rises and starts feeling its way round the berth. It plunges into a bunk and pulls out a bolster, nips it in half and drops it, then moves on. It is feeling along the deck. As it does so it comes across a half of the bolster. It seems to toy with it, then picks it up and takes it out through the port . . .

A wave of putrid air fills the berth. There is a grating sound, and something enters the port again—something white and tapering and set with teeth. Hither and thither it curls, rasping over the bunks, ceiling, and deck, with a noise like that of a great saw at work. Twice it flickers above my head, and I close my eyes. Then off it goes again. It sounds now on the opposite side of the berth and nearer to Joky. Suddenly the harsh, raspy noise becomes muffled, as though the teeth were passing across some soft substance. Joky gives a horrid little scream, that breaks off into a bubbling, whistling sound.

I open my eyes. The tip of the tongue is curled tightly round something that drips, then is quickly withdrawn, allowing the moonbeams to steal again into the berth. I rise to my feet. Looking round, I note a mechanical sort of way the wrecked state of the berth—the shattered chests, dismantled bunks, and something else—

"Joky!" I cry, and I tingle all over.

There is that awful Thing again at the port. I glance round for a weapon. I will revenge Joky. Ah! there, right under the lamp, where the wreck of the Carpenter's chest strews the floor, lies a small hatchet. I spring forward and seize it. It is small, but so keen—so keen! I feel its razor edge lovingly. Then I am back at the port. I stand to one side and raise my weapon. The great tongue is feeling its way to those fearsome remains. It reaches them. As it does so, with a scream of "Joky! Joky!" I strike savagely again and again and again, gasping as I strike; once more, and the monstrous mass falls to the deck, writhing like a hideous eel. A vast, warm flood rushes in through the porthole. There is a sound of breaking steel and an enormous bellowing. A singing comes in my ears and grows louder—louder. Then the berth grows indistinct and suddenly dark.

EXTRACT FROM THE LOG OF THE STEAMSHIP *HISPANOLA.*

June 24.–Lat–N. Long–W. 11 a.m.—Sighted four-masted barque about four points on the port bow, flying signal of distress. Ran down to her and sent a boat aboard. She proved to be the Glen Doon, homeward bound from Melbourne to London. Found things in a terrible state. Decks covered with blood and slime. Steel deckhouse stove in. Broke open door, and discovered youth of about nineteen in last stage of inanition, also part remains of boy about fourteen years of age. There was a great quantity of blood in the place, and a huge curled-up mass of whitish flesh, weighing about half a ton, one end of which appeared to have been hacked through with a sharp instrument. Found forecastle door open and hanging from one hinge. Doorway bulged, as though something had been forced through. Went inside. Terrible state of affairs, blood everywhere, broken chests, smashed bunks, but no men nor remains. Went aft again and found youth showing signs of recovery. When he came round, gave the name of Thompson. Said they had been attacked by a huge serpent–thought it must have been a sea serpent. He was too weak to say much, but told us there were some men up the main-mast. Sent a hand aloft, who reported them lashed to the royal mast, and quite dead. Went aft to the cabin. Here we found the bulkhead smashed to pieces, and the cabin-door lying on the deck near the after-hatch. Found body of Captain down lazarette, but no officers. Noticed amongst the wreckage part of the carriage of a small cannon. Came aboard again.

Have sent the Second Mate with six men to work her into port. Thompson is with us. He has written out his version of the affair. We certainly consider that the state of the ship, as we found her, bears out in every respect his story.

(Signed)

William Norton

William Norton (Master).

Tom Briggs

Tom Briggs (1st Mate).

PARIS, 1925.

THE HOSPITAL OF ST. MARY AND ST. JOSEPH.

...COMPLETELY SEVERED! WHAT KIND OF *MONSTER* COULD HAVE HACKED OFF HER *ARM* LIKE THIS?

WELL, WHOEVER IT IS IS KEEPING BUSY. THIS IS WHAT... THE THIRD ONE THIS MONTH?

TO WEAVE A LOVER
ARVID NELSON AND JUAN FERREYRA

IT'S THE *FOURTH.*

JOURNEYMAN PHYSICIAN JULIEN SAUNIÈRE.

JOURNEYMAN PHYSICIAN GENEVIEVE TOURNON.

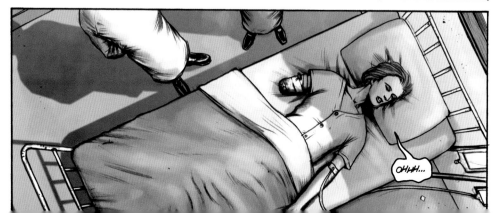

OHHH...

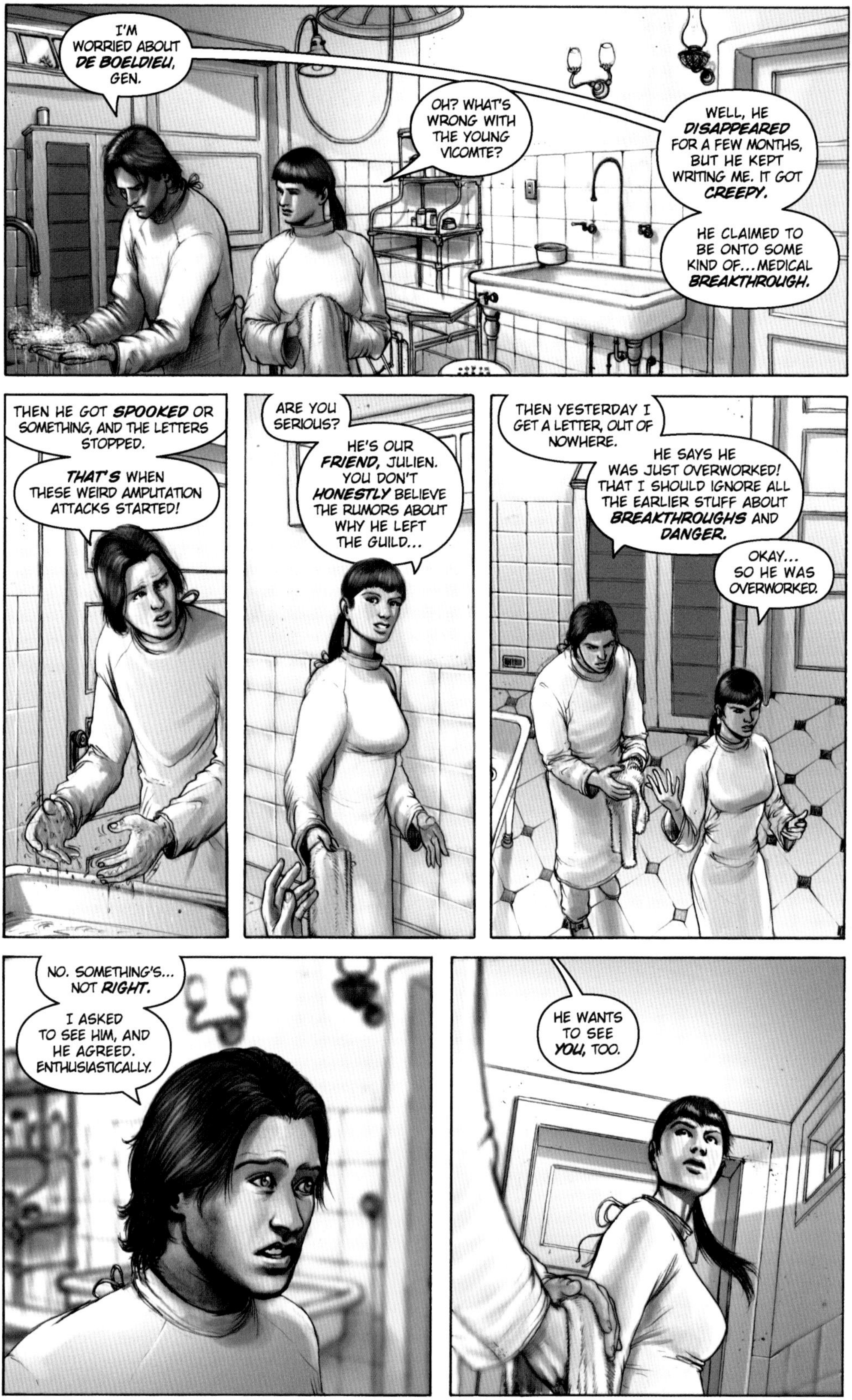
I'M WORRIED ABOUT DE BOELDIEU, GEN.
OH? WHAT'S WRONG WITH THE YOUNG VICOMTE?
WELL, HE DISAPPEARED FOR A FEW MONTHS, BUT HE KEPT WRITING ME. IT GOT CREEPY.
HE CLAIMED TO BE ONTO SOME KIND OF... MEDICAL BREAKTHROUGH.
THEN HE GOT SPOOKED OR SOMETHING, AND THE LETTERS STOPPED.
THAT'S WHEN THESE WEIRD AMPUTATION ATTACKS STARTED!
ARE YOU SERIOUS?
HE'S OUR FRIEND, JULIEN. YOU DON'T HONESTLY BELIEVE THE RUMORS ABOUT WHY HE LEFT THE GUILD...
THEN YESTERDAY I GET A LETTER, OUT OF NOWHERE.
HE SAYS HE WAS JUST OVERWORKED! THAT I SHOULD IGNORE ALL THE EARLIER STUFF ABOUT BREAKTHROUGHS AND DANGER.
OKAY... SO HE WAS OVERWORKED.
NO. SOMETHING'S... NOT RIGHT.
I ASKED TO SEE HIM, AND HE AGREED. ENTHUSIASTICALLY.
HE WANTS TO SEE YOU, TOO.

A NCESTRAL ESTATE OF HOUSE DE BOELDIEU, OUTSIDE PARIS.

GOOD TO SEE YOU, DE BOELDIEU.

YOU LOOK *DIFFERENT!* WHY THE LONG HAIR?

I NEVER PEGGED YOU FOR THE ROMANTIC TYPE!

HAH, YES! THOUGHT I MIGHT *TRY IT ON,* YOU KNOW.

SEE HOW IT LOOKS.

QUITE A COINCIDENCE, YOU WRITING! I'VE BEEN *WANTING* TO SEE YOUR FACES!

MAY I... OFFER YOU SOME COGNAC?

J EAN-PIERRE DE BOELDIEU, 16TH VICOMTE DE BOELDIEU.

PLOOP!

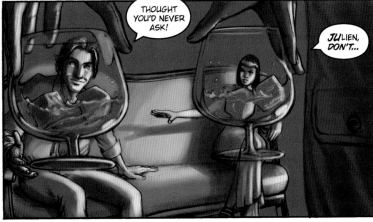

THOUGHT YOU'D NEVER ASK!

*JU*LIEN, *DON'T...*

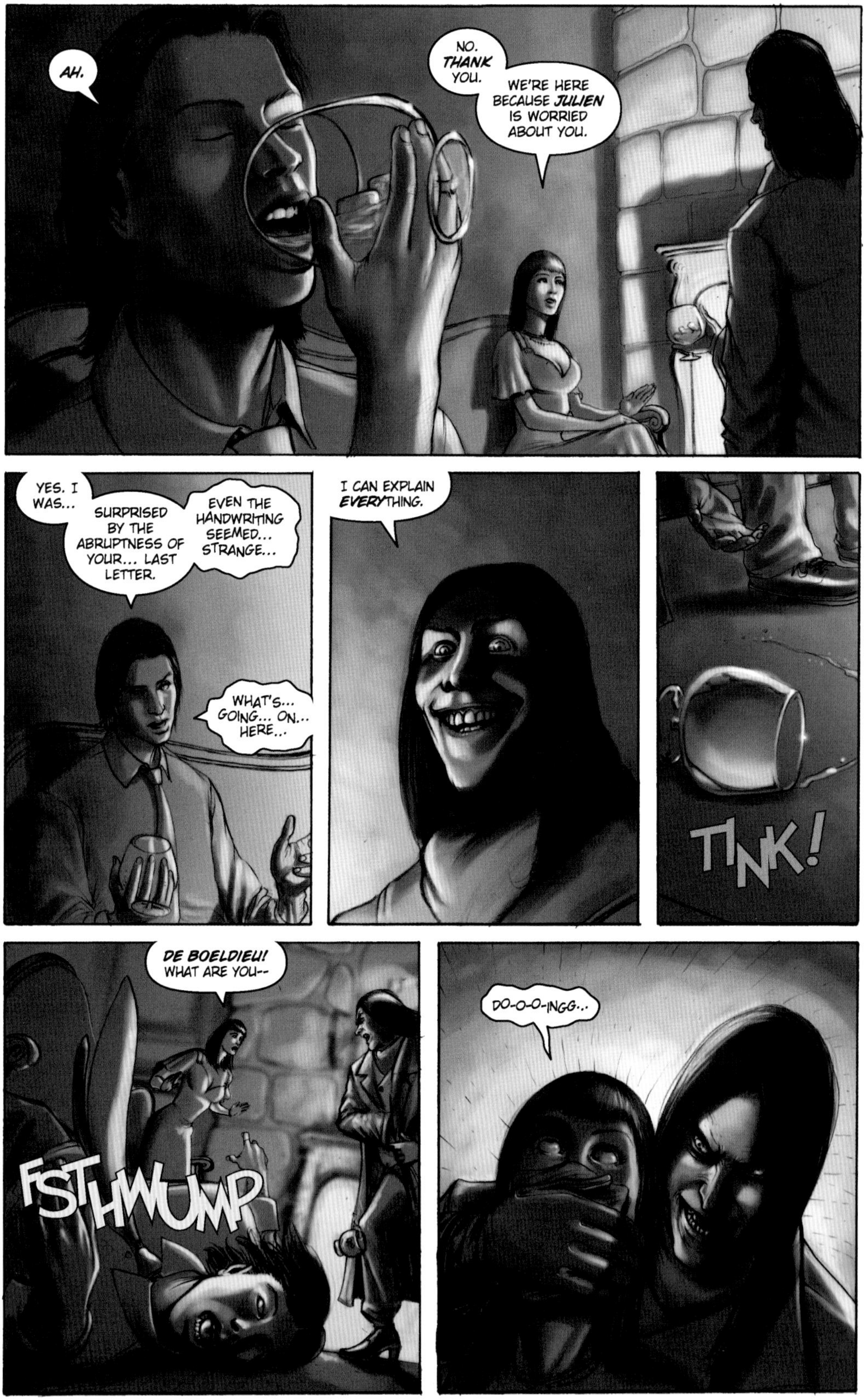
AH.
NO. THANK YOU.
WE'RE HERE BECAUSE JULIEN IS WORRIED ABOUT YOU.
YES. I WAS...
SURPRISED BY THE ABRUPTNESS OF YOUR... LAST LETTER.
EVEN THE HANDWRITING SEEMED... STRANGE...
WHAT'S... GOING... ON... HERE...
I CAN EXPLAIN EVERYTHING.
TINK!
DE BOELDIEU! WHAT ARE YOU--
FSTHWUMP
DO-O-O-INGG...

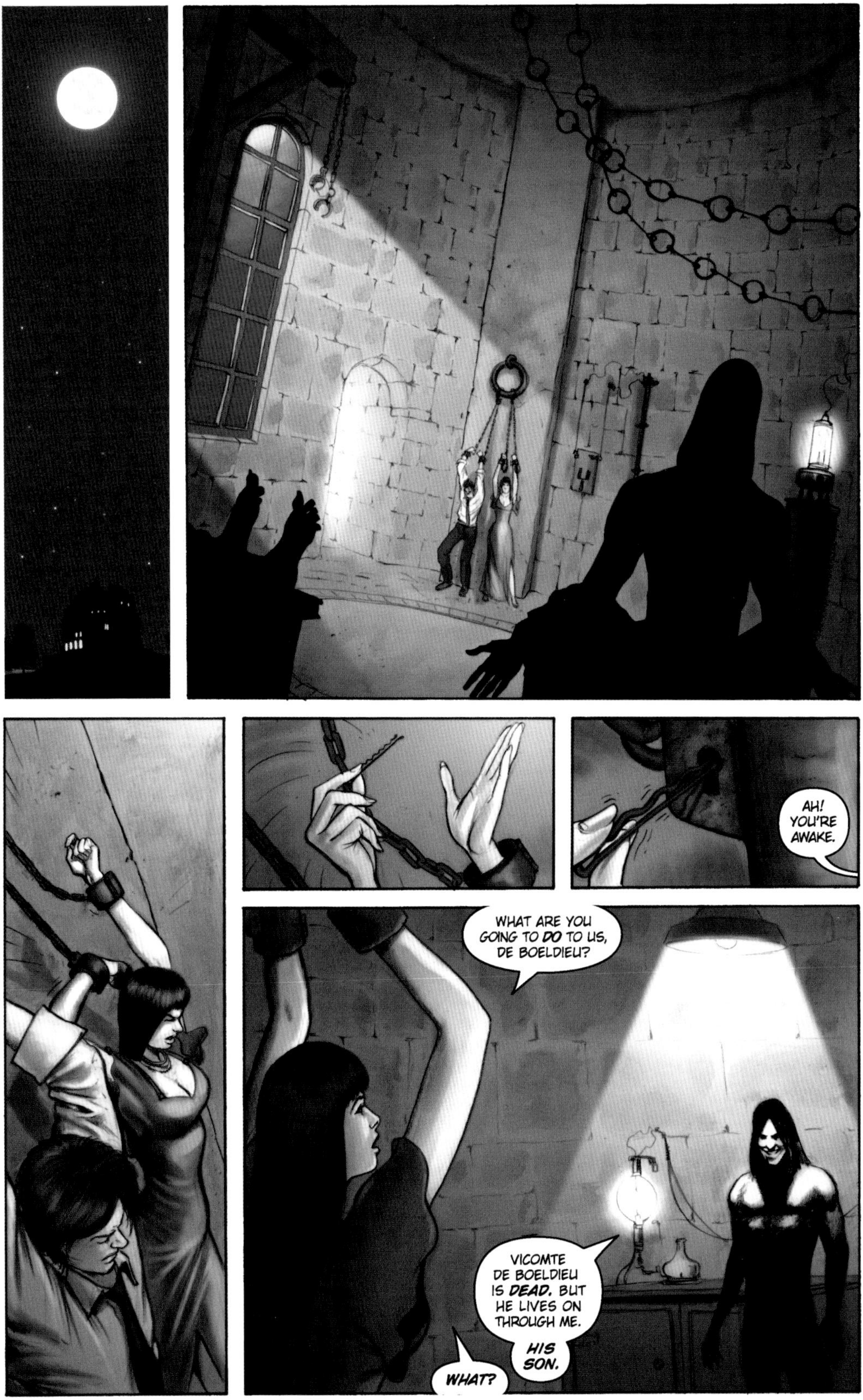
AH! YOU'RE AWAKE.
WHAT ARE YOU GOING TO DO TO US, DE BOELDIEU?
VICOMTE DE BOELDIEU IS DEAD. BUT HE LIVES ON THROUGH ME.
HIS SON.
WHAT?

VICOMTE DE BOELDIEU **CREATED** ME. STITCHED ME TOGETHER FROM THE REFUSE OF CHARNEL HOUSES.

HE UNCOVERED THE DEEPEST SECRETS OF **LIFE** AND **DEATH!**

AND THE **HIGH MASTERS** OF YOUR **PHYSICIANS'** GUILD THOUGHT HE WAS MAD.

OH NO, OH GOD...

IN SOME WAYS DE BOELDIEU **WAS** A GOD. HE TAUGHT ME EVERYTHING HE KNEW. ALL HIS **SECRETS.**

BUT I GET... **LONELY.**

GENEVIEVE? ISN'T THAT YOUR NAME? I SAW YOUR PICTURE AMONGST DE BOELDIEU'S EFFECTS.

HE... WOULDN'T LET ME HAVE YOU...

Y-YOUR FACE, YOU... YOU LOOK JUST **LIKE** HIM...

YES. I **KILLED** DE BOELDIEU. AND I **TOOK HIS FACE.**

I DON'T **FEEL** PAIN. I PERFORMED THE OPERATION MYSELF.

NOW **I** AM THE VICOMTE.

AND YOU. **YOU** WILL BE MY **BRIDE.**

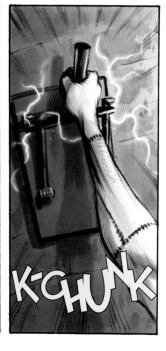

K-CHUNK

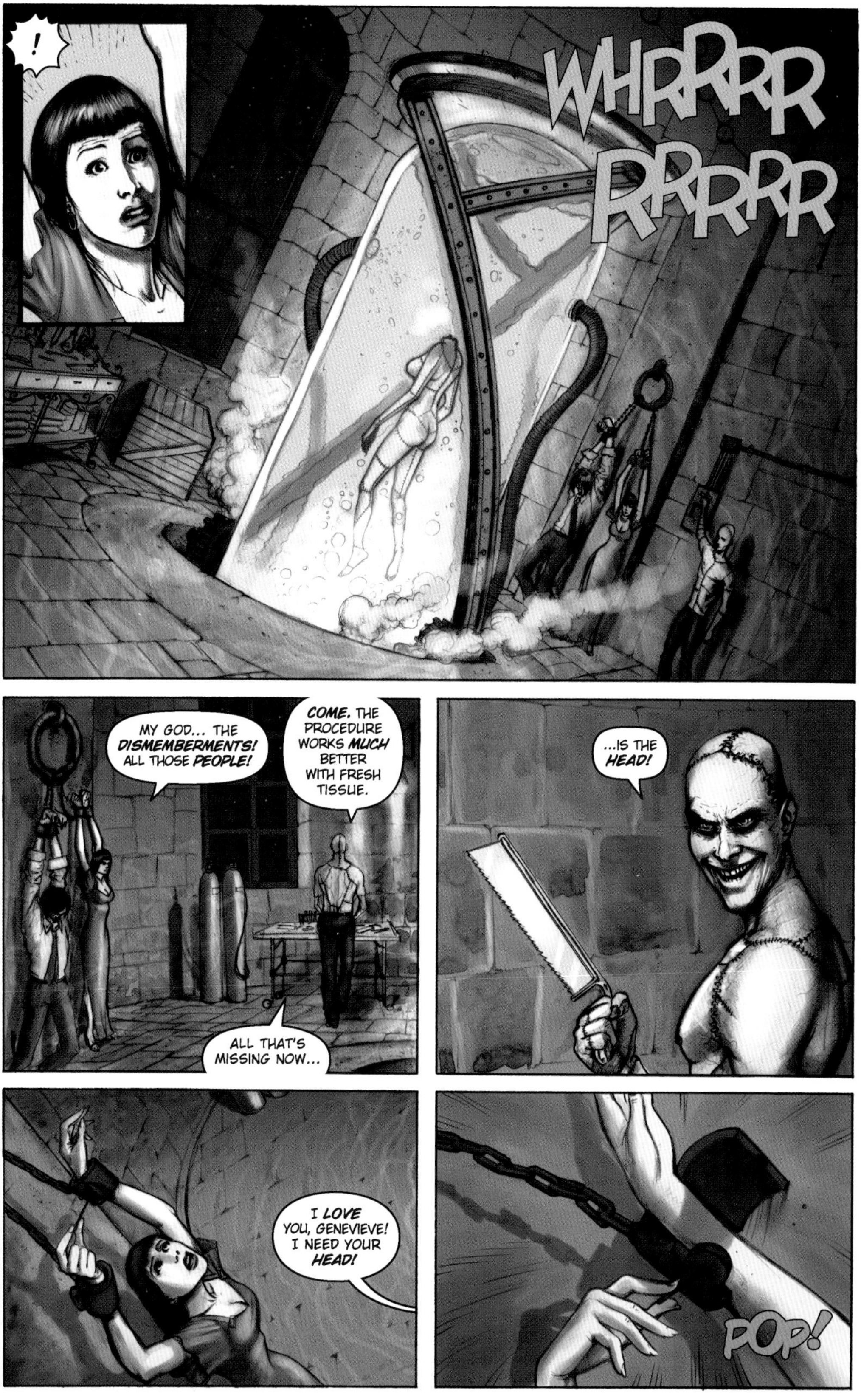
!
WHRRRR RRRRRR
MY GOD... THE DISMEMBERMENTS! ALL THOSE PEOPLE!
COME. THE PROCEDURE WORKS MUCH BETTER WITH FRESH TISSUE.
ALL THAT'S MISSING NOW...
...IS THE HEAD!
I LOVE YOU, GENEVIEVE! I NEED YOUR HEAD!
POP!

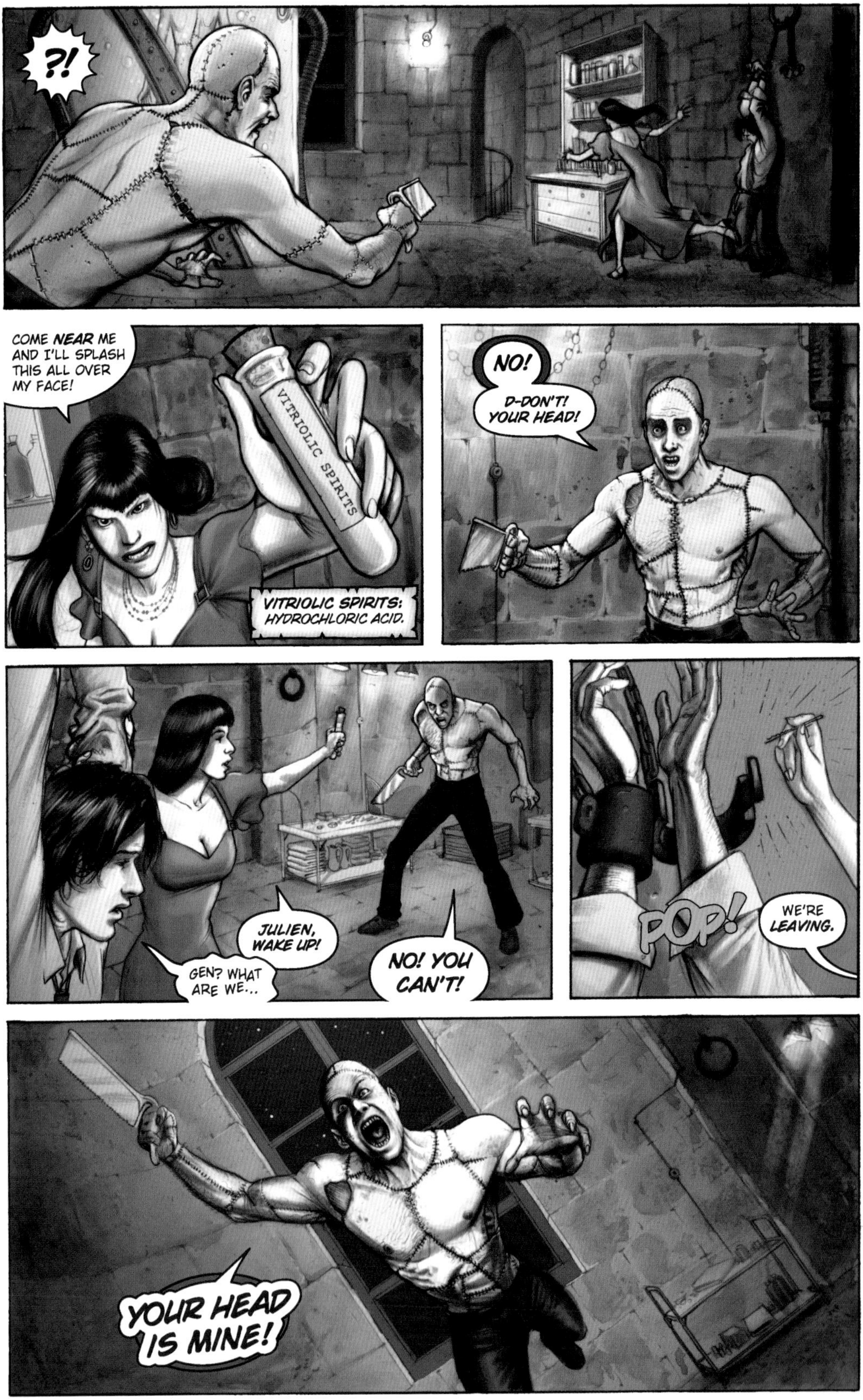
?!
COME NEAR ME AND I'LL SPLASH THIS ALL OVER MY FACE!
VITRIOLIC SPIRITS
VITRIOLIC SPIRITS: HYDROCHLORIC ACID.
NO!
D-DON'T! YOUR HEAD!
JULIEN, WAKE UP!
GEN? WHAT ARE WE...
NO! YOU CAN'T!
POP!
WE'RE LEAVING.
YOUR HEAD IS MINE!

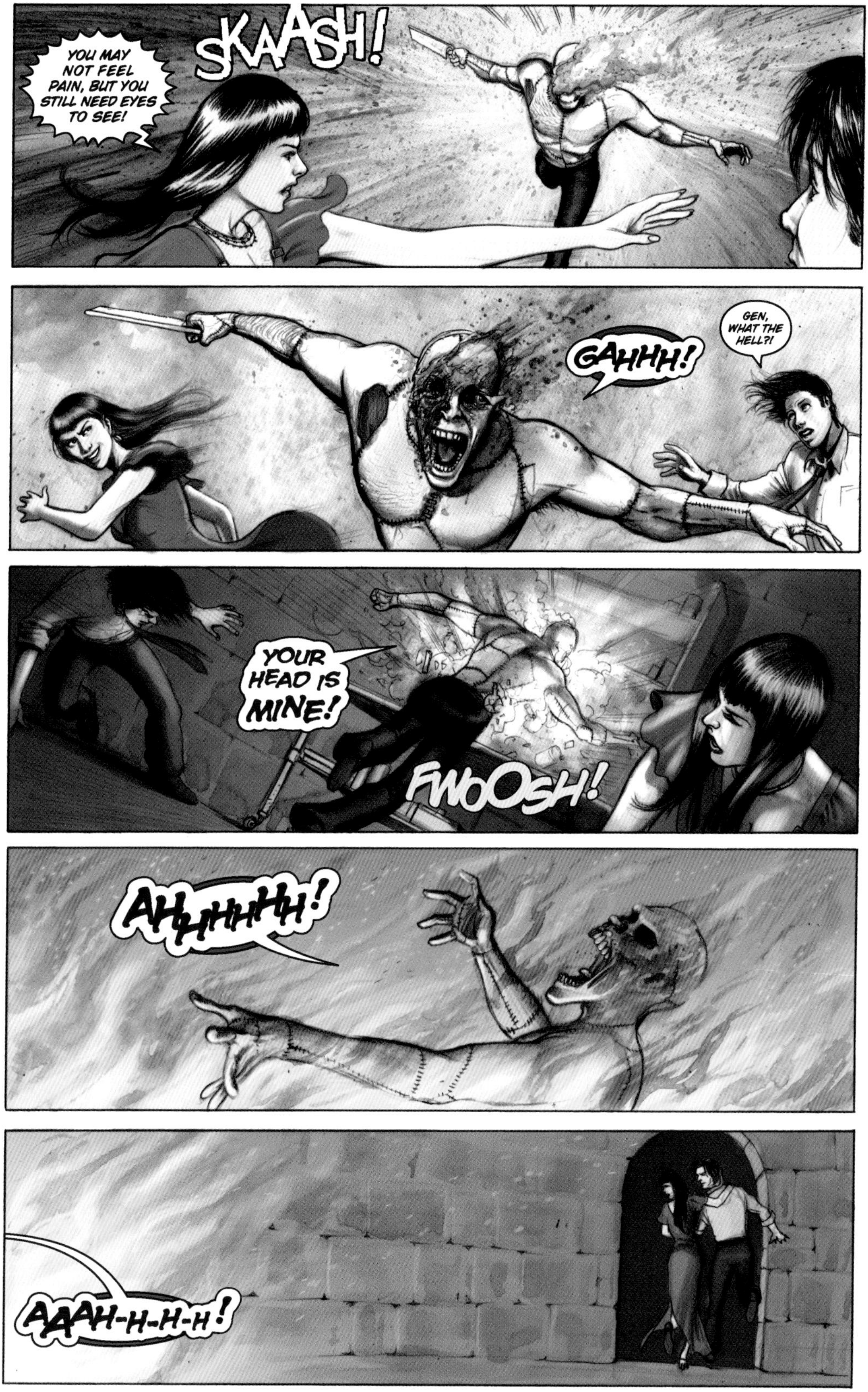
YOU MAY NOT FEEL PAIN, BUT YOU STILL NEED EYES TO SEE!
SKAASH!
GAHHH!
GEN, WHAT THE HELL?!
YOUR HEAD IS MINE!
FWOOSH!
AHHHHHH!
AAAH-H-H-H!

WHAT HAPPENED? THAT *THING*...

DE BOELDIEU IS *DEAD*, ISN'T HE?

YEAH. IT'S A *LONG* STORY, JULIEN.

I NEED A DRINK.

WHAT?

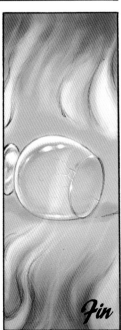

Fin

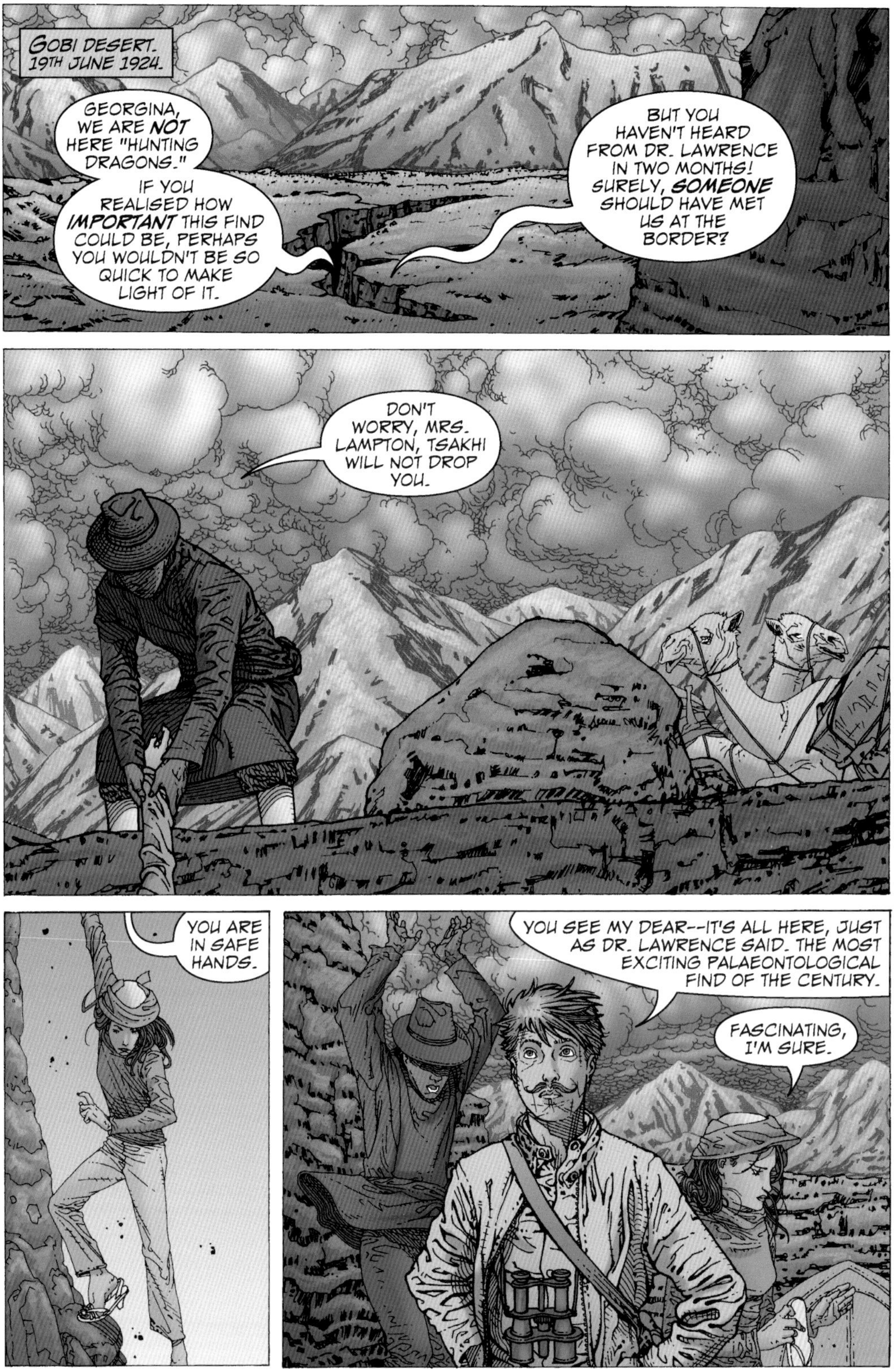
GOBI DESERT. 19TH JUNE 1924.
GEORGINA, WE ARE NOT HERE "HUNTING DRAGONS."
IF YOU REALISED HOW IMPORTANT THIS FIND COULD BE, PERHAPS YOU WOULDN'T BE SO QUICK TO MAKE LIGHT OF IT.
BUT YOU HAVEN'T HEARD FROM DR. LAWRENCE IN TWO MONTHS! SURELY, SOMEONE SHOULD HAVE MET US AT THE BORDER?
DON'T WORRY, MRS. LAMPTON, TSAKHI WILL NOT DROP YOU.
YOU ARE IN SAFE HANDS.
YOU SEE MY DEAR--IT'S ALL HERE, JUST AS DR. LAWRENCE SAID. THE MOST EXCITING PALAEONTOLOGICAL FIND OF THE CENTURY.
FASCINATING, I'M SURE.

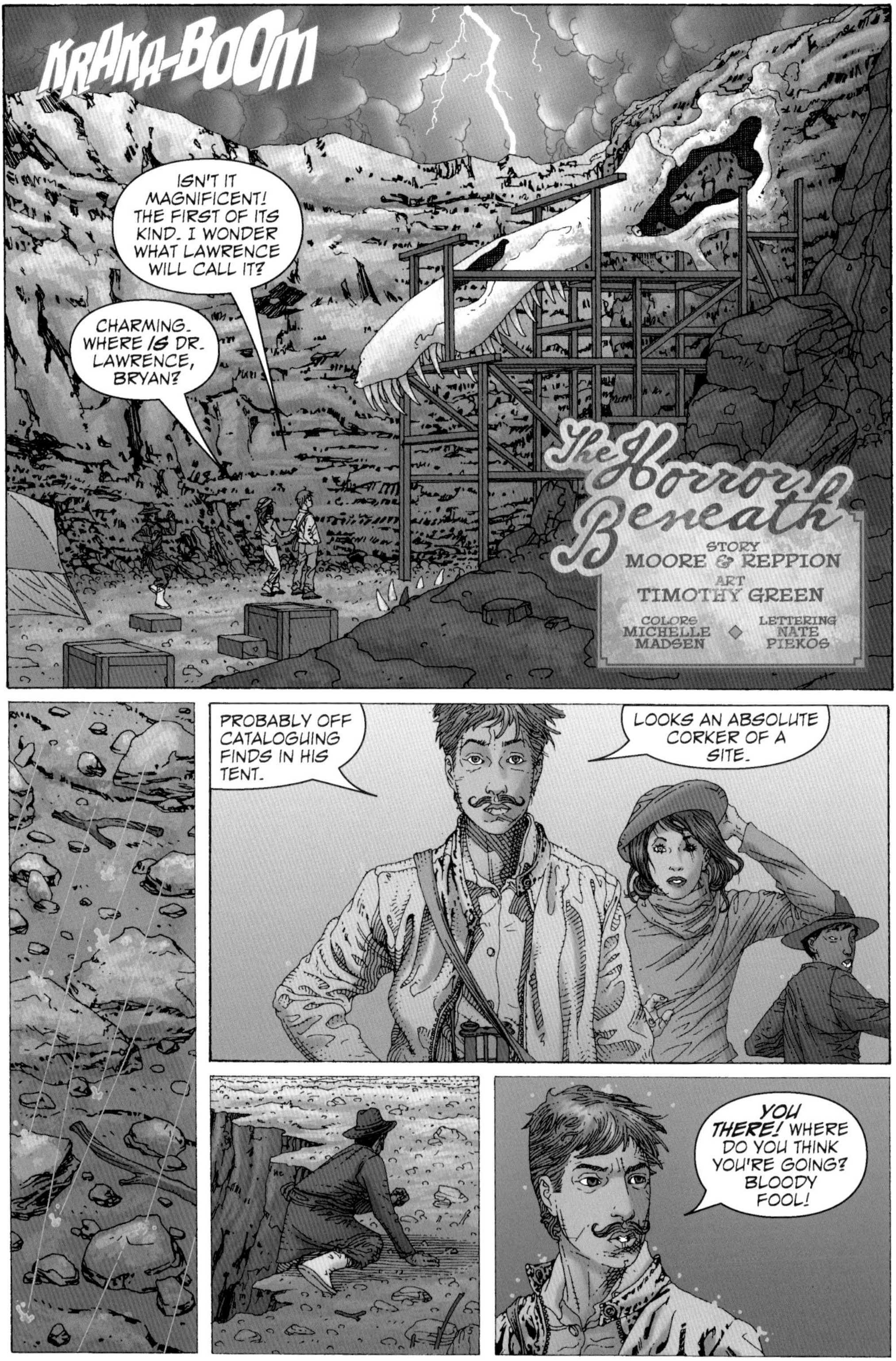
KRAKA-BOOM
ISN'T IT MAGNIFICENT! THE FIRST OF ITS KIND. I WONDER WHAT LAWRENCE WILL CALL IT?
CHARMING. WHERE IS DR. LAWRENCE, BRYAN?
The Horror Beneath
STORY MOORE & REPPION
ART TIMOTHY GREEN
COLORS MICHELLE MADSEN
LETTERING NATE PIEKOS
PROBABLY OFF CATALOGUING FINDS IN HIS TENT.
LOOKS AN ABSOLUTE CORKER OF A SITE.
YOU THERE! WHERE DO YOU THINK YOU'RE GOING? BLOODY FOOL!

HE DID NOTHING BUT GIBBER ABOUT MONSTERS THE WHOLE WAY HERE. CAN'T HE SEE IT'S ALREADY DEAD?

LOOKS LIKE SOMEONE LEFT IN A HURRY. MAYBE THE RESEARCH GRANT RAN OUT.

NOTHING MOVES A MAN OF SCIENCE QUICKER THAN FUNDING CUTS!

WHAT? HAVE THEY REALLY GONE? ARE WE ALONE HERE, BRYAN?

NOW IF I CAN JUST LAY MY HANDS ON A PARAFFIN LAMP...

COME ON, GEORGIE, WHERE'S YOUR PLUCK? THERE'S NOTHING TO WORRY ABOUT. *YOU'RE* NOT AFRAID OF FOSSILS NOW TOO, ARE YOU?

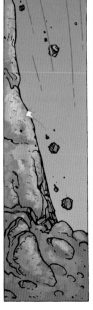

NO...NOT FOSSILS.

WELL STOP BEING SILLY THEN. LAWRENCE IS JUST WORKING IN THE CAVES FOR ALL WE KNOW. THEN YOU'LL FEEL A CHUMP!

OF COURSE, HE MIGHT HAVE HAD THE SENSE TO GO TO NIISLEL KHUREE FOR THE RAINY SEASON. OR ULAN BATOR, OR WHATEVER THEY CALL IT NEXT.

I RATHER WISH *WE* HAD.

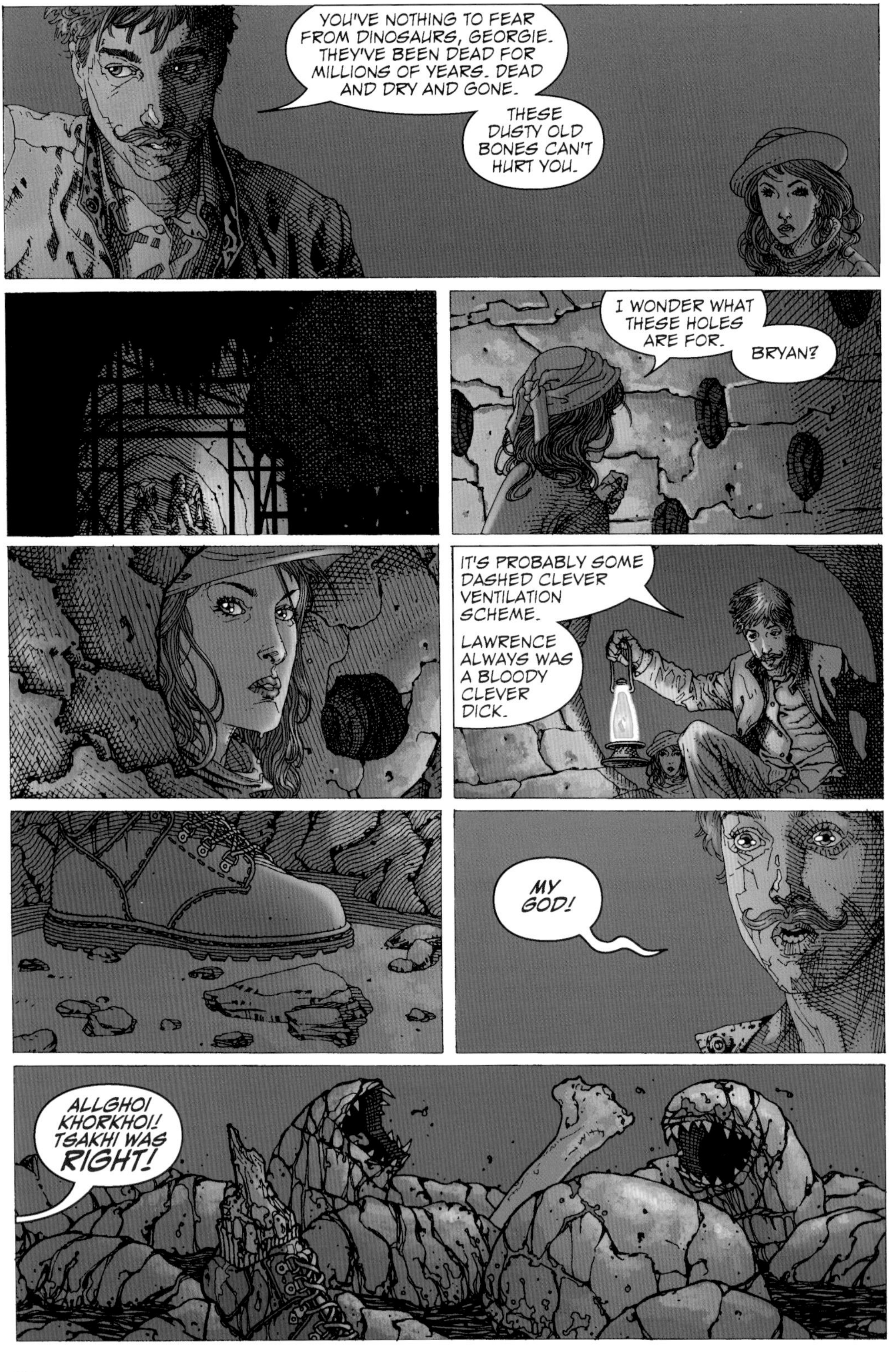
YOU'VE NOTHING TO FEAR FROM DINOSAURS, GEORGIE. THEY'VE BEEN DEAD FOR MILLIONS OF YEARS. DEAD AND DRY AND GONE.
THESE DUSTY OLD BONES CAN'T HURT YOU.
I WONDER WHAT THESE HOLES ARE FOR.
BRYAN?
IT'S PROBABLY SOME DASHED CLEVER VENTILATION SCHEME.
LAWRENCE ALWAYS WAS A BLOODY CLEVER DICK.
MY GOD!
ALLGHOI KHORKHOI! TSAKHI WAS RIGHT!

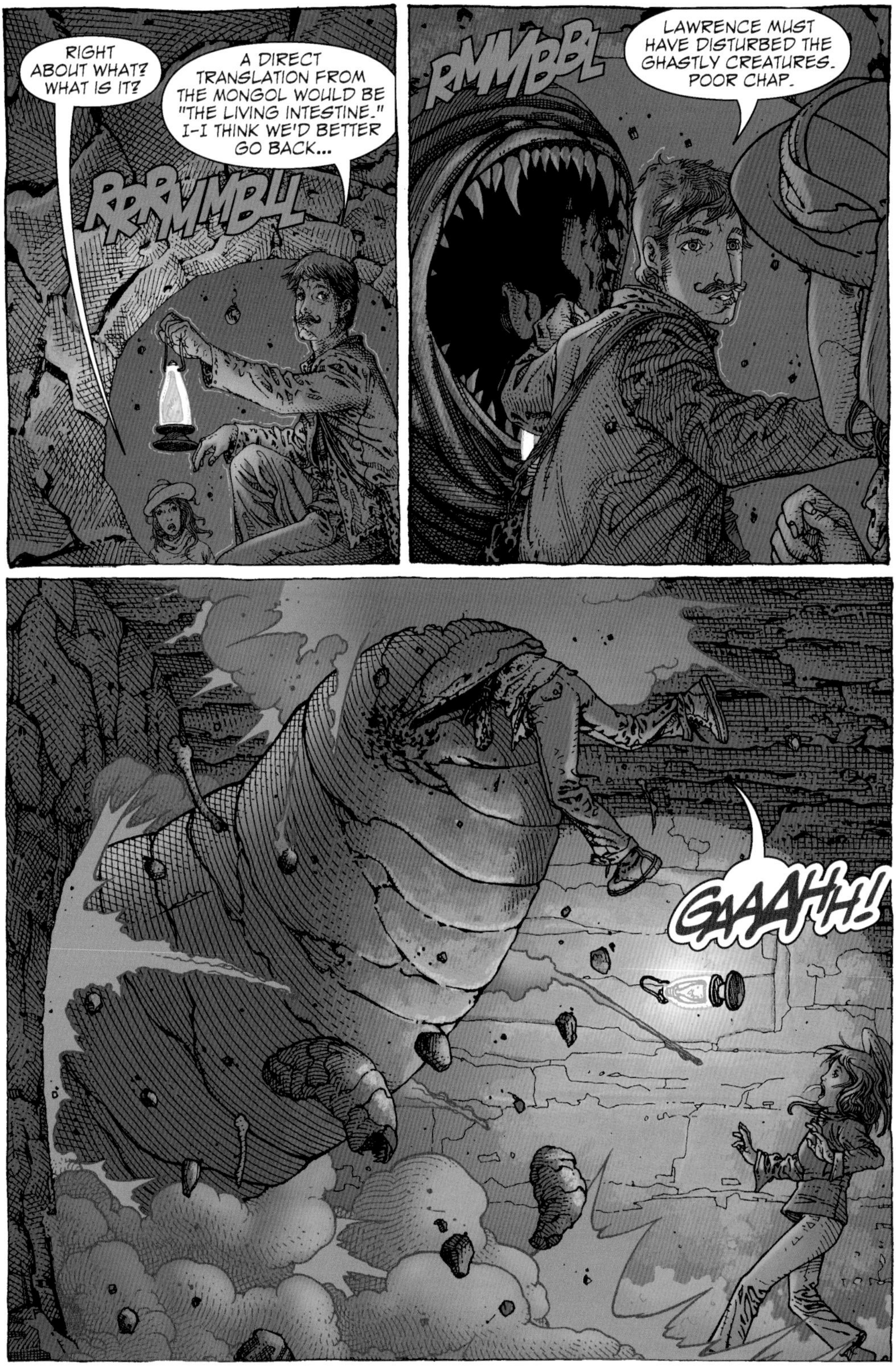
RIGHT ABOUT WHAT? WHAT IS IT?
A DIRECT TRANSLATION FROM THE MONGOL WOULD BE "THE LIVING INTESTINE." I-I THINK WE'D BETTER GO BACK...
RRRUMMBLL
RMMBBL
LAWRENCE MUST HAVE DISTURBED THE GHASTLY CREATURES. POOR CHAP.
GAAAHH!

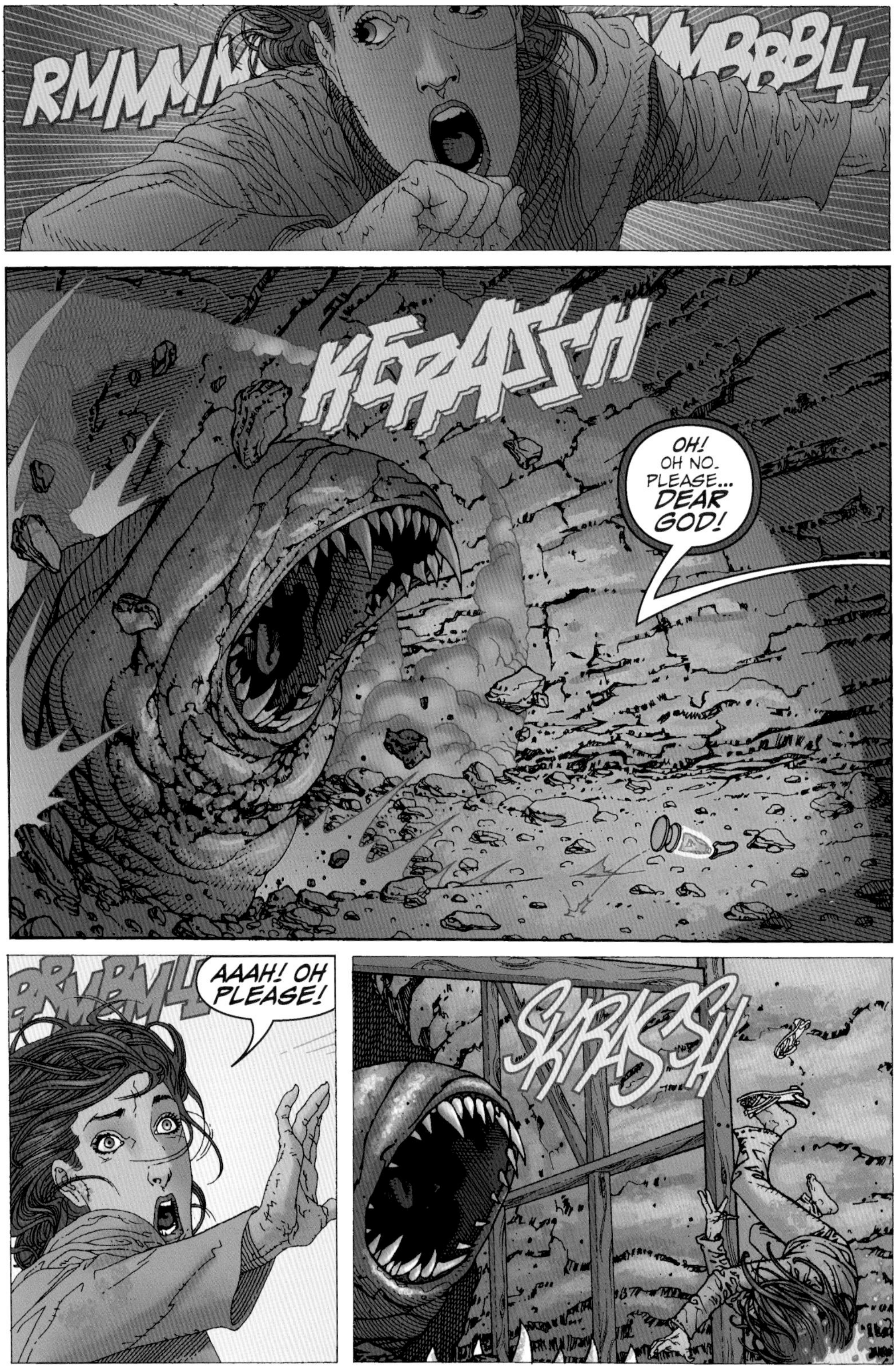
RMMMM
MMBBBLL
KERASH
OH! OH NO. PLEASE... DEAR GOD!
AAAH! OH PLEASE!
SKRASSH

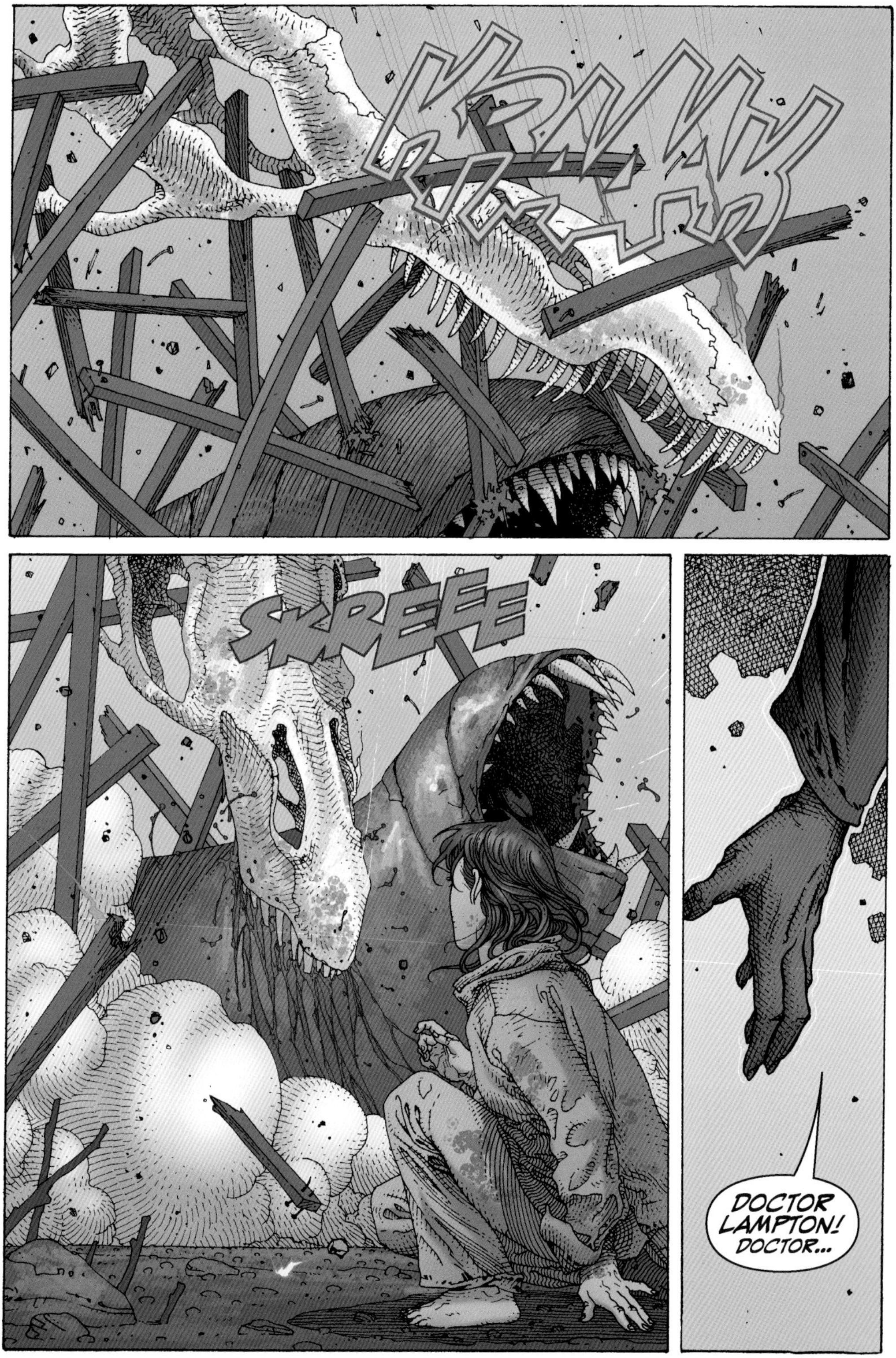
SKREEE
DOCTOR LAMPTON! DOCTOR...

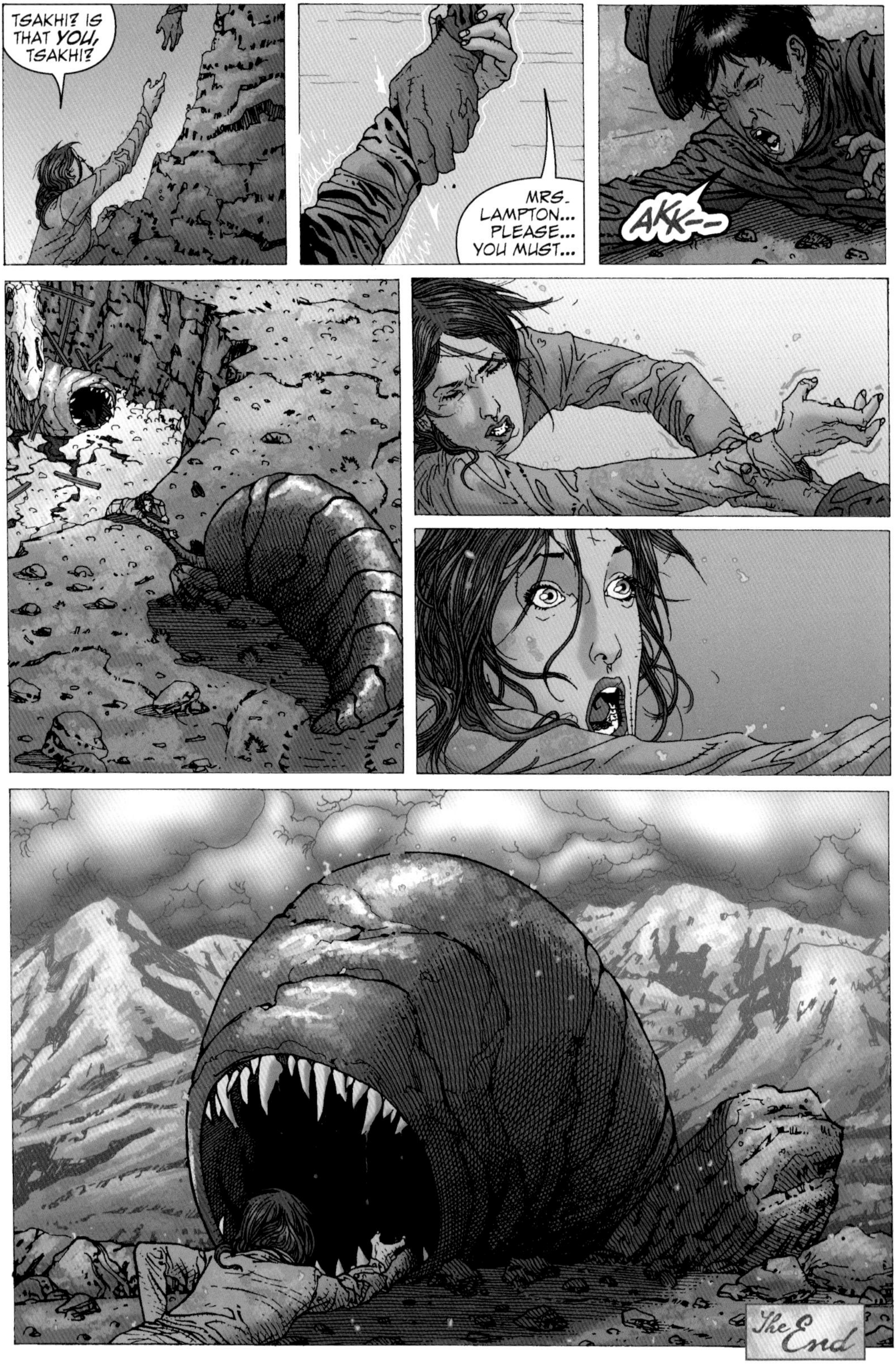
TSAKHI? IS THAT YOU, TSAKHI?
MRS. LAMPTON... PLEASE... YOU MUST...
AKK--
The End

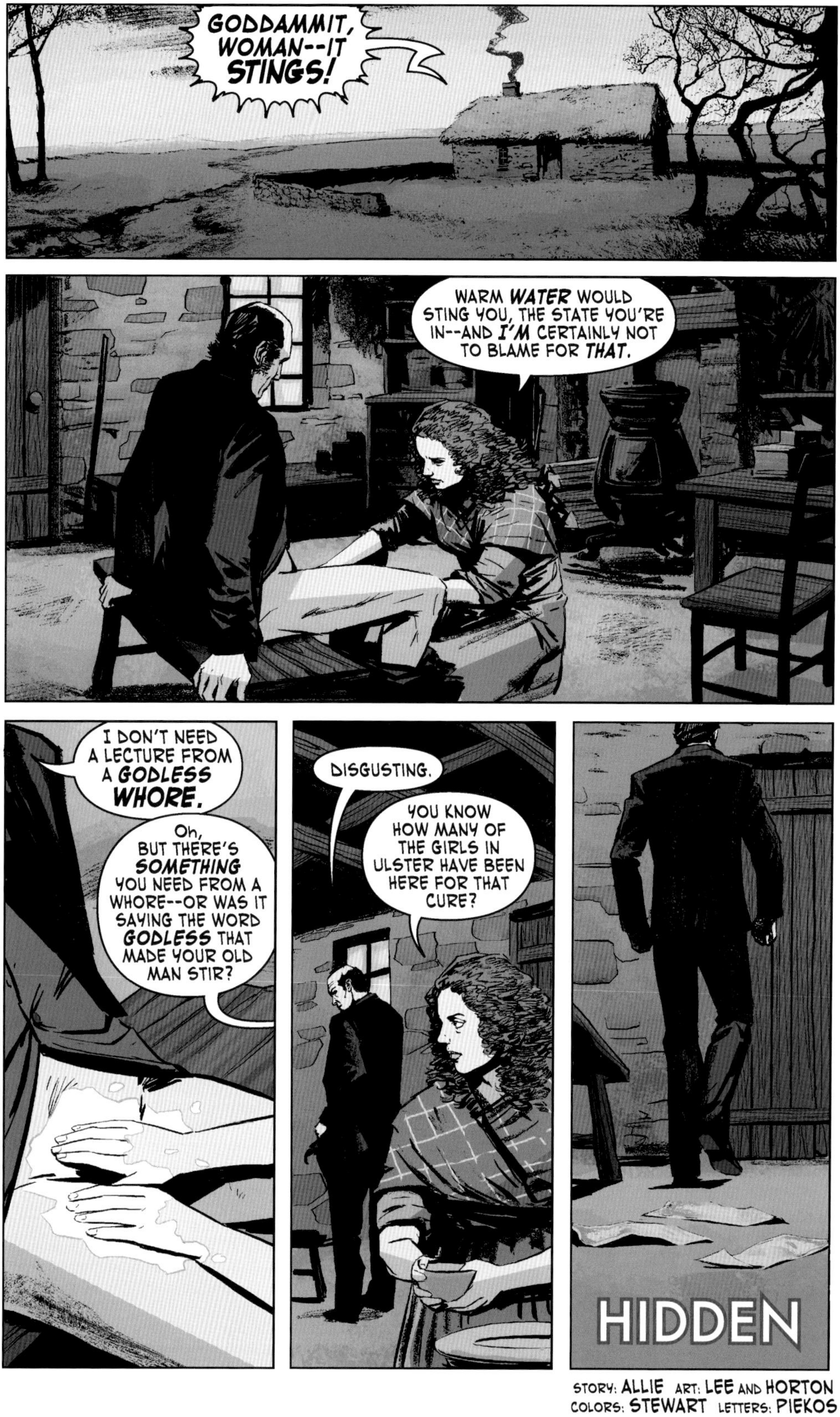
GODDAMMIT, WOMAN--IT STINGS!
WARM WATER WOULD STING YOU, THE STATE YOU'RE IN--AND I'M CERTAINLY NOT TO BLAME FOR THAT.
I DON'T NEED A LECTURE FROM A GODLESS WHORE.
Oh, BUT THERE'S SOMETHING YOU NEED FROM A WHORE--OR WAS IT SAYING THE WORD GODLESS THAT MADE YOUR OLD MAN STIR?
DISGUSTING.
YOU KNOW HOW MANY OF THE GIRLS IN ULSTER HAVE BEEN HERE FOR THAT CURE?
HIDDEN

STORY: ALLIE ART: LEE AND HORTON
COLORS: STEWART LETTERS: PIEKOS

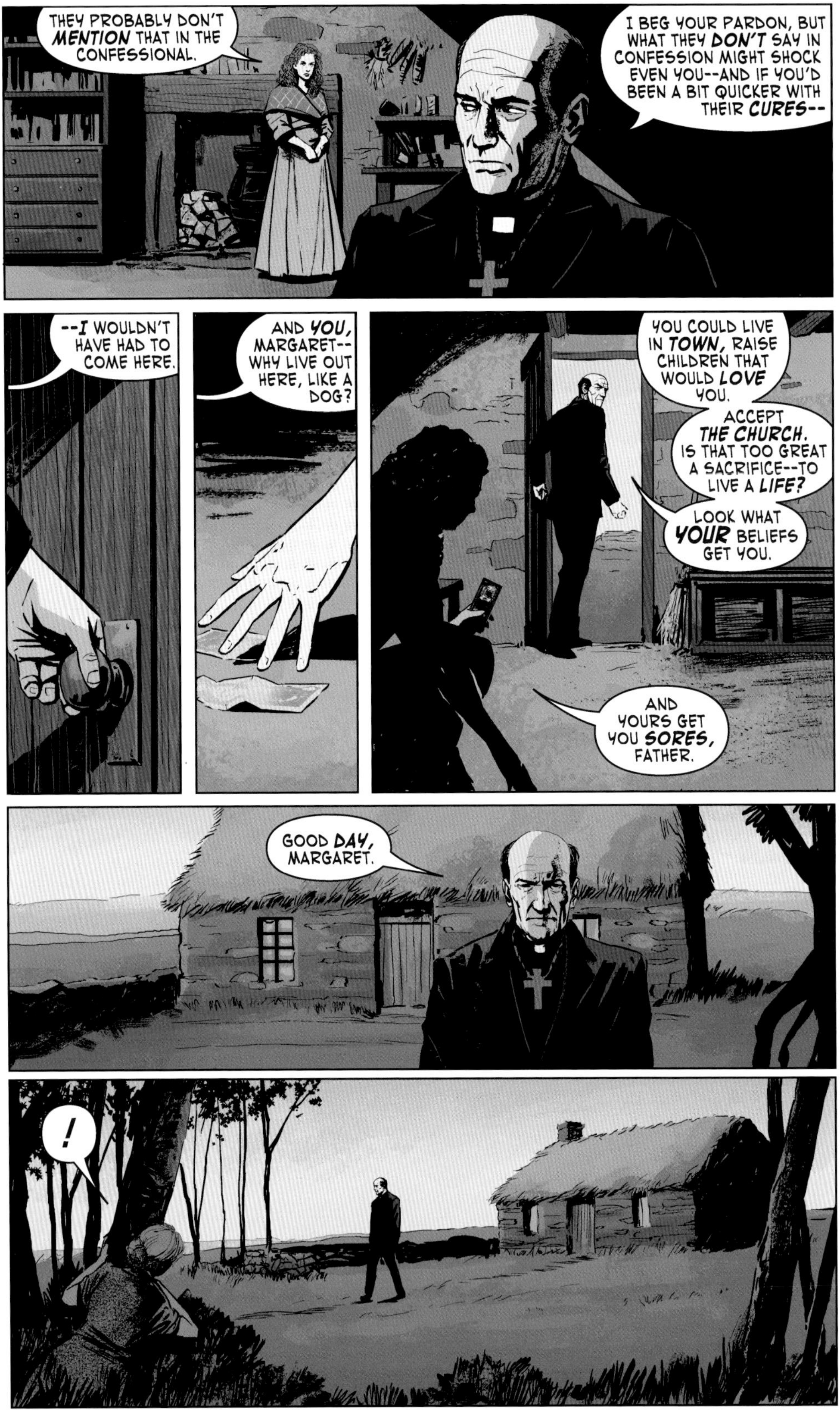
THEY PROBABLY DON'T MENTION THAT IN THE CONFESSIONAL.
I BEG YOUR PARDON, BUT WHAT THEY DON'T SAY IN CONFESSION MIGHT SHOCK EVEN YOU--AND IF YOU'D BEEN A BIT QUICKER WITH THEIR CURES--
--I WOULDN'T HAVE HAD TO COME HERE.
AND YOU, MARGARET--WHY LIVE OUT HERE, LIKE A DOG?
YOU COULD LIVE IN TOWN, RAISE CHILDREN THAT WOULD LOVE YOU.
ACCEPT THE CHURCH. IS THAT TOO GREAT A SACRIFICE--TO LIVE A LIFE?
LOOK WHAT YOUR BELIEFS GET YOU.
AND YOURS GET YOU SORES, FATHER.
GOOD DAY, MARGARET.
!

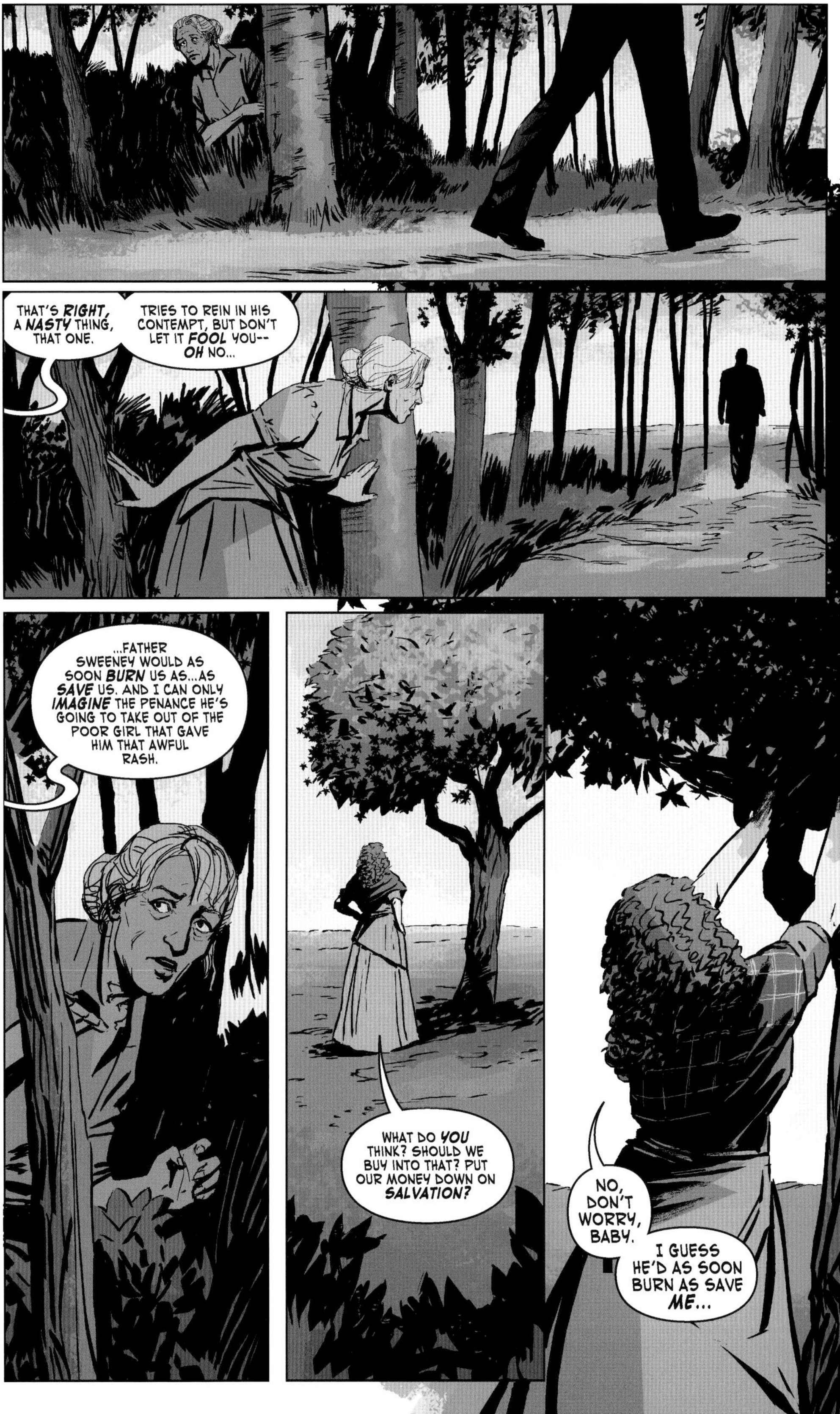
THAT'S RIGHT, A NASTY THING, THAT ONE.
TRIES TO REIN IN HIS CONTEMPT, BUT DON'T LET IT FOOL YOU-- OH NO...
...FATHER SWEENEY WOULD AS SOON BURN US AS...AS SAVE US. AND I CAN ONLY IMAGINE THE PENANCE HE'S GOING TO TAKE OUT OF THE POOR GIRL THAT GAVE HIM THAT AWFUL RASH.
WHAT DO YOU THINK? SHOULD WE BUY INTO THAT? PUT OUR MONEY DOWN ON SALVATION?
NO, DON'T WORRY, BABY.
I GUESS HE'D AS SOON BURN AS SAVE ME...

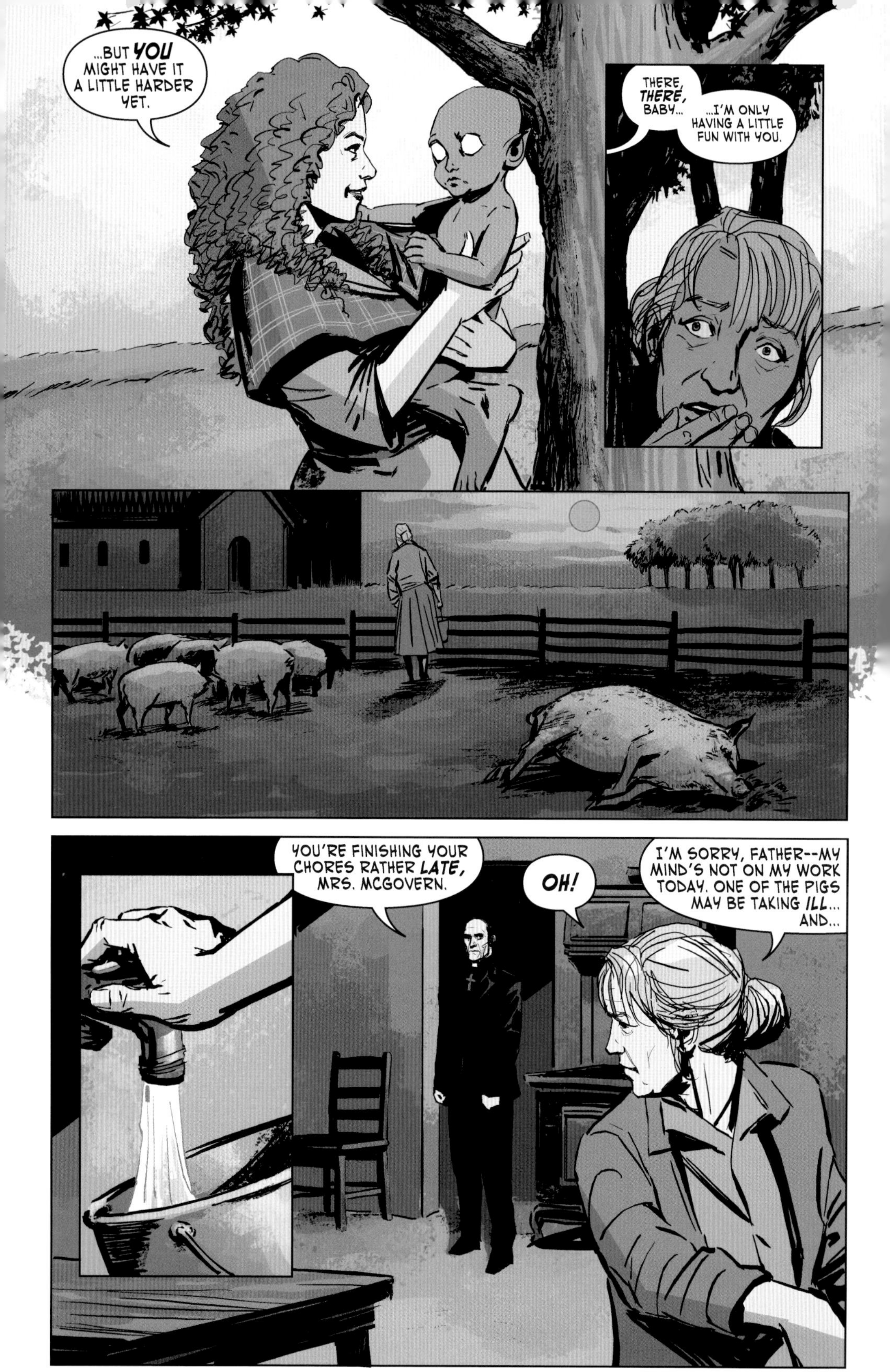
...BUT YOU MIGHT HAVE IT A LITTLE HARDER YET.
THERE, THERE, BABY...
...I'M ONLY HAVING A LITTLE FUN WITH YOU.
YOU'RE FINISHING YOUR CHORES RATHER LATE, MRS. MCGOVERN.
OH!
I'M SORRY, FATHER--MY MIND'S NOT ON MY WORK TODAY. ONE OF THE PIGS MAY BE TAKING ILL... AND...

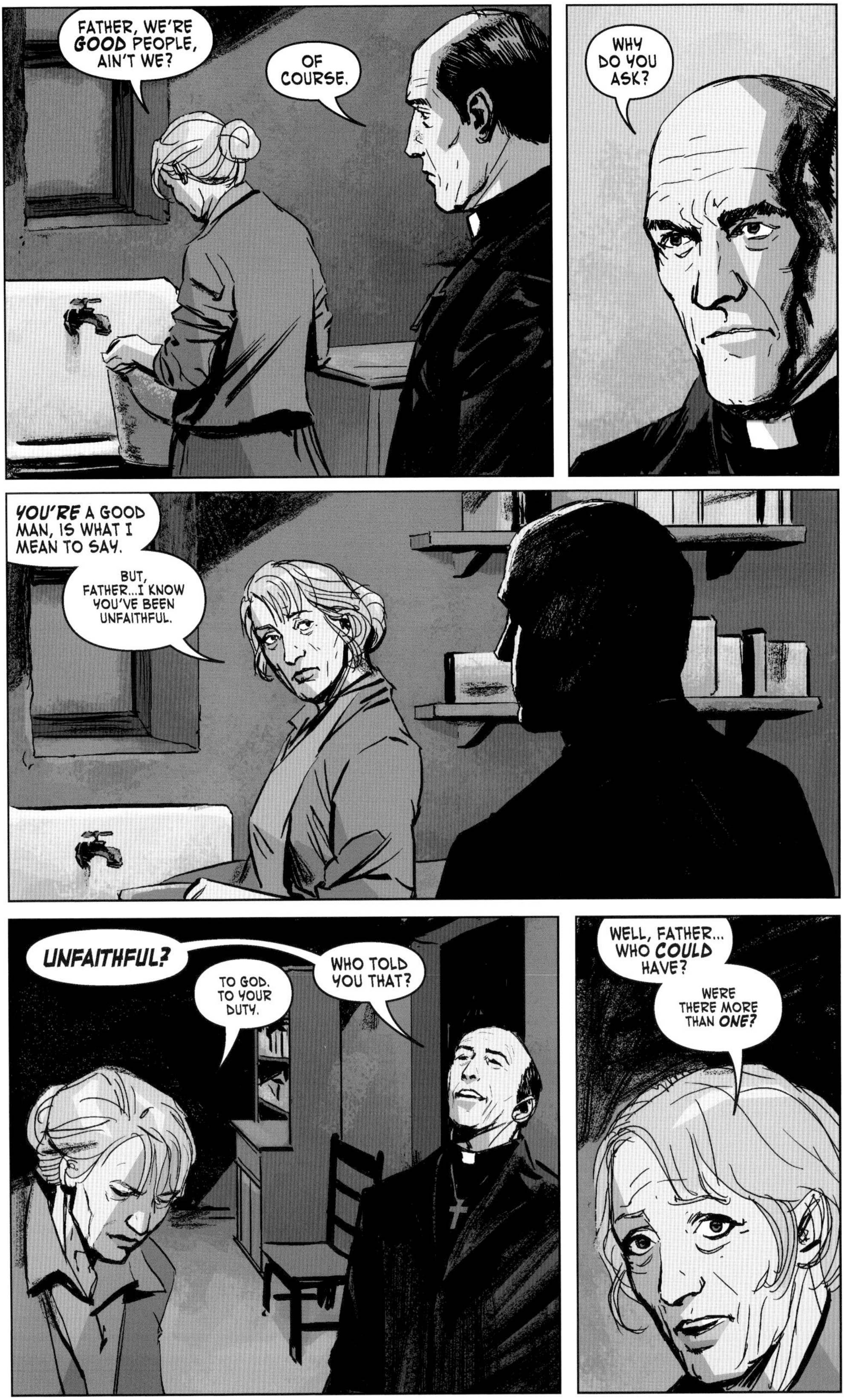
FATHER, WE'RE **GOOD** PEOPLE, AIN'T WE?
OF COURSE.
WHY DO YOU ASK?
YOU'RE A GOOD MAN, IS WHAT I MEAN TO SAY.
BUT, FATHER...I KNOW YOU'VE BEEN UNFAITHFUL.
UNFAITHFUL?
WHO TOLD YOU THAT?
TO GOD. TO YOUR DUTY.
WELL, FATHER... WHO **COULD** HAVE?
WERE THERE MORE THAN ***ONE?***

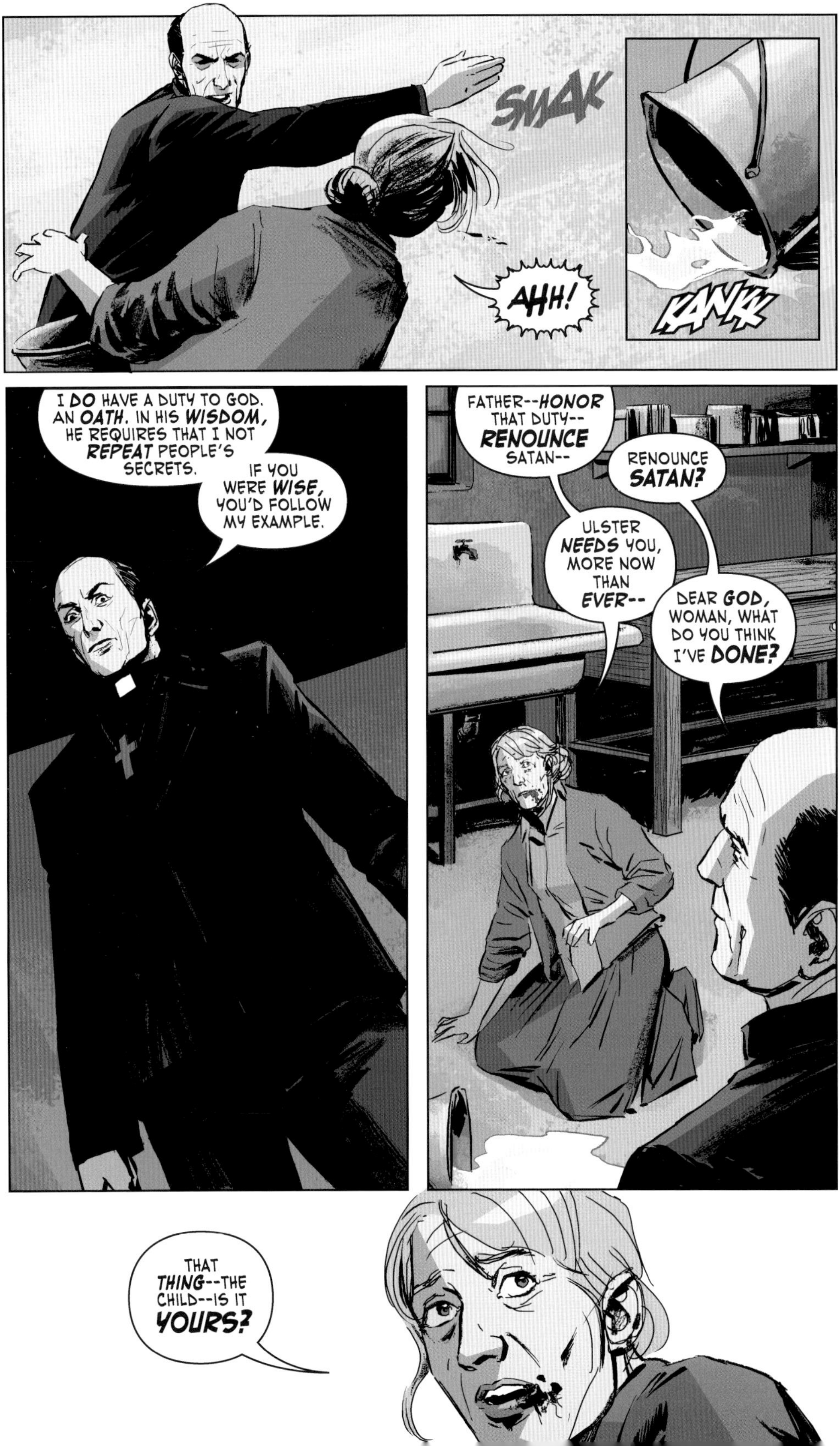
SMAK
AHH!
KANK
I DO HAVE A DUTY TO GOD. AN OATH. IN HIS WISDOM, HE REQUIRES THAT I NOT REPEAT PEOPLE'S SECRETS.
IF YOU WERE WISE, YOU'D FOLLOW MY EXAMPLE.
FATHER--HONOR THAT DUTY--RENOUNCE SATAN--
ULSTER NEEDS YOU, MORE NOW THAN EVER--
RENOUNCE SATAN?
DEAR GOD, WOMAN, WHAT DO YOU THINK I'VE DONE?
THAT THING--THE CHILD--IS IT YOURS?

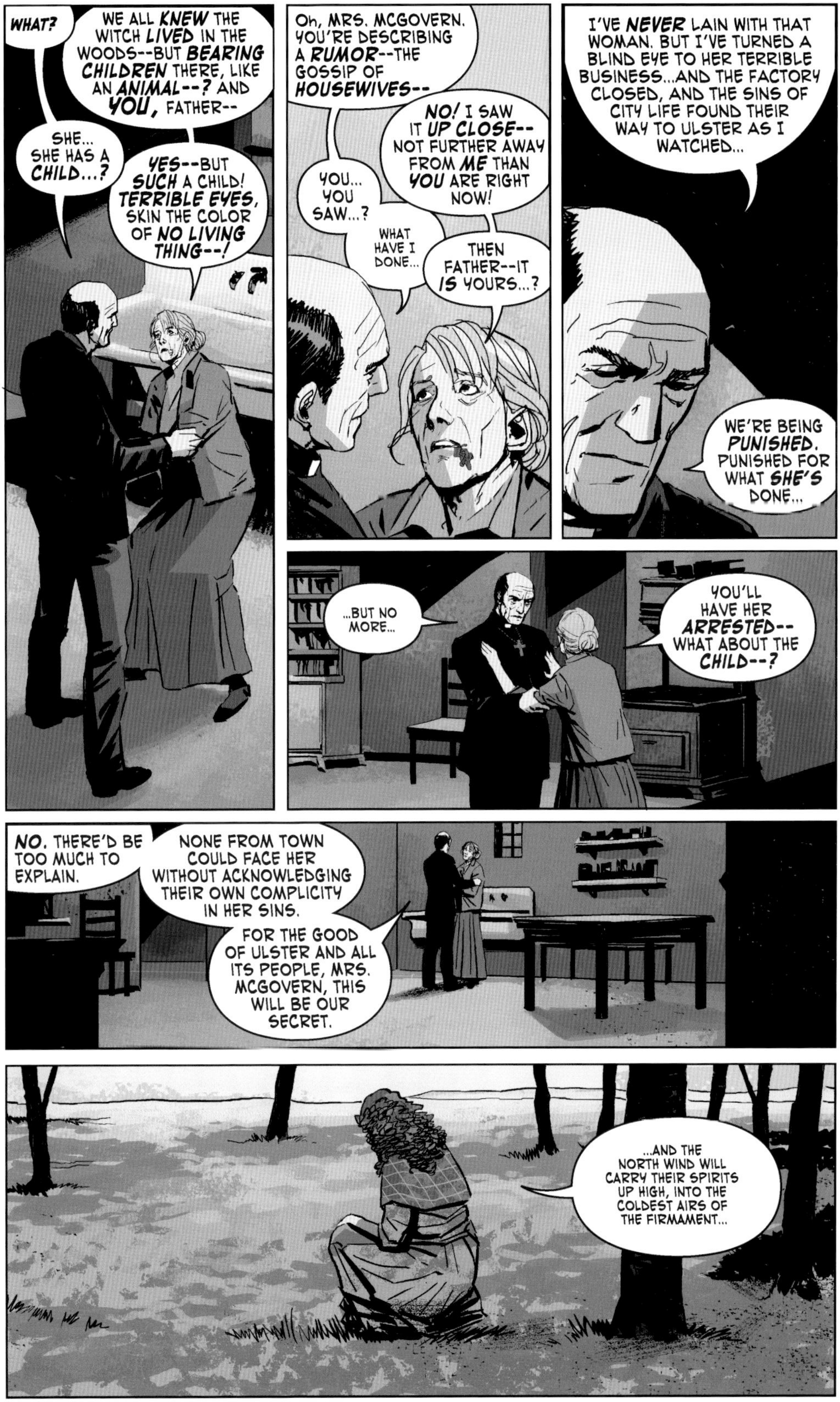
WHAT?
WE ALL KNEW THE WITCH LIVED IN THE WOODS--BUT BEARING CHILDREN THERE, LIKE AN ANIMAL--? AND YOU, FATHER--
SHE... SHE HAS A CHILD...?
YES--BUT SUCH A CHILD! TERRIBLE EYES, SKIN THE COLOR OF NO LIVING THING--!
Oh, MRS. MCGOVERN. YOU'RE DESCRIBING A RUMOR--THE GOSSIP OF HOUSEWIVES--
NO! I SAW IT UP CLOSE--NOT FURTHER AWAY FROM ME THAN YOU ARE RIGHT NOW!
YOU... YOU SAW...?
WHAT HAVE I DONE...
THEN FATHER--IT IS YOURS...?
I'VE NEVER LAIN WITH THAT WOMAN. BUT I'VE TURNED A BLIND EYE TO HER TERRIBLE BUSINESS...AND THE FACTORY CLOSED, AND THE SINS OF CITY LIFE FOUND THEIR WAY TO ULSTER AS I WATCHED...
WE'RE BEING PUNISHED. PUNISHED FOR WHAT SHE'S DONE...
...BUT NO MORE...
YOU'LL HAVE HER ARRESTED--WHAT ABOUT THE CHILD--?
NO. THERE'D BE TOO MUCH TO EXPLAIN.
NONE FROM TOWN COULD FACE HER WITHOUT ACKNOWLEDGING THEIR OWN COMPLICITY IN HER SINS.
FOR THE GOOD OF ULSTER AND ALL ITS PEOPLE, MRS. MCGOVERN, THIS WILL BE OUR SECRET.
...AND THE NORTH WIND WILL CARRY THEIR SPIRITS UP HIGH, INTO THE COLDEST AIRS OF THE FIRMAMENT...

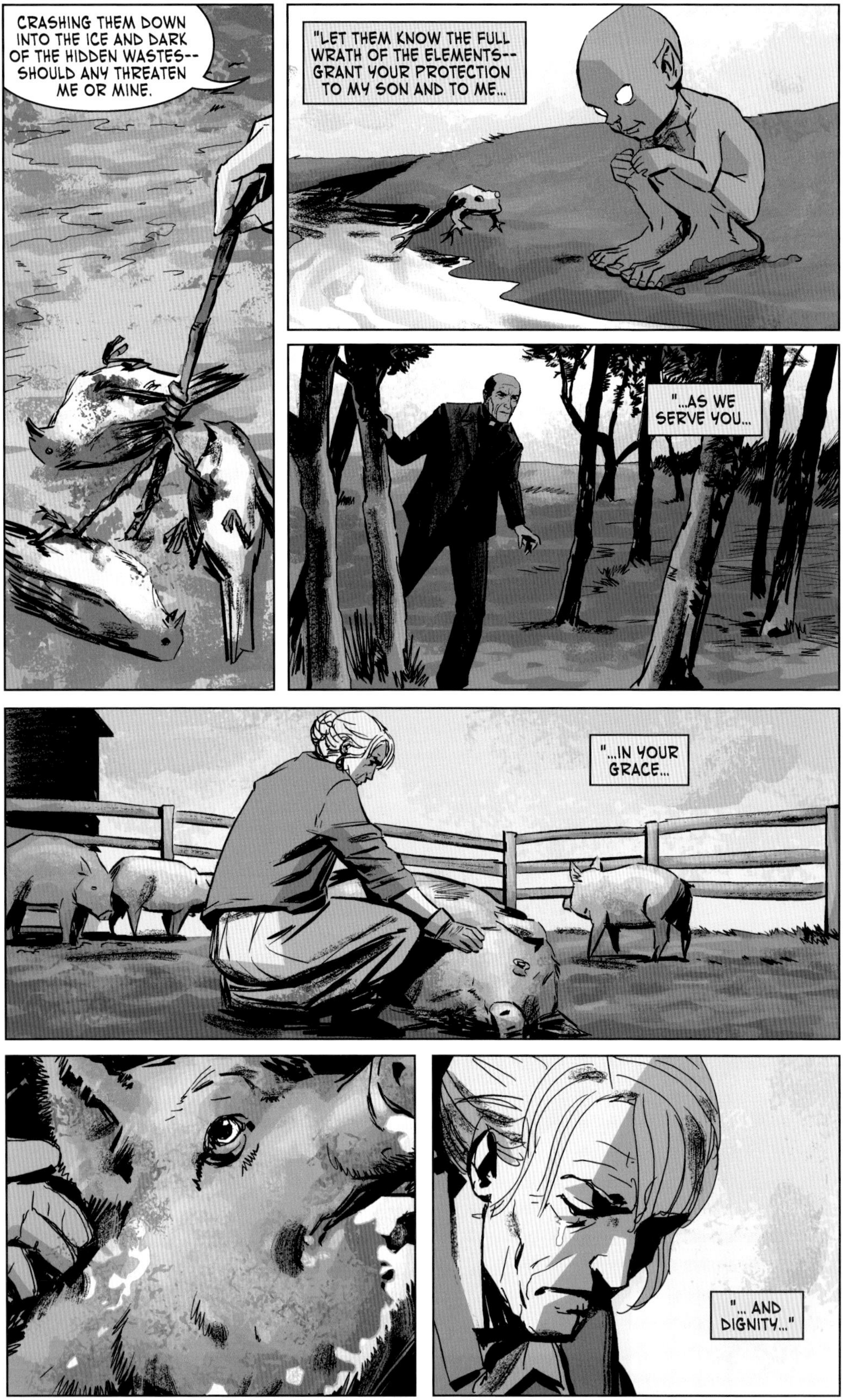
CRASHING THEM DOWN INTO THE ICE AND DARK OF THE HIDDEN WASTES-- SHOULD ANY THREATEN ME OR MINE.
"LET THEM KNOW THE FULL WRATH OF THE ELEMENTS-- GRANT YOUR PROTECTION TO MY SON AND TO ME...
"...AS WE SERVE YOU...
"...IN YOUR GRACE...
"... AND DIGNITY..."

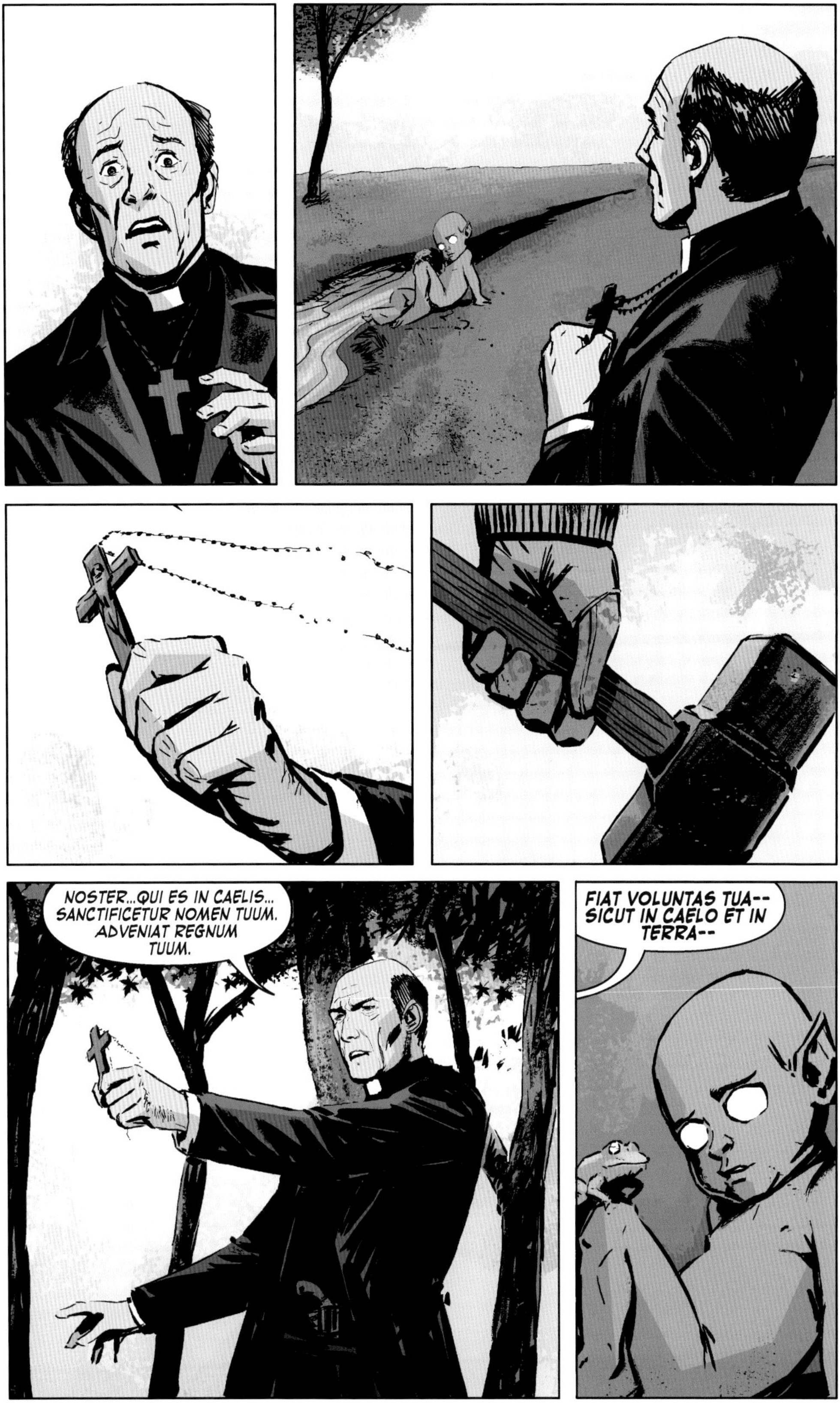
NOSTER...QUI ES IN CAELIS... SANCTIFICETUR NOMEN TUUM. ADVENIAT REGNUM TUUM.
FIAT VOLUNTAS TUA-- SICUT IN CAELO ET IN TERRA--

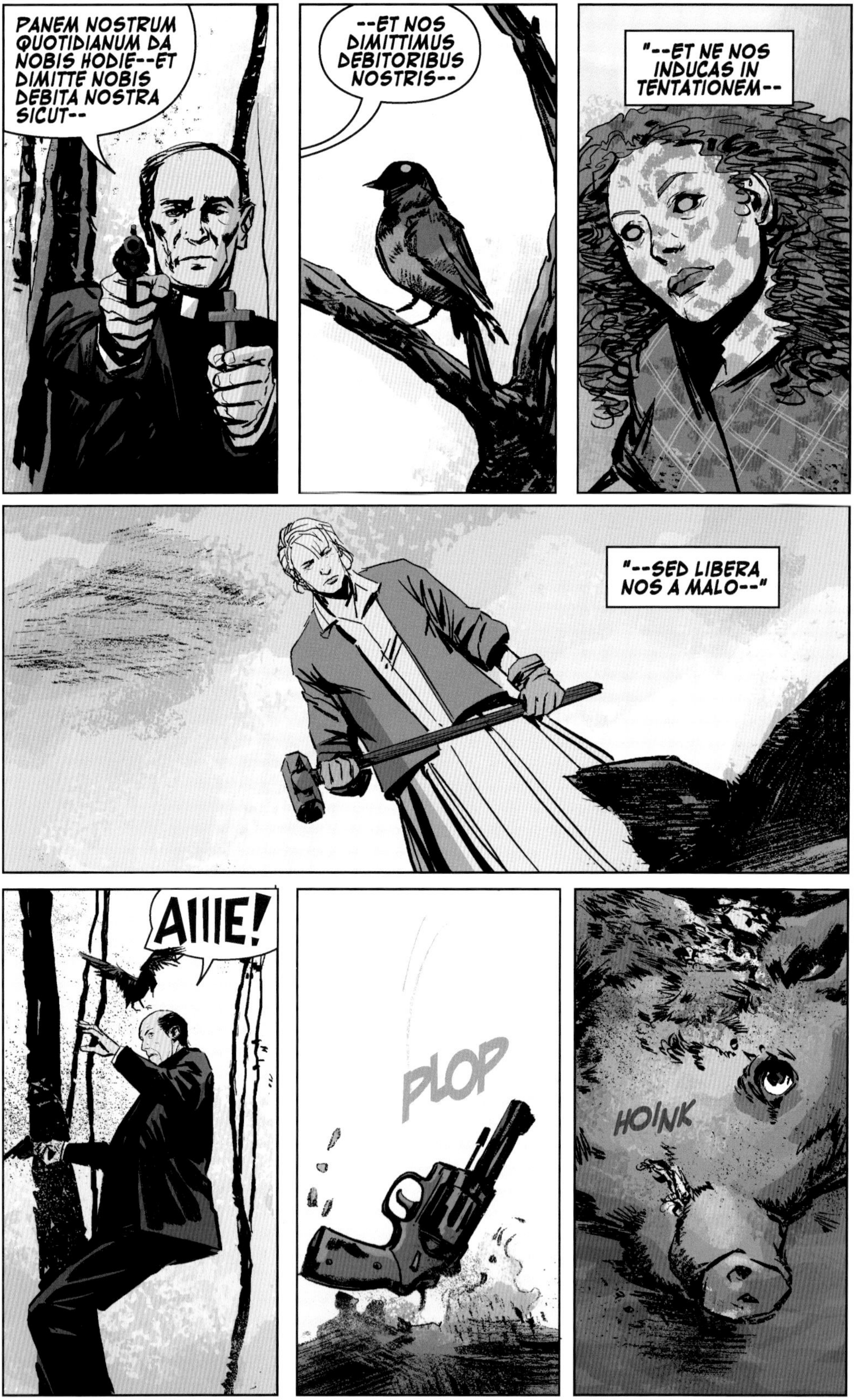
PANEM NOSTRUM QUOTIDIANUM DA NOBIS HODIE--ET DIMITTE NOBIS DEBITA NOSTRA SICUT--
--ET NOS DIMITTIMUS DEBITORIBUS NOSTRIS--
"--ET NE NOS INDUCAS IN TENTATIONEM--
"--SED LIBERA NOS A MALO--"
AIIIE!
PLOP
HOINK

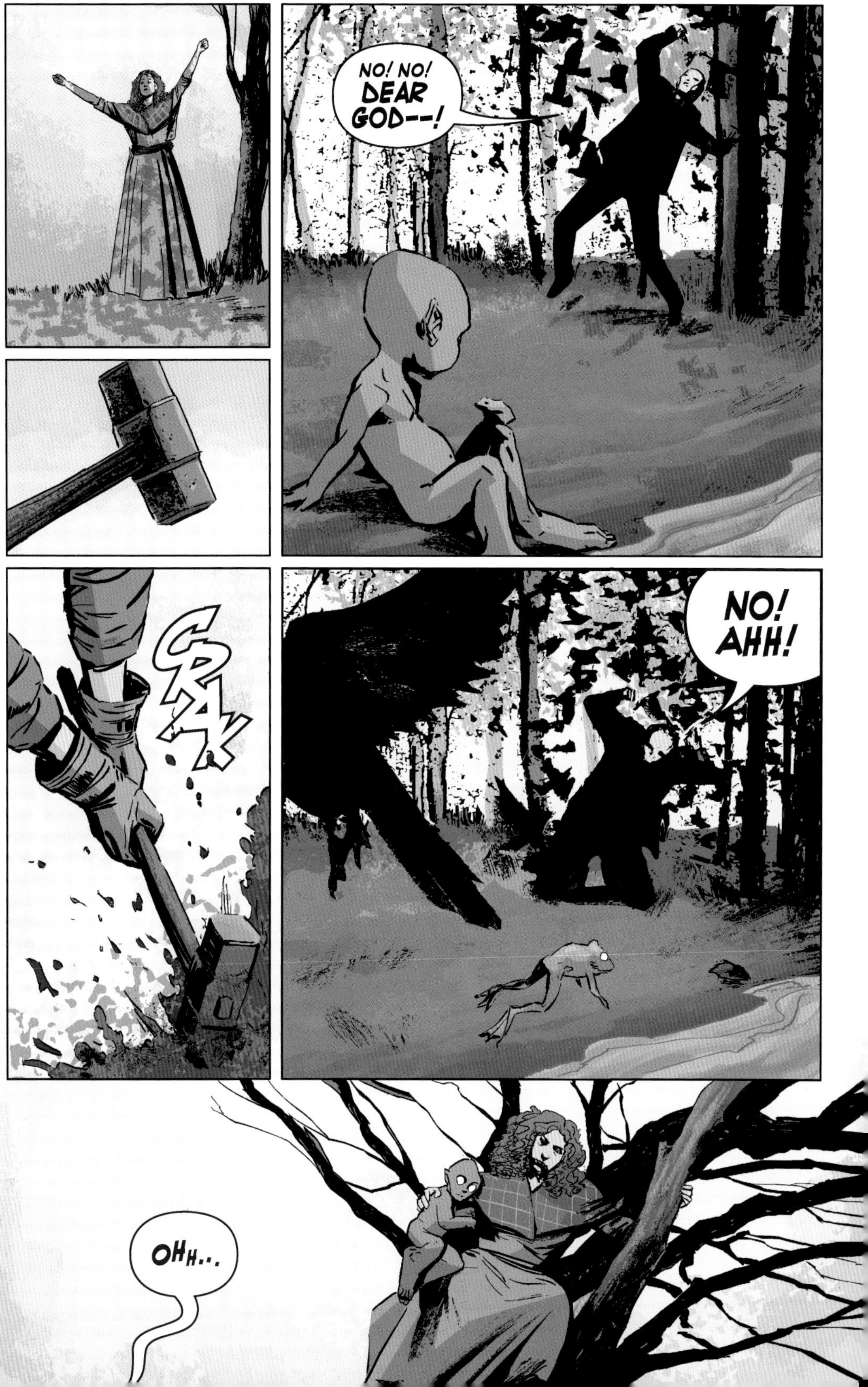
NO! NO! DEAR GOD--!
CRAK
NO! AHH!
OHH...

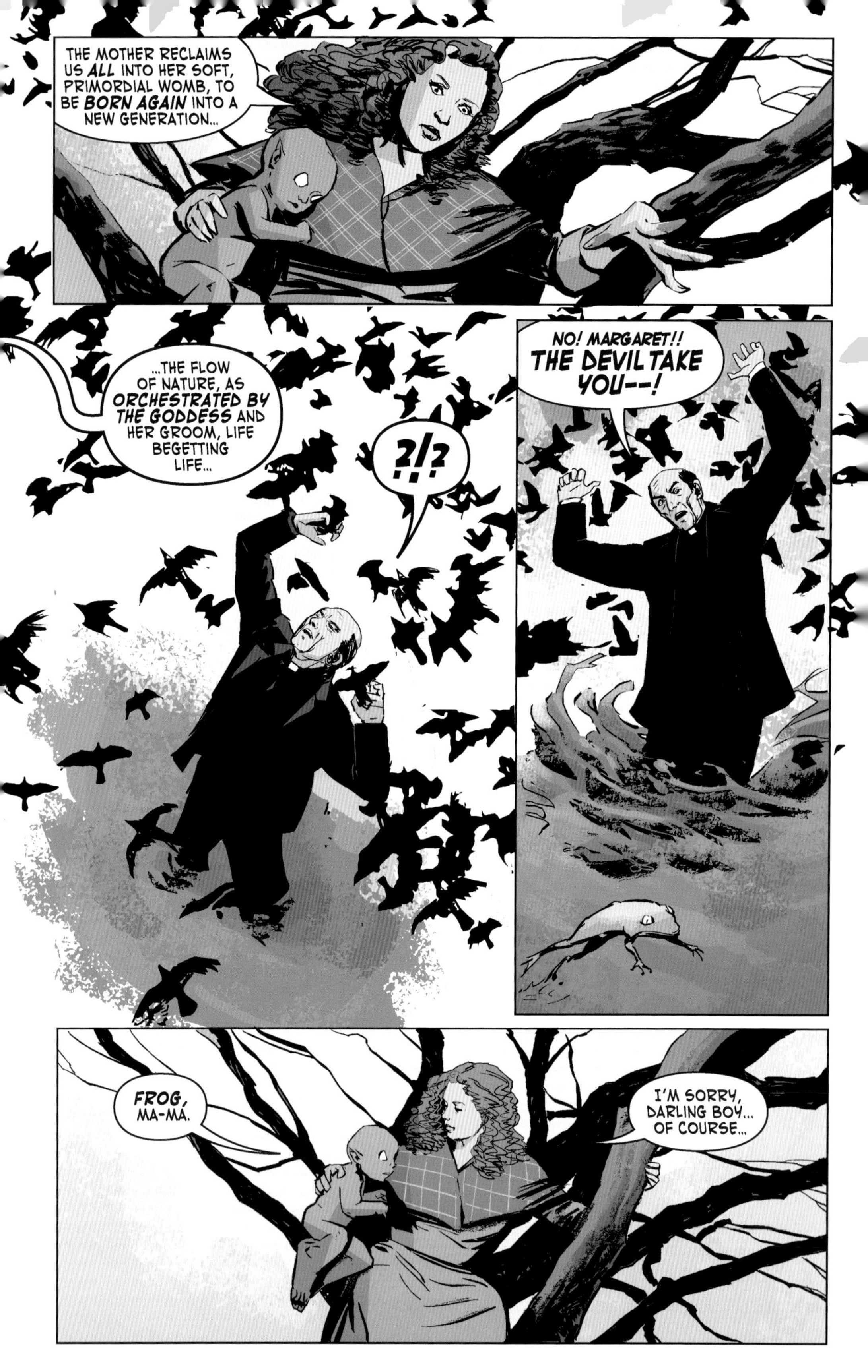
THE MOTHER RECLAIMS US ALL INTO HER SOFT, PRIMORDIAL WOMB, TO BE BORN AGAIN INTO A NEW GENERATION...
...THE FLOW OF NATURE, AS ORCHESTRATED BY THE GODDESS AND HER GROOM, LIFE BEGETTING LIFE...
?!?
NO! MARGARET!! THE DEVIL TAKE YOU--!
FROG, MA-MA.
I'M SORRY, DARLING BOY... OF COURSE...

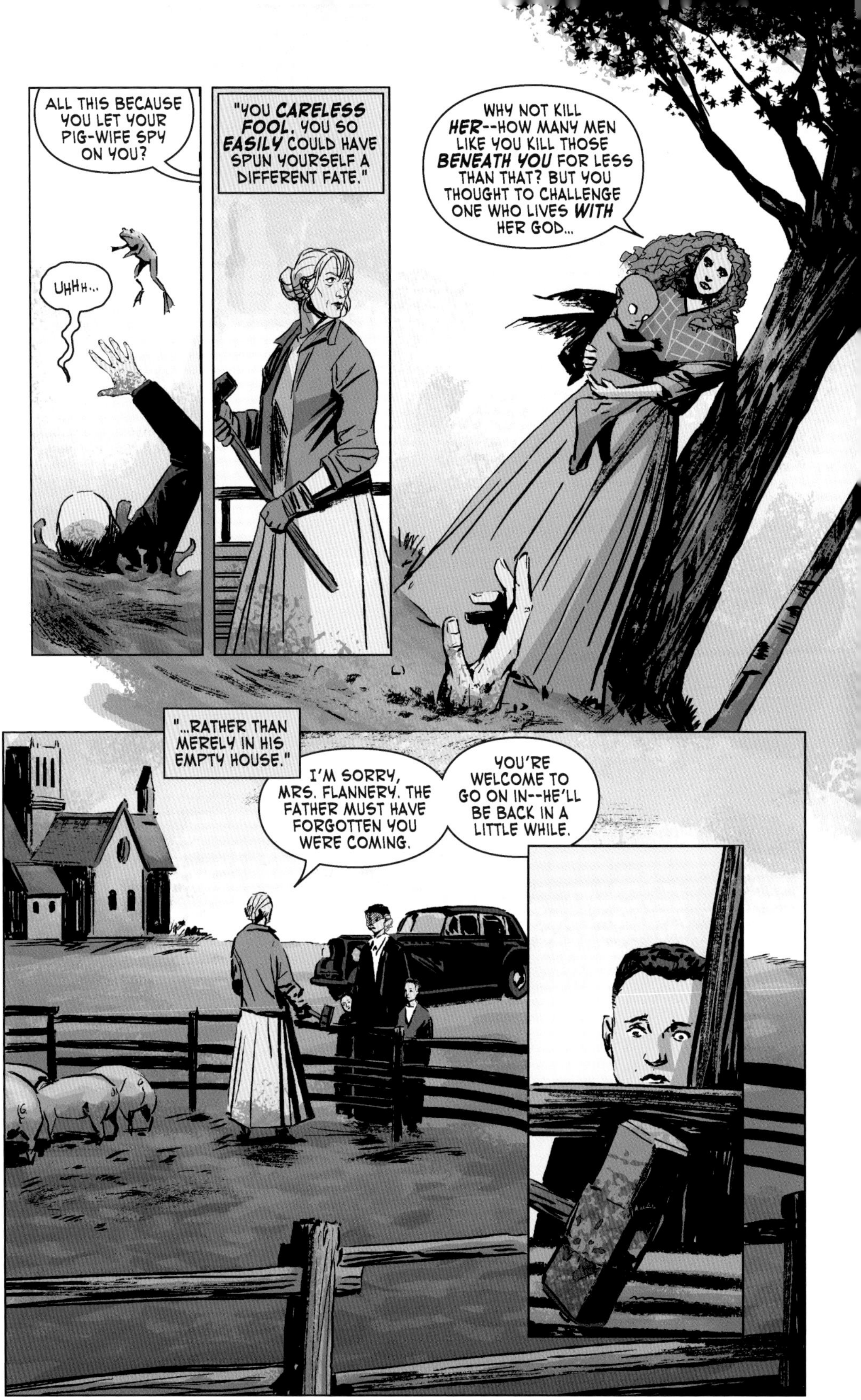
ALL THIS BECAUSE YOU LET YOUR PIG-WIFE SPY ON YOU?
UHHH...
"YOU CARELESS FOOL. YOU SO EASILY COULD HAVE SPUN YOURSELF A DIFFERENT FATE."
WHY NOT KILL HER--HOW MANY MEN LIKE YOU KILL THOSE BENEATH YOU FOR LESS THAN THAT? BUT YOU THOUGHT TO CHALLENGE ONE WHO LIVES WITH HER GOD...
"...RATHER THAN MERELY IN HIS EMPTY HOUSE."
I'M SORRY, MRS. FLANNERY. THE FATHER MUST HAVE FORGOTTEN YOU WERE COMING.
YOU'RE WELCOME TO GO ON IN--HE'LL BE BACK IN A LITTLE WHILE.

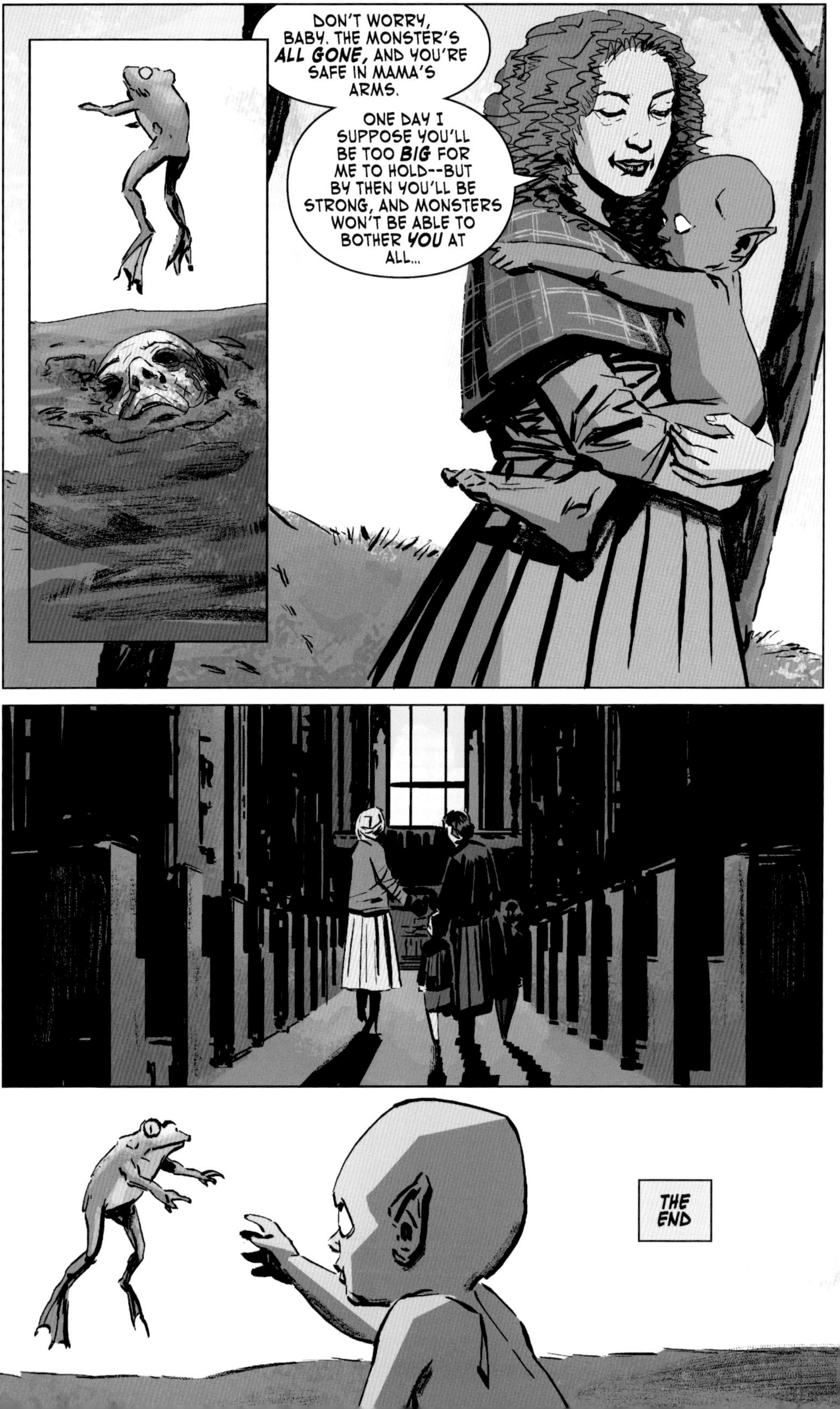

DON'T WORRY, BABY. THE MONSTER'S ALL GONE, AND YOU'RE SAFE IN MAMA'S ARMS.
ONE DAY I SUPPOSE YOU'LL BE TOO BIG FOR ME TO HOLD--BUT BY THEN YOU'LL BE STRONG, AND MONSTERS WON'T BE ABLE TO BOTHER YOU AT ALL...
THE END

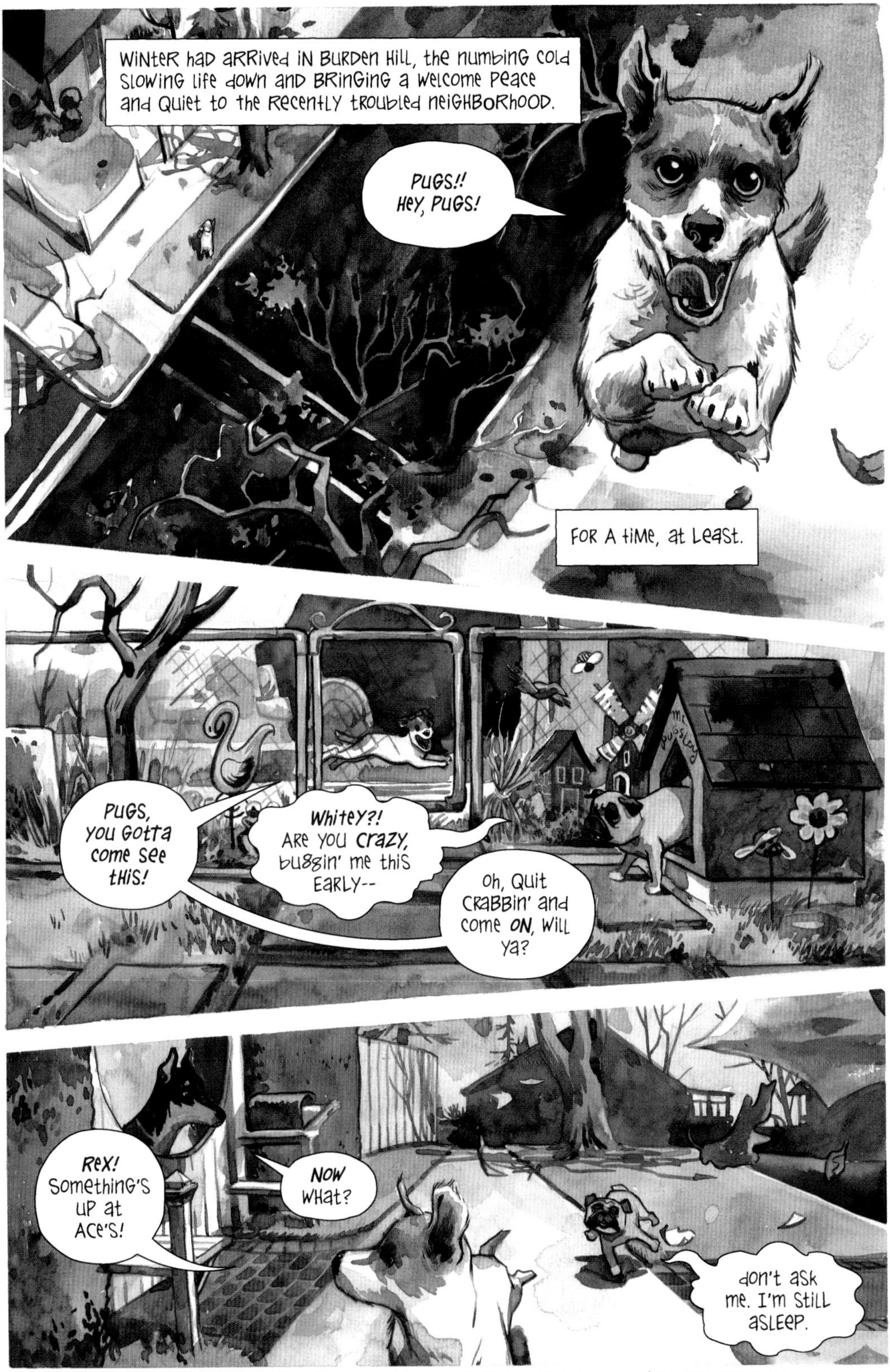
WINTER HAD ARRIVED IN BURDEN HILL, THE NUMBING COLD SLOWING LIFE DOWN AND BRINGING A WELCOME PEACE AND QUIET TO THE RECENTLY TROUBLED NEIGHBORHOOD.
PUGS!! HEY, PUGS!
FOR A TIME, AT LEAST.
PUGS, YOU GOTTA COME SEE THIS!
WHITEY?! ARE YOU CRAZY, BUGGIN' ME THIS EARLY--
OH, QUIT CRABBIN' AND COME ON, WILL YA?
REX! SOMETHING'S UP AT ACE'S!
NOW WHAT?
DON'T ASK ME. I'M STILL ASLEEP.

A DOG AND HIS BOY -BY EVAN DORKIN, SARAH DYER AND JILL THOMPSON 2006

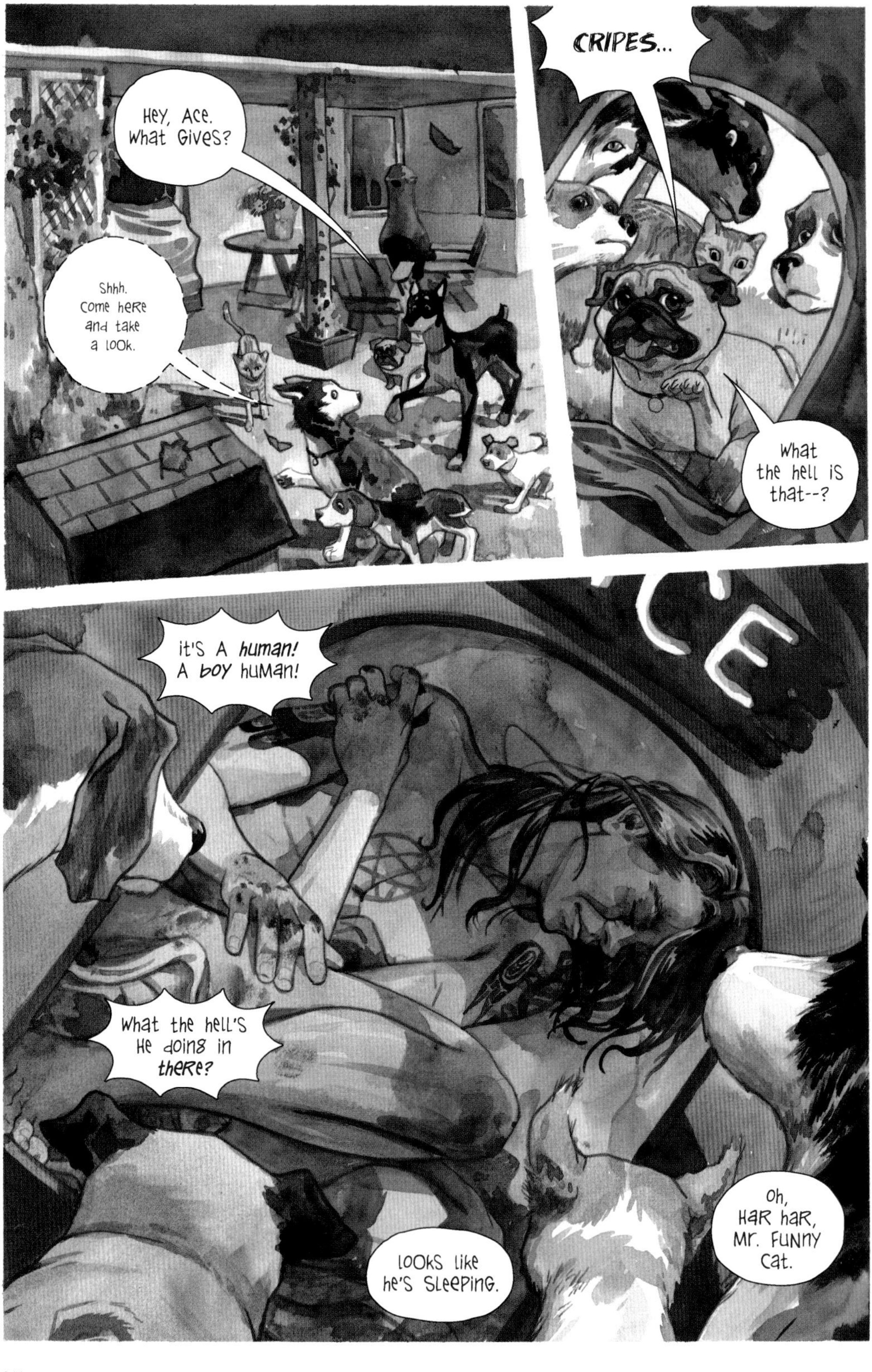
Hey, Ace. What Gives?
Shhh. Come here and take a look.
CRIPES...
What the hell is that--?
it's A *human!* A *boy* human!
What the hell's He doing in *there?*
looks like he's sleeping.
Oh, Har har, Mr. Funny Cat.

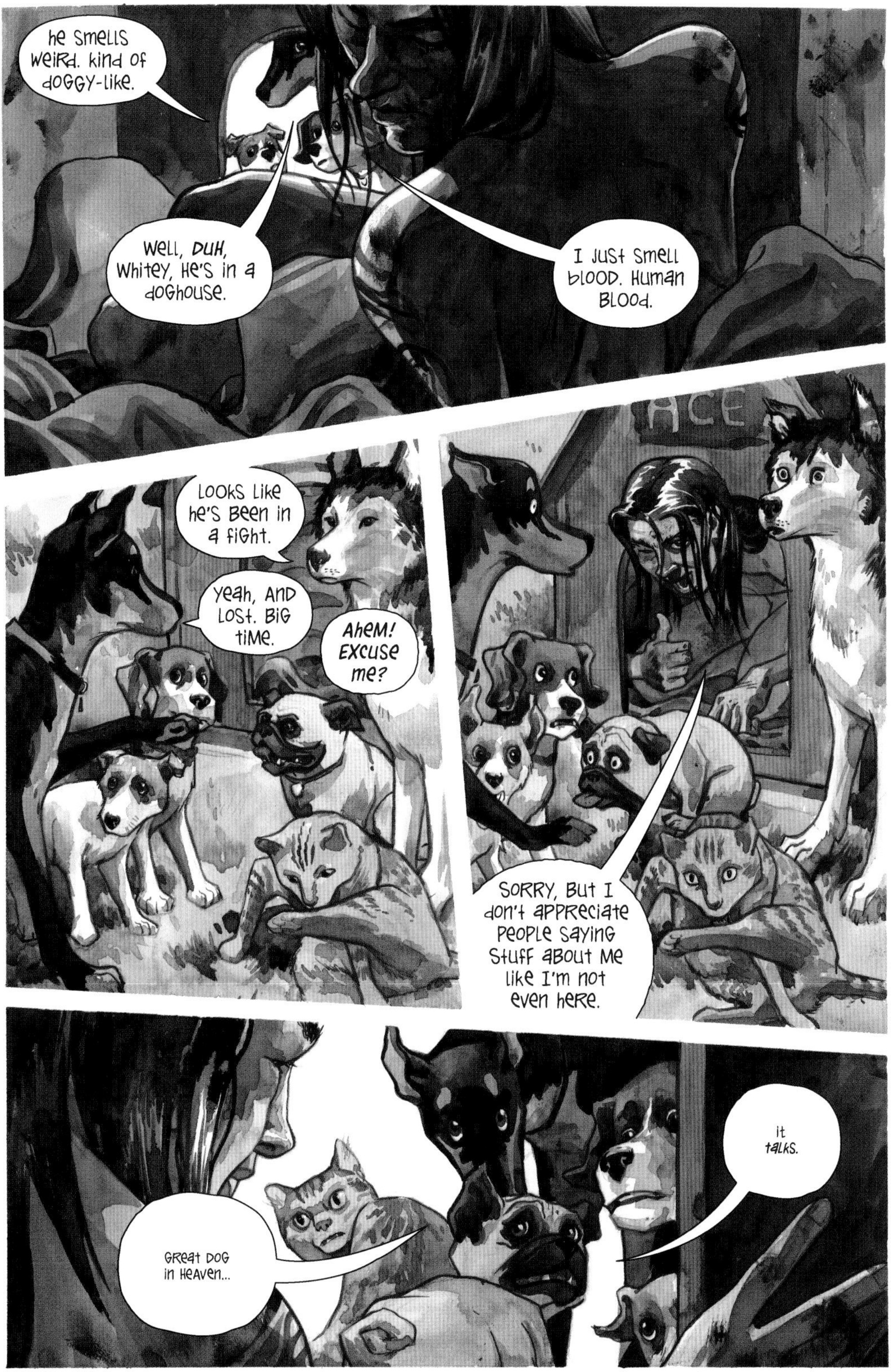
he smells weird. kind of doggy-like.
Well, DUH, Whitey, he's in a doghouse.
I just smell blood. Human Blood.
ACE
Looks like he's been in a fight.
Yeah, and lost. Big time.
Ahem! Excuse me?
Sorry, but I don't appreciate people saying stuff about me like I'm not even here.
Great dog in heaven...
it talks.

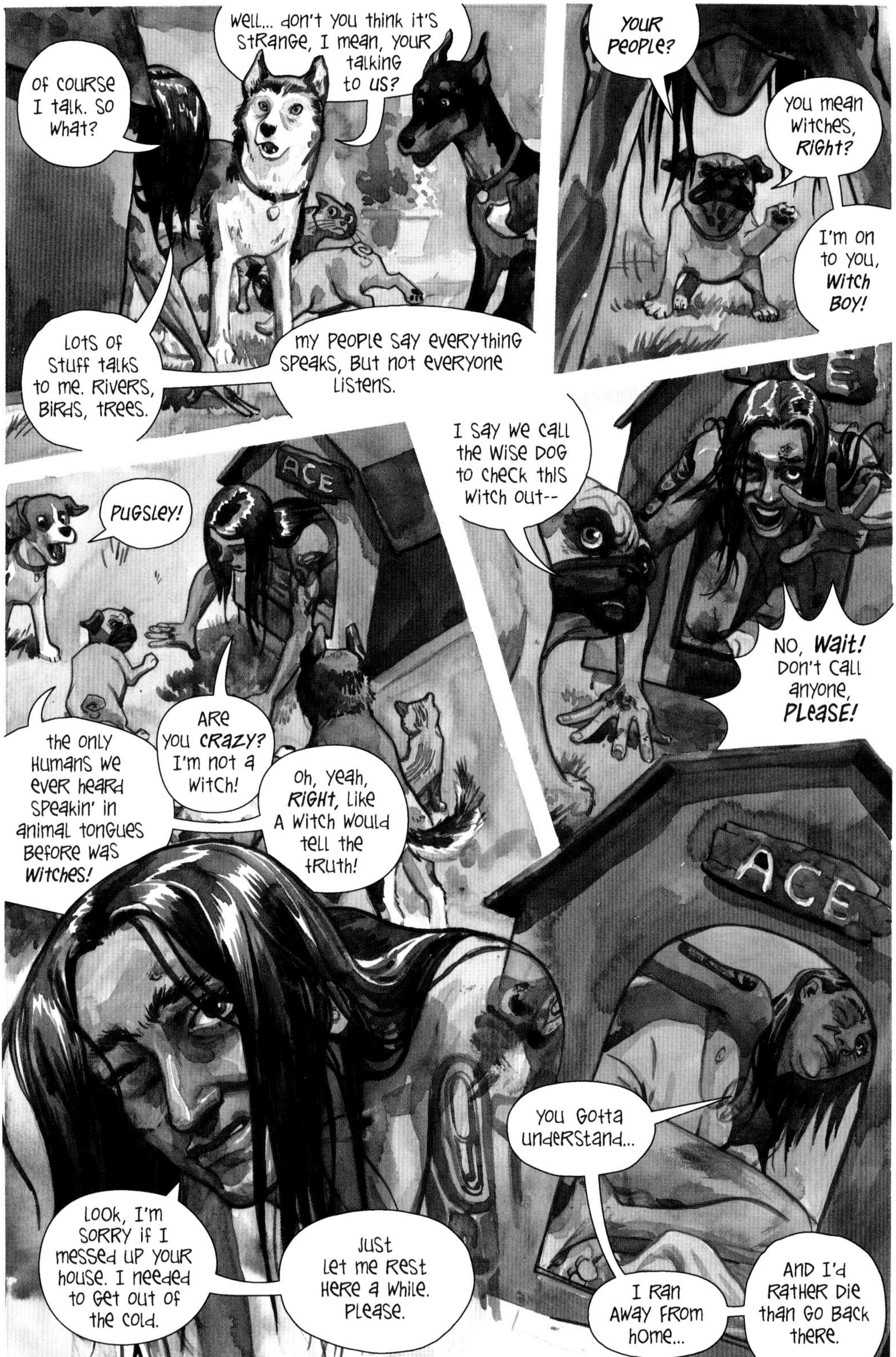
Of course I talk. So what?
Well... don't you think it's strange, I mean, your talking to us?
Lots of stuff talks to me. Rivers, birds, trees.
My people say everything speaks, but not everyone listens.
Your people?
You mean witches, right?
I'm on to you, witch boy!
Pugsley!
The only humans we ever heard speakin' in animal tongues before was witches!
Are you crazy? I'm not a witch!
Oh, yeah, right, like a witch would tell the truth!
I say we call the wise dog to check this witch out--
ACE
No, wait! Don't call anyone, please!
ACE
Look, I'm sorry if I messed up your house. I needed to get out of the cold.
Just let me rest here a while. Please.
You gotta understand...
I ran away from home...
And I'd rather die than go back there.
ACE

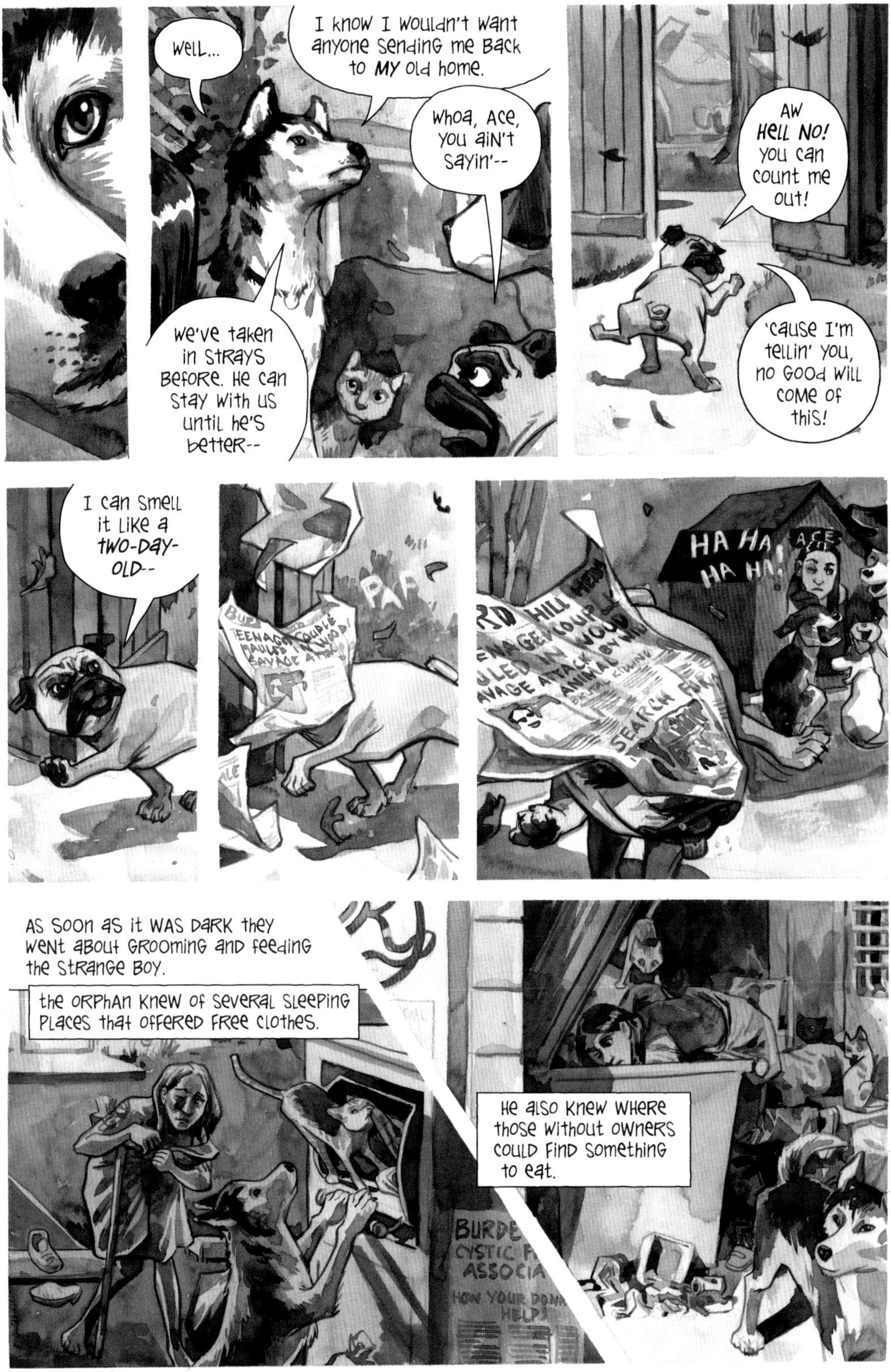
Well...
I know I wouldn't want anyone sending me back to MY old home.
Whoa, Ace, you ain't sayin'--
We've taken in strays before. He can stay with us until he's better--
AW HELL NO! You can count me out!
'cause I'm tellin' you, no good will come of this!
I can smell it like a TWO-DAY-OLD--
PAP
TEENAGE COUPLE MAULED IN WOOD
SAVAGE ATTACK
HA HA HA HA!
ACE
AS SOON AS IT WAS DARK THEY WENT ABOUT GROOMING AND FEEDING THE STRANGE BOY.
THE ORPHAN KNEW OF SEVERAL SLEEPING PLACES THAT OFFERED FREE CLOTHES.
HE ALSO KNEW WHERE THOSE WITHOUT OWNERS COULD FIND SOMETHING TO EAT.

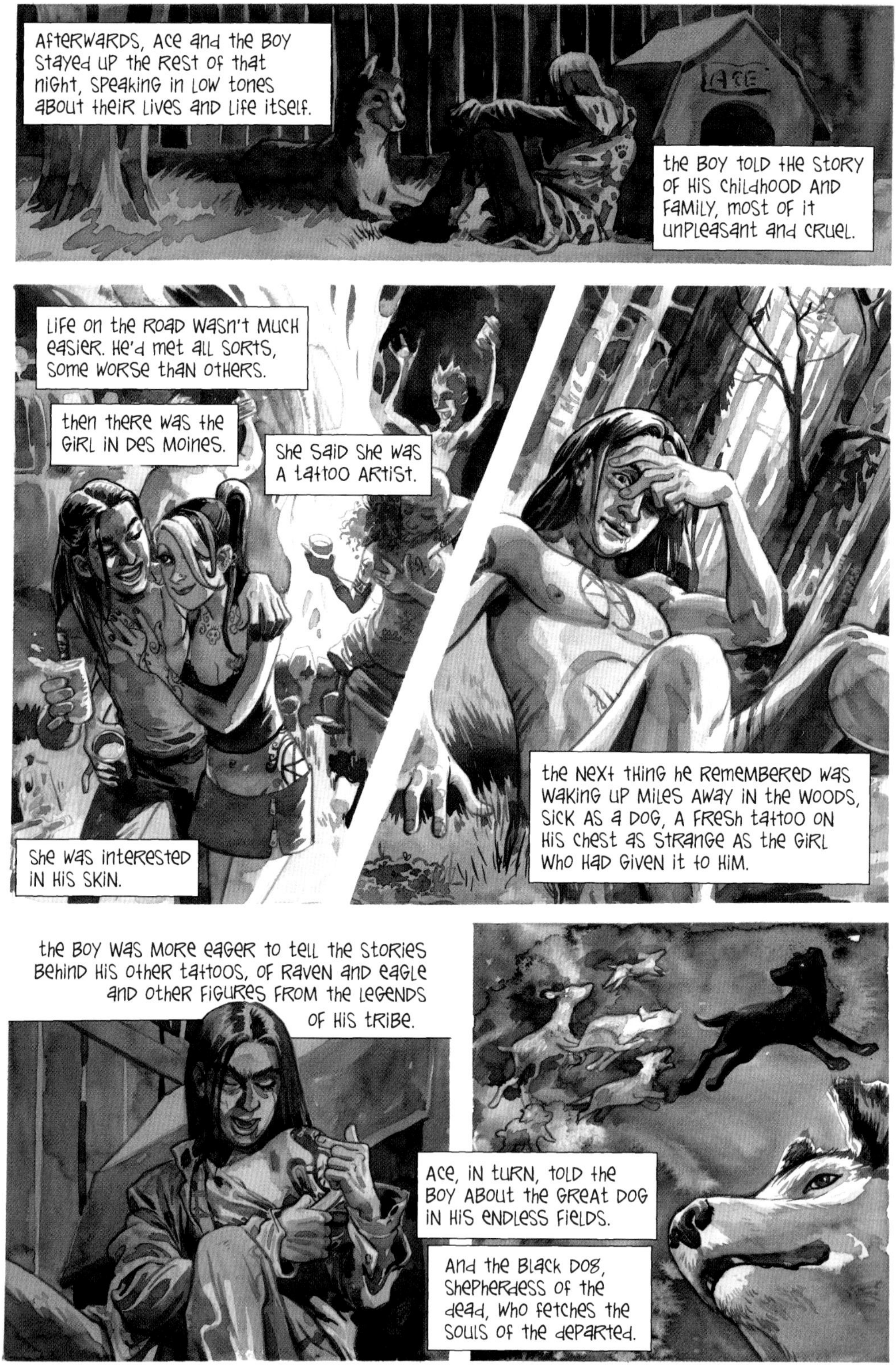
Afterwards, Ace and the Boy stayed up the rest of that night, speaking in low tones about their lives and life itself.
ACE
The Boy told the story of his childhood and family, most of it unpleasant and cruel.
Life on the road wasn't much easier. He'd met all sorts, some worse than others.
Then there was the girl in Des Moines.
She said she was a tattoo artist.
She was interested in his skin.
The next thing he remembered was waking up miles away in the woods, sick as a dog, a fresh tattoo on his chest as strange as the girl who had given it to him.
The Boy was more eager to tell the stories behind his other tattoos, of Raven and Eagle and other figures from the legends of his tribe.
Ace, in turn, told the Boy about the Great Dog in his endless fields.
And the Black Dog, shepherdess of the dead, who fetches the souls of the departed.

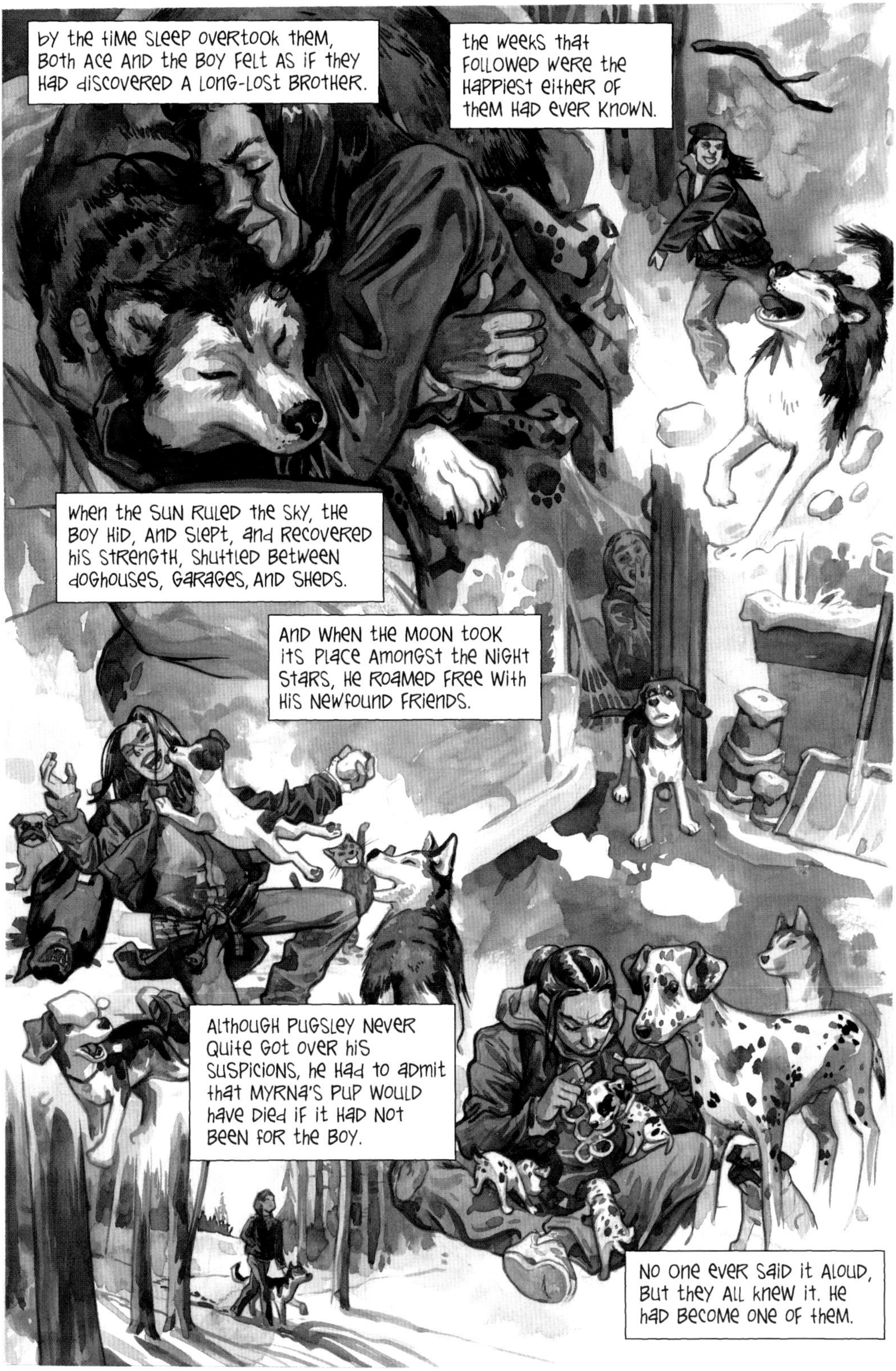
by the time sleep overtook them, Both Ace and the Boy felt as if they had discovered a long-lost brother.
the weeks that followed were the happiest either of them had ever known.
when the sun ruled the sky, the boy hid, and slept, and recovered his strength, shuttled between doghouses, garages, and sheds.
And when the moon took its place amongst the night stars, he roamed free with his newfound friends.
Although Pugsley never quite got over his suspicions, he had to admit that Myrna's pup would have died if it had not been for the boy.
No one ever said it aloud, but they all knew it. He had become one of them.

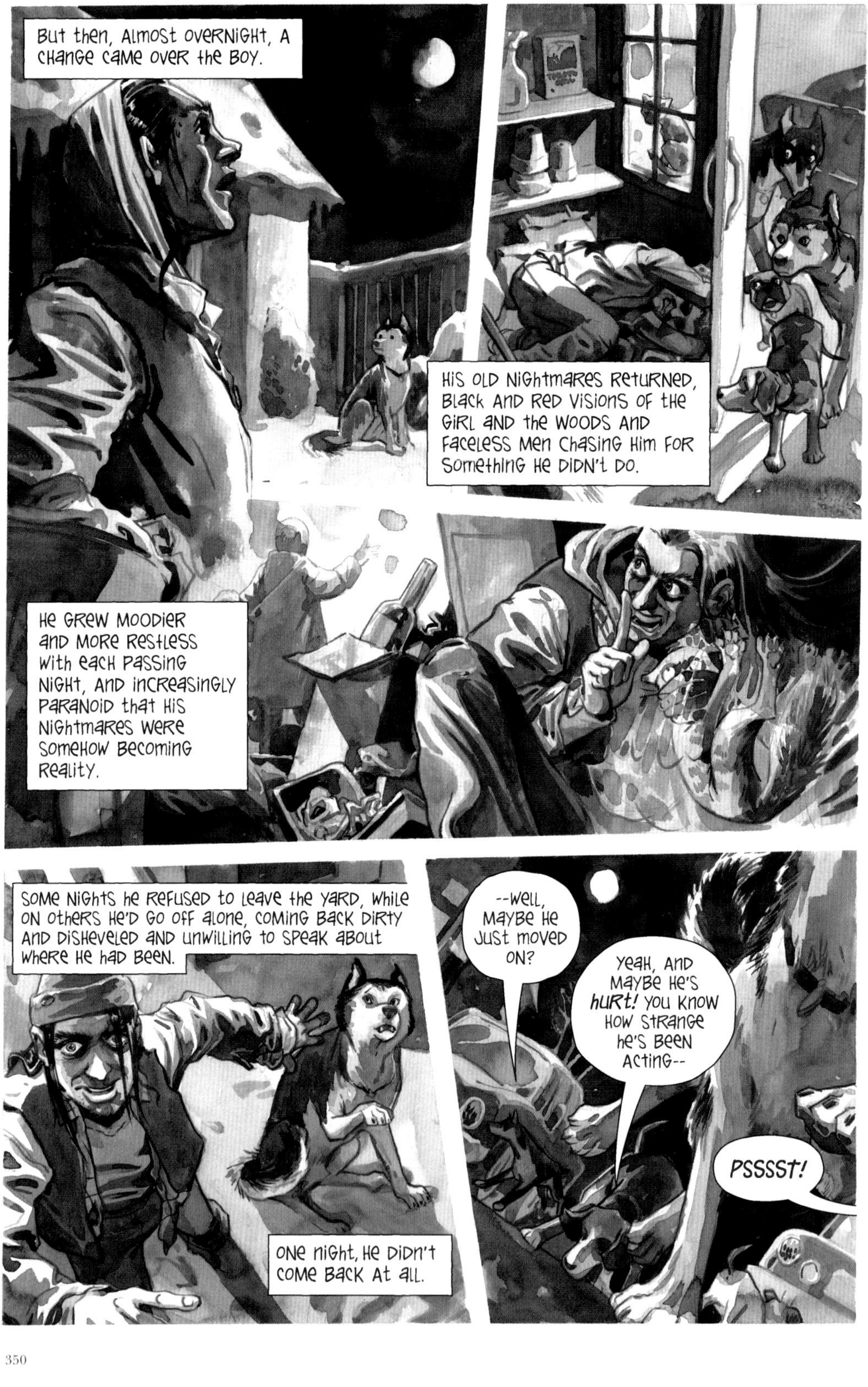
But then, almost overnight, a change came over the boy.
His old nightmares returned, black and red visions of the girl and the woods and faceless men chasing him for something he didn't do.
He grew moodier and more restless with each passing night, and increasingly paranoid that his nightmares were somehow becoming reality.
Some nights he refused to leave the yard, while on others he'd go off alone, coming back dirty and disheveled and unwilling to speak about where he had been.
One night, he didn't come back at all.
--Well, maybe he just moved on?
Yeah, and maybe he's hurt! You know how strange he's been acting--
PSSSST!

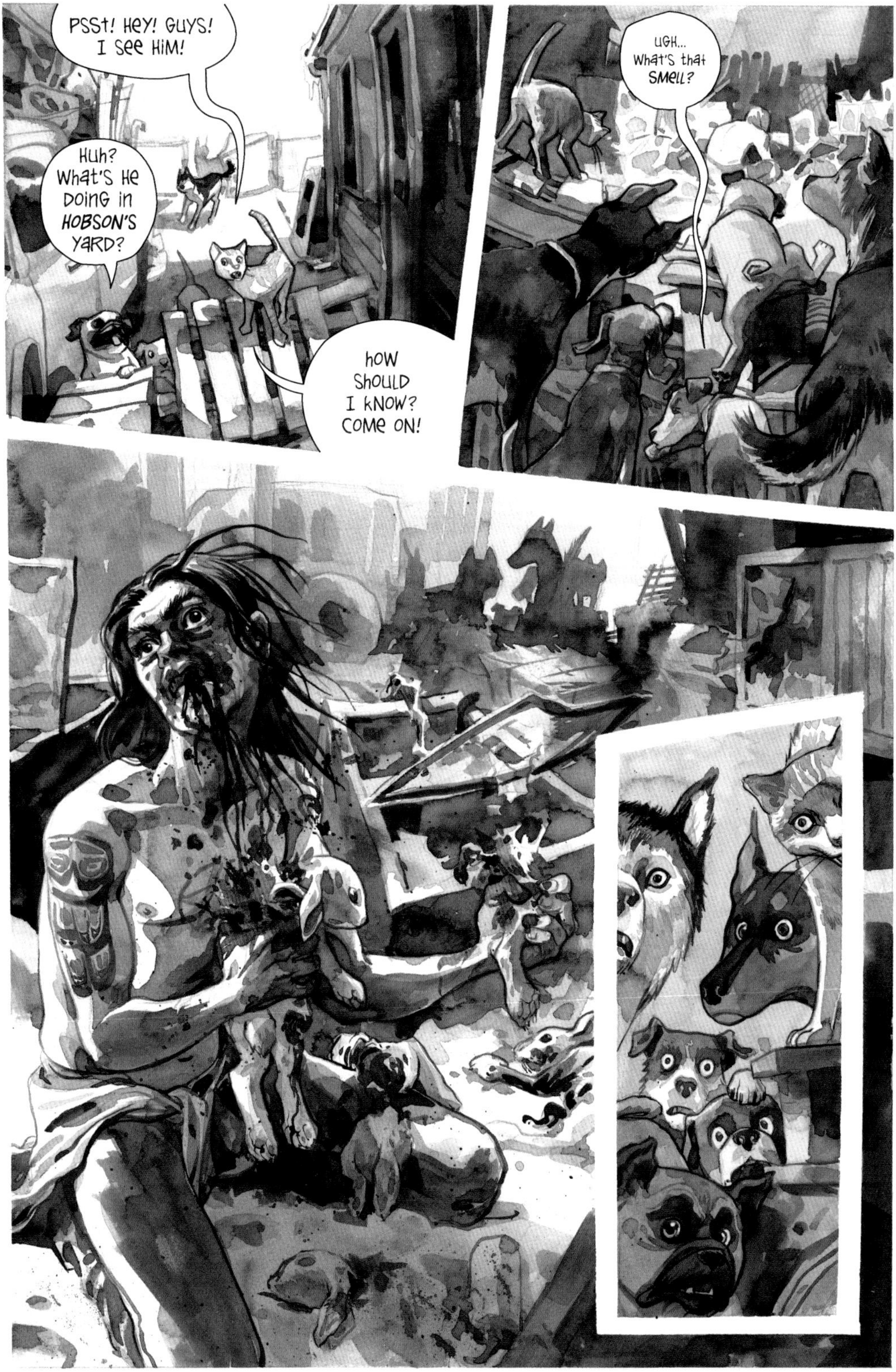
PSSt! HEY! GUYS! I SEE HIM!
Huh? What'S HE DOING in HOBSON'S YARD?
HOW SHOULD I KNOW? COME ON!
UGH... What'S that SMELL?

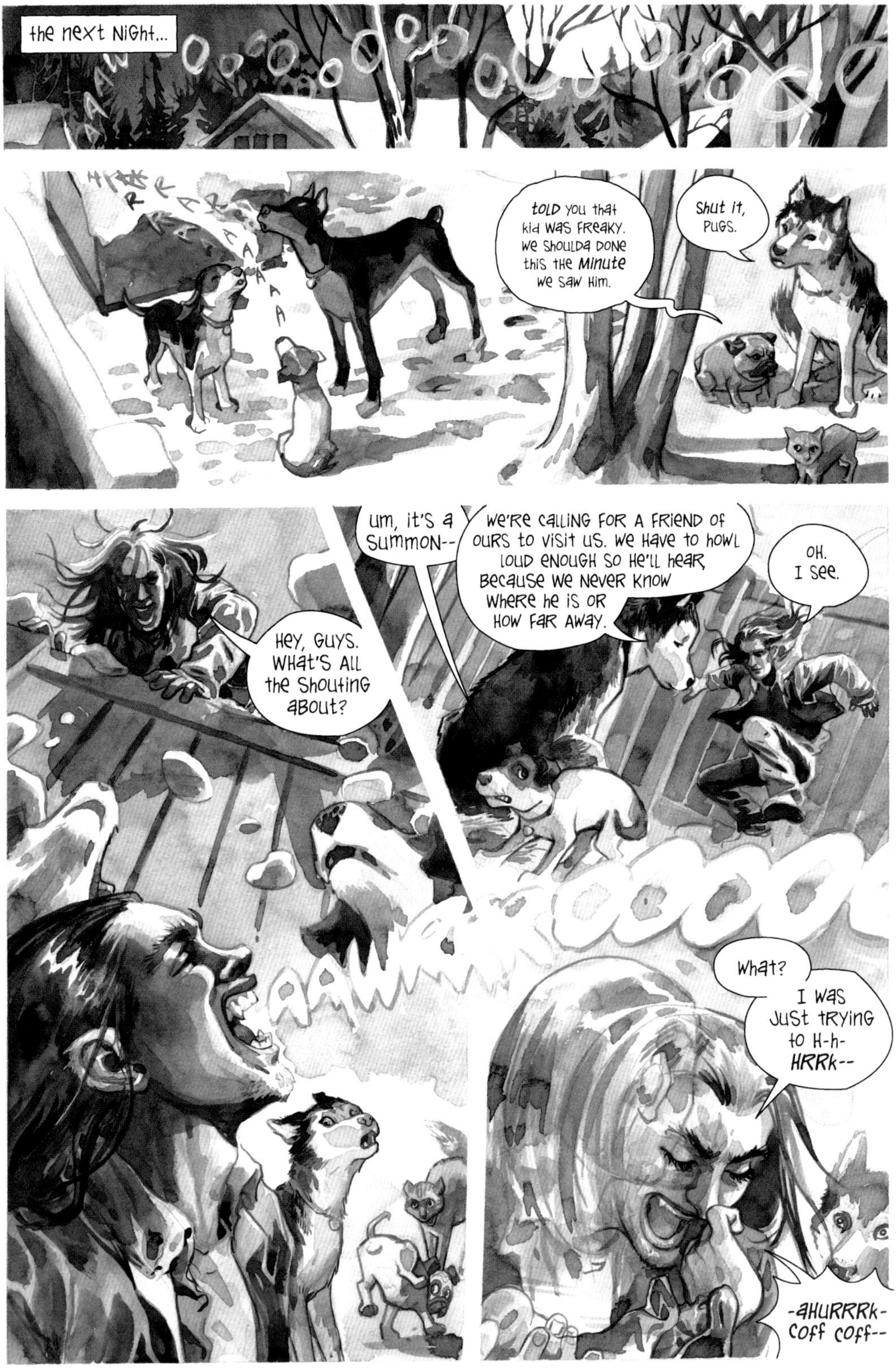

the next Night...
AAWOOOOOOOOOOOOOOOOOOOOOO
told you that kid was freaky. We shoulda done this the Minute we saw him.
Shut it, Pugs.
Hey, Guys. What's all the shouting about?
um, it's a summon--
We're calling for a friend of ours to visit us. We have to howl loud enough so he'll hear, because we never know where he is or how far away.
Oh. I see.
AAWOOOO
What?
I was just trying to H-h-HRRk--
-aHURRRk-
coff coff--

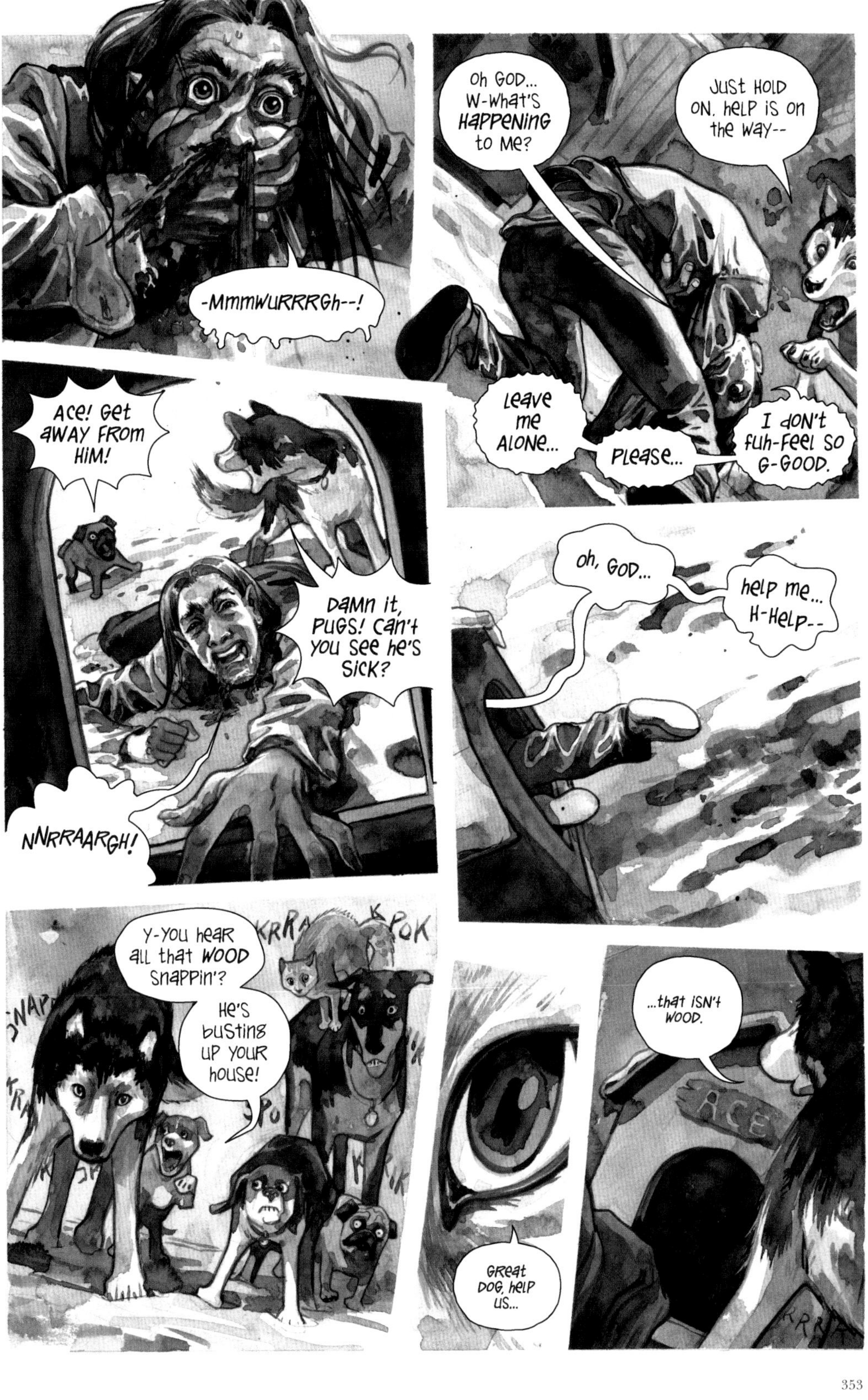
-MmmWURRRGh--!
Oh GOD... W-What's HAPPENING to me?
JUST HOLD ON. HELP IS ON THE WAY--
Leave me ALONE...
PLEASE...
I DON'T FUH-FEEL SO G-GOOD.
ACE! GET AWAY FROM HIM!
DAMN IT, PUGS! CAN'T YOU SEE HE'S SICK?
NNRRAARGH!
OH, GOD...
HELP ME... H-HELP--
Y-YOU HEAR ALL THAT WOOD SNAPPIN'?
HE'S BUSTING UP YOUR HOUSE!
KRRA
KPOK
SNAP
GREAT DOG, HELP US...
...THAT ISN'T WOOD.
ACE

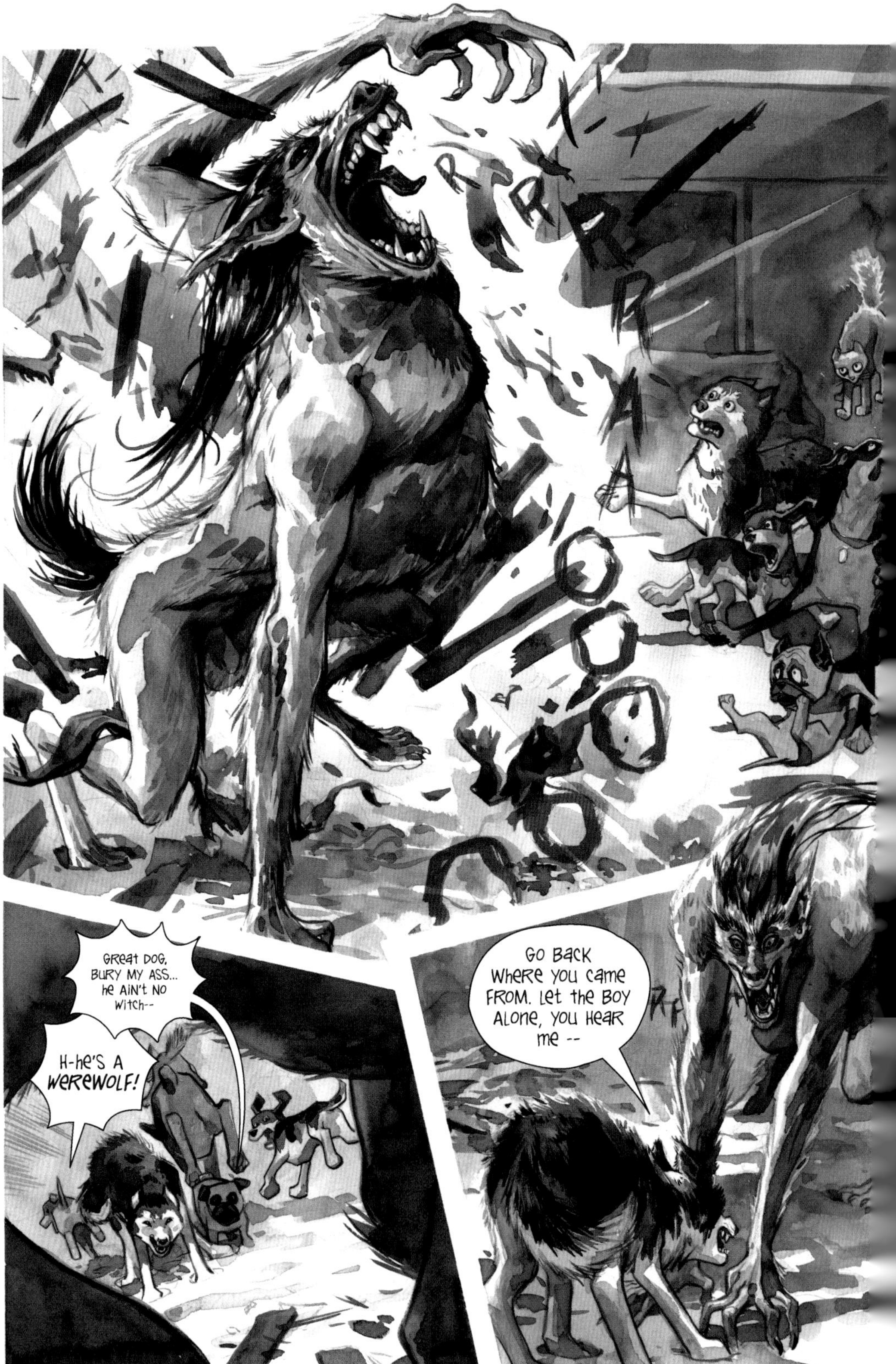
RRRAAOOOOO
Great dog, bury my ass... he ain't no witch--
H-he's a werewolf!
Go back where you came from. Let the boy alone, you hear me --

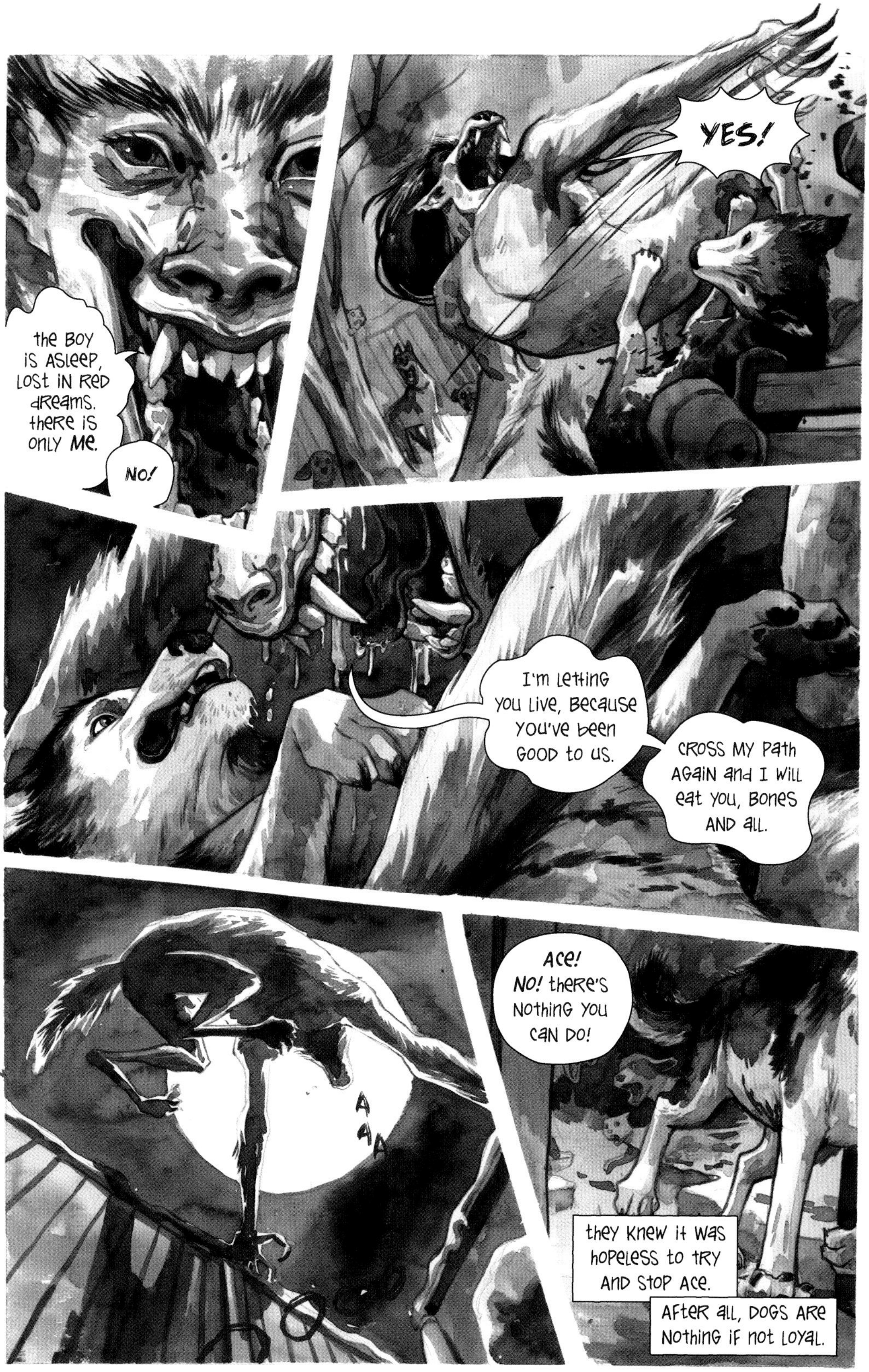
the Boy is Asleep, Lost in Red dreams. there is only Me.
No!
YES!
I'm Letting you Live, Because you've been Good to us.
CROSS MY Path Again and I will eat you, Bones AND all.
Ace! No! there's Nothing you can Do!
they Knew it was hopeless to try and Stop Ace.
After all, Dogs are Nothing if not Loyal.

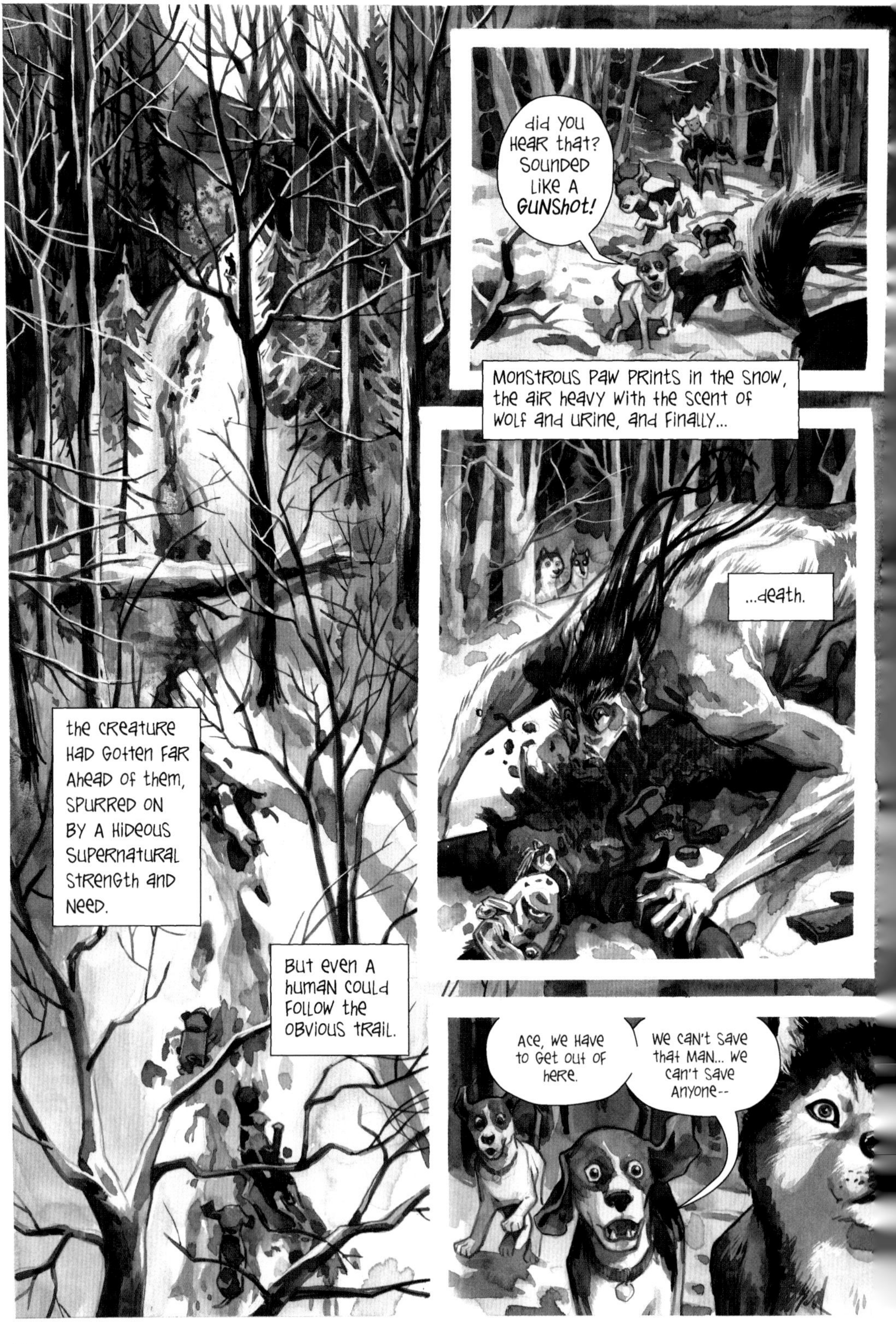
did you hear that? sounded like a GUNSHOT!
Monstrous paw prints in the snow, the air heavy with the scent of wolf and urine, and finally...
...death.
the creature had gotten far ahead of them, spurred on by a hideous supernatural strength and need.
But even a human could follow the obvious trail.
Ace, we have to get out of here.
We can't save that man... we can't save anyone--

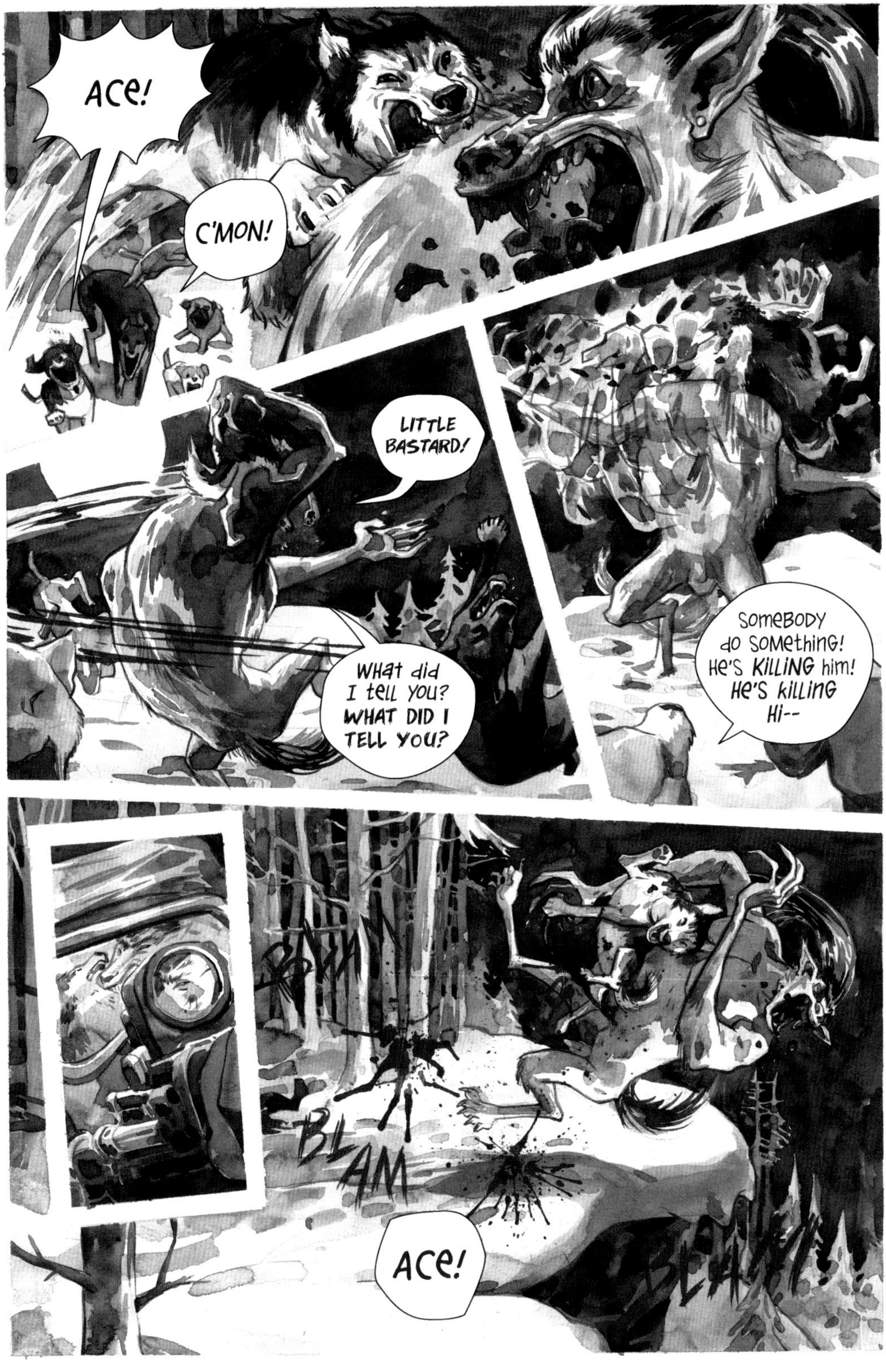
ACE!
C'MON!
LITTLE BASTARD!
What did I tell you? WHAT DID I TELL YOU?
SOMEBODY do Something! He's KILLING him! He's killing Hi--
BLAM
ACE!

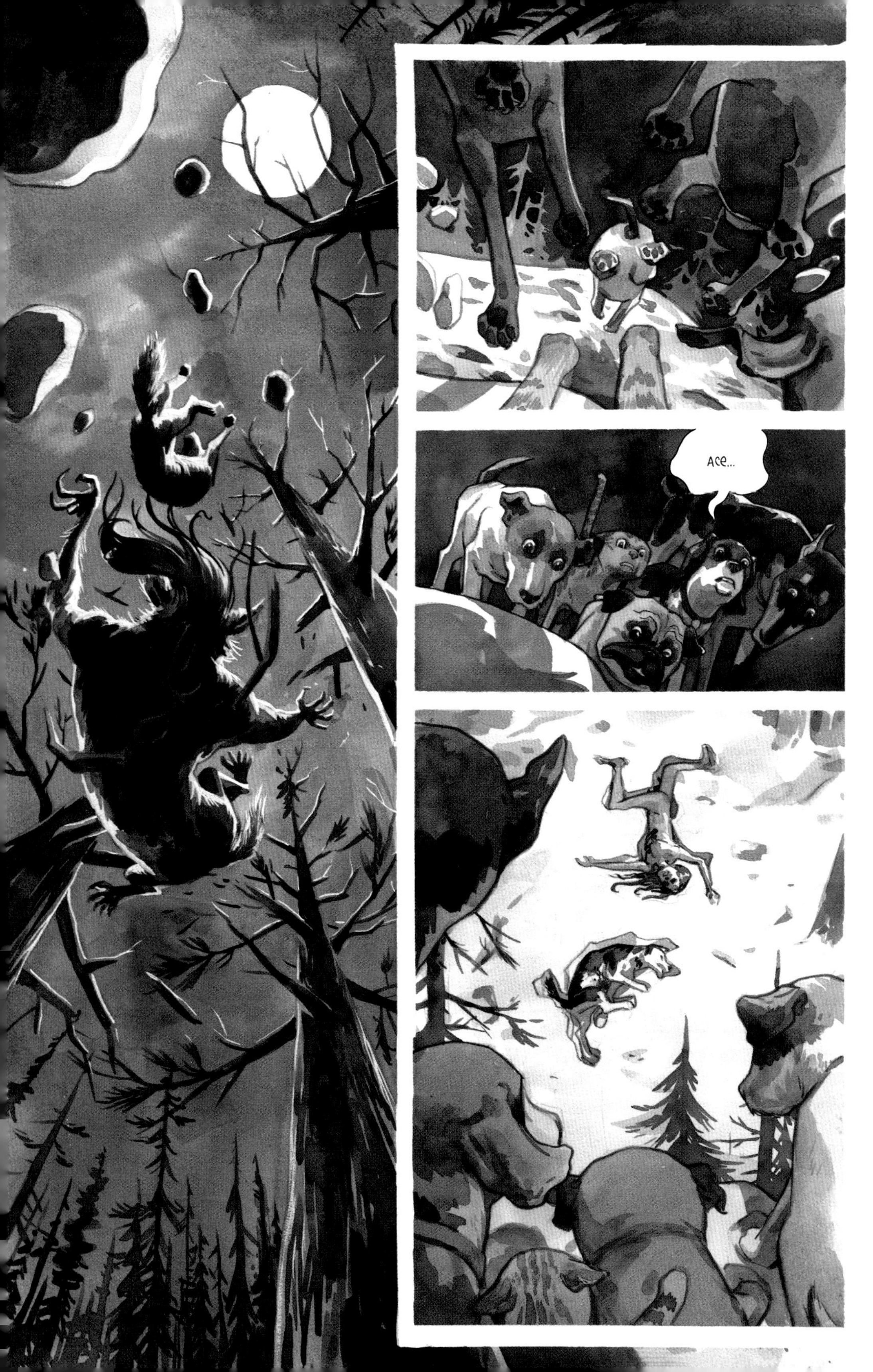
Ace...

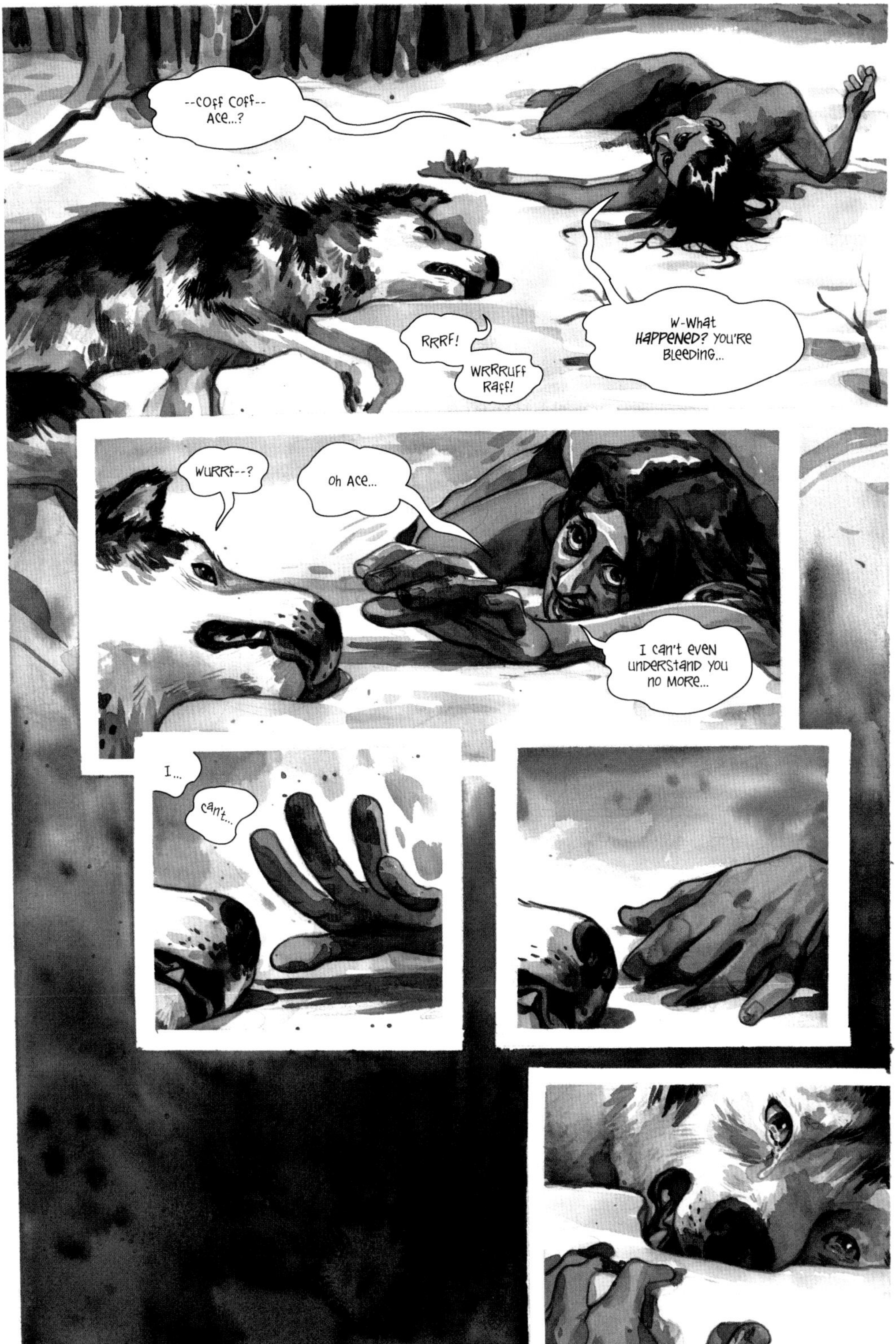
--COFF COFF--
ACE...?
RRRF!
WRRRUFF RAFF!
W-WHAT HAPPENED? YOU'RE BLEEDING...
WURRF--?
OH ACE...
I CAN'T EVEN UNDERSTAND YOU NO MORE...
I...
CAN'T...

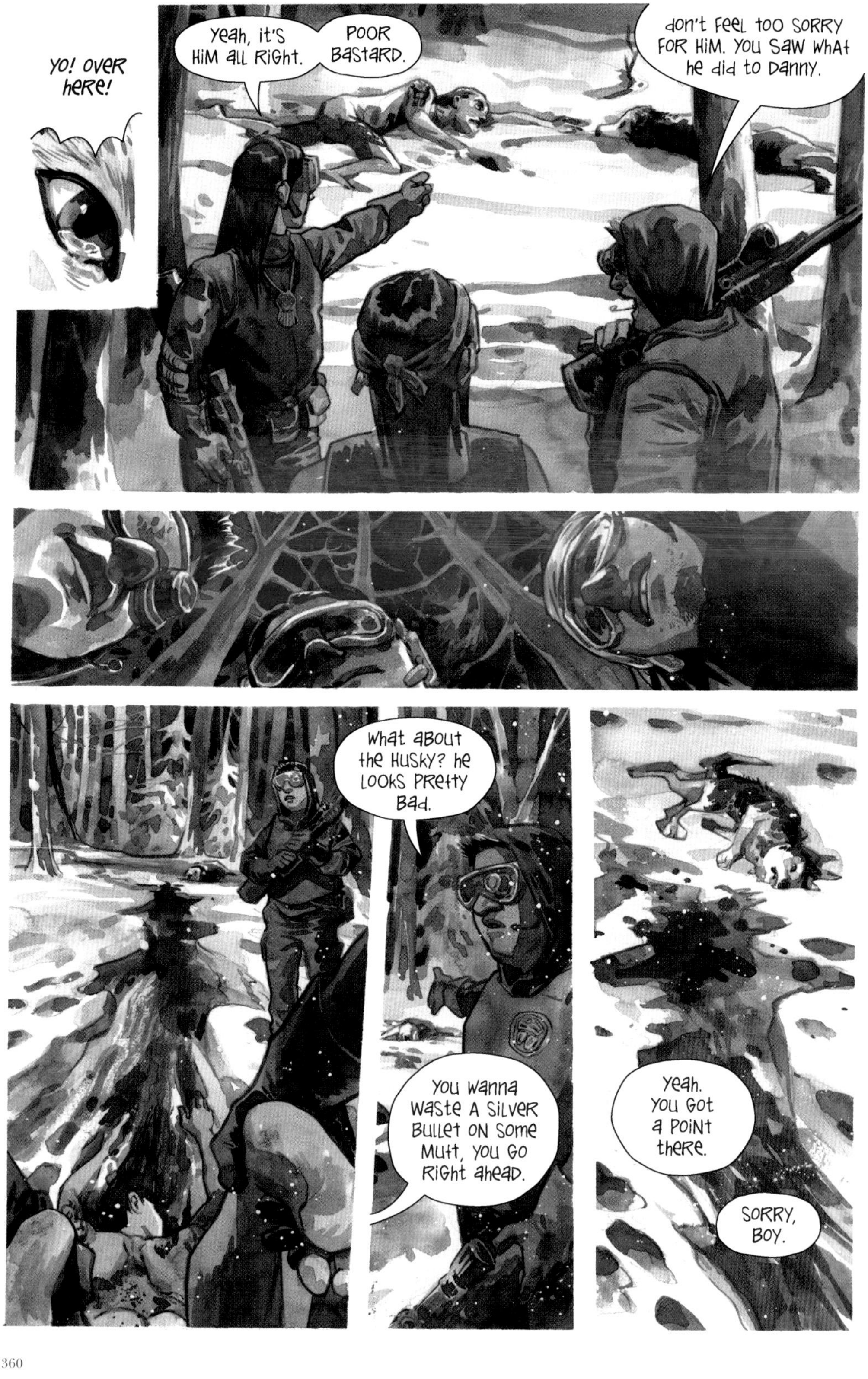
yo! over here!
Yeah, it's him all right.
Poor bastard.
don't feel too sorry for him. You saw what he did to danny.
What about the husky? he looks pretty bad.
You wanna waste a silver bullet on some mutt, you go right ahead.
Yeah. You got a point there.
Sorry, boy.

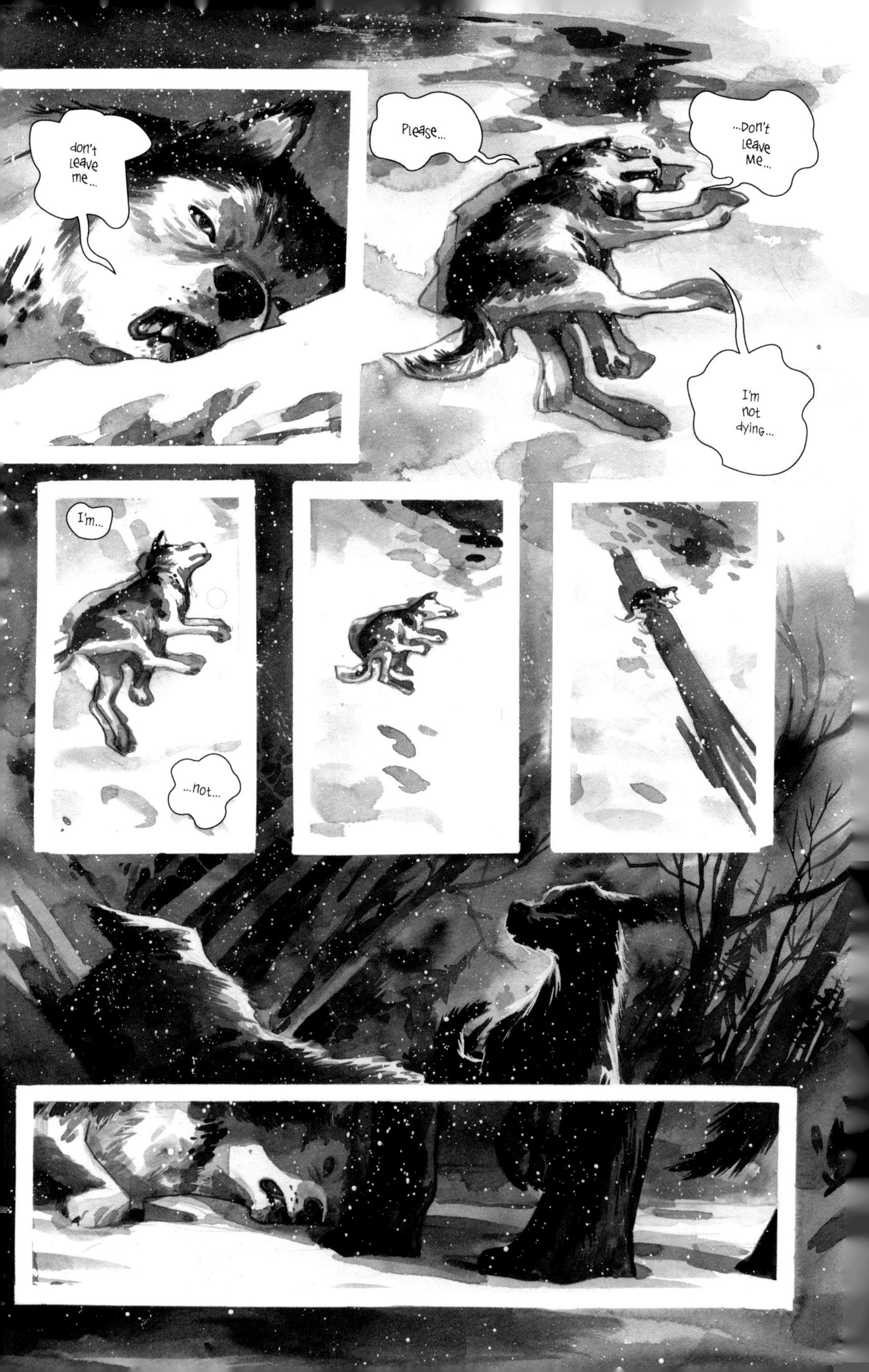
don't leave me...
Please...
...Don't leave me...
I'm not dying...
I'm...
...not...

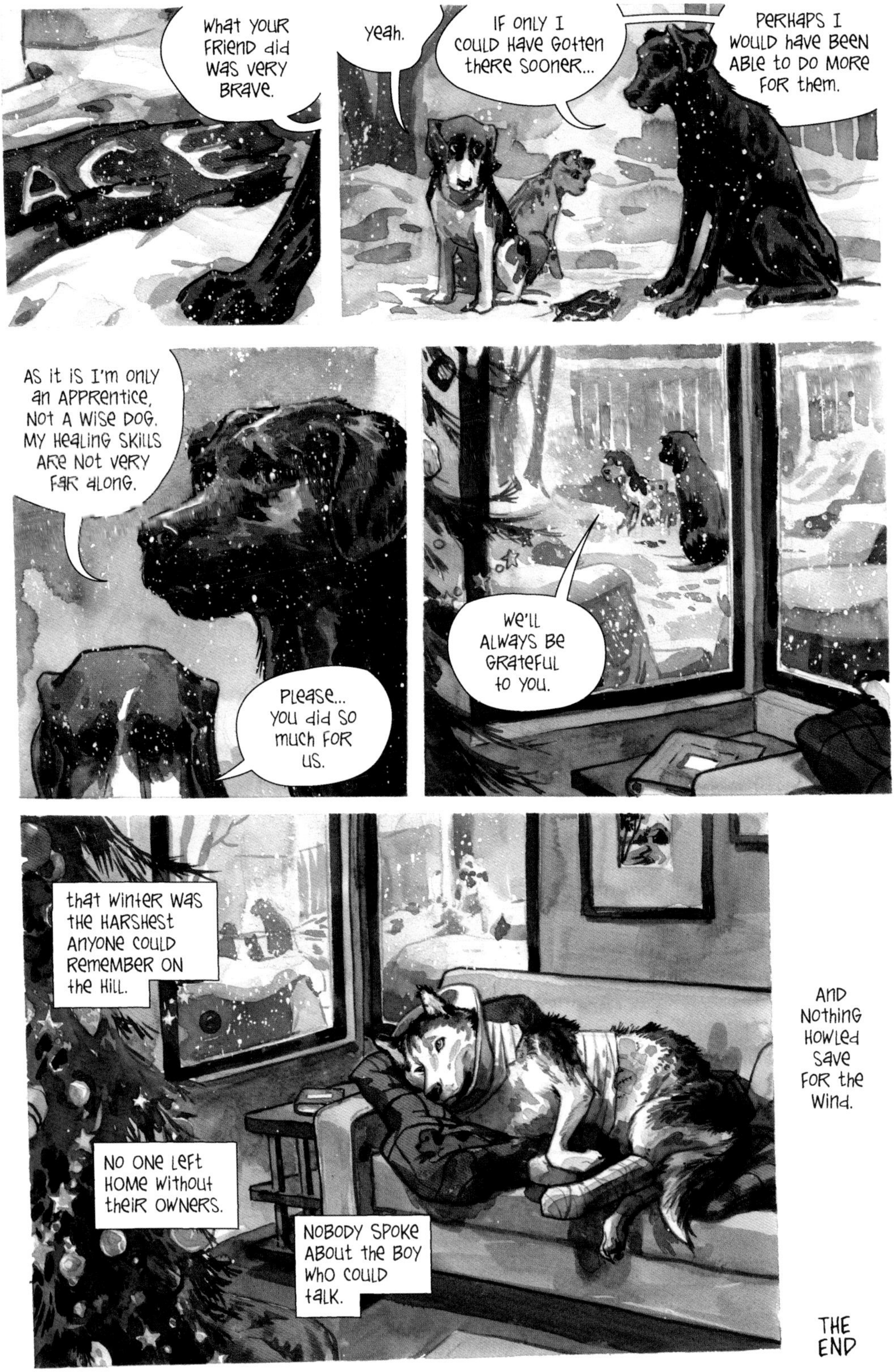
What your friend did was very brave.
Yeah.
If only I could have gotten there sooner...
Perhaps I would have been able to do more for them.
As it is I'm only an apprentice, not a wise dog. My healing skills are not very far along.
Please... you did so much for us.
We'll always be grateful to you.
That winter was the harshest anyone could remember on the Hill.
No one left home without their owners.
Nobody spoke about the boy who could talk.
And nothing howled save for the wind.
THE END

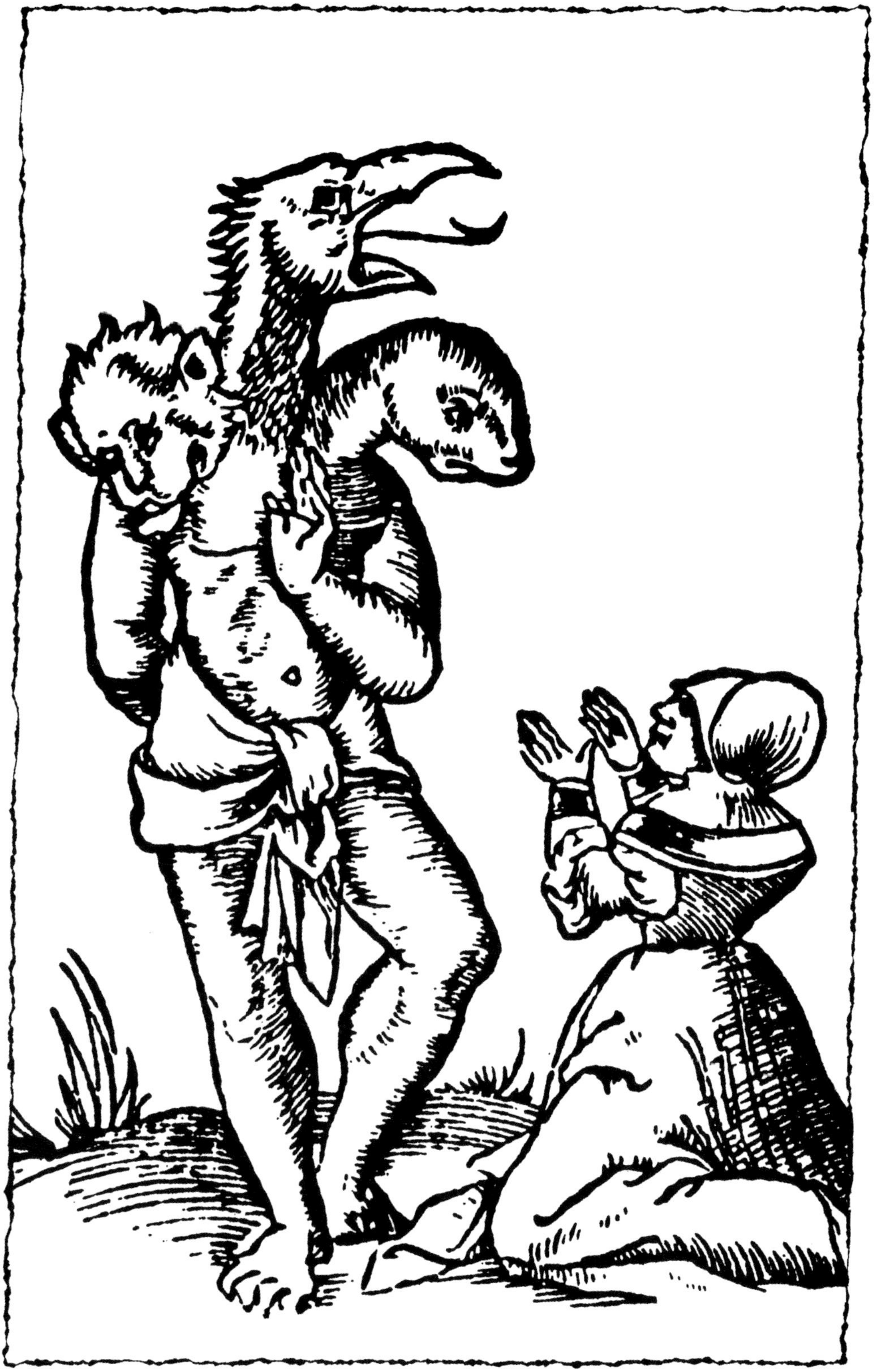

Further Reading

Rex Mundi Omnibus TPB
Story By: *Arvid Nelson*
Art By: *Juan Ferreyra and others*

When a medieval scroll disappears from a
Paris church, Dr. Julien Saunière uncovers
a series of horrific ritual murders connected
to the Catholic Church in this occult
murder mystery.

Vol. 1 | $24.99 | 978-1-59582-963-4
Vol. 2 | $24.99 | 978-1-61655-068-4

Calla Cthulhu TPB
Story By: *Evan Dorkin and Sarah Dyer*
Art By: *Erin Humiston, Mario A. Gonzalez,
and Bill Mudron*

Calla Tafali battles both monsters and the
internal struggle against her destiny in a
Lovecraftian all-ages adventure.

$12.99 | 978-1-50670-293-3

Colder Omnibus TPB
Story By: *Paul Tobin*
Art By: *Juan Ferreyra*

Declan Thomas, the former patient of an
insane asylum that was destroyed in a fire,
attempts to cure his own madness, but
demonic predators challenge him at
every turn.

$24.99 | 978-1-50670-479-1

The World Below TPB
Story By: *Paul Chadwick*
Art By: *Ron Randall*

Paul Chadwick delivers a fever-dream hybrid
of classic rip-roaring science-fiction adventure
and quirky, unsettling psychological drama.

$12.95 | 978-1-59307-360-2

Criminal Macabre
Omnibus Vol. 1 TPB
Story By: *Steve Niles*
Art By: *Kelley Jones and Ben Templesmith*

Hard-boiled and hard-living detective Cal
McDonald is the only line of defense between
Los Angeles and a growing horde of zombies,
vampires, possessed muscle cars, and much
more weirdness!

$24.99 | 978-1-59582-746-3

Murder Mysteries and Other
Stories Gallery Edition HC
Story and Art By: *P. Craig Russell and others*

This gallery edition features high-quality
scans of Russell's original art, printed at art-
board size, featuring collaborators such as
Neil Gaiman.

$125.00 | 978-1-61655-834-5

Lady Killer TPB
Story By: *Joëlle Jones and Jamie S. Rich*
Art By: *Joëlle Jones*

A picture-perfect homemaker, wife, and
mother, Josie Schuller is also a ruthless,
efficient killer! When she finds herself in the
crosshairs, her ideal American Dream hangs
in the balance.

$17.99 | 978-1-61655-757-7

The Marquis: Inferno TPB
Story and Art By: *Guy Davis*

In a Inquisition stronghold overrun with
damned souls, one man is blessed with the
ability to recognize the hidden demons, and
return them to hell.

$24.99 | 978-1-59582-368-7

Scary Godmother HC
Story and Art By: *Jill Thompson*

On Halloween night, Scary Godmother shows
little Hannah Marie just how much
fun spooky can be!

$24.99 | 978-1-59582-589-6

Lazarus Jack TPB
Story By: *Mark Ricketts*
Art By: *Horacio Domingues*

This spellbinding fantasy blends reality and
imagination, comedy and terror.

$14.99 | 978-1-59307-097-7

Concrete Vol. 1: Depths TPB
Story and Art By: *Paul Chadwick*

Over seven feet tall and weighing over a
thousand pounds, Concrete is trapped inside
a shell of stone. He has fantastic abilities, but
longs for the touch of a human hand.

$13.99 | 978-1-59307-343-5

Hellboy in Hell Library Edition
Story By: *Mike Mignola*
Art By: *Mike Mignola and Dave Stewart*

Mignola's tour of Hell reveals Hellboy's family and the strange workings of the capitol city of Pandemonium, leading to one of the most enigmatic finales in comics.

$49.99 | 978-1-50670-363-3

Hellboy: Into the Silent Sea HC
Story By: *Mike Mignola and Gary Gianni*
Art By: *Gary Gianni and Dave Stewart*

Hellboy sets sail from the wreckage of a deserted island only to be taken captive by the phantom crew of a ghost ship.

$14.99 | 978-1-50670-143-1

Hellboy Vol. 7: The Troll Witch and Others TPB
Story By: *Mike Mignola*
Art By: *Mike Mignola, P. Craig Russell, Richard Corben, and Dave Stewart*

A previously unpublished Hellboy story by Mike Mignola and P. Craig Russell headlines this collection of short comics stories.

$17.95 | 978-1-59307-860-7

Hellboy: Weird Tales HC
Story and Art By: *Mike Mignola, Evan Dorkin, Roger Langridge, Scott Morse, Mark Ricketts, P. Craig Russell, Jill Thompson, Bob Fingerman, and others*

Some of the best writers and artists in comics present stories featuring Hellboy and the B.P.R.D.

$24.99 | 978-1-61655-510-8

Hellboy Junior TPB
Story and Art By: *Mike Mignola, Pat McEown, and others*

Bill Wray joins Mignola and a lineup of cartoonists to reimagine a young, diaper-clad Hellboy and a host of twisted children's characters.

$14.95 | 978-1-56971-988-6

Abe Sapien Vol. 9: Lost Lives and Other Stories TPB
Story By: *Mike Mignola, Scott Allie, and John Arcudi*
Art By: *Juan Ferreyra, Dave Stewart, and others*

Trace the history of Abe Sapien, from his earliest days in the Bureau, through the frog war, to his current evolved form.

$19.99 | 978-1-50670-220-9

B.P.R.D: Plague of Frogs Vol. 1 HC
Story By: *Mike Mignola and others*
Art By: *Guy Davis and others*

After Hellboy's departure, the B.P.R.D. cracks open the secrets of Abe Sapien's origin, setting the war on frogs in motion.

$34.99 | 978-1-59582-609-1

Mr. Higgins Comes Home HC
Story By: *Mike Mignola*
Art By: *Warwick Johnson-Cadwell*

A pair of fearless vampire killers coerce a man who'd nearly been killed by the undead to return to the scene of the crime in order to end the only suffering he cares about— his own.

$14.99 | 978-1-50670-466-1

Conan Omnibus Vol. 1: Birth of Legend TPB
Story By: *Kurt Busiek*

Art By: *Cary Nord, Thomas Yeates, Tom Mandrake, Greg Ruth, and Dave Stewart*

Kurt Busiek's award-winning take on Conan's earliest adventures is now available in affordable omnibus format!

$24.99 | 978-1-50670-282-7

Conan: Book of Thoth TPB
Story By: *Kurt Busiek and Len Wein*
Art By: *Kelley Jones*

Kurt Busiek and Len Wein team with the grandmaster of horror art, Kelley Jones, for the horrifying origin of Conan's greatest adversary!

$17.95 | 978-1-59307-648-1

Conan and the Demons of Khitai TPB
Story By: *Akira Yoshida*
Art By: *Paul Lee*

King Conan travels to the Eastern land of Khitai, only to run afoul of an evil sorcerer and his demonic retainers.

$12.95 | 978-1-59307-543-9

Conan and the Midnight God TPB
Story By: *Joshua Dysart*
Art By: *Will Conrad and Juan Ferrerya*

King Conan strikes back at a sinister Stygian sorcerer with all his might, in a move that threatens to throw all Hyborea into chaos!

$14.95 | 978-1-59307-852-2

Conan and the Jewels of Gwahlur HC

Story and Art By: *P. Craig Russell and Lovern Kindzierski*

As an ally poses as the dead oracle of a primitive cult, Conan puts his experience as a thief and a soldier together in pursuit of the most prized jewels in the world!

$13.95 | 978-1-59307-491-3

Kull Vol. 1: The Shadow Kingdom

Story By: *Arvid Nelson*
Art By: *Will Conrad*

After crowning himself king, Kull uncovers layers of deception and reptilian treachery in the ancient halls of the Tower of Splendor.

$18.95 | 978-1-59582-385-4

Robert E. Howard's Savage Sword Vol. 1 TPB

By: *Scott Allie, Sean Phillips and others*

This collection features larger-than-life Howard heroes like Dark Agnes, El Borak, the Sonora Kid, and, of course, Conan.

$17.99 | 978-1-61655-075-2

Solomon Kane Vol. 1: The Castle of the Devil TPB

Story By: *Scott Allie*
Art By: *Mario Guevara and Dave Stewart*

When Solomon Kane stumbles upon the body of a boy hanged from a rickety gallows, he goes after the sorcerer responsible.

$15.99 | 978-1-59582-282-6

Tarzan: The Lost Adventure

Story By: *Edgar Rice Burroughs and Joe Lansdale*
Art By: *Gary Gianni and others*

Edgar Rice Burroughs' final, unfinished work is completed by Joe Lansdale in a densely illustrated novel.

$19.95 | 978-1-56971-083-8

Eerie Archives HC

Story By: *Al Milgrom and others*
Art By: *Estebon Maroto, Sanjulian, and others*

Dark Horse has restored these the famed horror comics of the sixties, seventies, and eighties for these massive hardcover editions.

Vol. 10 | $49.99 | 978-1-59582-774-6
Vol. 11 | $49.99 | 978-1-59582-775-3

Aliens/Predator: War TPB

Story By: *Randy Stradley*
Art By: *Jim Hall and others*

A human who has been inducted into the Predator clan is forced into a duel to claim her place in the upcoming hunt. The arrival of a new group of humans jeopardizes her shaky status.

$19.95 | 978-1-56971-158-3

Aliens vs. Predator TPB

Story By: *Randy Stradley*
Art By: *Phill Norwood and Karl Story*

A race of Predators' plan goes haywire when an Alien Queen turns the hunters into the hunted.

$19.95 | 978-1-56971-125-5

Prometheus: The Complete Fire and Stone HC

Story By: *Kelly Sue Deconnick and others*
Art By: *Juan Ferreyra and others*

A new generation of explorers hopes to uncover the mysteries of the lost vessel *Prometheus*, but what they find may lead to humanity's undoing.

$49.99 | 978-1-61655-772-0

Angel Omnibus

Story By: *Joss Whedon and others*
Art By: *Paul Lee, Brian Horton, and others*

Set during Seasons 1 and 2 of the Angel television series, LA's vampire detective agency delve into all that is dark, grotesque, strange, and unexplainable.

$24.99 | 978-1-59582-706-7

Buffy The Vampire Slayer Omnibus: Season 8 Vol. 1 TPB

Story By: *Joss Whedon and others*
Art By: *Georges Jeanty, Paul Lee and others*

Series creator Joss Whedon brought Buffy the Vampire Slayer back to life with this comics-only follow-up to Season 7 of the television show.

$24.99 | 978-1-63008-941-2

Grendel Omnibus Vol.1: Hunter Rose

Story and Art By: *Matt Wagner, Guy Davis, Paul Chadwick, Scott Morse, Jill Thompson, Kelley Jones, and others*

The first of four volumes of Matt Wagner's masterpiece introduces millionaire Hunter Rose and his alter ego, the criminal mastermind Grendel!

$24.99 | 978-1-59582-893-4

Beasts of Burden: Animal Rites HC
Story By: *Evan Dorkin*
Art By: *Jill Thompson*

Beneath its shiny exterior, Burden Hill harbors sinister secrets, and it's up to a heroic gang of dogs—and one cat—to protect the town from the evil forces at work.

$19.99 | 978-1-59582-513-1

47 Ronin
Story By: *Mike Richardson*
Art By: *Stan Sakai*

Opening with the tragic incident that sealed the fate of Lord Asano, *47 Ronin* follows a dedicated group of Asano's vassals on their years-long path of vengeance!

$19.99 | 978-1-59582-954-2

The Atomic Legion HC
Story By: *Mike Richardson*
Art By: *Bruce Zick*

A young boy rallies the rejected heroes of the past to save a kidnapped scientist.

$29.99 | 978-1-61655-312-8

Echoes TPB
Story By: *Mike Richardson*
Art By: *Gabriel Guzman*

Troubled pilot Fred Martin, after crashing from a bad storm, awakens thirty years in his past, with the opportunity to right the wrong that ruined him.

$14.99 | 978-1-50670-123-3

Cut
Story By: *Mike Richardson*
Art By: *Todd Herman*

Offers an original twist on horror movies like *Saw* and *Hostel*.

$9.95 | 978-1-59307-845-4

Living with the Dead: A Zombie Bromance TPB
Story By: *Mike Richardson*
Art By: *Ben Stenbeck*

Life in the big city has its problems, including the brain-hungry living dead. It only gets more complicated as Straw and Whip meet a gun-crazy vixen.

$9.99 | 978-1-50670-062-5

Father's Day
Story By: *Mike Richardson*
Art By: *Gabriel Guzman and Java Tartaglia*

Once a feared mob enforcer, Silas Smith has found peace in seclusion . . . until his estranged daughter shows up with a major axe to grind.

$14.99 | 978-1-61655-579-5

King Tiger: Song of the Dragon TPB
Story By: *Randy Stradley*
Art By: *Doug Wheatley and Rain Beredo*

A monstrous secret from King Tiger's past hunts the warrior mystic, but can Tiger's skills and sorcery overcome a supernatural obscenity linked to his own destiny?

$14.99 | 978-1-61655-817-8

Another Chance To Get It Right TPB
Story By: *Andrew Vachss*
Art By: *Geof Darrow, Brad Anderson, Tim Bradstreet, and others*

This work is an illumination of the realities of child abuse, juvenile violence . . . and a tribute to the power of imagination.

$14.99 | 978-1-50670-257-5

The Shaolin Cowboy Adventure Magazine TPB
Story By: *Geof Darrow and Mike Black*
Art By: *Andrew Vachss and Gary Gianni*

Celebrated author Andrew Vachss goes pulp with Geof Darrow's tight-lipped hero, combining hard-hitting prose with illustrated mayhem.

$15.99 | 978-1-61655-056-1

Michael Chabon Presents: The Amazing Adventures of the Escapist Vol. 1 TPB
Story and Art By: *Michael Chabon, Scott Morse, and others*

The Pulitzer Prize-winning novel *Kavalier & Clay* comes alive in comics.

$17.95 | 978-1-59307-171-4

The Eltingville Club HC
Story and Art By: *Evan Dorkin*

Definitive, complete, and unashamed, this is fandom at its fan-dumbest!

$19.99 | 978-1-61655-415-6

Milk and Cheese: Dairy Products Gone Bad
Story and Art By: *Evan Dorkin*

This deluxe hardcover collects every tale of the famed carton of hate and wedge of spit, along with a ton of supplemental awesomeness.

$19.99 | 978-1-59582-805-7

Kiss Me Satan! TPB
Story By: *Victor Gischler*
Art By: *Juan Ferreyra*

Cassian Steele, boss of the werewolf mafia in the Big Easy, puts out an open contract on the old witch Verona to protect his secret, but the hit isn't as simple as it seems.

$19.99 | 978-1-61655-436-1

R.I.P.D. TPB
Story By: *Peter Lenkov*
Art By: *Lucas Marangon, Randy Emberlin, and Dave Nestelle*

The original tale of the Rest in Peace Department.

$12.99 | 978-1-61655-071-4

The Devil's Footprints TPB
Story By: *Scott Allie*
Art By: *Paul Lee and Brian Horton*

The youngest son of a deceased sorcerer, desperate to protect his family, spirals into a world that puts his soul in jeopardy.

$14.95 | 978-1-56971-933-6

Gary Gianni's MonsterMen and Other Scary Stories
Story and Art By: *Gary Gianni*

Millionaire filmmaker Lawrence St. George and his mysterious associate Benedict battle unnatural horrors and bizarre monsters.

$19.99 | 978-1-50670-480-7

Visit our contributors!

Jason Arthur: pages.suddenlink.net/jasonarthur ~ **Kurt Busiek**: www.busiek.com

James Campbell: angryjim.com ~ *Paul Chadwick*: www.paulchadwick.net

David Crouse: davidcrousehouse.com ~ *Guy Davis*: www.guydavisartworks.com

Evan Dorkin & *Sarah Dyer*: houseoffunstudio.com ~ *Josh Dysart*: www.joshuadysart.com

Bob Fingerman: www.bobfingerman.com ~ *Jared Fletcher*: jaredkfletcher.com

Juan Ferreyra: jefandart.blogspot.com.ar ~ *Gary Gianni*: www.garygianni.com

Timothy Green II: timothygreenii.deviantart.com

Jim & Ruth Keegan: twogunblog.blogspot.com ~ *Roger Langridge*: hotelfred.blogspot.com

Lucas Marangon: lucasmarangon.deviantart.com ~ *Mike Mignola*: artofmikemignola.com

Tony Millionaire: www.maakies.com ~ *Scott Morse*: scottmorse.blogspot.com

Leah Moore & John Reppion: www.moorereppion.com ~ *Arvid Nelson*: www.arvidland.com

Uli Oesterle: www.oesterle-illustration.com ~ *Sean Phillips*: www.seanphillips.co.uk

Nate Piekos: www.blambot.com

AVAILABLE AT YOUR LOCAL COMICS SHOP OR BOOKSTORE
To find a comics shop in your area, call 1-888-266-4226.
For more information or to order direct, visit DarkHorse.com or call 1-800-862-0052. Mon.–Fri. 9 AM to 5 PM Pacific Time. Prices and availability subject to change without notice.

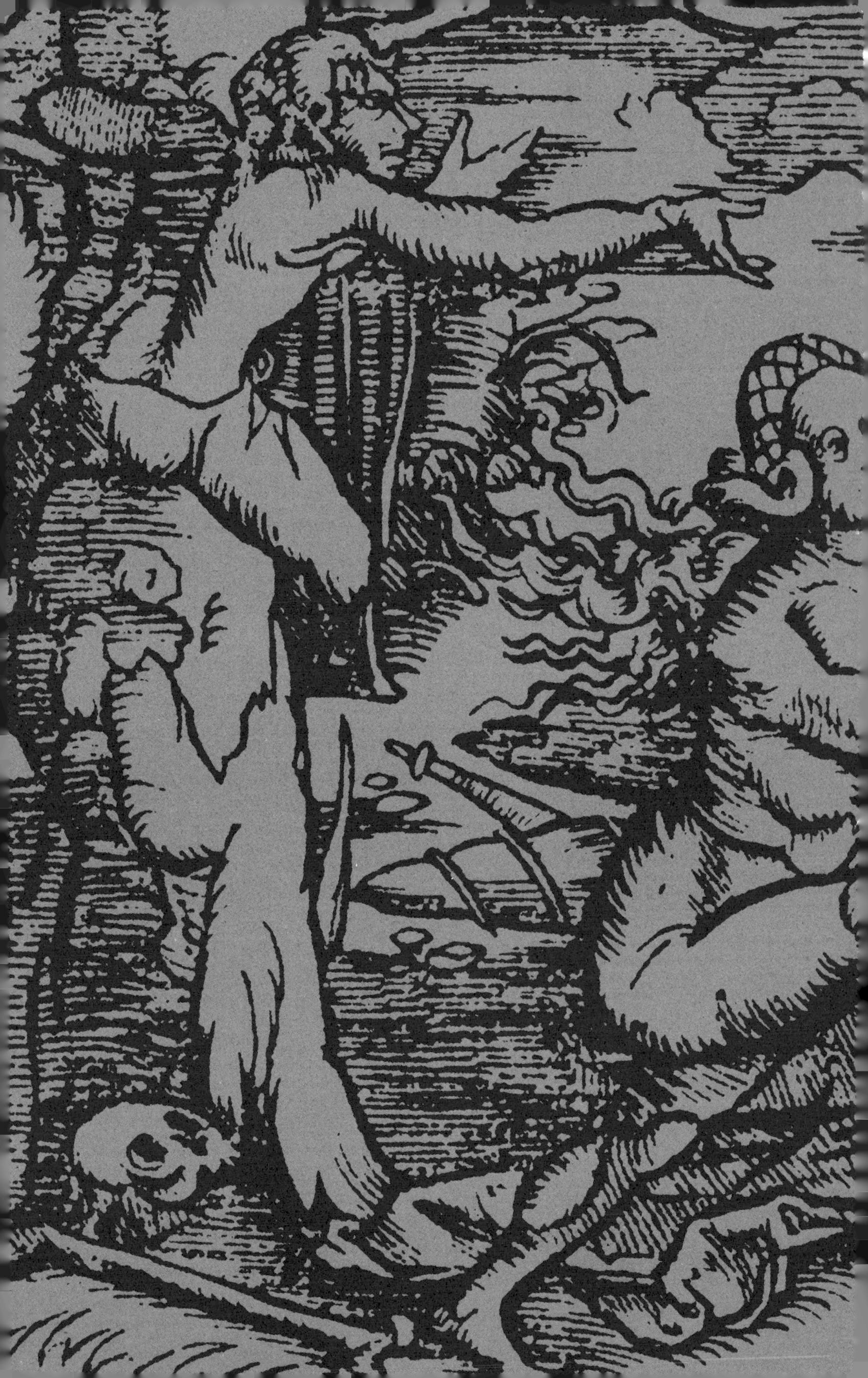